UNFINISHED TALES

tengwar inscription

PART I
THE FIRST AGE

PART II
THE SECOND AGE

PART III
THE THIRD AGE

PART IV
THE DRÚEDAIN, THE ISTARI, THE PALANTÍRI

tengwar inscription

Unfinished Tales

of Númenor and Middle-earth

by

J. R. R. TOLKIEN

edited with introduction, commentary, index and maps by

CHRISTOPHER TOLKIEN

HOUGHTON MIFFLIN COMPANY BOSTON

BOOKS BY J. R. R. TOLKIEN

The Lord of the Rings
The Fellowship of the Ring
The Two Towers
The Return of the King
The Hobbit
Farmer Giles of Ham
The Adventures of Tom Bombadil
Smith of Wootton Major
Tree and Leaf
Sir Gawain and the Green Knight,
Pearl *and* Sir Orfeo
The Father Christmas Letters
(edited by Baillie Tolkien)
The Silmarillion
(edited by Christopher Tolkien)
Unfinished Tales
(edited by Christopher Tolkien)

WITH DONALD SWANN
The Road Goes Ever On

ISBN: 0-395-29917-9
ISBN: 0-395-32441-6 pbk.

Library of Congress Catalogue Card Number: 80-83072

Printed in the United States of America

V 10 9 8 7 6 5 4 3 2 1

Houghton Mifflin Company paperback 1982

CONTENTS

NOTE

It has been necessary to distinguish author and editor in different ways in different parts of this book, since the incidence of commentary is very various. The author appears in larger type in the primary texts throughout; if the editor intrudes into one of these texts he is in smaller type indented from the margin (e.g. p. 294). In *The History of Galadriel and Celeborn*, however, where the editorial text is predominant, the reverse indentation is employed. In the Appendices (and also in *The Further Course of the Narrative* of 'Aldarion and Erendis', pp. 205 ff.) both author and editor are in the smaller type, with citations from the author indented (e.g. p. 154).

Notes to texts in the Appendices are given as footnotes rather than as numbered references; and the author's own annotation of a text at a particular point is indicated throughout by the words '[Author's note]'.

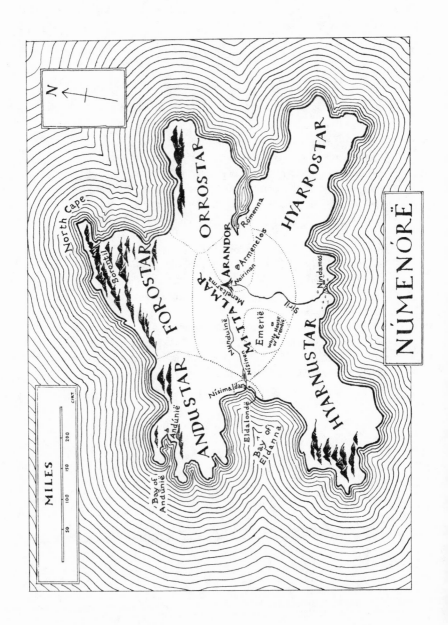

INTRODUCTION

The problems that confront one given responsibility for the writings of a dead author are hard to resolve. Some persons in this position may elect to make no material whatsoever available for publication, save perhaps for work that was in a virtually finished state at the time of the author's death. In the case of the unpublished writings of J. R. R. Tolkien this might seem at first sight the proper course; since he himself, peculiarly critical and exacting of his own work, would not have dreamt of allowing even the more completed narratives in this book to appear without much further refinement.

On the other hand, the nature and scope of his invention seems to me to place even his abandoned stories in a peculiar position. That *The Silmarillion* should remain unknown was for me out of the question, despite its disordered state, and despite my father's known if very largely unfulfilled intentions for its transformation; and in that case I presumed, after long hesitation, to present the work not in the form of an historical study, a complex of divergent texts interlinked by commentary, but as a completed and cohesive entity. The narratives in this book are indeed on an altogether different footing: taken together they constitute no whole, and the book is no more than a collection of writings, disparate in form, intent, finish, and date of composition (and in my own treatment of them), concerned with Númenor and Middle-earth. But the argument for their publication is not different in its nature, though it is of lesser force, from that which I held to justify the publication of *The Silmarillion*. Those who would not have forgone the images of Melkor with Ungoliant looking down from the summit of Hyarmentir upon 'the fields and pastures of Yavanna, gold beneath the tall wheat of the gods'; of the shadows of Fingolfin's host cast by the first moonrise in the West; of Beren lurking in wolf's shape beneath the throne of Morgoth; or of the light of the Silmaril suddenly revealed in the darkness of the Forest of Neldoreth – they will find, I believe, that imperfections of form in these tales are much outweighed by the voice (heard now for the last time) of Gandalf, teasing the lordly Saruman at the meeting of the White Council in the year 2851, or describing in Minas Tirith after the end of the War of the Ring how it was that he came to send the Dwarves to the celebrated party at Bag-End; by the arising of Ulmo Lord of Waters out of the sea at Vinyamar; by Mablung of Doriath hiding 'like a vole' beneath the ruins of the bridge at Nargothrond; or by the death of Isildur as he floundered up out of the mud of Anduin.

Many of the pieces in this collection are elaborations of matters told more briefly, or at least referred to, elsewhere; and it must be said at once that much in the book will be found unrewarding by readers of *The Lord of the Rings* who, holding that the historical structure of Middle-earth

is a means and not an end, the mode of the narrative and not its purpose,
feel small desire of further exploration for its own sake, do not wish to
know how the Riders of the Mark of Rohan were organised, and would
leave the Wild Men of the Drúadan Forest firmly where they found them.
My father would certainly not have thought them wrong. He said in a
letter written in March 1955, before the publication of the third volume of
The Lord of the Rings:

> I now wish that no appendices had been promised! For I think their
> appearance in truncated and compressed form will satisfy nobody:
> certainly not me; clearly from the (appalling mass of) letters I receive
> not those people who like that kind of thing – astonishingly many;
> while those who enjoy the book as an 'heroic romance' only, and find
> 'unexplained vistas' part of the literary effect, will neglect the appendices,
> very properly.
>
> I am not now at all sure that the tendency to treat the whole thing as
> a kind of vast game is really good – certainly not for me who find that
> kind of thing only too fatally attractive. It is, I suppose, a tribute to
> the curious effect that a story has, when based on very elaborate and
> detailed workings, of geography, chronology, and language, that so
> many should clamour for sheer 'information', or 'lore'.

In a letter of the following year he wrote:

> . . . while many like you demand maps, others wish for geological indi-
> cations rather than places; many want Elvish grammars, phonologies,
> and specimens; some want metrics and prosodies. . . . Musicians want
> tunes, and musical notation; archaeologists want ceramics and metal-
> lurgy; botanists want a more accurate description of the *mallorn*, of
> *elanor*, *niphredil*, *alfirin*, *mallos*, and *symbelmynë*; historians want more
> details about the social and political structure of Gondor; general
> enquirers want information about the Wainriders, the Harad, Dwarvish
> origins, the Dead Men, the Beornings, and the missing two wizards
> (out of five).

But whatever view may be taken of this question, for some, as for
myself, there is a value greater than the mere uncovering of curious detail
in learning that Vëantur the Númenórean brought his ship Entulessë, the
'Return', into the Grey Havens on the spring winds of the six hundredth
year of the Second Age, that the tomb of Elendil the Tall was set by
Isildur his son on the summit of the beacon-hill Halifirien, that the Black
Rider whom the Hobbits saw in the foggy darkness on the far side of
Bucklebury Ferry was Khamûl, chief of the Ringwraiths of Dol Guldur
– or even that the childlessness of Tarannon twelfth King of Gondor (a
fact recorded in an Appendix to *The Lord of the Rings*) was associated
with the hitherto wholly mysterious cats of Queen Berúthiel.

The construction of the book has been difficult, and in the result is somewhat complex. The narratives are all 'unfinished', but to a greater or lesser degree, and in different senses of the word, and have required different treatment; I shall say something below about each one in turn, and here only call attention to some general features.

The most important is the question of 'consistency', best illustrated from the section entitled 'The History of Galadriel and Celeborn'. This is an 'Unfinished Tale' in a larger sense: not a narrative that comes to an abrupt halt, as in 'Of Tuor and his Coming to Gondolin', nor a series of fragments, as in 'Cirion and Eorl', but a primary strand in the history of Middle-earth that never received a settled definition, let alone a final written form. The inclusion of the unpublished narratives and sketches of narrative on this subject therefore entails at once the acceptance of the history not as a fixed, independently-existing reality which the author 'reports' (in his 'persona' as translator and redactor), but as a growing and shifting conception in his mind. When the author has ceased to publish his works himself, after subjecting them to his own detailed criticism and comparison, the further knowledge of Middle-earth to be found in his unpublished writings will often conflict with what is already 'known'; and new elements set into the existing edifice will in such cases tend to contribute less to the history of the invented world itself than to the history of its invention. In this book I have accepted from the outset that this must be so; and except in minor details such as shifts in nomenclature (where retention of the manuscript form would lead to disproportionate confusion or disproportionate space in elucidation) I have made no alterations for the sake of consistency with published works, but rather drawn attention throughout to conflicts and variations. In this respect therefore 'Unfinished Tales' is essentially different from *The Silmarillion*, where a primary though not exclusive objective in the editing was to achieve cohesion both internal and external; and except in a few specified cases I have indeed treated the published form of *The Silmarillion* as a fixed point of reference of the same order as the writings published by my father himself, without taking into account the innumerable 'unauthorised' decisions between variants and rival versions that went into its making.

In content the book is entirely narrative (or descriptive): I have excluded all writings about Middle-earth and Aman that are of a primarily philosophic or speculative nature, and where such matters from time to time arise I have not pursued them. I have imposed a simple structure of convenience by dividing the texts into Parts corresponding to the first Three Ages of the World, there being in this inevitably some overlap, as with the legend of Amroth and its discussion in 'The History of Galadriel and Celeborn'. The fourth part is an appendage, and may require some excuse in a book called 'Unfinished Tales', since the pieces it contains are generalised and discursive essays with little or no element of 'story'. The section on the Drúedain did indeed owe its original inclusion to the story of 'The Faithful Stone' which forms a small part of it; and this section led me to introduce those on the Istari and the Palantíri, since they (especially the former) are matters about which many people have expressed curiosity, and this book seemed a convenient place to expound what there is to tell. The notes may seem to be in some places rather thick on the ground, but it will be seen that where clustered most densely (as in 'The Disaster of the Gladden Fields') they are due less to the editor than to the author, who in his later work tended to compose in this way, driving several subjects abreast by means of interlaced notes. I have throughout tried to make it clear what is editorial and what is not. And because of this abundance of original material appearing in the notes and appendices I have thought it best not to restrict the page-references in the Index to the texts themselves but to cover all parts of the book except the Introduction.

I have throughout assumed on the reader's part a fair knowledge of the published works of my father (more especially *The Lord of the Rings*), for to have done otherwise would have greatly enlarged the editorial element, which may well be thought quite sufficient already. I have, however, included short defining statements with almost all the primary entries in the Index, in the hope of saving the reader from constant reference elsewhere. If I have been inadequate in explanation or unintentionally obscure, Mr Robert Foster's *Complete Guide to Middle-earth* supplies, as I have found through frequent use, an admirable work of reference.

References to *The Silmarillion* are to the pages of the hardback edition; to *The Lord of the Rings* by title of the volume, book, and chapter.

There follow now primarily bibliographical notes on the individual pieces.

★ ★ ★

PART ONE

I

Of Tuor and his Coming to Gondolin

My father said more than once that 'The Fall of Gondolin' was the first of the tales of the First Age to be composed, and there is no evidence to set against his recollection. In a letter of 1964 he declared that he wrote it ' "out of my head" during sick-leave from the army in 1917', and at other times he gave the date as 1916 or 1916–17. In a letter to me written in 1944 he said: 'I first began to write [The Silmarillion] in army huts, crowded, filled with the noise of gramophones': and indeed some lines of verse in which appear the Seven Names of Gondolin are scribbled on the back of a piece of paper setting out 'the chain of responsibility in a battalion'. The earliest manuscript is still in existence, filling two small school exercise-books; it was written rapidly in pencil, and then, for much of its course, overlaid with writing in ink, and heavily emended. On the basis of this text my mother, apparently in 1917, wrote out a fair copy; but this in turn was further substantially emended, at some time that I cannot determine, but probably in 1919–20, when my father was in Oxford on the staff of the then still uncompleted Dictionary. In the spring of 1920 he was invited to read a paper to the Essay Club of his college (Exeter); and he read 'The Fall of Gondolin'. The notes of what he intended to say by way of introduction to his 'essay' still survive. In these he apologised for not having been able to produce a critical paper, and went on: 'Therefore I must read something already written, and in desperation I have fallen back on this Tale. It has of course never seen the light before. . . . A complete cycle of events in an Elfinesse of my own imagining has for some time past grown up (rather, has been constructed) in my mind. Some of the episodes have been scribbled down. . . . This tale is not the best of them, but it is the only one that has so far been revised at all and that, insufficient as that revision has been, I dare read aloud.'

The tale of Tuor and the Exiles of Gondolin (as 'The Fall of Gondolin' is entitled in the early MSS) remained untouched for many years, though my father at some stage, probably between 1926 and 1930, wrote a brief, compressed version of the story to stand as part of *The Silmarillion* (a title which, incidentally, first appeared in his letter to *The Observer* of 20 February 1938); and this was changed subsequently to bring it into harmony with altered conceptions in other parts of the book. Much later he began work on an entirely refashioned account, entitled 'Of Tuor and the Fall of Gondolin'. It seems very likely that this was written in 1951, when *The Lord of the Rings* was finished but its publication doubtful. Deeply changed in style and bearings, yet retaining many of the essentials of the story written in his youth, 'Of Tuor and the Fall of Gondolin' would have given in fine detail the whole legend that constitutes the brief 23rd chapter of the published *Silmarillion*; but, grievously, he went no further than the coming of Tuor and Voronwë to the last gate and Tuor's sight of Gondolin across the plain of Tumladen. To his reasons for abandoning it there is no clue.

This is the text that is given here. To avoid confusion I have retitled it 'Of Tuor and his Coming to Gondolin', since it tells nothing of the fall of the city. As always with my father's writings there are variant readings, and in one short section (the approach to and passage of the river Sirion by Tuor and Voronwë) several competing forms; some minor editorial work has therefore been necessary.

It is thus the remarkable fact that the only full account that my father ever wrote of the story of Tuor's sojourn in Gondolin, his union with Idril Celebrindal, the birth of Eärendil, the treachery of Maeglin, the sack of the city, and the escape of the fugitives – a story that was a central element in his imagination of the First Age – was the narrative composed in his youth. There is no question, however, that that (most remarkable) narrative is not suitable for inclusion in this book. It is written in the extreme archaistic style that my father employed at that time, and it inevitably embodies conceptions out of keeping with the world of *The Lord of the Rings* and *The Silmarillion* in its published form. It belongs with the rest of the earliest phase of the mythology, 'the Book of Lost Tales': itself a very substantial work, of the utmost interest to one concerned with the origins of Middle-earth, but requiring to be presented in a lengthy and complex study if at all.

II

The Tale of the Children of Húrin

The development of the legend of Túrin Turambar is in some respects the most tangled and complex of all the narrative elements in the story of the First Age. Like the tale of Tuor and the Fall of Gondolin it goes back to the very beginnings, and is extant in an early prose narrative (one of the 'Lost Tales') and in a long, unfinished poem in alliterative verse. But whereas the later 'long version' of *Tuor* never proceeded very far, my father carried the later 'long version' of *Túrin* much nearer completion. This is called *Narn i Hîn Húrin*; and this is the narrative that is given in the present book.

There are however great differences in the course of the long *Narn* in the degree to which the narrative approaches a perfected or final form. The concluding section (from The Return of Túrin to Dor-lómin to The Death of Túrin) has undergone only marginal editorial alteration; while the first section (to the end of Túrin in Doriath) required a good deal of revision and selection, and in some places some slight compression, the original texts being scrappy and disconnected. But the central section of the narrative (Túrin among the outlaws, Mîm the Petty-dwarf, the land of Dor-Cúarthol, the death of Beleg at Túrin's hand, and Túrin's life in Nargothrond) constituted a much more difficult editorial problem. The *Narn* is here at its least finished, and in places diminishes to outlines of possible turns in the story. My father was still evolving this part when he ceased to work on it; and the shorter version for *The Silmarillion* was to wait on the final development of the *Narn*. In preparing the text of *The Silmarillion* for publication I derived, by necessity, much of this section of the tale of Túrin from these very materials, which are of quite extraordinary complexity in their variety and interrelations.

For the first part of this central section, as far as the beginning of Túrin's sojourn in Mîm's dwelling on Amon Rûdh, I have contrived a narrative, in scale commensurate with other parts of the *Narn*, out of the existing materials (with one gap, see p. 96 and note 12); but from that point onwards (see p. 104) until Túrin's coming to Ivrin after the fall of Nargothrond I have found it unprofitable to attempt it. The gaps in the *Narn* are here too large, and could only be filled from the published text of *The Silmarillion*; but in an Appendix (pp. 150 ff.) I have cited isolated fragments from this part of the projected larger narrative. In the third section of the *Narn* (beginning with The Return of Túrin to Dor-lómin) a comparison with *The Silmarillion* (pp. 215–26) will show many close correspondences, and even identities of wording; while in the first section there are two extended passages that I have excluded from the present text (see p. 58 and note 1, and p. 66 and note 2), since they are close variants of passages that appear elsewhere and are included in the published *Silmarillion*. This overlapping and interrelation between one work and another may be explained in different ways, from different points of view. My father delighted in re-telling on different scales; but some parts did not call for more extended treatment in a larger version, and there was no need to rephrase for the sake of it. Again, when all was still fluid and the final organisation of the distinct narratives still a long way off, the same passage might be experimentally placed in either. But an explanation can be found at a different level. Legends like that of Túrin Turambar had been given a particular poetic form long ago – in this case, the *Narn i Hîn Húrin* of the poet Dírhavel – and phrases, or even whole passages, from it (especially at moments of great rhetorical intensity, such as Túrin's address to his sword before his death) would be preserved intact by those who afterwards made condensations of the history of the Elder Days (as *The Silmarillion* is conceived to be).

PART TWO

I

A Description of the Island of Númenor

Although descriptive rather than narrative, I have included selections from my father's account of Númenor, more especially as it concerns the physical nature of the Island, since it clarifies and naturally accompanies the tale of Aldarion and Erendis. This account was certainly in existence by 1965, and was probably written not long before that.

I have redrawn the map from a little rapid sketch, the only one, as it appears, that my father ever made of Númenor. Only names or features found on the original have been entered on the redrawing. In addition, the original shows another haven on the Bay of Andúnië, not far to the westward of Andúnië itself; the name is hard to read, but is almost certainly *Almaida*. This does not, so far as I am aware, occur elsewhere.

II

Aldarion and Erendis

This story was left in the least developed state of all the pieces in this collection, and has in places required a degree of editorial rehandling that made me doubt the propriety of including it. However, its very great interest as the single story (as opposed to records and annals) that survived at all from the long ages of Númenor before the narrative of its end (the *Akallabêth*), and as a story unique in its content among my father's writings, persuaded me that it would be wrong to omit it from this collection of 'Unfinished Tales'.

To appreciate the necessity for such editorial treatment it must be explained that my father made much use, in the composition of narrative, of 'plot-outlines', paying meticulous attention to the dating of events, so that these outlines have something of the appearance of annal-entries in a chronicle. In the present case there are no less than five of these schemes, varying constantly in their relative fullness at different points and not infrequently disagreeing with each other at large and in detail. But these schemes always had a tendency to move into pure narrative, especially by the introduction of short passages of direct speech; and in the fifth and latest of the outlines for the story of Aldarion and Erendis the narrative element is so pronounced that the text runs to some sixty manuscript pages.

This movement away from a staccato annalistic style in the present tense into fullblown narrative was however very gradual, as the writing of the outline progressed; and in the earlier part of the story I have rewritten much of the material in the attempt to give some degree of stylistic homogeneity throughout its course. This rewriting is entirely a matter of wording, and never alters meaning or introduces unauthentic elements.

The latest 'scheme', the text primarily followed, is entitled *The Shadow of the Shadow: the Tale of the Mariner's Wife; and the Tale of the Queen Shepherdess*. The manuscript ends abruptly, and I can offer no certain explanation of why my father abandoned it. A typescript made to this point was completed in January 1965. There exists also a typescript of two pages that I judge to be the latest of all these materials; it is evidently the beginning of what was to be a finished version of the whole story, and provides the text on pp. 173–5 in this book (where the plot-outlines are at their most scanty). It is entitled *Indis i · Kiryamo 'The Mariner's Wife': a tale of ancient Númenórë, which tells of the first rumour of the Shadow.*

At the end of this narrative (p. 205) I have set out such scanty indications as can be given of the further course of the story.

III

The Line of Elros: Kings of Númenor

Though in form purely a dynastic record, I have included this because it is an important document for the history of the Second Age, and a great part of the extant material concerning that Age finds a place in the texts and commentary in this book. It is a fine manuscript in which the dates of the Kings and Queens of Númenor and of their reigns have been copiously and sometimes obscurely emended: I have endeavoured to give the latest formulation. The text introduces several minor chronological puzzles, but also allows clarification of some apparent errors in the Appendices to *The Lord of the Rings*.

The genealogical table of the earlier generations of the Line of Elros is taken from several closely-related tables that derive from the same period as the discussion of the laws of succession in Númenor (pp. 208–9). There are some slight variations in minor names: thus *Vardilmë* appears also as *Vardilyë*, and *Yávien* as *Yávië*. The forms given in my table I believe to be later.

IV

The History of Galadriel and Celeborn

This section of the book differs from the others (save those in Part Four) in that there is here no single text but rather an essay incorporating citations. This treatment was enforced by the nature of the materials; as is made clear in the course of the essay, a history of Galadriel can only be a history of my father's changing conceptions, and the 'unfinished' nature of the tale is not in this case that of a particular piece of writing. I have restricted myself to the presentation of his unpublished writings on the subject, and forgone any discussion of the larger questions that underlie the development; for that would entail consideration of the entire relation between the Valar and the Elves, from the initial decision (described in *The Silmarillion*) to summon the Eldar to Valinor, and many other matters besides, concerning which my father wrote much that falls outside the scope of this book.

The history of Galadriel and Celeborn is so interwoven with other legends and histories – of Lothlórien and the Silvan Elves, of Amroth and Nimrodel, of Celebrimbor and the making of the Rings of Power, of the war against Sauron and the Númenórean intervention – that it cannot be treated in isolation, and thus this section of the book, together with its five Appendices, brings together virtually all the unpublished materials for the history of the Second Age in Middle-earth (and the discussion in places inevitably extends into the Third). It is said in the Tale of Years given in Appendix B to *The Lord of the Rings*: 'Those were the dark years for Men of Middle-earth, but the years of the glory of Númenor. Of events in Middle-earth the records are few and brief, and their dates are often uncertain.' But even that little surviving from the 'dark years' changed as my father's contemplation of it grew and changed; and I have made no attempt to smooth away inconsistency, but rather exhibited it and drawn attention to it.

Divergent versions need not indeed always be treated solely as a question of settling the priority of composition; and my father as 'author' or 'inventor' cannot always in these matters be distinguished from the 'recorder' of ancient traditions handed down in diverse forms among different peoples through long ages (when Frodo met Galadriel in Lórien, more than sixty centuries had passed since she went east over the Blue Mountains from the ruin of Beleriand). 'Of this two things are said, though which is true only those Wise could say who now are gone.'

In his last years my father wrote much concerning the etymology of names in Middle-earth. In these highly discursive essays there is a good deal of history and legend embedded; but being ancillary to the main philological purpose, and introduced as it were in passing, it has required extraction. It is for this reason that this part of the book is largely made up of short citations, with further material of the same kind placed in the Appendices.

PART THREE

I

The Disaster of the Gladden Fields

This is a 'late' narrative – by which I mean no more, in the absence of any indication of precise date, than that it belongs in the final period of my father's writing on Middle-earth, together with 'Cirion and Eorl', 'The Battles of the Fords of Isen', 'the Drúedain', and the philological essays excerpted in 'The History of Galadriel and Celeborn', rather than to the time of the publication of *The Lord of the Rings* and the years following it. There are two versions: a rough typescript of the whole (clearly the first stage of composition), and a good typescript incorporating many changes that breaks off at the point where Elendur urged Isildur to flee (p. 274). The editorial hand has here had little to do.

II

Cirion and Eorl and the Friendship of Gondor and Rohan

I judge these fragments to belong to the same period as 'The Disaster of the Gladden Fields', when my father was greatly interested in the earlier history of Gondor and Rohan; they were doubtless intended to form parts of a substantial history, developing in detail the summary accounts given in Appendix A to *The Lord of the Rings*. The material is in the first stage of composition, very disordered, full of variants, breaking off into rapid jottings that are in part illegible.

III

The Quest of Erebor

In a letter written in 1964 my father said:

> There are, of course, quite a lot of links between *The Hobbit* and *The Lord of the Rings* that are not clearly set out. They were mostly written or sketched out, but cut out to lighten the boat: such as Gandalf's exploratory journeys, his relations with Aragorn and Gondor; all the movements of Gollum, until he took refuge in Moria, and so on. I actually wrote in full an account of what really happened before Gandalf's visit to Bilbo and the subsequent 'Unexpected Party', as seen by Gandalf himself. It was to have come in during a looking-back conversation in Minas Tirith; but it had to go, and is only represented in brief in Appendix A pp. 358-60, though the difficulties that Gandalf had with Thorin are omitted.

This account of Gandalf's is given here. The complex textual situation is described in the Appendix to the narrative, where I have given substantial extracts from an earlier version.

IV

The Hunt for the Ring

There is much writing bearing on the events of the year 3018 of the Third Age, which are otherwise known from the Tale of Years and the reports of Gandalf and others to the Council of Elrond; and these writings are clearly those referred to as 'sketched out' in the letter just cited. I have given them the title 'The Hunt for the Ring'. The manuscripts themselves, in great though hardly exceptional confusion, are sufficiently described on p. 342; but the question of their date (for I believe them all, and also those of 'Concerning Gandalf, Saruman, and the Shire', given as the third element in this section, to derive from the same time) may be mentioned here. They were writtten after the publication of *The Lord of the Rings*, for there are references to the pagination of the printed text; but they differ in the dates they give for certain events from those in the Tale of Years in Appendix B. The explanation is clearly that they were written after the publication of the first volume but before that of the third, containing the Appendices.

V

The Battle of the Fords of Isen

This, together with the account of the military organisation of the Rohirrim and the history of Isengard given in an Appendix to the text, belongs with other late pieces of severe historical analysis; it presented relatively little difficulty of a textual kind, and is only unfinished in the most obvious sense.

PART FOUR

I

The Drúedain

Towards the end of his life my father revealed a good deal more about the Wild Men of the Drúadan Forest in Anórien and the statues of the Púkel-men on the road up to Dunharrow. The account given here, telling of the Drúedain in Beleriand in the First Age, and containing the story of 'The Faithful Stone', is drawn from a long, discursive, and unfinished essay concerned primarily with the interrelations of the languages of Middle-earth. As will be seen, the Drúedain were to be drawn back into the history of the earlier Ages; but of this there is necessarily no trace in the published Silmarillion.

II

The Istari

It was proposed soon after the acceptance of The Lord of the Rings for publication that there should be an index at the end of the third volume, and it seems that my father began to work on it in the summer of 1954, after the first two volumes had gone to press. He wrote of the matter in a letter of 1956: 'An index of names was to be produced, which by etymological interpretation would provide quite a large Elvish vocabulary. . . . I worked at it for months, and indexed the first two volumes (it was the chief cause of the delay of Volume III), until it became clear that size and cost were ruinous.'

In the event there was no index to The Lord of the Rings until the second edition of 1966, but my father's original rough draft has been preserved. From it I derived the plan of my index to The Silmarillion, with translation of names and brief explanatory statements, and also, both there and in the index to this book, some of the translations and the wording of some of the 'definitions'. From it comes also the 'essay on the Istari' with which this section of the book opens – an entry wholly uncharacteristic of the original index in its length, if characteristic of the way in which my father often worked.

For the other citations in this section I have given in the text itself such indications of date as can be provided.

III

The Palantíri

For the second edition of *The Lord of the Rings* (1966) my father made substantial emendations to a passage in *The Two Towers*, III 11 'The Palantír' (three-volume hardback edition p. 203), and some others in the same connection in *The Return of the King*, V 7 'The Pyre of Denethor' (edition cited p. 132), though these emendations were not incorporated in the text until the second impression of the revised edition (1967). This section of the present book is derived from writings on the *palantíri* associated with this revision; I have done no more than assemble them into a continuous essay.

★ ★ ★

The Map of Middle-earth

My first intention was to include in this book the map that accompanies *The Lord of the Rings* with the addition to it of further names; but it seemed to me on reflection that it would be better to copy my original map and take the opportunity to remedy some of its minor defects (to remedy the major ones being beyond my powers). I have therefore re-drawn it fairly exactly, on a scale half as large again (that is to say, the new map as drawn is half as large again as the old map in its published dimensions). The area shown is smaller, but the only features lost are the Havens of Umbar and the Cape of Forochel.* This has allowed of a different and larger mode of lettering, and a great gain in clarity.

All the more important place-names that occur in this book but not in *The Lord of the Rings* are included, such as *Lond Daer*, *Drúwaith Iaur*, *Edhellond*, the *Undeeps*, *Greylin*; and a few others that might have been, or should have been, shown on the original map, such as the rivers *Harnen* and *Carnen*, *Annúminas*, *Eastfold*, *Westfold*, the *Mountains of Angmar*. The mistaken inclusion of *Rhudaur* alone has been corrected by the addition of *Cardolan* and *Arthedain*, and I have shown the little island of *Himling* off the far north-western coast, which appears on one of my father's sketch-maps and on my own first draft. *Himling* was the earlier form of *Himring* (the great hill on which Maedhros son of Fëanor

---

* I have little doubt now that the water marked on my original map as 'The Icebay of Forochel' was in fact only a small part of the Bay (referred to in *The Lord of the Rings*, Appendix A I iii, as 'immense'), which extended much further to the north-east: its northern and western shores being formed by the great Cape of Forochel, of which the tip, unnamed, appears on my original map. In one of my father's map-sketches the northern coast of Middle-earth is shown stretching in a great curve east-north-east from the Cape, the most northerly point being some 700 miles north of Carn Dûm.

had his fortress in *The Silmarillion*), and though the fact is nowhere referred to it is clear that Himring's top rose above the waters that covered drowned Beleriand. Some way to the west of it was a larger island named *Tol Fuin*, which must be the highest part of *Taur-nu-Fuin*. In general, but not in all cases, I have preferred the Sindarin name (if known), but I have usually given the translated name as well when that is much used. It may be noted that 'The Northern Waste', marked at the head of my original map, seems in fact certainly to have been intended as an equivalent to *Forodwaith*.*

I have thought it desirable to mark in the entire length of the Great Road linking Arnor and Gondor, although its course between Edoras and the Fords of Isen is conjectural (as also is the precise placing of Lond Daer and Edhellond).

Lastly, I would emphasize that the exact preservation of the style and detail (other than nomenclature and lettering) of the map that I made in haste twenty-five years ago does not argue any belief in the excellence of its conception or execution. I have long regretted that my father never replaced it by one of his own making. However, as things turned out it became, for all its defects and oddities, 'the Map', and my father himself always used it as a basis afterwards (while frequently noticing its inadequacies). The various sketch-maps that he made, and from which mine was derived, are now a part of the history of the writing of *The Lord of the Rings*. I have thought it best therefore, so far as my own contribution to these matters extends, to let my original design stand, since it does at least represent the structure of my father's conceptions with tolerable faithfulness.

Forodwaith only occurs once in *The Lord of the Rings* (Appendix A I iii) and there refers to ancient inhabitants of the Northlands, of whom the Snowmen of Forochel were a remnant; but the Sindarin word (*g*)*waith* was used both of regions and of the peoples inhabiting them (cf. *Enedwaith*). In one of my father's sketch-maps *Forodwaith* seems to be explicitly equated with 'The Northern Waste', and in another is translated 'Northerland'.

PART ONE

THE FIRST AGE

I

OF TUOR AND HIS
COMING TO GONDOLIN

Rían, wife of Huor, dwelt with the people of the House of Hador;
but when rumour came to Dor-lómin of the Nirnaeth Arnoediad,
and yet she could hear no news of her lord, she became distraught
and wandered forth into the wild alone. There she would have
perished, but the Grey-elves came to her aid. For there was a dwelling
of this people in the mountains westward of Lake Mithrim; and
thither they led her, and she was there delivered of a son before the
end of the Year of Lamentation.

And Rían said to the Elves: 'Let him be called *Tuor*, for that
name his father chose, ere war came between us. And I beg of you to
foster him, and to keep him hidden in your care; for I forebode that
great good, for Elves and Men, shall come from him. But I must go
in search of Huor, my lord.'

Then the Elves pitied her; but one Annael, who alone of all that
went to war from that people had returned from the Nirnaeth, said
to her: 'Alas, lady, it is known now that Huor fell at the side of
Húrin his brother; and he lies, I deem, in the great hill of slain that
the Orcs have raised upon the field of battle.'

Therefore Rían arose and left the dwelling of the Elves, and she
passed through the land of Mithrim and came at last to the Haudh-
en-Ndengin in the waste of Anfauglith, and there she laid her down
and died. But the Elves cared for the infant son of Huor, and Tuor
grew up among them; and he was fair of face, and golden-haired
after the manner of his father's kin, and he became strong and
tall and valiant, and being fostered by the Elves he had lore and
skill no less than the princes of the Edain, ere ruin came upon the
North.

But with the passing of the years the life of the former folk of
Hithlum, such as still remained, Elves or Men, became ever harder
and more perilous. For as is elsewhere told, Morgoth broke his
pledges to the Easterlings that had served him, and he denied to them
the rich lands of Beleriand which they had coveted, and he drove

away these evil folk into Hithlum, and there commanded them to dwell. And though they loved Morgoth no longer, they served him still in fear, and hated all the Elven-folk; and they despised the remnant of the House of Hador (the aged and women and children, for the most part), and they oppressed them, and wedded their women by force, and took their lands and goods, and enslaved their children. Orcs came and went about the land as they would, pursuing the lingering Elves into the fastnesses of the mountains, and taking many captive to the mines of Angband to labour as the thralls of Morgoth.

Therefore Annael led his small people to the caves of Androth, and there they lived a hard and wary life, until Tuor was sixteen years of age and was become strong and able to wield arms, the axe and bow of the Grey-elves; and his heart grew hot within him at the tale of the griefs of his people, and he wished to go forth and avenge them on the Orcs and Easterlings. But Annael forbade this.

'Far hence, I deem, your doom lies, Tuor son of Huor,' he said. 'And this land shall not be freed from the shadow of Morgoth until Thangorodrim itself be overthrown. Therefore we are resolved at last to forsake it, and to depart into the South; and with us you shall go.'

'But how shall we escape the net of our enemies?' said Tuor. 'For the marching of so many together will surely be marked.'

'We shall not march through the land openly,' said Annael; 'and if our fortune is good we shall come to the secret way which we call Annon-in-Gelydh, the Gate of the Noldor; for it was made by the skill of that people, long ago in the days of Turgon.'

At that name Tuor was stirred, though he knew not why; and he questioned Annael concerning Turgon. 'He is a son of Fingolfin,' said Annael, 'and is now accounted High King of the Noldor, since the fall of Fingon. For he lives yet, most feared of the foes of Morgoth, and he escaped from the ruin of the Nirnaeth, when Húrin of Dor-lómin and Huor your father held the passes of Sirion behind him.'

'Then I will go and seek Turgon,' said Tuor; 'for surely he will lend me aid for my father's sake?'

'That you cannot,' said Annael. 'For his stronghold is hidden from the eyes of Elves and Men, and we know not where it stands. Of the Noldor some, maybe, know the way thither, but they will speak of it to none. Yet if you would have speech with them, then come with me, as I bid you; for in the far havens of the South you may meet with wanderers from the Hidden Kingdom.'

Thus it came to pass that the Elves forsook the caves of Androth, and Tuor went with them. But their enemies kept watch upon their dwellings, and were soon aware of their march; and they had not gone far from the hills into the plain before they were assailed by a great force of Orcs and Easterlings, and they were scattered far and wide, fleeing into the gathering night. But Tuor's heart was kindled with the fire of battle, and he would not flee, but boy as he was he wielded the axe as his father before him, and for long he stood his ground and slew many that assailed him; but at the last he was overwhelmed and taken captive and led before Lorgan the Easterling. Now this Lorgan was held the chieftain of the Easterlings and claimed to rule all Dor-lómin as a fief under Morgoth; and he took Tuor to be his slave. Hard and bitter then was his life; for it pleased Lorgan to treat Tuor the more evilly as he was of the kin of the former lords, and he sought to break, if he could, the pride of the House of Hador. But Tuor saw wisdom, and endured all pains and taunts with watchful patience; so that in time his lot was somewhat lightened, and at the least he was not starved, as were many of Lorgan's unhappy thralls. For he was strong and skilful, and Lorgan fed his beasts of burden well, while they were young and could work.

But after three years of thraldom Tuor saw at last a chance of escape. He was come now almost to his full stature, taller and swifter than any of the Easterlings; and being sent with other thralls on an errand of labour into the woods he turned suddenly on the guards and slew them with an axe, and fled into the hills. The Easterlings hunted him with dogs, but without avail; for wellnigh all the hounds of Lorgan were his friends, and if they came up with him they would fawn upon him, and then run homeward at his command. Thus he came back at last to the caves of Androth and dwelt there alone. And for four years he was an outlaw in the land of his fathers, grim and solitary; and his name was feared, for he went often abroad, and slew many of the Easterlings that he came upon. Then they set a great price upon his head; but they did not dare to come to his hiding-place, even with strength of men, for they feared the Elven-folk, and shunned the caves where they had dwelt. Yet it is said that Tuor's journeys were not made for the purpose of vengeance; rather he sought ever for the Gate of the Noldor, of which Annael had spoken. But he found it not, for he knew not where to look, and such few of the Elves as lingered still in the mountains had not heard of it.

Now Tuor knew that, though fortune still favoured him, yet in the end the days of an outlaw are numbered, and are ever few and without hope. Nor was he willing to live thus for ever a wild man in the houseless hills, and his heart urged him ever to great deeds. Herein, it is said, the power of Ulmo was shown. For he gathered tidings of all that passed in Beleriand, and every stream that flowed from Middle-earth to the Great Sea was to him a messenger, both to and fro; and he remained also in friendship, as of old, with Círdan and the Shipwrights at the Mouths of Sirion.[1] And at this time most of all Ulmo gave heed to the fates of the House of Hador, for in his deep counsels he purposed that they should play great part in his designs for the succour of the Exiles; and he knew well of the plight of Tuor, for Annael and many of his folk had indeed escaped from Dor-lómin and come at last to Círdan in the far South.

Thus it came to pass that on a day in the beginning of the year (twenty and three since the Nirnaeth) Tuor sat by a spring that trickled forth near to the door of the cave where he dwelt; and he looked out westward towards the cloudy sunset. Then suddenly it came into his heart that he would wait no longer, but would arise and go. 'I will leave now the grey land of my kin that are no more,' he cried, 'and I will go in search of my doom! But whither shall I turn? Long have I sought the Gate and found it not.'

Then he took up the harp which he bore ever with him, being skilled in playing upon its strings, and heedless of the peril of his clear voice alone in the waste he sang an elven-song of the North for the uplifting of hearts. And even as he sang the well at his feet began to boil with great increase of water, and it overflowed, and a rill ran noisily down the rocky hillside before him. And Tuor took this as a sign, and he arose at once and followed after it. Thus he came down from the tall hills of Mithrim and passed out into the northward plain of Dor-lómin; and ever the stream grew as he followed it westward, until after three days he could descry in the west the long grey ridges of Ered Lómin that in those regions marched north and south, fencing off the far coastlands of the Western Shores. To those hills in all his journeys Tuor had never come.

Now the land became more broken and stony again, as it approached the hills, and soon it began to rise before Tuor's feet, and the stream went down into a cloven bed. But even as dim dusk came on the third day of his journey, Tuor found before him a wall of rock, and there was an opening therein like a great arch; and the stream passed in and was lost. Then Tuor was dismayed, and he said: 'So my hope has cheated me! The sign in the hills has led me only to a dark end in the midst of the land of my enemies.' And grey at heart he sat among the rocks on the high bank of the stream, keeping watch through a bitter fireless night; for it was yet but the month of Súlimë, and no stir of spring had come to that far northern land, and a shrill wind blew from the East.

But even as the light of the coming sun shone pale in the far mists of Mithrim, Tuor heard voices, and looking down he saw in amazement two Elves that waded in the shallow water; and as they climbed up steps hewn in the bank, Tuor stood up and called to them. At once they drew their bright swords and sprang towards him. Then he saw that they were grey-cloaked but mail-clad under; and he marvelled, for they were fairer and more fell to look upon, because of the light of their eyes, than any of the Elven-folk that he yet had known. He stood to his full height and awaited them; but when they saw that he drew no weapon, but stood alone and greeted them in the Elven-tongue, they sheathed their swords and spoke courteously to him. And one said: 'Gelmir and Arminas we are, of Finarfin's people. Are you not one of the Edain of old that dwelt in these lands ere the Nirnaeth? And indeed of the kindred of Hador and Húrin I deem you; for so the gold of your head declares you.'

And Tuor answered: 'Yea, I am Tuor, son of Huor, son of Galdor, son of Hador; but now at last I desire to leave this land where I am outlawed and kinless.'

'Then,' said Gelmir, 'if you would escape and find the havens in the South, already your feet have been guided on the right road.'

'So I thought,' said Tuor. 'For I followed a sudden spring of water in the hills, until it joined this treacherous stream. But now I know not whither to turn, for it has gone into darkness.'

'Through darkness one may come to the light,' said Gelmir.

'Yet one will walk under the Sun while one may,' said Tuor. 'But since you are of that people, tell me if you can where lies the Gate of the Noldor. For I have sought it long, ever since Annael my foster-father of the Grey-elves spoke of it to me.'

Then the Elves laughed, and said: 'Your search is ended; for we have ourselves just passed that Gate. There it stands before you!' And they pointed to the arch into which the water flowed. 'Come now! Through darkness you shall come to the light. We will set your feet on the road, but we cannot guide you far; for we are sent back to the lands whence we fled upon an urgent errand.' 'But fear not,' said Gelmir: 'a great doom is written upon your brow, and it shall lead you far from these lands, far indeed from Middle-earth, as I guess.'

Then Tuor followed the Noldor down the steps and waded in the cold water, until they passed into the shadow beyond the arch of stone. And then Gelmir brought forth one of those lamps for which the Noldor were renowned; for they were made of old in Valinor, and neither wind nor water could quench them, and when they were unhooded they sent forth a clear blue light from a flame imprisoned in white crystal.[2] Now by the light that Gelmir held above his head Tuor saw that the river began to go suddenly down a smooth slope into a great tunnel, but beside its rock-hewn course there ran long flights of steps leading on and downward into a deep gloom beyond the beam of the lamp.

When they had come to the foot of the rapids they stood under a great dome of rock, and there the river rushed over a steep fall with a great noise that echoed in the vault, and it passed then on again beneath another arch into a further tunnel. Beside the falls the Noldor halted, and bade Tuor farewell.

'Now we must return and go our ways with all speed,' said Gelmir; 'for matters of great peril are moving in Beleriand.'

'Is then the hour come when Turgon shall come forth?' said Tuor.

Then the Elves looked at him in amazement. 'That is a matter which concerns the Noldor rather than the sons of Men,' said Arminas. 'What know you of Turgon?'

'Little,' said Tuor; 'save that my father aided his escape from the Nirnaeth, and that in his hidden stronghold dwells the hope of the Noldor. Yet, though I know not why, ever his name stirs in my heart, and comes to my lips. And had I my will, I would go in search of him, rather than tread this dark way of dread. Unless, perhaps, this secret road is the way to his dwelling?'

'Who shall say?' answered the Elf. 'For since the dwelling of Turgon is hidden, so also are the ways thither. I know them not, though I have sought them long. Yet if I knew them, I would not reveal them to you, nor to any among Men.'

But Gelmir said: 'Yet I have heard that your House has the favour of the Lord of Waters. And if his counsels lead you to Turgon, then surely shall you come to him, withersoever you turn. Follow now the road to which the water has brought you from the hills, and fear not! You shall not walk long in darkness. Farewell! And think not that our meeting was by chance; for the Dweller in the Deep moves many things in this land still. *Anar kaluva tielyanna!*'[3]

With that the Noldor turned and went back up the long stairs; but Tuor stood still, until the light of their lamp was lost, and he was alone in a darkness deeper than night amid the roaring of the falls. Then summoning his courage he set his left hand to the rock-wall, and felt his way forward, slowly at first, and then more quickly, as he became more used to the darkness and found nothing to hinder him. And after a great while, as it seemed to him, when he was weary and yet unwilling to rest in the black tunnel, he saw far before him a light; and hastening on he came to a tall and narrow cleft, and followed the noisy stream between its leaning walls out into a golden evening. For he was come into a deep ravine with tall sheer sides, and it ran straight towards the West; and before him the setting sun, going down through a clear sky, shone into the ravine and kindled its walls with yellow fire, and the waters of the river glittered like gold as they broke and foamed upon many gleaming stones.

In that deep place Tuor went on now in great hope and delight, finding a path beneath the southern wall, where there lay a long and narrow strand. And when night came, and the river rushed on unseen, save for a glint of high stars mirrored in dark pools, then he rested, and slept; for he felt no fear beside that water, in which the power of Ulmo ran.

With the coming of day he went on again without haste. The sun rose behind his back and set before his face, and where the water foamed among the boulders or rushed over sudden falls, at morning and evening rainbows were woven across the stream. Wherefore he named that ravine Cirith Ninniach.

Thus Tuor journeyed slowly for three days, drinking the cold water but desiring no food, though there were many fish that shone as gold and silver, or gleamed with colours like to the rainbows in the spray above. And on the fourth day the channel grew wider, and its walls lower and less sheer; but the river ran deeper and more strongly, for high hills now marched on either side, and fresh waters spilled from them into Cirith Ninniach over shimmering falls. There long while Tuor sat, watching the swirling of the stream and listening to its endless voice, until night came again and stars shone cold and white in the dark lane of sky above him. Then he lifted up his voice, and plucked the strings of his harp, and above the noise of the water the sound of his song and the sweet thrilling of the harp were echoed in the stone and multiplied, and went forth and rang in the night-clad hills, until all the empty land was filled with music beneath the stars. For though he knew it not, Tuor was now come to the Echoing Mountains of Lammoth about the Firth of Drengist. There once long ago Fëanor had landed from the sea, and the voices of his host were swelled to a mighty clamour upon the coasts of the North ere the rising of the Moon.[4]

Then Tuor was filled with wonder and stayed his song, and slowly the music died in the hills, and there was silence. And then amid

the silence he heard in the air above him a strange cry; and he knew
not of what creature that cry came. Now he said: 'It is a fay-voice,'
now: 'Nay, it is a small beast that is wailing in the waste'; and then,
hearing it again, he said: 'Surely, it is the cry of some nightfaring
bird that I know not.' And it seemed to him a mournful sound, and
yet he desired nonetheless to hear it and follow it, for it called him,
he knew not whither.

The next morning he heard the same voice above his head, and
looking up he saw three great white birds beating down the ravine
against the westerly wind, and their strong wings shone in the new-
risen sun, and as they passed over him they wailed aloud. Thus for
the first time he beheld the great gulls, beloved of the Teleri. Then
Tuor arose to follow them, and so that he might better mark whither
they flew he climbed the cliff upon his left hand, and stood upon the
top, and felt a great wind out of the West rush against his face; and
his hair streamed from his head. And he drank deep of that new air,
and said: 'This uplifts the heart like the drinking of cool wine!'
But he knew not that the wind came fresh from the Great Sea.

Now Tuor went on once more, seeking the gulls, high above the
river; and as he went the sides of the ravine drew together again, and
he came to a narrow channel, and it was filled with a great noise of
water. And looking down Tuor saw a great marvel, as it seemed to
him; for a wild flood came up the narrows and strove with the river
that would still press on, and a wave like a wall rose up almost to the
cliff-top, crowned with foam-crests flying in the wind. Then the
river was thrust back, and the incoming flood swept roaring up the
channel, drowning it in deep water, and the rolling of the boulders
was like thunder as it passed. Thus Tuor was saved by the call of
the sea-birds from death in the rising tide; and that was very great
because of the season of the year and of the high wind from the sea.

But now Tuor was dismayed by the fury of the strange waters, and
he turned aside and went away southward, and so came not to the
long shores of the Firth of Drengist, but wandered still for some days
in a rugged country bare of trees; and it was swept by a wind from
the sea, and all that grew there, herb or bush, leaned ever to the dawn
because of the prevalence of that wind from the West. In this way
Tuor passed into the borders of Nevrast, where once Turgon had
dwelt; and at last at unawares (for the cliff-tops at the margin of the
land were higher than the slopes behind) he came suddenly to the
black brink of Middle-earth, and saw the Great Sea, Belegaer the
Shoreless. And at that hour the sun went down beyond the rim of

the world, as a mighty fire; and Tuor stood alone upon the cliff with outspread arms, and a great yearning filled his heart. It is said that he was the first of Men to reach the Great Sea, and that none, save the Eldar, have ever felt more deeply the longing that it brings.

Tuor tarried many days in Nevrast, and it seemed good to him, for that land, being fenced by mountains from the North and East and nigh to the sea, was milder and more kindly than the plains of Hithlum. He was long used to dwell alone as a hunter in the wild, and he found no lack of food; for spring was busy in Nevrast, and the air was filled with the noise of birds, both those that dwelt in multitudes upon the shores and those that teemed in the marshes of Linaewen in the midst of the hollow land; but in those days no voice of Elves or Men was heard in all the solitude.

To the borders of the great mere Tuor came, but its waters were beyond his reach, because of the wide mires and the pathless forests of reeds that lay all about; and soon he turned away, and went back to the coast, for the Sea drew him, and he was not willing to dwell long where he could not hear the sound of its waves. And in the shorelands Tuor first found traces of the Noldor of old. For among the tall and sea-hewn cliffs south of Drengist there were many coves and sheltered inlets, with beaches of white sand among the black gleaming rocks, and leading down to such places Tuor found often winding stairs cut in the living stone; and by the water-edge were ruined quays, built of great blocks hewn from the cliffs, where elven-ships had once been moored. In those regions Tuor long remained, watching the ever-changing sea, while through spring and summer the slow year wore on, and darkness deepened in Beleriand, and the autumn of the doom of Nargothrond drew near.

And, maybe, birds saw from afar the fell winter that was to come;[5] for those that were wont to go south gathered early to depart, and others that used to dwell in the North came from their homes to Nevrast. And one day, as Tuor sat upon the shore, he heard the rush and whine of great wings, and he looked up and saw seven white swans flying in a swift wedge southward. But as they came above him they wheeled and flew suddenly down, and alighted with a great plash and churning of water.

Now Tuor loved swans, which he knew on the grey pools of Mith-rim; and the swan moreover had been the token of Annael and his foster-folk. He rose therefore to greet the birds, and called to them, marvelling to behold that they were greater and prouder than any of their kind that he had seen before; but they beat their wings and uttered harsh cries, as if they were wroth with him and would drive him from the shore. Then with a great noise they rose again from the water and flew above his head, so that the rush of their wings blew upon him as a whistling wind; and wheeling in a wide circle they ascended into the high air and went away south.

Then Tuor cried aloud: 'Here now comes another sign that I have tarried too long!' And straightway he climbed to the cliff-top, and there he beheld the swans still wheeling on high; but when he turned southward and set out to follow them, they flew swiftly away.

Now Tuor journeyed south along the coast for full seven days, and each morning he was aroused by the rush of wings above him in the dawn, and each day the swans flew on as he followed after. And as he went the great cliffs became lower, and their tops were clothed deep with flowering turf; and away eastward there were woods turning yellow in the waning of the year. But before him, drawing ever nearer, he saw a line of great hills that barred his way, marching westward until they ended in a tall mountain: a dark and cloud-helmed tower reared upon mighty shoulders above a great green cape thrust out into the sea.

Those grey hills were indeed the western outliers of Ered Wethrin, the north-fence of Beleriand, and the mountain was Mount Taras, westernmost of all the towers of that land, whose head a mariner would first descry across the miles of the sea, as he drew near to the mortal shores. Beneath its long slopes in bygone days Turgon had dwelt in the halls of Vinyamar, eldest of all the works of stone that the Noldor built in the lands of their exile. There it still stood, desolate but enduring, high upon great terraces that looked towards the sea. The years had not shaken it, and the servants of Morgoth had passed it by; but wind and rain and frost had graven it, and upon the coping of its walls and the great shingles of its roof there was a deep growth of grey-green plants that, living upon the salt air, throve even in the cracks of barren stone.

Now Tuor came to the ruins of a lost road, and he passed amid green mounds and leaning stones, and so came as the day was waning to the old hall and its high and windy courts. No shadow of fear or evil lurked there, but an awe fell upon him, thinking of those that had dwelt there and had gone, none knew whither: the proud people, deathless but doomed, from far beyond the Sea. And he turned and looked, as often their eyes had looked, out across the glitter of the unquiet waters to the end of sight. Then he turned back again, and saw that the swans had alighted on the highest terrace, and stood before the west-door of the hall; and they beat their wings, and it seemed to him that they beckoned him to enter. Then Tuor went up the wide stairs, now half-hidden in thrift and campion, and he passed under the mighty lintel and entered the shadows of the house of Turgon; and he came at last to a high-pillared hall. If great it had appeared from without, now vast and wonderful it seemed to Tuor from within, and for awe he wished not to awake the echoes in its emptiness. Nothing could he see there, save at the eastern end a high seat upon a dais, and softly as he might he paced towards it; but the sound of his feet rang upon the paved floor as the steps of doom, and echoes ran before him along the pillared aisles.

As he stood before the great chair in the gloom, and saw that it was hewn of a single stone and written with strange signs, the sinking sun drew level with a high window under the westward gable, and a shaft of light smote the wall before him, and glittered as it were upon burnished metal. Then Tuor marvelling saw that on the wall behind the throne there hung a shield and a great hauberk, and a helm and a long sword in a sheath. The hauberk shone as it were wrought of silver untarnished, and the sunbeam gilded it with sparks of gold. But the shield was of a shape strange to Tuor's eyes, for it was long and tapering; and its field was blue, in the midst of which was wrought an emblem of a white swan's wing. Then Tuor spoke, and his voice rang as a challenge in the roof: 'By this token I will take these arms unto myself, and upon myself whatsoever doom they bear.'[6] And he lifted down the shield and found it light and wieldy beyond his guess; for it was wrought, it seemed, of wood, but overlaid by the craft of elven-smiths with plates of metal, strong yet thin as foil, whereby it had been preserved from worm and weather.

Then Tuor arrayed himself in the hauberk, and set the helm upon his head, and he girt himself with the sword; black were sheath and belt with clasps of silver. Thus armed he went forth from Turgon's hall, and stood upon the high terraces of Taras in the red light of the sun. None were there to see him, as he gazed westward, gleaming in silver and gold, and he knew not that in that hour he appeared as one of the Mighty of the West, and fit to be the father of the kings of the Kings of Men beyond the Sea, as it was indeed his doom to be;[7] but in the taking of those arms a change came upon Tuor son of Huor, and his heart grew great within him. And as he stepped down from the doors the swans did him reverence, and plucking each a great feather from their wings they proffered them to him, laying their long necks upon the stone before his feet; and he took

the seven feathers and set them in the crest of his helm, and straightway the swans arose and flew north in the sunset, and Tuor saw
them no more.

Now Tuor felt his feet drawn to the sea-strand, and he went down
by long stairs to a wide shore upon the north side of Taras-ness;
and as he went he saw that the sun was sinking low into a great
black cloud that came up over the rim of the darkening sea; and it
grew cold, and there was a stirring and murmur as of a storm to come.
And Tuor stood upon the shore, and the sun was like a smoky fire
behind the menace of the sky; and it seemed to him that a great
wave rose far off and rolled towards the land, but wonder held him,
and he remained there unmoved. And the wave came towards him,
and upon it lay a mist of shadow. Then suddenly as it drew near it
curled, and broke, and rushed forward in long arms of foam; but
where it had broken there stood dark against the rising storm a
living shape of great height and majesty.

Then Tuor bowed in reverence, for it seemed to him that he beheld
a mighty king. A tall crown he wore like silver, from which his long
hair fell down as foam glimmering in the dusk; and as he cast back
the grey mantle that hung about him like a mist, behold! he was clad
in a gleaming coat, close-fitted as the mail of a mighty fish, and in a
kirtle of deep green that flashed and flickered with sea-fire as he
strode slowly towards the land. In this manner the Dweller of the
Deep, whom the Noldor name Ulmo, Lord of Waters, showed
himself to Tuor son of Huor of the House of Hador beneath Vinyamar.

He set no foot upon the shore, but standing knee-deep in the
shadowy sea he spoke to Tuor, and then for the light of his eyes and
for the sound of his deep voice that came as it seemed from the
foundations of the world, fear fell upon Tuor and he cast himself
down upon the sand.

'Arise, Tuor, son of Huor!' said Ulmo. 'Fear not my wrath,
though long have I called to thee unheard; and setting out at last
thou hast tarried on thy journey hither. In the Spring thou shouldst
have stood here; but now a fell winter cometh soon from the land
of the Enemy. Haste thou must learn, and the pleasant road that I
designed for thee must be changed. For my counsels have been
scorned,[8] and a great evil creeps upon the Valley of Sirion, and
already a host of foes is come between thee and thy goal.'

'What then is my goal, Lord?' said Tuor.

'That which thy heart hath ever sought,' answered Ulmo: 'to find
Turgon, and look upon the hidden city. For thou art arrayed thus

to be my messenger, even in the arms which long ago I decreed for thee. Yet now thou must under shadow pass through peril. Wrap thyself therefore in this cloak, and cast it never aside, until thou come to thy journey's end.'

Then it seemed to Tuor that Ulmo parted his grey mantle, and cast to him a lappet, and as it fell about him it was for him a great cloak wherein he might wrap himself over all, from head to foot.

'Thus thou shalt walk under my shadow,' said Ulmo. 'But tarry no more; for in the lands of Anar and in the fires of Melkor it will not endure. Wilt thou take up my errand?'

'I will, Lord,' said Tuor.

'Then I will set words in thy mouth to say unto Turgon,' said Ulmo. 'But first I will teach thee, and some things thou shalt hear which no Man else hath heard, nay, not even the mighty among the Eldar.' And Ulmo spoke to Tuor of Valinor and its darkening, and the Exile of the Noldor, and the Doom of Mandos, and the hiding of the Blessed Realm. 'But behold!' said he, 'in the armour of Fate (as the Children of Earth name it) there is ever a rift, and in the walls of Doom a breach, until the full-making, which ye call the End. So it shall be while I endure, a secret voice that gainsayeth, and a light where darkness was decreed. Therefore, though in the days of this darkness I seem to oppose the will of my brethren, the Lords of the West, that is my part among them, to which I was appointed ere the making of the World. Yet Doom is strong, and the shadow of the Enemy lengthens; and I am diminished, until in Middle-earth I am become now no more than a secret whisper. The waters that run westward wither, and their springs are poisoned, and my power withdraws from the land; for Elves and Men grow blind and deaf to me because of the might of Melkor. And now the Curse of Mandos hastens to its fulfilment, and all the works of the Noldor shall perish, and every hope which they build shall crumble. The last hope alone is left, the hope that they have not looked for and have not prepared. And that hope lieth in thee; for so I have chosen.'

'Then shall Turgon not stand against Morgoth, as all the Eldar yet hope?' said Tuor. 'And what wouldst thou of me, Lord, if I come now to Turgon? For though I am indeed willing to do as my father and stand by that king in his need, yet of little avail shall I be, a mortal man alone, among so many and so valiant of the High Folk of the West.'

'If I choose to send thee, Tuor son of Huor, then believe not that thy one sword is not worth the sending. For the valour of the Edain the Elves shall ever remember as the ages lengthen, marvelling that they gave life so freely of which they had on earth so little. But it is not for thy valour only that I send thee, but to bring into the world a hope beyond thy sight, and a light that shall pierce the darkness.' And as Ulmo said these things the mutter of the storm rose to a great cry, and the wind mounted, and the sky grew black; and the mantle of the Lord of Waters streamed out like a flying cloud. 'Go now,' said Ulmo, 'lest the Sea devour thee! For Ossë obeys the will of Mandos, and he is wroth, being a servant of the Doom.'

'As thou commandest,' said Tuor. 'But if I escape the Doom, what words shall I say unto Turgon?'

'If thou come to him,' answered Ulmo, 'then the words shall arise in thy mind, and thy mouth shall speak as I would. Speak and fear not! And thereafter do as thy heart and valour lead thee. Hold fast to my mantle, for thus shalt thou be guarded. And I will send one to thee out of the wrath of Ossë, and thus shalt thou be guided: yea, the last mariner of the last ship that shall seek into the West until the rising of the Star. Go now back to the land!'

Then there was a noise of thunder, and lightning flared over the sea; and Tuor beheld Ulmo standing among the waves as a tower of silver flickering with darting flames; and he cried against the wind: 'I go, Lord! Yet now my heart yearneth rather to the Sea.'

And thereupon Ulmo lifted up a mighty horn, and blew upon it a single great note, to which the roaring of the storm was but a wind-flaw upon a lake. And as he heard that note, and was encompassed by it, and filled with it, it seemed to Tuor that the coasts of Middle-earth vanished, and he surveyed all the waters of the world in a great vision: from the veins of the lands to the mouths of the rivers, and from the strands and estuaries out into the deep. The Great Sea he saw through its unquiet regions teeming with strange forms, even to its lightless depths, in which amid the everlasting darkness there echoed voices terrible to mortal ears. Its measureless plains he surveyed with the swift sight of the Valar, lying windless under the eye of Anar, or glittering under the horned Moon, or lifted in hills of wrath that broke upon the Shadowy Isles,[9] until remote upon the edge of sight, and beyond the count of leagues, he glimpsed a mountain, rising beyond his mind's reach into a shining cloud, and at its feet a long surf glimmering. And even as he strained to hear the sound of those far waves, and to see clearer that distant light, the note ended, and he stood beneath the thunder of the storm, and lightning many-branched rent asunder the heavens above him. And Ulmo was gone, and the sea was in tumult, as the wild waves of Ossë rode against the walls of Nevrast.

Then Tuor fled from the fury of the sea, and with labour he won his way back to the high terraces; for the wind drove him against the cliff, and when he came out upon the top it bent him to his knees. Therefore he entered again the dark and empty hall for shelter, and he sat nightlong in the stone seat of Turgon. The very pillars trembled for the violence of the storm, and it seemed to Tuor that the wind was full of wailing and wild cries. Yet being weary he slept at times, and his sleep was troubled with many dreams, of which naught remained in waking memory save one: a vision of an isle, and in the midst of it was a steep mountain, and behind it the sun went down, and shadows sprang into the sky; but above it there shone a single dazzling star.

After this dream Tuor fell into a deep sleep, for before the night was over the tempest passed, driving the black clouds into the East of the world. He awoke at length in the grey light, and arose, and left the high seat, and as he went down the dim hall he saw that it was filled with sea-birds driven in by the storm; and he went out as the last stars were fading in the West before the coming day. Then he saw that the great waves in the night had ridden high upon the land, and had cast their crests above the cliff-tops, and weed and shingle-drift were flung even upon the terraces before the doors. And Tuor looked down from the lowest terrace and saw, leaning against its wall among the stones and the sea-wrack, an Elf, clad in a grey cloak sodden with the sea. Silent he sat, gazing beyond the ruin of the beaches out over the long ridges of the waves. All was still, and there was no sound save the roaring of the surf below.

As Tuor stood and looked at the silent grey figure he remembered the words of Ulmo, and a name untaught came to his lips, and he called aloud: 'Welcome, Voronwë! I await you.'[10]

Then the Elf turned and looked up, and Tuor met the piercing glance of his sea-grey eyes, and knew that he was of the high folk of the Noldor. But fear and wonder grew in his gaze as he saw Tuor standing high upon the wall above him, clad in his great cloak like a shadow out of which the elven-mail gleamed upon his breast.

A moment thus they stayed, each searching the face of the other, and then the Elf stood up and bowed low before Tuor's feet. 'Who are you, lord?' he said. 'Long have I laboured in the unrelenting sea. Tell me: have great tidings befallen since I walked the land? Is the Shadow overthrown? Have the Hidden People come forth?'

'Nay,' Tuor answered. 'The Shadow lengthens, and the Hidden remain hid.'

Then Voronwë looked at him long in silence. 'But who are you?'

he asked again. 'For many years ago my people left this land, and none have dwelt here since. And now I perceive that despite your raiment you are not of them, as I thought, but are of the kindred of Men.'

'I am,' said Tuor. 'And are you not the last mariner of the last ship that sought the West from the Havens of Círdan?'

'I am,' said the Elf. 'Voronwë son of Aranwë am I. But how you know my name and fate I understand not.'

'I know, for the Lord of Waters spoke to me yestereve,' answered Tuor, 'and he said that he would save you from the wrath of Ossë, and send you hither to be my guide.'

Then in fear and wonder Voronwë cried: 'You have spoken with Ulmo the Mighty? Then great indeed must be your worth and doom! But whither should I guide you, lord? For surely a king of Men you must be, and many must wait upon your word.'

'Nay, I am an escaped thrall,' said Tuor, 'and I am an outlaw alone in an empty land. But I have an errand to Turgon the Hidden King. Know you by what road I may find him?'

'Many are outlaw and thrall in these evil days who were not born so,' answered Voronwë. 'A lord of Men by right you are, I deem. But were you the highest of all your folk, no right would you have to seek Turgon, and vain would be your quest. For even were I to lead you to his gates, you could not enter in.'

'I do not bid you to lead me further than the gate,' said Tuor. 'There Doom shall strive with the Counsel of Ulmo. And if Turgon will not receive me, then my errand will be ended, and Doom shall prevail. But as for my right to seek Turgon: I am Tuor son of Huor and kin to Húrin, whose names Turgon will not forget. And I seek also by the command of Ulmo. Will Turgon forget that which he spoke to him of old: *Remember that the last hope of the Noldor cometh from the Sea*? Or again: *When peril is nigh one shall come from Nevrast to warn thee*?[11] I am he that should come, and I am arrayed thus in the gear that was prepared for me.'

Tuor marvelled to hear himself speak so, for the words of Ulmo to Turgon at his going from Nevrast were not known to him before, nor to any save the Hidden People. Therefore the more amazed was Voronwë; but he turned away, and looked toward the Sea, and he sighed.

'Alas!' he said. 'I wish never again to return. And often have I vowed in the deeps of the sea that, if ever I set foot on land again, I would dwell at rest far from the Shadow in the North, or by the Havens of Círdan, or maybe in the fair fields of Nan-tathren, where

the spring is sweeter than heart's desire. But if evil has grown while
I have wandered, and the last peril approaches them, then I must
go to my people.' He turned back to Tuor. 'I will lead you to the
hidden gates,' he said; 'for the wise will not gainsay the counsels of
Ulmo.'

'Then we will go together, as we are counselled,' said Tuor. 'But
mourn not, Voronwë! For my heart says to you that far from the
Shadow your long road shall lead you, and your hope shall return to
the Sea.'[12]

'And yours also,' said Voronwë. 'But now we must leave it, and go
in haste.'

'Yea,' said Tuor. 'But whither will you lead me, and how far?
Shall we not first take thought how we may fare in the wild, or if the
way be long, how pass the harbourless winter?'

But Voronwë would answer nothing clearly concerning the road.
'You know the strength of Men,' he said. 'As for me, I am of the
Noldor, and long must be the hunger and cold the winter that shall
slay the kin of those who passed the Grinding Ice. Yet how think
you that we could labour countless days in the salt wastes of the sea?
Or have you not heard of the waybread of the Elves? And I keep
still that which all mariners hold until the last.' Then he showed
beneath his cloak a sealed wallet clasped upon his belt. 'No water
nor weather will harm it while it is sealed. But we must husband it
until great need; and doubtless an outlaw and hunter may find other
food ere the year worsens.'

'Maybe,' said Tuor. 'But not in all lands is it safe to hunt, be the
game never so plentiful. And hunters tarry on the road.'

Now Tuor and Voronwë made ready to depart. Tuor took with
him the small bow and arrows that he had brought, beside the gear
that he had taken from the hall; but his spear, upon which his name
was written in the elven-runes of the North, he set upon the wall in
token that he had passed. No arms had Voronwë save a short sword
only.

Before the day was broad they left the ancient dwelling of Turgon,
and Voronwë led Tuor about, westward of the steep slopes of Taras,
and across the great cape. There once the road from Nevrast to
Brithombar had passed, that now was but a green track between old
turf-clad dikes. So they came into Beleriand, and the north region of
the Falas; and turning eastward they sought the dark eaves of Ered
Wethrin, and there they lay hid and rested until day had waned to
dusk. For though the ancient dwellings of the Falathrim, Brithombar

and Eglarest, were still far distant, Orcs now dwelt there and all the land was infested by the spies of Morgoth: he feared the ships of Círdan that would come at times raiding to the shores, and join with the forays sent forth from Nargothrond.

Now as they sat shrouded in their cloaks as shadows under the hills, Tuor and Voronwë spoke much together. And Tuor questioned Voronwë concerning Turgon, but Voronwë would tell little of such matters, and spoke rather of the dwellings upon the Isle of Balar, and of the Lisgardh, the land of reeds at the Mouths of Sirion.

'There now the numbers of the Eldar increase,' he said, 'for ever more flee thither of either kin from the fear of Morgoth, weary of war. But I forsook not my people of my own choice. For after the Bragollach and the breaking of the Siege of Angband doubt first came into Turgon's heart that Morgoth might prove too strong. In that year he sent out the first of his folk that passed his gates from within: a few only, upon a secret errand. They went down Sirion to the shores about the Mouths, and there built ships. But it availed them nothing, save to come to the great Isle of Balar and there establish lonely dwellings, far from the reach of Morgoth. For the Noldor have not the art of building ships that will long endure the waves of Belegaer the Great.[13]

'But when later Turgon heard of the ravaging of the Falas and the sack of the ancient Havens of the Shipwrights that lie away there before us, and it was told that Círdan had saved a remnant of his people and sailed away south to the Bay of Balar, then he sent out messengers anew. That was but a little while ago, yet it seems in memory the longest portion of my life. For I was one of those that he sent, being young in years among the Eldar. I was born here in Middle-earth in the land of Nevrast. My mother was of the Grey-elves of the Falas, and akin to Círdan himself – there was much mingling of the peoples in Nevrast in the first days of Turgon's kingship – and I have the sea-heart of my mother's people. Therefore I was among the chosen, since our errand was to Círdan, to seek his aid in our shipbuilding, that some message and prayer for aid might come to the Lords of the West ere all was lost. But I tarried on the way. For I had seen little of the lands of Middle-earth, and we came to Nan-tathren in the spring of the year. Lovely to heart's enchantment is that land, Tuor, as you shall find, if ever your feet go upon the southward roads down Sirion. There is the cure of all sea-longing, save for those whom Doom will not release. There Ulmo is but the servant of Yavanna, and the earth has brought to life a wealth of fair things that is beyond the thought of hearts in the hard hills of the North. In that land Narog joins Sirion, and they haste no more, but flow broad and quiet through living meads; and all about the shining river are flaglilies like a blossoming forest, and the grass is filled with flowers, like gems, like bells, like flames of red and gold, like a waste of many-coloured stars in a firmament of green. Yet fairest of all are the willows of Nan-tathren, pale green, or silver in the wind, and the rustle of their innumerable leaves is a spell of music: day and night would flicker by uncounted, while still I stood knee-deep in grass and listened. There I was enchanted, and forgot the Sea in my heart. There I wandered, naming new flowers, or lay adream amid the singing of the birds, and the humming of bees and flies; and there I might still dwell in delight, forsaking all my kin, whether the ships of the Teleri or the swords of the Noldor, but my doom would not so. Or the Lord of Waters himself, maybe; for he was strong in that land.

'Thus it came into my heart to make a raft of willow-boughs and move upon the bright bosom of Sirion; and so I did, and so I was taken. For on a day, as I was in the midst of the river, a sudden wind came and caught me, and bore me away out of the Land of Willows down to the Sea. Thus I came last of the messengers to Círdan; and of the seven ships that he built at Turgon's asking all but one were then full-wrought. And one by one they set sail into the West, and none yet has ever returned, nor has any news of them been heard.

'But the salt air of the sea now stirred anew the heart of my mother's kin within me, and I rejoiced in the waves, learning all ship-lore, as were it already stored in the mind. So when the last ship, and the greatest, was made ready, I was eager to be gone, saying within my thought: "If the words of the Noldor be true, then in the West there are meads with which the Land of Willows cannot compare. There is no withering nor any end of Spring. And perhaps even I, Voronwë, may come thither. And at the worst to wander on the waters is better far than the Shadow in the North." And I feared not, for the ships of the Teleri no water may drown.

'But the Great Sea is terrible, Tuor son of Huor; and it hates the Noldor, for it works the Doom of the Valar. Worse things it holds than to sink into the abyss and so perish: loathing, and loneliness, and madness; terror of wind and tumult, and silence, and shadows where all hope is lost and all living shapes pass away. And many shores evil and strange it washes, and many islands of danger and fear infest it. I will not darken your heart, son of Middle-earth, with the tale of my labour seven years in the Great Sea from the North even into the South, but never to the West. For that is shut against us.

'At the last, in black despair, weary of all the world, we turned and fled from the doom that so long had spared us, only to strike us the more cruelly. For even as we descried a mountain from afar, and I cried: "Lo! There is Taras, and the land of my birth," the wind awoke, and great clouds thunder-laden came up from the West. Then the waves hunted us like living things filled with malice, and the lightnings smote us; and when we were broken down to a helpless hull the seas leaped upon us in fury. But as you see, I was spared; for it seemed to me that there came a wave, greater and yet calmer than all the others, and it took me and lifted me from the ship, and bore me high upon its shoulders, and rolling to the land it cast me upon the turf, and then drained away, pouring back over the cliff in a great waterfall. There but one hour had I sat when you came upon me, still dazed by the sea. And still I feel the fear of it, and the bitter loss of all my friends that went with me so long and so far, beyond the sight of mortal lands.'

Voronwë sighed, and spoke then softly as if to himself. 'But very bright were the stars upon the margin of the world, when at times the clouds about the West were drawn aside. Yet whether we saw only clouds still more remote, or glimpsed indeed, as some held, the Mountains of the Pelóri about the lost strands of our long home, I know not. Far, far away they stand, and none from mortal lands shall come there ever again, I deem.' Then Voronwë fell silent; for night had come, and the stars shone white and cold.

Soon after Tuor and Voronwë arose and turned their backs toward the sea, and set out upon their long journey in the dark; of which there is little to tell, for the shadow of Ulmo was upon Tuor, and none saw them pass, by wood or stone, by field or fen, between the setting and the rising of the sun. But ever warily they went, shunning the night-eyed hunters of Morgoth, and forsaking the trodden ways of Elves and Men. Voronwë chose their path and Tuor followed. He asked no vain questions, but noted well that they went ever eastward along the march of the rising mountains, and turned never southward: at which he wondered, for he believed, as did well nigh all Elves and Men, that Turgon dwelt far from the battles of the North.

Slow was their going by twilight or by night in the pathless wilds, and the fell winter came down swiftly from the realm of Morgoth. Despite the shelter of the hills the winds were strong and bitter, and soon the snow lay deep upon the heights, or whirled through the passes, and fell upon the woods of Núath ere the full-shedding of their withered leaves.[14] Thus though they set out before the middle of

Narquelië, the Hísimë came in with biting frost even as they drew nigh to the Sources of Narog.

There at the end of a weary night in the grey of dawn they halted; and Voronwë was dismayed, looking about him in grief and fear. Where once the fair pool of Ivrin had lain in its great stone basin carved by falling waters, and all about it had been a tree-clad hollow under the hills, now he saw a land defiled and desolate. The trees were burned or uprooted; and the stone-marges of the pool were broken, so that the waters of Ivrin strayed and wrought a great barren marsh amid the ruin. All now was but a welter of frozen mire, and a reek of decay lay like a foul mist upon the ground.

'Alas! Has the evil come even here?' Voronwë cried. 'Once far from the threat of Angband was this place; but ever the fingers of Morgoth grope further.'

'It is even as Ulmo spoke to me,' said Tuor: '*The springs are poisoned, and my power withdraws from the waters of the land.*'

'Yet,' said Voronwë, 'a malice has been here with strength greater than that of Orcs. Fear lingers in this place.' And he searched about the edges of the mire, until suddenly he stood still and cried again: 'Yea, a great evil!' And he beckoned to Tuor, and Tuor coming saw a slot like a huge furrow that passed away southward, and at either side, now blurred, now sealed hard and clear by frost, the marks of great clawed feet. 'See!' said Voronwë, and his face was pale with dread and loathing. 'Here not long since was the Great Worm of Angband, most fell of all the creatures of the Enemy! Late already is our errand to Turgon. There is need of haste.'

Even as he spoke thus, they heard a cry in the woods, and they stood still as grey stones, listening. But the voice was a fair voice, though filled with grief, and it seemed that it called ever upon a name, as one that searches for another who is lost. And as they waited one came through the trees, and they saw that he was a tall Man, armed, clad in black, with a long sword drawn; and they wondered, for the blade of the sword also was black, but the edges shone bright and cold. Woe was graven in his face, and when he beheld the ruin of Ivrin he cried aloud in grief, saying: 'Ivrin, Faelivrin! Gwindor and Beleg! Here once I was healed. But now never shall I drink the draught of peace again.'

Then he went swiftly away towards the North, as one in pursuit, or on an errand of great haste, and they heard him cry *Faelivrin, Finduilas!* until his voice died away in the woods.[15] But they knew not that Nargothrond had fallen, and this was Túrin son of Húrin, the Blacksword. Thus only for a moment, and never again, did the paths of those kinsmen, Túrin and Tuor, draw together.

When the Blacksword had passed, Tuor and Voronwë held on their way for a while, though day had come; for the memory of his grief was heavy upon them, and they could not endure to remain beside the defilement of Ivrin. But before long they sought a hiding-place, for all the land was filled now with a foreboding of evil. They slept little and uneasily, and as the day wore it grew dark and a great snow fell, and with the night came a grinding frost. Thereafter the snow and ice relented not at all, and for five months the Fell Winter, long remembered, held the North in bonds. Now Tuor and Voronwë were tormented by the cold, and feared to be revealed by the snow to hunting enemies, or to fall into hidden dangers treacherously cloaked. Nine days they held on, ever slower and more painfully, and Voronwë turned somewhat north, until they crossed the three well-streams of Teiglin; and then he bore eastward again, leaving the mountains, and went warily, until they passed Glithui and came to the stream of Malduin, and it was frozen black.[16]

Then Tuor said to Voronwë: 'Fell is this frost, and death draws near to me, if not to you.' For they were now in evil case: it was long since they had found any food in the wild, and the waybread was dwindling; and they were cold and weary. 'Ill is it to be trapped between the Doom of the Valar and the Malice of the Enemy,' said Voronwë. 'Have I escaped the mouths of the sea but to lie under the snow?'

But Tuor said: 'How far is now to go? For at last, Voronwë, you must forgo your secrecy with me. Do you lead me straight, and whither? For if I must spend my last strength, I would know to what that may avail.'

'I have led you as straight as I safely might,' answered Voronwë. 'Know then now that Turgon dwells still in the north of the land of the Eldar, though that is believed by few. Already we draw nigh to him. Yet there are many leagues still to go, even as a bird might fly; and for us Sirion is yet to cross, and great evil, maybe, lies between. For we must come soon to the Highway that ran of old down from the Minas of King Finrod to Nargothrond.[17] There the servants of the Enemy will walk and watch.'

'I counted myself the hardiest of Men,' said Tuor, 'and I have endured many winters' woe in the mountains; but I had a cave at my back and fire then, and I doubt now my strength to go much further thus hungry through the fell weather. But let us go on as far as we may before hope fails.'

'No other choice have we,' said Voronwë, 'unless it be to lay us down here and seek the snow-sleep.'

Therefore all through that bitter day they toiled on, deeming the peril of foes less than the winter; but ever as they went they found less snow, for they were now going southward again down into the Vale of Sirion, and the Mountains of Dor-lómin were left far behind. In the deepening dusk they came to the Highway at the bottom of a tall wooded bank. Suddenly they were aware of voices, and looking out warily from the trees they saw a red light below. A company of Orcs was encamped in the midst of the road, huddled about a large wood-fire.

'*Gurth an Glamhoth!*' Tuor muttered.[18] 'Now the sword shall come from under the cloak. I will risk death for mastery of that fire, and even the meat of Orcs would be a prize.'

'Nay!' said Voronwë. 'On this quest only the cloak will serve. You must forgo the fire, or else forgo Turgon. This band is not alone in the wild: cannot your mortal sight see the far flame of other posts to the north and to the south? A tumult will bring a host upon us. Hearken to me, Tuor! It is against the law of the Hidden Kingdom that any should approach the gates with foes at their heels; and that law I will not break, neither for Ulmo's bidding, nor for death. Rouse the Orcs, and I leave you.'

'Then let them be,' said Tuor. 'But may I live yet to see the day when I need not sneak aside from a handful of Orcs like a cowed dog.'

'Come then!' said Voronwë. 'Debate no more, or they will scent us. Follow me!'

He crept then away through the trees, southward down the wind, until they were midway between that Orc-fire and the next upon the road. There he stood still a long while listening.

'I hear none moving on the road,' he said, 'but we know not what may be lurking in the shadows.' He peered forward into the gloom and shuddered. 'The air is evil,' he muttered. 'Alas! Yonder lies the land of our quest and hope of life, but death walks between.'

'Death is all about us,' said Tuor. 'But I have strength left only for the shortest road. Here I must cross, or perish. I will trust to the mantle of Ulmo, and you also it shall cover. Now I will lead!'

So saying he stole to the border of the road. Then clasping Voronwë close he cast about them both the folds of the grey cloak of the Lord of Waters, and stepped forth.

All was still. The cold wind sighed as it swept down the ancient road. Then suddenly it too fell silent. In the pause Tuor felt a change in the air, as if the breath from the land of Morgoth had failed a while, and faint as a memory of the Sea came a breeze from the West. As a grey mist on the wind they passed over the stony street and entered a thicket on its eastern brink.

All at once from near at hand there came a wild cry, and many others along the borders of the road answered it. A harsh horn blared, and there was the sound of running feet. But Tuor held on. He had learned enough of the tongue of the Orcs in his captivity to know the meaning of those cries: the watchers had scented them and heard them, but they were not seen. The hunt was out. Desperately he stumbled and crept forward with Voronwë at his side, up a long slope deep in whin and whortleberry among knots of rowan and low birch. At the top of the ridge they halted, listening to the shouts behind and the crashing of the Orcs in the undergrowth below.

Beside them was a boulder that reared its head out of a tangle of heath and brambles, and beneath it was such a lair as a hunted beast might seek and hope there to escape pursuit, or at the least with its back to stone to sell its life dearly. Down into the dark shadow Tuor drew Voronwë, and side by side under the grey cloak they lay and panted like tired foxes. No word they spoke; all their heed was in their ears.

The cries of the hunters grew fainter; for the Orcs thrust never deep into the wild lands at either hand, but swept rather down and up the road. They recked little of stray fugitives, but spies they feared and the scouts of armed foes; for Morgoth had set a guard on the highway, not to ensnare Tuor and Voronwë (of whom as yet he knew nothing) nor any coming from the West, but to watch for the Blacksword, lest he should escape and pursue the captives of Nargothrond, bringing help, it might be, out of Doriath.

The night passed, and the brooding silence lay again upon the empty lands. Weary and spent Tuor slept beneath Ulmo's cloak; but Voronwë crept forth and stood like a stone silent, unmoving, piercing the shadows with his Elvish eyes. At the break of day he woke Tuor, and he creeping out saw that the weather had indeed for a time relented, and the black clouds were rolled aside. There was a red dawn, and he could see far before him the tops of strange mountains glinting against the eastern fire.

Then Voronwë said in a low voice: '*Alae! Ered en Echoriath, ered e·mbar nin!*'[19] For he knew that he looked on the Encircling Mountains and the walls of the realm of Turgon. Below them, eastward, in a deep and shadowy vale lay Sirion the fair, renowned in song; and beyond, wrapped in mist, a grey land climbed from the river to the broken hills at the mountains' feet. 'Yonder lies Dimbar,' said Voronwë. 'Would we were there! For there our foes seldom dare to walk. Or so it was, while the power of Ulmo was strong in Sirion. But all may now be changed[20] – save the peril of the river: it is already deep and swift, and even for the Eldar dangerous to cross. But I have led you well; for there gleams the Ford of Brithiach, yet a little southward, where the East Road that of old ran all the way from Taras in the West made the passage of the river. None now dare to use it save in desperate need, neither Elf nor Man nor Orc, since that road leads to Dungortheb and the land of dread between the Gorgoroth and the Girdle of Melian; and long since has it faded into the wild, or dwindled to a track among weeds and trailing thorns.'[21]

Then Tuor looked as Voronwë pointed, and far away he caught the glimmer as of open waters under the brief light of dawn; but beyond loomed a darkness, where the great forest of Brethil climbed away southward into a distant highland. Now warily they made their way down the valley-side, until at last they came to the ancient road descending from the waymeet on the borders of Brethil, where it crossed the highway from Nargothrond. Then Tuor saw that they were come close to Sirion. The banks of its deep channel fell away in that place, and its waters, choked by a great waste of stones,[22] were spread out into broad shallows, full of the murmur of fretting streams. Then after a little the river gathered together again, and delving a new bed flowed away towards the forest, and far off vanished into a deep mist that his eye could not pierce; for there lay, though he knew it not, the north march of Doriath within the shadow of the Girdle of Melian.

At once Tuor would hasten to the ford, but Voronwë restrained him, saying: 'Over the Brithiach we may not go in open day, nor while any doubt of pursuit remains.'

'Then shall we sit here and rot?' said Tuor. 'For such doubt will remain while the realm of Morgoth endures. Come! Under the shadow of the cloak of Ulmo we must go forward.'

Still Voronwë hesitated, and looked back westward; but the track behind was deserted, and all about was quiet save for the rush of the waters. He looked up, and the sky was grey and empty, for not even a bird was moving. Then suddenly his face brightened with joy, and he cried aloud: 'It is well! The Brithiach is guarded still by the enemies of the Enemy. The Orcs will not follow us here; and under the cloak we may pass now without more doubt.'

'What new thing have you seen?' said Tuor.

'Short is the sight of Mortal Men!' said Voronwë. 'I see the Eagles of the Crissaegrim; and they are coming hither. Watch a while!'

Then Tuor stood at gaze; and soon high in the air he saw three shapes beating on strong wings down from the distant mountain-peaks now wreathed again in cloud. Slowly they descended in great circles, and then stooped suddenly upon the wayfarers; but before Voronwë could call to them they turned with a wide sweep and rush, and flew northward along the line of the river.

'Now let us go,' said Voronwë. 'If there be any Orc nearby, he will lie cowering nose to ground, until the eagles have gone far away.'

Swiftly down a long slope they hastened, and passed over the Brithiach, walking often dryfoot upon shelves of shingle, or wading in the shoals no more than knee-deep. The water was clear and very cold, and there was ice upon the shallow pools, where the wandering streams had lost their way among the stones; but never, not even in the Fell Winter of the Fall of Nargothrond, could the deadly breath of the North freeze the main flood of Sirion.[23]

On the far side of the ford they came to a gully, as it were the bed of an old stream, in which no water now flowed; yet once, it seemed, a torrent had cloven its deep channel, coming down from the north out of the mountains of the Echoriath, and bearing thence all the stones of the Brithiach down into Sirion.

'At last beyond hope we find it!' cried Voronwë. 'See! Here is the mouth of the Dry River, and that is the road we must take.'[24] Then they passed into the gully, and as it turned north and the slopes of the land went steeply up, so its sides rose upon either hand, and Tuor stumbled in the dim light among the stones with which its rough bed was strewn. 'If this is a road,' he said, 'it is an evil one for the weary.'

'Yet it is the road to Turgon,' said Voronwë.

'Then the more do I marvel,' said Tuor, 'that its entrance lies open and unguarded. I had looked to find a great gate, and strength of guard.'

'That you shall yet see,' said Voronwë. 'This is but the approach. A road I named it; yet upon it none have passed for more than three hundred years, save messengers few and secret, and all the craft of the Noldor has been expended to conceal it, since the Hidden People entered in. Does it lie open? Would you have known it, if you had not had one of the Hidden Kingdom for a guide? Or would you have guessed it to be but the work of the weathers and the waters of the wilderness? And are there not the Eagles, as you have seen? They are the folk of Thorondor, who dwelt once even on Thangorodrim ere Morgoth grew so mighty, and dwell now in the Mountains of Turgon since the fall of Fingolfin.[25] They alone save the Noldor know the Hidden Kingdom and guard the skies above it, though as yet no servant of the Enemy has dared to fly into the high airs; and they bring much news to the King of all that moves in the lands without. Had we been Orcs, doubt not that we should have been seized, and cast from a great height upon the pitiless rocks.'

'I doubt it not,' said Tuor. 'But it comes into my mind to wonder also whether news will not now come to Turgon of our approach swifter than we. And if that be good or ill, you alone can say.'

'Neither good nor ill,' said Voronwë. 'For we cannot pass the Guarded Gate unmarked, be we looked for or no; and if we come there the Guards will need no report that we are not Orcs. But to pass we shall need a greater plea than that. For you do not guess, Tuor, the peril that we then shall face. Blame me not, as one un-warned, for what may then betide; may the power of the Lord of Waters be shown indeed! For in that hope alone have I been willing to guide you, and if it fails then more surely shall we die than by all the perils of wild and winter.'

But Tuor said: 'Forebode no more. Death in the wild is certain; and death at the Gate is yet in doubt to me, for all your words. Lead me still on!'

Many miles they toiled on in the stones of the Dry River, until they could go no further, and the evening brought darkness into the deep cleft; they climbed out then on to the east bank, and they had now come into the tumbled hills that lay at the feet of the mountains. And looking up Tuor saw that they towered up in a fashion other than that of any mountains that he had seen; for their sides were like sheer walls, piled each one above and behind the lower, as were they great towers of many-storeyed precipices. But the day had waned, and all the lands were grey and misty, and the Vale of Sirion was shrouded in shadow. Then Voronwë led him to a shallow cave in a hillside that looked out over the lonely slopes of Dimbar, and they crept within, and there they lay hid; and they ate their last crumbs of food, and were cold, and weary, but slept not. Thus did Tuor and Voronwë come in the dusk of the eighteenth day of Hísimë, the thirty-seventh of their journey, to the towers of the Echoriath and the threshold of Turgon, and by the power of Ulmo escaped both the Doom and the Malice.

When the first glimmer of day filtered grey amid the mists of Dimbar they crept back into the Dry River, and soon after its course turned eastward, winding up to the very walls of the mountains; and straight before them there loomed a great precipice, rising sheer and sudden from a steep slope upon which grew a tangled thicket of thorn-trees. Into this thicket the stony channel entered, and there it was still dark as night; and they halted, for the thorns grew far down the sides of the gully, and their lacing branches were a dense roof above it, so low that often Tuor and Voronwë must crawl under like beasts stealing back to their lair.

But at last, as with great labour they came to the very foot of the cliff, they found an opening, as it were the mouth of a tunnel worn in the hard rock by waters flowing from the heart of the mountains. They entered, and within there was no light, but Voronwë went steadily forward, while Tuor followed with his hand upon his shoulder, bending a little, for the roof was low. Thus for a time they went on blindly, step by step, until presently they felt the ground beneath their feet had become level and free from loose stones. Then they halted and breathed deeply, as they stood listening. The air seemed fresh and wholesome, and they were aware of a great space around and above them; but all was silent, and not even the drip of water could be heard. It seemed to Tuor that Voronwë was troubled and in doubt, and he whispered: 'Where then is the Guarded Gate? Or have we indeed now passed it?'

'Nay,' said Voronwë. 'Yet I wonder, for it is strange that any incomer should creep thus far unchallenged. I fear some stroke in the dark.'

But their whispers aroused the sleeping echoes, and they were enlarged and multiplied, and ran in the roof and the unseen walls, hissing and murmuring as the sound of many stealthy voices. And even as the echoes died in the stone, Tuor heard out of the heart of the darkness a voice speak in the Elven-tongues: first in the High Speech of the Noldor, which he knew not; and then in the tongue of Beleriand, though in a manner somewhat strange to his ears, as of a people long sundered from their kin.[26]

'Stand!' it said. 'Stir not! Or you will die, be you foes or friends.'

'We are friends,' said Voronwë.

'Then do as we bid,' said the voice.

The echo of their voices rolled into silence. Voronwë and Tuor stood still, and it seemed to Tuor that many slow minutes passed, and a fear was in his heart such as no other peril of his road had brought. Then there came the beat of feet, growing to a tramping loud as the march of trolls in that hollow place. Suddenly an elven-lantern was unhooded, and its bright ray was turned upon Voronwë before him, but nothing else could Tuor see save a dazzling star in the darkness; and he knew that while that beam was upon him he could not move, neither to flee nor to run forward.

For a moment they were held thus in the eye of the light, and then the voice spoke again, saying: 'Show your faces!' And Voronwë cast back his hood, and his face shone in the ray, hard and clear, as if graven in stone; and Tuor marvelled to see its beauty. Then he spoke proudly, saying: 'Know you not whom you see? I am Voronwë son of Aranwë of the House of Fingolfin. Or am I forgotten in my own land after a few years? Far beyond the thought of Middle-earth I have wandered, yet I remember your voice, Elemmakil.'

'Then Voronwë will remember also the laws of his land,' said the voice. 'Since by command he went forth, he has the right to return. But not to lead hither any stranger. By that deed his right is void, and he must be led as a prisoner to the king's judgement. As for the stranger, he shall be slain or held captive at the judgement of the Guard. Lead him hither that I may judge.'

Then Voronwë led Tuor towards the light, and as they drew near many Noldor, mail-clad and armed, stepped forward out of the darkness and surrounded them with drawn swords. And Elemmakil, captain of the Guard, who bore the bright lamp, looked long and closely at them.

'This is strange in you, Voronwë,' he said. 'We were long friends. Why then would you set me thus cruelly between the law and my friendship? If you had led hither unbidden one of the other houses of the Noldor, that were enough. But you have brought to knowledge of the Way a mortal Man – for by his eyes I perceive his kin. Yet free can he never again go, knowing the secret; and as one of alien kin that has dared to enter, I should slay him – even though he be your friend and dear to you.'

'In the wide lands without, Elemmakil, many strange things may befall one, and tasks unlooked for be laid on one,' Voronwë answered. 'Other shall the wanderer return than as he set forth. What I have done, I have done under command greater than the law of the Guard. The King alone should judge me, and him that comes with me.'

Then Tuor spoke, and feared no longer. 'I come with Voronwë son of Aranwë, because he was appointed to be my guide by the Lord of Waters. To this end was he delivered from the wrath of the Sea and the Doom of the Valar. For I bear from Ulmo an errand to the son of Fingolfin, and to him will I speak it.'

Thereat Elemmakil looked in wonder upon Tuor. 'Who then are you?' he said. 'And whence come you?'

'I am Tuor son of Huor of the House of Hador and the kindred of Húrin, and these names, I am told, are not unknown in the Hidden Kingdom. From Nevrast I have come through many perils to seek it.'

'From Nevrast?' said Elemmakil. 'It is said that none dwell there, since our people departed.'

'It is said truly,' answered Tuor. 'Empty and cold stand the courts of Vinyamar. Yet thence I come. Bring me now to him that built those halls of old.'

'In matters so great judgement is not mine,' said Elemmakil. 'Therefore I will lead you to the light where more may be revealed, and I will deliver you to the Warden of the Great Gate.'

Then he spoke in command, and Tuor and Voronwë were set between tall guards, two before and three behind them; and their captain led them from the cavern of the Outer Guard, and they passed, as it seemed, into a straight passage, and there walked long upon a level floor, until a pale light gleamed ahead. Thus they came at length to a wide arch with tall pillars upon either hand, hewn in the rock, and between hung a great portcullis of crossed wooden bars, marvellously carved and studded with nails of iron.

Elemmakil touched it, and it rose silently, and they passed through; and Tuor saw that they stood at the end of a ravine, the like of which he had never before beheld or imagined in his thought, long though he had walked in the wild mountains of the North; for beside the Orfalch Echor Cirith Ninniach was but a groove in the rock. Here the hands of the Valar themselves, in ancient wars of the world's beginning, had wrested the great mountains asunder, and the sides of the rift were sheer as if axe-cloven, and they towered up to heights unguessable. There far aloft ran a ribbon of sky, and against its deep blue stood black peaks and jagged pinnacles, remote but hard, cruel as spears. Too high were those mighty walls for the winter sun to overlook, and though it was now full morning faint stars glimmered above the mountain-tops, and down below all was dim, but for the pale light of lamps set beside the climbing road. For the floor of the ravine sloped steeply up, eastward, and upon the left hand Tuor saw beside the stream-bed a wide way, laid and paved with stone, winding upward till it vanished into shadow.

'You have passed the First Gate, the Gate of Wood,' said Elemmakil. 'There lies the way. We must hasten.'

How far that deep road ran Tuor could not guess, and as he stared onward a great weariness came upon him like a cloud. A chill wind hissed over the faces of the stones, and he drew his cloak close about him. 'Cold blows the wind from the Hidden Kingdom!' he said.

'Yea, indeed,' said Voronwë; 'to a stranger it might seem that pride has made the servants of Turgon pitiless. Long and hard seem the leagues of the Seven Gates to the hungry and wayworn.'

'If our law were less stern, long ago guile and hatred would have entered and destroyed us. That you know well,' said Elemmakil. 'But we are not pitiless. Here there is no food, and the stranger may not go back through a gate that he has passed. Endure then a little, and at the Second Gate you shall be eased.'

'It is well,' said Tuor, and he went forward as he was bidden. After a little he turned, and saw that Elemmakil alone followed with Voronwë. 'There is no need more of guards,' said Elemmakil, reading his thought. 'From the Orfalch there is no escape for Elf or Man, and no returning.'

Thus they went on up the steep way, sometimes by long stairs, sometimes by winding slopes, under the daunting shadow of the cliff, until some half-league from the Wooden Gate Tuor saw that the way was barred by a great wall built across the ravine from side to side, with stout towers of stone at either hand. In the wall was a great archway above the road, but it seemed that masons had blocked it with a single mighty stone. As they drew near its dark and polished face gleamed in the light of a white lamp that hung above the midst of the arch.

'Here stands the Second Gate, the Gate of Stone,' said Elemmakil; and going up to it he thrust lightly upon it. It turned upon an unseen pivot, until its edge was towards them, and the way was open upon either side; and they passed through, into a court where stood many armed guards clad in grey. No word was spoken, but Elemmakil led his charges to a chamber beneath the northern tower; and there food and wine was brought to them, and they were permitted to rest a while.

'Scant may the fare seem,' said Elemmakil to Tuor. 'But if your claim be proved, hereafter it shall richly be amended.'

'It is enough,' said Tuor. 'Faint were the heart that needed better healing.' And indeed such refreshment did he find in the drink and food of the Noldor that soon he was eager to go on.

After a little space they came to a wall yet higher and stronger than before, and in it was set the Third Gate, the Gate of Bronze: a great twofold door hung with shields and plates of bronze, wherein were wrought many figures and strange signs. Upon the wall above its lintel were three square towers, roofed and clad with copper that by some device of smith-craft were ever bright and gleamed as fire in the rays of the red lamps ranged like torches along the wall. Again silently they passed the gate, and saw in the court beyond a yet greater company of guards in mail that glowed like dull fire; and the blades of their axes were red. Of the kindred of the Sindar of Nevrast for the most part were those that held this gate.

Now they came to the most toilsome road, for in the midst of the Orfalch the slope was at the steepest, and as they climbed Tuor saw the mightiest of the walls looming dark above him. Thus at last they drew near the Fourth Gate, the Gate of Writhen Iron. High and black was the wall, and lit with no lamps. Four towers of iron stood upon it, and between the two inner towers was set an image of a great eagle wrought in iron, even the likeness of King Thorondor himself, as he would alight upon a mountain from the high airs. But as Tuor stood before the gate it seemed to his wonder that he was looking through boughs and stems of imperishable trees into a pale glade of the Moon. For a light came through the traceries of the gate, which were wrought and hammered into the shapes of trees with writhing roots and woven branches laden with leaves and flowers. And as he passed through he saw how this could be; for the wall was of great thickness, and there was not one grill but three in line, so set that to one who approached in the middle of the way each formed part of the device; but the light beyond was the light of day.

For they had climbed now to a great height above the lowlands where they began, and beyond the Iron Gate the road ran almost level. Moreover, they had passed the crown and heart of the Echoriath, and the mountain-towers now fell swiftly down towards the inner hills, and the ravine opened wider, and its sides became less sheer. Its long shoulders were mantled with white snow, and the light of the sky snow-mirrored came white as moonlight through a glimmering mist that filled the air.

Now they passed through the lines of the Iron Guards that stood behind the Gate; black were their mantles and their mail and long shields, and their faces were masked with vizors bearing each an eagle's beak. Then Elemmakil went before them and they followed him into the pale light; and Tuor saw beside the way a sward of grass, where like stars bloomed the white flowers of *uilos*, the Evermind that knows no season and withers not;[27] and thus in wonder and lightening of heart he was brought to the Gate of Silver.

The wall of the Fifth Gate was built of white marble, and was low

and broad, and its parapet was a trellis of silver between five great
globes of marble; and there stood many archers robed in white.
The gate was in shape as three parts of a circle, and wrought of
silver and pearl of Nevrast in likenesses of the Moon; but above the
Gate upon the midmost globe stood an image of the White Tree
Telperion, wrought of silver and malachite, with flowers made of
great pearls of Balar.[28] And beyond the Gate in a wide court paved
with marble, green and white, stood archers in silver mail and white-
crested helms, a hundred upon either hand. Then Elemmakil led
Tuor and Voronwë through their silent ranks, and they entered
upon a long white road, that ran straight towards the Sixth Gate;
and as they went the grass-sward became wider, and among the
white stars of *uilos* there opened many small flowers like eyes of
gold.

So they came to the Golden Gate, the last of the ancient gates of
Turgon that were wrought before the Nirnaeth; and it was much
like the Gate of Silver, save that the wall was built of yellow marble,
and the globes and parapet were of red gold; and there were six
globes, and in the midst upon a golden pyramid was set an image of
Laurelin, the Tree of the Sun, with flowers wrought of topaz in long
clusters upon chains of gold. And the Gate itself was adorned with
discs of gold, many-rayed, in likenesses of the Sun, set amid devices
of garnet and topaz and yellow diamonds. In the court beyond were
arrayed three hundred archers with long bows, and their mail was
gilded, and tall golden plumes rose from their helmets; and their
great round shields were red as flame.

Now sunlight fell upon the further road, for the walls of the hills
were low on either side, and green, but for the snows upon their
tops; and Elemmakil hastened forward, for the way was short to the
Seventh Gate, named the Great, the Gate of Steel that Maeglin
wrought after the return from the Nirnaeth, across the wide entrance
to the Orfalch Echor.

No wall stood there, but on either hand were two round towers
of great height, many-windowed, tapering in seven storeys to a turret
of bright steel, and between the towers there stood a mighty fence of
steel that rusted not, but glittered cold and white. Seven great
pillars of steel there were, tall with the height and girth of strong
young trees, but ending in a bitter spike that rose to the sharpness
of a needle; and between the pillars were seven cross-bars of steel,
and in each space seven times seven rods of steel upright, with heads
like the broad blades of spears. But in the centre, above the midmost
pillar and the greatest, was raised a mighty image of the king-helm

of Turgon, the Crown of the Hidden Kingdom, set about with diamonds.

No gate or door could Tuor see in this mighty hedge of steel, but as he drew near through the spaces between its bars there came, as it seemed to him, a dazzling light, and he shaded his eyes, and stood still in dread and wonder. But Elemmakil went forward, and no gate opened to his touch; but he struck upon a bar, and the fence rang like a harp of many strings, giving forth clear notes in harmony that ran from tower to tower.

Straightway there issued riders from the towers, but before those of the north tower came one upon a white horse; and he dismounted and strode towards them. And high and noble as was Elemmakil, greater and more lordly was Ecthelion, Lord of the Fountains, at that time Warden of the Great Gate.[29] All in silver was he clad, and upon his shining helm there was set a spike of steel pointed with a diamond; and as his esquire took his shield it shimmered as if it were bedewed with drops of rain, that were indeed a thousand studs of crystal.

Elemmakil saluted him and said: 'Here have I brought Voronwë Aranwion, returning from Balar; and here is the stranger that he has led hither, who demands to see the King.'

Then Ecthelion turned to Tuor, but he drew his cloak about him and stood silent, facing him; and it seemed to Voronwë that a mist mantled Tuor and his stature was increased, so that the peak of his high hood over-topped the helm of the Elf-lord, as it were the crest of a grey sea-wave riding to the land. But Ecthelion bent his bright glance upon Tuor, and after a silence he spoke gravely, saying:[30] 'You have come to the Last Gate. Know then that no stranger who passes it shall ever go out again, save by the door of death.'

'Speak not ill-boding! If the messenger of the Lord of Waters go by that door, then all those who dwell here will follow him. Lord of the Fountains, hinder not the messenger of the Lord of Waters!'

Then Voronwë and all those who stood near looked again in wonder at Tuor, marvelling at his words and voice. And to Voronwë it seemed as if he heard a great voice, but as of one who called from afar off. But to Tuor it seemed that he listened to himself speaking, as if another spoke with his mouth.

For a while Ecthelion stood silent, looking at Tuor, and slowly awe filled his face, as if in the grey shadow of Tuor's cloak he saw visions from far away. Then he bowed, and went to the fence and laid hands upon it, and gates opened inward on either side of the pillar of the Crown. Then Tuor passed through, and coming to a high sward that looked out over the valley beyond, he beheld a vision of Gondolin amid the white snow. And so entranced was he that for long he could look at nothing else; for he saw before him at last the vision of his desire out of dreams of longing. Thus he stood and spoke no word. Silent upon either hand stood a host of the army of Gondolin; all of the seven kinds of the Seven Gates were there represented; but their captains and chieftains were upon horses, white and grey. Then even as they gazed on Tuor in wonder, his cloak fell down, and he stood there before them in the mighty livery of Nevrast. And many were there who had seen Turgon himself set these things upon the wall behind the High Seat of Vinyamar.

Then Ecthelion said at last: 'Now no further proof is needed; and even the name he claims as son of Huor matters less than this clear truth, that he comes from Ulmo himself.'[31]

NOTES

1 In *The Silmarillion* p. 196 it is said that when the Havens of Brithombar and Eglarest were destroyed in the year after the Nirnaeth Arnoediad those of the Elves of the Falas that escaped went with Círdan to the Isle of Balar, 'and they made a refuge for all that could come thither; for they kept a foothold also at the Mouths of Sirion, and there many light and swift ships lay hid in the creeks and waters where the reeds were dense as a forest'.

2 The blue-shining lamps of the Noldorin Elves are referred to elsewhere, though they do not appear in the published text of *The Silmarillion*. In earlier versions of the tale of Túrin Gwindor, the Elf of Nargothrond who escaped from Angband and was found by Beleg in the forest of Taur-nu-Fuin, possessed one of these lamps (it can be seen in my father's painting of that meeting, see *Pictures by J. R. R. Tolkien*, 1979, no. 37); and it was the overturning and uncovering of Gwindor's lamp so that its light shone out that showed Túrin the face of Beleg whom he had killed. In a note on the story of Gwindor they are called 'Fëanorian lamps', of which the Noldor themselves did not know the secret; and they are there described as 'crystals hung in a fine chain net, the crystals being ever shining with an inner blue radiance'.

3 'The sun shall shine upon your path.' – In the very much briefer story told in *The Silmarillion*, there is no account of how Tuor found the Gate of the Noldor, nor any mention of the Elves Gelmir and Arminas. They appear however in the tale of Túrin (*The Silmarillion* p. 212) as the messengers who brought Ulmo's warning to Nargoth-

rond; and there they are said to be of the people of Finarfin's son
Angrod, who after the Dagor Bragollach dwelt in the south with
Círdan the Shipwright. In a longer version of the story of their
coming to Nargothrond, Arminas, comparing Túrin unfavourably
with his kinsman, speaks of having met Tuor 'in the wastes of
Dor-lómin'; see p. 161.

4 In *The Silmarillion* pp. 80–1 it is told that when Morgoth and
   Ungoliant struggled in this region for possession of the Silmarils
   'Morgoth sent forth a terrible cry, that echoed in the mountains.
   Therefore that region was called Lammoth; for the echoes of his
   voice dwelt there ever after, so that any who cried aloud in that land
   awoke them, and all the waste between the hills and the sea was
   filled with a clamour as of voices in anguish.' Here, on the other hand,
   the conception is rather that any sound uttered there was magnified
   in its own nature; and this idea is clearly also present at the beginning
   of ch. 13 of *The Silmarillion*, where (in a passage very similar to the
   present) 'even as the Noldor set foot upon the strand their cries were
   taken up into the hills and multiplied, so that a clamour as of countless mighty voices filled all the coasts of the North'. It seems that
   according to the one 'tradition' Lammoth and Ered Lómin (Echoing
   Mountains) were so named from their retaining the echoes of
   Morgoth's dreadful cry in the toils of Ungoliant; while according to
   the other the names are simply descriptive of the nature of sounds
   in that region.

5 Cf. *The Silmarillion* p. 215: 'And Túrin hastened along the ways to
   the north, through the lands now desolate between Narog and Teiglin,
   and the Fell Winter came down to meet him; for in that year snow
   fell ere autumn was passed, and spring came late and cold.'

6 In *The Silmarillion* p. 126 it is told that when Ulmo appeared to
   Turgon at Vinyamar and bade him go to Gondolin, he said: 'Thus
   it may come to pass that the curse of the Noldor shall find thee too
   ere the end, and treason awake within thy walls. Then they shall be
   in peril of fire. But if this peril draweth nigh indeed, then even from
   Nevrast one shall come to warn thee, and from him beyond ruin
   and fire hope shall be born for Elves and Men. Leave therefore in
   this house arms and a sword, that in years to come he may find them,
   and thus shalt thou know him, and not be deceived.' And Ulmo
   declared to Turgon of what kind and stature should be the helm
   and mail and sword that he left behind.

7 Tuor was the father of Eärendil, who was the father of Elros Tar-
   Minyatur, the first King of Númenor.

8 This must refer to the warning of Ulmo brought to Nargothrond by
   Gelmir and Arminas; see pp. 159 ff.

9 The Shadowy Isles are very probably the Enchanted Isles described
   at the end of *The Silmarillion* ch. 11, which were 'strung as a net

in the Shadowy Seas from the north to the south' at the time of the Hiding of Valinor.

10 Cf. *The Silmarillion* p. 196: 'At the bidding of Turgon [after the Nirnaeth Arnoediad] Círdan built seven swift ships, and they sailed out into the West; but no tidings of them came ever back to Balar, save of one, and the last. The mariners of that ship toiled long in the sea, and returning at last in despair they foundered in a great storm within sight of the coasts of Middle-earth; but one of them was saved by Ulmo from the wrath of Ossë, and the waves bore him up, and cast him ashore in Nevrast. His name was Voronwë; and he was one of those that Turgon sent forth as messengers from Gondolin.' Cf. also *The Silmarillion* p. 239.

11 The words of Ulmo to Turgon appear in *The Silmarillion* ch. 15 in the form: 'Remember that the true hope of the Noldor lieth in the West and cometh from the Sea,' and 'But if this peril draweth nigh indeed, then even from Nevrast one shall come to warn thee.'

12 Nothing is told in *The Silmarillion* of the further fate of Voronwë after his return to Gondolin with Tuor; but in the original story ('Of Tuor and the Exiles of Gondolin') he was one of those who escaped from the sack of the city – as is implied by the words of Tuor here.

13 Cf. *The Silmarillion* p. 159: '[Turgon] believed also that the ending of the Siege was the beginning of the downfall of the Noldor, unless aid should come; and he sent companies of the Gondolindrim in secret to the mouths of Sirion and the Isle of Balar. There they built ships, and set sail into the uttermost West upon Turgon's errand, seeking for Valinor, to ask for pardon and aid of the Valar; and they besought the birds of the sea to guide them. But the seas were wild and wide, and shadow and enchantment lay upon them; and Valinor was hidden. Therefore none of the messengers of Turgon came into the West, and many were lost and few returned.'

In one of the 'constituent texts' of *The Silmarillion* it is said that although the Noldor 'had not the art of shipbuilding, and all the craft that they built foundered or were driven back by the winds', yet after the Dagor Bragollach 'Turgon ever maintained a secret refuge upon the Isle of Balar', and when after the Nirnaeth Arnoediad Círdan and the remnant of his people fled from Brithombar and Eglarest to Balar 'they mingled with Turgon's outpost there'. But this element in the story was rejected, and thus in the published text of *The Silmarillion* there is no reference to the establishment of dwellings on Balar by Elves from Gondolin.

14 The woods of Núath are not mentioned in *The Silmarillion* and are not marked on the map that accompanies it. They extended westward from the upper waters of the Narog towards the source of the river Nenning.

15 Cf. *The Silmarillion* pp. 209–10: 'Finduilas daughter of Orodreth the King knew [Gwindor] and welcomed him, for she had loved him before the Nirnaeth, and so greatly did Gwindor love her beauty that he named her Faelivrin, which is the gleam of the sun on the pools of Ivrin.'

16 The river Glithui is not mentioned in *The Silmarillion* and is not named on the map, though it is shown: a tributary of the Teiglin joining that river some way north of the inflowing of the Malduin.

17 This road is referred to in *The Silmarillion*, p. 205: 'The ancient road . . . that led through the long defile of Sirion, past the isle where Minas Tirith of Finrod had stood, and so through the land between Malduin and Sirion, and on through the eaves of Brethil to the Crossings of Teiglin.'

18 'Death to the *Glamhoth*!' This name, though it does not occur in *The Silmarillion* or in *The Lord of the Rings*, was a general term in the Sindarin language for Orcs. The meaning is 'din-horde', 'host of tumult'; cf. Gandalf's sword *Glamdring*, and *Tol-in-Gaurhoth*, the Isle of (the host of) Werewolves.

19 *Echoriath*: the Encircling Mountains about the plain of Gondolin. *ered e·mbar nin*: the mountains of my home.

20 In *The Silmarillion*, pp. 200–1, Beleg of Doriath said to Túrin (at a time some years before that of the present narrative) that Orcs had made a road through the Pass of Anach, 'and Dimbar which used to be at peace is falling under the Black Hand'.

21 By this road Maeglin and Aredhel fled to Gondolin pursued by Eöl (*The Silmarillion* ch. 16); and afterwards Celegorm and Curufin took it when they were expelled from Nargothrond (*ibid.* p. 176). Only in the present text is there any mention of its westward extension to Turgon's ancient home at Vinyamar under Mount Taras; and its course is not marked on the map from its junction with the old south road to Nargothrond at the north-western edge of Brethil.

22 The name *Brithiach* contains the element *brith* 'gravel', as also in the river *Brithon* and the haven of *Brithombar*.

23 In a parallel version of the text at this point, almost certainly rejected in favour of the one printed, the travellers did not cross the Sirion by the Ford of Brithiach, but reached the river several leagues to the north of it. 'They trod a toilsome path to the brink of the river, and there Voronwë cried: "See a wonder! Both good and ill does it forebode. Sirion is frozen, though no tale tells of the like since the coming of the Eldar out of the East. Thus we may pass and save many weary miles, too long for our strength. Yet thus also others may have passed, or may follow."' They crossed the river on the ice unhindered, and 'thus did the counsels of Ulmo turn the malice of the Enemy to avail, for the way was shortened, and at the end of

their hope and strength Tuor and Voronwë came at last to the Dry River at its issuing from the skirts of the mountains'.

24 Cf. *The Silmarillion* p. 125: 'But there was a deep way under the mountains delved in the darkness of the world by waters that flowed out to join the streams of Sirion; and this way Turgon found, and so came to the green plain amid the mountains, and saw the island-hill that stood there of hard smooth stone; for the vale had been a great lake in ancient days.'

25 It is not said in *The Silmarillion* that the great eagles ever dwelt on Thangorodrim. In ch. 13 (p. 110) Manwë 'sent forth the race of Eagles, commanding them to dwell in the crags of the North, and to keep watch upon Morgoth'; while in ch. 18 (p. 154) Thorondor 'came hasting from his eyrie among the peaks of the Crissaegrim' for the rescue of Fingolfin's body before the gates of Angband. Cf. also *The Return of the King* VI 4: 'Old Thorondor, who built his eyries in the inaccessible peaks of the Encircling Mountains when Middle-earth was young.' In all probability the conception of Thorondor's dwelling at first upon Thangorodrim, which is found also in an early Silmarillion text, was later abandoned.

26 In *The Silmarillion* nothing is said specifically concerning the speech of the Elves of Gondolin; but this passage suggests that for some of them the High Speech (Quenya) was in ordinary use. It is stated in a late linguistic essay that Quenya was in daily use in Turgon's house, and was the childhood speech of Eärendil; but that 'for most of the people of Gondolin it had become a language of books, and as the other Noldor they used Sindarin in daily speech'. Cf. *The Silmarillion* p. 129: after the edict of Thingol 'the Exiles took the Sindarin tongue in all their daily uses, and the High Speech of the West was spoken only by the lords of the Noldor among themselves. Yet that speech lived ever as a language of lore, wherever any of that people dwelt.'

27 These were the flowers that bloomed abundantly on the burial mounds of the Kings of Rohan below Edoras, and which Gandalf named in the language of the Rohirrim (as translated into Old English) *simbelmynë*, that is 'Evermind', 'for they blossom in all the seasons of the year, and grow where dead men rest'. (*The Two Towers* III 6.) The Elvish name *uilos* is only given in this passage, but the word is found also in *Amon Uilos*, as the Quenya name *Oiolossë* ('Ever-snow-white', the Mountain of Manwë) was rendered into Sindarin. In 'Cirion and Eorl' the flower is given another Elvish name, *alfirin* (p. 303).

28 In *The Silmarillion* p. 92 it is said that Thingol rewarded the Dwarves of Belegost with many pearls: 'These Círdan gave to him, for they were got in great number in the shallow waters about the Isle of Balar.'

29 Ecthelion of the Fountain is mentioned in *The Silmarillion* as one of Turgon's captains who guarded the flanks of the host of Gondolin

in their retreat down Sirion from the Nirnaeth Arnoediad, and as the slayer of Gothmog Lord of Balrogs, by whom he himself was slain, in the assault on the city.

30 From this point the carefully-written, though much-emended, manuscript ceases, and the remainder of the narrative is hastily scribbled on a scrap of paper.

31 Here the narrative finally comes to an end, and there remain only some hasty jottings indicating the course of the story:

Tuor asked the name of the City, and was told its seven names. (It is notable, and no doubt intentional, that the name Gondolin is never once used in the narrative until the very end (p. 51): always it is called the Hidden Kingdom or the Hidden City). Ecthelion gave orders for the sounding of the signal, and trumpets were blown on the towers of the Great Gate, echoing in the hills. After a hush, they heard far off answering trumpets blown upon the city walls. Horses were brought (a grey horse for Tuor); and they rode to Gondolin.

A description of Gondolin was to follow, of the stairs up to its high platform, and its great gate; of the mounds (this word is uncertain) of mallorns, birches, and evergreen trees; of the Place of the Fountain, the King's tower on a pillared arcade, the King's house, and the banner of Fingolfin. Now Turgon himself would appear, 'tallest of all the Children of the World, save Thingol', with a white and gold sword in a ruel-bone (ivory) sheath, and welcome Tuor. Maeglin would be seen standing on the right of the throne, and Idril the King's daughter seated on the left; and Tuor would speak the message of Ulmo either 'in the hearing of all' or 'in the council-chamber'.

Other disjointed notes indicate that there was to be a description of Gondolin as seen by Tuor from far off; that Ulmo's cloak would vanish when Tuor spoke the message of Turgon; that it would be explained why there was no Queen of Gondolin; and that it was to be emphasized, either when Tuor first set eyes upon Idril or at some earlier point, that he had known or even seen few women in his life. Most of the women and all the children of Annael's company in Mithrim were sent away south; and as a thrall Tuor had seen only the proud and barbaric women of the Easterlings, who treated him as a beast, or the unhappy slaves forced to labour from childhood, for whom he had only pity.

It may be noted that later mentions of mallorns in Númenor, Lindon, and Lothlórien do not suggest, though they do not deny, that those trees flourished in Gondolin in the Elder Days (see pp. 167–8), and that the wife of Turgon, Elenwë, was lost long before in the crossing of the Helcaraxë by the host of Fingolfin (*The Silmarillion* p. 90).

II

NARN I HÎN HÚRIN

The Tale of the Children of Húrin

The Childhood of Túrin

Hador Goldenhead was a lord of the Edain and well-beloved by the Eldar. He dwelt while his days lasted under the lordship of Fingolfin, who gave to him wide lands in that region of Hithlum which was called Dor-lómin. His daughter Glóredhel wedded Haldir son of Halmir, lord of the Men of Brethil; and at the same feast his son Galdor the Tall wedded Hareth, the daughter of Halmir.

Galdor and Hareth had two sons, Húrin and Huor. Húrin was by three years the elder, but he was shorter in stature than other men of his kin; in this he took after his mother's people, but in all else he was like Hador his grandfather, fair of face and golden-haired, strong in body and fiery of mood. But the fire in him burned steadily, and he had great endurance of will. Of all Men of the North he knew most of the counsels of the Noldor. Huor his brother was tall, the tallest of all the Edain save his own son Tuor only, and a swift runner; but if the race were long and hard Húrin would be the first home, for he ran as strongly at the end of the course as at the beginning. There was great love between the brothers, and they were seldom apart in their youth.

Húrin wedded Morwen, the daughter of Baragund son of Bregolas of the House of Bëor; and she was thus of close kin to Beren One-hand. Morwen was dark-haired and tall, and for the light of her glance and the beauty of her face men called her Eledhwen, the elven-fair; but she was somewhat stern of mood and proud. The sorrows of the House of Bëor saddened her heart; for she came as an exile to Dor-lómin from Dorthonion after the ruin of the Bragollach.

Túrin was the name of the eldest child of Húrin and Morwen, and he was born in that year in which Beren came to Doriath and found Lúthien Tinúviel, Thingol's daughter. Morwen bore a daughter also to Húrin, and she was named Urwen; but she was called Lalaith, which is Laughter, by all that knew her in her short life.

Huor wedded Rían, the cousin of Morwen; she was the daughter of

Belegund son of Bregolas. By hard fate was she born into such days, for she was gentle of heart and loved neither hunting nor war. Her love was given to trees and to the flowers of the wild, and she was a singer and a maker of songs. Two months only had she been wedded to Huor when he went with his brother to the Nirnaeth Arnoediad, and she never saw him again.[1]

In the years after the Dagor Bragollach and the fall of Fingolfin the shadow of the fear of Morgoth lengthened. But in the four hundred and sixty-ninth year after the return of the Noldor to Middle-earth there was a stirring of hope among Elves and Men; for the rumour ran among them of the deeds of Beren and Lúthien, and the putting to shame of Morgoth even upon his throne in Angband, and some said that Beren and Lúthien yet lived, or had returned from the Dead. In that year also the great counsels of Maedhros were almost complete, and with the reviving strength of the Eldar and the Edain the advance of Morgoth was stayed, and the Orcs were driven back from Beleriand. Then some began to speak of victories to come, and of redressing the Battle of the Bragollach, when Maedhros should lead forth the united hosts, and drive Morgoth underground, and seal the Doors of Angband.

But the wiser were uneasy still, fearing that Maedhros revealed his growing strength too soon, and that Morgoth would be given time enough to take counsel against him. 'Ever will some new evil be hatched in Angband beyond the guess of Elves and Men,' they said. And in the autumn of that year, to point their words, there came an ill wind from the North under leaden skies. The Evil Breath it was called, for it was pestilent; and many sickened and died in the fall of the year in the northern lands that bordered on the Anfauglith, and they were for the most part the children or the rising youth in the houses of Men.

In that year Túrin son of Húrin was yet only five years old, and Urwen his sister was three in the beginning of spring. Her hair was like the yellow lilies in the grass as she ran in the fields, and her laughter was like the sound of the merry stream that came singing out of the hills past the walls of her father's house. Nen Lalaith it was named, and after it all the people of the household called the child Lalaith, and their hearts were glad while she was among them.

But Túrin was loved less than she. He was dark-haired as his mother, and promised to be like her in mood also; for he was not merry, and spoke little, though he learned to speak early and ever seemed older than his years. Túrin was slow to forget injustice or mockery; but the fire of his father was also in him, and he could be sudden and fierce. Yet he was quick to pity, and the hurts or sadness of living things might move him to tears; and he was like his father in this also, for Morwen was stern with others as with herself. He loved his mother, for her speech to him was forthright and plain; but his father he saw little, for Húrin was often long away from home with the host of Fingon that guarded Hithlum's eastern borders, and when he returned his quick speech, full of strange words and jests and half-meanings, bewildered Túrin and made him uneasy. At that time all the warmth of his heart was for Lalaith his sister; but he played with her seldom, and liked better to guard her unseen and to watch her going upon grass or under tree, as she sang such songs as the children of the Edain made long ago when the tongue of the Elves was still fresh upon their lips.

'Fair as an Elf-child is Lalaith,' said Húrin to Morwen; 'but briefer, alas! And so fairer, maybe, or dearer.' And Túrin hearing these words pondered them, but could not understand them. For he had seen no Elf-children. None of the Eldar at that time dwelt in his father's lands, and once only had he seen them, when King Fingon and many of his lords had ridden through Dor-lómin and passed over the bridge of Nen Lalaith, glittering in silver and white.

But before the year was out the truth of his father's words was shown; for the Evil Breath came to Dor-lómin, and Túrin took sick, and lay long in a fever and dark dream. And when he was healed, for such was his fate and the strength of life that was in him, he asked for Lalaith. But his nurse answered: 'Speak no more of Lalaith, son of Húrin; but of your sister Urwen you must ask tidings of your mother.'

And when Morwen came to him, Túrin said to her: 'I am no longer sick, and I wish to see Urwen; but why must I not say Lalaith any more?'

'Because Urwen is dead, and laughter is stilled in this house,' she answered. 'But you live, son of Morwen; and so does the Enemy who has done this to us.'

She did not seek to comfort him any more than herself; for she met her grief in silence and coldness of heart. But Húrin mourned openly, and he took up his harp and would make a song of lamentation; but he could not, and he broke his harp, and going out he lifted up his hand towards the North, crying: 'Marrer of Middle-earth, would that I might see thee face to face, and mar thee as my lord Fingolfin did!'

But Túrin wept bitterly at night alone, though to Morwen he

never again spoke the name of his sister. To one friend only he turned at that time, and to him he spoke of his sorrow and the emptiness of the house. This friend was named Sador, a house-man in the service of Húrin; he was lame, and of small account. He had been a woodman, and by ill-luck or the mishandling of his axe he had hewn his right foot, and the footless leg had shrunken; and Túrin called him Labadal, which is 'Hopafoot', though the name did not displease Sador, for it was given in pity and not in scorn. Sador worked in the outbuildings, to make or mend things of little worth that were needed in the house, for he had some skill in the working of wood; and Túrin would fetch him what he lacked, to spare his leg, and sometimes he would carry off secretly some tool or piece of timber that he found unwatched, if he thought his friend might use it. Then Sador smiled, but bade him return the gifts to their places; 'Give with a free hand, but give only your own,' he said. He rewarded as he could the kindness of the child, and carved for him the figures of men and beasts; but Túrin delighted most in Sador's tales, for he had been a young man in the days of the Bragollach, and loved now to dwell upon the short days of his full manhood before his maiming.

'That was a great battle, they say, son of Húrin. I was called from my tasks in the wood in the need of that year; but I was not in the Bragollach, or I might have got my hurt with more honour. For we came too late, save to bear back the bier of the old lord, Hador, who fell in the guard of King Fingolfin. I went for a soldier after that, and I was in Eithel Sirion, the great fort of the Elf-kings, for many years; or so it seems now, and the dull years since have little to mark them. In Eithel Sirion I was when the Black King assailed it, and Galdor your father's father was the captain there in the King's stead. He was slain in that assault; and I saw your father take up his lordship and his command, though but new-come to manhood. There was a fire in him that made the sword hot in his hand, they said. Behind him we drove the Orcs into the sand; and they have not dared to come within sight of the walls since that day. But alas! my love of battle was sated, for I had seen spilled blood and wounds enough; and I got leave to come back to the woods that I yearned for. And there I got my hurt; for a man that flies from his fear may find that he has only taken a short cut to meet it.'

In this way Sador would speak to Túrin as he grew older; and Túrin began to ask many questions that Sador found hard to answer, thinking that others nearer akin should have had the teaching. And one day Túrin said to him: 'Was Lalaith indeed like an Elf-child, as my father said? And what did he mean, when he said that she was briefer?'

'Very like,' said Sador; 'for in their first youth the children of Men and Elves seem close akin. But the children of Men grow more swiftly, and their youth passes soon; such is our fate.'

Then Túrin asked him: 'What is fate?'

'As to the fate of Men,' said Sador, 'you must ask those that are wiser than Labadal. But as all can see, we weary soon and die; and by mischance many meet death even sooner. But the Elves do not weary, and they do not die save by great hurt. From wounds and griefs that would slay Men they may be healed; and even when their bodies are marred they return again, some say. It is not so with us.'

'Then Lalaith will not come back?' said Túrin. 'Where has she gone?'

'She will not come back,' said Sador. 'But where she has gone no man knows; or I do not.'

'Has it always been so? Or do we suffer some curse of the wicked King, perhaps, like the Evil Breath?'

'I do not know. A darkness lies behind us, and out of it few tales have come. The fathers of our fathers may have had things to tell, but they did not tell them. Even their names are forgotten. The Mountains stand between us and the life that they came from, flying from no man now knows what.'

'Were they afraid?' said Túrin.

'It may be,' said Sador. 'It may be that we fled from the fear of the Dark, only to find it here before us, and nowhere else to fly to but the Sea.'

'We are not afraid any longer,' said Túrin, 'not all of us. My father is not afraid, and I will not be; or at least, as my mother, I will be afraid and not show it.'

It seemed then to Sador that Túrin's eyes were not like the eyes of a child, and he thought: 'Grief is a hone to a hard mind.' But aloud he said: 'Son of Húrin and Morwen, how it will be with your heart Labadal cannot guess; but seldom and to few will you show what is in it.'

Then Túrin said: 'Perhaps it is better not to tell what you wish, if you cannot have it. But I wish, Labadal, that I were one of the Eldar. Then Lalaith might come back, and I should still be here, even if she were long away. I shall go as a soldier with an Elf-king as soon as I am able, as you did, Labadal.'

'You may learn much of them,' said Sador, and he sighed. 'They are a fair folk and wonderful, and they have a power over the hearts of Men. And yet I think sometimes that it might have been better if we had never met them, but had walked in lowlier ways. For already they are ancient in knowledge; and they are proud and enduring. In their light we are dimmed, or we burn with too quick a flame, and the weight of our doom lies the heavier on us.'

'But my father loves them,' said Túrin, 'and he is not happy without them. He says that we have learned nearly all that we know from them, and have been made a nobler people; and he says that the Men that have lately come over the Mountains are hardly better than Orcs.'

'That is true,' answered Sador; 'true at least of some of us. But the up-climbing is painful, and from high places it is easy to fall low.'

At this time Túrin was almost eight years old, in the month of Gwaeron in the reckoning of the Edain, in the year that cannot be forgotten. Already there were rumours among his elders of a great mustering and gathering of arms, of which Túrin heard nothing; and Húrin, knowing her courage and her guarded tongue, often spoke with Morwen of the designs of the Elven-kings, and of what might befall, if they went well or ill. His heart was high with hope, and he had little fear for the outcome of the battle; for it did not seem to him that any strength in Middle-earth could overthrow the might and splendour of the Eldar. 'They have seen the Light in the West,' he said, 'and in the end Darkness must flee from their faces.' Morwen did not gainsay him; for in Húrin's company the hopeful ever seemed the more likely. But there was knowledge of Elven-lore in her kindred also, and to herself she said: 'And yet did they not leave the Light, and are they not now shut out from it? It may be that the Lords of the West have put them out of their thought; and how then can even the Elder Children overcome one of the Powers?'

No shadow of such doubt seemed to lie upon Húrin Thalion; yet one morning in the spring of that year he awoke as after unquiet sleep, and a cloud lay on his brightness that day; and in the evening he said suddenly: 'When I am summoned, Morwen Eledhwen, I shall leave in your keeping the heir of the House of Hador. The lives of Men are short, and in them there are many ill chances, even in time of peace.'

'That has ever been so,' she answered. 'But what lies under your words?'

'Prudence, not doubt,' said Húrin; yet he looked troubled. 'But one who looks forward must see this: that things will not remain as they were. This will be a great throw, and one side must fall lower than it now stands. If it be the Elven-kings that fall, then it must go evilly with the Edain; and we dwell nearest to the Enemy. But if things do go ill, I will not say to you: *Do not be afraid!* For you fear what should be feared, and that only; and fear does not dismay you. But I say: *Do not wait!* I shall return to you as I may, but do not wait! Go south as swiftly as you can; and I shall follow, and I shall find you, though I have to search through all Beleriand.'

'Beleriand is wide, and houseless for exiles,' said Morwen. 'Whither should I flee, with few or with many?'

Then Húrin thought for a while in silence. 'There is my mother's kin in Brethil,' he said. 'That is some thirty leagues, as the eagle flies.'

'If such an evil time should indeed come, what help would there be in Men?' said Morwen. 'The House of Bëor has fallen. If the great House of Hador falls, in what holes shall the little Folk of Haleth creep?'

'They are few and unlearned, but do not doubt their valour,' said Húrin. 'Where else is hope?'

'You do not speak of Gondolin,' said Morwen.

'No, for that name has never passed my lips,' said Húrin. 'Yet the word is true that you have heard: I have been there. But I tell you now truly, as I have told no other, and will not: I do not know where it stands.'

'But you guess, and guess near, I think,' said Morwen.

'It may be so,' said Húrin. 'But unless Turgon himself released me from my oath, I could not tell that guess, even to you; and therefore your search would be vain. But were I to speak, to my shame, you would at best but come at a shut gate; for unless Turgon comes out to war (and of that no word has been heard, and it is not hoped) no one will come in.'

'Then if your kin are not hopeful, and your friends deny you,' said Morwen, 'I must take counsel for myself; and to me now comes the thought of Doriath. Last of all defences will the Girdle of Melian be broken, I think; and the House of Bëor will not be despised in Doriath. Am I not now kin of the king? For Beren son of Barahir was grandson of Bregor, as was my father also.'

'My heart does not lean to Thingol,' said Húrin. 'No help will come from him to King Fingon; and I know not what shadow falls on my spirit when Doriath is named.'

'At the name of Brethil my heart also is darkened,' said Morwen.

Then suddenly Húrin laughed, and he said: 'Here we sit debating things beyond our reach, and shadows that come out of dream. Things will not go so ill; but if they do, then to your courage and counsel all is committed. Do then what your heart bids you; but do it swiftly. And if we gain our ends, then the Elven-kings are resolved to restore all the fiefs of Bëor's house to his heirs; and a high inheritance will come to our son.'

That night Túrin half-woke, and it seemed to him that his father and mother stood beside his bed, and looked down on him in the light of the candles that they held; but he could not see their faces.

On the morning of Túrin's birthday Húrin gave his son a gift, an Elf-wrought knife, and the hilt and the sheath were silver and black; and he said: 'Heir of the House of Hador, here is a gift for the day. But have a care! It is a bitter blade, and steel serves only those that can wield it. It will cut your hand as willingly as aught else.' And setting Túrin on a table he kissed his son, and said: 'You overtop me already, son of Morwen; soon you will be as high on your own feet. In that day many may fear your blade.'

Then Túrin ran from the room and went away alone, and in his heart there was a warmth like the warmth of the sun upon the cold earth that sets growth astir. He repeated to himself his father's words, Heir of the House of Hador; but other words came also to his mind: Give with a free hand, but give of your own. And he went to Sador and cried: 'Labadal, it is my birthday, the birthday of the heir of the House of Hador! And I have brought you a gift to mark the day. Here is a knife, just such as you need; it will cut anything that you wish, as fine as a hair.'

Then Sador was troubled, for he knew well that Túrin had himself received the knife that day; but men held it a grievous thing to refuse a free-given gift from any hand. He spoke then to him gravely: 'You come of a generous kin, Túrin son of Húrin. I have done nothing to equal your gift, and I cannot hope to do better in the days that are left to me; but what I can do, I will.' And when Sador drew the knife from the sheath he said: 'This is a gift indeed: a blade of elven steel. Long have I missed the feel of it.'

Húrin soon marked that Túrin did not wear the knife, and he asked him whether his warning had made him fear it. Then Túrin answered: 'No; but I gave the knife to Sador the woodwright.'

'Do you then scorn your father's gift?' said Morwen; and again Túrin answered: 'No; but I love Sador, and I feel pity for him.'

Then Húrin said: 'All three gifts were your own to give, Túrin: love, pity, and the knife the least.'

'Yet I doubt if Sador deserves them,' said Morwen. 'He is self-maimed by his own want of skill, and he is slow with his tasks, for he spends much time on trifles unbidden.'

'Give him pity nonetheless,' said Húrin. 'An honest hand and a true heart may hew amiss; and the harm may be harder to bear than the work of a foe.'

'But you must wait now for another blade,' said Morwen. 'Thus the gift shall be a true gift and at your own cost.'

Nonetheless Túrin saw that Sador was treated more kindly thereafter, and was set now to the making of a great chair for the lord to sit on in his hall.

There came a bright morning in the month of Lothron when Túrin was roused by sudden trumpets; and running to the doors he saw in the court a great press of men on foot and on horse, and all fully armed as for war. There also stood Húrin, and he spoke to the men and gave commands; and Túrin learned that they were setting out that day for Barad Eithel. These were Húrin's guards and household men; but all the men of his land were summoned. Some had gone already with Huor his father's brother; and many others would join the Lord of Dor-lómin on the road, and go behind his banner to the great muster of the King.

Then Morwen bade farewell to Húrin without tears; and she said: 'I will guard what you leave in my keeping, both what is and what shall be.'

And Húrin answered her: 'Farewell, Lady of Dor-lómin; we ride now with greater hope than ever we have known before. Let us think that at this midwinter the feast shall be merrier than in all our years yet, with a fearless spring to follow after!' Then he lifted Túrin to his shoulder, and cried to his men: 'Let the heir of the House of Hador see the light of your swords!' And the sun glittered on fifty blades as they leaped forth, and the court rang with the battle-cry of the Edain of the North: *Lacho calad! Drego morn!* Flame Light! Flee Night!

Then at last Húrin sprang into his saddle, and his golden banner was unfurled, and the trumpets sang again in the morning; and thus Húrin Thalion rode away to the Nirnaeth Arnoediad.

But Morwen and Túrin stood still by the doors, until far away they heard the faint call of a single horn on the wind: Húrin had passed over the shoulder of the hill, beyond which he could see his house no more.

The Words of Húrin and Morgoth

Many songs are sung and many tales are told by the Elves of the Nirnaeth Arnoediad, the Battle of Unnumbered Tears, in which

Fingon fell and the flower of the Eldar withered. If all were retold a man's life would not suffice for the hearing;[2] but now is to be told only of what befell Húrin son of Galdor, Lord of Dor-lómin, when beside the stream of Rivil he was taken at last alive by the command of Morgoth, and carried off to Angband.

Húrin was brought before Morgoth, for Morgoth knew by his arts and his spies that Húrin had the friendship of the King of Gondolin; and he sought to daunt him with his eyes. But Húrin could not yet be daunted, and he defied Morgoth. Therefore Morgoth had him chained and set in slow torment; but after a while he came to him, and offered him his choice to go free whither he would, or to receive power and rank as the greatest of Morgoth's captains, if he would but reveal where Turgon had his stronghold, and aught else that he knew of the King's counsels. But Húrin the Steadfast mocked him, saying: 'Blind you are Morgoth Bauglir, and blind shall ever be, seeing only the dark. You know not what rules the hearts of Men, and if you knew you could not give it. But a fool is he who accepts what Morgoth offers. You will take first the price and then withhold the promise; and I should get only death, if I told you what you ask.'

Then Morgoth laughed, and he said: 'Death you may yet crave from me as a boon.' Then he took Húrin to the Haudh-en-Nirnaeth, and it was then new-built and the reek of death was upon it; and Morgoth set Húrin upon its top and bade him look west towards Hithlum, and think of his wife and his son and other kin. 'For they dwell now in my realm,' said Morgoth, 'and they are at my mercy.'

'You have none,' answered Húrin. 'But you will not come at Turgon through them; for they do not know his secrets.'

Then wrath mastered Morgoth, and he said: 'Yet I may come at you, and all your accursed house; and you shall be broken on my will, though you all were made of steel.' And he took up a long sword that lay there and broke it before the eyes of Húrin, and a splinter wounded his face; but Húrin did not blench. Then Morgoth stretching out his long arm towards Dor-lómin cursed Húrin and Morwen and their offspring, saying: 'Behold! The shadow of my thought shall lie upon them wherever they go, and my hate shall pursue them to the ends of the world.'

But Húrin said: 'You speak in vain. For you cannot see them, nor govern them from afar: not while you keep this shape, and desire still to be a King visible upon earth.'

Then Morgoth turned upon Húrin, and he said: 'Fool, little

among Men, and they are the least of all that speak! Have you seen
the Valar, or measured the power of Manwë and Varda? Do you know
the reach of their thought? Or do you think, perhaps, that their
thought is upon you, and that they may shield you from afar?'

'I know not,' said Húrin. 'Yet so it might be, if they willed. For
the Elder King shall not be dethroned while Arda endures.'

'You say it,' said Morgoth. 'I am the Elder King: Melkor, first
and mightiest of all the Valar, who was before the world, and made it.
The shadow of my purpose lies upon Arda, and all that is in it bends
slowly and surely to my will. But upon all whom you love my thought
shall weigh as a cloud of Doom, and it shall bring them down into
darkness and despair. Wherever they go, evil shall arise. Whenever
they speak, their words shall bring ill counsel. Whatsoever they do
shall turn against them. They shall die without hope, cursing both
life and death.'

But Húrin answered: 'Do you forget to whom you speak? Such
things you spoke long ago to our fathers; but we escaped from your
shadow. And now we have knowledge of you, for we have looked on
the faces that have seen the Light, and heard the voices that have
spoken with Manwë. Before Arda you were, but others also; and you
did not make it. Neither are you the most mighty; for you have
spent your strength upon yourself and wasted it in your own emptiness. No more are you now than an escaped thrall of the Valar, and
their chain still awaits you.'

'You have learned the lessons of your masters by rote,' said
Morgoth. 'But such childish lore will not help you, now they are all
fled away.'

'This last then I will say to you, thrall Morgoth,' said Húrin, 'and
it comes not from the lore of the Eldar, but is put into my heart in
this hour. You are not the Lord of Men, and shall not be, though all
Arda and Menel fall in your dominion. Beyond the Circles of the
World you shall not pursue those who refuse you.'

'Beyond the Circles of the World I will not pursue them,' said
Morgoth. 'For beyond the Circles of the World there is Nothing.
But within them they shall not escape me, until they enter into
Nothing.'

'You lie,' said Húrin.

'You shall see and you shall confess that I do not lie,' said Morgoth.
And taking Húrin back to Angband he set him in a chair of stone
upon a high place of Thangorodrim, from which he could see afar
the land of Hithlum in the west and the lands of Beleriand in the
south. There he was bound by the power of Morgoth; and Morgoth

standing beside him cursed him again and set his power upon him, so that he could not move from that place, nor die, until Morgoth should release him.

'Sit now there,' said Morgoth, 'and look out upon the lands where evil and despair shall come upon those whom you have delivered to me. For you have dared to mock me, and have questioned the power of Melkor, Master of the fates of Arda. Therefore with my eyes you shall see, and with my ears you shall hear, and nothing shall be hidden from you.'

The Departure of Túrin

To Brethil three men only found their way back at last through Taur-nu-Fuin, an evil road; and when Glóredhel Hador's daughter learned of the fall of Haldir she grieved and died.

To Dor-lómin no tidings came. Rían wife of Huor fled into the wild distraught; but she was aided by the Grey-elves of the hills of Mithrim, and when her child, Tuor, was born they fostered him. But Rían went to the Haudh-en-Nirnaeth, and laid herself down there, and died.

Morwen Eledhwen remained in Hithlum, silent in grief. Her son Túrin was only in his ninth year, and she was again with child. Her days were evil. The Easterlings came into the land in great numbers, and they dealt cruelly with the people of Hador, and robbed them of all that they possessed and enslaved them. All the people of Húrin's homelands that could work or serve any purpose they took away, even young girls and boys, and the old they killed or drove out to starve. But they dared not yet lay hands on the Lady of Dor-lómin, or thrust her from her house; for the word ran among them that she was perilous, and a witch who had dealings with the white-fiends: for so they named the Elves, hating them, but fearing them more.[3] For this reason they also feared and avoided the mountains, in which many of the Eldar had taken refuge, especially in the south of the land; and after plundering and harrying the Easterlings drew back northwards. For Húrin's house stood in the south-east of Dor-lómin, and the mountains were near; Nen Lalaith indeed came down from a spring under the shadow of Amon Darthir, over whose shoulder there was a steep pass. By this the hardy could cross Ered Wethrin and come down by the wells of Glithui into Beleriand. But this was not known to the Easterlings, nor to Morgoth yet; for all that country, while the House of Fingolfin stood, was secure from him, and none of his servants had ever come there. He trusted that Ered Wethrin was a wall insurmountable, both against escape from the north and against assault from the south; and there was indeed no other pass, for the unwinged, between Serech and far westward where Dor-lómin marched with Nevrast.

Thus it came to pass that after the first inroads Morwen was let be, though there were men that lurked in the woods about, and it was perilous to stir far abroad. There still remained under Morwen's shelter Sador the woodwright and a few old men and women, and Túrin, whom she kept close within the garth. But the homestead of Húrin soon fell into decay, and though Morwen laboured hard she was poor, and would have gone hungry but for the help that was sent to her secretly by Aerin, Húrin's kinswoman; for a certain Brodda, one of the Easterlings, had taken her by force to be his wife. Alms were bitter to Morwen; but she took this aid for the sake of Túrin and her unborn child, and because, as she said, it came of her own. For it was this Brodda who had seized the people, the goods, and the cattle of Húrin's homelands, and carried them off to his own dwellings. He was a bold man, but of small account among his own people before they came to Hithlum; and so, seeking wealth, he was ready to hold lands that others of his sort did not covet. Morwen he had seen once, when he rode to her house on a foray; but a great dread of her had seized him. He thought that he had looked in the fell eyes of a white-fiend, and he was filled with a mortal fear lest some evil should overtake him; and he did not ransack her house, nor discover Túrin, else the life of the heir of the true lord would have been short.

Brodda made thralls of the Strawheads, as he named the people of Hador, and set them to build him a wooden hall in the land to the northward of Húrin's house; and within a stockade his slaves were herded like cattle in a byre, but ill guarded. Among them some could still be found uncowed and ready to help the Lady of Dor-lómin, even at their peril; and from them came secretly tidings of the land to Morwen, though there was little hope in the news they brought. But Brodda took Aerin as a wife and not a slave, for there were few women amongst his own following, and none to compare with the daughters of the Edain; and he hoped to make himself a lordship in that country, and have an heir to hold it after him.

Of what had happened and of what might happen in the days to come Morwen said little to Túrin; and he feared to break her silence with questions. When the Easterlings first came into Dor-lómin he said to his mother: 'When will my father come back, to cast out these ugly thieves? Why does he not come?'

Morwen answered: 'I do not know. It may be that he was slain, or that he is held captive; or again it may be that he was driven far away, and cannot yet return through the foes that surround us.'

'Then I think that he is dead,' said Túrin, and before his mother he restrained his tears; 'for no one could keep him from coming back to help us, if he were alive.'

'I do not think that either of those things are true, my son,' said Morwen.

As the time lengthened the heart of Morwen grew darker with fear for her son Túrin, heir of Dor-lómin and Ladros; for she could see no hope for him better than to become a slave of the Easterling men, before he was much older. Therefore she remembered her words with Húrin, and her thought turned again to Doriath; and she resolved at last to send Túrin away in secret, if she could, and to beg King Thingol to harbour him. And as she sat and pondered how this might be done, she heard clearly in her thought the voice of Húrin saying to her: *Go swiftly! Do not wait for me!* But the birth of her child was drawing near, and the road would be hard and perilous; the more that went the less hope of escape. And her heart still cheated her with hope unadmitted; her inmost thought foreboded that Húrin was not dead, and she listened for his footfall in the sleepless watches of the night, or would wake thinking that she had heard in the courtyard the neigh of Arroch his horse. Moreover, though she was willing that her son should be fostered in the halls of another, after the manner of that time, she would not yet humble her pride to be an alms-guest, not even of a king. Therefore the voice of Húrin, or the memory of his voice, was denied, and the first strand of the fate of Túrin was woven.

Autumn of the Year of Lamentation was drawing on before Morwen came to this resolve, and then she was in haste; for the time for journeying was short, but she dreaded that Túrin would be taken, if she waited over winter. Easterlings were prowling round the garth and spying on the house. Therefore she said suddenly to Túrin: 'Your father does not come. So you must go, and go soon. It is as he would wish.'

'Go?' cried Túrin. 'Whither shall we go? Over the Mountains?'

'Yes,' said Morwen, 'over the Mountains, away south. South – that way some hope may lie. But I did not say *we*, my son. You must go, but I must stay.'

'I cannot go alone!' said Túrin. 'I will not leave you. Why should we not go together?'

'I cannot go,' said Morwen. 'But you will not go alone. I shall send Gethron with you, and Grithnir too, perhaps.'

'Will you not send Labadal?' said Túrin.

'No, for Sador is lame,' said Morwen, 'and it will be a hard road. And since you are my son and the days are grim, I will not speak softly: you may die on that road. The year is getting late. But if you stay, you will come to a worse end: to be a thrall. If you wish to be a man, when you come to a man's age, you will do as I bid, bravely.'

'But I shall leave you only with Sador, and blind Ragnir, and the old women,' said Túrin. 'Did not my father say that I am the heir of Hador? The heir should stay in Hador's house to defend it. Now I wish that I still had my knife!'

'The heir should stay, but he cannot,' said Morwen. 'But he may return one day. Now take heart! I will follow you, if things grow worse; if I can.'

'But how will you find me, lost in the wild?' said Túrin; and suddenly his heart failed him, and he wept openly.

'If you wail, other things will find you first,' said Morwen. 'But I know whither you are going, and if you come there, and if you remain there, there I will find you, if I can. For I am sending you to King Thingol in Doriath. Would you not rather be a king's guest than a thrall?'

'I do not know,' said Túrin. 'I do not know what a thrall is.'

'I am sending you away so that you need not learn it,' Morwen answered. Then she set Túrin before her and looked into his eyes, as if she were trying to read some riddle there. 'It is hard, Túrin, my son,' she said at length. 'Not hard for you only. It is heavy on me in evil days to judge what is best to do. But I do as I think right; for why else should I part with the thing most dear that is left to me?'

They spoke no more of this together, and Túrin was grieved and bewildered. In the morning he went to find Sador, who had been hewing sticks for firing, of which they had little, for they dared not stray out in the woods; and now he leant on his crutch and looked at the great chair of Húrin, which had been thrust unfinished in a corner. 'It must go,' he said, 'for only bare needs can be served in these days.'

'Do not break it yet,' said Túrin. 'Maybe he will come home, and then it will please him to see what you have done for him while he was away.'

'False hopes are more dangerous than fears,' said Sador, 'and they will not keep us warm this winter.' He fingered the carving on the chair, and sighed. 'I wasted my time,' he said, 'though the hours seemed pleasant. But all such things are short-lived; and the joy in the making is their only true end, I guess. And now I might as well give you back your gift.'

Túrin put out his hand, and quickly withdrew it. 'A man does not take back his gifts,' he said.

'But if it is my own, may I not give it as I will?' said Sador.

'Yes,' said Túrin, 'to any man but me. But why should you wish to give it?'

'I have no hope of using it for worthy tasks,' Sador said. 'There will be no work for Labadal in days to come but thrall-work.'

'What is a thrall?' said Túrin.

'A man who was a man but is treated as a beast,' Sador answered. 'Fed only to keep alive, kept alive only to toil, toiling only for fear of pain or death. And from these robbers he may get pain or death just for their sport. I hear that they pick some of the fleet-footed and hunt them with hounds. They have learned quicker from the Orcs than we learnt from the Fair Folk.'

'Now I understand things better,' said Túrin.

'It is a shame that you should have to understand such things so soon,' said Sador; then seeing the strange look on Túrin's face: 'What do you understand now?'

'Why my mother is sending me away,' said Túrin, and tears filled his eyes.

'Ah!' said Sador, and he muttered to himself: 'But why so long delayed?' Then turning to Túrin he said: 'That does not seem news for tears to me. But you should not speak your mother's counsels aloud to Labadal, or to any one. All walls and fences have ears these days, ears that do not grow on fair heads.'

'But I must speak with someone!' said Túrin. 'I have always told things to you. I do not want to leave you, Labadal. I do not want to leave this house or my mother.'

'But if you do not,' said Sador, 'soon there will be an end of the House of Hador for ever, as you must understand now. Labadal does not want you to go; but Sador servant of Húrin will be happier when Húrin's son is out of the reach of the Easterlings. Well, well, it cannot be helped: we must say farewell. Now will you not take my knife as a parting gift?'

'No!' said Túrin. 'I am going to the Elves, to the King of Doriath, my mother says. There I may get other things like it. But I shall not be able to send you any gifts, Labadal. I shall be far away and all alone.' Then Túrin wept; but Sador said to him: 'Hey now! Where is Húrin's son? For I heard him say, not long ago: *I shall go as a soldier with an Elf-king, as soon as I am able.*'

Then Túrin stayed his tears, and he said: 'Very well: if those were the words of the son of Húrin, he must keep them, and go. But whenever I say that I will do this or that, it looks very different when the time comes. Now I am unwilling. I must take care not to say such things again.'

'It would be best indeed,' said Sador. 'So most men teach, and few men learn. Let the unseen days be. Today is more than enough.'

Now Túrin was made ready for the journey, and he bade farewell to his mother, and departed in secret with his two companions. But when they bade Túrin turn and look back upon the house of his father, then the anguish of parting smote him like a sword, and he cried: 'Morwen, Morwen, when shall I see you again?' But Morwen standing on her threshold heard the echo of that cry in the wooded hills, and she clutched the post of the door so that her fingers were torn. This was the first of the sorrows of Túrin.

Early in the year after Túrin was gone Morwen gave birth to her child, and she named her Nienor, which is Mourning; but Túrin was already far away when she was born. Long and evil was his road, for the power of Morgoth was ranging far abroad; but he had as guides Gethron and Grithnir, who had been young in the days of Hador, and though they were now aged they were valiant, and they knew well the lands, for they had journeyed often through Beleriand in former times. Thus by fate and courage they passed over the Shadowy Mountains, and coming down into the Vale of Sirion they passed into the Forest of Brethil; and at last, weary and haggard, they reached the confines of Doriath. But there they became bewildered, and were enmeshed in the mazes of the Queen, and wandered lost amid the pathless trees, until all their food was spent. There they came near to death, for winter came cold from the North; but not so light was Túrin's doom. Even as they lay in despair they heard a horn sounded. Beleg the Strongbow was hunting in that region, for he dwelt ever upon the marches of Doriath, and he was the greatest woodsman of those days. He heard their cries and came to them, and when he had given them food and drink he learned their names and whence they came, and he was filled with wonder and pity. And he looked with liking upon Túrin, for he had the beauty of his mother and the eyes of his father, and he was sturdy and strong.

'What boon would you have of King Thingol?' said Beleg to the boy.

'I would be one of his knights, to ride against Morgoth, and avenge my father,' said Túrin.

'That may well be, when the years have increased you,' said Beleg. 'For though you are yet small you have the makings of a valiant man, worthy to be a son of Húrin the Steadfast, if that were possible.' For the name of Húrin was held in honour in all the lands of the Elves. Therefore Beleg gladly became the guide of the wanderers, and he led them to a lodge where he dwelt at that time with other hunters, and there they were housed while a messenger went to Menegroth. And when word came back that Thingol and Melian would receive the son of Húrin and his guardians, Beleg led them by secret ways into the Hidden Kingdom.

Thus Túrin came to the great bridge over the Esgalduin, and passed the gates of Thingol's halls; and as a child he gazed upon the marvels of Menegroth, which no mortal Man before had seen, save Beren only. Then Gethron spoke the message of Morwen before Thingol and Melian; and Thingol received them kindly, and set Túrin upon his knee in honour of Húrin, mightiest of Men, and of Beren his kinsman. And those that saw this marvelled, for it was a sign that Thingol took Túrin as his foster-son; and that was not at that time done by kings, nor ever again by Elf-lord to a Man. Then Thingol said to him: 'Here, son of Húrin, shall your home be; and in all your life you shall be held as my son, Man though you be. Wisdom shall be given you beyond the measure of mortal Men, and the weapons of the Elves shall be set in your hands. Perhaps the time may come when you shall regain the lands of your father in Hithlum; but dwell now here in love.'

Thus began the sojourn of Túrin in Doriath. With him for a while remained Gethron and Grithnir his guardians, though they yearned to return again to their lady in Dor-lómin. Then age and sickness came upon Grithnir, and he stayed beside Túrin until he died; but Gethron departed, and Thingol sent with him an escort to guide him and guard him, and they brought words from Thingol to Morwen. They came at last to Húrin's house, and when Morwen learned that Túrin was received with honour in the halls of Thingol her grief was lightened; and the Elves brought also rich gifts from Melian, and a message bidding her return with Thingol's folk to

Doriath. For Melian was wise and foresighted, and she hoped thus to avert the evil that was prepared in the thought of Morgoth. But Morwen would not depart from her house, for her heart was yet unchanged and her pride still high; moreover Nienor was a babe in arms. Therefore she dismissed the Elves of Doriath with her thanks, and gave them in gift the last small things of gold that remained to her, concealing her poverty; and she bade them take back to Thingol the Helm of Hador. But Túrin watched ever for the return of Thingol's messengers; and when they came back alone he fled into the woods and wept, for he knew of Melian's bidding and he had hoped that Morwen would come. This was the second sorrow of Túrin.

When the messengers spoke Morwen's answer, Melian was moved with pity, perceiving her mind; and she saw that the fate which she foreboded could not lightly be set aside.

The Helm of Hador was given into Thingol's hands. That helm was made of grey steel adorned with gold, and on it were graven runes of victory. A power was in it that guarded any who wore it from wound or death, for the sword that hewed it was broken, and the dart that smote it sprang aside. It was wrought by Telchar, the smith of Nogrod, whose works were renowned. It had a visor (after the manner of those that the Dwarves used in their forges for the shielding of their eyes), and the face of one that wore it struck fear into the hearts of all beholders, but was itself guarded from dart and fire. Upon its crest was set in defiance a gilded image of the head of Glaurung the dragon; for it had been made soon after he first issued from the gates of Morgoth. Often Hador, and Galdor after him, had borne it in war; and the hearts of the host of Hithlum were uplifted when they saw it towering high amid the battle, and they cried: 'Of more worth is the Dragon of Dor-lómin than the gold-worm of Angband!'

But in truth this helm had not been made for Men, but for Azaghâl Lord of Belegost, he who was slain by Glaurung in the Year of Lamentation.[4] It was given by Azaghâl to Maedhros, as guerdon for the saving of his life and treasure, when Azaghâl was waylaid by Orcs upon the Dwarf-road in East Beleriand.[5] Maedhros afterwards sent it as a gift to Fingon, with whom he often exchanged tokens of friendship, remembering how Fingon had driven Glaurung back to Angband. But in all Hithlum no head and shoulders were found stout enough to bear the dwarf-helm with ease, save those of Hador and his son Galdor. Fingon therefore gave it to Hador, when he received the lordship of Dor-lómin. By ill-fortune Galdor did not wear it when he defended Eithel Sirion, for the assault was sudden, and he ran barehead to the walls, and an orc-arrow pierced his eye. But Húrin did not wear the Dragon-helm with ease, and in any case he would not use it, for he said: 'I would rather look on my foes with my true face.' Nonetheless he accounted the helm among the greatest heirlooms of his house.

Now Thingol had in Menegroth deep armouries filled with great wealth of weapons: metal wrought like fishes' mail and shining like water in the moon; swords and axes, shields and helms, wrought by Telchar himself or by his master Gamil Zirak the old, or by elven-wrights more skilful still. For some things he had received in gift that came out of Valinor and were wrought by Fëanor in his mastery, than whom no craftsman was greater in all the days of the world. Yet Thingol handled the Helm of Hador as though his hoard were scanty, and he spoke courteous words, saying: 'Proud were the head that bore this helm, which the sires of Húrin bore.'

Then a thought came to him, and he summoned Túrin, and told him that Morwen had sent to her son a mighty thing, the heirloom of his fathers. 'Take now the Dragonhead of the North,' he said, 'and when the time comes wear it well.' But Túrin was yet too young to lift the helm, and he heeded it not because of the sorrow of his heart.

Túrin in Doriath

In the years of his childhood in the kingdom of Doriath Túrin was watched over by Melian, though he saw her seldom. But there was a maiden named Nellas, who lived in the woods; and at Melian's bidding she would follow Túrin if he strayed in the forest, and often she met him there, as it were by chance. From Nellas Túrin learned much concerning the ways and the wild things of Doriath, and she taught him to speak the Sindarin tongue after the manner of the ancient realm, older, and more courteous, and richer in beautiful words.[6] Thus for a little while his mood was lightened, until he fell again under shadow, and that friendship passed like a morning of spring. For Nellas did not go to Menegroth, and was unwilling ever to walk under roofs of stone; so that as Túrin's boyhood passed and he turned his thoughts to the deeds of men, he saw her less and less often, and at last called for her no more. But she watched over him still, though now she remained hidden.[7]

Nine years Túrin dwelt in the halls of Menegroth. His heart and thought turned ever to his own kin, and at times he had tidings of them for his comfort. For Thingol sent messengers to Morwen as often as he might, and she sent back words for her son; thus Túrin heard that his sister Nienor grew in beauty, a flower in the grey North, and that Morwen's plight was eased. And Túrin grew in stature until he became tall among Men, and his strength and hardihood were renowned in the realm of Thingol. In those years he learned much lore, hearing eagerly the histories of ancient days; and he became thoughtful, and sparing in speech. Often Beleg Strongbow came to Menegroth to seek him, and led him far afield, teaching him woodcraft and archery and (which he loved best) the handling of swords; but in crafts of making he had less skill, for he was slow to learn his own strength, and often marred what he made with some sudden stroke. In other matters also it seemed that fortune was unfriendly to him, so that often what he designed went awry, and what he desired he did not gain; neither did he win friendship easily, for he was not merry, and laughed seldom, and a shadow lay on his youth. Nonetheless he was held in love and esteem by those who knew him well, and he had honour as the fosterling of the King.

Yet there was one that begrudged him this, and ever the more as Túrin drew nearer to manhood: Saeros, son of Ithilbor, was his name. He was of the Nandor, being one of those who took refuge in Doriath after the fall of their lord Denethor upon Amon Ereb, in the first battle of Beleriand. These Elves dwelt for the most part in Arthórien, between Aros and Celon in the east of Doriath, wandering at times over Celon into the wild lands beyond; and they were no friends to the Edain since their passage through Ossiriand and settlement in Estolad. But Saeros dwelt mostly in Menegroth, and won the esteem of the king; and he was proud, dealing haughtily with those whom he deemed of lesser state and worth than himself. He became a friend of Daeron the minstrel,[8] for he also was skilled in song; and he had no love for Men, and least of all for any kinsman of Beren Erchamion. 'Is it not strange,' said he, 'that this land should be opened to yet another of this unhappy race? Did not the other do harm enough in Doriath?' Therefore he looked askance on Túrin and on all that he did, saying what ill he could of it; but his words were cunning and his malice veiled. If he met with Túrin alone, he spoke haughtily to him and showed plain his contempt; and Túrin grew weary of him, though for long he returned ill words with silence, for Saeros was great among the people of Doriath and a counsellor of the King. But the silence of Túrin displeased Saeros as much as his words.

In the year that Túrin was seventeen years old, his grief was renewed; for all tidings from his home ceased at that time. The power of Morgoth had grown yearly, and all Hithlum was now under his shadow. Doubtless he knew much of the doings of Húrin's kin, and had not molested them for a while, so that his design might be fulfilled; but now in pursuit of this purpose he set a close watch upon all the passes of the Shadowy Mountains, so that none might come out of Hithlum nor enter it, save at great peril, and the Orcs swarmed about the sources of Narog and Teiglin and the upper waters of Sirion. Thus there came a time when the messengers of Thingol did not return, and he would send no more. He was ever loath to let any stray beyond the guarded borders, and in nothing had he shown greater good will to Húrin and his kin than in sending his people on the dangerous roads to Morwen in Dor-lómin.

Now Túrin grew heavy-hearted, not knowing what new evil was afoot, and fearing that an ill fate had befallen Morwen and Nienor; and for many days he sat silent, brooding on the downfall of the House of Hador and the Men of the North. Then he rose up and went to seek Thingol; and he found him sitting with Melian under Hírilorn, the great beech of Menegroth.

Thingol looked on Túrin in wonder, seeing suddenly before him in the place of his fosterling a Man and a stranger, tall, dark-haired, looking at him with deep eyes in a white face. Then Túrin asked Thingol for mail, sword, and shield, and he reclaimed now the Dragon-helm of Dor-lómin; and the king granted him what he sought, saying: 'I will appoint you a place among my knights of the sword; for the sword will ever be your weapon. With them you may make trial of war upon the marches, if that is your desire.'

But Túrin said: 'Beyond the marches of Doriath my heart urges me; I long rather for assault upon the Enemy, than for defence of the borderlands.'

'Then you must go alone,' said Thingol. 'The part of my people in the war with Angband I rule according to my wisdom, Túrin son of Húrin. No force of the arms of Doriath will I send out at this time; nor in any time that I can yet foresee.'

'Yet you are free to go as you will, son of Morwen,' said Melian. 'The Girdle of Melian does not hinder the going of those that passed in with our leave.'

'Unless wise counsel will restrain you,' said Thingol.

'What is your counsel, lord?' said Túrin.

'A Man you seem in stature,' Thingol answered, 'but nonetheless you have not come to the fullness of your manhood that shall be. When that time comes, then, maybe, you can remember your kin; but there is little hope that one Man alone can do more against the

Dark Lord than to aid the Elf-lords in their defence, as long as that
may last.'

Then Túrin said: 'Beren my kinsman did more.'

'Beren, and Lúthien,' said Melian. 'But you are over-bold to
speak so to the father of Lúthien. Not so high is your destiny, I
think, Túrin son of Morwen, though your fate is twined with that of
the Elven-folk, for good or for ill. Beware of yourself, lest it be ill.'
Then after a silence she spoke to him again, saying: 'Go now,
fosterson; and heed the counsel of the king. Yet I do not think that
you will long abide with us in Doriath after the coming of manhood.
If in days to come you remember the words of Melian, it will be for
your good: fear both the heat and the cold of your heart.'

Then Túrin bowed before them, and took his leave. And soon
after he put on the Dragon-helm, and took arms, and went away to
the north-marches, and was joined to the elven-warriors who there
waged unceasing war upon the Orcs and all servants and creatures of
Morgoth. Thus while yet scarcely out of his boyhood his strength
and courage were proved; and remembering the wrongs of his kin
he was ever forward in deeds of daring, and he received many wounds
by spear or arrow or the crooked blades of the Orcs. But his doom
delivered him from death; and word ran through the woods, and
was heard far beyond Doriath, that the Dragon-helm of Dor-lómin
was seen again. Then many wondered, saying: 'Can the spirit of
Hador or of Galdor the Tall return from death; or has Húrin of
Hithlum escaped indeed from the pits of Angband?'

One only was mightier in arms among the march-wardens of
Thingol at that time than Túrin, and that was Beleg Cúthalion; and
Beleg and Túrin were companions in every peril, and walked far and
wide in the wild woods together.

Thus three years passed, and in that time Túrin came seldom to
Thingol's halls; and he cared no longer for his looks or his attire,
but his hair was unkempt, and his mail covered with a grey cloak
stained with the weather. But it chanced in the third summer, when
Túrin was twenty years old, that desiring rest and needing smith-
work for the repair of his arms he came unlooked for to Menegroth
in the evening; and he went into the hall. Thingol was not there,
for he was abroad in the greenwood with Melian, as was his delight
at times in the high summer. Túrin went to a seat without heed, for
he was wayworn, and filled with thought; and by ill-luck he set
himself at a board among the elders of the realm, and in that very
place where Saeros was accustomed to sit. Saeros, entering late, was

angered, believing that Túrin had done this in pride, and with intent to affront him; and his anger was not lessened to find that Túrin was not rebuked by those that sat there, but welcomed among them.

For a while therefore Saeros feigned to be of like mind, and took another seat, facing Túrin across the board. 'Seldom does the march-warden favour us with his company,' he said; 'and I gladly yield my accustomed seat for the chance of speech with him.' And much else he said to Túrin, questioning him concerning the news from the borders, and his deeds in the wild; but though his words seemed fair, the mockery in his voice could not be mistaken. Then Túrin became weary, and he looked about him, and knew the bitterness of exile; and for all the light and laughter of the Elven-halls his thought turned to Beleg and their life in the woods, and thence far away, to Morwen in Dor-lómin in the house of his father; and he frowned, because of the darkness of his thoughts, and made no answer to Saeros. At this, believing the frown aimed at himself, Saeros re-strained his anger no longer; and he took out a golden comb, and cast it on the board before Túrin, saying: 'Doubtless, Man of Hithlum, you came in haste to this table, and may be excused your ragged cloak; but you have no need to leave your head untended as a thicket of brambles. And perhaps if your ears were uncovered you would hear better what is said to you.'

Túrin said nothing, but turned his eyes upon Saeros, and there was a glint in their darkness. But Saeros did not heed the warning, and returned the gaze with scorn, saying for all to hear: 'If the Men of Hithlum are so wild and fell, of what sort are the women of that land? Do they run like deer clad only in their hair?'

Then Túrin took up a drinking-vessel and cast it in Saeros' face, and he fell backward with great hurt; and Túrin drew his sword and would have run at him, but Mablung the Hunter, who sat at his side, restrained him. Then Saeros rising spat blood upon the board, and spoke from a broken mouth: 'How long shall we harbour this wood-wose?[9] Who rules here tonight? The king's law is heavy upon those who hurt his lieges in the hall; and for those who draw blades there outlawry is the least doom. Outside the hall I could answer you, Woodwose!'

But when Túrin saw the blood upon the table his mood became cold; and releasing himself from Mablung's grasp he left the hall without a word.

Then Mablung said to Saeros: 'What ails you tonight? For this evil I hold you to blame; and it may be that the King's law will judge a broken mouth a just return for your taunting.'

'If the cub has a grievance, let him bring it to the King's judgement,' answered Saeros. 'But the drawing of swords here is not to be excused for any such cause. Outside the hall, if the woodwose draws on me, I shall kill him.'

'That seems to me less certain,' said Mablung; 'but if either be slain it will be an evil deed, more fit for Angband than Doriath, and more evil will come of it. Indeed I think that some shadow of the North has reached out to touch us tonight. Take heed, Saeros son of Ithilbor, lest you do the will of Morgoth in your pride, and remember that you are of the Eldar.'

'I do not forget it,' said Saeros; but he did not abate his wrath, and through the night his malice grew, nursing his injury.

In the morning, when Túrin left Menegroth to return to the north-marches, Saeros waylaid him, running out upon him from behind with drawn sword and shield on arm. But Túrin, trained in the wild to wariness, saw him from the corner of his eye, and leaping aside he drew swiftly and turned upon his foe. 'Morwen!' he cried, 'now your mocker shall pay for his scorn!' And he clove Saeros' shield, and then they fought together with swift blades. But Túrin had been long in a hard school, and had grown as agile as any Elf, but stronger. He soon had the mastery, and wounding Saeros' sword-arm he had him at his mercy. Then he set his foot on the sword that Saeros had let fall. 'Saeros,' he said, 'there is a long race before you, and clothes will be a hindrance; hair must suffice.' And suddenly throwing him to the ground he stripped him, and Saeros felt Túrin's great strength, and was afraid. But Túrin let him up, and then 'Run!' he cried. 'Run! And unless you go as swift as the deer I shall prick you on from behind.' And Saeros fled into the wood, crying wildly for help; but Túrin came after him like a hound, and however he ran, or swerved, still the sword was behind him to egg him on.

The cries of Saeros brought many others to the chase, and they followed after, but only the swiftest could keep up with the runners. Mablung was in the forefront of these, and he was troubled in mind, for though the taunting had seemed evil to him, 'malice that wakes in the morning is the mirth of Morgoth ere night'; and it was held moreover a grievous thing to put any of the Elven-folk to shame, self-willed, without the matter being brought to judgement. None knew at that time that Túrin had been assailed first by Saeros, who would have slain him.

'Hold, hold, Túrin!' he cried. 'This is Orc-work in the woods!' But Túrin called back: 'Orc-work in the woods for Orc-words in the hall!' and sprang again after Saeros; and he, despairing of aid and

thinking his death close behind, ran wildly on, until he came suddenly
to a brink where a stream that fed Esgalduin flowed in a deep cleft
through high rocks, and it was wide for a deer-leap. There Saeros
in his great fear attempted the leap; but he failed of his footing on
the far side and fell back with a cry, and was broken on a great stone
in the water. So he ended his life in Doriath; and long would Mandos
hold him.

Túrin looked down on his body lying in the stream, and he thought:
'Unhappy fool! From here I would have let him walk back to
Menegroth. Now he has laid a guilt upon me undeserved.' And he
turned and looked darkly on Mablung and his companions, who now
came up and stood near him on the brink. Then after a silence
Mablung said: 'Alas! But come back now with us, Túrin, for the
King must judge these deeds.'

But Túrin said: 'If the King were just, he would judge me guiltless.
But was not this one of his counsellors? Why should a just king
choose a heart of malice for his friend? I abjure his law and his
judgement.'

'Your words are unwise,' said Mablung, though in his heart he
felt pity for Túrin. 'You shall not turn runagate. I bid you return
with me, as a friend. And there are other witnesses. When the King
learns the truth you may hope for his pardon.'

But Túrin was weary of the Elven-halls, and he feared lest he be
held captive; and he said to Mablung: 'I refuse your bidding. I will
not seek King Thingol's pardon for nothing; and I will go now where
his doom cannot find me. You have but two choices: to let me go
free, or to slay me, if that would fit your law. For you are too few
to take me alive.'

They saw in his eyes that this was true, and they let him pass;
and Mablung said: 'One death is enough.'

'I did not will it, but I do not mourn it,' said Túrin. 'May Mandos
judge him justly; and if ever he return to the lands of the living,
may he prove wiser. Farewell!'

'Fare free!' said Mablung; 'for that is your wish. But well I do
not hope for, if you go in this way. A shadow is on your heart.
When we meet again, may it be no darker.'

To that Túrin made no answer, but left them, and went swiftly
away, none knew whither.

It is told that when Túrin did not return to the north-marches
of Doriath and no tidings could be heard of him, Beleg Strongbow
came himself to Menegroth to seek him; and with heavy heart he

gathered news of Túrin's deeds and flight. Soon afterwards Thingol and Melian came back to their halls, for the summer was waning; and when the King heard report of what had passed he sat upon his throne in the great hall of Menegroth, and about him were all the lords and counsellors of Doriath.

Then all was searched and told, even to the parting words of Túrin; and at the last Thingol sighed, and he said: 'Alas! How has this shadow stolen into my realm? Saeros I accounted faithful and wise; but if he lived he would feel my anger, for his taunting was evil, and I hold him to blame for all that chanced in the hall. So far Túrin has my pardon. But the shaming of Saeros and the hounding of him to his death were wrongs greater than the offence, and these deeds I cannot pass over. They show a hard heart, and proud.' Then Thingol fell silent, but at last he spoke again in sadness. 'This is an ungrateful fosterson, and a Man too proud for his state. How shall I harbour one who scorns me and my law, or pardon one who will not repent? Therefore I will banish Túrin son of Húrin from the kingdom of Doriath. If he seeks entry he shall be brought to judgement before me; and until he sues for pardon at my feet he is my son no longer. If any here accounts this unjust, let him speak.'

Then there was silence in the hall, and Thingol lifted up his hand to pronounce his doom. But at that moment Beleg entered in haste, and cried: 'Lord, may I yet speak?'

'You come late,' said Thingol. 'Were you not bidden with the others?'

'Truly, lord,' answered Beleg, 'but I was delayed; I sought for one whom I knew. Now I bring at last a witness who should be heard, ere your doom falls.'

'All were summoned who had aught to tell,' said the King. 'What can he tell now of more weight than those to whom I have listened?'

'You shall judge when you have heard,' said Beleg. 'Grant this to me, if I have ever deserved your grace.'

'To you I grant it,' said Thingol. Then Beleg went out, and led in by the hand the maiden Nellas, who dwelt in the woods, and came never into Menegroth; and she was afraid, both for the great pillared hall and the roof of stone, and for the company of many eyes that watched her. And when Thingol bade her speak, she said: 'Lord, I was sitting in a tree'; but then she faltered in awe of the King, and could say no more.

At that the King smiled, and said: 'Others have done this also, but have felt no need to tell me of it.'

'Others indeed,' said she, taking courage from his smile. 'Even

Lúthien! And of her I was thinking that morning, and of Beren the Man.'

To that Thingol said nothing, and he smiled no longer, but waited until Nellas should speak again.

'For Túrin reminded me of Beren,' she said at last. 'They are akin, I am told, and their kinship can be seen by some: by some that look close.'

Then Thingol grew impatient. 'That may be,' he said. 'But Túrin son of Húrin is gone in scorn of me, and you will see him no more to read his kindred. For now I will speak my judgement.'

'Lord King!' she cried then. 'Bear with me, and let me speak first. I sat in a tree to look on Túrin as he went away; and I saw Saeros come out from the wood with sword and shield, and spring on Túrin at unawares.'

At that there was a murmur in the hall; and the King lifted his hand, saying: 'You bring graver news to my ear than seemed likely. Take heed now to all that you say; for this is a court of doom.'

'So Beleg has told me,' she answered, 'and only for that have I dared to come here, so that Túrin shall not be ill judged. He is valiant, but he is merciful. They fought, lord, these two, until Túrin had bereft Saeros of both shield and sword; but he did not slay him. Therefore I do not believe that he willed his death in the end. If Saeros were put to shame, it was shame that he had earned.'

'Judgement is mine,' said Thingol. 'But what you have told shall govern it.' Then he questioned Nellas closely; and at last he turned to Mablung, saying: 'It is strange to me that Túrin said nᵣ thing of this to you.'

'Yet he did not,' said Mablung. 'And had he spoken of it, other-wise would my words have been to him at parting.'

'And otherwise shall my doom now be,' said Thingol. 'Hear me! Such fault as can be found in Túrin I now pardon, holding him wronged and provoked. And since it was indeed, as he said, one of my council who so misused him, he shall not seek for this pardon, but I will send it to him, wherever he may be found; and I will recall him in honour to my halls.'

But when the doom was pronounced, suddenly Nellas wept. 'Where can he be found?' she said. 'He has left our land, and the world is wide.'

'He shall be sought,' said Thingol. Then he rose, and Beleg led Nellas forth from Menegroth; and he said to her: 'Do not weep; for if Túrin lives or walks still abroad, I shall find him, though all others fail.'

On the next day Beleg came before Thingol and Melian, and the King said to him: 'Counsel me, Beleg; for I am grieved. I took Húrin's son as my son, and so he shall remain, unless Húrin himself should return out of the shadows to claim his own. I would not have any say that Túrin was driven forth unjustly into the wild, and gladly would I welcome him back; for I loved him well.'

And Beleg answered: 'I will seek Túrin until I find him, and I will bring him back to Menegroth, if I can; for I love him also.' Then he departed; and far across Beleriand he sought in vain for tidings of Túrin, through many perils; and that winter passed away, and the spring after.

Túrin among the Outlaws

Now the tale turns again to Túrin. He, believing himself an outlaw whom the king would pursue, did not return to Beleg on the north-marches of Doriath, but went away westward, and passing secretly out of the Guarded Realm came into the woodlands south of Teiglin. There before the Nirnaeth many Men had dwelt in scattered home-steads; they were of Haleth's folk for the most part, but owned no lord, and they lived both by hunting and by husbandry, keeping swine in the mast-lands, and tilling clearings in the forest which were fenced from the wild. But most were now destroyed, or had fled into Brethil, and all that region lay under the fear of Orcs, and of outlaws. For in that time of ruin houseless and desperate Men went astray: remnants of battle and defeat, and lands laid waste; and some were Men driven into the wild for evil deeds. They hunted and gathered such food as they could; but in winter when hunger drove them they were to be feared as wolves, and Gaurwaith, the Wolf-men, they were called by those who still defended their homes. Some fifty of these Men had joined in one band, wandering in the woods beyond the western marches of Doriath; and they were hated scarcely less than Orcs, for there were among them outcasts hard of heart, bearing a grudge against their own kind. The grimmest among them was one named Andróg, hunted from Dor-lómin for the slaying of a woman; and others also came from that land: old Algund, the oldest of the fellowship, who had fled from the Nirnaeth, and Forweg, as he named himself, the captain of the band, a man with fair hair and unsteady glittering eyes, big and bold, but far fallen from the ways of the Edain of the people of Hador. They were become very wary, and they set scouts or a watch about them, whether moving or at rest; and thus they were quickly aware of Túrin when he strayed into their haunts. They trailed him, and they drew a ring about him; and suddenly, as he came out into a glade beside a stream, he found himself within a circle of men with bent bows and drawn swords.

Then Túrin halted, but he showed no fear. 'Who are you?' he said. 'I thought that only Orcs waylaid Men; but I see that I am mistaken.'

'You may rue the mistake,' said Forweg, 'for these are our haunts, and we do not allow other Men to walk in them. We take their lives as forfeit, unless they can ransom them.'

Then Túrin laughed. 'You will get no ransom from me,' he said, 'an outcast and an outlaw. You may search me when I am dead, but it will cost you dearly to prove my words true.'

Nonetheless his death seemed near, for many arrows were notched to the string, waiting for the word of the captain; and none of his enemies stood within reach of a leap with drawn sword. But Túrin, seeing some stones at the stream's edge before his feet, stooped suddenly; and in that instant one of the men, angered by his words, let fly a shaft. But it passed over Túrin, and he springing up cast a stone at the bowman with great force and true aim; and he fell to the ground with broken skull.

'I might be of more service to you alive, in the place of that luckless man,' said Túrin; and turning to Forweg he said: 'If you are the captain here, you should not allow your men to shoot without command.'

'I do not,' said Forweg; 'but he has been rebuked swiftly enough. I will take you in his stead, if you will heed my words better.'

Then two of the outlaws cried out against him; and one was a friend of the fallen man. Ulrad was his name. 'A strange way to gain entry to a fellowship,' he said: 'the slaying of one of the best men.'

'Not unchallenged,' said Túrin. 'But come then! I will endure you both together, with weapons or with strength alone; and then you shall see if I am fit to replace one of your best men.' Then he strode towards them; but Ulrad gave back and would not fight. The other threw down his bow, and looked Túrin up and down; and this man was Andróg of Dor-lómin.

'I am not your match,' he said at length, shaking his head. 'There is none here, I think. You may join us, for my part. But there is a strange look about you; you are a dangerous man. What is your name?'

'Neithan, the Wronged, I call myself,' said Túrin, and Neithan he was afterwards called by the outlaws; but though he told them that he had suffered injustice (and to any who claimed the like he ever lent too ready an ear), no more would he reveal concerning his life or his home. Yet they saw that he had fallen from some high state, and that though he had nothing but his arms, those were made by elvensmiths. He soon won their praise, for he was strong and valiant, and had more skill in the woods than they, and they trusted him, for he was not greedy, and took little thought for himself; but they feared him, because of his sudden angers, which they seldom understood. To Doriath Túrin could not, or in pride would not, return; to Nargothrond since the fall of Felagund none were admitted. To the lesser folk of Haleth in Brethil he did not deign to go; and to Dor-lómin he did not dare, for it was closely beset, and one man alone could not hope at that time, as he thought, to come through the passes of the Mountains of Shadow. Therefore Túrin abode with the outlaws, since the company of any men made the hardship of the wild more easy to endure; and because he wished to live and could not be ever at strife with them, he did little to restrain their evil deeds. Yet at times pity and shame would wake in him, and then he was perilous in his anger. In this way he lived to that year's end, and through the need and hunger of winter, until Stirring came and then a fair spring.

Now in the woods south of Teiglin, as has been told, there were still some homesteads of Men, hardy and wary, though now few in number. Though they loved them not at all and pitied them little, they would in bitter winter put out such food as they could well spare where the Gaurwaith might find it; and so they hoped to avoid the banded attack of the famished. But they earned less gratitude so from the outlaws than from beasts and birds, and they were saved rather by their dogs and their fences. For each homestead had great hedges about its cleared land, and about the houses was a ditch and a stockade; and there were paths from stead to stead, and men could summon help and need by horn-calls.

But when spring was come it was perilous for the Gaurwaith to linger so near to the houses of the Woodmen, who might gather and hunt them down; and Túrin wondered therefore that Forweg did not lead them away. There was more food and game, and less peril, away South where no Men remained. Then one day Túrin missed Forweg, and also Andróg his friend; and he asked where they were, but his companions laughed.

'Away on business of their own, I guess,' said Ulrad. 'They will be back before long, and then we shall move. In haste, maybe; for we shall be lucky if they do not bring the hive-bees after them.'

The sun shone and the young leaves were green; and Túrin was irked by the squalid camp of the outlaws, and he wandered away alone far into the forest. Against his will be remembered the Hidden Kingdom, and he seemed to hear the names of the flowers of Doriath as echoes of an old tongue almost forgotten. But on a sudden he heard cries, and from a hazel-thicket a young women ran out; her clothes were rent by thorns, and she was in great fear, and stumbling she fell gasping to the ground. Then Túrin springing towards the thicket with drawn sword hewed down a man that burst from the hazels in pursuit; and he saw only in the very stroke that it was Forweg.

But as he stood looking down in amaze at the blood upon the grass, Andróg came out, and halted also astounded. 'Evil work, Neithan!' he cried, and drew his sword; but Túrin's mood ran cold, and he said to Andróg: 'Where are the Orcs, then? Have you outrun them to help her?'

'Orcs?' said Andróg. 'Fool! You call yourself an outlaw. Outlaws know no law but their needs. Look to your own, Neithan, and leave us to mind ours.'

'I will do so,' said Túrin. 'But today our paths have crossed. You will leave the woman to me, or you will join Forweg.'

Andróg laughed. 'If that is the way of it, have your will,' he said. 'I make no claim to match you, alone; but our fellows may take this slaying ill.'

Then the woman rose to her feet and laid her hand on Túrin's arm. She looked at the blood and she looked at Túrin, and there was delight in her eyes. 'Kill him, lord!' she said. 'Kill him too! And then come with me. If you bring their heads, Larnach my father will not be displeased. For two "wolf-heads" he has rewarded men well.'

But Túrin said to Andróg: 'Is it far to her home?'

'A mile or so,' he answered, 'in a fenced homestead yonder. She was straying outside.'

'Go then quickly,' said Túrin, turning back to the woman. 'Tell your father to keep you better. But I will not cut off the heads of my fellows to buy his favour, or aught else.'

Then he put up his sword. 'Come!' he said to Andróg. 'We will return. But if you wish to bury your captain, you must do so yourself. Make haste, for a hue and cry may be raised. Bring his weapons!'

Then Túrin went on his way without more words, and Andróg watched him go, and he frowned as one pondering a riddle.

When Túrin came back to the camp of the outlaws he found

them restless and ill at ease; for they had stayed too long already in one place, near to homesteads well-guarded, and they murmured against Forweg. 'He runs hazards to our cost,' they said; 'and others may have to pay for his pleasures.'

'Then choose a new captain!' said Túrin, standing before them. 'Forweg can lead you no longer; for he is dead.'

'How do you know that?' said Ulrad. 'Did you seek honey from the same hive? Did the bees sting him?'

'No,' said Túrin. 'One sting was enough. I slew him. But I spared Andróg, and he will soon return.' Then he told all that was done, rebuking those that did such deeds; and while he yet spoke Andróg returned bearing Forweg's weapons. 'See, Neithan!' he cried. 'No alarm has been raised. Maybe she hopes to meet you again.'

'If you jest with me,' said Túrin, 'I shall regret that I grudged her your head. Now tell your tale, and be brief.'

Then Andróg told truly enough all that had befallen. 'What business Neithan had there I now wonder,' he said. 'Not ours, it seems. For when I came up, he had already slain Forweg. The woman liked that well, and offered to go with him, begging our heads as a bride-price. But he did not want her, and sped her off; so what grudge he had against the captain I cannot guess. He left my head on my shoulders, for which I am grateful, though much puzzled.'

'Then I deny your claim to come of the People of Hador,' said Túrin. 'To Uldor the Accursed you belong rather, and should seek service with Angband. But hear me now!' he cried to them all. 'These choices I give you. You must take me as your captain in Forweg's place, or else let me go. I will govern this fellowship now, or leave it. But if you wish to kill me, set to! I will fight you all until I am dead – or you.'

Then many men seized their weapons, but Andróg cried out: 'Nay! The head that he spared is not witless. If we fight, more than one will die needlessly, before we kill the best man among us.' Then he laughed. 'As it was when he joined us, so it is again. He kills to make room. If it proved well before, so may it again; and he may lead us to better fortune than prowling about other men's middens.'

And old Algund said: 'The best man among us. Time was when we would have done the same, if we dared; but we have forgotten much. He may bring us home in the end.'

At that the thought came to Túrin that from this small band he might rise to build himself a free lordship of his own. But he looked

at Algund and Andróg, and he said: 'Home, do you say? Tall and
cold stand the Mountains of Shadow between. Behind them are the
people of Uldor, and about them the legions of Angband. If such
things do not daunt you, seven times seven men, then I may lead
you homewards. But how far, before we die?'

All were silent. Then Túrin spoke again. 'Do you take me to be
your captain? Then I will lead you first away into the wild, far from
the homes of Men. There we may find better fortune, or not; but at
the least we shall earn less hatred of our own kind.'

Then all those that were of the People of Hador gathered to him,
and took him as their captain; and the others with less good will
agreed. And at once he led them away out of that country.[10]

Many messengers had been sent out by Thingol to seek Túrin
within Doriath and in the lands near its borders; but in the year of
his flight they searched for him in vain, for none knew or could guess
that he was with the outlaws and enemies of Men. When winter
came on they returned to the king, save Beleg only. After all others
had departed still he went on alone.

But in Dimbar and along the north-marches of Doriath things had
gone ill. The Dragon-helm was seen there in battle no longer, and
the Strongbow also was missed; and the servants of Morgoth were
heartened and increased ever in numbers and in daring. Winter came
and passed, and with Spring their assault was renewed: Dimbar was
overrun, and the Men of Brethil were afraid, for evil roamed now
upon all their borders, save in the south.

It was now almost a year since Túrin had fled, and still Beleg
sought for him, with ever lessening hope. He passed northwards in
his wanderings to the Crossings of Teiglin, and there, hearing ill
news of a new inroad of Orcs out of Taur-nu-Fuin, he turned back,
and came as it chanced to the homes of the Woodmen soon after
Túrin had left that region. There he heard a strange tale that went
among them. A tall and lordly Man, or an Elf-warrior, some said,
had appeared in the woods, and had slain one of the Gaurwaith, and
rescued the daughter of Larnach whom they were pursuing. 'Very
proud he was,' said Larnach's daughter to Beleg, 'with bright eyes
that scarcely deigned to look at me. Yet he called the Wolf-men his
fellows, and would not slay another that stood by, and knew his name.
Neithan, he called him.'

'Can you read this riddle?' asked Larnach of the Elf.

'I can, alas,' said Beleg. 'The Man that you tell of is one whom I
seek.' No more of Túrin did he tell the Woodmen; but he warned

them of evil gathering northwards. 'Soon the Orcs will come ravening in this country in strength too great for you to withstand,' he said. 'This year at last you must give up your freedom or your lives. Go to Brethil while there is time!'

Then Beleg went on his way in haste, and sought for the lairs of the outlaws, and such signs as might show him whither they had gone. These he soon found; but Túrin was now several days ahead, and moved swiftly, fearing the pursuit of the Woodmen, and he used all the arts that he knew to defeat or mislead any that tried to follow them. Seldom did they remain two nights in one camp, and they left little trace of their going or staying. So it was that even Beleg hunted them in vain. Led by signs that he could read, or by the rumour of the passing of Men among the wild things with whom he could speak, he came often near, but always their lair was deserted when he came to it; for they kept a watch about them by day and night, and at any rumour of approach they were swiftly up and away. 'Alas!' he cried. 'Too well did I teach this child of Men craft in wood and field! An Elvish band almost one might think this to be.' But they for their part became aware that they were trailed by some tireless pursuer, whom they could not see, and yet could not shake off; and they grew uneasy.[11]

Not long afterwards, as Beleg had feared, the Orcs came across the Brithiach, and being resisted with all the force that he could muster by Handir of Brethil they passed south over the Crossings of Teiglin in search of plunder. Many of the Woodmen had taken Beleg's counsel and sent their women and children to ask for refuge in Brethil. These and their escort escaped, passing over the Crossings in time; but the armed men that came behind were met by the Orcs, and the men were worsted. A few fought their way through and came to Brethil, but many were slain or captured; and the Orcs passed on to the homesteads, and sacked them and burned them. Then at once they turned back westwards, seeking the Road, for they wished now to return North as swiftly as they could with their booty and their captives.

But the scouts of the outlaws were soon aware of them; and though they cared little enough for the captives, the plunder of the Woodmen aroused their greed. To Túrin it seemed perilous to reveal themselves to the Orcs, until their numbers were known; but the outlaws would not heed him, for they had need of many things in the wild, and already some began to regret his leading. Therefore taking one Orleg as his only companion Túrin went forth to spy upon the Orcs; and giving command of the band to Andróg he charged him to lie close and well hid while they were gone.

Now the Orc-host was far greater than the band of the outlaws, but they were in lands to which Orcs had seldom dared to come, and they knew also that beyond the Road lay the Talath Dirnen, the Guarded Plain, upon which the scouts and spies of Nargothrond kept watch; and fearing danger they were wary, and their scouts went creeping through the trees on either side of the marching lines. Thus it was that Túrin and Orleg were discovered, for three scouts stumbled upon them as they lay hid; and though they slew two the third escaped, crying as he ran *Golug! Golug!* Now that was a name which they had for the Noldor. At once the forest was filled with Orcs, scattering silently and hunting far and wide. Then Túrin, seeing that there was small hope of escape, thought at least to deceive them and to lead them away from the hiding-place of his men; and perceiving from the cry of *Golug!* that they feared the spies of Nargothrond, he fled with Orleg westward. The pursuit came swiftly after them, until turn and dodge as they would they were driven at last out of the forest; and then they were espied, and as they sought to cross the Road Orleg was shot down by many arrows. But Túrin was saved by his elven-mail, and escaped alone into the wilds beyond; and by speed and craft he eluded his enemies, fleeing far into lands that were strange to him. Then the Orcs, fearing that the Elves of Nargothrond might be aroused, slew their captives and made haste away into the North.

Now when three days had passed, and yet Túrin and Orleg did not return, some of the outlaws wished to depart from the cave where they lay hid; but Andróg spoke against it. And while they were in the midst of this debate, suddenly a grey figure stood before them. Beleg had found them at last. He came forward with no weapon in his hands, and held the palms turned towards them; but they leapt up in fear, and Andróg coming behind cast a noose over him, and drew it so that it pinioned his arms.

'If you do not wish for guests, you should keep better watch,' said Beleg. 'Why do you welcome me thus? I come as a friend, and seek only a friend. Neithan I hear that you call him.'

'He is not here,' said Ulrad. 'But unless you have long spied on us, how know you that name?'

'He has long spied on us,' said Andróg. 'This is the shadow that has dogged us. Now perhaps we shall learn his true purpose.' Then he bade them tie Beleg to a tree beside the cave; and when he was hard bound hand and foot they questioned him. But to all their questions Beleg would give one answer only: 'A friend I have been to this Neithan since I first met him in the woods, and he was then but a child. I seek him only in love, and to bring him good tidings.'

'Let us slay him, and be rid of his spying,' said Andróg in wrath; and he looked on the great bow of Beleg and coveted it, for he was an archer. But some of better heart spoke against him, and Algund said to him: 'The captain may return yet; and then you will rue it, if he learns that he has been robbed at once of a friend and of good tidings.'

'I do not believe the tale of this Elf,' said Andróg. 'He is a spy of the King of Doriath. But if he has indeed any tidings, he shall tell them to us; and we shall judge if they give us reason to let him live.'

'I shall wait for your captain,' said Beleg.

'You shall stand there until you speak,' said Andróg.

Then at the egging of Andróg they left Beleg tied to the tree without food or water, and they sat near eating and drinking; but he said no more to them. When two days and nights had passed in this way they became angry and fearful, and were eager to be gone; and most were now ready to slay the Elf. As night drew down they were all gathered about him, and Ulrad brought a brand from the little fire that was lit in the cave-mouth. But at that moment Túrin returned. Coming silently, as was his custom, he stood in the shadows beyond the ring of men, and he saw the haggard face of Beleg in the light of the brand.

Then he was stricken as with a shaft, and as if at the sudden melting of a frost tears long unshed filled his eyes. He sprang out and ran to the tree. 'Beleg! Beleg!' he cried. 'How have you come hither? And why do you stand so?' At once he cut the bonds from his friend, and Beleg fell forward into his arms.

When Túrin heard all that the men would tell, he was angry and grieved; but at first he gave heed only to Beleg. While he tended him with what skill he had, he thought of his life in the woods, and his anger turned upon himself. For often strangers had been slain, when caught near the lairs of the outlaws, or waylaid by them, and he had not hindered it; and often he himself had spoken ill of King Thingol and of the Grey-elves, so that he must share the blame, if they were treated as foes. Then with bitterness he turned to the men. 'You were cruel,' he said, 'and cruel without need. Never until now have we tormented a prisoner; but to such Orc-work such a life as we lead has brought us. Lawless and fruitless all our deeds have been, serving only ourselves, and feeding hate in our hearts.'

But Andróg said: 'Whom shall we serve, if not ourselves? Whom shall we love, when all hate us?'

'At least my hands shall not again be raised against Elves or Men,' said Túrin. 'Angband has servants enough. If others will not take this vow with me, I will walk alone.'

Then Beleg opened his eyes and raised his head. 'Not alone!' he said. 'Now at last I can tell my tidings. You are no outlaw, and Neithan is a name unfit. Such fault as was found in you is pardoned. For a year you have been sought, to recall you to honour and to the service of the king. The Dragon-helm has been missed too long.'

But Túrin showed no joy in this news, and sat long in silence; for at Beleg's words a shadow fell upon him again. 'Let this night pass,' he said at length. 'Then I will choose. However it goes, we must leave this lair tomorrow; for not all who seek us wish us well.'

'Nay, none,' said Andróg, and he cast an evil look at Beleg.

In the morning Beleg, being swiftly healed of his pains, after the manner of the Elven-folk of old, spoke to Túrin apart.

'I looked for more joy at my tidings,' he said. 'Surely you will return now to Doriath?' And he begged Túrin to do this in all ways that he could; but the more he urged it, the more Túrin hung back. Nonetheless he questioned Beleg closely concerning the judgement of Thingol. Then Beleg told him all that he knew, and at the last Túrin said: 'Then Mablung proved my friend, as he once seemed?'

'The friend of truth, rather,' said Beleg, 'and that was best, in the end. But why, Túrin, did you not speak to him of Saeros' assault upon you? All otherwise might things have gone. And,' he said, looking at the men sprawled near the mouth of the cave, 'you might have held your helm still high, and not fallen to this.'

'That may be, if fall you call it,' said Túrin. 'That may be. But so it went; and words stuck in my throat. There was reproof in his eyes, without question asked of me, for a deed I had not done. My Man's heart was proud, as the Elf-king said. And so it still is, Beleg Cúthalion. Not yet will it suffer me to go back to Menegroth and bear looks of pity and pardon, as for a wayward boy amended. I should give pardon, not receive it. And I am a boy no longer, but a man, according to my kind; and a hard man by my fate.'

Then Beleg was troubled. 'What will you do, then?' he asked.

'Fare free,' said Túrin. 'That wish Mablung gave me at our parting. The grace of Thingol will not stretch to receive these companions of my fall, I think; but I will not part with them now, if they do not wish to part with me. I love them in my way, even the

worst a little. They are of my own kind, and there is some good in
each that might grow. I think that they will stand by me.'

'You see with other eyes than mine,' said Beleg. 'If you try to
wean them from evil, they will fail you. I doubt them, and one most
of all.'

'How shall an Elf judge of Men?' said Túrin.

'As he judges all deeds, by whomsoever done,' answered Beleg,
but he said no more, and did not speak of Andróg's malice, to which
his evil handling had been chiefly due; for perceiving Túrin's mood
he feared to be disbelieved and to hurt their old friendship, driving
Túrin back to his evil ways.

'Fare free, you say, Túrin, my friend,' he said. 'What is your
meaning?'

'I would lead my own men, and make war in my own way,' Túrin
answered. 'But in this at least my heart is changed: I repent every
stroke save those dealt against the Enemy of Men and Elves. And
above all else I would have you beside me. Stay with me!'

'If I stayed beside you, love would lead me, not wisdom,' said
Beleg. 'My heart warns me that we should return to Doriath.'

'Nonetheless, I will not go there,' said Túrin.

Then Beleg strove once more to persuade him to return to the
service of King Thingol, saying that there was great need of his
strength and valour on the north-marches of Doriath, and he spoke
to him of the new inroads of the Orcs, coming down into Dimbar out
of Taur-nu-Fuin by the Pass of Anach. But all his words were of no
avail, and at last he said: 'A hard man you have called yourself,
Túrin. Hard you are, and stubborn. Now the turn is mine. If you
wish indeed to have the Strongbow beside you, look for me in
Dimbar; for thither I shall return.'

Then Túrin sat in silence, and strove with his pride, which would
not let him turn back; and he brooded on the years that lay behind
him. But coming suddenly out of his thought he said to Beleg:
'The elf-maiden whom you named: I owe her well for her timely
witness; yet I cannot recall her. Why did she watch my ways?'

Then Beleg looked strangely at him. 'Why indeed?' he said.
'Túrin, have you lived always with your heart and half your mind
far away? You walked with Nellas in the woods of Doriath, when
you were a boy.'

'That was long ago,' said Túrin. 'Or so my childhood now seems,
and a mist is over it – save only the memory of my father's house in
Dor-lómin. But why should I have walked with an elf-maiden?'

'To learn what she could teach, maybe,' said Beleg. 'Alas, child of Men! There are other griefs in Middle-earth than yours, and wounds made by no weapon. Indeed, I begin to think that Elves and Men should not meet or meddle.'

Túrin said nothing, but looked long in Beleg's face, as if he would read in it the riddle of his words. But Nellas of Doriath never saw him again, and his shadow passed from her.[12]

Of Mim the Dwarf

After the departure of Beleg (and that was in the second summer after the flight of Túrin from Doriath)[13] things went ill for the outlaws. There were rains out of season, and Orcs in greater numbers than before came down from the North and along the old South Road over Teiglin, troubling all the woods on the west borders of Doriath. There was little safety or rest, and the company were more often hunted than hunters.

One night as they lay lurking in the fireless dark, Túrin looked on his life, and it seemed to him that it might well be bettered. 'I must find some secure refuge,' he thought, 'and make provision against winter and hunger'; and the next day he led his men away, further than they had yet come from the Teiglin and the marches of Doriath. After three days' journeying they halted at the western edge of the woods of Sirion's Vale. There the land was drier and more bare, as it began to climb up into the moorlands.

Soon after, it chanced that as the grey light of a day of rain was failing Túrin and his men were sheltering in a holly-thicket; and beyond it was a treeless space, in which there were many great stones, leaning or tumbled together. All was still, save for the drip of rain from the leaves. Suddenly a watchman gave a call, and leaping up they saw three hooded shapes, grey-clad, going stealthily among the stones. They were burdened each with a great sack, but they went swiftly for all that.

Túrin cried out to them to halt, and the men ran out on them like hounds; but they held on their way, and though Andróg shot arrows after them two vanished in the dusk. One lagged behind, being slower or more heavily burdened; and he was soon seized and thrown down, and held by many hard hands, though he struggled and bit like a beast. But Túrin came up, and rebuked his men. 'What have you there?' he said. 'What need to be so fierce? It is old and small. What harm is in it?'

'It bites,' said Andróg, showing his hand that bled. 'It is an Orc, or of Orc-kin. Kill it!'

'It deserved no less, for cheating our hope,' said another, who had taken the sack. 'There is nothing here but roots and small stones.'

'Nay,' said Túrin, 'it is bearded. It is only a dwarf, I guess. Let him up, and speak.'

So it was that Mîm came in to the Tale of the Children of Húrin. For he stumbled up on his knees before Túrin's feet and begged for his life. 'I am old,' he said, 'and poor. Only a dwarf, as you say, and not an Orc. Mîm is my name. Do not let them slay me, lord, for no cause, as would the Orcs.'

Then Túrin pitied him in his heart, but he said: 'Poor you seem, Mîm, though that is strange in a dwarf; but we are poorer, I think: houseless and friendless Men. If I said that we do not spare for pity's sake only, being in great need, what would you offer for ransom?'

'I do not know what you desire, lord,' said Mîm warily.

'At this time, little enough!' said Túrin, looking about him bitterly with rain in his eyes. 'A safe place to sleep in out of the damp woods. Doubtless you have such for yourself.'

'I have,' said Mîm; 'but I cannot give it in ransom. I am too old to live under the sky.'

'You need grow no older,' said Andróg, stepping up with a knife in his unharmed hand. 'I can spare you that.'

'Lord!' cried Mîm then in great fear. 'If I lose my life, you will lose the dwelling; for you will not find it without Mîm. I cannot give it, but I will share it. There is more room in it than once there was: so many have gone for ever,' and he began to weep.

'Your life is spared, Mîm,' said Túrin.

'Till we come to his lair, at least,' said Andróg.

But Túrin turned upon him, and said: 'If Mîm brings us to his home without trickery, and it is good, then his life is ransomed; and he shall not be slain by any man who follows me. So I swear.'

Then Mîm clasped Túrin about his knees, saying: 'Mîm will be your friend, lord. At first I thought you were an Elf, by your speech and your voice; but if you are a Man, that is better. Mîm does not love Elves.'

'Where is this house of yours?' said Andróg. 'It must be good indeed if Andróg is to share it with a Dwarf. For Andróg does not like Dwarves. His people brought few good tales of that race out of the East.'

'Judge my home when you see it,' said Mîm. 'But you will need light on the way, you stumbling Men. I will return in good time and lead you.'

'No, no!' said Andróg. 'You will not allow this, surely, captain? You would never see the old rascal again.'

'It is growing dark,' said Túrin. 'Let him leave us some pledge. Shall we keep your sack and its load, Mîm?'

But at this the Dwarf fell on his knees again in great trouble. 'If Mîm did not mean to return, he would not return for an old sack of roots,' he said. 'I will come back. Let me go!'

'I will not,' said Túrin. 'If you will not part with your sack, you must stay with it. A night under the leaves will make you pity us in your turn, maybe.' But he marked, and others also, that Mîm set more value on his load than it seemed worth to the eye.

They led the old Dwarf away to their dismal camp, and as he went he muttered in a strange tongue that seemed harsh with ancient hatred; but when they put bonds on his legs he went suddenly quiet. And those who were on the watch saw him sitting on through the night silent and still as stone, save for his sleepless eyes that glinted as they roved in the dark.

Before morning the rain ceased, and a wind stirred in the trees. Dawn came more brightly than for many days, and light airs from the South opened the sky, pale and clear about the rising of the sun. Mîm sat on without moving, and he seemed as if dead; for now the heavy lids of his eyes were closed, and the morning-light showed him withered and shrunken with age. Túrin stood and looked down on him. 'There is light enough now,' he said.

Then Mîm opened his eyes and pointed to his bonds; and when he was released he spoke fiercely. 'Learn this, fools!' he said. 'Do not put bonds on a Dwarf! He will not forgive it. I do not wish to die, but for what you have done my heart is hot. I repent my promise.'

'But I do not,' said Túrin. 'You will lead me to your home. Till then we will not speak of death. That is *my* will.' He looked steadfastly in the eyes of the Dwarf, and Mîm could not endure it; few indeed could challenge the eyes of Túrin in set will or in wrath. Soon he turned away his head, and rose. 'Follow me, lord!' he said.

'Good!' said Túrin. 'But now I will add this: I understand your pride. You may die, but you shall not be set in bonds again.'

Then Mîm led them back to the place where he had been captured, and he pointed westward. 'There is my home!' he said. 'You have often seen it, I guess, for it is tall. Sharbhund we called it, before the Elves changed all the names.' Then they saw that he was pointing to Amon Rûdh, the Bald Hill, whose bare head watched over many leagues of the wild.

'We have seen it, but never nearer,' said Andróg. 'For what safe lair can be there, or water, or any other thing that we need? I guessed that there was some trick. Do men hide on a hill-top?'

'Long sight may be safer than lurking,' said Túrin. 'Amon Rûdh gazes far and wide. Well, Mîm, I will come and see what you have to show. How long will it take us, stumbling Men, to come thither?'

'All this day until dusk,' Mîm answered.

The company set out westward, and Túrin went at the head with Mîm at his side. They walked warily when they left the woods, but all the land was empty and quiet. They passed over the tumbled stones, and began to climb; for Amon Rûdh stood upon the eastern edge of the high moorlands that rose between the vales of Sirion and Narog, and even above the stony heath at its base its crown was reared up a thousand feet and more. Upon the eastern side a broken land climbed slowly up to the high ridges among knots of birch and rowan, and ancient thorn-trees rooted in rock. About the lower slopes of Amon Rûdh there grew thickets of *aeglos*; but its steep grey head was bare, save for the red *seregon* that mantled the stone.[14]

As the afternoon was waning the outlaws drew near to the roots of the hill. They came now from the north, for so Mîm had led them, and the light of the westering sun fell upon the crown of Amon Rûdh, and the *seregon* was all in flower.

'See! There is blood on the hill-top,' said Andróg.

'Not yet,' said Túrin.

The sun was sinking and light was failing in the hollows. The hill now loomed up before them and above them, and they wondered what need there could be of a guide to so plain a mark. But as Mîm led them on, and they began to climb the last steep slopes, they perceived that he was following some path by secret signs or old custom. Now his course wound to and fro, and if they looked aside they saw that at either hand dark dells and chines opened, or the land ran down into wastes of great stones, with falls and holes masked by bramble and thorn. There without a guide they might have laboured and clambered for days to find a way.

At length they came to steeper but smoother ground. They passed under the shadows of ancient rowan-trees into aisles of long-legged *aeglos*: a gloom filled with a sweet scent.[15] Then suddenly there was a rock-wall before them, flat-faced and sheer, towering high above them in the dusk.

'Is this the door of your house?' said Túrin. 'Dwarves love stone, it is said.' He drew close to Mîm, lest he should play them some trick at the last.

'Not the door of the house, but the gate of the garth,' said Mîm. Then he turned to the right along the cliff-foot, and after twenty paces halted suddenly; and Túrin saw that by the work of hands or of weather there was a cleft so shaped that two faces of the wall overlapped, and an opening ran back to the left between them. Its entrance was shrouded by long-trailing plants rooted in crevices above, but within there was a steep stony path going upwards in the dark. Water trickled down it, and it was dank. One by one they filed up. At the top the path turned right and south again, and brought them through a thicket of thorns out upon a green flat, through which it ran on into the shadows. They had come to Mîm's house, Bar-en-Nibin-noeg,[16] which only ancient tales in Doriath and Nargothrond remembered, and no Men had seen. But night was falling, and the east was starlit, and they could not yet see how this strange place was shaped.

Amon Rûdh had a crown: a great mass like a steep cap of stone with a bare flattened top. Upon its north side there stood out from it a shelf, level and almost square, which could not be seen from below; for behind it stood the hill-crown like a wall, and west and east from its brink sheer cliffs fell. Only from the north, as they had come, could it be reached with ease by those who knew the way.[17] From the cleft a path led, and passed soon into a little grove of dwarfed birches growing about a clear pool in a rock-hewn basin. This pool was fed by a spring at the foot of the wall behind, and through a runnel it spilled like a white thread over the western brink of the shelf. Behind the screen of the trees near the spring, between two tall buttresses of rock, there was a cave. No more than a shallow grot it looked, with a low broken arch; but further in it had been deepened and bored far under the hill by the slow hands of the Petty-dwarves, in the long years that they had dwelt there, untroubled by the Grey-elves of the woods.

Through the deep dusk Mîm led them past the pool, where now the faint stars were mirrored among the shadows of the birch-boughs. At the mouth of the cave he turned and bowed to Túrin. 'Enter,' he said, 'Bar-en-Danwedh, the House of Ransom; for so it shall be called.'

'That may be,' said Túrin. 'I will look first.' Then he went in with Mîm, and the others, seeing him unafraid, followed behind, even Andróg, who most misdoubted the Dwarf. They were soon in a black dark; but Mîm clapped his hands, and a little light appeared, coming round a corner: from a passage at the back of the outer grot there stepped another Dwarf bearing a small torch.

'Ha! I missed him, as I feared!' said Andróg. But Mîm spoke quickly with the other in their own harsh tongue, and seeming troubled or angered by what he heard, he darted into the passage and disappeared. Then Andróg was all for going forward. 'Attack first!' he said. 'There may be a hive of them; but they are small.'

'Three only, I guess,' said Túrin; and he led the way, while behind him the outlaws groped along the passage by the feel of the rough walls. Many times it bent this way and that at sharp angles; but at last a faint light gleamed ahead, and they came into a small but lofty hall, dim-lit by lamps hanging down out of the roof-shadow upon fine chains. Mîm was not there, but his voice could be heard, and led by it Túrin came to the door of a chamber opening at the back of the hall. Looking in, he saw Mîm kneeling on the floor. Beside him stood silent the Dwarf with the torch; but on a stone couch by the further wall there lay another. 'Khîm, Khîm, Khîm!' the old Dwarf wailed, tearing at his beard.

'Not all your shafts went wild,' said Túrin to Andróg. 'But this may prove an ill hit. You loose shaft too lightly; but you may not live long enough to learn wisdom.' Then entering softly Túrin stood behind Mîm, and spoke to him. 'What is the trouble, Mîm?' he said. 'I have some healing arts. Can I give you aid?'

Mîm turned his head, and there was a red light in his eyes. 'Not unless you can turn back time, and then cut off the cruel hands of your men,' he answered. 'This is my son, pierced by an arrow. Now he is beyond speech. He died at sunset. Your bonds held me from healing him.'

Again pity long hardened welled in Túrin's heart as water from rock. 'Alas!' he said. 'I would recall that shaft, if I could. Now Bar-en-Danwedh, House of Ransom, shall this be called in truth. For whether we dwell here or no, I will hold myself in your debt; and if ever I come to any wealth, I will pay you a ransom of heavy gold for your son, in token of sorrow, though it gladden your heart no more.'

Then Mîm rose, and looked long at Túrin. 'I hear you,' he said. 'You speak like a dwarf-lord of old; and at that I marvel. Now my heart is cooled, though it is not glad. My own ransom I will pay, therefore: you may dwell here, if you will. But this I will add: he that loosed the shaft shall break his bow and his arrows and lay them at my son's feet; and he shall never take arrow nor bear bow again. If he does, he shall die by it. That curse I lay on him.'

Andróg was afraid when he heard of this curse; and though he did so with great grudge, he broke his bow and his arrows and laid them at the dead Dwarf's feet. But as he came out from the chamber, he glanced evilly at Mîm, and muttered: 'The curse of a Dwarf never dies, they say; but a Man's too may come home. May he die with a dart in his throat!'[18]

That night they lay in the hall and slept uneasily for the wailing of Mîm and of Ibun, his other son. When that ceased they could not tell; but when they woke at last the Dwarves were gone, and the chamber was closed by a stone. The day was fair again, and in the morning sun the outlaws washed in the pool and prepared such food as they had; and as they ate Mîm stood before them.

He bowed to Túrin. 'He is gone, and all is done,' he said. 'He lies with his fathers. Now we turn to such life as is left, though the days before us may be short. Does Mîm's home please you? Is the ransom paid and accepted?'

'It is,' said Túrin.

'Then all is yours, to order your dwelling here as you will, save this: the chamber that is closed, none shall open it but me.'

'We hear you,' said Túrin. 'But as for our life here, we are secure, or so it seems; but still we must have food, and other things. How shall we go out; or still more, how shall we return?'

To their disquiet Mîm laughed in his throat. 'Do you fear that you have followed a spider to the heart of his web?' he said. 'Mîm does not eat Men! And a spider could ill deal with thirty wasps at a time. See, you are armed, and I stand here bare. No, we must share, you and I: house, food, and fire, and maybe other winnings. The house, I think, you will guard and keep secret for your own good, even when you know the ways in and out. You will learn them in time. But in the meanwhile Mîm must guide you, or Ibun his son.'

To this Túrin agreed, and he thanked Mîm, and most of his men were glad; for under the sun of morning, while summer was yet high, it seemed a fair place to dwell in. Andróg alone was ill-content. 'The sooner we are masters of our goings and comings the better,' he said. 'Never before have we taken a prisoner with a grievance to and fro on our ventures.'

That day they rested, and cleaned their arms and mended their gear; for they had food to last for a day or two yet, and Mîm added to what they had. Three great cooking-pots he lent to them, and firing also; and he brought out a sack. 'Rubbish,' he said. 'Not worth the stealing. Only wild roots.'

But when they were cooked these roots proved good to eat, somewhat like bread; and the outlaws were glad of them, for they had long lacked bread save when they could steal it. 'Wild Elves know them not; Grey-elves have not found them; the proud ones from over the Sea are too proud to delve,' said Mîm.

'What is their name?' said Túrin.

Mîm looked at him sidelong. 'They have no name, save in the dwarf-tongue, which we do not teach,' he said. 'And we do not teach Men to find them, for Men are greedy and thriftless, and would not spare till all the plants had perished; whereas now they pass them by as they go blundering in the wild. No more will you learn of me; but you may have enough of my bounty, as long as you speak fair and do not spy or steal.' Then again he laughed in his throat. 'They are of great worth,' he said. 'More than gold in the hungry winter, for they may be hoarded like the nuts of a squirrel, and already we were building our store from the first that are ripe. But you are fools, if you think that I would not be parted from one small load even for the saving of my life.'

'I hear you,' said Ulrad, who had looked in the sack when Mîm was taken. 'Yet you would not be parted, and your words only make me wonder the more.'

Mîm turned and looked at him darkly. 'You are one of the fools that spring would not mourn if you perished in winter,' he said. 'I had spoken my word, and so must have returned, willing or not, with sack or without, let a lawless and faithless man think what he will! But I like not to be parted from my own by force of the wicked, be it no more than a shoe-thong. Do I not remember that your hands were among those that put bonds on me, and so held me that I did not speak again with my son? Ever when I deal out the earth-bread from my store you shall be counted out, and if you eat it, you shall eat by the bounty of your fellows, not of me.'

Then Mîm went away; but Ulrad, who had quailed under his anger, spoke to his back: 'High words! Nonetheless the old rogue had other things in his sack, of like shape but harder and heavier. Maybe there are other things beside earth-bread in the wild which Elves have not found and Men must not know!'[19]

'That may be,' said Túrin. 'Nonetheless the Dwarf spoke the truth in one point at least, calling you a fool. Why must you speak your thoughts? Silence, if fair words stick in your throat, would serve all our ends better.'

The day passed in peace, and none of the outlaws desired to go abroad. Túrin paced much upon the green sward of the shelf, from brink to brink; and he looked out east, and west, and north, and wondered to find how far were the views in the clear air. Northward he looked, and descried the Forest of Brethil climbing green about Amon Obel in its midst, and thither his eyes were drawn ever and again, he knew not why; for his heart was set rather to the north-west, where league upon league away on the skirts of the sky it seemed to him that he could glimpse the Mountains of Shadow, the walls of his home. But at evening Túrin looked west into the sunset, as the sun rode down red into the hazes above the distant coasts, and the Vale of Narog lay deep in the shadows between.

So began the abiding of Túrin son of Húrin in the halls of Mîm, in Bar-en-Danwedh, the House of Ransom.

For the story of Túrin from his coming to Bar-en-Danwedh to the fall of Nargothrond see The Silmarillion, pp. 204-15, and the Appendix to the Narn i Hîn Húrin, p. 150 below.

The Return of Túrin to Dor-lómin

At last worn by haste and the long road (for forty leagues and more had he journeyed without rest) Túrin came with the first ice of winter to the pools of Ivrin, where before he had been healed. But they were now only a frozen mire, and he could drink there no more.

Thence he came to the passes into Dor-lómin;[20] and snow came bitterly from the North, and the ways were perilous and cold. Though three and twenty years were gone since he had trodden that path it was graven in his heart, so great was the sorrow of each step at the parting from Morwen. Thus at last he came back to the land of his childhood. It was bleak and bare; and the people there were few and churlish, and they spoke the harsh tongue of the Easterlings, and the old tongue was become the language of serfs, or of foes.

Therefore Túrin walked warily, hooded and silent, and he came at last to the house that he sought. It stood empty and dark, and no living thing dwelt near it; for Morwen was gone, and Brodda the Incomer (he that took by force Aerin, Húrin's kinswoman, to wife) had plundered her house, and taken all that was left to her of goods or of servants. Brodda's house stood nearest to the old house of Húrin, and thither Túrin came, spent with wandering and grief, begging for shelter; and it was granted to him, for some of the kindlier manners of old were still kept there by Aerin. He was given a seat by a fire among the servants, and a few vagabonds well-nigh as grim and wayworn as he; and he asked news of the land.

At that the company fell silent, and some drew away, looking askance at the stranger. But one old vagabond man, with a crutch, said: 'If you must speak the old tongue, master, speak it softer, and ask for no tidings. Would you be beaten for a rogue, or hung for a spy? For both you may well be by the looks of you. Which is but to say,' he said, coming near and speaking low in Túrin's ear, 'one of the kindly folk of old that came with Hador in the days of gold, before heads wore wolf-hair. Some here are of that sort, though now made beggars and slaves, and but for the Lady Aerin would get neither this fire nor this broth. Whence are you, and what news would you have?'

'There was a lady called Morwen,' answered Túrin, 'and long ago I lived in her house. Thither after far wandering I came to seek welcome, but neither fire nor folk are there now.'

'Nor have been this long year and more,' answered the old man. 'But scant were both fire and folk in that house since the deadly war; for she was of the old people – as doubtless you know, the widow of our lord, Húrin Galdor's son. They dared not touch her, though, for they feared her; proud and fair as a queen, before sorrow marred her. Witchwife they called her, and shunned her. Witchwife: it is but "elf-friend" in the new language. Yet they robbed her. Often would she and her daughter have gone hungry, but for the Lady Aerin. She aided them in secret, it is said, and was often beaten for it by the churl Brodda, her husband by need.'

'And this long year and more?' said Túrin. 'Are they dead or made thralls? Or have the Orcs assailed her?'

'It is not known for sure,' said the old man. 'But she is gone with her daughter; and this Brodda has plundered her and stripped what remained. Not a dog is left, and her few folk made his slaves; save some that have gone begging, as have I. I served her many a year, and the great Master before, Sador Onefoot: a cursed axe in the woods long ago, or I would be lying in the Great Mound now. Well I remember the day Húrin's boy was sent away, and how he wept; and she, when he was gone. To the Hidden Kingdom he went, it was said.'

With that the old man stayed his tongue, and eyed Túrin doubt-
fully. 'I am old and I babble,' he said. 'Mind me not! But though it
is pleasant to speak the old tongue with one that speaks it fair as in
time past, the days are ill, and one must be wary. Not all that speak
the fair tongue are fair at heart.'

'Truly,' said Túrin. 'My heart is grim. But if you fear that I am
a spy of the North or the East, then you have little more wisdom
than you had long ago, Sador Labadal.'

The old man eyed him agape; then trembling he spoke. 'Come
outside! It is colder, but safer. You speak too loud, and I too much,
for an Easterling's hall.'

When they were come into the court he clutched at Túrin's cloak.
'Long ago you dwelt in that house, you say. Lord Túrin, son of
Húrin, why have you come back? My eyes are opened, and my ears
at last; you have the voice of your father. But young Túrin alone ever
gave me that name, Labadal. He meant no ill: we were merry friends
in those days. What does he seek here now? Few are we left; and we
are old and weaponless. Happier are those in the Great Mound.'

'I did not come with thought of battle,' said Túrin, 'though your
words have waked the thought in me now, Labadal. But it must
wait. I came seeking the Lady Morwen and Nienor. What can you
tell me, and swiftly?'

'Little, lord,' said Sador. 'They went away secretly. It was
whispered among us that they were summoned by the Lord Túrin;
for we did not doubt that he had grown great in the years, a king or
a lord in some south country. But it seems that is not so.'

'It is not,' answered Túrin. 'A lord I was in a south country,
though now I am a vagabond. But I did not summon them.'

'Then I know not what to tell you,' said Sador. 'But the Lady
Aerin will know, I doubt not. She knew all the counsel of your mother.'

'How can I come to her?'

'That I know not. It would cost her much pain were she caught
whispering at a door with a wandering wretch of the downtrod
people, even could any message call her forth. And such a beggar
as you are will not walk far up the hall towards the high board, before
the Easterlings seize him and beat him, or worse.'

Then in anger Túrin cried: 'May I not walk up Brodda's hall,
and will they beat me? Come, and see!'

Thereupon he went into the hall, and cast back his hood, and
thrusting aside all in his path he strode towards the board where sat
the master of the house and his wife, and other Easterling lords.
Then some ran to seize him, but he flung them to the ground, and

cried: 'Does no one rule this house, or is it an Orc-hold? Where is the master?'

Then Brodda rose in wrath. 'I rule this house,' said he.

But before he could say more, Túrin said: 'Then you have not learned the courtesy that was in this land before you. Is it now the manner of men to let lackeys mishandle the kinsmen of their wives? Such am I, and I have an errand to the Lady Aerin. Shall I come freely, or shall I come as I will?'

'Come!' said Brodda, and he scowled; but Aerin turned pale.

Then Túrin strode to the high board, and stood before it, and bowed. 'Your pardon, Lady Aerin,' he said, 'that I break in upon you thus; but my errand is urgent and has brought me far. I seek Morwen, Lady of Dor-lómin, and Nienor her daughter. But her house is empty and plundered. What can you tell me?'

'Nothing,' said Aerin in great fear, for Brodda watched her narrowly. 'Nothing, save that she is gone.'

'That I do not believe,' said Túrin.

Then Brodda sprang forth, and he was red with drunken rage. 'No more!' he cried. 'Shall my wife be gainsaid before me, by a beggar that speaks the serf-tongue? There is no Lady of Dor-lómin. But as for Morwen, she was of the thrall-folk, and has fled as thralls will. Do you likewise, and swiftly, or I will have you hung on a tree!'

Then Túrin leapt at him, and drew his black sword, and seized Brodda by the hair and laid back his head. 'Let no one stir,' said he, 'or this head will leave its shoulders! Lady Aerin, I would beg your pardon once more, if I thought that this churl had ever done you anything but wrong. But speak now, and do not deny me! Am I not Túrin, Lord of Dor-lómin? Shall I command you?'

'Command me,' she answered.

'Who plundered the house of Morwen?'

'Brodda,' she answered.

'When did she flee, and whither?'

'A year and three months gone,' said Aerin. 'Master Brodda and others of the Incomers of the East hereabout oppressed her sorely. Long ago she was bidden to the Hidden Kingdom; and she went forth at last. For the lands between were then free of evil for a while, because of the prowess of the Blacksword of the south country, it is said; but that now is ended. She looked to find her son there awaiting her. But if you are he, then I fear that all has gone awry.'

Then Túrin laughed bitterly. 'Awry, awry?' he cried. 'Yes, ever awry: as crooked as Morgoth!' And suddenly a black wrath shook him; for his eyes were opened, and the spell of Glaurung loosed its last threads, and he knew the lies with which he had been cheated. 'Have I been cozened, that I might come and die here dishonoured, who might at least have ended valiantly before the Doors of Nargothrond?' And out of the night about the hall it seemed to him that he heard the cries of Finduilas.

'Not first will I die here!' he cried. And he seized Brodda, and with the strength of his great anguish and wrath he lifted him on high and shook him, as if he were a dog. 'Morwen of the thrall-folk, did you say? You son of dastards, thief, slave of slaves!' Thereupon he flung Brodda head foremost across his own table, full in the face of an Easterling that rose to assail Túrin.

In that fall Brodda's neck was broken; and Túrin leapt after his cast and slew three more that cowered there, for they were caught weaponless. There was tumult in the hall. The Easterlings that sat there would have come against Túrin, but many others were gathered there of the elder people of Dor-lómin: long had they been tame servants, but now they rose with shouts in rebellion. Soon there was great fighting in the hall, and though the thralls had but meat-knives and such things as they could snatch up against daggers and swords, many were quickly slain on either hand, before Túrin leapt down among them and slew the last of the Easterlings that remained in the hall.

Then he rested, leaning against a pillar, and the fire of his rage was as ashes. But old Sador crept up to him and clutched him about the knees, for he was wounded to the death. 'Thrice seven years and more, it was long to wait for this hour,' he said. 'But now go, go, lord! Go, and do not come back, unless with greater strength. They will raise the land against you. Many have run from the hall. Go, or you will end here. Farewell!' Then he slipped down and died.

'He speaks with the truth of death,' said Aerin. 'You have learned what you would. Now go swiftly! But go first to Morwen and comfort her, or I will hold all the wrack you have wrought here hard to forgive. For ill though my life was, you have brought death to me with your violence. The Incomers will avenge this night on all that were here. Rash are your deeds, son of Húrin, as if you were still but the child that I knew.'

'And faint heart is yours, Aerin Indor's daughter, as it was when I called you aunt, and a rough dog frightened you,' said Túrin. 'You were made for a kinder world. But come away! I will bring you to Morwen.'

'The snow lies on the land, but deeper upon my head,' she answered. 'I should die as soon in the wild with you, as with the brute

Easterlings. You cannot mend what you have done. Go! To stay will make all the worse, and rob Morwen to no purpose. Go, I beg you!'

Then Túrin bowed low to her, and turned, and left the hall of Brodda; but all the rebels that had the strength followed him. They fled towards the mountains, for some among them knew well the ways of the wild, and they blessed the snow that fell behind them and covered their trail. Thus though soon the hunt was up, with many men and dogs and braying of horses, they escaped south into the hills. Then looking back they saw a red light far off in the land they had left.

'They have fired the hall,' said Túrin. 'To what purpose is that?'

'They? No, lord: she, I guess,' said one, Asgon by name. 'Many a man of arms misreads patience and quiet. She did much good among us at much cost. Her heart was not faint, and patience will break at the last.'

Now some of the hardiest that could endure the winter stayed with Túrin and led him by strange paths to a refuge in the mountains, a cave known to outlaws and runagates; and some store of food was hidden there. There they waited until the snow ceased, and then they gave him food and took him to a pass little used that led south to Sirion's Vale, where the snow had not come. On the downward path they parted.

'Farewell now, Lord of Dor-lómin,' said Asgon. 'But do not forget us. We shall be hunted men now; and the Wolf-folk will be crueller because of your coming. Therefore go, and do not return, unless you come with strength to deliver us. Farewell!'

The Coming of Túrin into Brethil

Now Túrin went down towards Sirion, and he was torn in mind. For it seemed to him that whereas before he had two bitter choices, now there were three, and his oppressed people called him, upon whom he had brought only increase of woe. This comfort only he had: that beyond doubt Morwen and Nienor had come long since to Doriath, and only by the prowess of the Blacksword of Nargothrond had their road been made safe. And he said in his thought: 'Where else better might I have bestowed them, had I come indeed sooner? If the Girdle of Melian be broken, then is all ended. Nay, it is better as things be; for by my wrath and rash deeds I cast a shadow wherever I dwell. Let Melian keep them! And I will leave them in peace unshadowed for a while.'

But too late Túrin now sought for Finduilas, roaming the woods under the eaves of Ered Wethrin, wild and wary as a beast; and he waylaid all the roads that went north to the Pass of Sirion. Too late. For all trails had been washed away by the rains and the snows. But thus it was that Túrin passing down Teiglin came upon some of the People of Haleth from the Forest of Brethil. They were dwindled now by war to a small people, and dwelt for the most part secretly within a stockade upon Amon Obel deep in the forest. Ephel Brandir that place was named; for Brandir son of Handir was now their lord, since his father was slain. And Brandir was no man of war, being lamed by a leg broken in a misadventure in childhood; and he was moreover gentle in mood, loving wood rather than metal, and the knowledge of things that grow in the earth rather than other lore.

But some of the woodmen still hunted the Orcs on their borders; and thus it was that as Túrin came thither he heard the sound of an affray. He hastened towards it, and coming warily through the trees he saw a small band of men surrounded by Orcs. They defended themselves desperately, with their backs to a knot of trees that grew apart in a glade; but the Orcs were in great number, and they had little hope of escape, unless help came. Therefore, out of sight in the underwood, Túrin made a great noise of stamping and crashing, and then he cried in a loud voice, as if leading many men: 'Ha! Here we find them! Follow me all! Out now, and slay!'

At that many of the Orcs looked back in dismay, and then out came Túrin leaping, waving as if to men behind, and the edges of Gurthang flickered like flame in his hand. Too well was that blade known to the Orcs, and even before he sprang among them many scattered and fled. Then the woodmen ran to join him, and together they hunted their foes into the river: few came across.

At last they halted on the bank, and Dorlas, leader of the woodmen, said: 'You are swift in the hunt, lord; but your men are slow to follow.'

'Nay,' said Túrin, 'we all run together as one man, and will not be parted.'

Then the Men of Brethil laughed, and said: 'Well, one such is worth many. And we owe you great thanks. But who are you, and what do you here?'

'I do but follow my trade, which is Orc-slaying,' said Túrin. 'And I dwell where my trade is. I am Wildman of the Woods.'

'Then come and dwell with us,' said they. 'For we dwell in the woods, and we have need of such craftsmen. You would be welcome!'

Then Túrin looked at them strangely, and said: 'Are there then any left who will suffer me to darken their doors? But, friends, I have still a grievous errand: to find Finduilas, daughter of Orodreth of Nargothrond, or at least to learn news of her. Alas! Many weeks is it since she was taken from Nargothrond, but still I must go seeking.'

Then they looked on him with pity, and Dorlas said: 'Seek no more. For an Orc-host came up from Nargothrond towards the Crossings of Teiglin, and we had long warning of it: it marched very slow, because of the number of captives that were led. Then we thought to deal our small stroke in the war, and we ambushed the Orcs with all the bowmen we could muster, and hoped to save some of the prisoners. But alas! as soon as they were assailed the foul Orcs slew first the women among their captives; and the daughter of Orodreth they fastened to a tree with a spear.'

Túrin stood as one mortally stricken. 'How do you know this?' he said.

'Because she spoke to me, before she died,' said Dorlas. 'She looked upon us as though seeking one whom she had expected, and she said: "Mormegil. Tell the Mormegil that Finduilas is here." She said no more. But because of her latest words we laid her where she died. She lies in a mound beside Teiglin. It is a month now ago.'

'Bring me there,' said Túrin; and they led him to a hillock by the Crossings of Teiglin. There he laid himself down, and a darkness fell on him, so that they thought he was dead. But Dorlas looked down at him as he lay, and then he turned to his men and said: 'Too late! This is a piteous chance. But see: here lies the Mormegil himself, the great captain of Nargothrond. By his sword we should have known him, as did the Orcs.' For the fame of the Blacksword of the South had gone far and wide, even into the deeps of the wood.

Now therefore they lifted him with reverence and bore him to Ephel Brandir; and Brandir coming out to meet them wondered at the bier that they bore. Then drawing back the coverlet he looked on the face of Túrin son of Húrin; and a dark shadow fell on his heart.

'O cruel Men of Haleth!' he cried. 'Why did you hold back death from this man? With great labour you have brought hither the last bane of our people.'

But the woodmen said: 'Nay, it is the Mormegil of Nargothrond,[21] a mighty Orc-slayer, and he shall be a great help to us, if he lives. And were it not so, should we leave a man woe-stricken to lie as carrion by the way?'

'You should not indeed,' said Brandir. 'Doom willed it not so.' And he took Túrin into his house and tended him with care.

But when at last Túrin shook off the darkness, spring was returning;

and he awoke and saw sun on the green buds. Then the courage of
the House of Hador awoke in him also, and he arose, and said in his
heart: 'All my deeds and past days were dark and full of evil. But a
new day is come. Here I will stay at peace, and renounce name and
kin; and so I will put my shadow behind me, or at the least not lay
it upon those that I love.'

Therefore he took a new name, calling himself Turambar, which
in the High-elven speech signified Master of Doom; and he dwelt
among the woodmen, and was loved by them, and he charged them
to forget his name of old, and to count him as born in Brethil. Yet
with the change of a name he could not change wholly his temper,
nor wholly forget his old griefs against the servants of Morgoth; and
he would go hunting the Orcs with a few of the same mind, though
this was displeasing to Brandir. For he hoped rather to preserve his
people by silence and secrecy.

'The Mormegil is no more,' said he, 'yet have a care lest the valour
of Turambar bring a like vengeance on Brethil!'

Therefore Turambar laid his black sword by, and took it no more
to battle, and wielded rather the bow and the spear. But he would
not suffer the Orcs to use the Crossings of Teiglin or draw near the
mound where Finduilas was laid. Haudh-en-Elleth it was named, the
Mound of the Elfmaid, and soon the Orcs learned to dread that place,
and shunned it. And Dorlas said to Turambar: 'You have renounced
the name, but the Blacksword you are still; and does not rumour
say truly that he was the son of Húrin of Dor-lómin, lord of the
House of Hador?'

And Turambar answered: 'So I have heard. But publish it not, I
beg you, as you are my friend.'

The Journey of Morwen and Nienor to Nargothrond

When the Fell Winter withdrew new tidings of Nargothrond came to
Doriath. For some that escaped from the sack, and had survived the
winter in the wild, came at last seeking refuge with Thingol, and the
march-wards brought them to the King. And some said that all the
enemy had withdrawn northwards, and others that Glaurung abode
still in the halls of Felagund; and some said that the Mormegil was
slain, and others that he was cast under a spell by the Dragon and
dwelt there yet, as one changed to stone. But all declared that it was
known in Nargothrond ere the end that the Blacksword was none
other than Túrin son of Húrin of Dor-lómin.

Then great was the fear and sorrow of Morwen and of Nienor;

and Morwen said: 'Such doubt is the very work of Morgoth! May we not learn the truth, and know surely the worst that we must endure?'

Now Thingol himself desired greatly to know more of the fate of Nargothrond, and had in mind already the sending out of some that might go warily thither, but he believed that Túrin was indeed slain or beyond rescue, and he was loath to see the hour when Morwen should know this clearly. Therefore he said to her: 'This is a perilous matter, Lady of Dor-lómin, and must be pondered. Such doubt may in truth be the work of Morgoth, to draw us on to some rashness.'

But Morwen being distraught cried: 'Rashness, lord! If my son lurks in the woods hungry, if he lingers in bonds, if his body lies unburied, then I would be rash. I would lose no hour to go to seek him.'

'Lady of Dor-lómin,' said Thingol, 'that surely the son of Húrin would not desire. Here would he think you better bestowed than in any other land that remains: in the keeping of Melian. For Húrin's sake and Túrin's I will not have you wander abroad in the black peril of these days.'

'You did not hold Túrin from peril, but me you will hold from him,' cried Morwen. 'In the keeping of Melian! Yes, a prisoner of the Girdle. Long did I hold back before I entered it, and now I rue it.'

'Nay, if you speak so, Lady of Dor-lómin,' said Thingol, 'know this: the Girdle is open. Free you came hither; free you shall stay – or go.'

Then Melian, who had remained silent, spoke: 'Go not hence, Morwen. A true word you said: this doubt is of Morgoth. If you go, you go at his will.'

'Fear of Morgoth will not withhold me from the call of my kin,' Morwen answered. 'But if you fear for me, lord, then lend me some of your people.'

'I command you not,' said Thingol. 'But my people are my own to command. I will send them at my own advice.'

Then Morwen said no more, but wept; and she left the presence of the King. Thingol was heavy-hearted, for it seemed to him that the mood of Morwen was fey; and he asked Melian whether she would not restrain her by her power.

'Against the coming in of evil I may do much,' she answered. 'But against the going out of those who will go, nothing. That is your part. If she is to be held here, you must hold her with strength. Yet maybe thus you will overthrow her mind.'

Now Morwen went to Nienor, and said: 'Farewell, daughter of

Húrin. I go to seek my son, or true tidings of him, since none here will do aught, but will tarry until too late. Await me here until haply I return.'

Then Nienor in dread and distress would restrain her, but Morwen answered nothing, and went to her chamber; and when morning came she had taken horse and gone.

Now Thingol had commanded that none should stay her, or seem to waylay her. But as soon as she went forth, he gathered a company of the hardiest and most skilled of his march-wards, and he set Mablung in charge.

'Follow now speedily,' he said, 'yet let her not be aware of you. But when she is come into the wild, if danger threatens, then show yourselves; and if she will not return, then guard her as you may. But some of you I would have go forward as far as you can, and learn all that you may.'

Thus it was that Thingol sent out a larger company than he had at first intended, and there were ten riders among them with spare horses. They followed after Morwen, and she went south through Region, and so came to the shores of Sirion above the Twilit Meres; there she halted, for Sirion was wide and swift, and she did not know the way. Therefore now the guards must needs reveal themselves; and Morwen said: 'Will Thingol stay me? Or late does he send me the help that he denied?'

'Both,' answered Mablung. 'Will you not return?'

'No!' she said.

'Then I must help you,' said Mablung, 'though it is against my own will. Wide and deep here is Sirion, and perilous to swim for beast or man.'

'Then bring me over by whatever way the Elven-folk are used to cross,' said Morwen; 'or else I will try the swimming.'

Therefore Mablung led her to the Twilit Meres. There amid the creeks and reeds ferries were kept hidden and guarded on the east shore; for by that way messengers would pass to and fro between Thingol and his kin in Nargothrond.²² Now they waited until the starlit night was late, and they passed over in the white mists before the dawn. And even as the sun rose red beyond the Blue Mountains, and a strong morning-wind blew and scattered the mists, the guards went up on to the west shore, and left the Girdle of Melian. Tall Elves of Doriath they were, grey-clad, and cloaked over their mail. Morwen from the ferry watched them as they passed silently, and then suddenly she gave a cry, and pointed to the last of the company that went by.

'Whence came he?' she said. 'Thrice ten you came to me. Thrice ten and one you go ashore!'

Then the others turned, and saw that the sun shone upon a head of gold: for it was Nienor, and her hood was blown back by the wind. Thus it was revealed that she had followed the company, and joined them in the dark before they crossed the river. They were dismayed, and none more than Morwen. 'Go back, go back! I command you!' she cried.

'If the wife of Húrin can go forth against all counsel at the call of kindred,' said Nienor, 'then so also can Húrin's daughter. Mourning you named me, but I will not mourn alone, for father, brother, and mother. But of these you only have I known, and above all do I love. And nothing that you fear not do I fear.'

In truth little fear was seen in her face or her bearing. Tall and strong she seemed; for of great stature were those of Hador's House, and thus clad in Elvish raiment she matched well with the guards, being smaller only than the greatest among them.

'What would you do?' said Morwen.

'Go where you go,' said Nienor. 'This choice indeed I bring. To lead me back and bestow me safely in the keeping of Melian; for it is not wise to refuse her counsel. Or to know that I shall go into peril, if you go.' For in truth Nienor had come most in the hope that for fear and love of her her mother would turn back; and Morwen was indeed torn in mind.

'It is one thing to refuse counsel,' said she. 'It is another to refuse the command of your mother. Go now back!'

'No,' said Nienor. 'It is long since I was a child. I have a will and wisdom of my own, though until now it has not crossed yours. I go with you. Rather to Doriath, for reverence of those that rule it; but if not, then westward. Indeed, if either of us should go on, it is I rather, in the fullness of strength.'

Then Morwen saw in the grey eyes of Nienor the steadfastness of Húrin; and she wavered, but she could not overcome her pride, and would not seem thus (save the fair words) to be led back by her daughter, as one old and doting.

'I go on, as I have purposed,' she said. 'Come you also, but against my will.'

'Let it be so,' said Nienor.

Then Mablung said to his company: 'Truly, it is by lack of counsel not of courage that Húrin's folk bring woe to others! Even so with Túrin; yet not so with his fathers. But now they are all fey, and I like it not. More do I dread this errand of the King than the hunting of the Wolf. What is to be done?'

But Morwen, who had come ashore and now drew near, heard the last of his words. 'Do as you are bidden by the King,' said she. 'Seek for tidings of Nargothrond, and of Túrin. For this end are we all come together.'

'It is yet a long way and dangerous,' said Mablung. 'If you go further, you shall both be ho sed and go among the riders, and stray no foot from them.'

Thus it was that with the full day they set forth, and passed slowly and warily out of the country of reeds and low willows, and came to the grey woods that covered much of the southern plain before Nargothrond. All day they went due west, and saw nothing but desolation, and heard nothing; for the lands were silent, and it seemed to Mablung that a present fear lay upon them. That same way had Beren trodden years before, and then the woods were filled with the hidden eyes of the hunters; but now all the people of Narog were gone, and the Orcs, as it seemed, were not yet roaming so far southward. That night they encamped in the grey wood without fire or light.

The next two days they went on, and by evening of the third day from Sirion they were come across the plain and were drawing near to the east shores of Narog. Then so great an unease came upon Mablung that he begged Morwen to go no further. But she laughed, and said: 'You will be glad soon to be rid of us, as is likely enough. But you must endure us a little longer. We are come too near now to turn back in fear.'

Then Mablung cried: 'Fey are you both, and foolhardy. You help not but hinder any gathering of news. Now hear me! I was bidden not to stay you with strength; but I was bidden also to guard you, as I might. In this pass, one only can I do. And I will guard you. Tomorrow I will lead you to Amon Ethir, the Spyhill, which is near; and there you shall sit under guard, and go no further while I command here.'

Now Amon Ethir was a mound as great as a hill that long ago Felagund had caused to be raised with great labour in the plain before his Doors, a league east of Narog. It was tree-grown, save on the summit, where a wide view might be had all ways, of the roads that led to the great bridge of Nargothrond, and of the lands round about. To this hill they came late in the morning and climbed up from the east. Then looking out towards the High Faroth, brown and bare beyond the river,[23] Mablung saw with elven-sight the terraces of Nargothrond on the steep west bank, and as a small black hole in the hill-wall the gaping Doors of Felagund. But he could hear no sound, and he could see no sign of any foe, nor any token of the Dragon, save the burning about the Doors that he had wrought in the day of the sack. All lay quiet under a pale sun.

Now therefore Mablung, as he had said, commanded his ten riders to keep Morwen and Nienor on the hill-top, and not to stir thence until he returned, unless some great peril arose: and if that befell, the riders should set Morwen and Nienor in their midst and flee as swiftly as they might, east-away towards Doriath, sending one ahead to bring news and seek aid.

Then Mablung took the other score of his company, and they crept down from the hill; and then passing into the fields westward, where trees were few, they scattered and made each his way, daring but stealthy, to the banks of Narog. Mablung himself took the middle way, going towards the bridge, and so came to its hither end and found it all broken down; and the deep-cloven river, running wild after rains far away northward, was foaming and roaring among the fallen stones.

But Glaurung lay there, just within the shadow of the great passage that led inward from the ruined Doors, and he had long been aware of the spies, though few other eyes in Middle-earth would have discerned them. But the glance of his fell eyes was keener than that of eagles, and outreached the far sight of the Elves; and indeed he knew also that some remained behind and sat upon the bare top of Amon Ethir.

Thus, even as Mablung crept among the rocks seeking whether he could ford the wild river upon the fallen stones of the bridge, suddenly Glaurung came forth with a great blast of fire, and crawled down into the stream. Then straightway there was a vast hissing and huge vapours arose, and Mablung and his followers that lurked near were engulfed in a blinding steam and foul stench; and the most fled as best they could guess towards the Spyhill. But as Glaurung was passing over Narog, Mablung drew aside and lay under a rock, and remained; for it seemed to him that he had an errand yet to do. He knew now indeed that Glaurung abode in Nargothrond, but he was bidden also to learn the truth concerning Húrin's son, if he might; and in the stoutness of his heart, therefore, he purposed to cross the river, as soon as Glaurung was gone, and search the halls of Felagund. For he thought that all had been done that could be for the keeping of Morwen and Nienor: the coming of Glaurung would be marked, and even now the riders should be speeding towards Doriath.

Glaurung therefore passed Mablung by, a vast shape in the mist; and he went swiftly, for he was a mighty Worm, and yet lithe. Then

Mablung behind him forded Narog in great peril; but the watchers upon Amon Ethir beheld the issuing of the Dragon, and were dismayed. At once they bade Morwen and Nienor mount, without debate, and prepared to flee eastward as they were bidden. But even as they came down from the hill into the plain, an ill wind blew the great vapours upon them, bringing a stench that no horses would endure. Then, blinded by the fog and in mad terror of the dragon-reek, the horses soon became ungovernable, and went wildly this way and that; and the guards were dispersed, and were dashed against trees to great hurt, or sought vainly one for another. The neighing of the horses and the cries of the riders came to the ears of Glaurung; and he was well pleased.

One of the Elf-riders, striving with his horse in the fog, saw the Lady Morwen passing near, a grey wraith upon a mad steed; but she vanished into the mist, crying *Nienor*, and they saw her no more.

But when the blind terror came upon the riders, Nienor's horse, running wild, stumbled, and she was thrown. Falling softly into grass she was unhurt; but when she got to her feet she was alone: lost in the mist without horse or companion. Her heart did not fail her, and she took thought; and it seemed to her vain to go towards this cry or that, for cries were all about her, but growing ever fainter. Better it seemed to her in such case to seek again for the hill: thither doubtless Mablung would come before he went away, if only to be sure that none of his company had remained there.

Therefore walking at guess she found the hill, which was indeed close at hand, by the rising of the ground before her feet; and slowly she climbed the path that led up from the east. And as she climbed so the fog grew thinner, until she came at last out into the sunlight on the bare summit. Then she stepped forward and looked westward. And there right before her was the great head of Glaurung, who had even then crept up from the other side; and before she was aware her eyes looked in his eyes, and they were terrible, being filled with the fell spirit of Morgoth, his master.

Then Nienor strove against Glaurung, for she was strong in will; but he put forth his power against her. 'What seek you here?' he said.

And constrained to answer she said: 'I do but seek one Túrin that dwelt here a while. But he is dead, maybe.'

'I know not,' said Glaurung. 'He was left here to defend the women and weaklings; but when I came he deserted them, and fled. A boaster but a craven, it seems. Why seek you such a one?'

'You lie,' said Nienor. 'The children of Húrin at least are not craven. We fear you not.'

Then Glaurung laughed, for so was Húrin's daughter revealed to his malice. 'Then you are fools, both you and your brother,' said he. 'And your boast shall be made vain. For I am Glaurung!'

Then he drew her eyes unto his, and her will swooned. And it seemed to her that the sun sickened and all became dim about her; and slowly a great darkness drew down on her and in that darkness there was emptiness; she knew nothing, and heard nothing, and remembered nothing.

Long Mablung explored the halls of Nargothrond, as well he might for the darkness and the stench; but he found no living thing there: nothing stirred amid the bones, and none answered his cries. At last, being oppressed by the horror of the place, and fearing the return of Glaurung, he came back to the Doors. The sun was sinking west, and the shadows of the Faroth behind lay dark on the terraces and the wild river below; but away beneath Amon Ethir he descried, as it seemed, the evil shape of the Dragon. Harder and more perilous was the return over Narog in such haste and fear; and scarcely had he reached the east shore and crept aside under the bank when Glaurung drew nigh. But he was slow now and stealthy; for all the fires in him were burned low: great power had gone out of him, and he would rest and sleep in the dark. Thus he writhed through the water and slunk up to the Doors like a huge snake, ashen-grey, sliming the ground with his belly.

But he turned before he went in and looked back eastward, and there came from him the laughter of Morgoth, dim but horrible, as an echo of malice out of the black depths far away. And this voice, cold and low, came after: 'There you lie like a vole under the bank, Mablung the mighty! Ill do you run the errands of Thingol. Haste you now to the hill and see what is become of your charge!'

Then Glaurung passed into his lair, and the sun went down and grey evening came chill over the land. But Mablung hastened back to Amon Ethir; and as he climbed to the top the stars came out in the East. Against them he saw there standing, dark and still, a figure as it were an image of stone. Thus Nienor stood, and heard nothing that he said, and made him no answer. But when at last he took her hand, she stirred, and suffered him to lead her away; and while he held her she followed, but if he loosed her, she stood still.

Then great was Mablung's grief and bewilderment; but no other choice had he but to lead Nienor so upon the long eastward way, without help or company. Thus they passed away, walking like dreamers, out into the night-shadowed plain. And when morning returned Nienor stumbled and fell, and lay still; and Mablung sat beside her in despair.

'Not for nothing did I dread this errand,' he said. 'For it will be my last, it seems. With this unlucky child of Men I shall perish in the wilderness, and my name shall be held in scorn in Doriath: if any tidings indeed are ever heard of our fate. All else doubtless are slain, and she alone spared, but not in mercy.'

Thus they were found by three of the company that had fled from Narog at the coming of Glaurung, and after much wandering when the mist had passed went back to the hill; and finding it empty they had begun to seek their way home. Hope then returned to Mablung; and they went on now together steering northward and eastward, for there was no road back into Doriath in the south, and since the fall of Nargothrond the ferry-wards were forbidden to set any across save those that came from within.

Slow was their journey, as for those that lead a weary child. But ever as they passed further from Nargothrond and drew nearer to Doriath, so little by little strength returned to Nienor, and she would walk hour by hour obediently, led by the hand. Yet her wide eyes saw nothing, and her ears heard no words, and her lips spoke no words.

And now at length after many days they came nigh to the west border of Doriath, somewhat south of Teiglin; for they intended to pass the fences of the little land of Thingol beyond Sirion and so come to the guarded bridge near the inflowing of Esgalduin. There a while they halted; and they laid Nienor on a couch of grass, and she closed her eyes as she had not yet done, and it seemed that she slept. Then the Elves rested also, and for very weariness were unheedful. Thus they were assailed at unawares by a band of Orc-hunters, such as now roamed much in that region, as nigh to the fences of Doriath as they dared to go. In the midst of the affray suddenly Nienor leapt up from her couch, as one waking out of sleep to an alarm by night, and with a cry she sped away into the forest. Then the Orcs turned and gave chase, and the Elves after them. But a strange change came upon Nienor and now she outran them all, flying like a deer among the trees with her hair streaming in the wind of her speed. The Orcs indeed Mablung and his companions swiftly overtook and they slew them one and all, and hastened on. But by then Nienor had passed away like a wraith; and neither sight nor slot of her could they find, though they hunted for many days.

Then at last Mablung returned to Doriath bowed with grief and

with shame. 'Choose you a new master of your hunters, lord,' he said
to the King. 'For I am dishonoured.'

But Melian said: 'It is not so, Mablung. You did all that you
could, and none other among the King's servants would have done
so much. But by ill chance you were matched against a power too
great for you: too great indeed for all that now dwell in Middle-
earth.'

'I sent you to win tidings, and that you have done,' said Thingol.
'It is no fault of yours that those whom the tidings touch nearest are
now beyond hearing. Grievous indeed is this end of all Húrin's kin,
but it lies not at your door.'

For not only was Nienor now run witless into the wild, but Morwen
also was lost. Neither then nor after did any certain news of her fate
come to Doriath or to Dor-lómin. Nonetheless Mablung would not
rest, and with a small company he went out into the wild and for
three years wandered far, from Ered Wethrin even to the Mouths of
Sirion, seeking for sign or tidings of the lost.

Nienor in Brethil

But as for Nienor, she ran on into the wood, hearing the shouts of
pursuit come behind; and her clothing she tore off, casting away her
garments as she fled, until she went naked; and all that day still she
ran, as a beast that is hunted to heart-bursting, and dare not stay or
draw breath. But at evening suddenly her madness passed. She stood
still a moment as in wonder, and then, in a swoon of utter weariness,
she fell as one stricken down into a deep brake of fern. And there
amid the old bracken and the swift fronds of spring she lay and
slept, heedless of all.

In the morning she woke, and rejoiced in the light as one first
called to life; and all things that she saw seemed to her new and
strange, and she had no names for them. For behind her lay only an
empty darkness, through which came no memory of anything she had
ever known, nor any echo of any word. A shadow of fear only she
remembered, and so she was wary, and sought ever for hidings: she
would climb into trees or slip into thickets, swift as squirrel or fox,
if any sound or shadow frightened her; and thence she would peer
long through the leaves before she went on again.

Thus going forward in the way she first ran, she came to the river
Teiglin, and stayed her thirst; but no food she found, nor knew how
to seek it, and she was famished and cold. And since the trees across
the water seemed closer and darker (as indeed they were, being the

eaves of Brethil forest) she crossed over at last, and came to a green mound and there cast herself down: for she was spent, and it seemed to her that the darkness that lay behind her was overtaking her again, and the sun going dark.

But indeed it was a black storm that came up out of the South, laden with lightning and great rain; and she lay there cowering in terror of the thunder, and the dark rain smote her nakedness.

Now it chanced that some of the woodmen of Brethil came by in that hour from a foray against Orcs, hastening over the Crossings of Teiglin to a shelter that was near; and there came a great flash of lightning, so that the Haudh-en-Elleth was lit as with a white flame. Then Turambar who led the men started back and covered his eyes, and trembled; for it seemed that he saw the wraith of a slain maiden that lay upon the grave of Finduilas.

But one of the men ran to the mound, and called to him: 'Hither, lord! Here is a young woman lying, and she lives!' and Turambar coming lifted her, and the water dripped from her drenched hair, but she closed her eyes and quivered and strove no more. Then marvelling that she lay thus naked Turambar cast his cloak about her and bore her away to the hunters' lodge in the woods. There they lit a fire and wrapped coverlets about her, and she opened her eyes and looked upon them; and when her glance fell on Turambar a light came in her face and she put out a hand towards him, for it seemed to her that she had found at last something that she had sought in the darkness, and she was comforted. But Turambar took her hand, and smiled, and said: 'Now, lady, will you not tell us your name and your kin, and what evil has befallen you?'

Then she shook her head, and said nothing, but began to weep; and they troubled her no more, until she had eaten hungrily of what food they could give her. And when she had eaten she sighed, and laid her hand again in Turambar's; and he said: 'With us you are safe. Here you may rest this night, and in the morning we will lead you to our homes up in the high forest. But we would know your name and your kin, so that we may find them, maybe, and bring them news of you. Will you not tell us?'

But again she made no answer, and wept.

'Do not be troubled!' said Turambar. 'Maybe the tale is too sad yet to tell. But I will give you a name, and call you Níniel, Maid of Tears.' And at that name she looked up, and she shook her head, but said: Níniel. And that was the first word that she spoke after her darkness, and it was her name among the woodmen ever after.

In the morning they bore Níniel towards Ephel Brandir, and the road went steeply upward towards Amon Obel until it came to a place where it must cross the tumbling stream of Celebros. There a bridge of wood had been built, and below it the stream went over a lip of worn stone, and fell down by many foaming steps into a rocky bowl far below; and all the air was filled with spray like rain. There was a wide greensward at the head of the falls, and birches grew about it, but over the bridge there was a wide view towards the ravines of Teiglin some two miles to the west. There the air was cool and there wayfarers in summer would rest and drink of the cold water. Dimrost, the Rainy Stair, those falls were called, but after that day Nen Girith, the Shuddering Water; for Turambar and his men halted there, but as soon as Níniel came to that place she grew cold and shivered, and they could not warm her or comfort her.[24] Therefore they hastened on their way; but before they came to Ephel Brandir Níniel was already wandering in a fever.

Long she lay in her sickness, and Brandir used all his skill in her healing, and the wives of the woodmen watched over her by night and by day. But only when Turambar stayed near her would she lie at peace, or sleep without moaning; and this thing all marked that watched her: throughout all her fever, though often she was much troubled, she murmured never a word in any tongue of Elves or of Men. And when health slowly returned to her, and she walked and began to eat again, then as with a child the women of Brethil must teach her to speak, word by word. But in this learning she was quick and took great delight, as one that finds again treasures great and small that were mislaid; and when at length she had learned enough to speak with her friends she would say: 'What is the name of this thing? For in my darkness I lost it.' And when she was able to go about again, she would seek the house of Brandir; for she was most eager to learn the names of all living things, and he knew much of such matters; and they would walk together in the gardens and the glades.

Then Brandir grew to love her; and when she grew strong she would lend him an arm for his lameness, and she called him her brother. But to Turambar her heart was given, and only at his coming would she smile, and only when he spoke gaily would she laugh.

One evening of the golden autumn they sat together, and the sun set the hillside and the houses of Ephel Brandir aglow, and there was a deep quiet. Then Níniel said to him: 'Of all things I have now asked the name, save you. What are you called?'

'Turambar,' he answered.

Then she paused as if listening for some echo; but she said: 'And what does that say, or is it just the name for you alone?'

'It means,' said he, 'Master of the Dark Shadow. For I also, Níniel, had my darkness, in which dear things were lost; but now I have overcome it, I deem.'

'And did you also flee from it, running, until you came to these fair woods?' she said. 'And when did you escape, Turambar?'

'Yes,' he answered, 'I fled for many years. And I escaped when you did so. For it was dark when you came, Níniel, but ever since it has been light. And it seems to me that what I long sought in vain has come to me.' And as he went back to his house in the twilight, he said to himself: 'Haudh-en-Elleth! From the green mound she came. Is that a sign, and how shall I read it?'

Now that golden year waned and passed to a gentle winter, and there came another bright year. There was peace in Brethil, and the woodmen held themselves quiet and went not abroad, and they heard no tidings of the lands that lay about them. For the Orcs that at that time came southward to the dark reign of Glaurung, or were sent to spy on the borders of Doriath, shunned the Crossings of Teiglin, and passed westward far beyond the river.

And now Níniel was fully healed, and was grown fair and strong; and Turambar restrained himself no longer, but asked her in marriage. Then Níniel was glad; but when Brandir learned of it his heart was sick within him, and he said to her: 'Be not in haste! Think me not unkindly, if I counsel you to wait.'

'Nothing that you do is done unkindly,' she said. 'But why then do you give me such counsel, wise brother?'

'Wise brother?' he answered. 'Lame brother, rather, unloved and unlovely. And I scarce know why. Yet there lies a shadow on this man, and I am afraid.'

'There was a shadow,' said Níniel, 'for so he told me. But he has escaped from it, even as I. And is he not worthy of love? Though he now holds himself at peace, was he not once the greatest captain, from whom all our enemies would flee, if they saw him?'

'Who told you this?' said Brandir.

'It was Dorlas,' she said. 'Does he not speak truth?'

'Truth indeed,' said Brandir, but he was ill pleased, for Dorlas was chief of that party that wished for war on the Orcs. And yet he sought still for reasons to delay Níniel; and he said therefore: 'The truth, but not the whole truth; for he was the Captain of Nargothrond, and came before out of the North, and was (it is said) son of Húrin of Dor-lómin of the warlike House of Hador.' And Brandir, seeing the shadow that passed over her face at that name, misread her, and said more: 'Indeed, Níniel, well may you think that such a one is likely ere long to go back to war, far from this land, maybe. And if so, how will you endure it? Have a care, for I forebode that if Turambar goes again to battle, then not he but the Shadow shall have the mastery.'

'Ill would I endure it,' she answered; 'but unwedded no better than wedded. And a wife, maybe, would better restrain him, and hold off the shadow.' Nonetheless she was troubled by the words of Brandir, and she bade Turambar wait yet a while. And he wondered and was downcast; but when he learned from Níniel that Brandir had counselled her to wait, he was ill pleased.

But when the next spring came he said to Níniel: 'Time passes. We have waited, and now I will wait no longer. Do as your heart bids you, Níniel most dear, but see: this is the choice before me. I will go back now to war in the wild; or I will wed you, and go never to war again – save only to defend you, if some evil assails our home.'

Then she was glad indeed, and she plighted her troth, and at the mid-summer they were wedded; and the woodmen made a great feast, and they gave them a fair house which they had built for them upon Amon Obel. There they dwelt in happiness, but Brandir was troubled, and the shadow on his heart grew deeper.

The Coming of Glaurung

Now the power and malice of Glaurung grew apace, and he waxed fat, and he gathered Orcs to him, and ruled as a dragon-King, and all the realm of Nargothrond that had been was laid under him. And before this year ended, the third of Turambar's dwelling among the woodmen, he began to assail their land, which for a while had had peace; for indeed it was well known to Glaurung and to his Master that in Brethil there abode still a remnant of free men, the last of the Three Houses to defy the power of the North. And this they would not brook; for it was the purpose of Morgoth to subdue all Beleriand and to search out its every corner, so that none in any hole or hiding might live that were not thrall to him. Thus, whether Glaurung guessed where Túrin was hidden, or whether (as some hold) he had indeed for that time escaped from the eye of Evil that pursued him, is of little matter. For in the end the counsels of Brandir must prove vain, and at the last two choices only could there be for Turambar: to sit deedless until he was found, driven forth like a rat; or to go forth soon to battle, and be revealed.

But when tidings of the coming of the Orcs were first brought to Ephel Brandir, he did not go forth and yielded to the prayers of Níniel. For she said: 'Our homes are not yet assailed, as your word was. It is said that the Orcs are not many. And Dorlas has told me that before you came such affrays were not seldom, and the woodmen held them off.'

But the woodmen were worsted, for these Orcs were of a fell breed, fierce and cunning; and they came indeed with a purpose to invade the Forest of Brethil, not as before passing through its eaves on other errands, or hunting in small bands. Therefore Dorlas and his men were driven back with loss, and the Orcs came over Teiglin and roamed far into the woods. And Dorlas came to Turambar and showed his wounds, and he said: 'See, lord, now is the time of our need come upon us, after a false peace, even as I foreboded. Did you not ask to be counted one of our people, and no stranger? Is this peril not yours also? For our homes will not remain hidden, if the Orcs come further into our land.'

Therefore Turambar arose, and took up again his sword Gurthang, and he went to battle; and when the woodmen learned this they were greatly heartened, and they gathered to him, till he had a force of many hundreds. Then they hunted through the forest and slew all the Orcs that crept there, and hung them on the trees near the Crossings of Teiglin. And when a new host came against them, they trapped it, and being surprised both by the numbers of the woodmen and by the terror of the Black Sword that had returned, the Orcs were routed and slain in great number. Then the woodmen made great pyres and burned the bodies of the soldiers of Morgoth in heaps, and the smoke of their vengeance rose black into heaven, and the wind bore it away westward. But few living went back to Nargothrond with these tidings.

Then Glaurung was wrathful indeed; but for a while he lay still and pondered what he had heard. Thus the winter passed in peace, and men said: 'Great is the Black Sword of Brethil, for all our enemies are overcome.' And Níniel was comforted, and she rejoiced in the renown of Turambar; but he sat in thought, and he said in his heart: 'The die is cast. Now comes the test, in which my boast shall be made good, or fail utterly. I will flee no more. Turambar indeed I will be, and by my own will and prowess I will surmount my doom – or fall. But falling or riding, Glaurung at least I will slay.'

Nonetheless he was unquiet, and he sent out men of daring as scouts far afield. For indeed though no word was said he now ordered things as he would, as if he were lord of Brethil, and no man heeded Brandir.

Spring came hopefully, and men sang at their work. But in that spring Níniel conceived, and she became pale and wan, and all her happiness was dimmed. And soon there came strange tidings, from the men that had gone abroad beyond Teiglin, that there was a great burning far out in the woods of the plain towards Nargothrond, and men wondered what it might be.

Before long there came more reports: that the fires drew ever northward, and that indeed Glaurung himself made them. For he had left Nargothrond, and was abroad again on some errand. Then the more foolish or more hopeful said: 'His army is destroyed, and now at last he sees wisdom and is going back whence he came.' And others said: 'Let us hope that he will pass us by.' But Turambar had no such hope, and knew that Glaurung was coming to seek him. Therefore though he masked his mind because of Níniel, he pondered ever by day and by night what counsel he should take; and spring turned towards summer.

A day came when two men returned to Ephel Brandir in terror, for they had seen the Great Worm himself. 'In truth, lord,' they said to Turambar, 'he draws now near to Teiglin, and turns not aside. He lay in the midst of a great burning, and the trees smoked about him. The stench of him is scarce to be endured. And all the long leagues back to Nargothrond his foul swath lies, we deem, in a line that swerves not, but points straight to us. What is to be done?'

'Little,' said Turambar, 'but to that little I have already given thought. The tidings you bring give me hope rather than dread; for if indeed he goes straight, as you say, and will not swerve, then I have some counsel for hardy hearts.' The men wondered, for he said no more at that time; but they took heart from his steadfast bearing.[25]

Now the river Teiglin ran in this manner. It flowed down from Ered Wethrin swift as Narog, but at first between low shores, until after the Crossings, gathering power from other streams, it clove a way through the feet of the highlands upon which stood the Forest of Brethil. Thereafter it ran in deep ravines, whose great sides were like walls of rock, but pent at the bottom the waters flowed with great force and noise. And right in the path of Glaurung there lay now one of these gorges, by no means the deepest, but the narrowest, just north of the inflow of Celebros. Therefore Turambar sent out three hardy men to keep watch from the brink on the movements of the Dragon; but he himself would ride to the high fall of Nen Girith, where news could find him swiftly, and whence he himself could look far across the lands.

But first he gathered the woodmen together in Ephel Brandir and spoke to them, saying:

'Men of Brethil, a deadly peril has come upon us which only great hardihood shall turn aside. But in this matter numbers will avail little; we must use cunning, and hope for good fortune. If we went up against the Dragon with all our strength, as against an army of Orcs, we should but offer ourselves all to death, and so leave our wives and kin defenceless. Therefore I say that you should stay here, and prepare for flight. For if Glaurung comes, then you must abandon this place, and scatter far and wide; and so may some escape and live. For certainly, if he can, he will come to our stronghold and dwelling, and he will destroy it, and all that he espies; but afterwards he will not abide here. In Nargothrond lies all his treasure, and there are the deep halls in which he can lie safe, and grow.'

Then the men were dismayed, and were utterly downcast, for they trusted in Turambar, and had looked for more hopeful words. But he said: 'Nay, that is the worst. And it shall not come to pass, if my counsel and fortune is good. For I do not believe that this Dragon is unconquerable, though he grows greater in strength and malice with the years. I know somewhat of him. His power is rather in the evil spirit that dwells within him than in the might of his body, great though that be. For hear now this tale that I was told by some that fought in the year of the Nirnaeth, when I and most that hear me were children. In that field the Dwarves withstood him and Azaghâl of Belegost pricked him so deep that he fled back to Angband. But here is a thorn sharper and longer than the knife of Azaghâl.'

And Turambar swept Gurthang from its sheath and stabbed with it up above his head, and it seemed to those that looked on that a flame leapt from Turambar's hand many feet into the air. Then they gave a great cry: 'The Black Thorn of Brethil!'

'The Black Thorn of Brethil,' said Turambar: 'well may he fear it. For know this: it is the doom of this Dragon (and all his brood, it is said) that how great so ever be his armour of horn, harder than iron, below he must go with the belly of a snake. Therefore, Men of Brethil, I go now to seek the belly of Glaurung, by what means I may. Who will come with me? I need but a few with strong arms and stronger hearts.'

Then Dorlas stood forth and said: 'I will go with you, lord; for I would ever go forward rather than wait for a foe.'

But no others were so swift to the call, for the dread of Glaurung lay on them, and the tale of the scouts that had seen him had gone about and grown in the telling. Then Dorlas cried out: 'Hearken, Men of Brethil, it is now well seen that for the evil of our times the counsels of Brandir were vain. There is no escape by hiding. Will none of you take the place of the son of Handir, that the House of Haleth be not put to shame?' Thus Brandir, who sat indeed in the high-seat of the lord of the assembly, but unheeded, was scorned, and he was bitter in his heart; for Turambar did not rebuke Dorlas. But one Hunthor, Brandir's kinsman, arose and said: 'You do evilly, Dorlas, to speak thus to the shame of your lord, whose limbs by ill hazard cannot do as his heart would. Beware lest the contrary be seen in you at some turn! And how can it be said that his counsels were vain, when they were never taken? You, his liege, have ever set them at naught. I say to you that Glaurung comes now to us, as to Nargothrond before, because our deeds have betrayed us, as he feared. But since this woe is now come, with your leave, son of Handir, I will go on behalf of Haleth's house.'

Then Turambar said: 'Three is enough! You twain will I take. But, lord, I do not scorn you. See! We must go in great haste, and our task will need strong limbs. I deem that your place is with your people. For you are wise, and are a healer; and it may be that there will be great need of wisdom and healing ere long.' But these words, though fair spoken, did but embitter Brandir the more, and he said to Hunthor: 'Go then, but not with my leave. For a shadow lies on this man, and it will lead you to evil.'

Now Turambar was in haste to go; but when he came to Níniel, to bid her farewell, she clung to him, weeping grievously. 'Go not forth, Turambar, I beg!' she said. 'Challenge not the shadow that you have fled from! Nay, nay, flee still, and take me with you, far away!'

'Níniel most dear,' he answered, 'we cannot flee further, you and I. We are hemmed in this land. And even should I go, deserting the people that befriended us, I could but take you forth into the houseless wild, to your death and the death of our child. A hundred leagues lie between us and any land that is yet beyond the reach of the Shadow. But take heart, Níniel. For I say to you: neither you nor I shall be slain by this Dragon, nor by any foe of the North.' Then Níniel ceased to weep and fell silent, but her kiss was cold as they parted.

Then Turambar with Dorlas and Hunthor went away hotfoot to Nen Girith, and when they came there the sun was westering and shadows were long; and the last two of the scouts were there awaiting them.

'You come not too soon, lord,' said they. 'For the Dragon has come on, and already when we left he had reached the brink of Teiglin, and glared across the water. He moves ever by night, and we may look then for some stroke before tomorrow's dawn.'

Turambar looked out over the falls of Celebros and saw the sun going down to its setting, and black spires of smoke rising by the borders of the river. 'There is no time to lose,' he said; 'yet these tidings are good. For my fear was that he would seek about; and if he passed northward and came to the Crossings and so to the old road in the lowland, then hope would be dead. But now some fury of pride and malice drives him headlong.' But even as he spoke, he wondered, and mused in his mind: 'Or can it be that one so evil and fell shuns the Crossings, even as the Orcs? Haudh-en-Elleth! Does Finduilas lie still between me and my doom?'

Then he turned to his companions and said: 'This task now lies before us. We must wait yet a little; for too soon in this case were as ill as too late. When dusk falls, we must creep down, with all stealth, to Teiglin. But beware! For the ears of Glaurung are as keen as his eyes – and they are deadly. If we reach the river unmarked, we must climb then down into the ravine, and cross the water, and so come in the path that he will take when he stirs.'

'But how can he come forward so?' said Dorlas. 'Lithe he may be, but he is a great Dragon, and how shall he climb down the one cliff and up the other, when part must again be climbing before the hinder is yet descended? And if he can so, what will it avail us to be in the wild water below?'

'Maybe he can so,' answered Turambar, 'and indeed if he does, it will go ill with us. But it is my hope from what we learn of him, and from the place where he now lies, that his purpose is otherwise. He is come to the brink of Cabed-en-Aras, over which, as you tell, a deer once leaped from the huntsmen of Haleth. So great is he now that I think he will seek to cast himself across there. That is all our hope, and we must trust to it.'

Dorlas' heart sank at these words; for he knew better than any all the land of Brethil, and Cabed-en-Aras was a grim place indeed. On the east side was a sheer cliff of some forty feet, bare but tree-grown at the crown; on the other side was a bank somewhat less sheer and less high, shrouded with hanging trees and bushes, but between them the water ran fiercely among rocks, and though a man bold and sure-footed might ford it by day, it was perilous to dare it at night. But this was the counsel of Turambar, and it was useless to gainsay him.

They set out therefore at dusk, and they did not go straight towards the Dragon, but took first the path to the Crossings; then, before they came so far, they turned southward by a narrow track and passed into the twilight of the woods above Teiglin.[26] And as they drew near to Cabed-en-Aras, step by step, halting often to listen, the reek of burning came to them, and a stench that sickened them. But all was deadly still, and there was no stir of air. The first stars glimmered in the East behind them, and faint spires of smoke rose straight and unwavering against the last light in the West.

Now when Turambar was gone Níniel stood silent as stone; but Brandir came to her and said: 'Níniel, fear not the worst until you must. But did I not counsel you to wait?'

'You did so,' she answered. 'Yet how would that profit me now? For love may abide and suffer unwedded.'

'That I know,' said Brandir. 'Yet wedding is not for nothing.'

'I am two months gone with his child,' said Níniel. 'But it does not seem to me that my fear of loss is the more heavy to bear. I understand you not.'

'Nor I myself,' said he. 'And yet I am afraid.'

'What a comforter are you!' she cried. 'But Brandir, friend: wedded or unwedded, mother or maid, my dread is beyond enduring. The Master of Doom is gone to challenge his doom far hence, and how shall I stay here and wait for the slow coming of tidings, good or ill? This night, it may be, he will meet with the Dragon, and how shall I stand, or sit, or pass the dreadful hours?'

'I know not,' said he, 'but somehow the hours must pass, for you and for the wives of those that went with him.'

'Let them do as their hearts bid!' she cried. 'But for me, I shall go. The miles shall not lie between me and my lord's peril. I will go to meet the tidings!'

Then Brandir's dread grew black at her words, and he cried: 'That you shall not do, if I may hinder it. For thus will you endanger all counsel. The miles that lie between may give time for escape, if ill befall.'

'If ill befall, I shall not wish to escape,' she said. 'And now your wisdom is vain, and you shall not hinder me.' And she stood forth before the people that were still gathered in the open place of the Ephel, and she cried: 'Men of Brethil! I will not wait here. If my lord fails, then all hope is false. Your land and woods shall be burned utterly, and all your houses laid in ashes, and none, none, shall escape. Therefore why tarry here? Now I go to meet the tidings and whatever doom may send. Let all those of like mind come with me!'

Then many were willing to go with her: the wives of Dorlas and Hunthor because those whom they loved were gone with Turambar; others for pity of Níniel and desire to befriend her; and many more that were lured by the very rumour of the Dragon, in their hardihood or their folly (knowing little of evil) thinking to see strange and glorious deeds. For indeed so great in their minds had the Black Sword become that few could believe that even Glaurung could conquer him. Therefore they set forth soon in haste, a great company, towards a peril that they did not understand; and going with little rest they came wearily at last, just at nightfall, to Nen Girith but a little while after Turambar had departed. But night is a cold counsellor, and many were now amazed at their own rashness; and when they heard from the scouts that remained there how near Glaurung was come, and the desperate purpose of Turambar, their hearts were chilled, and they dared go no further. Some looked out towards Cabed-en-Aras with anxious eyes, but nothing could they see, and nothing hear save the cold voice of the falls. And Níniel sat apart, and a great shuddering seized her.

When Níniel and her company had gone, Brandir said to those that remained: 'Behold how I am scorned, and all my counsel disdained! Let Turambar be your lord in name, since already he has taken all my authority. For here I renounce both lordship and people. Let none seek of me ever again either counsel or healing!' And he broke his staff. To himself he thought: 'Now nothing is left to me, save only my love of Níniel: therefore where she goes, in wisdom or folly, I must go. In this dark hour nothing can be foreseen; but it may well chance that even I could ward off some evil from her, if I were near.'

He girt himself therefore with a short sword, as seldom before, and took his crutch, and went with what speed he might out of the gate of the Ephel, limping after the others down the long path to the west march of Brethil.

The Death of Glaurung

At last, even as full night closed over the land, Turambar and his companions came to Cabed-en-Aras, and they were glad of the great noise of the water; for though it promised peril below, it covered all other sounds. Then Dorlas led them a little aside, southwards, and they climbed down by a cleft to the cliff-foot; but there his heart quailed, for many rocks and great stones lay in the river, and the water ran wild about them, grinding its teeth. 'This is a sure way to death,' said Dorlas.

'It is the only way, to death or to life,' said Turambar, 'and delay will not make it seem more hopeful. Therefore follow me!' And he went on before them, and by skill and hardihood, or by fate, he came across, and in the deep dark he turned to see who came after. A dark form stood beside him. 'Dorlas?' he said.

'No, it is I,' said Hunthor. 'Dorlas failed at the crossing. For a man may love war, and yet dread many things. He sits shivering on the shore, I guess; and may shame take him for his words to my kinsman.'

Now Turambar and Hunthor rested a little, but soon the night chilled them, for they were both drenched with water, and they began to seek a way along the stream northwards towards the lodgement of Glaurung. There the chasm grew darker and narrower, and as they felt their way forward they could see a flicker above them as of smouldering fire, and they heard the snarling of the Great Worm in his watchful sleep. Then they groped for a way up, to come nigh under the brink; for in that lay all their hope to come at their enemy beneath his guard. But so foul now was the reek that their heads were dizzy, and they slipped as they clambered, and clung to the tree-stems, and retched, forgetting in their misery all fear save the dread of falling into the teeth of Teiglin.

Then Turambar said to Hunthor: 'We spend our waning strength to no avail. For till we be sure where the Dragon will pass, it is vain to climb.'

'But when we know,' said Hunthor, 'then there will be no time to seek a way up out of the chasm.'

'Truly,' said Turambar. 'But where all lies on chance, to chance we must trust.' They halted therefore and waited, and out of the dark ravine they watched a white star far above creep across the faint strip of sky; and then slowly Turambar sank into a dream, in which all his will was given to clinging, though a black tide sucked and gnawed at his limbs.

Suddenly there was a great noise and the walls of the chasm quivered and echoed. Turambar roused himself, and said to Hunthor: 'He stirs. The hour is upon us. Strike deep, for two must strike now for three!'

And with that Glaurung began his assault upon Brethil; and all passed much as Turambar had hoped. For now the Dragon crawled with slow weight to the edge of the cliff, and he did not turn aside, but made ready to spring over the chasm with his great forelegs and then draw his bulk after. Terror came with him; for he did not begin his passage right above, but a little to the northward, and the watchers from beneath could see the huge shadow of his head against the stars; and his jaws gaped, and he had seven tongues of fire. Then he sent forth a blast, so that all the ravine was filled with a red light, and black shadows flying among the rocks; but the trees before him withered and went up in smoke, and stones crashed down into the river. And thereupon he hurled himself forward, and grappled the further cliff with his mighty claws, and began to heave himself across.

Now there was need to be bold and swift, for though Turambar and Hunthor had escaped the blast, since they were not standing right in Glaurung's path, they yet had to come at him, before he passed over, or all their hope failed. Heedless of peril Turambar clambered along the water-edge to come beneath him; but there so deadly was the heat and the stench that he tottered and would have fallen if Hunthor, following stoutly behind, had not seized his arm and steadied him.

'Great heart!' said Turambar. 'Happy was the choice that took you for a helper!' But even as he spoke, a great stone hurtled from above and smote Hunthor on the head, and he fell into the water, and so ended: not the least valiant of the House of Haleth. Then Turambar cried: 'Alas! It is ill to walk in my shadow! Why did I seek aid? For now you are alone, O Master of Doom, as you should have known it must be. Now conquer alone!'

Then he summoned to him all his will, and all his hatred of the Dragon and his Master, and it seemed that suddenly he found a strength of heart and of body that he had not known before; and he climbed the cliff, from stone to stone, and root to root, until he seized at last a slender tree that grew a little beneath the lip of the chasm, and though its top was blasted, it held still fast by its roots. And even as he steadied himself in a fork of its boughs, the midmost parts of the Dragon came above him, and swayed down with their weight almost upon his head, ere Glaurung could heave them up. Pale and wrinkled was their underside, and all dank with a grey slime, to which clung all manner of dropping filth; and it stank of death. Then Turambar drew the Black Sword of Beleg and stabbed upwards with all the might of his arm, and of his hate, and the deadly blade, long and greedy, went into the belly even to its hilts.

Then Glaurung, feeling his death-pang, gave forth a scream,

whereat all the woods were shaken, and the watchers at Nen Girith were aghast. Turambar reeled as from a blow, and slipped down, and his sword was torn from his grasp, and clave to the belly of the Dragon. For Glaurung in a great spasm bent up all his shuddering bulk and hurled it over the ravine, and there upon the further shore he writhed, screaming, lashing and coiling himself in his agony, until he had broken a great space all about him, and lay there at last in a smoke and a ruin, and was still.

Now Turambar clung to the roots of the tree, stunned and well-nigh overcome. But he strove against himself and drove himself on, and half sliding and half climbing he came down to the river, and dared again the perilous crossing, crawling now on hands and feet, clinging, blinded with spray, until he came over at last, and climbed wearily up by the cleft by which they had descended. Thus he came at length to the place of the dying Dragon, and he looked on his stricken enemy without pity, and was glad.

There now Glaurung lay, with jaws agape; but all his fires were burned out, and his evil eyes were closed. He was stretched out in his length, and had rolled upon one side, and the hilts of Gurthang stood in his belly. Then the heart of Turambar rose high within him, and though the Dragon still breathed he would recover his sword, which if he prized it before was now worth to him all the treasure of Nargothrond. True proved the words spoken at its forging that nothing, great or small, should live that once it had bitten.

Therefore going up to his foe he set foot upon his belly, and seizing the hilts of Gurthang he put forth his strength to withdraw it. And he cried in mockery of Glaurung's words at Nargothrond: 'Hail, Worm of Morgoth! Well met again! Die now and the darkness have thee! Thus is Túrin son of Húrin avenged.' Then he wrenched out the sword, and even as he did so a spout of black blood followed it, and fell upon his hand, and his flesh was burned by the venom, so that he cried aloud at the pain. Thereat Glaurung stirred and opened his baleful eyes and looked upon Turambar with such malice that it seemed to him that he was smitten by an arrow; and for that and for the anguish of his hand he fell in a swoon, and lay as one dead beside the Dragon, and his sword was beneath him.

Now the screams of Glaurung came to the people at Nen Girith, and they were filled with terror; and when the watchers beheld from afar the great breaking and burning that the Dragon made in his throes, they believed that he was trampling and destroying those that had assailed him. Then indeed they wished the miles longer that lay between them; but they dared not leave the high place where they were gathered, for they remembered the words of Turambar that, if Glaurung conquered, he would go first to Ephel Brandir. Therefore they watched in fear for any sign of his movement, but none were so hardy as to go down and seek for tidings in the place of the battle. And Níniel sat, and did not move, save that she shuddered and could not still her limbs; for when she heard the voice of Glaurung her heart died within her, and she felt her darkness creeping upon her again.

Thus Brandir found her. For he came at last to the bridge over Celebros, slow and weary; all the long way alone he had limped on his crutch, and it was five leagues at the least from his home. Fear for Níniel had driven him on, and now the tidings that he learned were no worse than he had dreaded. 'The Dragon has crossed the river,' men told him, 'and the Black Sword is surely dead, and those that went with him.' Then Brandir stood by Níniel, and guessed her misery, and he yearned to her; but he thought nonetheless: 'The Black Sword is dead, and Níniel lives.' And he shuddered, for suddenly it seemed cold by the waters of Nen Girith; and he cast his cloak about Níniel. But he found no words to say; and she did not speak.

Time passed, and still Brandir stood silent beside her, peering into the night and listening; but he could see nothing, and could hear no sound but the falling of the waters of Nen Girith, and he thought: 'Now surely Glaurung is gone and has passed into Brethil.' But he pitied his people no more, fools that had flouted his counsel, and had scorned him. 'Let the Dragon go to Amon Obel, and there will be time then to escape, to lead Níniel away.' Whither, he scarce knew, for he had never journeyed beyond Brethil.

At last he bent down and touched Níniel on the arm, and said to her: 'Time passes, Níniel! Come! It is time to go. If you will let me, I will lead you.'

Then silently she arose, and took his hand, and they passed over the bridge and went down the path that led to the Crossings of Teiglin. But those that saw them moving as shadows in the dark knew not who they were, and cared not. And when they had gone some little way through the silent trees, the moon rose beyond Amon Obel, and the glades of the forest were filled with a grey light. Then Níniel halted and said to Brandir: 'Is this the way?'

And he answered: 'What is the way? For all our hope in Brethil is ended. We have no way, save to escape the Dragon, and flee far from him while there is yet time.'

Níniel looked at him in wonder and said: 'Did you not offer to lead me to him? Or would you deceive me? The Black Sword was my beloved and my husband, and only to find him do I go. What else could you think? Now do as you will, but I must hasten.'

And even as Brandir stood a moment amazed, she sped from him; and he called after her, crying: 'Wait, Níniel! Go not alone! You know not what you will find. I will come with you!' But she paid no heed to him, and went now as though her blood burned her, which before had been cold; and though he followed as he could she passed soon out of his sight. Then he cursed his fate and his weakness; but he would not turn back.

Now the moon rose white in the sky, and was near the full, and as Níniel came down from the upland towards the land near the river, it seemed to her that she remembered it, and feared it. For she was come to the Crossings of Teiglin, and Haudh-en-Elleth stood there before her, pale in the moonlight, with a black shadow cast athwart it; and out of the mound came a great dread.

Then she turned with a cry and fled south along the river, and cast her cloak as she ran, as though casting off a darkness that clung to her; and beneath she was all clad in white, and she shone in the moon as she flitted among the trees. Thus Brandir above on the hill-side saw her, and turned to cross her course, if he could; and finding by fortune the narrow path that Turambar had used, for it left the more beaten road and went steeply down southward to the river, he came at last close behind her again. But though he called, she did not heed, or did not hear, and soon once more she passed on ahead; and so they drew near to the woods beside Cabed-en-Aras and the place of the agony of Glaurung.

The moon then was riding in the South unclouded, and the light was cold and clear. Coming to the edge of the ruin that Glaurung had wrought, Níniel saw his body lying there, and his belly grey in the moon-sheen; but beside him lay a man. Then forgetting her fear she ran on amid the smouldering wrack and so came to Turambar. He was fallen on his side, and his sword lay beneath him, but his face was wan as death in the white light. Then she threw herself down by him weeping, and kissed him; and it seemed to her that he breathed faintly, but she thought it but a trickery of false hope, for he was cold, and did not move, nor did he answer her. And as she caressed him she found that his hand was blackened as if it had been scorched, and she washed it with her tears, and tearing a strip from her raiment she bound it about. But still he did not move at her touch, and she kissed him again, and cried aloud: 'Turambar,

Turambar, come back! Hear me! Awake! For it is Níniel. The Dragon is dead, dead, and I alone am here by you.' But he answered nothing.

Her cry Brandir heard, for he had come to the edge of the ruin; but even as he stepped forward towards Níniel, he was halted, and stood still. For at the cry of Níniel Glaurung stirred for the last time, and a quiver ran through all his body; and he opened his baleful eyes a slit, and the moon gleamed in them, as gasping he spoke:

'Hail, Nienor, daughter of Húrin. We meet again ere the end. I give thee joy that thou hast found thy brother at last. And now thou shalt know him: a stabber in the dark, treacherous to foes, faithless to friends, and a curse unto his kin, Túrin son of Húrin! But the worst of all his deeds thou shalt feel in thyself.'

Then Nienor sat as one stunned, but Glaurung died; and with his death the veil of his malice fell from her, and all her memory grew clear before her, from day unto day, neither did she forget any of those things that had befallen her since she lay on Haudh-en-Elleth. And her whole body shook with horror and anguish. But Brandir, who had heard all, was stricken, and leaned against a tree.

Then suddenly Nienor started to her feet, and stood pale as a wraith in the moon, and looked down on Túrin, and cried: 'Farewell, O twice beloved! *A Túrin Turambar turún' ambartanen*: master of doom by doom mastered! O happy to be dead!' Then distraught with woe and the horror that had overtaken her she fled wildly from that place; and Brandir stumbled after her, crying: 'Wait! Wait, Níniel!'

One moment she paused, looking back with staring eyes. 'Wait?' she cried. 'Wait? That was ever your counsel. Would that I had heeded! But now it is too late. And now I will wait no more upon Middle-earth.' And she sped on before him.[27]

Swiftly she came to the brink of Cabed-en-Aras, and there stood and looked on the loud water crying: 'Water, water! Take now Níniel Nienor daughter of Húrin; Mourning, Mourning daughter of Morwen! Take me and bear me down to the Sea!' With that she cast herself over the brink: a flash of white swallowed in the dark chasm, a cry lost in the roaring of the river.

The waters of Teiglin flowed on, but Cabed-en-Aras was no more: Cabed Naeramarth thereafter it was named by men; for no deer would ever leap there again, and all living things shunned it, and no man would walk upon its shore. Last of men to look down into its darkness was Brandir son of Handir; and he turned away in horror, for his heart quailed, and though he hated now his life, he could not there take the death that he desired.[28] Then his thought turned to

Túrin Turambar, and he cried: 'Do I hate you, or do I pity you? But you are dead. I owe you no thanks, taker of all that I had or would have. But my people owe you a debt. It is fitting that from me they should learn it.'

And so he began to limp back to Nen Girith, avoiding the place of the Dragon with a shudder; and as he climbed the steep path again he came on a man that peered through the trees, and seeing him drew back. But he had marked his face in a gleam of the sinking moon.

'Ha, Dorlas!' he cried. 'What news can you tell? How came you off alive? And what of my kinsman?'

'I know not,' answered Dorlas sullenly.

'Then that is strange,' said Brandir.

'If you will know,' said Dorlas, 'the Black Sword would have us ford the races of Teiglin in the dark. Is it strange that I could not? I am a better man with an axe than some, but I am not goat-footed.'

'So they went on without you to come at the Dragon?' said Brandir. 'But how when he passed over? At the least you would stay near, and would see what befell.'

Bur Dorlas made no answer, and stared only at Brandir with hatred in his eyes. Then Brandir understood, perceiving suddenly that this man had deserted his companions, and unmanned by shame had then hidden in the woods. 'Shame on you, Dorlas!' he said. 'You are the begetter of our woes: egging on the Black Sword, bringing the Dragon upon us, putting me to scorn, drawing Hunthor to his death, and then you flee to skulk in the woods!' And as he spoke another thought entered his mind, and he said in great anger: 'Why did you not bring tidings? It was the least penance that you could do. Had you done so, the Lady Níniel would have had no need to seek them herself. She need never have seen the Dragon. She might have lived. Dorlas, I hate you!'

'Keep your hate!' said Dorlas. 'It is as feeble as all your counsels. But for me the Orcs would have come and hung you as a scarecrow in your own garden. Take the name skulker to yourself!' And with that, being for his shame the readier to wrath, he aimed a blow at Brandir with his great fist, and so ended his life, before the look of amazement left his eyes: for Brandir drew his sword and hewed him his death-blow. Then for a moment he stood trembling, sickened by the blood; and casting down his sword he turned, and went on his way, bowed upon his crutch.

As Brandir came to Nen Girith the pallid moon was gone down, and the night was fading; morning was opening in the East. The people that cowered there still by the bridge saw him come like a grey shadow in the dawn, and some called to him in wonder: 'Where have you been? Have you seen her? For the Lady Níniel is gone.'

'Yes, she is gone,' he said. 'Gone, gone, never to return! But I am come to bring you tidings. Hear now, people of Brethil, and say if there was ever such a tale as the tale that I bear! The Dragon is dead, but dead also is Turambar at his side. And those are good tidings: yes, both are good indeed.'

Then the people murmured, wondering at his speech, and some said that he was mad; but Brandir cried: 'Hear me to the end! Níniel too is dead, Níniel the fair whom you loved, whom I loved dearest of all. She leaped from the brink of the Deer's Leap,[29] and the teeth of Teiglin have taken her. She is gone, hating the light of day. For this she learned before she fled: Húrin's children were they both, sister and brother. The Morgemil he was called, Turambar he named himself, hiding his past: Túrin son of Húrin. Níniel we named her, not knowing her past: Nienor she was, daughter of Húrin. To Brethil they brought their dark doom's shadow. Here their doom has fallen, and of grief this land shall never again be free. Call it not Brethil, not the land of the Halethrim, but *Sarch nia Hîn Húrin*, Grave of the Children of Húrin!'

Then though they did not understand yet how this evil had come to pass, the people wept as they stood, and some said: 'A grave there is in Teiglin for Níniel the beloved, a grave there shall be for Turambar, most valiant of men. Our deliverer shall not be left to lie under the sky. Let us go to him.'

The Death of Túrin

Now even as Níniel fled away, Túrin stirred, and it seemed to him that out of his deep darkness he heard her call to him far away; but as Glaurung died, the black swoon left him, and he breathed deep again, and sighed, and passed into a slumber of great weariness. But ere dawn it grew bitter cold, and he turned in his sleep, and the hilts of Gurthang drove into his side, and suddenly he awoke. Night was going, and there was a breath of morning in the air; and he sprang to his feet, remembering his victory, and the burning venom on his hand. He raised it up, and looked at it, and marvelled. For it was bound about with a strip of white cloth, yet moist, and it was at ease; and he said to himself: 'Why should one tend me so, and yet leave me here to lie cold amid the wrack and the dragon-stench? What strange things have chanced?'

Then he called aloud, but there was no answer. All was black and drear about him, and there was a reek of death. He stooped and lifted his sword, and it was whole, and the light of its edges was undimmed. 'Foul was the venom of Glaurung,' he said, 'but you are stronger than I, Gurthang! All blood will you drink. Yours is the victory. But come! I must go seek for aid. My body is weary, and there is a chill in my bones.'

Then he turned his back upon Glaurung and left him to rot; but as he passed from that place each step seemed more heavy, and he thought: 'At Nen Girith, maybe, I will find one of the scouts awaiting me. But would I were soon in my own house, and might feel the gentle hands of Níniel, and the good skill of Brandir!' And so at last, walking wearily, leaning on Gurthang, through the grey light of early day he came to Nen Girith, and even as men were setting forth to seek his dead body, he stood before the people.

Then they gave back in terror, believing that it was his unquiet spirit, and the women wailed and covered their eyes. But he said: 'Nay, do not weep, but be glad! See! Do I not live? And have I not slain the Dragon that you feared?'

Then they turned upon Brandir, and cried: 'Fool, with your false tales, saying that he lay dead. Did we not say that you were mad?' But Brandir was aghast, and stared at Túrin with fear in his eyes, and he could say nothing.

But Túrin said to him: 'It was you then that were there, and tended my hand? I thank you. But your skill is failing, if you cannot tell swoon from death.' Then he turned to the people: 'Speak not so to him, fools all of you. Which of you would have done better? At least he had the heart to come down to the place of battle, while you sit wailing!

'But now, son of Handir, come! There is more that I would learn. Why are you here, and all this people, whom I left at the Ephel? If I may go into the peril of death for your sakes, may I not be obeyed when I am gone? And where is Níniel? At the least I may hope that you did not bring her hither, but left her where I bestowed her, in my house, with true men to guard it?'

And when no one answered him, 'Come, say where is Níniel?' he cried. 'For her first I would see; and to her first will I tell the tale of the deeds in the night.'

But they turned their faces from him, and Brandir said at last: 'Níniel is not here.'

'That is well then,' he said. 'Then I will go to my home. Is there a horse to bear me? Or a bier would be better. I faint with my labours.'

'Nay, nay!' said Brandir in anguish. 'Your house is empty. Níniel is not there. She is dead.'

But one of the women – the wife of Dorlas, who loved Brandir little – cried shrilly: 'Pay no heed to him, lord! For he is crazed. He came crying that you were dead, and called it good tidings. But you live. Why then should his tale of Níniel be true: that she is dead, and yet worse?'

Then Túrin strode towards Brandir: 'So my death was good tidings?' he cried. 'Yes, ever you did begrudge her to me, that I knew. Now she is dead, you say. And yet worse? What lie have you begotten in your malice, Club-foot? Would you slay us then with foul words, since you can wield no other weapon?'

Then anger drove pity from Brandir's heart, and he cried: 'Crazed? Nay, crazed are you, Black Sword of black doom! And all this dotard people. I do not lie! Níniel is dead, dead, dead! Seek her in Teiglin!'

Then Túrin stood still and cold. 'How do you know?' he said softly. 'How did you contrive it?'

'I know because I saw her leap,' answered Brandir. 'But the contriving was yours. She fled from you, Túrin son of Húrin, and in Cabed-en-Aras she cast herself, that she might never see you again. Níniel! Níniel? Nay, Nienor daughter of Húrin.'

Then Túrin seized him and shook him; for in those words he heard the feet of his doom overtaking him, but in horror and fury his heart would not receive them, as a beast hurt to death that will wound ere it dies all that are near it.

'Yes, I am Túrin son of Húrin,' he cried. 'So long ago you guessed. But nothing do you know of Nienor my sister. Nothing! She dwells in the Hidden Kingdom, and is safe. It is a lie of your own vile mind, to drive my wife witless, and now me. You limping evil – would you dog us both to death?'

But Brandir shook him off. 'Touch me not!' he said. 'Stay your raving. She that you name wife came to you and tended you, and you did not answer her call. But one answered for you. Glaurung the Dragon, who I deem bewitched you both to your doom. So he spoke, before he ended: "Nienor daughter of Húrin, here is thy brother: treacherous to foes, faithless to friends, a curse unto his kin, Túrin son of Húrin".' Then suddenly a fey laughter seized on Brandir. 'On their deathbed men will speak true, they say,' he cackled. 'And even a Dragon too, it seems! Túrin son of Húrin, a curse unto thy kin and unto all that harbour thee!'

Then Túrin grasped Gurthang and a fell light was in his eyes. 'And what shall be said of you, Club-foot?' he said slowly. 'Who told her secretly behind my back my right name? Who brought her to the malice of the Dragon? Who stood by and let her die? Who came hither to publish this horror at the swiftest? Who would now gloat upon me? Do men speak true before death? Then speak it now quickly.'

Then Brandir, seeing his death in Túrin's face, stood still and did not quail, though he had no weapon but his crutch; and he said: 'All that has chanced is a long tale to tell, and I am weary of you. But you slander me, son of Húrin. Did Glaurung slander you? If you slay me, then all shall see that he did not. Yet I do not fear to die, for then I will go to seek Níniel whom I loved, and perhaps I may find her again beyond the Sea.'

'Seek Níniel!' cried Túrin. 'Nay, Glaurung you shall find, and breed lies together. You shall sleep with the Worm, your soul's mate, and rot in one darkness!' Then he lifted up Gurthang and hewed Brandir, and smote him to death. But the people hid their eyes from that deed, and as he turned and went from Nen Girith they fled from him in terror.

Then Túrin went as one witless through the wild woods, now cursing Middle-earth and all the life of Men, now calling upon Níniel. But when at last the madness of his grief left him he sat awhile and pondered all his deeds, and he heard himself crying: 'She dwells in the Hidden Kingdom, and is safe!' And he thought that now, though all his life was in ruin, he must go thither; for all the lies of Glaurung had ever led him astray. Therefore he arose and went to the Crossings of Teiglin, and as he passed by Haudh-en-Elleth he cried: 'Bitterly have I paid, O Finduilas! that ever I gave heed to the Dragon. Send me now counsel!'

But even as he cried out he saw twelve huntsmen well-armed that came over the Crossings, and they were Elves; and as they drew near he knew one, for it was Mablung, chief huntsman of Thingol. And Mablung hailed him, crying: 'Túrin! Well met at last. I seek you, and glad I am to see you living, though the years have been heavy on you.'

'Heavy!' said Túrin. 'Yes, as the feet of Morgoth. But if you are glad to see me living, you are the last in Middle-earth. Why so?'

'Because you were held in honour among us,' answered Mablung; 'and though you have escaped many perils, I feared for you at the last. I watched the coming forth of Glaurung, and I thought that he had fulfilled his wicked purpose and was returning to his Master. But he turned towards Brethil, and at the same time I learned from wanderers in the land that the Black Sword of Nargothrond had appeared there again, and the Orcs shunned its borders as death. Then I was filled with dread, and I said: "Alas! Glaurung goes where his Orcs dare not, to seek out Túrin. Therefore I came hither as swift as might be, to warn you and aid you."'

'Swift, but not swift enough,' said Túrin. 'Glaurung is dead.'

Then the Elves looked at him in wonder, and said: 'You have slain the Great Worm! Praised for ever shall your name be among Elves and Men!'

'I care not,' said Túrin. 'For my heart also is slain. But since you come from Doriath, give me news of my kin. For I was told in Dor-lómin that they had fled to the Hidden Kingdom.'

The Elves made no answer, but at length Mablung spoke: 'They did so indeed, in the year before the coming of the Dragon. But they are not there now, alas!' Then Túrin's heart stood still, hearing the feet of doom that would pursue him to the end. 'Say on!' he cried. 'And be swift!'

'They went out into the wild seeking you,' said Mablung. 'It was against all counsel; but they would go to Nargothrond, when it was known that you were the Black Sword; and Glaurung came forth, and all their guard were scattered. Morwen none have seen since that day; but Nienor had a spell of dumbness upon her, and fled north into the woods like a wild deer, and was lost.' Then to the wonder of the Elves Túrin laughed loud and shrill. 'Is not that a jest?' he cried. 'O the fair Nienor! So she ran from Doriath to the Dragon, and from the Dragon unto me. What a sweet grace of fortune! Brown as a berry she was, dark was her hair; small and slim as an Elf-child, none could mistake her!'

Then Mablung was amazed, and he said: 'But some mistake is here. Not such was your sister. She was tall, and her eyes were blue, her hair fine gold, the very likeness in woman's form of Húrin her father. You cannot have seen her!'

'Can I not, can I not, Mablung?' cried Túrin. 'But why no! For see, I am blind! Did you not know? Blind, blind, groping since childhood in a dark mist of Morgoth! Therefore leave me! Go, go! Go back to Doriath, and may winter shrivel it! A curse upon Menegroth! And a curse on your errand! This only was wanting. Now comes the night!'

Then he fled from them, like the wind, and they were filled with wonder and fear. But Mablung said: 'Some strange and dreadful thing has chanced that we know not. Let us follow him and aid him if we may: for now he is fey and witless.'

But Túrin sped far before them, and came to Cabed-en-Aras, and stood still; and he heard the roaring of the water, and saw that all the trees near and far were withered, and their sere leaves fell mournfully, as though winter had come in the first days of summer.

'Cabed-en-Aras, Cabed Naeramarth!' he cried. 'I will not defile your waters where Níniel was washed. For all my deeds have been ill, and the latest the worst.'

Then he drew forth his sword, and said: 'Hail Gurthang, iron of death, thou alone now remainest! But what lord or loyalty dost thou know, save the hand that wieldeth thee? From no blood wilt thou shrink! Wilt thou take Túrin Turambar? Wilt thou slay me swiftly?'

And from the blade rang a cold voice in answer: 'Yea, I will drink thy blood, that I may forget the blood of Beleg my master, and the blood of Brandir slain unjustly. I will slay thee swiftly.'

Then Túrin set the hilts upon the ground, and cast himself upon the point of Gurthang, and the black blade took his life.

But Mablung came and looked on the hideous shape of Glaurung lying dead, and he looked upon Túrin and was grieved, thinking of Húrin as he had seen him in the Nirnaeth Arnoediad, and the dreadful doom of his kin. As the Elves stood there, men came down from Nen Girith to look upon the Dragon, and when they saw to what end the life of Túrin Turambar had come they wept; and the Elves learning at last the reason of Túrin's words to them were aghast. Then Mablung said bitterly: 'I also have been meshed in the doom of the Children of Húrin, and thus with words have slain one that I loved.'

Then they lifted up Túrin, and saw that his sword was broken asunder. So passed all that he possessed.

With toil of many hands they gathered wood and piled it high and made a great burning, and destroyed the body of the Dragon, until he was but black ash and his bones beaten to dust, and the place of that burning was ever bare and barren thereafter. But Túrin they laid in a high mound where he had fallen, and the shards of Gurthang were set beside him. And when all was done, and the minstrels of Elves and Men had made lament, telling of the valour of Turambar and the beauty of Níniel, a great grey stone was brought and set upon the mound; and thereon the Elves carved in the Runes of Doriath:

TÚRIN TURAMBAR DAGNIR GLAURUNGA

and beneath they wrote also:

NIENOR NÍNIEL

But she was not there, nor was it ever known whither the cold waters of Teiglin had taken her.

Thus ends the Tale of the Children of Húrin, longest of all the lays of Beleriand.

NOTES

In an introductory note, existing in different forms, it is said that though made in Elvish speech and using much Elvish lore, especially of Doriath, the *Narn i Hîn Húrin* was the work of a Mannish poet, Dírhavel, who lived at the Havens of Sirion in the days of Eärendil, and there gathered all the tidings that he could of the House of Hador, whether among Men or Elves, remnants and fugitives of Dor-lómin, of Nargothrond, of Gondolin, or of Doriath. In one version of this note Dírhavel is said to have come himself of the House of Hador. This lay, longest of all the lays of Beleriand, was all that he ever made, but it was prized by the Eldar, for Dírhavel used the Grey-elven tongue, in which he had great skill. He used that mode of Elvish verse which was called *Minlamed thent / estent*, and was of old proper to the *narn* (a tale that is told in verse, but to be spoken and not sung). Dírhavel perished in the raid of the Sons of Fëanor upon the Havens of Sirion.

1   At this point in the text of the *Narn* there is a passage describing the sojourn of Húrin and Huor in Gondolin. This is very closely based on the story told in one of the 'constituent texts' of *The Silmarillion* – so closely as to be no more than a variant, and I have not given it again here. The story can be read in *The Silmarillion* pp. 158–9.

2   Here in the text of the *Narn* there is a passage, giving an account of the Nirnaeth Arnoediad, that I have excluded for the same reason as that given in Note 1; see *The Silmarillion* pp. 190–5.

3   In another version of the text it is made explicit that Morwen did indeed have dealings with the Eldar who had secret dwellings in the mountains not far from her house. 'But they could tell her no news. None had seen Húrin's fall. "He was not with Fingon," they said; "he was driven south with Turgon, but if any of his folk escaped it was in the wake of the host of Gondolin. But who knows? For the Orcs have piled all the slain together, and search is vain, even if any dared to go to the Haudh-en-Nirnaeth." '

4   With this description of the Helm of Hador compare the 'great masks hideous to look upon' worn by the Dwarves of Belegost in the Nirnaeth Arnoediad, which 'stood them in good stead against the dragons' (*The Silmarillion* p. 193). Túrin afterwards wore a dwarf-mask when he went into battle out of Nargothrond, 'and his enemies fled before his face' (*ibid.* p. 210). See further the Appendix to the *Narn*, pp. 154–5 below.

5 The Orc-raid into East Beleriand in which Maedhros saved Azaghâl is nowhere else referred to.

6 Elsewhere my father remarked that the speech of Doriath, whether of the King or others, was even in the days of Túrin more antique than that used elsewhere; and also that Mîm observed (though the extant writings concerning Mîm do not mention this) that one thing of which Túrin never rid himself, despite his grievance against Doriath, was the speech he had acquired during his fostering.

7 A marginal note in one text says here: 'Always he sought in all faces of women the face of Lalaith.'

8 In one variant text of this section of the narrative Saeros is said to have been the kinsman of Daeron, and in another Daeron's brother; the text printed is probably the latest.

9 *Woodwose*: 'wild man of the woods'; see note 14 to *The Drúedain*, p. 387 below.

10 In a variant text of this part of the story Túrin at this time declared to the outlaws his true name; and he claimed that, being by right the lord and judge of the People of Hador, he had slain Forweg justly, since he was a man of Dor-lómin. Then Algund, the old outlaw who had fled down Sirion from the Nirnaeth Arnoediad, said that Túrin's eyes had long reminded him of another whom he could not recall, and that now he knew him for the son of Húrin. ' "But he was a smaller man, small for his kin, though filled with fire; and his hair gold-red. You are dark, and tall. I see your mother in you, now that I look closer; she was of Bëor's people. What fate was hers, I wonder." "I do not know," said Túrin. "No word comes out of the North." ' In this version it was the knowledge that Neithan was Túrin son of Húrin that led those outlaws who came originally from Dor-lómin to accept him as the leader of the band.

11 The last-written versions of this part of the story agree that when Túrin became captain of the outlaw band he led them away from the homes of the Woodmen in the forest south of Teiglin, and that Beleg came there soon after they had gone; but the geography is unclear and the accounts of the outlaws' movements conflicting. It seems necessary to suppose, in view of the subsequent course of the narrative, that they remained in the Vale of Sirion, and indeed that they were not far from their previous haunts at the time of the Orc-raid on the homes of the Woodmen. In one tentative version they went away southwards and came to the country 'above the Aelin-uial and the Fens of Sirion'; but the men becoming discontented in that 'harbourless land', Túrin was persuaded to lead them back to the woodlands south of Teiglin where he first encountered them. This would fit the requirements of the narrative.

12 In *The Silmarillion* the narrative continues (pp. 201–2) with Beleg's farewell to Túrin, Túrin's strange foreknowledge that his fate would

lead him to Amon Rûdh, Beleg's coming to Menegroth (where he received the sword Anglachel from Thingol and *lembas* from Melian), and his return to warfare against the Orcs in Dimbar. There is no other text to supplement this, and the passage is omitted here.

13 Túrin fled from Doriath in the summer; he passed the autumn and winter among the outlaws, and he slew Forweg and became their captain in the spring of the next year. The events described here took place in the summer following.

14 *Aeglos*, 'snowthorn', is said to have been like furze (gorse), but larger, and with white flowers. *Aeglos* was also the name of the spear of Gil-galad. *Seregon*, 'blood of stone', was a plant of the kind called in English 'stonecrop'; it had flowers of a deep red.

15 So also the yellow-flowered gorse bushes encountered by Frodo, Sam and Gollum in Ithilien were 'gaunt and leggy below but thick above', so that they could walk upright under them, 'passing through long dry aisles', and they bore flowers that 'glimmered in the gloom and gave a faint sweet scent' (*The Two Towers* IV 7).

16 Elsewhere the Sindarin name of the Petty-Dwarves is given as *Noegyth Nibin* (so in *The Silmarillion* p. 204) and *Nibin-Nogrim*. The 'high moorlands that rose between the Vales of Sirion and Narog', north-east of Nargothrond (p. 99 above) are more than once referred to as the Moors of the Nibin-noeg (or variants of this name).

17 The tall cliff through which Mîm led them by the cleft that he called 'the gate of the garth' was (it appears) the north edge of the shelf; the cliffs on the eastern and western sides were much more precipitous.

18 Andróg's curse is also recorded in the form: 'May he lack a bow at need ere his end.' In the event Mîm met his death from Húrin's sword before the Doors of Nargothrond (*The Silmarillion* p. 230).

19 The mystery of the other things in Mîm's sack is not explained. The only other statement on the subject is in a hastily scribbled note, which suggests that there were ingots of gold disguised as roots, and refers to Mîm seeking 'for old treasures of a dwarf-house near the "flat stones"'. These were no doubt those referred to in the text (p. 96) as 'great stones, leaning or tumbled together', at the place where Mîm was captured. But there is nowhere any indication of what part this treasure was to play in the story of Bar-en-Danwedh.

20 It is said on p. 69 that the pass over the shoulder of Amon Darthir was the only pass 'between Serech and far westward where Dor-lómin marched with Nevrast'.

21 In the story as told in *The Silmarillion* (p. 216) Brandir's foreboding of evil came upon him after he had heard 'the tidings that Dorlas brought', and therefore (as it appears) after he knew that the man

on the bier was the Black Sword of Nargothrond, rumoured to be the son of Húrin of Dor-lómin.

22 See p. 153, where there is a reference to Orodreth's exchanging messages with Thingol 'by secret ways'.

23 In *The Silmarillion* (p. 122) the High Faroth, or Taur-en-Faroth, are 'great wooded highlands'. The description of them here as 'brown and bare' perhaps refers to the leaflessness of the trees in the beginning of spring.

24 One might suppose that it was only when all was over, and Túrin and Nienor dead, that her shuddering fit was recalled and its meaning seen, and Dimrost renamed Nen Girith; but in the legend Nen Girith is used as the name throughout.

25 If Glaurung's intention had indeed been to return to Angband it might be thought that he would have taken the old road to the Crossings of Teiglin, a course not greatly different from that which brought him to Cabed-en-Aras. Perhaps the assumption was that he would return to Angband by the way that he came south to Nargothrond, going up Narog to Ivrin. Cf. also Mablung's words (p. 143): 'I watched the coming forth of Glaurung, and I thought that he . . . was returning to his Master. But he turned towards Brethil . . .'

When Turambar spoke of his hope that Glaurung would go straight and not swerve, he meant that if the Dragon went up along Teiglin to the Crossings he would be able to enter Brethil without having to pass over the gorge, where he would be vulnerable: see his words to the men at Nen Girith, p. 130.

26 I have found no map to illustrate my father's conception of the lie of the land in detail, but this sketch seems at least to fit the references in the narrative:

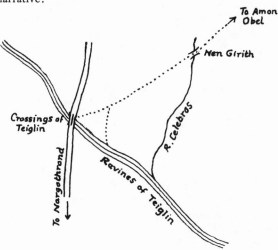

27 The phrases 'fled wildly from that place' and 'sped on before him'
    suggest that there was some distance between the place where Túrin
    lay beside Glaurung's corpse and the edge of the ravine. It may be
    that the Dragon's death-leap carried him some way beyond the further
    brink.

28 Later in the narrative (p. 145) Túrin himself, before his death,
    called the place Cabed Naeramarth, and it may be supposed that it
    was from the tradition of his last words that the later name was
    derived.
        The apparent discrepancy that, although Brandir is said (both
    here and in *The Silmarillion*) to have been the last man to look on
    Cabed-en-Aras, Túrin came there soon afterwards, and indeed the
    Elves also and all those who raised the mound over him, may perhaps
    be explained by taking the words of the *Narn* concerning Brandir in
    a narrow sense: he was the last man actually to 'look down into its
    darkness'. It was indeed my father's intention to alter the narrative
    so that Túrin slew himself not at Cabed-en-Aras but on the mound
    of Finduilas by the Crossings of Teiglin; but this never received
    written form.

29 It seems from this that 'The Deer's Leap' was the original name of
    the place, and indeed the meaning of Cabed-en-Aras.

APPENDIX

From the point in the story where Túrin and his men established themselves in the ancient dwelling of the Petty-dwarves on Amon Rûdh there
is no completed narrative on the same detailed plan, until the *Narn* takes
up again with Túrin's journey northwards after the fall of Nargothrond.
From many tentative or exploratory outlines and notes, however, some
further glimpses can be gained beyond the more summary account in
The Silmarillion, and even some short stretches of connected narrative on
the scale of the *Narn*.

An isolated fragment describes the life of the outlaws on Amon Rûdh
in the time that followed their settlement there, and gives some further
description of Bar-en-Danwedh.

For a long while the life of the outlaws went well to their liking.
Food was not scarce, and they had good shelter, warm and dry, with
room enough and to spare; for they found that the caves could have
housed a hundred or more at need. There was another smaller hall
further in. It had a hearth at one side, above which a smoke-shaft ran
up through the rock to a vent cunningly hidden in a crevice on the
hillside. There were also many other chambers, opening out of the halls
or the passage between them, some for dwelling, some for works or for

stores. In storage Mîm had more arts than they, and he had many vessels and chests of stone and wood that looked to be of great age. But most of the chambers were now empty: in the armouries hung axes and other gear rusted and dusty, shelves and aumbries were bare; and the smithies were idle. Save one: a small room that led out of the inner hall and had a hearth which shared the smoke-vent of the hearth in the hall. There Mîm would work at times, but would not allow others to be with him.

During the rest of that year they went on no more raids, and if they stirred abroad for hunting or gathering of food they went for the most part in small parties. But for a long while they found it hard to retrace their road, and beside Túrin not more than six of his men became ever sure of the way. Nonetheless, seeing that those skilled in such things could come to their lair without Mîm's help, they set a watch by day and night near to the cleft in the north-wall. From the south they expected no enemies, nor was there fear of any climbing Amon Rûdh from that quarter; but by day there was at most times a watchman set on the top of the crown, who could look far all about. Steep as were the sides of the crown, the summit could be reached, for to the east of the cave-mouth rough steps had been hewn leading up to slopes where men could clamber unaided.

So the year wore on without hurt or alarm. But as the days drew in, and the pool became grey and cold and the birches bare, and great rains returned, they had to pass more time in shelter. Then they soon grew weary of the dark under hill, or the dim halflight of the halls; and to most it seemed that life would be better if it were not shared with Mîm. Too often he would appear out of some shadowy corner or doorway when they thought him elsewhere; and when Mîm was near unease fell on their talk. They took to speaking one to another ever in whispers.

Yet, and strange it seemed to them, with Túrin it went otherwise; and he became ever more friendly with the old Dwarf, and listened more and more to his counsels. In the winter that followed he would sit for long hours with Mîm, listening to his lore and the tales of his life; nor did Túrin rebuke him if he spoke ill of the Eldar. Mîm seemed well pleased, and showed much favour to Túrin in return; him only would he admit to his smithy at times, and there they would talk softly together. Less pleased were the Men; and Andróg looked on with a jealous eye.

The text followed in *The Silmarillion* gives no indication of how Beleg found his way into Bar-en-Danwedh: he 'appeared suddenly among them' 'in the dim dusk of a winter's day'. In other brief outlines the story is that through the improvidence of the outlaws food became short in Bar-en-Danwedh during the winter, and Mîm begrudged them the edible roots from his store; therefore in the beginning of the year they went out on a hunting foray from the stronghold. Beleg, approaching Amon Rûdh, came upon their tracks, and either trailed them to a camp which they were forced to make in a sudden snowstorm, or followed them back to Bar-en-Danwedh and slipped in after them.

At this time Andróg, seeking for Mîm's secret store of food, became lost in the caves, and found a hidden stair that led out on to the flat summit of Amon Rûdh (it was by this stair that some of the outlaws fled from Bar-en-Danwedh when it was attacked by the Orcs: *The Silmarillion* p. 206). And either during the foray just mentioned, or on a later occasion, Andróg, having taken up again bow and arrows in defiance of Mîm's curse, was wounded by a poisoned shaft – in one only of several references to the event said to have been an Orc-arrow.

Andróg was cured of this wound by Beleg, but it seems that his dislike and distrust of the Elf was not thereby mitigated; and Mîm's hatred of Beleg became all the fiercer, for he had thus 'undone' his curse upon Andróg. 'It will bite again,' he said. It came into Mîm's mind that if he also ate the *lembas* of Melian he would renew his youth and grow strong again; and since he could not come at it by stealth he feigned sickness and begged it of his enemy. When Beleg refused it to him the seal was set upon Mîm's hatred, and all the more because of Túrin's love for the Elf.

It may be mentioned here that when Beleg brought out the *lembas* from his pack (see *The Silmarillion* pp. 202, 204) Túrin refused it:

The silver leaves were red in the firelight; and when Túrin saw the seal his eyes darkened. 'What have you there?' he said.

'The greatest gift that one who loves you still has to give,' answered Beleg. 'Here is *lembas*, the waybread of the Eldar, that no Man yet has tasted.'

'The Helm of my fathers I take,' said Túrin, 'with good will for your keeping; but I will not receive gifts out of Doriath.'

'Then send back your sword and your arms,' said Beleg. 'Send back also the teaching and fostering of your youth. And let your men die in the desert to please your mood. Nonetheless, this waybread was a gift not to you but to me, and I may do with it as I will. Eat it not, if it sticks in your throat; but others here may be more hungry and less proud.'

Then Túrin was abashed, and in that matter overcame his pride.

Some slight further indications are found concerning Dor-Cúarthol, the Land of Bow and Helm, where Beleg and Túrin for a time became from their stronghold on Amon Rûdh the leaders of a strong force in the lands south of Teiglin (*The Silmarillion* p. 205).

Túrin received gladly all who came to him, but by the counsel of

Beleg he admitted no newcomer to his refuge upon Amon Rûdh (and that was now named Echad i Sedryn, Camp of the Faithful); the way thither only those of the Old Company knew and no others were admitted. But other guarded camps and forts were established round about: in the forest eastward, or in the highlands, or in the southward fens, from Methed-en-glad ('the End of the Wood') to Bar-erib some leagues south of Amon Rûdh; and from all these places men could see the summit of Amon Rûdh, and by signals receive tidings and commands.

In this way, before the summer had passed, the following of Túrin was swelled to a great force; and the power of Angband was thrown back. Word of this came even to Nargothrond, and many there grew restless, saying that if an Outlaw could do such hurt to the Enemy, what might not the Lord of Narog do. But Orodreth would not change his counsels. In all things he followed Thingol, with whom he exchanged messengers by secret ways; and he was a wise lord, according to the wisdom of those who considered first their own people, and how long they might preserve their life and wealth against the lust of the North. Therefore he allowed none of his people to go to Túrin, and he sent messengers to say to him that in all that he might do or devise in his war he should not set foot in the land of Nargothrond, nor drive Orcs thither. But help other than in arms he offered to the Two Captains, should they have need (and in this, it is thought, he was moved by Thingol and Melian).

It is several times emphasized that Beleg remained throughout opposed to Túrin's grand design, although he supported him; that it seemed to him that the Dragon-helm had worked otherwise with Túrin than he had hoped; and that he foresaw with a troubled mind what the days to come would bring. Scraps of his words with Túrin on these matters are preserved. In one of these, they sat in the stronghold of Echad i Sedryn together, and Túrin said to Beleg:

'Why are you sad, and thoughtful? Does not all go well, since you returned to me? Has not my purpose proved good?'

'All is well now,' said Beleg. 'Our enemies are still surprised, and afraid. And still good days lie before us; for a while.'

'And what then?'

'Winter. And after that another year, for those who live to see it.'

'And what then?'

'The wrath of Angband. We have burned the finger tips of the Black Hand – no more. It will not withdraw.'

'But is not the wrath of Angband our purpose and delight?' said Túrin. 'What else would you have me do?'

'You know full well,' said Beleg. 'But of that road you have forbidden me to speak. But hear me now. The lord of a great host has many needs. He must have a secure refuge; and he must have wealth, and many whose work is not in war. With numbers comes the need of food, more than the wild will furnish; and there comes the passing of secrecy. Amon Rûdh is a good place for a few – it has eyes and ears. But it stands alone, and is seen far off; and no great force is needed to surround it.'

'Nonetheless, I will be the captain of my own host,' said Túrin; 'and if I fall, then I fall. Here I stand in the path of Morgoth, and while I so stand he cannot use the southward road. For that in Nargothrond there should be some thanks; and even help with needful things.'

In another brief passage of speech between them Túrin replied to Beleg's warnings of the frailty of his power in these words:

'I wish to rule a land; but not this land. Here I desire only to gather strength. To my father's land in Dor-lómin my heart turns, and thither I shall go when I may.'

It is also asserted that Morgoth for a time withheld his hand and made mere feints of attack, 'so that by easy victory the confidence of these rebels might become overweening; as it proved indeed'.

Andróg appears again in an outline of the course of the assault on Amon Rûdh. It was only then that he revealed to Túrin the existence of the inner stair; and he was one of those who came by that way to the summit. There he is said to have fought more valiantly than any, but he fell at last mortally wounded by an arrow; and thus the curse of Mîm was fulfilled.

To the tale in *The Silmarillion* of Beleg's journey in pursuit of Túrin, his meeting with Gwindor in Taur-nu-Fuin, the rescue of Túrin, and Beleg's death at Túrin's hands, there is nothing of any moment to add. For Gwindor's possession of one of the blue-shining 'Fëanorian lamps' and the part that this lamp played in a version of the story see p. 51 above, Note 2.

It may be noted here that it was my father's intention to extend the history of the Dragon-helm of Dor-lómin into the period of Túrin's sojourn in Nargothrond and even beyond; but this was never incorporated into the narratives. In the existing versions the Helm disappears with the end of Dor-Cúarthol, in the destruction of the outlaws' stronghold on Amon Rûdh; but in some way it was to reappear in Túrin's possession at Nargothrond. It could only have come there if it had been taken by the Orcs that carried Túrin off to Angband; but its recovery from them at the time of Túrin's rescue by Beleg and Gwindor would have required some development of the narrative at that point.

An isolated scrap of writing tells that in Nargothrond Túrin would not wear the Helm again 'lest it reveal him', but that he wore it when he went to the Battle of Tumhalad (*The Silmarillion* p. 212, where he is said to have worn the dwarf-mask that he found in the armouries of Nargothrond). This note continues:

> For fear of that helm all foes avoided him, and thus it was that he came off unhurt from that deadly field. It was thus that he came back to Nargothrond wearing the Dragon-helm, and Glaurung, desiring to rid Túrin of its aid and protection (since he himself feared it), taunted him, saying that surely Túrin claimed to be his vassal and retainer, since he bore his master's likeness on the crest of his helm.
>
> But Túrin answered: 'Thou liest, and knowest it. For this image was made in scorn of thee; and while there is one to bear it doubt shall ever assail thee, lest the bearer deal thee thy doom.'
>
> 'Then it must await a master of another name,' said Glaurung; 'for Túrin son of Húrin I do not fear. Otherwise is it. For he has not the hardihood to look me in the face, openly.'
>
> And indeed so great was the terror of the Dragon that Túrin dared not look straight upon his eye, but had kept the visor of his helmet down, shielding his face, and in his parley had looked no higher than Glaurung's feet. But being thus taunted, in pride and rashness he thrust up the visor and looked Glaurung in the eye.

In another place there is a note that it was when Morwen heard in Doriath of the appearance of the Dragon-helm at the Battle of Tumhalad that she knew that the tale was true that the Mormegil was indeed Túrin her son.

Finally, there is a suggestion that Túrin was to wear the Helm when he slew Glaurung, and would taunt the Dragon at his death with his words at Nargothrond about 'a master of another name'; but there is no indication of how the narrative was to be managed to bring this about.

There is an account of the nature and substance of Gwindor's opposition to Túrin's policies in Nargothrond, which in *The Silmarillion* is only very briefly referred to (p. 211). This account is not fully formed into narrative, but may be represented thus:

> Gwindor spoke ever against Túrin in the council of the King, saying that he had been in Angband, and knew somewhat of the might of Morgoth, and of his designs. 'Petty victories will prove profitless at the last,' he said; 'for thus Morgoth learns where the boldest of his enemies are to be found, and gathers strength great enough to destroy them. All the might of the Elves and the Edain united sufficed only to contain him, and to gain the peace of a siege; long indeed, but only so long as Morgoth bided his time before he broke the leaguer; and never again can such a union be made. In secrecy only lies now any hope; until the Valar come.'

'The Valar!' said Túrin. 'They have forsaken you, and they hold Men in scorn. What use to look westward across the endless Sea? There is but one Vala with whom we have to do, and that is Morgoth; and if in the end we cannot overcome him, at the least we can hurt him and hinder him. For victory is victory, however small, nor is its worth only in what follows from it. But it is expedient also; for if you do nothing to halt him, all Beleriand will fall beneath his shadow before many years are passed, and then one by one he will smoke you out of your earths. And what then? A pitiable remnant will fly south and west, to cower on the shores of the Sea, caught between Morgoth and Ossë. Better then to win a time of glory, though it be shortlived; for the end will be no worse. You speak of secrecy, and say that therein lies the only hope; but could you ambush and waylay every scout and spy of Morgoth to the last and least, so that none came ever back with tidings to Angband, yet from that he would learn that you lived and guess where. And this also I say: though mortal Men have little life beside the span of the Elves, they would rather spend it in battle than fly or submit. The defiance of Húrin Thalion is a great deed; and though Morgoth slay the doer he cannot make the deed not to have been. Even the Lords of the West will honour it; and is it not written into the history of Arda, which neither Morgoth nor Manwë can unwrite?'

'You speak of high things,' Gwindor answered, 'and plain it is that you have lived among the Eldar. But a darkness is on you if you set Morgoth and Manwë together, or speak of the Valar as the foes of Elves or Men; for the Valar scorn nothing, and least of all the Children of Ilúvatar. Nor do you know all the hopes of the Eldar. It is a prophecy among us that one day a messenger from Middle-earth will come through the shadows to Valinor, and Manwë will hear, and Mandos relent. For that time shall we not attempt to preserve the seed of the Noldor, and of the Edain also? And Círdan dwells now in the South, and there is building of ships; but what know you of ships, or of the Sea? You think of yourself and of your own glory, and bid us each do likewise; but we must think of others beside ourselves, for not all can fight and fall, and those we must keep from war and ruin, while we can.'

'Then send them to your ships, while there is yet time,' said Túrin.

'They will not be parted from us,' said Gwindor, 'even could Círdan sustain them. We must abide together as long as we may, and not court death.'

'All this I have answered,' said Túrin. 'Valiant defence of the borders and hard blows ere the enemy gathers: in that course lies the best hope of your long abiding together. And do those that you speak of love such skulkers in the woods, hunting always like a wolf, better than one who puts on his helm and figured shield, and drives away the foe, be they far greater than all his host? At least the women of the Edain do not. They did not hold back the men from the Nirnaeth Arnoediad.'

'But they suffered greater woe than if that field had not been fought,' said Gwindor.

The love of Finduilas for Túrin was also to be more fully treated:

Finduilas the daughter of Orodreth was golden-haired after the manner of the house of Finarfin, and Túrin began to take pleasure in the sight of her and in her company; for she reminded him of his kindred and the women of Dor-lómin in his father's house. At first he met her only when Gwindor was by; but after a while she sought him out, and they met at times alone, though it seemed to be chance. Then she would question him about the Edain, of whom she had seen few and seldom, and about his country and his kin.

Then Túrin spoke freely to her concerning these things, though he did not name the land of his birth nor any of his kindred; and on a time he said to her: 'I had a sister, Lalaith, or so I named her; and of her you put me in mind. But Lalaith was a child, a yellow flower in the green grass of spring; and had she lived she would now, maybe, have become dimmed with grief. But you are queenly, and as a golden tree; I would I had a sister so fair.'

'But you are kingly,' said she, 'even as the lords of the people of Fingolfin; I would I had a brother so valiant. And I do not think that Agarwaen is your true name, nor is it fit for you, Adanedhel. I call you Thurin, the Secret.'

At this Túrin started, but he said: 'That is not my name; and I am not a king, for our kings are of the Eldar, as I am not.'

Now Túrin marked that Gwindor's friendship grew cooler towards him; and he wondered also that whereas at first the woe and horror of Angband had begun to be lifted from him, now he seemed to slip back into care and sorrow. And he thought, it may be that he is grieved that I oppose his counsels, and have overcome him; I would it were not so. For he loved Gwindor as his guide and healer, and was filled with pity for him. But in those days the radiance of Finduilas also became dimmed, her footsteps slow and her face grave; and Túrin perceiving this surmised that the words of Gwindor had set fear in her heart of what might come to pass.

In truth Finduilas was torn in mind. For she honoured Gwindor and pitied him, and wished not to add one tear to his suffering; but against her will her love for Túrin grew day by day, and she thought of Beren and Lúthien. But Túrin was not like Beren! He did not scorn her, and was glad in her company; yet she knew that he had no love of the kind she wished. His mind and heart were elsewhere, by rivers in springs long past.

Then Túrin spoke to Finduilas, and said: 'Do not let the words of Gwindor affright you. He has suffered in the darkness of Angband;

and it is hard for one so valiant to be thus crippled and backward perforce. He needs all solace, and a longer time for healing.'

'I know it well,' she said.

'But we will win that time for him!' said Túrin. 'Nargothrond shall stand! Never again will Morgoth the Craven come forth from Angband, and all his reliance must be on his servants; thus says Melian of Doriath. They are the fingers of his hands; and we will smite them, and cut them off, till he draws back his claws. Nargothrond shall stand!'

'Perhaps,' said Finduilas. 'It shall stand, if you can achieve it. But have a care, Adenedhel; my heart is heavy when you go out to battle, lest Nargothrond be bereaved.'

And afterwards Túrin sought out Gwindor, and said to him: 'Gwindor, dear friend, you are falling back into sadness; do not so! For your healing will come in the houses of your kin, and in the light of Finduilas.'

Then Gwindor stared at Túrin, but he said nothing, and his face was clouded.

'Why do you look upon me so?' said Túrin. 'Often your eyes have gazed strangely at me of late. How have I grieved you? I have opposed your counsels; but a man must speak as he sees, nor hide the truth that he believes, for any private cause. I would that we were one in mind; for to you I owe a great debt, and I shall not forget it.'

'Will you not?' said Gwindor. 'Nonetheless your deeds and your counsels have changed my home and my kin. Your shadow lies upon them. Why should I be glad, who have lost all to you?'

But Túrin did not understand these words, and did but guess that Gwindor begrudged him his place in the heart and counsels of the King.

A passage follows in which Gwindor warned Finduilas against her love for Túrin, telling her who Túrin was, and this is closely based on the text given in *The Silmarillion* (pp. 210–11). But at the end of Gwindor's speech Finduilas answers him at greater length than in the other version:

'Your eyes are dimmed, Gwindor,' she said. 'You do not see or understand what is here come to pass. Must I now be put to double shame to reveal the truth to you? For I love you, Gwindor, and I am ashamed that I love you not more, but have taken a love even greater, from which I cannot escape. I did not seek it, and long I put it aside. But if I have pity for your hurts, have pity on mine. Túrin loves me not; nor will.'

'You say this,' said Gwindor, 'to take the blame from him whom you love. Why does he seek you out, and sit long with you, and come ever more glad away?'

'Because he also needs solace,' said Finduilas, 'and is bereaved of his kin. You both have your needs. But what of Finduilas? Now is it not enough that I must confess myself to you unloved, but that you should say that I speak so to deceive?'

'Nay, a woman is not easily deceived in such a case,' said Gwindor. 'Nor will you find many who will deny that they are loved, if that is true.'

'If any of us three be faithless, it is I: but not in will. But what of your doom and rumours of Angband? What of death and destruction? The Adanedhel is mighty in the tale of the World, and his stature shall reach yet to Morgoth in some far day to come.'

'He is proud,' said Gwindor.

'But also he is merciful,' said Finduilas. 'He is not yet awake, but still pity can ever pierce his heart, and he will never deny it. Pity maybe shall be ever the only entry. But he does not pity me. He holds me in awe, as were I both his mother and a queen!'

Maybe Finduilas spoke truly, seeing with the keen eyes of the Eldar. And now Túrin, not knowing what had passed between Gwindor and Finduilas, was ever gentler towards her as she seemed more sad. But on a time Finduilas said to him: 'Thurin Adanedhel, why did you hide your name from me? Had I known who you were I should not have honoured you less, but I should better have understood your grief.'

'What do you mean?' he said. 'Whom do you make me?'

'Túrin son of Húrin Thalion, captain of the North.'

Then Túrin rebuked Gwindor for revealing his true name, as is told in *The Silmarillion* (p. 211).

One other passage in this part of the narrative exists in a fuller form than in *The Silmarillion* (of the battle of Tumhalad and the sack of Nargothrond there is no other account; while the speeches of Túrin and the Dragon are so fully recorded in *The Silmarillion* that it seems unlikely that they would have been further expanded). This passage is a much fuller account of the coming of the Elves Gelmir and Arminas to Nargothrond in the year of its fall (*The Silmarillion* pp. 211–12); for their earlier encounter with Tuor in Dor-lómin, which is referred to here, see pp. 21–2 above.

In the spring there came two Elves, and they named themselves Gelmir and Arminas of the people of Finarfin, and said that they had an errand to the Lord of Nargothrond. They were brought before Túrin; but Gelmir said: 'It is to Orodreth, Finarfin's son, that we would speak.'

And when Orodreth came, Gelmir said to him: 'Lord, we were of Angrod's people, and we have wandered far since the Dagor Bragollach; but of late we have dwelt among Círdan's following by the Mouths of

Sirion. And on a day he called us, and bade us go to you; for Ulmo himself, the Lord of Waters, had appeared to him and warned him of great peril that draws near to Nargothrond.'

But Orodreth was wary, and he answered: 'Why then do you come hither out of the North? Or perhaps you had other errands also?'

Then Arminas said: 'Lord, ever since the Nirnaeth I have sought for the hidden kingdom of Turgon, and I have found it not; and in this search I fear now that I have delayed our errand hither over long. For Círdan sent us along the coast by ship, for secrecy and speed, and we were put ashore in Drengist. But among the sea-folk were some that came south in past years as messengers from Turgon, and it seemed to me from their guarded speech that maybe Turgon dwells still in the North, and not in the South, as most believe. But we have found neither sign nor rumour of what we sought.'

'Why do you seek Turgon?' said Orodreth.

'Because it is said that his kingdom shall stand longest against Morgoth,' answered Arminas. And those words seemed to Orodreth ill-omened, and he was displeased.

'Then tarry not in Nargothrond,' he said; 'for here you will hear no news of Turgon. And I need none to teach me that Nargothrond stands in peril.'

'Be not angered, lord,' said Gelmir, 'if we answer your questions with truth. And our wandering from the straight path hither has not been fruitless, for we have passed beyond the reach of your furthest scouts; we have traversed Dor-lómin and all the lands under the eaves of Ered Wethrin, and we have explored the Pass of Sirion, spying out the ways of the Enemy. There is a great gathering of Orcs and evil creatures in those regions, and a host is mustering about Sauron's Isle.'

'I know it,' said Túrin. 'Your news is stale. If the message of Círdan was to any purpose, it should have come sooner.'

'At least, lord, you shall hear the message now,' said Gelmir to Orodreth. 'Hear then the words of the Lord of Waters! Thus he spoke to Círdan the Shipwright: "The Evil of the North has defiled the springs of Sirion, and my power withdraws from the fingers of the flowing waters. But a worse thing is yet to come forth. Say therefore to the Lord of Nargothrond: Shut the doors of the fortress and go not abroad. Cast the stones of your pride into the loud river, that the creeping evil may not find the gate." '

These words seemed dark to Orodreth, and he turned as he ever did to Túrin for counsel. But Túrin mistrusted the messengers, and he said in scorn: 'What does Círdan know of our wars, who dwell nigh to the Enemy? Let the mariner look to his ships! But if in truth the Lord of Waters would send us counsel, let him speak more plainly. For otherwise it will seem better in our case to muster our strength, and go boldly to meet our foes, ere they come too nigh.'

Then Gelmir bowed before Orodreth, and said: 'I have spoken as I was bidden, lord'; and he turned away. But Arminas said to Túrin: 'Are you indeed of the House of Hador, as I have heard said?'

'Here I am named Agarwaen, the Black Sword of Nargothrond,' said Túrin. 'You deal much, it seems, in guarded speech, friend Arminas; and it is well that Turgon's secret is hid from you, or soon it would be heard in Angband. A man's name is his own, and should the son of Húrin learn that you have betrayed him when he would be hid, then may Morgoth take you and burn out your tongue!'

Then Arminas was dismayed by the black wrath of Túrin; but Gelmir said: 'He shall not be betrayed by us, Agarwaen. Are we not in council behind closed doors, where speech may be plainer? And Arminas asked this thing, I deem, because it is known to all that dwell by the Sea that Ulmo has great love for the House of Hador, and some say that Húrin and Huor his brother came once into the Hidden Realm.'

'If that were so, then he would speak of it to none, neither the great nor the less, and least of all to his son in childhood,' answered Túrin. 'Therefore I do not believe that Arminas asked this of me in hope to learn aught of Turgon. I mistrust such messengers of mischief.'

'Save your mistrust!' said Arminas in anger. 'Gelmir mistakes me. I asked because I doubted what here seems believed; for little indeed do you resemble the kin of Hador, whatever your name.'

'And what do you know of them?' said Túrin.

'Húrin I have seen,' answered Arminas, 'and his fathers before him. And in the wastes of Dor-lómin I met with Tuor, son of Huor, Húrin's brother; and he is like his fathers, as you are not.'

'That may be,' said Túrin, 'though of Tuor I have heard no word ere now. But if my head be dark and not golden, of that I am not ashamed. For I am not the first of sons in the likeness of his mother; and I come through Morwen Eledhwen of the House of Bëor and the kindred of Beren Camlost.'

'I spoke not of the difference between the black and the gold,' said Arminas. 'But others of the House of Hador bear themselves otherwise, and Tuor among them. For they use courtesy, and they listen to good counsel, holding the Lords of the West in awe. But you, it seems, will take counsel with your own wisdom, or with your sword only; and you speak haughtily. And I say to you, Agarwaen Mormegil, that if you do so, other shall be your doom than one of the Houses of Hador and Bëor might look for.'

'Other it has ever been,' answered Túrin. 'And if, as it seems, I must bear the hate of Morgoth because of the valour of my father, shall I also endure the taunts and ill-boding of a runagate, though he claim the kinship of kings? I counsel you: get you back to the safe shores of the Sea.'

Then Gelmir and Arminas departed, and went back to the South:

but despite Túrin's taunts they would gladly have awaited battle beside their kin, and they went only because Círdan had bidden them under the command of Ulmo to bring back word to him of Nargothrond and of the speeding of their errand there. And Orodreth was much troubled by the words of the messengers; but all the more fell became the mood of Túrin, and he would by no means listen to their counsels, and least of all would he suffer the great bridge to be cast down. For so much at least of the words of Ulmo were read aright.

It is nowhere explained why Gelmir and Arminas on an urgent errand to Nargothrond were sent by Círdan all the length of the coast to the Firth of Drengist. Arminas said that it was done for speed and secrecy; but greater secrecy could surely have been achieved by journeying up Narog from the South. It might be supposed that Círdan did this in obedience to Ulmo's command (so that they should meet Tuor in Dor-lómin and guide him through the Gate of the Noldor), but this is nowhere suggested.

PART TWO

THE SECOND AGE

I

A DESCRIPTION OF
THE ISLAND OF NÚMENOR

The account of the Island of Númenor that here follows is derived
from descriptions and simple maps that were long preserved in the
archives of the Kings of Gondor. These represent indeed but a small
part of all that was once written, for many natural histories and
geographies were composed by learned men in Númenor; but these,
like nearly all else of the arts and sciences of Númenor at its high
tide, disappeared in the Downfall.

Even such documents as were preserved in Gondor, or in Imladris
(where in the care of Elrond were deposited the surviving treasures of
the Northern Númenórean kings) suffered from loss and destruction
by neglect. For though the survivors in Middle-earth 'yearned', as
they said, for Akallabêth, the Downfallen, and never even after long
ages ceased to regard themselves as in a measure exiles, when it
became clear that the Land of Gift was taken away and that Númenor
had disappeared for ever, all but a few regarded study of what was
left of its history as vain, breeding only useless regret. The story of
Ar-Pharazôn and his impious armada was all that remained generally
known in later ages.

★

The land of Númenor resembled in outline a five-pointed star, or
pentangle, with a central portion some two hundred and fifty miles
across, north and south, and east and west, from which extended five
large peninsular promontories. These promontories were regarded
as separate regions, and they were named Forostar (Northlands),
Andustar (Westlands), Hyarnustar (Southwestlands), Hyarrostar
(Southeastlands), and Orrostar (Eastlands). The central portion was
called Mittalmar (Inlands), and it had no coast, except the land
about Rómenna and the head of its firth. A small part of the Mittalmar
was, however, separated from the rest, and called Arandor, the
Kingsland. In Arandor were the haven of Rómenna, the Meneltarma,
and Armenelos, the City of the Kings; and it was at all times the
most populous region of Númenor.

The Mittalmar was raised above the promontories (not reckoning

the height of their mountains and hills); it was a region of grasslands
and low downs, and few trees grew there. Near to the centre of the
Mittalmar stood the tall mountain called Meneltarma, Pillar of the
Heavens, sacred to the worship of Eru Ilúvatar. Though the lower
slopes of the mountain were gentle and grass-covered, it grew ever
steeper, and towards the summit it could not be scaled; but a winding
spiral road was made upon it, beginning at its foot upon the south,
and ending below the lip of the summit upon the north. For the
summit was somewhat flattened and depressed, and could contain a
great multitude; but it remained untouched by hands throughout the
history of Númenor. No building, no raised altar, not even a pile of
undressed stones, ever stood there; and no other likeness of a temple
did the Númenóreans possess in all the days of their grace, until the
coming of Sauron. There no tool or weapon had ever been borne;
and there none might speak any word, save the King only. Thrice
only in each year the King spoke, offering prayer for the coming
year at the *Erukyermë* in the first days of spring, praise of Eru
Ilúvatar at the *Erulaitalë* in midsummer, and thanksgiving to him
at the *Eruhantalë* at the end of autumn. At these times the King
ascended the mountain on foot followed by a great concourse of the
people, clad in white and garlanded, but silent. At other times the
people were free to climb to the summit alone or in company; but
it is said that the silence was so great that even a stranger ignorant
of Númenor and all its history, if he were transported thither, would
not have dared to speak aloud. No bird ever came there, save only
eagles. If anyone approached the summit, at once three eagles
would appear and alight upon three rocks near to the western edge;
but at the times of the Three Prayers they did not descend, remaining
in the sky and hovering above the people. They were called the
Witnesses of Manwë, and they were believed to be sent by him from
Aman to keep watch upon the Holy Mountain and upon all the land.

The base of the Meneltarma sloped gently into the surrounding
plain, but it extended, after the fashion of roots, five long low ridges
outwards in the direction of the five promontories of the land; and
these were called Tarmasundar, the Roots of the Pillar. Along the
crest of the south-western ridge the climbing road approached the
mountain; and between this ridge and that on the south-east the
land went down into a shallow valley. That was named Noirinan,
the Valley of the Tombs; for at its head chambers were cut in the
rock at the base of the mountain, in which were the tombs of the
Kings and Queens of Númenor.

But for the most part the Mittalmar was a region of pastures. In the south-west there were rolling downs of grass; and there, in the Emerië, was the chief region of the Shepherds.

The Forostar was the least fertile part; stony, with few trees, save that on the westward slopes of the high heather-covered moors there were woods of fir and larch. Towards the North Cape the land rose to rocky heights, and there great Sorontil rose sheer from the sea in tremendous cliffs. Here was the abode of many eagles; and in this region Tar-Meneldur Elentirmo built a tall tower, from which he could observe the motions of the stars.

The Andustar was also rocky in its northern parts, with high fir-woods looking out upon the sea. Three small bays it had, facing west, cut back into the highlands; but here the cliffs were in many places not at the sea's edge, and there was a shelving land at their feet. The northmost of these was called the Bay of Andúnië, for there was the great haven of Andúnië (Sunset), with its town beside the shore and many other dwellings climbing up the steep slopes behind. But much of the southerly part of the Andustar was fertile, and there also were great woods, of birch and beech upon the upper ground, and in the lower vales of oaks and elms. Between the promontories of the Andustar and the Hyarnustar was the great Bay that was called Eldanna, because it faced towards Eressëa; and the lands about it, being sheltered from the north and open to the western seas, were warm, and the most rain fell there. At the centre of the Bay of Eldanna was the most beautiful of all the havens of Númenor, Eldalondë the Green; and hither in the earlier days the swift white ships of the Eldar of Eressëa came most often.

All about that place, up the seaward slopes and far into the land, grew the evergreen and fragrant trees that they brought out of the West, and so throve there that the Eldar said that almost it was fair as a haven in Eressëa. They were the greatest delight of Númenor, and they were remembered in many songs long after they had perished for ever, for few ever flowered east of the Land of Gift: *oiolairë* and *lairelossë*, *nessamelda*, *vardarianna*, *taniquelassë*, and *yavannamirë* with its globed and scarlet fruits. Flower, leaf, and rind of those trees exuded sweet scents, and all that country was full of blended fragrance; therefore it was called Nísimaldar, the Fragrant Trees. Many of them were planted and grew, though far less abundantly, in other regions of Númenor; but only here grew the mighty golden tree *malinornë*, reaching after five centuries a height scarce less than it achieved in Eressëa itself. Its bark was silver and smooth, and its boughs somewhat upswept after the manner of the beech; but it never grew save with a single trunk. Its leaves, like those of the beech but greater, were pale green above and beneath were silver, glistering in the sun; in the autumn they did not fall, but turned to pale gold. In the spring it bore golden blossom in clusters like a cherry, which bloomed on during the summer; and as soon as the flowers opened the leaves fell, so that through spring and summer a grove of *malinorni* was carpeted and roofed with gold, but its pillars were of grey silver.[1] Its fruit was a nut with a silver shale; and some were given as a gift by Tar-Aldarion, the sixth King of Númenor, to King Gil-galad of Lindon. They did not take root in that land; but Gil-galad gave some to his kinswoman Galadriel, and under her power they grew and flourished in the guarded land of Lothlórien beside the River Anduin, until the High Elves at last left Middle-earth; but they did not reach the height or girth of the great groves of Númenor.

The river Nunduinë flowed into the sea at Eldalondë, and on its way made the little lake of Nísinen, that was so named from the abundance of sweet-smelling shrubs and flowers that grew upon its banks.

The Hyarnustar was in its western part a mountainous region, with great cliffs on the western and southern coasts; but eastwards were great vineyards in a warm and fertile land. The promontories of the Hyarnustar and the Hyarrostar were splayed wide apart, and on those long shores sea and land came gently together, as nowhere else in Númenor. Here flowed down Siril, the chief river of the land (for all others, save for the Nunduinë in the west, were short and swift torrents hurrying to the sea), that rose in springs under the Menel-tarma in the valley of Noirinan, and running through the Mittalmar southwards became in its lower course a slow and winding stream. It issued at last into the sea amid wide marshes and reedy flats, and its many small mouths found their changing paths through great sands; for many miles on either side were wide white beaches and grey shingles, and here the fisherfolk mostly dwelt, in villages upon the hards among the marshes and meres, of which the chief was Nindamos.

In the Hyarrostar grew an abundance of trees of many kinds, and among them the *laurinquë* in which the people delighted for its flowers, for it had no other use. This name they gave it because of its long-hanging clusters of yellow flowers; and some who had heard from the Eldar of Laurelin, the Golden Tree of Valinor, believed that it came from that great Tree, being brought in seed thither by the Eldar; but it was not so. From the days of Tar-Aldarion there were great plantations in the Hyarrostar to furnish timber for ship-building.

The Orrostar was a cooler land, but it was protected from the cold north-east winds by highlands that rose towards the end of the promontory; and in the inner regions of the Orrostar much grain was grown, especially in those parts near to the borders of Arandor.

The whole land of Númenor was so posed as if it had been thrust upward out of the sea, but tilted southward and a little eastward; and save upon the south the land in nearly all places fell towards the sea in steep cliffs. In Númenor birds that dwell near the sea, and swim or dive in it, abode in multitudes beyond reckoning. The mariners said that were they blind they still would know that their ship was drawing near to Númenor because of the great clamour of the birds of the shore; and when any ship approached the land seabirds in great flocks would arise and fly above it in welcome and gladness, for they were never killed or molested by intent. Some would accompany ships on their voyages, even those that went to Middle-earth. Likewise within the lands the birds of Númenor were beyond count, from the *kirinki* that were no bigger than wrens, but all scarlet, with piping voices on the edge of human hearing, to the great eagles that were held sacred to Manwë, and never afflicted, until the days of evil and the hatred of the Valar began. For two thousand years, from the days of Elros Tar-Minyatur until the time of Tar-Ancalimon son of Tar-Atanamir, there was an eyrie in the summit of the tower of the King's palace in Armenelos; and there one pair ever dwelt and lived on the bounty of the King.

In Númenor all journeyed from place to place on horseback; for in riding the Númenóreans, both men and women, took delight, and all the people of the land loved horses, treating them honourably and housing them nobly. They were trained to hear and answer calls from a great distance, and it is said in old tales that where there was great love between men and women and their favourite steeds they could be summoned at need by thought alone. Therefore the roads of Númenor were for the most part unpaved, made and tended for riding, since coaches and carriages were little used in the earlier centuries, and heavy cargoes were borne by sea. The chief and most ancient road, suitable for wheels, ran from the greatest port, Rómenna in the east, to the royal city of Armenelos, and thence on to the Valley of the Tombs and the Meneltarma; and this road was early extended to Ondosto within the borders of the Forostar, and thence to Andúnië in the west. Along it passed wains bearing stone from the Northlands that was most esteemed for building, and timber in which the Westlands were rich.

The Edain brought with them to Númenor the knowledge of many crafts, and many craftsmen who had learned from the Eldar, besides preserving lore and traditions of their own. But they could bring with them few materials, save for the tools of their crafts; and for long all metals in Númenor were precious metals. They brought with them many treasures of gold and silver, and gems also; but they did not find these things in Númenor. They loved them for their beauty, and it was this love that first aroused in them cupidity, in later days when they fell under the Shadow and became proud and unjust in their dealings with lesser folk of Middle-earth. Of the Elves of Eressëa in the days of their friendship they had at times gifts of gold and silver and jewels; but such things were rare and prized in all the earlier centuries, until the power of the Kings was spread to the coasts of the East.

Some metals they found in Númenor, and as their cunning in mining and in smelting and smithying swiftly grew things of iron and copper became common. Among the wrights of the Edain were weaponsmiths, and they had with the teaching of the Noldor acquired great skill in the forging of swords, of axe-blades, and of spearheads and knives. Swords the Guild of Weaponsmiths still made, for the preservation of the craft, though most of their labour was spent on the fashioning of tools for the uses of peace. The King and most of the great chieftains possessed swords as heirlooms of their fathers;[2] and at times they would still give a sword as a gift to their heirs. A new sword was made for the King's Heir to be given to him on the day on which this title was conferred. But no man wore a sword in Númenor, and for long years few indeed were the weapons of warlike intent that were made in the land. Axes and spears and bows they had, and shooting with bows on foot and on horseback was a chief sport and pastime of the Númenóreans. In later days, in the wars upon Middle-earth, it was the bows of the Númenóreans that were most greatly feared. 'The Men of the Sea', it was said, 'send before them a great cloud, as a rain turned to serpents, or a black hail tipped with steel'; and in those days the great cohorts of the King's Archers used bows made of hollow steel, with black-feathered arrows a full ell long from point to notch.

But for long the crews of the great Númenórean ships came unarmed among the men of Middle-earth; and though they had axes and bows aboard for the felling of timber and the hunting for food upon wild shores owned by no man, they did not bear these when they sought out the men of the lands. It was indeed their grievance, when the Shadow crept along the coasts and men whom they had befriended became afraid or hostile, that iron was used against them by those to whom they had revealed it.

Beyond all other pursuits the strong men of Númenor took delight in the Sea, in swimming, in diving, or in small craft for contests of speed in rowing or sailing. The hardiest of the people were the fisherfolk; fish were abundant all about the coasts, and were at all times a chief source of food in Númenor; and all the towns where many people congregated were set by the shores. From the fisherfolk were mostly drawn the Mariners, who as the years passed grew greatly in importance and esteem. It is said that when the Edain first set sail upon the Great Sea, following the Star to Númenor, the Elvish ships that bore them were each steered and captained by one of the Eldar deputed by Círdan; and after the Elvish steersmen departed and took with them the most part of their ships it was long before the Númenóreans themselves ventured far to sea. But there were shipwrights among them who had been instructed by the Eldar; and by their own study and devices they improved their art until they dared to sail ever further into the deep waters. When six hundred years had passed from the beginning of the Second Age Vëantur, Captain of the King's Ships under Tar-Elendil, first achieved the voyage to Middle-earth. He brought his ship *Entulessë* (which signifies 'Return') into Mithlond on the spring winds blowing from the west; and he returned in the autumn of the following year. Thereafter seafaring became the chief enterprise for daring and hardihood among the men of Númenor; and Aldarion son of Meneldur, whose wife was Vëantur's daughter, formed the Guild of Venturers, in which were joined all the tried mariners of Númenor; as is told in the tale that follows here.

NOTES

1   This description of the mallorn is much like that given by Legolas to his companions as they approached Lothlórien (*The Fellowship of the Ring* II 6).

2   The King's sword was indeed Aranrúth, the sword of Elu Thingol of Doriath in Beleriand, that had descended to Elros from Elwing his mother. Other heirlooms there were beside: the Ring of Barahir; the great Axe of Tuor, father of Eärendil; and the Bow of Bregor of the House of Bëor. Only the Ring of Barahir father of Beren One-hand survived the Downfall; for it was given by Tar-Elendil to his daughter Silmarien and was preserved in the House of the Lords of Andúnië, of whom the last was Elendil the Faithful who fled from the wrack of

Númenor to Middle-earth. [Author's note.] – The story of the Ring
of Barahir is told in *The Silmarillion*, Chapter XIX, and its later
history in *The Lord of the Rings* Appendix A (I, iii and v). Of 'the
great Axe of Tuor' there is no mention in *The Silmarillion*, but it is
named and described in the original 'Fall of Gondolin' (1916–17,
see p. iv), where it is said that in Gondolin Tuor carried an axe
rather than a sword, and that he named it in the speech of the people
of Gondolin *Dramborleg*. In a list of names accompanying the tale
Dramborleg is translated 'Thudder-Sharp': 'the axe of Tuor that
smote both a heavy dint as of a club and cleft as a sword'.

II

ALDARION AND ERENDIS

The Mariner's Wife

Meneldur was the son of Tar-Elendil, the fourth King of Númenor. He was the King's third child, for he had two sisters, named Silmarien and Isilmë. The elder of these was wedded to Elatan of Andúnië, and their son was Valandil, Lord of Andúnië, from whom came long after the lines of the Kings of Gondor and Arnor in Middle-earth.

Meneldur was a man of gentle mood, without pride, whose exercise was rather in thought than in deeds of the body. He loved dearly the land of Númenor and all things in it, but he gave no heed to the Sea that lay all about it; for his mind looked further than Middle-earth: he was enamoured of the stars and the heavens. All that he could gather of the lore of the Eldar and Edain concerning Eä and the deeps that lay about the Kingdom of Arda he studied, and his chief delight was in the watching of the stars. He built a tower in the Forostar (the northernmost region of the island) where the airs were clearest, from which by night he would survey the heavens and observe all the movements of the lights of the firmament.[1]

When Meneldur received the Sceptre he removed, as he must, from the Forostar, and dwelt in the great house of the Kings in Armenelos. He proved a good and wise king, though he never ceased to yearn for days in which he might enrich his knowledge of the heavens. His wife was a woman of great beauty, named Almarian. She was the daughter of Vëantur, Captain of the King's Ships under Tar-Elendil; and though she herself loved ships and the sea no more than most women of the land her son followed after Vëantur her father, rather than after Meneldur.

The son of Meneldur and Almarian was Anardil, afterwards renowned among the Kings of Númenor as Tar-Aldarion. He had two sisters, younger than he: Ailinel and Almiel, of whom the elder married Orchaldor, a descendant of the House of Hador, son of Hatholdir, who was close in friendship with Meneldur; and the son of Orchaldor and Ailinel was Soronto, who comes later into the tale.[2]

Aldarion, for so he is called in all tales, grew swiftly to a man of great stature, strong and vigorous in mind and body, golden-haired as his mother, ready to mirth and generous, but prouder than his father and ever more bent on his own will. From the first he loved the Sea, and his mind was turned to the craft of ship-building. He had little liking for the north country, and spent all the time that his father would grant by the shores of the sea, especially near Rómenna, where was the chief haven of Númenor, the greatest shipyards, and the most skilled shipwrights. His father did little to hinder him for many years, being well-pleased that Aldarion should have exercise for his hardihood and work for thought and hand.

Aldarion was much loved by Vëantur his mother's father, and he dwelt often in Vëantur's house on the southern side of the firth of Rómenna. That house had its own quay, to which many small boats were always moored, for Vëantur would never journey by land if he could by water; and there as a child Aldarion learned to row, and later to manage sail. Before he was full grown he could captain a ship of many men, sailing from haven to haven.

It happened on a time that Vëantur said to his grandson: 'Anardilya, the spring is drawing nigh, and also the day of your full age' (for in that April Aldarion would be twenty-five years old). 'I have in mind a way to mark it fittingly. My own years are far greater, and I do not think that I shall often again have the heart to leave my fair house and the blest shores of Númenor; but once more at least I would ride the Great Sea and face the North wind and the East. This year you shall come with me, and we will go to Mithlond and see the tall blue mountains of Middle-earth and the green land of the Eldar at their feet. Good welcome you will find from Círdan the Shipwright and from King Gil-galad. Speak of this to your father.'[3]

When Aldarion spoke of this venture, and asked leave to go as soon as the spring winds should be favourable, Meneldur was loath to grant it. A chill came upon him, as though his heart guessed that more hung upon this than his mind could foresee. But when he looked upon the eager face of his son he let no sign of this be seen. 'Do as your heart calls, *onya*,' he said. 'I shall miss you sorely; but with Vëantur as captain, under the grace of the Valar, I shall live in good hope of your return. But do not become enamoured of the Great Lands, you who one day must be King and Father of this Isle!'

Thus it came to pass that on a morning of fair sun and white wind, in the bright spring of the seven hundred and twenty-fifth year of the Second Age, the son of the King's Heir of Númenor[4] sailed from the land; and ere day was over he saw it sink shimmering into

the sea, and last of all the peak of the Meneltarma as a dark finger
against the sunset.

It is said that Aldarion himself wrote records of all his journeys
to Middle-earth, and they were long preserved in Rómenna, though
all were afterwards lost. Of his first journey little is known, save
that he made the friendship of Círdan and Gil-galad, and journeyed
far in Lindon and the west of Eriador, and marvelled at all that he
saw. He did not return for more than two years, and Meneldur was
in great disquiet. It is said that his delay was due to the eagerness
he had to learn all that he could of Círdan, both in the making and
management of ships, and in the building of walls to withstand the
hunger of the sea.

There was joy in Rómenna and Armenelos when men saw the
great ship *Númerrámar* (which signifies 'West-wings') coming up
from the sea, her golden sails reddened in the sunset. The summer
was nearly over and the *Eruhantalë* was nigh.[5] It seemed to Meneldur
when he welcomed his son in the house of Vëantur that he had grown
in stature, and his eyes were brighter; but they looked far away.

'What did you see, *onya*, in your far journeys that now lives most
in memory?'

But Aldarion, looking east towards the night, was silent. At last
he answered, but softly, as one that speaks to himself: 'The fair
people of the Elves? The green shores? The mountains wreathed in
cloud? The regions of mist and shadow beyond guess? I do not know.'
He ceased, and Meneldur knew that he had not spoken his full mind.
For Aldarion had become enamoured of the Great Sea, and of a ship
riding there alone without sight of land, borne by the winds with
foam at its throat to coasts and havens unguessed; and that love and
desire never left him until his life's end.

Vëantur did not again voyage from Númenor; but the *Númerrámar*
he gave in gift to Aldarion. Within three years Aldarion begged leave
to go again, and he set sail for Lindon. He was three years abroad;
and not long after another voyage he made, that lasted for four years,
for it is said that he was no longer content to sail to Mithlond, but
began to explore the coasts southwards, past the mouths of Baranduin
and Gwathló and Angren, and he rounded the dark cape of Ras
Morthil and beheld the great Bay of Belfalas, and the mountains of the
country of Amroth where the Nandor Elves still dwell.[6]

In the thirty-ninth year of his age Aldarion returned to Númenor,
bringing gifts from Gil-galad to his father; for in the following year,
as he had long proclaimed, Tar-Elendil relinquished the Sceptre to his
son, and Tar-Meneldur became the King. Then Aldarion restrained

his desire, and remained at home for a while for the comfort of his father; and in those days he put to use the knowledge he had gained of Círdan concerning the making of ships, devising much anew of his own thought, and he began also to set men to the improvement of the havens and the quays, for he was ever eager to build greater vessels. But the sea-longing came upon him anew, and he departed again and yet again from Númenor; and his mind turned now to ventures that might not be compassed with one vessel's company. Therefore he formed the Guild of Venturers, that afterwards was renowned; to that brotherhood were joined all the hardiest and most eager mariners, and young men sought admission to it even from the inland regions of Númenor, and Aldarion they called the Great Captain. At that time he, having no mind to live upon land in Armenelos, had a ship built that should serve as his dwelling-place; he named it therefore *Eämbar*, and at times he would sail in it from haven to haven of Númenor, but for the most part it lay at anchor off Tol Uinen: and that was a little isle in the bay of Rómenna that was set there by Uinen the Lady of the Seas.[7] Upon Eämbar was the guildhouse of the Venturers, and there were kept the records of their great voyages;[8] for Tar-Meneldur looked coldly on the enterprises of his son, and cared not to hear the tale of his journeys, believing that he sowed the seeds of restlessness and the desire of other lands to hold.

In that time Aldarion became estranged from his father, and ceased to speak openly of his designs and his desires; but Almarian the Queen supported her son in all that he did, and Meneldur perforce let matters go as they must. For the Venturers grew in numbers and in the esteem of men, and they called them *Uinendili*, the lovers of Uinen; and their Captain became the less easy to rebuke or restrain. The ships of the Númenóreans became ever larger and of greater draught in those days, until they could make far voyages, carrying many men and great cargoes; and Aldarion was often long gone from Númenor. Tar-Meneldur ever opposed his son, and he set a curb on the felling of trees in Númenor for the building of vessels; and it came therefore into Aldarion's mind that he would find timber in Middle-earth, and seek there for a haven for the repair of his ships. In his voyages down the coasts he looked with wonder on the great forests; and at the mouth of the river that the Númenóreans called Gwathir, River of Shadow, he established Vinyalondë, the New Haven.[9]

But when nigh on eight hundred years had passed since the

beginning of the Second Age, Tar-Meneldur commanded his son to remain now in Númenor and to cease for a time his eastward voyaging; for he desired to proclaim Aldarion the King's Heir, as had been done at that age of the Heir by the Kings before him. Then Meneldur and his son were reconciled, for that time, and there was peace between them; and amid joy and feasting Aldarion was proclaimed Heir in the hundredth year of his age, and received from his father the title and power of Lord of the Ships and Havens of Númenor. To the feasting in Armenelos came one Beregar from his dwelling in the west of the Isle, and with him came Erendis his daughter. There Almarian the Queen observed her beauty, of a kind seldom seen in Númenor; for Beregar came of the House of Bëor by ancient descent, though not of the royal line of Elros, and Erendis was dark-haired and of slender grace, with the clear grey eyes of her kin.[10] But Erendis looked upon Aldarion as he rode by, and for his beauty and splendour of bearing she had eyes for little else. Thereafter Erendis entered the household of the Queen, and found favour also with the King; but little did she see of Aldarion, who busied himself in the tending of the forests, being concerned that in days to come timber should not lack in Númenor. Ere long the mariners of the Guild of Venturers became restless, for they were ill content to voyage more briefly and more rarely under lesser commanders; and when six years had passed since the proclamation of the King's Heir Aldarion determined to sail again to Middle-earth. Of the King he got but grudging leave, for he refused his father's urging that he abide in Númenor and seek a wife; and he set sail in the spring of the year. But coming to bid farewell to his mother he saw Erendis amid the Queen's company; and looking on her beauty he divined the strength that lay concealed in her.

Then Almarian said to him: 'Must you depart again, Aldarion, my son? Is there nothing that will hold you in the fairest of all mortal lands?'

'Not yet,' he answered; 'but there are fairer things in Armenelos than a man could find elsewhere, even in the lands of the Eldar. But mariners are men of two minds, at war with themselves; and the desire of the Sea still holds me.'

Erendis believed that these words were spoken also for her ears; and from that time forth her heart was turned wholly to Aldarion, though not in hope. In those days there was no need, by law or custom, that those of the royal house, not even the King's Heir, should wed only with descendants of Elros Tar-Minyatur; but Erendis deemed that Aldarion was too high. Yet she looked on no man with favour thereafter, and every suitor she dismissed.

Seven years passed before Aldarion came back, bringing with him ore of silver and gold; and he spoke with his father of his voyage and his deeds. But Meneldur said: 'Rather would I have had you beside me, than any news or gifts from the Dark Lands. This is the part of merchants and explorers, not of the King's Heir. What need have we of more silver and gold, unless to use in pride where other things would serve as well? The need of the King's house is for a man who knows and loves this land and people, which he will rule.'

'Do I not study men all my days?' said Aldarion. 'I can lead and govern them as I will.'

'Say rather, some men, of like mind with yourself,' answered the King. 'There are also women in Númenor, scarce fewer than men; and save your mother, whom indeed you can lead as you will, what do you know of them? Yet one day you must take a wife.'

'One day!' said Aldarion. 'But not before I must; and later, if any try to thrust me towards marriage. Other things I have to do more urgent to me, for my mind is bent on them. "Cold is the life of a mariner's wife"; and the mariner who is single of purpose and not tied to the shore goes further, and learns better how to deal with the sea.'

'Further, but not with more profit,' said Meneldur. 'And you do not "deal with the sea", Aldarion, my son. Do you forget that the Edain dwell here under the grace of the Lords of the West, that Uinen is kind to us, and Ossë is restrained? Our ships are guarded, and other hands guide them than ours. So be not overproud, or the grace may wane; and do not presume that it will extend to those who risk themselves without need upon the rocks of strange shores or in the lands of men of darkness.'

'To what purpose then is the gracing of our ships,' said Aldarion, 'if they are to sail to no shores, and may seek nothing not seen before?'

He spoke no more to his father of such matters, but passed his days upon the ship Eämbar in the company of the Venturers, and in the building of a vessel greater than any made before: that ship he named *Palarran*, the Far-Wanderer. Yet now he met Erendis often (and that was by contrivance of the Queen); and the King learning of their meetings felt disquiet, yet he was not displeased. 'It would be more kind to cure Aldarion of his restlessness,' said he, 'before he win the heart of any woman.' 'How else will you cure him, if not by love?' said the Queen. 'Erendis is yet young,' said Meneldur. But Almarian answered: 'The kin of Erendis have not the length of life that is granted to the descendants of Elros; and her heart is already won.'[11]

Now when the great ship Palarran was built Aldarion would depart once more. At this Meneldur became wrathful, though by the persuasions of the Queen he would not use the King's power to stay him. Here must be told of the custom that when a ship departed from Númenor over the Great Sea to Middle-earth a woman, most often of the captain's kin, should set upon the vessel's prow the Green Bough of Return; and that was cut from the tree *oiolairë*, that signifies 'Ever-summer', which the Eldar gave to the Númenóreans,[12] saying that they set it upon their own ships in token of friendship with Ossë and Uinen. The leaves of that tree were evergreen, glossy and fragrant; and it throve upon sea-air. But Meneldur forbade the Queen and the sisters of Aldarion to bear the bough of *oiolairë* to Rómenna where lay the Palarran, saying that he refused his blessing to his son, who was venturing forth against his will; and Aldarion hearing this said: 'If I must go without blessing or bough, then so I will go.'

Then the Queen was grieved; but Erendis said to her: '*Tarinya*, if you will cut the bough from the Elven-tree, I will bear it to the haven, by your leave; for the King has not forbidden it to me.'

The mariners thought it an ill thing that the Captain should depart thus; but when all was made ready and men prepared to weigh anchor Erendis came there, little though she loved the noise and bustle of the great harbour and the crying of the gulls. Aldarion greeted her with amazement and joy; and she said: 'I have brought you the Bough of Return, lord: from the Queen.' 'From the Queen?' said Aldarion, in a changed manner. 'Yes, lord,' said she; 'but I asked for her leave to do so. Others beside your own kin will rejoice at your return, as soon as may be.'

At that time Aldarion first looked on Erendis with love; and he stood long in the stern looking back as the Palarran passed out to sea. It is said that he hastened his return, and was gone less time than he had designed; and coming back he brought gifts for the Queen and the ladies of her house, but the richest gift he brought for Erendis, and that was a diamond. Cold now were the greetings between the King and his son; and Meneldur rebuked him, saying that such a gift was unbecoming in the King's Heir unless it were a betrothal gift, and he demanded that Aldarion declare his mind.

'In gratitude I brought it,' said he, 'for a warm heart amid the coldness of others.'

'Cold hearts may not kindle others to give them warmth at their goings and comings,' said Meneldur; and again he urged Aldarion to take thought of marriage, though he did not speak of Erendis. But Aldarion would have none of it, for he was ever and in every course the more opposed as those about him urged it; and treating Erendis now with greater coolness he determined to leave Númenor and further his designs in Vinyalondë. Life on land was irksome to him, for aboard his ship he was subject to no other will, and the Venturers who accompanied him knew only love and admiration for the Great Captain. But now Meneldur forbade his going; and Aldarion, before the winter was fully gone, set sail with a fleet of seven ships and the greater part of the Venturers in defiance of the King. The Queen did not dare incur Meneldur's wrath; but at night a cloaked woman came to the haven bearing a bough, and she gave it into the hands of Aldarion, saying: 'This comes from the Lady of the Westlands' (for so they called Erendis), and went away in the dark.

At the open rebellion of Aldarion the King rescinded his authority as Lord of the Ships and Havens of Númenor; and he caused the Guildhouse of the Venturers on Eämbar to be shut, and the shipyards of Rómenna to be closed, and forbade the felling of all trees for shipbuilding. Five years passed; and Aldarion returned with nine ships, for two had been built in Vinyalondë, and they were laden with fine timber from the forests of the coasts of Middle-earth. The anger of Aldarion was great when he found what had been done; and to his father he said: 'If I am to have no welcome in Númenor, and no work for my hands to do, and if my ships may not be repaired in its havens, then I will go again and soon; for the winds have been rough,[13] and I need refitment. Has not a King's son aught to do but study women's faces to find a wife? The work of forestry I took up, and I have been prudent in it; there will be more timber in Númenor ere my day ends than there is under your sceptre.' And true to his word Aldarion left again in the same year with three ships and the hardiest of the Venturers, going without blessing or bough; for Meneldur set a ban on all the women of his house and of the Venturers, and put a guard about Rómenna.

On that voyage Aldarion was away so long that the people feared for him; and Meneldur himself was disquieted, despite the grace of the Valar that had ever protected the ships of Númenor.[14] When ten years were gone since his sailing Erendis at last despaired, and believing that Aldarion had met with disaster, or else that he had determined to dwell in Middle-earth, and also in order to escape the importuning of suitors, she asked the Queen's leave, and departing from Armenelos she returned to her own kindred in the Westlands. But after four years more Aldarion at last returned, and his ships were battered and broken by the seas. He had sailed first to the haven of Vinyalondë, and thence he had made a great coastwise journey southwards, far beyond any place yet reached by the ships of the Númenóreans; but returning northwards he had met contrary winds and great storms, and scarce escaping shipwreck in the Harad found Vinyalondë overthrown by great seas and plundered by hostile men. Three times he was driven back from the crossing of the Great Sea by high winds out of the West, and his own ship was struck by lightning and dismasted; and only with labour and hardship in the deep waters did he come at last to haven in Númenor. Greatly was Meneldur comforted at Aldarion's return; but he rebuked him for his rebellion against king and father, thus forsaking the guardianship of the Valar, and risking the wrath of Ossë not only for himself but for men whom he had bound to himself in devotion. Then Aldarion was chastened in mood, and he received the pardon of Meneldur, who restored to him the Lordship of the Ships and Havens, and added thereto the title of Master of the Forests.

Aldarion was grieved to find Erendis gone from Armenelos, but he was too proud to seek her; and indeed he could not well do so save to ask for her in marriage, and he was still unwilling to be bound. He set himself to the repairing of the neglects of his long absence, for he had been nigh on twenty years away; and at that time great harbour works were put in hand, especially at Rómenna. He found that there had been much felling of trees for building and the making of many things, but all was done without foresight, and little had been planted to replace what was taken; and he journeyed far and wide in Númenor to view the standing woods.

Riding one day in the forests of the Westlands he saw a woman, whose dark hair flowed in the wind, and about her was a green cloak clasped at the throat with a bright jewel; and he took her for one of the Eldar, who came at times to those parts of the Island. But she approached, and he knew her for Erendis, and saw that the jewel was the one that he had given her; then suddenly he knew in himself the love that he bore her, and he felt the emptiness of his days. Erendis seeing him turned pale and would ride off, but he was too quick, and he said: 'Too well have I deserved that you should flee from me, who have fled so often and so far! But forgive me, and stay now.' They rode then together to the house of Beregar her father, and there Aldarion made plain his desire for betrothal to Erendis; but now Erendis was reluctant, though according to custom and the life of her people it was now full time for her marriage. Her love for him was not lessened, nor did she retreat out of guile; but she feared now in her heart that in the war between herself and the Sea for the keeping of Aldarion she would not conquer. Never would Erendis take less, that she might not lose all; and fearing the Sea, and begrudging to all ships the felling of trees which she loved, she determined that she must utterly defeat the Sea and the ships, or else be herself defeated utterly.

But Aldarion wooed Erendis in earnest, and wherever she went he would go; he neglected the havens and the shipyards and all the concerns of the Guild of Venturers, felling no trees but setting himself to their planting only, and he found more contentment in those days than in any others of his life, though he did not know it until he looked back long after when old age was upon him. At length he sought to persuade Erendis to sail with him on a voyage about the Island in the ship Eämbar; for one hundred years had now passed since Aldarion founded the Guild of Venturers, and feasts were to be held in all the havens of Númenor. To this Erendis consented, concealing her distaste and fear; and they departed from Rómenna and came to Andúnië in the west of the Isle. There Valandil, Lord of Andúnië and close kin of Aldarion,[15] held a great feast; and at that feast he drank to Erendis, naming her *Uinéniel*, Daughter of Uinen, the new Lady of the Sea. But Erendis, who sat beside the wife of Valandil, said aloud: 'Call me by no such name! I am no daughter of Uinen: rather is she my foe.'

Thereafter for a while doubt again assailed Erendis, for Aldarion turned his thoughts again to the works at Rómenna, and busied himself with the building of great sea-walls, and the raising of a tall tower upon Tol Uinen: *Calmindon*, the Light-tower, was its name. But when these things were done Aldarion returned to Erendis and besought her to be betrothed; yet still she delayed, saying: 'I have journeyed with you by ship, lord. Before I give you my answer, will you not journey with me ashore, to the places that I love? You know too little of this land, for one who shall be its King.' Therefore they departed together, and came to Emerië, where were rolling downs of grass, and it was the chief place of sheep pasturage in Númenor; and they saw the white houses of the farmers and shepherds, and heard the bleating of the flocks.

There Erendis spoke to Aldarion and said: 'Here could I be at ease!'

'You shall dwell where you will, as wife of the King's Heir,' said Aldarion. 'And as Queen in many fair houses, such as you desire.'

'When you are King, I shall be old,' said Erendis. 'Where will the King's Heir dwell meanwhile?'

'With his wife,' said Aldarion, 'when his labours allow, if she cannot share in them.'

'I will not share my husband with the Lady Uinen,' said Erendis.

'That is a twisted saying,' said Aldarion. 'As well might I say that I would not share my wife with the Lord Oromë of Forests, because she loves trees that grow wild.'

'Indeed you would not,' said Erendis; 'for you would fell any wood as a gift to Uinen, if you had a mind.'

'Name any tree that you love and it shall stand till it dies,' said Aldarion.

'I love all that grow in this Isle,' said Erendis.

Then they rode a great while in silence; and after that day they parted, and Erendis returned to her father's house. To him she said nothing, but to her mother Núneth she told the words that had passed between herself and Aldarion.

'All or nothing, Erendis,' said Núneth. 'So you were as a child. But you love this man, and he is a great man, not to speak of his rank; and you will not cast out your love from your heart so easily, nor without great hurt to yourself. A woman must share her husband's love with his work and the fire of his spirit, or make him a thing not loveable. But I doubt that you will ever understand such counsel. Yet I am grieved, for it is full time that you were wed; and having borne a fair child I had hoped to see fair grandchildren; nor if they were cradled in the King's house would that displease me.'

This counsel did not indeed move the mind of Erendis; nevertheless she found that her heart was not under her will, and her days were empty: more empty than in the years when Aldarion had been gone. For he still abode in Númenor, and yet the days passed, and he did not come again into the west.

Now Almarian the Queen, being acquainted by Núneth with what had passed, and fearing lest Aldarion should seek solace in voyaging again (for he had been long ashore), sent word to Erendis asking that she return to Armenelos; and Erendis being urged by Núneth and by her own heart did as she was bid. There she was reconciled to Aldarion; and in the spring of the year, when the time of the *Erukyermë* was come, they ascended in the retinue of the King to the summit of the Meneltarma, which was the Hallowed Mountain of the Númenóreans.[16] When all had gone down again Aldarion and Erendis remained behind; and they looked out, seeing all the Isle of Westernesse laid green beneath them in the spring, and they saw the glimmer of light in the West where far away was Avallóne,[17] and the shadows in the East upon the Great Sea; and the Menel was blue above them. They did not speak, for no one, save only the King, spoke upon the height of Meneltarma; but as they came down Erendis stood a moment, looking towards Emerië, and beyond, towards the woods of her home.

'Do you not love the Yôzâyan?' she said.

'I love it indeed,' he answered, 'though I think that you doubt it. For I think also of what it may be in time to come, and the hope and splendour of its people; and I believe that a gift should not lie idle in hoard.'

But Erendis denied his words, saying: 'Such gifts as come from the Valar, and through them from the One, are to be loved for themselves now, and in all nows. They are not given for barter, for more or for better. The Edain remain mortal Men, Aldarion, great though they be: and we cannot dwell in the time that is to come, lest we lose our now for a phantom of our own design.' Then taking suddenly the jewel from her throat she asked him: 'Would you have me trade this to buy me other goods that I desire?'

'No!' said he. 'But you do not lock it in hoard. Yet I think you set it too high; for it is dimmed by the light of your eyes.' Then he kissed her on the eyes, and in that moment she put aside fear, and accepted him; and their troth was plighted upon the steep path of the Meneltarma.

They went back then to Armenelos, and Aldarion presented Erendis to Tar-Meneldur as the betrothed of the King's Heir; and the King was rejoiced, and there was merrymaking in the city and in all the Isle. As betrothal gift Meneldur gave to Erendis a fair portion of land in Emerië, and there he had built for her a white house. But Aldarion said to her: 'Other jewels I have in hoard, gifts of kings in far lands to whom the ships of Númenor have brought aid. I have gems as green as the light of the sun in the leaves of trees which you love.'

'No!' said Erendis. 'I have had my betrothal gift, though it came beforehand. It is the only jewel that I have or would have; and I will set it yet higher.' Then he saw that she had caused the white gem to be set as a star in a silver fillet; and at her asking he bound it on her forehead. She wore it so for many years, until sorrow befell; and thus she was known far and wide as Tar-Elestirnë, the Lady of the Star-brow.[18] Thus there was for a time peace and joy in Armenelos in the house of the King, and in all the Isle, and it is recorded in ancient books that there was great fruitfulness in the golden summer of that year, which was the eight hundred and fifty-eighth of the Second Age.

But alone among the people the mariners of the Guild of Venturers were not well content. For fifteen years Aldarion had remained in Númenor, and led no expedition abroad; and though there were gallant captains who had been trained by him, without the wealth and authority of the King's son their voyages were fewer and more brief, and went but seldom further than the land of Gil-galad. Moreover timber was become scarce in the shipyards, for Aldarion neglected the forests; and the Venturers besought him to turn again to this work. At their prayer Aldarion did so, and at first Erendis would go about with him in the woods; but she was saddened by the sight of trees felled in their prime, and afterwards hewn and sawn. Soon therefore Aldarion went alone, and they were less in company.

Now the year came in, in which all looked for the marriage of the King's Heir; for it was not the custom that betrothal should last much longer than three years. One morning in that spring Aldarion rode up from the haven of Andúnië, to take the road to the house of Beregar; for there he was to be guest, and thither Erendis had preceded him, going from Armenelos by the roads of the land. As he came to the top of the great bluff that stood out from the land and sheltered the haven from the north, he turned and looked back over the sea. A west wind was blowing, as often at that season, beloved by those who had a mind to sail to Middle-earth, and white-crested waves marched towards the shore. Then suddenly the sea-longing took him as though a great hand had been laid on his throat, and his heart hammered, and his breath was stopped. He strove for the mastery, and at length turned his back and continued on his journey; and by design he took his way through the wood where he had seen Erendis riding as one of the Eldar, now fifteen years gone. Almost he looked to see her so once more; but she was not there, and desire to see her face again hastened him, so that he came to Beregar's house before evening.

There she welcomed him gladly, and he was merry; but he said nothing touching their wedding, though all had thought that this was a part of his errand to the Westlands. As the days passed Erendis marked that he now often fell silent in company when others were gay; and if she looked towards him suddenly she saw his eyes upon her. Then her heart was shaken; for the blue eyes of Aldarion seemed to her now grey and cold, yet she perceived as it were a hunger in his gaze. That look she had seen too often before, and feared what it boded; but she said nothing. At that Núneth, who marked all that passed, was glad; for 'words may open wounds', as she said. Ere long Aldarion and Erendis rode away, returning to Armenelos, and as they drew further from the sea he grew merrier again. Still he said nothing to her of his trouble: for indeed he was at war within himself, and irresolute.

So the year drew on, and Aldarion spoke neither of the sea nor of wedding; but he was often in Rómenna, and in the company of the Venturers. At length, when the next year came in, the King called him to his chamber; and they were at ease together, and the love they bore one another was no longer clouded.

'My son,' said Tar-Meneldur, 'when will you give me the daughter that I have so long desired? More than three years have now passed, and that is long enough. I marvel that you could endure so long a delay.'

Then Aldarion was silent, but at length he said: 'It has come upon me again, Atarinya. Eighteen years is a long fast. I can scarce lie still in a bed, or hold myself upon a horse, and the hard ground of stone wounds my feet.'

Then Meneldur was grieved, and pitied his son; but he did not understand his trouble, for he himself had never loved ships, and he said: 'Alas! But you are betrothed. And by the laws of Númenor and the right ways of the Eldar and Edain a man shall not have two wives. You cannot wed the Sea, for you are affianced to Erendis.'

Then Aldarion's heart was hardened, for these words recalled his speech with Erendis as they passed through Emerië; and he thought (but untruly) that she had consulted with his father. It was ever his mood, if he thought that others combined to urge him on some path of their choosing, to turn away from it. 'Smiths may smithy, and horsemen ride, and miners delve, when they are betrothed,' said he. 'Therefore why may not mariners sail?'

'If smiths remained five years at the anvil few would be smiths' wives,' said the King. 'And mariners' wives are few, and they endure what they must, for such is their livelihood and their necessity. The King's Heir is not a mariner by trade, nor is he under necessity.'

'There are other needs than livelihood that drive a man,' said Aldarion. 'And there are yet many years to spare.'

'Nay, nay,' said Meneldur, 'you take your grace for granted: Erendis has shorter hope than you, and her years wane swifter. She is not of the line of Elros; and she has loved you now many years.'

'She held back well nigh twelve years, when I was eager,' said Aldarion. 'I do not ask for a third of such a time.'

'She was not then betrothed,' said Meneldur. 'But neither of you are now free. And if she held back, I doubt not that it was in fear of what now seems likely to befall, if you cannot master yourself. In some way you must have stilled that fear; and though you may have spoken no plain word, yet you are beholden, as I judge.'

Then Aldarion said in anger: 'It were better to speak with my betrothed myself, and not hold parley by proxy.' And he left his father. Not long after he spoke to Erendis of his desire to voyage again upon the great waters, saying that he was robbed of all sleep and rest. But she sat pale and silent. At length she said: 'I thought that you were come to speak of our wedding.'

'I will,' said Aldarion. 'It shall be as soon as I return, if you will wait.' But seeing the grief in her face he was moved, and a thought came to him. 'It shall be now,' he said. 'It shall be before this year is done. And then I will fit out such a ship as the Venturers made never yet, a Queen's house on the water. And you shall sail with me, Erendis, under the grace of the Valar, of Yavanna and of Oromë whom you love; you shall sail to lands where I shall show you such woods as you have never seen, where even now the Eldar sing; or forests wider than Númenor, free and wild since the beginning of days, where still you may hear the great horn of Oromë the Lord.'

But Erendis wept. 'Nay, Aldarion,' she said. 'I rejoice that the world yet holds such things as you tell of; but I shall never see them. For I do not desire it: to the woods of Númenor my heart is given. And, alas! if for love of you I took ship, I should not return. It is beyond my strength to endure; and out of sight of land I should die. The Sea hates me; and now it is revenged that I kept you from it and yet fled from you. Go, my lord! But have pity, and take not so many years as I lost before.'

Then Aldarion was abashed; for as he had spoken in heedless anger to his father, so now she spoke with love. He did not sail that year; but he had little peace or joy. 'Out of sight of land she will die!' he said. 'Soon I shall die, if I see it longer. Then if we are to spend any years together I must go alone, and go soon.' He made ready therefore at last for sailing in the spring; and the Venturers were glad, if none else in the Isle who knew of what was done. Three ships were manned, and in the month of Víressë they departed. Erendis herself set the green bough of *oiolairë* on the prow of the Palarran, and hid her tears, until it passed out beyond the great new harbour-walls.

Six years and more passed away before Aldarion returned to Númenor. He found even Almarian the Queen colder in welcome, and the Venturers were fallen out of esteem; for men thought that he had treated Erendis ill. But indeed he was longer gone than he had purposed; for he had found the haven of Vinyalondë now wholly ruined, and great seas had brought to nothing all his labours to restore it. Men near the coasts were growing afraid of the Númenóreans, or were become openly hostile; and Aldarion heard rumours of some lord in Middle-earth who hated the men of the ships. Then when he would turn for home a great wind came out of the south, and he was borne far to the northward. He tarried a while at Mithlond, but when his ships stood out to sea once more they were again swept away north, and driven into wastes perilous with ice, and they suffered cold. At last the sea and wind relented, but even as Aldarion looked out in longing from the prow of the Palarran and saw far off the Meneltarma, his glance fell upon the green bough, and he saw that it was withered. Then Aldarion was dismayed, for such a thing had never befallen the bough of *oiolairë*, so long as it was washed with the spray. 'It is frosted, Captain,' said a mariner who stood beside him. 'It has been too cold. Glad am I to see the Pillar.'

When Aldarion sought out Erendis she looked at him keenly but did not come forward to meet him; and he stood for a while at a loss for words, as was not his wont. 'Sit, my lord,' said Erendis, 'and first tell me of all your deeds. Much must you have seen and done in these long years!'

Then Aldarion began haltingly, and she sat silent, listening, while he told all the tale of his trials and delays; and when he ended she said: 'I thank the Valar by whose grace you have returned at last. But I thank them also that I did not come with you; for I should have withered sooner than any green bough.'

'Your green bough did not go into the bitter cold by will,' he answered. 'But dismiss me now, if you will, and I think that men will not blame you. Yet dare I not to hope that your love will prove stronger to endure even than fair *oiolairë*?'

'So it does prove indeed,' said Erendis. 'It is not yet chilled to the death, Aldarion. Alas! How can I dismiss you, when I look on you again, returning as fair as the sun after winter!'

'Then let spring and summer now begin!' he said.

'And let not winter return,' said Erendis.

Then to the joy of Meneldur and Almarian the wedding of the King's Heir was proclaimed for the next spring; and so it came to pass. In the eight hundred and seventieth year of the Second Age

Aldarion and Erendis were wedded in Armenelos, and in every house there was music, and in all the streets men and women sang. And afterwards the King's Heir and his bride rode at their leisure through all the Isle, until at midsummer they came to Andúnië, where the last feast was prepared by Valandil its lord; and all the people of the Westlands were gathered there, for love of Erendis and pride that a Queen of Númenor should come from among them.

In the morning before the feast Aldarion gazed out from the window of the bedchamber, which looked west-over-sea. 'See, Erendis!' he cried. 'There is a ship speeding to haven; and it is no ship of Númenor, but one such as neither you nor I shall ever set foot upon, even if we would.' Then Erendis looked forth, and she saw a tall white ship, with white birds turning in the sunlight all about it; and its sails glimmered with silver as with foam at the stem it rode towards the harbour. Thus the Eldar graced the wedding of Erendis, for love of the people of the Westlands, who were closest in their friendship.[19] Their ship was laden with flowers for the adornment of the feast, so that all that sat there, when evening was come, were crowned with *elanor*[20] and sweet *lissuin* whose fragrance brings heart's ease. Minstrels they brought also, singers who re-membered songs of Elves and Men in the days of Nargothrond and Gondolin long ago; and many of the Eldar high and fair were seated among Men at the tables. But the people of Andúnië, looking upon the blissful company, said that none were more fair than Erendis; and they said that her eyes were as bright as were the eyes of Morwen Eledhwen of old,[21] or even as those of Avallónë.

Many gifts the Eldar brought also. To Aldarion they gave a sapling tree, whose bark was snow-white, and its stem straight, strong and pliant as it were of steel; but it was not yet in leaf. 'I thank you,' said Aldarion to the Elves. 'The wood of such a tree must be precious indeed.'

'Maybe; we know not,' said they. 'None has ever been hewn. It bears cool leaves in summer, and flowers in winter. It is for this that we prize it.'

To Erendis they gave a pair of birds, grey, with golden beaks and feet. They sang sweetly one to another with many cadences never repeated through a long thrill of song; but if one were separated from the other, at once they flew together, and they would not sing apart.

'How shall I keep them?' said Erendis.

'Let them fly and be free,' answered the Eldar. 'For we have spoken to them and named you; and they will stay wherever you dwell. They mate for their life, and that is long. Maybe there will be many such birds to sing in the gardens of your children.'

That night Erendis awoke, and a sweet fragrance came through the lattice; but the night was light, for the full moon was westering. Then leaving their bed Erendis looked out and saw all the land sleeping in silver; but the two birds sat side by side upon her sill.

When the feasting was ended Aldarion and Erendis went for a while to her home; and the birds again perched upon the sill of her window. At length they bade Beregar and Núneth farewell, and they rode back at last to Armenelos; for there by the King's wish his Heir would dwell, and a house was prepared for them amidst a garden of trees. There the Elven-tree was planted, and the Elven-birds sang in its boughs.

Two years later Erendis conceived, and in the spring of the year after she bore to Aldarion a daughter. Even from birth the child was fair, and grew ever in beauty: the woman most beautiful, as old tales tell, that ever was born in the line of Elros, save Ar-Zimraphel, the last. When her first naming was due they called her Ancalimë. In heart Erendis was glad, for she thought: 'Surely now Aldarion will desire a son, to be his heir; and he will abide with me long yet.' For in secret she still feared the Sea and its power upon his heart; and though she strove to hide it, and would talk with him of his old ventures and of his hopes and designs, she watched jealously if he went to his house-ship or was much with the Venturers. To Eämbar Aldarion once asked her to come, but seeing swiftly in her eyes that she was not full-willing he never pressed her again. Not without cause was Erendis' fear. When Aldarion had been five years ashore he began to be busy again with his Mastership of Forests, and was often many days away from his house. There was now indeed sufficient timber in Númenor (and that was chiefly owing to his prudence); yet since the people were now more numerous there was ever need of wood for building and for the making of many things beside. For in those ancient days, though many had great skill with stone and with metals (since the Edain of old had learned much of the Noldor), the Númenóreans loved things fashioned of wood, whether for daily use, or for beauty of carving. At that time Aldarion again gave most heed to the future, planting always where there was felling, and he had new woods set to grow where there was room, a free land that was suited to trees of different kinds. It was then that he became most widely known as Aldarion, by which name he is remembered among those who held the sceptre in Númenor. Yet to many beside Erendis it seemed that he had little love for trees in themselves, caring for them rather as timber that would serve his designs. Not far otherwise was it with the Sea. For as Núneth had said to Erendis long before: 'Ships he may love, my daughter, for those are made by men's minds and hands; but I think that it is not the winds or the great waters that so burn his heart, nor yet the sight of strange lands, but some heat in his mind, or some dream that pursues him.' And it may be that she struck near the truth; for Aldarion was a man long-sighted, and he looked forward to days when the people would need more room and greater wealth; and whether he himself knew this clearly or no, he dreamed of the glory of Númenor and the power of its kings, and he sought for footholds whence they could step to wider dominion. So it was that ere long he turned again from forestry to the building of ships, and a vision came to him of a mighty vessel like a castle with tall masts and great sails like clouds, bearing men and stores enough for a town. Then in the yards of Rómenna the saws and hammers were busy, while among many lesser craft a great ribbed hull took shape; at which men wondered. *Turuphanto*, the Wooden Whale, they called it, but that was not its name.

Erendis learned of these things, though Aldarion had not spoken to her of them, and she was unquiet. Therefore one day she said to him: 'What is all this busyness with ships, Lord of the Havens? Have we not enough? How many fair trees have been cut short of their lives in this year?' She spoke lightly, and smiled as she spoke.

'A man must have work to do upon land,' he answered, 'even though he have a fair wife. Trees spring and trees fall. I plant more than are felled.' He spoke also in a light tone, but he did not look her in the face; and they did not speak again of these matters.

But when Ancalimë was close on four years old Aldarion at last declared openly to Erendis his desire to sail again from Númenor. She sat silent, for he said nothing that she did not already know; and words were in vain. He tarried until the birthday of Ancalimë, and made much of her that day. She laughed and was merry, though others in that house were not so; and as she went to her bed she said to her father: 'Where will you take me this summer, *tatanya*? I should like to see the white house in the sheep-land that *mamil* tells of.' Aldarion did not answer; and the next day he left the house, and was gone for some days. When all was ready he returned, and bade Erendis farewell. Then against her will tears were in her eyes. They grieved him, and yet irked him, for his mind was resolved, and he hardened his heart. 'Come, Erendis!' he said. 'Eight years I have stayed. You cannot bind for ever in soft bonds the son of the King, of the blood of Tuor and Eärendil! And I am not going to my death. I shall soon return.'

'Soon?' she said. 'But the years are unrelenting, and you will not bring them back with you. And mine are briefer than yours. My youth runs away; and where are my children, and where is your heir? Too long and often of late is my bed cold.'[22]

'Often of late I have thought that you preferred it so,' said Aldarion. 'But let us not be wroth, even if we are not of like mind. Look in your mirror, Erendis. You are beautiful, and no shadow of age is there yet. You have time to spare to my deep need. Two years! Two years is all that I ask!'

But Erendis answered: 'Say rather: "Two years I will take, whether you will or no." Take two years, then! But no more. A King's son of the blood of Eärendil should also be a man of his word.'

Next morning Aldarion hastened away. He lifted up Ancalimë and kissed her; but though she clung to him he set her down quickly and rode off. Soon after the great ship set sail from Rómenna. *Hirilondë* he named it, Haven-finder; but it went from Númenor without the blessing of Tar-Meneldur; and Erendis was not at the harbour to set the green Bough of Return, nor did she send. Aldarion's face was dark and troubled as he stood at the prow of Hirilondë, where the wife of his captain had set a great branch of *oiolairë*; but he did not look back until the Meneltarma was far off in the twilight.

All that day Erendis sat in her chamber alone, grieving; but deeper in her heart she felt a new pain of cold anger, and her love of Aldarion was wounded to the quick. She hated the Sea; and now even trees, that once she had loved, she desired to look upon no more, for they recalled to her the masts of great ships. Therefore ere long she left Armenelos, and went to Emerië in the midst of the Isle, where ever, far and near, the bleating of sheep was borne upon the wind. 'Sweeter it is to my ears than the mewing of gulls,' she said, as she stood at the doors of her white house, the gift of the King; and that was upon a downside, facing west, with great lawns all about that merged without wall or hedge into the pastures. Thither she took Ancalimë, and they were all the company that either had. For Erendis would have only servants in her household, and they were all women; and she sought ever to mould her daughter to her own mind, and to feed her upon her own bitterness against men. Ancalimë seldom indeed saw any man, for Erendis kept no state, and her few farm-servants and shepherds had a homestead at a distance. Other men did not come there, save rarely some messenger from the King; and he would ride away soon, for to men there seemed a chill in the house that put them to flight, and while there they felt constrained to speak half in whisper.

One morning soon after Erendis came to Emerië she awoke to the song of birds, and there on the sill of her window were the Elven-birds that long had dwelt in her garden in Armenelos, but which she had left behind forgotten. 'Sweets fools, fly away!' she said. 'This is no place for such joy as yours.'

Then their song ceased, and they flew up over the trees; thrice they wheeled above the roofs, and then they went away westwards. That evening they settled upon the sill of the chamber in the house of her father, where she had lain with Aldarion on their way from the feast in Andúnië; and there Núneth and Beregar found them on the morning of the next day. But when Núneth held out her hands to them they flew steeply up and fled away, and she watched them until they were specks in the sunlight, speeding to the sea, back to the land whence they came.

'He has gone again, then, and left her,' said Núneth.

'Then why has she not sent news?' said Beregar. 'Or why has she not come home?'

'She has sent news enough,' said Núneth. 'For she has dismissed the Elven-birds, and that was ill done. It bodes no good. Why, why, my daughter? Surely you knew what you must face? But let her alone, Beregar, wherever she may be. This is her home no longer, and she will not be healed here. He will come back. And then may the Valar send her wisdom – or guile, at the least!'

When the second year after Aldarion's sailing came in, by the King's wish Erendis ordered the house in Armenelos to be arrayed and made ready; but she herself made no preparation for return. To the King she sent answer saying: 'I will come if you command me, *atar aranya*. But have I a duty now to hasten? Will it not be time enough when his sail is seen in the East?' And to herself she said: 'Will the King have me wait upon the quays like a sailor's lass? Would that I were, but I am so no longer. I have played that part to the full.'

But that year passed, and no sail was seen; and the next year came, and waned to autumn. Then Erendis grew hard and silent. She ordered that the house in Armenelos be shut, and she went never more than a few hours' journey from her house in Emerië. Such love as she had was all given to her daughter, and she clung to her, and would not have Ancalimë leave her side, not even to visit Núneth and her kin in the Westlands. All Ancalimë's teaching was from her mother; and she learned well to write and to read, and to speak the Elven-tongue with Erendis, after the manner in which high men of Númenor used it. For in the Westlands it was a daily speech in such houses as Beregar's, and Erendis seldom used the Númenórean tongue, which Aldarion loved the better. Much Ancalimë also learned of Númenor and the ancient days in such books and scrolls as were in the house which she could understand; and lore of other kinds, of the people and the land, she heard at times from the women of the household, though of this Erendis knew nothing. But the women were chary of their speech to the child, fearing their mistress; and there was little enough of laughter for Ancalimë in the white house in Emerië. It was hushed and without music, as if one had died there not long since; for in Númenor in those days it was the part of men to play upon instruments, and the music that Ancalimë heard in childhood was the singing of women at work, out of doors, and away from the hearing of the White Lady of Emerië. But now Ancalimë was seven years old, and as often as she could get leave she would go out of the house and on to the wide downs where she could run free; and at times she would go with a shepherdess, tending the sheep, and eating under the sky.

One day in the summer of that year a young boy, but older than herself, came to the house on an errand from one of the distant farms; and Ancalimë came upon him munching bread and drinking milk in the farm-courtyard at the rear of the house. He looked at her without deference, and went on drinking. Then he set down his mug.

'Stare, if you must, great eyes!' he said. 'You're a pretty girl, but too thin. Will you eat?' He took a loaf out of his bag.

'Be off, Îbal!' cried an old woman, coming from the dairy-door. 'And use your long legs, or you'll forget the message I gave you for your mother before you get home!'

'No need for a watch-dog where you are, mother Zamîn!' cried the boy, and with a bark and a shout he leapt over the gate and went off at a run down the hill. Zamîn was an old country-woman, free-tongued, and not easily daunted, even by the White Lady.

'What noisy thing was that?' said Ancalimë.

'A boy,' said Zamîn, 'if you know what that is. But how should you? They're breakers and eaters, mostly. That one is ever eating – but not to no purpose. A fine lad his father will find when he comes back; but if that is not soon, he'll scarce know him. I might say that of others.'

'Has the boy then a father too?' asked Ancalimë.

'To be sure,' said Zamîn. 'Ulbar, one of the shepherds of the great lord away south: the Sheep-lord we call him, a kinsman of the King.'

'Then why is the boy's father not at home?'

'Why, *hérinkë*,' said Zamîn, 'because he heard of those Venturers, and took up with them, and went away with your father, the Lord Aldarion: but the Valar know whither, or why.'

That evening Ancalimë said suddenly to her mother: 'Is my father also called the Lord Aldarion?'

'He was,' said Erendis. 'But why do you ask?' Her voice was quiet and cool, but she wondered and was troubled; for no word concerning Aldarion had passed between them before.

Ancalimë did not answer the question. 'When will he come back?' she said.

'Do not ask me!' said Erendis. 'I do not know. Never, perhaps. But do not trouble yourself; for you have a mother, and she will not run away, while you love her.'

Ancalimë did not speak of her father again.

The days passed bringing in another year, and then another; in that spring Ancalimë was nine years old. Lambs were born and grew; shearing came and passed; a hot summer burned the grass. Autumn turned to rain. Then out of the East upon a cloudy wind Hirilondë came back over the grey seas, bearing Aldarion to Rómenna; and word was sent to Emerië, but Erendis did not speak of it. There were none to greet Aldarion upon the quays. He rode through the rain to Armenelos; and he found his house shut. He was dismayed, but he would ask news of no man; first he would seek the King, for he thought he had much to say to him.

He found his welcome no warmer than he looked for; and Meneldur spoke to him as King to a captain whose conduct is in question. 'You have been long away,' he said coldly. 'It is more than three years now since the date that you set for your return.'

'Alas!' said Aldarion. 'Even I have become weary of the sea, and for long my heart has yearned westward. But I have been detained against my heart: there is much to do. And all things go backward in my absence.'

'I do not doubt it,' said Meneldur. 'You will find it true here also in your right land, I fear.'

'That I hope to redress,' said Aldarion. 'But the world is changing again. Outside nigh on a thousand years have passed since the Lords of the West sent their power against Angband; and those days are forgotten, or wrapped in dim legend among Men of Middle-earth. They are troubled again, and fear haunts them. I desire greatly to consult with you, to give account of my deeds, and my thought concerning what should be done.'

'You shall do so,' said Meneldur. 'Indeed I expect no less. But there are other matters which I judge more urgent. "Let a King first rule well his own house ere he correct others", it is said. It is true of all men. I will now give you counsel, son of Meneldur. You have also a life of your own. Half of yourself you have ever neglected. To you I say now: Go home!'

Aldarion stood suddenly still, and his face was stern. 'If you know, tell me,' he said. 'Where is my home?'

'Where your wife is,' said Meneldur. 'You have broken your word to her, whether by necessity or no. She dwells now in Emerië, in her own house, far from the sea. Thither you must go at once.'

'Had any word been left for me, whither to go, I would have gone directly from the haven,' said Aldarion. 'But at least I need not now ask tidings of strangers.' He turned then to go, but paused, saying: 'Captain Aldarion has forgotten somewhat that belongs to his other half, which in his waywardness he also thinks urgent. He has a letter that he was charged to deliver to the King in Armenelos.' Presenting it to Meneldur he bowed and left the chamber; and within an hour he took horse and rode away, though night was falling. With him he had but two companions, men from his ship: Henderch of the Westlands, and Ulbar who came from Emerië.

Riding hard they came to Emerië at nightfall of the next day, and men and horses were weary. Cold and white looked the house on the hill in a last gleam of sunset under cloud. He blew a horn-call as soon as he saw it from afar.

As he leapt from his horse in the forecourt he saw Erendis: clad in white she stood upon the steps that went up to the pillars before the door. She held herself high, but as he drew near he saw that she was pale and her eyes over-bright.

'You come late, my lord,' she said. 'I had long ceased to expect you. I fear that there is no such welcome prepared for you as I had made when you were due.'

'Mariners are not hard to please,' he said.

'That is well,' she said; and she turned back into the house and left him. Then two women came forward, and an old crone who went down the steps. As Aldarion went in she said to the men in a loud voice so that he could hear her: 'There is no lodging for you here. Go down to the homestead at the hill's foot!'

'No, Zamîn,' said Ulbar. 'I'll not stay. I am for home, by the Lord Aldarion's leave. Is all well there?'

'Well enough,' said she. 'Your son has eaten himself out of your memory. But go, and find your own answers! You'll be warmer there than your Captain.'

Erendis did not come to the table at his late evening-meal, and Aldarion was served by women in a room apart. But before he was done she entered, and said before the women: 'You will be weary, my lord, after such haste. A guest-room is made ready for you, when you will. My women will wait on you. If you are cold, call for fire.'

Aldarion made no answer. He went early to the bedchamber, and being now weary indeed he cast himself on the bed and forgot soon the shadows of Middle-earth and of Númenor in a heavy sleep. But at cockcrow he awoke to a great disquiet and anger. He rose at once, and thought to go without noise from the house: he would find his man Henderch and the horses, and ride to his kinsman Hallatan, the sheep-lord of Hyarastorni. Later he would summon Erendis to bring his daughter to Armenelos, and not have dealings with her upon her own ground. But as he went out towards the doors Erendis came forward. She had not lain in bed that night, and she stood before him on the threshold.

'You leave more promptly than you came, my lord,' she said. 'I hope that (being a mariner) you have not found this house of women irksome already, to go thus before your business is done. Indeed, what business brought you hither? May I learn it before you leave?'

'I was told in Armenelos that my wife was here, and had removed my daughter hither,' he answered. 'As to the wife I am mistaken, it seems, but have I not a daughter?'

'You had one some years ago,' she said. 'But my daughter has not yet risen.'

'Then let her rise, while I go for my horse,' said Aldarion.

Erendis would have withheld Ancalimë from meeting him at that time; but she feared to go so far as to lose the King's favour, and the Council[23] had long shown their displeasure at the upbringing of the child in the country. Therefore when Aldarion rode back, with Henderch beside him, Ancalimë stood beside her mother on the threshold. She stood erect and stiff as her mother, and made him no courtesy as he dismounted and came up the steps towards her. 'Who are you?' she said. 'And why do you bid me to rise so early, before the house is stirring?'

Aldarion looked at her keenly, and though his face was stern he smiled within: for he saw there a child of his own, rather than of Erendis, for all her schooling.

'You knew me once, Lady Ancalimë,' he said, 'but no matter. Today I am but a messenger from Armenelos, to remind you that you are the daughter of the King's Heir; and (so far as I can now see) you shall be his Heir in your turn. You will not always dwell here. But go back to your bed now, my lady, until your maidservant wakes, if you will. I am in haste to see the King. Farewell!' He kissed the hand of Ancalimë and went down the steps; then he mounted and rode away with a wave of his hand.

Erendis alone at a window watched him riding down the hill, and she marked that he rode towards Hyarastorni and not towards Armenelos. Then she wept, from grief, but still more from anger. She had looked for some penitence, that she might extend after rebuke pardon if prayed for; but he had dealt with her as if she were the offender, and ignored her before her daughter. Too late she remembered the words of Núneth long before, and she saw Aldarion now as something large and not to be tamed, driven by a fierce will, more perilous when chill. She rose, and turned from the window, thinking of her wrongs. 'Perilous!' she said. 'I am steel hard to break. So he would find even were he the King of Númenor.'

Aldarion rode on to Hyarastorni, the house of Hallatan his cousin; for he had a mind to rest there a while and take thought. When he came near, he heard the sound of music, and he found the shepherds making merry for the homecoming of Ulbar, with many marvellous tales and many gifts; and the wife of Ulbar garlanded was dancing with him to the playing of pipes. At first none observed him, and he sat on his horse watching with a smile; but then suddenly Ulbar cried out 'The Great Captain!' and Îbal his son ran forward to Aldarion's stirrup. 'Lord Captain!' he said eagerly.

'What is it? I am in haste,' said Aldarion; for now his mood was changed, and he felt wrathful and bitter.

'I would but ask,' said the boy, 'how old must a man be, before he may go over sea in a ship, like my father?'

'As old as the hills, and with no other hope in life,' said Aldarion. 'Or whenever he has a mind! But your mother, Ulbar's son: will she not greet me?'

When Ulbar's wife came forward Aldarion took her hand. 'Will you receive this of me?' he said. 'It is but little return for six years of a good man's aid that you gave me.' Then from a wallet under his tunic he took a jewel red like fire, upon a band of gold, and he pressed it into her hand. 'From the King of the Elves it came,' he said. 'But he will think it well-bestowed, when I tell him.' Then Aldarion bade farewell to the people there, and rode away, having no mind now to stay in that house. When Hallatan heard of his strange coming and going he marvelled, until more news ran through the countryside.

Aldarion rode only a short way from Hyarastorni and then he stayed his horse, and spoke to Henderch his companion. 'Whatever welcome awaits you, friend, out West, I will not keep you from it. Ride now home with my thanks. I have a mind to go alone.'

'It is not fitting, Lord Captain,' said Henderch.

'It is not,' said Aldarion. 'But that is the way of it. Farewell!'

Then he rode on alone to Armenelos, and never again set foot in Emerië.

When Aldarion left the chamber, Meneldur looked at the letter that his son had given him, wondering; for he saw that it came from King Gil-galad in Lindon. It was sealed and bore his device of white stars upon a blue rondure.[24] Upon the outer fold was written:

Given at Mithlond to the hand of the Lord Aldarion King's Heir of Númenórë, to be delivered to the High King at Armenelos in person.

Then Meneldur broke the seal and read:

Ereinion Gil-galad son of Fingon to Tar-Meneldur of the line of Eärendil, greeting: the Valar keep you and may no shadow fall upon the Isle of Kings.

Long I have owed you thanks, for you have so many times sent to me your son Anardil Aldarion: the greatest Elf-friend that now is among Men, as I deem. At this time I ask your pardon, if I have detained him overlong in my service; for I had great need of the knowledge of Men and their tongues which he alone possesses. He has dared many perils to bring me counsel. Of my need he will speak to you; yet he does not guess how great it is, being young and full of hope. Therefore I write this for the eyes of the King of Númenórë only.

A new shadow arises in the East. It is no tyranny of evil Men, as your son believes; but a servant of Morgoth is stirring, and evil things wake again. Each year it gains in strength, for most Men are ripe to its purpose. Not far off is the day, I judge, when it will become too great for the Eldar unaided to withstand. Therefore, whenever I behold a tall ship of the Kings of Men, my heart is eased. And now I make bold to seek your help. If you have any strength of Men to spare, lend it to me, I beg.

Your son will report to you, if you will, all our reasons. But in fine it is his counsel (and that is ever wise) that when assault comes, as it surely will, we should seek to hold the Westlands, where still the Eldar dwell, and Men of your race, whose hearts are not yet darkened. At the least we must defend Eriador about the long rivers west of the mountains that we name Hithaeglir: our chief defence. But in that mountain-wall there is a great gap southward in the land of Calenardhon; and by that way inroad from the East must come. Already enmity creeps along the coast towards it. It could be defended and assault hindered, did we hold some seat of power upon the nearer shore.

So the Lord Aldarion long has seen. At Vinyalondë by the mouth of Gwathló he has long laboured to establish such a haven, secure against sea and land; but his mighty works have been in vain. He has great knowledge in such matters, for he has learned much of Círdan, and he understands better than any the needs of your great ships. But he has never had men enough; whereas Círdan has no wrights or masons to spare.

The King will know his own needs; but if he will listen with favour to the Lord Aldarion, and support him as he may, then hope will be greater in the world. The memories of the First Age are dim, and all things in Middle-earth grow colder. Let not the ancient friendship of Eldar and Dúnedain wane also.

Behold! The darkness that is to come is filled with hatred for us, but it hates you no less. The Great Sea will not be too wide for its wings, if it is suffered to come to full growth.

Manwë keep you under the One, and send fair wind to your sails.

Meneldur let the parchment fall into his lap. Great clouds borne upon a wind out of the East brought darkness early, and the tall candles at his side seemed to dwindle in the gloom that filled his chamber.

'May Eru call me before such a time comes!' he cried aloud. Then to himself he said: 'Alas! that his pride and my coolness have kept our minds apart so long. But sooner now than I had resolved it will be the course of wisdom to resign the Sceptre to him. For these things are beyond my reach.

'When the Valar gave to us the Land of Gift they did not make us their vice-gerents: we were given the Kingdom of Númenor, not of the world. They are the Lords. Here we were to put away hatred and war; for war was ended, and Morgoth thrust forth from Arda. So I deemed, and so was taught.

'Yet if the world grows again dark, the Lords must know; and they have sent me no sign. Unless this be the sign. What then? Our fathers were rewarded for the aid they gave in the defeat of the Great Shadow. Shall their sons stand aloof, if evil finds a new head?

'I am in too great doubt to rule. To prepare or to let be? To prepare for war, which is yet only guessed: train craftsmen and tillers in the midst of peace for bloodspilling and battle: put iron in the hands of greedy captains who will love only conquest, and count the slain as their glory? Will they say to Eru: *At least your enemies were amongst them*? Or to fold hands, while friends die unjustly: let men live in blind peace, until the ravisher is at the gate? What then will they do: match naked hands against iron and die in vain, or flee leaving the cries of women behind them? Will they say to Eru: *At least I spilled no blood*?

'When either way may lead to evil, of what worth is choice? Let the Valar rule under Eru! I will resign the Sceptre to Aldarion. Yet that also is a choice, for I know well which road he will take. Unless Erendis . . .'

Then Meneldur's thought turned in disquiet to Erendis in Emerië. 'But there is little hope there (if it should be called hope). He will not bend in such grave matters. I know her choice – even were she to listen long enough to understand. For her heart has no wings beyond Númenor, and she has no guess of the cost. If her choice should lead to death in her own time, she would die bravely. But what will she do with life, and other wills? The Valar themselves, even as I, must wait to discover.'

Aldarion came back to Rómenna on the fourth day after Hirilondë had returned to haven. He was way-stained and weary, and he went at once to Eämbar, upon which he now intended to dwell. By that time, as he found to his embitterment, many tongues were already wagging in the City. On the next day he gathered men in Rómenna and brought them to Armenelos. There he bade some fell all the trees, save one, in his garden, and take them to the shipyards; others he commanded to raze his house to the ground. The white Elven-tree alone he spared; and when the woodcutters were gone he looked at it, standing amid the desolation, and he saw for the first time that it was in itself beautiful. In its slow Elven growth it was yet but twelve feet high, straight, slender, youthful, now budded with its winter flowers upon upheld branches pointing to the sky. It recalled to him his daughter, and he said: 'I will call you also Ancalimë. May you and she stand so in long life, unbent by wind or will, and unclipped!'

On the third day after his return from Emerië Aldarion sought the King. Tar-Meneldur sat still in his chair and waited. Looking at his son he was afraid; for Aldarion was changed: his face was become grey, cold, and hostile, as the sea when the sun is suddenly veiled in dull cloud. Standing before his father he spoke slowly with tone of contempt rather than of wrath.

'What part you have played in this you yourself know best,' he said. 'But a King should consider how much a man will endure, though he be a subject, even his son. If you would shackle me to this Island, then you choose your chain ill. I have now neither wife, nor love of this land, left. I will go from this misenchanted isle of daydreams where women in their insolence would have men cringe. I will use my days to some purpose, elsewhere, where I am not scorned, more welcome in honour. Another Heir you may find more fit for a house-servant. Of my inheritance I demand only this: the ship Hirilondë and as many men as it will hold. My daughter I would take also, were she older; but I will commend her to my mother. Unless you dote upon sheep, you will not hinder this, and will not suffer the child to be stunted, reared among mute women in cold insolence and contempt of her kin. She is of the Line of Elros, and no other descendant will you have through your son. I have done. I will go now about business more profitable.'

Thus far Meneldur had sat in patience with downcast eyes and made no sign. But now he sighed, and looked up. 'Aldarion, my son,' he said sadly, 'the King would say that you also show cold insolence and contempt of your kin, and yourself condemn others unheard; but your father who loves you and grieves for you will remit that. The fault is not mine only that I have not ere now understood your purposes. But as for what you have suffered (of which, alas! too many now speak): I am guiltless. Erendis I have loved, and since our hearts lean the same way I have thought that she had much to endure that was hard. Your purposes are now become clear to me, though if you are in mood to hear aught but praise I would say that at first your own pleasure also led you. And it may be that things would have been otherwise if you had spoken more openly long ago.'

'The King may have some grievance in this,' cried Aldarion, now more hotly, 'but not the one you speak of! To her at least I spoke long and often: to cold ears uncomprehending. As well might a truant boy talk of tree-climbing to a nurse anxious only about the tearing of clothes and the due time of meals! I love her, or I should care less. The past I will keep in my heart; the future is dead. She does not love me, or aught else. She loves herself with Númenor as a setting, and myself as a tame hound, to drowse by the hearth until she has a mind to walk in her own fields. But since hounds now seem too gross, she will have Ancalimë to pipe in a cage. But enough of this. Have I the King's leave to depart? Or has he some command?'

'The King,' answered Tar-Meneldur, 'has thought much about these matters, in what seem the long days since last you were in Armenelos. He has read the letter of Gil-galad, which is earnest and grave in tone. Alas! To his prayer and your wishes the King of Númenor must say *nay*. He cannot do otherwise, according to his understanding of the perils of either course: to prepare for war, or not to prepare.'

Aldarion shrugged his shoulders, and took a step as if to go. But Meneldur held up his hand commanding attention, and continued: 'Nevertheless, the King, though he has now ruled the land of Númenor for one hundred and forty-two years, has no certainty that his understanding of the matter is sufficient for a just decision in matters of such high import and peril.' He paused, and taking up a parchment written in his own hand he read from it in a clear voice:

Therefore: first for the honour of his well-beloved son; and second for the better direction of the realm in courses which his son more clearly understands, the King has resolved: that he will forthwith resign the Sceptre to his son, who shall now become Tar-Aldarion, the King.

'This,' said Meneldur, 'when it is proclaimed, will make known to all my thought concerning this present pass. It will raise you above scorn; and it will set free your powers so that other losses may seem more easy to endure. The letter of Gil-galad, when you are King, you shall answer as seems fit to the holder of the Sceptre.'

Aldarion stood still for a moment in amaze. He had braced himself to face the King's anger, which wilfully he had endeavoured to kindle. Now he stood confounded. Then, as one swept from his feet by a sudden wind from a quarter unexpected, he fell to his knees before his father; but after a moment he raised his bowed head and laughed – so he always did, when he heard of any deed of great generosity, for it gladdened his heart.

'Father,' he said, 'ask the King to forget my insolence to him. For he is a great King, and his humility sets him far above my pride. I am conquered: I submit myself wholly. That such a King should resign the Sceptre while in vigour and wisdom is not to be thought.'

'Yet so it is resolved,' said Meneldur. 'The Council shall be summoned forthwith.'

When the Council came together, after seven days had passed, Tar-Meneldur acquainted them with his resolve, and laid the scroll before them. Then all were amazed, not yet knowing what were the courses of which the King spoke; and all demurred, begging him to delay his decision, save only Hallatan of Hyarastorni. For he had long held his kinsman Aldarion in esteem, though his own life and likings were far otherwise; and he judged the King's deed to be noble, and timed with shrewdness, if it must be.

But to those others who urged this or that against his resolve Meneldur answered: 'Not without thought did I come to this resolution, and in my thought I have considered all the reasons that you wisely argue. Now and not later is the time most fit for my will to be published, for reasons which though none here has uttered all must guess. Forthwith then let this decree be proclaimed. But if you will, it shall not take effect until the time of the *Erukyermë* in the Spring. Till then, I will hold the Sceptre.'

When news came to Emerië of the proclamation of the decree Erendis was dismayed; for she read therein a rebuke by the King in whose favour she had trusted. In this she saw truly, but that anything else of greater import lay behind she did not conceive. Soon afterwards there came a message from Tar-Meneldur, a command indeed, though graciously worded. She was bidden to come to Armenelos and to bring with her the lady Ancalimë, there to abide at least until the *Erukyermë* and the proclamation of the new King.

'He is swift to strike,' she thought. 'So I should have foreseen. He will strip me of all. But myself he shall not command, though it be by the mouth of his father.'

Therefore she returned answer to Tar-Meneldur: 'King and father, my daughter Ancalimë must come indeed, if you command it. I beg that you will consider her years, and see to it that she is lodged in quiet. For myself, I pray you to excuse me. I learn that my house in Armenelos has been destroyed; and I would not at this time willingly be a guest, least of all upon a house-ship among mariners. Here then permit me to remain in my solitude, unless it be the King's will also to take back this house.'

This letter Tar-Meneldur read with concern, but it missed its mark in his heart. He showed it to Aldarion, to whom it seemed chiefly aimed. Then Aldarion read the letter; and the King, regarding the face of his son, said: 'Doubtless you are grieved. But for what else did you hope?'

'Not for this, at least,' said Aldarion. 'It is far below my hope of her. She has dwindled; and if I have wrought this, then black is my blame. But do the large shrink in adversity? This was not the way, not even in hate or revenge! She should have demanded that a great house be prepared for her, called for a Queen's escort, and come back to Armenelos with her beauty adorned, royally, with the star on her brow; then well nigh all the Isle of Númenor she might have bewitched to her part, and made me seem madman and churl. The Valar be my witness, I would rather have had it so: rather a beautiful Queen to thwart me and flout me, than freedom to rule while the Lady Elestirnë falls down dim into her own twilight.'

Then with a bitter laugh he gave back the letter to the King. 'Well: so it is,' he said. 'But if one has a distaste to dwell on a ship among mariners, another may be excused dislike of a sheep-farm among serving-women. But I will not have my daughter so schooled. At least she shall choose by knowledge.' He rose, and begged leave to go.

The Further Course of the Narrative

From the point where Aldarion read the letter from Erendis, refusing to return to Armenelos, the story can only be traced in glimpses and snatches, from notes and jottings: and even those do not constitute the fragments of a wholly consistent story, being composed at different times and often at odds with themselves.

It seems that when Aldarion became King of Númenor in the year 883 he determined to revisit Middle-earth at once, and departed for Mithlond either in the same year or the next. It is recorded that on the prow of Hirilondë he set no bough of *orolairë*, but the image of an eagle with golden beak and jewelled eyes, which was the gift of Círdan.

It perched there, by the craft of its maker, as if poised for flight unerring to some far mark that it espied. 'This sign shall lead us to our aim,' he said. 'For our return let the Valar care – if our deeds do not displease them.'

It is also stated that 'no records are now left of the later voyages that Aldarion made', but that 'it is known that he went much on land as well as sea, and went up the River Gwathló as far as Tharbad, and there met Galadriel'. There is no mention elsewhere of this meeting; but at that time Galadriel and Celeborn were dwelling in Eregion, at no great distance from Tharbad (see p. 235).

But all Aldarion's labours were swept away. The works that he began again at Vinyalondë were never completed, and the sea gnawed them.[25] Nevertheless he laid the foundation for the achievement of Tar-Minastir long years after, in the first war with Sauron, and but for his works the fleets of Númenor could not have brought their power in time to the right place – as he foresaw. Already the hostility was growing and dark men out of the mountains were thrusting into Enedwaith. But in Aldarion's day the Númenóreans did not yet desire more room, and his Venturers remained a small people, admired but little emulated.

There is no mention of any further development of the alliance with Gil-galad, or of the sending of the aid that he requested in his letter to Tar-Meneldur; it is said indeed that

Aldarion was too late, or too early. Too late: for the power that hated Númenor had already waked. Too early: for the time was not yet ripe for Númenor to show its power or to come back into the battle for the world.

There was a stir in Númenor when Tar-Aldarion determined to return to Middle-earth in 883 or 884, for no King had ever before left the Isle, and the Council had no precedent. It seems that Meneldur was offered but refused the regency, and that Hallatan of Hyarastorni became regent, either appointed by the Council or by Tar-Aldarion himself.

Of the history of Ancalimë during those years when she was growing up there is no certain form. There is less doubt concerning her somewhat ambiguous character, and the influence that her mother exerted on her. She was less prim than Erendis, and natively liked display, jewels, music, admiration, and deference; but she liked them at will and not unceasingly, and she made her mother and the white house in Emerië an excuse for escape. She approved, as it were, both Erendis' treatment of Aldarion on his late return, but also Aldarion's anger, impenitence, and subsequent relentless dismissal of Erendis from his heart and concern. She had a profound dislike of obligatory marriage, and in marriage of any constraint on her will. Her mother had spoken unceasingly against men, and indeed a remarkable example of Erendis' teaching in this respect is preserved:

Men in Númenor are half-Elves (said Erendis), especially the high men; they are neither the one nor the other. The long life that they were granted deceives them, and they dally in the world, children in mind, until age finds them – and then many only forsake play out of doors for play in their houses. They turn their play into great matters and great matters into play. They would be craftsmen and loremasters and heroes all at once; and women to them are but fires on the hearth – for others to tend, until they are tired of play in the evening. All things were made for their service: hills are for quarries, rivers to furnish water or to turn wheels, trees for boards, women for their body's need, or if fair to adorn their table and hearth; and children to be teased when nothing else is to do – but they would as soon play with their hounds' whelps. To all they are gracious and kind, merry as larks in the morning (if the sun shines); for they are never wrathful if they can avoid it. Men should be gay, they hold, generous as the rich, giving away what they do not need. Anger they show only when they become aware, suddenly, that there are other wills in the world beside their own. Then they will be as ruthless as the seawind if anything dare to withstand them.

Thus it is, Ancalimë, and we cannot alter it. For men fashioned Númenor: men, those heroes of old that they sing of – of their women we hear less, save that they wept when their men were slain. Númenor was to be a rest after war. But if they weary of rest and the plays of peace, soon they will go back to their great play, manslaying and war. Thus it is; and we are set here among them. But we need not assent. If we love Númenor also, let us enjoy it before they ruin it. We also are daughters of the great, and we have wills and courage of our own. Therefore do not bend, Ancalimë. Once bend a little, and they will bend you further until you are bowed down. Sink your roots into the rock, and face the wind, though it blow away all your leaves.

Moreover, and more potently, Erendis had made Ancalimë accustomed to the society of women: the cool, quiet, gentle life of Emerië without interruptions or alarms. Boys, like Îbal, shouted. Men rode up blowing horns at strange hours, and were fed with great noise. They begot children and left them in the care of women when they were troublesome. And though childbirth had less of ills and peril, Númenor was not an 'earthly paradise', and the weariness of labour or of all making was not taken away.

Ancalimë, like her father, was resolute in pursuing her policies; and like him she was obstinate, taking the opposite course to any that was counselled. She had something of her mother's coldness and sense of personal injury; and deep in her heart, almost but not quite forgotten, was the firmness with which Aldarion had unclasped her hand and set her down when he was in haste to be gone. She loved dearly the downlands of her home, and never (as she said) in her life could she sleep at peace far from the sound of sheep. But she did not refuse the Heirship, and determined that when her day came she would be a powerful Ruling Queen; and when so, to live where and how she pleased.

It seems that for some eighteen years after Aldarion became King he was often gone from Númenor; and during that time Ancalimë passed her days both in Emerië and in Armenelos, for Queen Almarian took a great liking to her, and indulged her as she had indulged Aldarion in his youth. In Armenelos she was treated with deference by all, and not least by Aldarion; and though at first she was ill at ease, missing the wide airs of her home, in time she ceased to be abashed, and became aware that men looked with wonder upon her beauty, now come to its full. As she grew older she became ever more wilful, and she found irksome the company of Erendis, who behaved like a widow and would not be Queen; but she continued to return to Emerië, both as a retreat from Armenelos and because she desired thus to vex Aldarion. She was clever, and malicious, and saw promise of sport as the prize for which her mother and her father did battle.

Now in the year 892, when Ancalimë was nineteen years old, she was proclaimed the King's Heir (at a far earlier age than had previously been the case, see p. 177); and at that time Tar-Aldarion caused the law of succession in Númenor to be changed. It is said specifically that Tar-Aldarion did this 'for reasons of private concern, rather than policy', and out of 'his long resolve to defeat Erendis'. The change of the law is referred to in *The Lord of the Rings*, Appendix A (I i):

> The sixth King [Tar-Aldarion] left only one child, a daughter. She became the first Queen [i.e. Ruling Queen]; for it was then made a law of the royal house that the eldest child of the King, whether man or woman, should receive the sceptre.

But elsewhere the new law is formulated differently from this. The fullest and clearest account states in the first place that the 'old law', as it was afterwards called, was not in fact a Númenórean 'law', but an inherited custom which circumstances had not yet called in question; and according to that custom the Ruler's eldest son inherited the Sceptre. It was understood that if there were no son the nearest male kinsman *of male descent* from Elros Tar-Minyatur would be the Heir. Thus if Tar-Meneldur had had no son the Heir would not have been Valandil his nephew (son of his sister Silmarien), but Malantur his cousin (grandson of Tar-Elendil's younger brother Eärendur). But by the 'new law' the (eldest) daughter of the Ruler inherited the Sceptre, if he had no son (this being, of course, in contradiction to what is said in *The Lord of the Rings*). By the advice of the Council it was added that she was free to refuse.[26] In such a case, according to the 'new law', the heir of the Ruler was the nearest male kinsman whether by male or female descent. Thus if Ancalimë had refused the Sceptre Tar-Aldarion's heir would have been Soronto, the son of his sister Ailinel; and if Ancalimë had resigned the Sceptre or died childless Soronto would likewise have been her heir.

It was also ordained at the instance of the Council that a female heir must resign, if she remained unwed beyond a certain time; and to these provisions Tar-Aldarion added that the King's Heir should not wed save in the Line of Elros, and that any who did so should cease to be eligible for the Heirship. It is said that this ordinance arose directly from Aldarion's disastrous marriage to Erendis and his reflections upon it; for she was not of the Line of Elros, and had a lesser life-span, and he believed that therein lay the root of all their troubles.

Beyond question these provisions of the 'new law' were recorded in such detail because they were to bear closely on the later history of these reigns; but unhappily very little can now be said of it.

At some later date Tar-Aldarion rescinded the law that a Ruling Queen must marry, or resign (and this was certainly due to Ancalimë's reluctance to countenance either alternative); but the marriage of the Heir to another member of the Line of Elros remained the custom ever after.[27]

At all events, suitors for Ancalimë's hand soon began to appear in Emerië, and not only because of the change in her position, for the fame of her beauty, of her aloofness and disdain, and of the strangeness of her upbringing had run through the land. In that time the people began to speak of her as Emerwen Aranel, the Princess Shepherdess. To escape from importunity Ancalimë, aided by the old woman Zamîn, went into hiding at a farm on the borders of the lands of Hallatan of Hyarastorni, where she lived for a time the life of a shepherdess. The accounts (which are indeed no more than hasty jottings) vary as to how her parents responded to this state of affairs. According to one, Erendis herself knew where Ancalimë was, and approved the reason for her flight, while Aldarion prevented the Council from searching for her, since it was to his mind that his daughter should act thus independently. According to another, however, Erendis was disturbed at Ancalimë's flight and the King was wrathful; and at this time Erendis attempted some reconciliation with him, at least in respect of Ancalimë. But Aldarion was unmoved, declaring that the King had no wife, but that he had a daughter and an heir; and that he did not believe that Erendis was ignorant of her hiding-place.

What is certain is that Ancalimë fell in with a shepherd who was minding flocks in the same region; and to her this man named himself Mámandil. Ancalimë was all unused to such company as his, and she took delight in his singing, in which he was skilled; and he sang to her songs that came out of far-off days, when the Edain pastured their flocks in Eriador long ago, before ever they met the Eldar. They met thus in the pastures often and often, and he altered the songs of the lovers of old and brought into them the names of Emerwen and Mámandil; and Ancalimë feigned not to understand the drift of the words. But at length he declared his love for her openly, and she drew back, and refused him, saying that her fate lay between them, for she was the Heir of the King. But Mámandil was

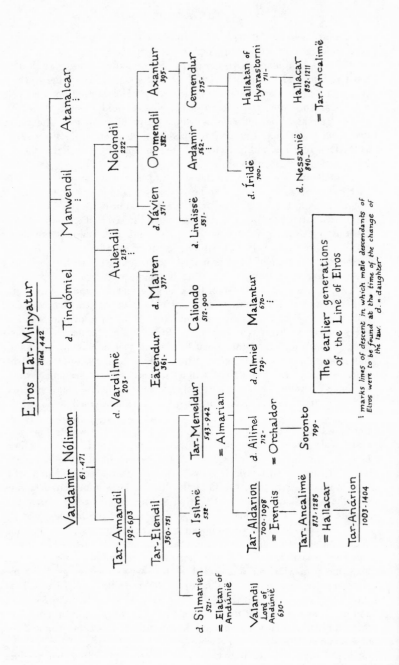

Elros Tar-Minyatur

The earlier generations of the Line of Elros

not abashed, and he laughed, and told her that his right name was Hallacar, son of Hallatan of Hyarastorni, of the line of Elros Tar-Minyatur. 'And how else could any wooer find you?' he said. Then Ancalimë was angry, because he had deceived her, knowing from the first who she was; but he answered: 'That is true in part. I contrived indeed to meet the Lady whose ways were so strange that I was curious to see more of her. But then I loved Emerwen, and I care not now who she may be. Do not think that I pursue your high place; for far rather would I have it that you were Emerwen only. I rejoice but in this, that I also am of the Line of Elros, because otherwise I deem that we could not wed.'

'We could,' said Ancalimë, 'if I had any mind to such a state. I could lay down my royalty, and be free. But if I were to do so, I should be free to wed whom I will; and that would be Úner (which is "Noman"), whom I prefer above all others.'

It was however to Hallacar that Ancalimë was wedded in the end. From one version it appears that the persistence of Hallacar in his suit despite her rejection of him, and the urging of the Council that she choose a husband for the quiet of the realm, led to their marriage not many years after their first meeting among the flocks in Emerië. But elsewhere it is said that she remained unmarried so long that her cousin Soronto, relying on the provision of the new law, called upon her to surrender the Heirship, and that she then married Hallacar in order to spite Soronto. In yet another brief notice it is implied that she wedded Hallacar after Aldarion had rescinded the provision, in order to put an end to Soronto's hopes of becoming King if Ancalimë died childless.

However this may be, the story is clear that Ancalimë did not desire love, nor did she wish for a son; and she said: 'Must I become like Queen Almarian, and dote upon him?' Her life with Hallacar was unhappy, and she begrudged him her son Anárion, and there was strife between them thereafter. She sought to subject him, claiming to be the owner of his land, and forbidding him to dwell upon it, for she would not, as she said, have her husband a farm-steward. From this time comes the last tale that is recorded of those unhappy things. For Ancalimë would let none of her women wed, and although for fear of her most were restrained, they came from the country about and had lovers whom they wished to marry. But Hallacar in secret arranged for them to be wedded; and he declared that he would give a last feast at his own house, before he left it. To this feast he invited Ancalimë, saying that it was the house of his kindred, and should be given a farewell of courtesy.

Ancalimë came, attended by all her women, for she did not care to be waited on by men. She found the house all lit and arrayed as for a great feast, and men of the household attired in garlands as for their weddings, and each with another garland in his hands for a bride. 'Come!' said Hallacar. 'The weddings are prepared, and the bride-chambers ready.

But since it cannot be thought that we should ask the Lady Ancalimë, King's Heir, to lie with a farm-steward, then, alas! she must sleep alone tonight.' And Ancalimë perforce remained there, for it was too far to ride back, nor would she go unattended. Neither men nor women hid their smiles; and Ancalimë would not come to the feast, but lay abed listening to the laughter far off and thinking it aimed at herself. Next day she rode off in a cold rage, and Hallacar sent three men to escort her. Thus he was revenged, for she came never back to Emerië, where the very sheep seemed to make scorn of her. But she pursued Hallacar with hatred afterwards.

Of the later years of Tar-Aldarion nothing can now be said, save that he seems to have continued his voyages to Middle-earth, and more than once left Ancalimë as his regent. His last voyage took place about the end of the first millennium of the Second Age; and in the year 1075 Ancalimë became the first Ruling Queen of Númenor. It is told that after the death of Tar-Aldarion in 1098 Tar-Ancalimë neglected all her father's policies and gave no further aid to Gil-galad in Lindon. Her son Anárion, who was afterwards the eighth Ruler of Númenor, first had two daughters. They disliked and feared the Queen, and refused the Heirship, remaining unwed, since the Queen would not in revenge allow them to marry.[28] Anárion's son Súrion was born the last, and was the ninth Ruler of Númenor.

Of Erendis it is said that when old age came upon her, neglected by Ancalimë and in bitter loneliness, she longed once more for Aldarion; and learning that he was gone from Númenor on what proved to be his last voyage but that he was soon expected to return, she left Emerië at last and journeyed unrecognised and unknown to the haven of Rómenna. There, it seems, she met her fate; but only the words 'Erendis perished in water in the year 985' remain to suggest how it came to pass.

NOTES

Chronology

Anardil (Aldarion) was born in the year 700 of the Second Age, and his first voyage to Middle-earth took place in 725–7. Meneldur his father became King of Númenor in 740. The Guild of Venturers was founded in 750, and Aldarion was proclaimed King's Heir in 800. Erendis was born in 771. Aldarion's seven year voyage (p. 178) covered the years 806–13, the first voyage of the Palarran (p. 179) 816–20, the voyage of seven ships in defiance of Tar-Meneldur (p. 180) 824–9, and the voyage of fourteen years that followed immediately on the last (pp. 180–1) 829–43.

Aldarion and Erendis were betrothed in 858; the years of the voyage undertaken by Aldarion after his betrothal (p. 187) were 863–9, and the wedding was in 870. Ancalimë was born in the Spring of 873. The Hirilondë sailed in the Spring of 877 and Aldarion's return, followed by the breach with Erendis, took place in 882; he received the Sceptre of Númenor in 883.

1 In the 'Description of Númenor' (p. 167) he is called Tar-Meneldur Elentirmo (Star-watcher). See also his entry in 'The Line of Elros' (p. 219).

2 Soronto's part in the story can now only be glimpsed; see p. 211.

3 As is told in the 'Description of Númenor' (p. 171) it was Vëantur who first achieved the voyage to Middle-earth in the year 600 of the Second Age (he was born in 451). In the Tale of Years in Appendix B to *The Lord of the Rings* the annal entry for the year 600 states: 'The first ships of the Númenóreans appear off the coasts.'

There is a description in a late philological essay of the first meeting of the Númenóreans with Men of Eriador at that time: 'It was six hundred years after the departure of the survivors of the Atani [Edain] over the sea to Númenor that a ship first came again out of the West to Middle-earth and passed up the Gulf of Lhûn. Its captain and mariners were welcomed by Gil-galad; and thus was begun the friendship and alliance of Númenor with the Eldar of Lindon. The news spread swiftly and Men in Eriador were filled with wonder. Although in the First Age they had dwelt in the East, rumours of the terrible war "beyond the Western Mountains" [i.e. Ered Luin] had reached them; but their traditions preserved no clear account of it, and they believed that all the Men who dwelt in the lands beyond had been destroyed or drowned in great tumults of fire and inrushing seas. But since it was still said among them that those Men had in years beyond memory been kinsmen of their own, they sent messages to Gil-galad asking leave to meet the shipmen "who had returned from death in the deeps of the Sea". Thus it came about that there was a meeting between them on the Tower Hills; and to that meeting with the Númenóreans came twelve Men only out of Eriador, Men of high heart and courage, for most of their people feared that the newcomers were perilous spirits of the Dead. But when they looked on the shipmen fear left them, though for a while they stood silent in awe; for mighty as they were themselves accounted among their kin, the shipmen resembled rather Elvish lords than mortal Men in bearing and apparel. Nonetheless they felt no doubt of their ancient kinship; and likewise the shipmen looked with glad surprise upon the Men of Middle-earth, for it had been believed in Númenor that the

Men left behind were descended from the evil Men who in the last days of the war against Morgoth had been summoned by him out of the East. But now they looked upon faces free from the Shadow and Men who could have walked in Númenor and not been thought aliens save in their clothes and their arms. Then suddenly, after the silence, both the Númenóreans and the Men of Eriador spoke words of welcome and greeting in their own tongues, as if addressing friends and kinsmen after a long parting. At first they were disappointed, for neither side could understand the other; but when they mingled in friendship they found that they shared very many words still clearly recognisable, and others that could be understood with attention, and they were able to converse haltingly about simple matters.' Elsewhere in this essay it is explained that these Men dwelt about Lake Evendim, in the North Downs and the Weather Hills, and in the lands between as far as the Brandywine, west of which they often wandered though they did not dwell there. They were friendly with the Elves, though they held them in awe; and they feared the Sea and would not look upon it. It appears that they were in origin Men of the same stock as the Peoples of Bëor and Hador who had not crossed the Blue Mountains into Beleriand during the First Age.

4   The son of the King's Heir: Aldarion son of Meneldur. Tar-Elendil did not resign the sceptre to Meneldur until a further fifteen years had passed.

5   *Eruhantalë*: 'Thanksgiving to Eru', the autumn feast in Númenor; see the 'Description of Númenor' p. 166.

6   (Sîr) Angren was the Elvish name of the river Isen. Ras Morthil, a name not otherwise found, must be the great headland at the end of the northern arm of the Bay of Belfalas, which was also called Andrast (Long Cape).
     The reference to 'the country of Amroth where the Nandor Elves still dwell' can be taken to imply that the tale of Aldarion and Erendis was written down in Gondor before the departure of the last ship from the haven of the Silvan Elves near Dol Amroth in the year 1981 of the Third Age; see pp. 240 ff.

7   For Uinen the spouse of Ossë (Maiar of the Sea) see *The Silmarillion* p. 30. There it is said that 'the Númenóreans lived long in her protection, and held her in reverence equal to the Valar'.

8   It is stated that the Guildhouse of the Venturers 'was confiscated by the Kings, and removed to the western haven of Andúnië; all its records perished' (i.e. in the Downfall), including all the accurate charts of Númenor. But it is not said when this confiscation of Eämbar took place.

9   The river was afterwards called Gwathló or Greyflood, and the haven Lond Daer; see pp. 261 ff.

10   Cf. *The Silmarillion* p. 148: 'The Men of that House [i.e. of Bëor]

were dark or brown of hair, with grey eyes.' According to a genealogical table of the House of Bëor Erendis was descended from Bereth, who was the sister of Baragund and Belegund, and thus the aunt of Morwen mother of Túrin Turambar and of Rían the mother of Tuor.

11 On different life-spans among the Númenóreans see Note 1 to 'The Line of Elros', p. 224.

12 On the tree *oiolairë* see the 'Description of Númenor', p. 167.

13 This is to be understood as a portent.

14 Cf. the *Akallabêth* (*The Silmarillion* p. 277), where it is told that in the days of Ar-Pharazôn 'ever and anon a great ship of the Númenóreans would founder and not return to haven, though such a grief had not till then befallen them since the rising of the Star'.

15 Valandil was Aldarion's cousin, for he was the son of Silmarien, daughter of Tar-Elendil and sister of Tar-Meneldur. Valandil, first of the Lords of Andúnië, was the ancestor of Elendil the Tall, father of Isildur and Anárion.

16 *Erukyermë*: 'Prayer to Eru', the feast of the Spring in Númenor; see the 'Description of Númenor' p. 166.

17 It is said in the *Akallabêth* (*The Silmarillion* pp. 262–3) that 'at times, when all the air was clear and the sun was in the east, they would look out and descry far off in the west a city white-shining on a distant shore, and a great harbour and a tower. For in those days the Númenóreans were far-sighted; yet even so it was only the keenest eyes among them that could see this vision, from the Meneltarma maybe, or from some tall ship that lay off their western coast. . . . But the wise among them knew that this distant land was not indeed the Blessed Realm of Valinor, but was Avallónë, the haven of the Eldar upon Eressëa, easternmost of the Undying Lands.'

18 Thus came, it is said, the manner of the Kings and Queens afterward to wear as a star a white jewel upon the brow, and they had no crown. [Author's note.]

19 In the Westlands and in Andúnië the Elven-tongue [Sindarin] was spoken by high and low. In that tongue Erendis was nurtured; but Aldarion spoke the Númenórean speech, although as all high men of Númenor he knew also the tongue of Beleriand. [Author's note.] – Elsewhere, in a note on the languages of Númenor, it is said that the general use of Sindarin in the north-west of the Isle was due to the fact that those parts were largely settled by people of 'Bëorian' descent; and the People of Bëor had in Beleriand early abandoned their own speech and adopted Sindarin. (Of this there is no mention in *The Silmarillion*, though it is said there (p. 148) that in Dor-lómin in the days of Fingolfin the people of Hador did not forget their own speech, 'and from it came the common tongue of Númenor'.) In other regions of Númenor Adûnaic was the native language of the

people, though Sindarin was known in some degree to nearly all; and
in the royal house, and in most of the houses of the noble or learned,
Sindarin was usually the native tongue, until after the days of Tar-
Atanamir. (It is said later in the present narrative (p. 194) that Aldarion
actually preferred the Númenórean speech; it may be that in this
he was exceptional.) This note further states that although Sindarin
as used for a long period by mortal Men tended to become divergent
and dialectal, this process was largely checked in Númenor, at least
among the nobles and the learned, by their contact with the Eldar
of Eressëa and Lindon. Quenya was not a spoken tongue in Númenor.
It was known only to the learned and to the families of high descent,
to whom it was taught in their early youth. It was used in official
documents intended for preservation, such as the Laws, and the
Scroll and Annals of the Kings (cf. the *Akallabêth* p. 267: 'in the
Scroll of Kings the name Herunúmen was inscribed in the High-
elven speech'), and often in more recondite works of lore. It was also
largely used in nomenclature: the official names of all places, regions,
and geographical features in the land were of Quenya form (though
they usually had also local names, generally of the same meaning, in
either Sindarin or Adúnaic). The personal names, and especially the
official and public names, of all members of the royal house, and of
the Line of Elros in general, were given in Quenya form.

In a reference to these matters in *The Lord of the Rings*, Appendix
F, I (section *Of Men*), a somewhat different impression is given of the
place of Sindarin among the languages of Númenor: 'The *Dúnedain*
alone of all races of Men knew and spoke an Elvish tongue; for their
forefathers had learned the Sindarin tongue, and this they handed
on to their children as a matter of lore, changing little with the
passing of the years.'

20   *Elanor* was a small golden star-shaped flower; it grew also upon the
mound of Cerin Amroth in Lothlórien (*The Fellowship of the Ring*
II 6). Sam Gamgee gave its name to his daughter, on Frodo's suggestion (*The Return of the King* VI 9).

21   See note 10 above for Erendis' descent from Bereth, the sister of
Morwen's father Baragund.

22   It is stated that the Númenóreans, like the Eldar, avoided the be-
getting of children if they foresaw any separation likely between
husband and wife between the conception of the child and at least
its very early years. Aldarion stayed in his house for a very brief time
after the birth of his daughter, according to the Númenóreans' idea
of the fitness of things.

23   In a note on the 'Council of the Sceptre' at this time in the history of
Númenor it is said that this Council had no powers to govern the
King save by advice; and no such powers had yet been desired or
dreamed of as needful. The Council was composed of members from

each of the divisions of Númenor; but the King's Heir when proclaimed was also a member, so that he might learn of the government of the land, and others also the King might summon, or ask to be chosen, if they had special knowledge of matters at any time in debate. At this time there were only two members of the Council (other than Aldarion) who were of the Line of Elros: Valandil of Andúnië for the Andustar, and Hallatan of Hyarastorni for the Mittalmar; but they owed their place not to their descent or their wealth, but to the esteem and love in which they were held in their countries. (In the *Akallabêth* (p. 268) it is said that 'the Lord of Andúnië was ever among the chief councillors of the Sceptre'.)

24 It is recorded that Ereinion was given the name Gil-galad 'Star of Radiance' 'because his helm and mail, and his shield overlaid with silver and set with a device of white stars, shone from afar like a star in sunlight or moonlight, and could be seen by Elvish eyes at a great distance if he stood upon a height'.

25 See p. 265.

26 A legitimate male heir, on the other hand, could not refuse; but since a King could always resign the Sceptre, a male heir could in fact immediately resign to *his* natural heir. He was then himself deemed also to have reigned for at least one year; and this was the case (the only case) with Vardamir, the son of Elros, who did not ascend the throne but gave the Sceptre to his son Amandil.

27 It is said elsewhere that this rule of 'royal marriage' was never a matter of law, but it became a custom of pride: 'a symptom of the growth of the Shadow, since it only became rigid when the distinction between the Line of Elros and other families, in life-span, vigour, or ability, had diminished or altogether disappeared.'

28 This is strange, because Anárion was the Heir in Ancalimë's lifetime. In 'The Line of Elros' (p. 220) it is said only that Anárion's daughters 'refused the sceptre'.

III

THE LINE OF ELROS:
KINGS OF NÚMENOR

*from the Founding of the City of Armenelos
to the Downfall*

The Realm of Númenor is held to have begun in the thirty-second
year of the Second Age, when Elros son of Eärendil ascended the
throne in the City of Armenelos, being then ninety years of age.
Thereafter he was known in the Scroll of the Kings by the name of
Tar-Minyatur; for it was the custom of the Kings to take their titles
in the forms of the Quenya or High-elven tongue, that being the
noblest tongue of the world, and this custom endured until the days
of Ar-Adûnakhôr (Tar-Herunúmen). Elros Tar-Minyatur ruled the
Númenóreans for four hundred years and ten. For to the Númenóreans long life had been granted, and they remained unwearied for
thrice the span of mortal Men in Middle-earth; but to Eärendil's
son the longest life of any Man was given, and to his descendants a
lesser span, and yet one greater than to others even of the Númenóreans; and so it was until the coming of the Shadow, when the years
of the Númenóreans began to wane.[1]

I *Elros Tar-Minyatur*
He was born fifty-eight years before the Second Age began: he
remained unwearied until he was five hundred years old and then
laid down his life, in the year 442, having ruled for 410 years.

II *Vardamir Nólimon*
He was born in the year 61 of the Second Age and died in 471. He
was called Nólimon for his chief love was for ancient lore, which he
gathered from Elves and Men. Upon the departure of Elros, being
then 381 years of age, he did not ascend the throne, but gave the
sceptre to his son. He is nonetheless accounted the second of the
Kings, and is deemed to have reigned one year.[2] It remained the
custom thereafter until the days of Tar-Atanamir that the King
should yield the sceptre to his successor before he died; and the
Kings died of free will while yet in vigour of mind.

III *Tar-Amandil*

He was the son of Vardamir Nólimon, and he was born in the year 192. He ruled for 148 years,[3] and surrendered the sceptre in 590; he died in 603.

IV *Tar-Elendil*

He was the son of Tar-Amandil, and he was born in the year 350. He ruled for 150 years, and surrendered the sceptre in 740; he died in 751. He was also called Parmaitë, for with his own hand he made many books and legends of the lore gathered by his grandfather. He married late in his life, and his eldest child was a daughter, Silmarien, born in the year 521,[4] whose son was Valandil. Of Valandil came the Lords of Andúnië, of whom the last was Amandil father of Elendil the Tall, who came to Middle-earth after the Downfall. In Tar-Elendil's reign the ships of the Númenóreans first came back to Middle-earth.

V *Tar-Meneldur*

He was the only son and third child of Tar-Elendil, and he was born in the year 543. He ruled for 143 years, and surrendered the sceptre in 883; he died in 942. His 'right name' was Írimon; he took his title Meneldur from his love of star-lore. He married Almarian daughter of Vëantur, Captain of Ships under Tar-Elendil. He was wise, but gentle and patient. He resigned to his son, suddenly and long before due time, as a stroke of policy, in troubles that arose, owing to the disquiet of Gil-galad in Lindon, when he first became aware that an evil spirit, hostile to Eldar and Dúnedain, was stirring in Middle-earth.

VI *Tar-Aldarion*

He was the eldest child and only son of Tar-Meneldur, and he was born in the year 700. He ruled for 192 years, and surrendered the sceptre to his daughter in 1075; he died in 1098. His 'right name' was Anardil; but he was early known by the name of Aldarion, because he was much concerned with trees, and planted great woods to furnish timber for the ship-yards. He was a great mariner and ship-builder; and himself sailed often to Middle-earth, where he became the friend and counsellor of Gil-galad. Owing to his long absences abroad his wife Erendis became angered, and they separated in the year 882. His only child was a daughter, very beautiful, Ancalimë. In her favour Aldarion altered the law of succession, so that the (eldest) daughter of a King should succeed, if he had no sons. This change displeased the descendants of Elros, and especially the heir under the old law, Soronto, Aldarion's nephew, son of his elder sister Ailinel.[5]

VII   Tar-Ancalimë

She was the only child of Tar-Aldarion, and the first Ruling Queen of Númenor. She was born in the year 873, and she reigned for 205 years, longer than any ruler after Elros; she surrendered the sceptre in 1280, and died in 1285. She long remained unwed; but when pressed by Soronto to resign, in his despite she married in the year 1000 Hallacar son of Hallatan, a descendant of Vardamir.[6] After the birth of her son Anárion there was strife between Ancalimë and Hallacar. She was proud and wilful. After Aldarion's death she neglected all his policies, and gave no further aid to Gil-galad.

VIII   Tar-Anárion

He was the son of Tar-Ancalimë, and he was born in the year 1003. He ruled for 114 years, and surrendered the sceptre in 1394; he died in 1404.

IX   Tar-Súrion

He was the third child of Tar-Anárion; his sisters refused the sceptre.[7] He was born in the year 1174, and ruled for 162 years; he surrendered the sceptre in 1556, and died in 1574.

X   Tar-Telperien

She was the second Ruling Queen of Númenor. She was long-lived (for the women of the Númenóreans had the longer life, or laid down their lives less easily), and she would wed with no man. Therefore after her day the sceptre passed to Minastir; he was the son of Isilmo, the second child of Tar-Súrion.[8] Tar-Telperien was born in the year 1320; she ruled for 175 years, until 1731, and died in that same year.[9]

XI   Tar-Minastir

This name he had because he built a high tower upon the hill of Oromet, nigh to Andúnië and the west shores, and thence would spend great part of his days gazing westward. For the yearning was grown strong in the hearts of the Númenóreans. He loved the Eldar but envied them. He it was who sent a great fleet to the aid of Gil-galad in the first war against Sauron. He was born in the year 1474, and ruled for 138 years; he surrendered the sceptre in 1869, and died in 1873.

XII   *Tar-Ciryatan*

He was born in the year 1634, and ruled for 160 years; he surrendered the sceptre in 2029, and died in 2035. He was a mighty King, but greedy of wealth; he built a great fleet of royal ships, and his servants brought back great store of metals and gems, and oppressed the men of Middle-earth. He scorned the yearnings of his father, and eased the restlessness of his heart by voyaging, east, and north, and south, until he took the sceptre. It is said that he constrained his father to yield to him ere of his free will he would. In this way (it is held) might the first coming of the Shadow upon the bliss of Númenor be seen.

XIII   *Tar-Atanamir the Great*

He was born in the year 1800, and ruled for 192 years, until 2221, which was the year of his death. Much is said of this King in the Annals, such as now survive the Downfall. For he was like his father proud and greedy of wealth, and the Númenóreans in his service exacted heavy tribute from the men of the coasts of Middle-earth. In his time the Shadow fell upon Númenor; and the King, and those that followed his lore, spoke openly against the ban of the Valar, and their hearts were turned against the Valar and the Eldar; but wisdom they still kept, and they feared the Lords of the West, and did not defy them. Atanamir is called also the Unwilling, for he was the first of the Kings to refuse to lay down his life, or to renounce the sceptre; and he lived until death took him perforce in dotage.[10]

XIV   *Tar-Ancalimon*

He was born in the year 1986, and ruled for 165 years, until his death in 2386. In his time the rift became wider between the King's Men (the larger part) and those who maintained their ancient friendship with the Eldar. Many of the King's Men began to forsake the use of the Elven-tongues, and to teach them no longer to their children. But the royal titles were still given in Quenya, out of ancient custom rather than love, for fear lest the breaking of the old usage should bring ill-fortune.

XV   *Tar-Telemmaitë*

He was born in the year 2136, and ruled for 140 years, until his death in 2526. Hereafter the Kings ruled in name from the death of their father to their own death, though the actual power passed often to their sons or counsellors; and the days of the descendants of Elros waned under the Shadow. This King was so called because of his love of silver, and he bade his servants to seek ever for *mithril*.

XVI   *Tar-Vanimeldë*

She was the third Ruling Queen; she was born in the year 2277, and ruled for 111 years until her death in 2637. She gave little heed to ruling, loving rather music and dance; and the power was wielded by her husband Herucalmo, younger than she, but a descendant of the same degree from Tar-Atanamir. Herucalmo took the sceptre upon his wife's death, calling himself Tar-Anducal, and withholding the rule from his son Alcarin; yet some do not reckon him in the Line of Kings as seventeenth, and pass to Alcarin. Tar-Anducal was born in the year 2286, and he died in 2657.

XVII   *Tar-Alcarin*

He was born in the year 2406, and he ruled for 80 years until his death in 2737, being rightful King for one hundred years.

XVIII   *Tar-Calmacil*

He was born in the year 2516, and he ruled for 88 years until his death in 2825. This name he took, for in his youth he was a great captain, and won wide lands along the coasts of Middle-earth. Thus he kindled the hate of Sauron, who nonetheless withdrew, and built his power in the East, far from the shores, biding his time. In the days of Tar-Calmacil the name of the King was first spoken in Adûnaic; and by the King's Men he was called Ar-Belzagar.

XIX   *Tar-Ardamin*

He was born in the year 2618, and he ruled for 74 years until his death in 2899. His name in Adûnaic was Ar-Abattârik.[11]

XX   *Ar-Adûnakhôr* (*Tar-Herunúmen*)

He was born in the year 2709, and he ruled for 63 years until his death in 2962. He was the first King to take the sceptre with a title in the Adûnaic tongue; though out of fear (as aforesaid) a name in Quenya was inscribed in the Scrolls. But these titles were held by the Faithful to be blasphemous, for they signified 'Lord of the West', by which title they had been wont to name one of the great Valar only, Manwë in especial. In this reign the Elven-tongues were no longer used, nor permitted to be taught, but were maintained in secret by the Faithful; and the ships from Eressëa came seldom and secretly to the west shores of Númenor thereafter.

XXI   *Ar-Zimrathon* (*Tar-Hostamir*)

He was born in the year 2798, and he ruled for 71 years until his death in 3033.

XXII   *Ar-Sakalthôr (Tar-Falassion)*
He was born in the year 2876, and he ruled for 69 years until his death in 3102.

XXIII   *Ar-Gimilzôr (Tar-Telemnar)*
He was born in the year 2960, and he ruled for 75 years until his death in 3177. He was the greatest enemy of the Faithful that had yet arisen; and he forbade utterly the use of the Eldarin tongues, and would not permit any of the Eldar to come to the land, and punished those that welcomed them. He revered nothing, and went never to the Hallow of Eru. He was wedded to Inzilbêth, a lady descended from Tar-Calmacil;[12] but she was secretly of the Faithful, for her mother was Lindórië of the House of the Lords of Andúnië, and there was small love between them, and strife between their sons. For Inziladûn[13] the elder was beloved of his mother and of like mind with her; but Gimilkhâd the younger was his father's son, and him Ar-Gimilzôr would fain have appointed his Heir, had the laws allowed. Gimilkhâd was born in the year 3044, and he died in 3243.[14]

XXIV   *Tar-Palantir (Ar-Inziladûn)*
He was born in the year 3035, and he ruled for 78 years until his death in 3255. Tar-Palantir repented of the ways of the Kings before him, and would fain have returned to the friendship of the Eldar and the Lords of the West. This name Inziladûn took, because he was far-sighted both in eye and in mind, and even those who hated him feared his words as those of a true-seer. He also would spend much of his days in Andúnië, since Lindórië his mother's mother was of the kin of the Lords, being sister indeed of Eärendur, the fifteenth Lord and grandfather of Númendil, who was Lord of Andúnië in the days of Tar-Palantir his cousin; and Tar-Palantir would ascend often to the ancient tower of King Minastir, and gaze westward in yearning, hoping to see, maybe, some sail coming from Eressëa. But no ship came ever again out of the West, because of the insolence of the Kings, and because the hearts of the most part of the Númenóreans were still hardened. For Gimilkhâd followed the ways of Ar-Gimilzôr, and became leader of the King's Party, and resisted the will of Tar-Palantir as openly as he dared, and yet more in secret. But for a while the Faithful had peace; and the King went ever at due times to the Hallow upon the Meneltarma, and the White Tree was again given tendance and honour. For Tar-Palantir prophesied, saying that when the Tree died then the line of the Kings also would perish.

Tar-Palantir married late and had no son, and his daughter he named Míriel in the Elven-tongue. But when the King died, she was taken to wife by Pharazôn son of Gimilkhâd (who also was dead) against her will, and against the law of Númenor, since she was the child of his father's brother. And he then seized the sceptre into his own hand, taking the title of Ar-Pharazôn (Tar-Calion); and Míriel was named Ar-Zimraphel.[15]

XXV *Ar-Pharazôn (Tar-Calion)*
The mightiest and last King of Númenor. He was born in the year 3118, and ruled for 64 years, and died in the Downfall in the year 3319, usurping the sceptre of

Tar-Míriel (Ar-Zimraphel)
She was born in the year 3117, and died in the Downfall.

Of the deeds of Ar-Pharazôn, of his glory and his folly, more is told in the tale of the Downfall of Númenor, which Elendil wrote, and which was preserved in Gondor.[16]

NOTES

1 There are several references to the greater life-span of the descendants of Elros than that of any others among the Númenóreans, in addition to those in the tale of Aldarion and Erendis. Thus in the *Akallabêth* (*The Silmarillion* p. 261) it is said that all the line of Elros 'had long life even according to the measure of the Númenóreans'; and in an isolated note the difference in longevity is given a precise range: the 'end of vigour' for the descendants of Elros came (before the waning of their life-span set in) about the four hundredth year, or somewhat earlier, whereas for those not of that line it came towards the two hundredth year, or somewhat later. It may be noted that almost all the Kings from Vardamir to Tar-Ancalimon lived to or a little beyond their four hundredth year, and the three who did not died within one or two years of it.
　　But in the latest writing on this subject (which derives, however, from about the same time as the latest work on the tale of Aldarion and Erendis) the distinction in longevity is greatly diminished. To the Númenórean people as a whole is ascribed a life-span some five times the length of that of other Men (although this is in contradiction to the statement in *The Lord of the Rings* Appendix A (I, i) that the Númenóreans were granted a span 'in the beginning thrice that of lesser Men', a statement made again in the preface to the present text); and the difference of the Line of Elros from others in

this respect is less a distinct mark and attribute than a mere tendency to live to a greater age. Though the case of Erendis, and the somewhat shorter lives of the 'Bëorians' of the West, are mentioned, there is no suggestion here, as there is in the tale of Aldarion and Erendis, that the difference in their expectation of life was both very great and also something inherent in their destinies, and recognised to be so.

In this account, only Elros was granted a peculiar longevity, and it is said here that he and his brother Elrond were not differently endowed in the physical potential of life, but that since Elros elected to remain among the kindred of Men he retained the chief characteristic of Men as opposed to the Quendi: the 'seeking elsewhither', as the Eldar called it, the 'weariness' or desire to depart from the world. It is further expounded that the increase in the Númenórean span was brought about by assimilation of their mode of life to that of the Eldar: though they were expressly warned that they had not become Eldar, but remained mortal Men, and had been granted only an extension of the period of their vigour of mind and body. Thus (as the Eldar) they grew at much the same rate as other Men, but when they had achieved 'full-growth' they then aged, or 'wore out', very much more slowly. The first approach of 'world-weariness' was indeed for them a sign that their period of vigour was nearing its end. When it came to an end, if they persisted in living, then decay would proceed, as growth had done, no more slowly than among other Men. Thus a Númenórean would pass quickly, in ten years maybe, from health and vigour of mind to decrepitude and senility. In the earlier generations they did not 'cling to life', but resigned it voluntarily. 'Clinging to life', and so in the end dying perforce and involuntarily, was one of the changes brought about by the Shadow and the rebellion of the Númenóreans; it was also accompanied by a shrinking of their natural life-span.

2 See p. 217, note 26.

3 The figure of 148 (rather than 147) must represent the years of Tar-Amandil's actual rule, and not take the notional year of Vardamir's reign into account.

4 There is no question but that Silmarien was the eldest child of Tar-Elendil; and her birth-date is several times given as Second Age 521, while that of her brother Tar-Meneldur is fixed at 543. In the Tale of Years (Appendix B to *The Lord of the Rings*), however, Silmarien's birth is given in the annal entry 548; a date that goes back to the first drafts of that text. I think it very likely that this should have been revised but escaped notice.

5 This is not in agreement with the account of the earlier and later laws of succession given on pp. 208–9, according to which Soronto only became Ancalimë's heir (if she died childless) by virtue of the new

law, for he was a descendant in the female line. – 'His elder sister' undoubtedly means 'the elder of his two sisters'.

6 See p. 211.

7 See p. 212 and note 28 on p. 217.

8 It is curious that the sceptre passed to Tar-Telperien when Tar-Súrion had a son, Isilmo. It may well be that the succession here depends on the formulation of the new law given in *The Lord of the Rings*, i.e. simple primogeniture irrespective of sex (see p. 208), rather than inheritance by a daughter only if the Ruler had no son.

9 The date 1731 here given for the end of the rule of Tar-Telperien and the accession of Tar-Minastir is strangely at variance with the dating, fixed by many references, of the first war against Sauron; for the great Númenórean fleet sent by Tar-Minastir reached Middle-earth in the year 1700. I cannot in any way account for the discrepancy.

10 In the Tale of Years (Appendix B to *The Lord of the Rings*) occurs the entry: '2251 Tar-Atanamir takes the sceptre. Rebellion and division of the Númenóreans begins.' This is altogether discrepant with the present text, according to which Tar-Atanamir died in 2221. This date 2221 is, however, itself an emendation from 2251; and his death is given elsewhere as 2251. Thus the same year appears in different texts as both the date of his accession and the date of his death; and the whole structure of the chronology shows clearly that the former must be wrong. Moreover, in the *Akallabêth* (*The Silmarillion* p. 266) it is said that it was in the time of Atanamir's son Ancalimon that the people of Númenor became divided. I have little doubt therefore that the entry in the Tale of Years is in error for a correct reading: '2251 Death of Tar-Atanamir. Tar-Ancalimon takes the sceptre. Rebellion and division of the Númenóreans begins.' But if so, it remains strange that the date of Atanamir's death should have been altered in 'The Line of Elros' if it were fixed by an entry in the Tale of Years.

11 In the list of the Kings and Queens of Númenor in Appendix A (I, i) to *The Lord of the Rings* the ruler following Tar-Calmacil (the eighteenth) was Ar-Adûnakhôr (the nineteenth). In the Tale of Years in Appendix B Ar-Adûnakhôr is said to have taken the sceptre in the year 2899; and on this basis Mr Robert Foster in *The Complete Guide to Middle-earth* gives the death-date of Tar-Calmacil as 2899. On the other hand, at a later point in the account of the rulers of Númenor in Appendix A, Ar-Adûnakhôr is called the twentieth king; and in 1964 my father replied to a correspondent who had enquired about this: 'As the genealogy stands he should be called the sixteenth king and nineteenth ruler. Nineteen should possibly be read for twenty; but it is also possible that a name has been left out.' He explained that he could not be certain because at the time of writing this letter his papers on the subject were not available to him.

When editing the *Akallabêth* I changed the actual reading 'And the twentieth king took the sceptre of his fathers, and he ascended the throne in the name of Adûnakhôr' to 'And the nineteenth king . . .' (*The Silmarillion* p. 267), and similarly 'four and twenty' to 'three and twenty' (*ibid.* p. 270). At that time I had not observed that in 'The Line of Elros' the ruler following Tar-Calmacil was not Ar-Adûnakhôr but Tar-Ardamin; but it now seems perfectly clear, from the fact alone that Tar-Ardamin's death-date is here given as 2899, that he was omitted in error from the list in *The Lord of the Rings*.

On the other hand, it is a certainty of the tradition (stated in Appendix A, in the *Akallabêth*, and in 'The Line of Elros') that Ar-Adûnakhôr was the first King to take the sceptre in a name of the Adûnaic tongue. On the assumption that Tar-Ardamin dropped out of the list in Appendix A by a mere oversight, it is surprising that the change in the style of the royal names should there be attributed to the first ruler after Tar-Calmacil. It may be that a more complex textual situation underlies the passage than a mere error of omission.

12   In two genealogical tables her father is shown as Gimilzagar, the second son (born in 2630) of Tar-Calmacil, but this is clearly impossible: Inzilbêth must have been descended from Tar-Calmacil at more removes.

13   There is a highly formalised floral design of my father's, similar in style to that shown in *Pictures by J. R. R. Tolkien* (1979) no. 45, bottom right, which bears the title *Inziladûn*, and beneath it is written both in Fëanorian script and transliterated *Númellótë* ['Flower of the West'].

14   According to the *Akallabêth* (*The Silmarillion* p. 269) Gimilkhâd 'died two years before his two hundredth year, which was accounted an early death for one of Elros' line even in its waning'.

15   As noted in Appendix A to *The Lord of the Rings* Míriel should have been the fourth Ruling Queen.

A final discrepancy between 'The Line of Elros' and the Tale of Years arises in the dates of Tar-Palantir. It is said in the *Akallabêth* (p. 269) that 'when Inziladûn acceded to the sceptre, he took again a title in the Elven-tongue as of old, calling himself Tar-Palantir'; and in the Tale of Years occurs the entry: '3175 Repentance of Tar-Palantir. Civil war in Númenor.' It would seem almost certain from these statements that 3175 was the year of his accession; and this is borne out by the fact that in 'The Line of Elros' the death-date of his father Ar-Gimilzôr was originally given as 3175, and only later emended to 3177. As with the death-date of Tar-Atanamir (note 10 above) it is hard to understand why this small change was made, in contradiction to the Tale of Years.

16   The statement that Elendil was the author of the *Akallabêth* is made only here. It is also said, elsewhere, that the story of Aldarion and Erendis, 'one of the few detailed histories preserved from Númenor', owed its preservation to its being of interest to Elendil.

IV

THE HISTORY OF
GALADRIEL AND CELEBORN

and of Amroth King of Lórien

There is no part of the history of Middle-earth more full of problems than the story of Galadriel and Celeborn, and it must be admitted that there are severe inconsistencies 'embedded in the traditions'; or, to look at the matter from another point of view, that the role and importance of Galadriel only emerged slowly, and that her story underwent continual refashionings.

Thus, at the outset, it is certain that the earlier conception was that Galadriel went east over the mountains from Beleriand alone, before the end of the First Age, and met Celeborn in his own land of Lórien; this is explicitly stated in unpublished writing, and the same idea underlies Galadriel's words to Frodo in *The Fellowship of the Ring* II 7, where she says of Celeborn that 'He has dwelt in the West since the days of dawn, and I have dwelt with him years uncounted; for ere the fall of Nargothrond or Gondolin I passed over the mountains, and together through ages of the world we have fought the long defeat.' In all probability Celeborn was in this conception a Nandorin Elf (that is, one of the Teleri who refused to cross the Misty Mountains on the Great Journey from Cuiviénen).

On the other hand, in Appendix B to *The Lord of the Rings* appears a later version of the story; for it is stated there that at the beginning of the Second Age 'In Lindon south of the Lune dwelt for a time Celeborn, kinsman of Thingol; his wife was Galadriel, greatest of Elven women.' And in the notes to *The Road Goes Ever On* (1968, p. 60) it is said that Galadriel 'passed over the Mountains of Eredluin with her husband Celeborn (one of the Sindar) and went to Eregion'.

In *The Silmarillion* there is mention of the meeting of Galadriel and Celeborn in Doriath, and of his kinship with Thingol (p. 115); and of their being among the Eldar who remained in Middle-earth after the end of the First Age (p. 254).

The reasons and motives given for Galadriel's remaining in Middle-earth are various. The passage just cited from *The Road Goes Ever On* says explicitly: 'After the overthrow of Morgoth at the end of the First Age a ban was set upon her return, and she had replied proudly that she had no wish to do so.' There is no such explicit statement in *The Lord of the Rings*; but in a letter written in 1967 my father declared:

The Exiles were allowed to return – save for a few chief actors in the rebellion, of whom at the time of *The Lord of the Rings* only Galadriel remained. At the time of her Lament in Lórien she believed this to be perennial, as long as the Earth endured. Hence she concludes her lament with a wish or prayer that Frodo may as a special grace be granted a purgatorial (but not penal) sojourn in Eressëa, the solitary isle in sight of Aman, though for her the way is closed. Her prayer was granted – but also her personal ban was lifted, in reward for her services against Sauron, and above all for her rejection of the temptation to take the Ring when offered to her. So at the end we see her taking ship.

This statement, very positive in itself, does not however demonstrate that the conception of a ban on Galadriel's return into the West was present when the chapter 'Farewell to Lórien' was composed, many years before; and I am inclined to think that it was not (see p. 234).

In a very late and primarily philological essay, certainly written after the publication of *The Road Goes Ever On*, the story is distinctively different:

Galadriel and her brother Finrod were the children of Finarfin, the second son of Indis. Finarfin was of his mother's kind in mind and body, having the golden hair of the Vanyar, their noble and gentle temper, and their love of the Valar. As well as he could he kept aloof from the strife of his brothers and their estrangement from the Valar, and he often sought peace among the Teleri, whose language he learned. He wedded Eärwen, the daughter of King Olwë of Alqualondë, and his children were thus the kin of King Elu Thingol of Doriath in Beleriand, for he was the brother of Olwë; and this kinship influenced their decision to join in the Exile, and proved of great importance later in Beleriand. Finrod was like his father in his fair face and golden hair, and also in noble and generous heart, though he had the high courage of the Noldor and in his youth their eagerness and unrest; and he had also from his Telerin mother a love of the sea and dreams of far lands that he had never seen. Galadriel was the greatest of the Noldor, except Fëanor maybe, though she was wiser than he, and her wisdom increased with the long years.

Her mother-name was Nerwen ('man-maiden'),[1] and she grew to be tall beyond the measure even of the women of the Noldor; she was strong of body, mind, and will, a match for both the loremasters and the athletes of the Eldar in the days of their youth. Even among the Eldar she was accounted beautiful, and her hair was held a marvel unmatched. It was golden like the hair of her father and of her foremother Indis, but richer and more radiant, for its gold was touched by some memory of the starlike silver of her mother; and the Eldar said that the light of the Two Trees, Laurelin and Telperion, had been snared in her tresses. Many thought that this saying first gave to Fëanor the thought of imprisoning and blending the light of the Trees that later took shape in his hands as the Silmarils. For Fëanor beheld the hair of Galadriel with wonder and delight. He begged three times for a tress, but Galadriel would not give him even one hair. These two kinsfolk, the greatest of the Eldar of Valinor, were unfriends for ever.

Galadriel was born in the bliss of Valinor, but it was not long, in the reckoning of the Blessed Realm, before that was dimmed; and thereafter she had no peace within. For in that testing time amid the strife of the Noldor she was drawn this way and that. She was proud, strong, and selfwilled, as were all the descendants of Finwë save Finarfin; and like her brother Finrod, of all her kin the nearest to her heart, she had dreams of far lands and dominions that might be her own to order as she would without tutelage. Yet deeper still there dwelt in her the noble and generous spirit of the Vanyar, and a reverence for the Valar that she could not forget. From her earliest years she had a marvellous gift of insight into the minds of others, but judged them with mercy and understanding, and she withheld her goodwill from none save only Fëanor. In him she perceived a darkness that she hated and feared, though she did not perceive that the shadow of the same evil had fallen upon the minds of all the Noldor, and upon her own.

So it came to pass that when the light of Valinor failed, for ever as the Noldor thought, she joined the rebellion against the Valar who commanded them to stay; and once she had set foot upon that road of exile she would not relent, but rejected the last message of the Valar, and came under the Doom of Mandos. Even after the merciless assault upon the Teleri and the rape of their ships, though she fought fiercely against Fëanor in defence of her mother's kin, she did not turn back. Her pride was unwilling to return, a defeated suppliant for pardon; but now she burned with desire to follow Fëanor with her anger to whatever lands he might come, and to thwart him in all ways that she could. Pride still moved her when, at the end of the Elder Days after the final overthrow of Morgoth, she refused the pardon of the Valar for all who had fought against him, and remained in Middle-earth. It was not until two long ages more had passed, when at last all that she had desired in her youth came to her hand, the Ring of Power and the dominion of Middle-earth of which she had dreamed, that her wisdom was full grown and she rejected it, and passing the last test departed from Middle-earth for ever.

This last sentence relates closely to the scene in Lothlórien when Frodo offered the One Ring to Galadriel (*The Fellowship of the Ring* II 7): 'And now at last it comes. You will give me the Ring freely! In place of the Dark Lord you will set up a Queen.'

In *The Silmarillion* it is told (p. 84) that at the time of the rebellion of the Noldor in Valinor Galadriel

was eager to be gone. No oaths she swore, but the words of Fëanor concerning Middle-earth had kindled in her heart, for she longed to see the wide unguarded lands and to rule there a realm at her own will.

There are however in the present account several features of which there is no trace in *The Silmarillion*: the kinship of Finarfin's children with Thingol as a factor influencing their decision to join in Fëanor's rebellion; Galadriel's peculiar dislike and distrust of Fëanor from the beginning, and the effect she had on him; and the fighting at Alqualondë among the Noldor themselves – Angrod asserted to Thingol in Menegroth no more than that the kin of Finarfin were guiltless of the slaying of the Teleri (*The Silmarillion* p. 129). Most notable however in the passage just cited is the explicit statement that Galadriel *refused the pardon of the Valar* at the end of the First Age.

Later in this essay it is said that though called Nerwen by her mother and Artanis ('noble woman') by her father, the name she chose to be her Sindarin name was Galadriel, 'for it was the most beautiful of her names, and had been given to her by her lover, Teleporno of the Teleri, whom she wedded later in Beleriand'. Teleporno is Celeborn, here given a different history, as discussed further below (p. 233); on the name itself see Appendix E, p. 266.

A wholly different story, adumbrated but never told, of Galadriel's conduct at the time of the rebellion of the Noldor appears in a very late and partly illegible note: the last writing of my father's on the subject of Galadriel and Celeborn, and probably the last on Middle-earth and Valinor, set down in the last month of his life. In this he emphasized the commanding stature of Galadriel already in Valinor, the equal if unlike in endowments of Fëanor; and it is said here that so far from joining in

Fëanor's revolt she was in every way opposed to him. She did indeed wish to depart from Valinor and to go into the wide world of Middle-earth for the exercise of her talents; for 'being brilliant in mind and swift in action she had early absorbed all of what she was capable of the teaching which the Valar thought fit to give the Eldar', and she felt confined in the tutelage of Aman. This desire of Galadriel's was, it seems, known to Manwë, and he had not forbidden her; but nor had she been given formal leave to depart. Pondering what she might do Galadriel's thoughts turned to the ships of the Teleri, and she went for a while to dwell with her mother's kindred in Alqualondë. There she met Celeborn, who is here again a Telerin prince, the grandson of Olwë of Alqualondë and thus her close kinsman. Together they planned to build a ship and sail in it to Middle-earth; and they were about to seek leave from the Valar for their venture when Melkor fled from Valmar and returning with Ungoliant destroyed the light of the Trees. In Fëanor's revolt that followed the Darkening of Valinor Galadriel had no part: indeed she with Celeborn fought heroically in defence of Alqualondë against the assault of the Noldor, and Celeborn's ship was saved from them. Galadriel, despairing now of Valinor and horrified by the violence and cruelty of Fëanor, set sail into the darkness without waiting for Manwë's leave, which would undoubtedly have been withheld in that hour, however legitimate her desire in itself. It was thus that she came under the ban set upon all departure, and Valinor was shut against her return. But together with Celeborn she reached Middle-earth somewhat sooner than Fëanor, and sailed into the haven where Círdan was lord. There they were welcomed with joy, as being of the kin of Elwë (Thingol). In the years after they did not join in the war against Angband, which they judged to be hopeless under the ban of the Valar and without their aid; and their counsel was to withdraw from Beleriand and to build up a power to the eastward (whence they feared that Morgoth would draw reinforcement), befriending and teaching the Dark Elves and Men of those regions. But such a policy having no hope of acceptance among the Elves of Beleriand, Galadriel and Celeborn departed over Ered Lindon before the end of the First Age; and when they received the permission of the Valar to return into the West they rejected it.

This story, withdrawing Galadriel from all association with the rebellion of Fëanor, even to the extent of giving her a separate departure (with Celeborn) from Aman, is profoundly at variance with all that is said elsewhere. It arose from 'philosophical' (rather than 'historical') considerations, concerning the precise nature of Galadriel's disobedience in Valinor on the one hand, and her status and power in Middle-earth on the other. That it would have entailed a good deal of alteration in the narrative of *The Silmarillion* is evident; but that my father doubtless intended to do. It may be noted here that Galadriel did not appear in the original story of the rebellion and flight of the Noldor, which existed long before she did; and also, of course, that after her entry into the stories of the First Age her actions could still be transformed radically, since *The Silmarillion* had not been published. The book as published was however formed from completed narratives, and I could not take into account merely projected revisions.

On the other hand, the making of Celeborn into a Telerin Elf of Aman contradicts not only statements in *The Silmarillion*, but also those cited already (p. 228) from *The Road Goes Ever On* and Appendix B to *The Lord of the Rings*, where Celeborn is a Sindarin Elf of Beleriand. As to why this fundamental alteration in his history was to be made, it might be answered that it arose from the new narrative element of Galadriel's departure from Aman *separately* from the hosts of the rebel Noldor; but Celeborn is already transformed into a Telerin Elf in the text cited on p. 231, where Galadriel did take part in Fëanor's revolt and march from Valinor, and where there is no indication of how Celeborn came to Middle-earth.

The earlier story (apart from the question of the ban and the pardon), to which the statements in *The Silmarillion*, *The Road Goes Ever On*, and Appendix B to *The Lord of the Rings* refer, is fairly clear: Galadriel, coming to Middle-earth as one of the leaders of the second host of the Noldor, met Celeborn in Doriath, and was later wedded to him; he was the grandson of Thingol's brother Elmo – a shadowy figure about whom nothing is told save that he was the younger brother of Elwë (Thingol) and Olwë, and was 'beloved of Elwë with whom he remained'. (Elmo's son was named Galadhon, and his sons were Celeborn and Galathil; Galathil was the father of Nimloth, who wedded Dior Thingol's Heir and was the mother of Elwing. By this genealogy Celeborn was a kinsman of Galadriel, the grand-daughter of Olwë of Alqualondë, but not so close as by that in which he became Olwë's grandson.) It is a natural assumption that Celeborn and Galadriel were present at the ruin of Doriath (it is said in one place that Celeborn 'escaped the sack of Doriath'), and perhaps aided the escape of Elwing to the Havens of Sirion with the Silmaril – but this is nowhere stated. Celeborn is mentioned in Appendix B to *The Lord of the Rings* as dwelling for a time in Lindon south of the Lune;[2] but early in the Second Age they passed over the Mountains into Eriador. Their subsequent history, in the same phase (so to call it) of my father's writing, is told in the short narrative that follows here.

Concerning Galadriel and Celeborn

The text bearing this title is a short and hasty outline, very roughly composed, which is nonetheless almost the sole narrative source for the events in the West of Middle-earth up to the defeat and expulsion of Sauron from Eriador in the year 1701 of the Second Age. Other than this there is little beyond the brief and infrequent entries in the Tale of Years, and the much more generalised and selective account in *Of the Rings of Power and the Third Age* (published in *The Silmarillion*). It is certain that this present text was composed after the publication of *The Lord of the Rings*, both from there being a reference to the book and from the fact that Galadriel is called the daughter of Finarfin and the sister of Finrod Felagund (for these are the later names of those princes, introduced in the revised edition: see p. 255, note 20). The text is much emended, and it is not always possible to see what belongs to the time of composition of the manuscript and what is indefinitely later. This is the case with those references to Amroth that make him the son of Galadriel and Celeborn; but whenever these references were inserted, I think it is virtually certain that this was a new construction, later than the writing of *The Lord of the Rings*. Had he been supposed to be their son when it was written, the fact would surely have been mentioned.

It is very notable that not only is there no mention in this text of a ban on Galadriel's return into the West, but it even seems from a passage at the beginning of the account that no such idea was present; while later in the narrative Galadriel's remaining in Middle-earth after the defeat of Sauron in Eriador is ascribed to her sense that it was her duty not to depart while he was still finally unconquered. This is a chief support of the (hesitant) view expressed above (p. 229) that the story of the ban was later than the writing of *The Lord of the Rings*; cf. also a passage in the story of the Elessar, given on p. 249.

What follows here is retold from this text, with some interspersed comments, indicated by square brackets.

Galadriel was the daughter of Finarfin, and sister of Finrod Felagund. She was welcome in Doriath, because her mother Eärwen, daughter of Olwë, was Telerin and the niece of Thingol, and because the people of Finarfin had had no part in the Kinslaying of Alqualondë; and she became a friend of Melian. In Doriath she met Celeborn, grandson of Elmo the brother of Thingol. For love of Celeborn, who would not leave Middle-earth (and probably with some pride of her own, for she had been one of those eager to adventure there), she did not go West at the Downfall of Melkor, but crossed Ered Lindon with Celeborn and came into Eriador. When they entered that region there were many Noldor in their following, together with Grey-elves and Green-elves; and for a while they dwelt in the country about Lake Nenuial (Evendim, north of the Shire). Celeborn and Galadriel came to be regarded as Lord and Lady of the Eldar in Eriador, including the wandering companies of Nandorin origin who had never passed west over Ered Lindon and come down into Ossiriand [see *The Silmarillion* p. 94]. During their sojourn near Nenuial was born, at some time between the years 350 and 400, their son Amroth. [The time and place of Celebrían's birth, whether here or later in Eregion, or even later in Lórien, is not made definite.]

But eventually Galadriel became aware that Sauron again, as in the ancient days of the captivity of Melkor [see *The Silmarillion* p. 51], had been left behind. Or rather, since Sauron had as yet no single name, and his operations had not been perceived to proceed from a single evil spirit, prime servant of Melkor, she perceived that there was an evil controlling purpose abroad in the world, and that it seemed to proceed from a source further to the East, beyond Eriador and the Misty Mountains.

Celeborn and Galadriel therefore went eastwards, about the year 700 of the Second Age, and established the (primarily but by no means solely) Noldorin realm of Eregion. It may be that Galadriel chose it because she knew of the Dwarves of Khazad-dûm (Moria). There were and always remained some Dwarves on the eastern side of Ered Lindon,[3] where the very ancient mansions of Nogrod and Belegost had been – not far from Nenuial; but they had transferred most of their strength to Khazad-dûm. Celeborn had no liking for Dwarves of any race (as he showed to Gimli in Lothlórien), and never forgave them for their part in the destruction of Doriath; but it was only the host of Nogrod that took part in that assault, and it was destroyed in the battle of Sarn Athrad [*The Silmarillion* pp. 233–5]. The Dwarves of Belegost were filled with dismay at the calamity and fear for its outcome, and this hastened their departure eastwards to Khazad-dûm.[4] Thus the Dwarves of Moria may be presumed to have been innocent of the ruin of Doriath and not hostile to the Elves. In any case, Galadriel was more far-sighted in this than Celeborn; and she perceived from the beginning that Middle-earth could not be saved from 'the residue of evil' that Morgoth had left behind him save by a union of all the peoples who were in their way and in their measure opposed to him. She looked upon the Dwarves also with the eye of a commander, seeing in them the finest warriors to pit against the Orcs. Moreover Galadriel was a Noldo, and she had a natural sympathy with their minds and their passionate love of crafts of hand, a sympathy much greater than that found among many of the Eldar: the Dwarves were 'the Children of Aulë', and Galadriel, like others of the Noldor, had been a pupil of Aulë and Yavanna in Valinor.

Galadriel and Celeborn had in their company a Noldorin craftsman named Celebrimbor. [He is here said to have been one of the survivors of Gondolin, who had been among Turgon's greatest artificers; but the text is emended to the later story that made him a descendant of Fëanor, as is mentioned in Appendix B to *The Lord of the Rings* (in the revised edition only), and more fully detailed in *The Silmarillion* (pp. 176, 276), where he is said to have been the son of Curufin, the fifth son of Fëanor, who was estranged from his father and remained in Nargothrond when Celegorm and Curufin were driven forth.] Celebrimbor had 'an almost "dwarvish" obsession with crafts'; and he soon became the chief artificer of Eregion, entering into a close relationship with the Dwarves of Khazad-dûm, among whom his greatest friend was Narvi. [In the inscription on the West-gate of Moria Gandalf read the words: *Im Narvi hain echant: Celebrimbor o Eregion teithant i thiw hin:* 'I, Narvi, made them. Celebrimbor of Hollin drew these signs.' *The Fellowship of the Ring* II 4.] Both Elves and Dwarves had great profit from this association: so that Eregion became far stronger, and Khazad-dûm far more beautiful, than either would have done alone. [This account of the origin of Eregion agrees with what is told in *Of the Rings of Power* (*The Silmarillion* p. 286), but neither there nor in the brief references in Appendix B to *The Lord of the Rings* is there any mention of the presence of Galadriel and Celeborn; indeed in the latter (again, in the revised edition only) Celebrimbor is called the Lord of Eregion.]

The building of the chief city of Eregion, Ost-in-Edhil, was begun in about the year 750 of the Second Age [the date that is given in the Tale of Years for the founding of Eregion by the Noldor]. News of these things came to the ears of Sauron, and increased the fears that he felt concerning the coming of the Númenóreans to Lindon and the coasts further south, and their friendship with Gil-galad; and he heard tell also of Aldarion, son of Tar-Meneldur the King of Númenor, now become a great ship-builder who brought his vessels to haven far down into the Harad. Sauron therefore left Eriador alone for a while, and he chose the land of Mordor, as it was afterwards called, for a stronghold as a counter to the threat of the Númenórean landings [this is dated c. 1000 in the Tale of Years]. When he felt himself to be secure he sent emissaries to Eriador, and finally, in about the year 1200 of the Second Age, came himself, wearing the fairest form that he could contrive.

But in the meantime the power of Galadriel and Celeborn had grown, and Galadriel, assisted in this by her friendship with the Dwarves of Moria, had come into contact with the Nandorin realm of Lórinand on the other side of the Misty Mountains.[5] This was peopled by those Elves who forsook the Great Journey of the Eldar from Cuiviénen and settled in the woods of the Vale of Anduin [*The Silmarillion* p. 94]; and it extended into the forests on both sides of the Great River, including the region where afterwards was Dol Guldur. These Elves had no princes or rulers, and led their lives free of care while all Morgoth's power was concentrated in the North-west of Middle-earth;[6] 'but many Sindar and Noldor came to dwell among them, and their "Sindarizing" under the impact of Beleriandic culture began'. [It is not made clear when this movement into Lórinand took place; it may be that they came from Eregion by way of Khazad-dûm and under the auspices of Galadriel.] Galadriel, striving to counteract the machinations of Sauron, was successful in Lórinand; while in Lindon Gil-galad shut out Sauron's emissaries and even Sauron himself [as is more fully reported in *Of the Rings of Power* (*The Silmarillion* p. 287)]. But Sauron had better fortune with the Noldor of Eregion and especially with Celebrimbor, who desired in his heart to rival the skill and fame of Fëanor. [The cozening of the smiths of Eregion by Sauron, and his giving himself the name Annatar, Lord of Gifts, is told in *Of the Rings of Power*; but there is there no mention of Galadriel.]

In Eregion Sauron posed as an emissary of the Valar, sent by them to

Middle-earth ('thus anticipating the Istari') or ordered by them to remain there to give aid to the Elves. He perceived at once that Galadriel would be his chief adversary and obstacle, and he endeavoured therefore to placate her, bearing her scorn with outward patience and courtesy. [No explanation is offered in this rapid outline of why Galadriel scorned Sauron, unless she saw through his disguise, or of why, if she did perceive his true nature, she permitted him to remain in Eregion.][7] Sauron used all his arts upon Celebrimbor and his fellow-smiths, who had formed a society or brotherhood, very powerful in Eregion, the Gwaith-i-Mírdain; but he worked in secret, unknown to Galadriel and Celeborn. Before long Sauron had the Gwaith-i-Mírdain under his influence, for at first they had great profit from his instruction in secret matters of their craft.[8] So great became his hold on the Mírdain that at length he persuaded them to revolt against Galadriel and Celeborn and to seize power in Eregion; and that was at some time between 1350 and 1400 of the Second Age. Galadriel thereupon left Eregion and passed through Khazad-dûm to Lórinand, taking with her Amroth and Celebrían; but Celeborn would not enter the mansions of the Dwarves, and he remained behind in Eregion, disregarded by Celebrimbor. In Lórinand Galadriel took up rule, and defence against Sauron.

Sauron himself departed from Eregion about the year 1500, after the Mírdain had begun the making of the Rings of Power. Now Celebrimbor was not corrupted in heart or faith, but had accepted Sauron as what he posed to be; and when at length he discovered the existence of the One Ring he revolted against Sauron, and went to Lórinand to take counsel once more with Galadriel. They should have destroyed all the Rings of Power at this time, 'but they failed to find the strength'. Galadriel counselled him that the Three Rings of the Elves should be hidden, never used, and dispersed, far from Eregion where Sauron believed them to be. It was at that time that she received Nenya, the White Ring, from Celebrimbor, and by its power the realm of Lórinand was strengthened and made beautiful; but its power upon her was great also and unforeseen, for it increased her latent desire for the Sea and for return into the West, so that her joy in Middle-earth was diminished.[9] Celebrimbor followed her counsel that the Ring of Air and the Ring of Fire should be sent out of Eregion; and he entrusted them to Gil-galad in Lindon. (It is said here that at this time Gil-galad gave Narya, the Red Ring, to Círdan Lord of the Havens, but later in the narrative there is a marginal note that he kept it himself until he set out for the War of the Last Alliance.)

When Sauron learned of the repentance and revolt of Celebrimbor his disguise fell and his wrath was revealed; and gathering a great force he moved over Calenardhon (Rohan) to the invasion of Eriador in the year 1695. When news of this reached Gil-galad he sent out a force under Elrond Half-elven; but Elrond had far to go, and Sauron turned north and made at once for Eregion. The scouts and vanguard of Sauron's host were already approaching when Celeborn made a sortie and drove them back; but though he was able to join his force to that of Elrond they could not return to Eregion, for Sauron's host was far greater than theirs, great enough both to hold them off and closely to invest Eregion. At last the attackers broke into Eregion with ruin and devastation, and captured the chief object of Sauron's assault, the House of the Mírdain, where were their smithies and their treasures. Celebrimbor, desperate, himself withstood Sauron on the steps of the great door of the Mírdain; but he was grappled and taken captive, and the House was ransacked. There Sauron took the Nine Rings and other lesser works of the Mírdain; but the Seven and the Three he could not find. Then Celebrimbor was put to torment, and Sauron learned from him where the Seven were bestowed. This Celebrimbor revealed, because neither the Seven nor the Nine did he value as he valued the Three; the Seven and the Nine were made with Sauron's aid, whereas the Three were made by Celebrimbor alone, with a different power and purpose. [It is not actually said here that Sauron at this time took possession of the Seven Rings, though the implication seems clear that he did so. In Appendix A (III) to *The Lord of the Rings* it is said that there was a belief among the Dwarves of Durin's Folk that the Ring of Durin III, King of Khazad-dûm, was given to him by the Elven-smiths themselves, and not by Sauron; but nothing is said in the present text about the way in which the Seven Rings came into the possession of the Dwarves.] Concerning the Three Rings Sauron could learn nothing from Celebrimbor; and he had him put to death. But he guessed the truth, that the Three had been committed to Elvish guardians: and that must mean to Galadriel and Gil-galad.

In black anger he turned back to battle; and bearing as a banner Celebrimbor's body hung upon a pole, shot through with Orc-arrows, he turned upon the forces of Elrond. Elrond had gathered such few of the Elves of Eregion as had escaped, but he had no force to withstand the onset. He would indeed have been overwhelmed had not Sauron's host been attacked in the rear; for Durin sent out a force of Dwarves from Khazad-dûm, and with them came Elves of Lórinand led by Amroth. Elrond was able to extricate himself, but he was forced away northwards, and it was at that time [in the year 1697, according to the Tale of Years] that he established a refuge and stronghold at Imladris (Rivendell). Sauron withdrew the pursuit of Elrond and turned upon the Dwarves and the Elves of Lórinand, whom he drove back; but the Gates of Moria were shut, and he could not enter. Ever afterwards Moria had Sauron's hate, and all Orcs were commanded to harry Dwarves whenever they might.

But now Sauron attempted to gain the mastery of Eriador: Lórinand could wait. But as he ravaged the lands, slaying or drawing off all the small groups of Men and hunting the remaining Elves, many fled to swell Elrond's host to the northward. Now Sauron's immediate purpose was to take Lindon, where he believed that he had most chance of seizing one, or more, of the Three Rings; and he called in therefore his scattered forces and marched west towards the land of Gil-galad, ravaging as he went. But his force was weakened by the necessity of leaving a strong detachment to contain Elrond and prevent him coming down upon his rear. Now for long years the Númenóreans had brought in their ships to the Grey Havens, and there they were welcome. As soon as Gil-galad began to fear that Sauron would come with open war into Eriador he sent messages to Númenor; and on the shores of Lindon the Númenóreans began to build up a force and supplies for war. In 1695, when Sauron invaded Eriador, Gil-galad called on Númenor for aid. Then Tar-Minastir the King sent out a great navy; but it was delayed, and did not reach the coasts of Middle-earth until the year 1700. By that time Sauron had mastered all Eriador, save only besieged Imladris, and had reached the line of the River Lhûn. He had summoned more forces, which were approaching from the south-east, and were indeed in Enedwaith at the Crossing of Tharbad, which was only lightly held. Gil-galad and the Númenóreans were holding the Lhûn in desperate defence of the Grey Havens, when in the very nick of time the great armament of Tar-Minastir came in; and Sauron's host was heavily defeated and driven back. The Númenórean admiral Ciryatur sent part of his ships to make a landing further to the south.

Sauron was driven away south-east after great slaughter at Sarn Ford (the crossing of the Baranduin); and though strengthened by his force at Tharbad he suddenly found a host of the Númenóreans again in his rear, for Ciryatur had put a strong force ashore at the mouth of the Gwathló (Greyflood), 'where there was a small Númenórean harbour'. [This was Vinyalondë of Tar-Aldarion, afterwards called Lond Daer; see Appendix D, p. 261.] In the Battle of the Gwathló Sauron was routed utterly and he himself only narrowly escaped. His small remaining force was assailed in the east of Calenardhon, and he with no more than a bodyguard fled to the region afterwards called Dagorlad (Battle Plain), whence broken and humiliated he returned to Mordor, and vowed vengeance upon Númenor. The army that was besieging Imladris was caught between Elrond and Gil-galad, and utterly destroyed. Eriador was cleared of the enemy, but lay largely in ruins.

At this time the first Council was held,[10] and it was there determined that an Elvish stronghold in the east of Eriador should be maintained at Imladris rather than in Eregion. At that time also Gil-galad gave Vilya, the Blue Ring, to Elrond, and appointed him to be his vice-regent in Eriador; but the Red Ring he kept, until he gave it to Círdan when he set out from Lindon in the days of the Last Alliance.[11] For many years the Westlands had peace, and time in which to heal their wounds; but the Númenóreans had tasted power in Middle-earth, and from that time forward they began to make permanent settlements on the western coasts [dated 'c. 1800' in the Tale of Years], becoming too powerful for Sauron to attempt to move west out of Mordor for a long time.

In its concluding passage the narrative returns to Galadriel, telling that the sea-longing grew so strong in her that (though she deemed it her duty to remain in Middle-earth while Sauron was still unconquered) she determined to leave Lórinand and to dwell near the sea. She committed Lórinand to Amroth, and passing again through Moria with Celebrían she came to Imladris, seeking Celeborn. There (it seems) she found him, and there they dwelt together for a long time; and it was then that Elrond first saw Celebrían, and loved her, though he said nothing of it. It was while Galadriel was in Imladris that the Council referred to above was held. But at some later time [there is no indication of the date] Galadriel and Celeborn together with Celebrían departed from Imladris and went to the little-inhabited lands between the mouth of the Gwathló and Ethir Anduin. There they dwelt in Belfalas, at the place that was afterwards called Dol Amroth; there Amroth their son at times visited them, and their company was swelled by Nandorin Elves from Lórinand. It was not until far on in the Third Age, when Amroth was lost and Lórinand was in peril, that Galadriel returned there, in the year 1981. Here the text 'Concerning Galadriel and Celeborn' comes to an end.

It may be noted here that the absence of any indication to the contrary in *The Lord of the Rings* had led commentators to the natural assumption that Galadriel and Celeborn passed the latter half of the Second Age and all the Third in Lothlórien; but this was not so, though their story as outlined in 'Concerning Galadriel and Celeborn' was greatly modified afterwards, as will be shown below.

Amroth and Nimrodel

I have said earlier (p. 234) that if Amroth were indeed thought of as the son of Galadriel and Celeborn when *The Lord of the Rings* was written, so important a connection could hardly have escaped mention. But whether he was or not, this view of his parentage was later rejected. I give next a short tale (dating from 1969 or later) entitled 'Part of the Legend of Amroth and Nimrodel recounted in brief'.

Amroth was King of Lórien, after his father Amdír was slain in the Battle of Dagorlad [in the year 3434 of the Second Age]. His land had peace for many years after the defeat of Sauron. Though Sindarin in descent he lived after the manner of the Silvan Elves and housed in the tall trees of a great green mound, ever after called Cerin Amroth. This he did because of his love for Nimrodel. For long years he had loved her, and taken no wife, since she would not wed with him. She loved him indeed, for he was beautiful even for one of the Eldar, and valiant and wise; but she was of the Silvan Elves, and regretted the incoming of the Elves from the West, who (as she said) brought wars and destroyed the peace of old. She would speak only the Silvan tongue, even after it had fallen into disuse among the folk of Lórien;[12] and she dwelt alone beside the falls of the river Nimrodel to which she gave her name. But when the terror came out of Moria and the Dwarves were driven out, and in their stead Orcs crept in, she fled distraught alone south into empty lands [in the year 1981 of the Third Age]. Amroth followed her, and at last he found her under the eaves of Fangorn, which in those days drew much nearer to Lórien.[13] She dared not enter the wood, for the trees, she said, menaced her, and some moved to bar her way.

There Amroth and Nimrodel held a long debate; and at the last they plighted their troth. 'To this I will be true,' she said, 'and we shall be wedded when you bring me to a land of peace.' Amroth vowed that for her sake he would leave his people, even in their time of need, and with her seek for such a land. 'But there is none now in Middle-earth,' he said, 'and will not be for the Elven-folk ever again. We must seek for a passage over the Great Sea to the ancient West.' Then he told her of the haven in the south, where many of his own people had come long ago. 'They are now diminished, for most have set sail into the West; but the remnant of them still build ships and offer passage to any of their kin that come to them, weary of Middle-earth. It is said that the grace that the Valar gave to us to pass over the Sea is granted also now to any of those who made the Great Journey, even if they did not come in ages past to the shores and have not yet beheld the Blessed Land.'

There is not here the place to tell of their journey into the land of Gondor. It was in the days of King Eärnil the Second, the last but one of the Kings of the Southern Realm, and his lands were troubled. [Eärnil II reigned in Gondor from 1945 to 2043.] Elsewhere it is told [but not in any extant writing] how they became separated, and how Amroth after seeking her in vain went to the Elf-haven and found that only a few still lingered there. Less than a ship-load; and they had only one seaworthy ship. In this they were now preparing to depart, and to leave Middle-earth. They welcomed Amroth, being glad to strengthen their small company; but they were unwilling to await Nimrodel, whose coming seemed to them now beyond hope. 'If she came through the settled lands of Gondor,' they said, 'she would not be molested, and might receive help; for the Men of Gondor are good, and they are ruled by descendants of the Elf-friends of old who can still speak our tongue, after a fashion; but in the mountains are many unfriendly Men and evil things.'

The year was waning to autumn, and before long great winds were to be expected, hostile and dangerous, even to Elven-ships while they were still near to Middle-earth. But so great was the grief of Amroth that nonetheless they stayed their going for many weeks; and they lived on the ship, for their houses on the shore were stripped and empty. Then in the autumn there came a great night of storm, one of the fiercest in the annals of Gondor. It came from the cold Northern Waste, and roared down through Eriador into the lands of Gondor, doing great havoc; the White Mountains were no shield against it, and many of the ships of Men were swept out into the Bay of Belfalas and lost. The light Elven-ship was torn from its moorings and driven into the wild waters towards the coasts of Umbar. No tidings of it were ever heard in Middle-earth; but the Elven-ships made for this journey did not founder, and doubtless it left the Circles of the World and came at last to Eressëa. But it did not bring Amroth thither. The storm fell upon the coasts of Gondor just as dawn was peering through the flying clouds; but when Amroth woke the ship was already far from land. Crying aloud in despair *Nimrodel!* he leapt into the sea and swam towards the fading shore. The mariners with their Elvish sight for a long time could see him battling with the waves, until the rising sun gleamed through the clouds and far off lit his bright hair like a spark of gold. No eyes of Elves or Men ever saw him again in Middle-earth. Of what befell Nimrodel nothing is said here, though there were many legends concerning her fate.

The foregoing narrative was actually composed as an offshoot from an etymological discussion of the names of certain rivers in Middle-earth, in this case the Gilrain, a river of Lebennin in Gondor that flowed into the Bay of Belfalas west of Ethir Anduin, and another facet of the legend of Nimrodel emerges from the discussion of the element *rain*. This was probably derived from the stem *ran-* 'wander, stray, go on uncertain course' (as in *Mithrandir*, and in the name *Rána* of the Moon).

This would not seem suitable to any of the rivers of Gondor; but the names of rivers may often apply only to part of their course, to their source, or to their lower reaches, or to other features that struck explorers who named them. In this case, however, the fragments of the legend of Amroth and Nimrodel offer an explanation. The Gilrain came swiftly down from the mountains as did the other rivers of that region; but as it reached the end of the outlier of Ered Nimrais that separated it from the Celos [see the map accompanying Volume III of *The Lord of the Rings*] it ran into a wide shallow depression. In this it wandered for a while, and formed a small mere at the southern end before it cut through a ridge and went on swiftly again to join the Serni. When Nimrodel fled from Lórien it is said that seeking for the sea she became lost in the White Mountains, until at last (by what road or pass is not told) she came to a river that reminded her of her own stream in Lórien. Her heart was lightened, and she sat by a mere, seeing the stars reflected in its dim waters, and listening to the waterfalls by which the river went again on its journey down to the sea. There she fell into a deep sleep of weariness, and so long she slept that she did not come down into Belfalas until Amroth's ship had been blown out to sea, and he was lost trying to swim back to Belfalas. This legend was well known in the Dor-en-Ernil (the Land of the Prince),[14] and no doubt the name was given in memory of it.

The essay continues with a brief explanation of how Amroth as King of Lórien related to the rule there of Celeborn and Galadriel:

The people of Lórien were even then [i.e. at the time of the loss of Amroth] much as they were at the end of the Third Age: Silvan Elves in origin, but ruled by princes of Sindarin descent (as was the realm of Thranduil in the northern parts of Mirkwood; though whether Thranduil and Amroth were akin is not now known.)[15] They had however been much mingled with Noldor (of Sindarin speech), who passed through Moria after the destruction of Eregion by Sauron in the year 1697 of the Second Age. At that time Elrond went westward [*sic*; probably meaning simply that he did not cross the Misty Mountains] and established the refuge of Imladris; but Celeborn went at first to Lórien and fortified it against any further attempts of Sauron to cross the Anduin. When however Sauron withdrew to Mordor, and was (as reported) wholly concerned with conquests in the East, Celeborn rejoined Galadriel in Lindon.

Lórien had then long years of peace and obscurity under the rule of its own king Amdír, until the Downfall of Númenor and the sudden return of Sauron to Middle-earth. Amdír obeyed the summons of Gil-galad and brought as large a force as he could muster to the Last Alliance, but he was slain in the Battle of

Dagorlad and most of his company with him. Amroth, his son, became king.

This account is of course greatly at variance with that contained in 'Concerning Galadriel and Celeborn'. Amroth is no longer the son of Galadriel and Celeborn, but of Amdír, a prince of Sindarin origin. The older story of the relations of Galadriel and Celeborn with Eregion and Lórien seems to have been modified in many important respects, but how much of it would have been retained in any fully written narrative cannot be said. Celeborn's association with Lórien is now placed much further back (for in 'Concerning Galadriel and Celeborn' he never went to Lórien at all during the Second Age); and we learn here that many Noldorin Elves passed through Moria to Lórien *after* the destruction of Eregion. In the earlier account there is no suggestion of this, and the movement of 'Beleriandic' Elves into Lórien took place under peaceful conditions many years before (p. 236). The implication of the extract just given is that after Eregion's fall Celeborn led this migration to Lórien, while Galadriel joined Gil-galad in Lindon; but elsewhere, in a writing contemporary with this, it is said explicitly that they both at that time 'passed through Moria with a considerable following of Noldorin exiles and dwelt for many years in Lórien'. It is neither asserted nor denied in these late writings that Galadriel (or Celeborn) had relations with Lórien before 1697, and there are no other references outside 'Concerning Galadriel and Celeborn' to Celebrimbor's revolt (at some time between 1350 and 1400) against their rule in Eregion, nor to Galadriel's departure at that time to Lórien and her taking up rule there, while Celeborn remained behind in Eregion. It is not made clear in the late accounts where Galadriel and Celeborn passed the long years of the Second Age after the defeat of Sauron in Eriador; there are at any rate no further mentions of their agelong sojourn in Belfalas (p. 240).

The discussion of Amroth continues:

But during the Third Age Galadriel became filled with foreboding, and with Celeborn she journeyed to Lórien and stayed there long with Amroth, being especially concerned to learn all news and rumours of the growing shadow in Mirkwood and the dark stronghold in Dol Guldur. But his people were content with Amroth; he was valiant and wise, and his little kingdom was yet prosperous and beautiful. Therefore after long journeys of enquiry in Rhovanion, from Gondor and the borders of Mordor to Thranduil in the north, Celeborn and Galadriel passed over the mountains to Imladris, and there dwelt for many years; for Elrond was their kinsman, since he had early in the Third Age [in the year 109, according to the Tale of Years] wedded their daughter Celebrían.

After the disaster in Moria [in the year 1980] and the sorrows of Lórien, which was now left without a ruler (for Amroth was drowned in the sea in the Bay of Belfalas and left no heir), Celeborn and Galadriel returned to Lórien, and were welcomed by the people. There they dwelt while the Third Age lasted, but they took no title of King or Queen; for they said that they were only guardians of this small but fair realm, the last eastward outpost of the Elves.

Elsewhere there is one other reference to their movements during those years:

To Lórien Celeborn and Galadriel returned twice before the Last Alliance and the end of the Second Age; and in the Third Age, when the shadow of Sauron's recovery arose, they dwelt there again for a long time. In her wisdom Galadriel saw that Lórien would be a stronghold and point of power to prevent the Shadow from crossing the Anduin in the war that must inevitably come before it was again defeated (if that were possible); but that it needed a rule of greater strength and wisdom than the Silvan folk possessed. Nevertheless, it was not until the disaster in Moria, when by means beyond the foresight of Galadriel Sauron's power actually crossed the Anduin and Lórien was in great peril, its king lost, its people fleeing and likely to leave it deserted to be occupied by Orcs, that Galadriel and Celeborn took up their permanent abode in Lórien, and its government. But they took no title of King or Queen, and were the guardians that in the event brought it unviolated through the War of the Ring.

In another etymological discussion of the same period the name Amroth is explained as being a nickname derived from his living in a high *talan* or *flet*, the wooden platforms built high up in the trees of Lothlórien in which the Galadhrim dwelt (see *The Fellowship of the Ring* II 6): it meant 'upclimber, high climber'.[16] It is said here that the custom of dwelling in trees was not a habit of the Silvan Elves in general, but was developed in Lórien by the nature and situation of the land: a flat land with no good stone, except what might be quarried in the mountains westward and brought with difficulty down the Silverlode. Its chief wealth was in its trees, a remnant of the great forests of the Elder Days. But the dwelling in trees was not universal even in Lórien, and the *telain* or *flets* were in origin either refuges to be used in the event of attack, or most often (especially those high up in great trees) outlook posts from which the land and its borders could be surveyed by Elvish eyes: for Lórien after the end of the first millennium of the Third Age became a land of uneasy vigilance, and Amroth must have dwelt in growing disquiet ever since Dol Guldur was established in Mirkwood.

Such an outlook post, used by the wardens of the north marches, was the *flet* in which Frodo spent the night. The abode of Celeborn in Caras Galadhon was also of the same origin: its highest *flet*, which the Fellowship of the Ring did not see, was the highest point in the land. Earlier the *flet* of Amroth at the top of the great mound or hill of Cerin Amroth, piled by the labour of many hands, had been the highest, and was principally designed to watch Dol Guldur across the Anduin. The conversion of these *telain* into permanent dwellings was a later development, and only in Caras Galadhon were such dwellings numerous. But Caras Galadhon was itself a fortress, and only a small part of the Galadhrim dwelt within its walls. Living in such lofty houses was no doubt at first thought remarkable, and Amroth was probably the first to do so. It was thus from his living in a high *talan* that his name – the only one that was later remembered in legend – was most probably derived.

A note to the words 'Amroth was probably the first to do so' states:

> Unless it was Nimrodel. Her motives were different. She loved the waters and the falls of Nimrodel from which she would not long be parted; but as times darkened the stream was too near the north borders, and in a part where few of the Galadhrim now dwelt. Maybe it was from her that Amroth took the idea of living in a high *flet*.[17]

Returning to the legend of Amroth and Nimrodel given above, what was the 'haven in the south' where Amroth awaited for Nimrodel, and where (as he told her) 'many of his own people had come long ago' (p. 241)? Two passages in *The Lord of the Rings* bear on this question. One is in *The Fellowship of the Ring* II 6, where Legolas, after singing the song of Amroth and Nimrodel, speaks of 'the Bay of Belfalas, whence the Elves of Lórien set sail'. The other is in *The Return of the King* V 9, where Legolas, looking on Prince Imrahil of Dol Amroth, saw that he was 'one who had elven-blood in his veins', and said to him: 'It is long since the people of Nimrodel left the woodlands of Lórien, and yet still one may see that not all sailed from Amroth's haven west over water.' To which Prince Imrahil replied: 'So it is said in the lore of my land.'

Late and fragmentary notes go some way to explaining these references. Thus in a discussion of linguistic and political interrelations in Middle-earth (dating from 1969 or later) there is a passing reference to the fact that in the days of the earlier settlements of Númenor the shores of the Bay of Belfalas were still mainly desolate 'except for a haven and small settlement of Elves at the south of the confluence of Morthond and Ringló' (i.e. just north of Dol Amroth).

This, according to the traditions of Dol Amroth, had been established by seafaring Sindar from the west havens of Beleriand who fled in three small ships when the power of Morgoth overwhelmed the Eldar and the Atani; but it was later increased by adventurers of the Silvan Elves seeking for the sea who came down Anduin.

The Silvan Elves (it is remarked here) 'were never wholly free of an unquiet and a yearning for the Sea which at times drove some of them to wander from their homes'. To relate this story of the 'three small ships' to the traditions recorded in *The Silmarillion* we would probably have to assume that they escaped from Brithombar or Eglarest (the Havens of the Falas on the west coast of Beleriand) when they were destroyed in the year after the Nirnaeth Arnoediad (*The Silmarillion* p. 196), but that whereas Círdan and Gil-galad made a refuge on the Isle of Balar these three ships' companies sailed far further south down the coasts, to Belfalas.

But a quite different account, making the establishment of the Elvish haven later, is given in an unfinished scrap on the origin of the name *Belfalas*. It is said here that while the element *Bel-* is certainly derived from a pre-Númenórean name, its source was in fact Sindarin. The note peters out before any further information is given about *Bel-*, but the reason given for its Sindarin origin is that 'there was one small but important element in Gondor of quite exceptional kind: an Eldarin settlement'. After the breaking of Thangorodrim the Elves of Beleriand, if they did not take ship over the Great Sea or remain in Lindon, wandered east over the Blue Mountains into Eriador; but there appears nonetheless to have been a group of Sindar who in the beginning of the Second Age went south. They were a remnant of the people of Doriath who harboured still their grudge against the Noldor; and having remained a while at the Grey Havens, where they learned the craft of shipbuilding, 'they went in the course of years seeking a place for lives of their own, and at last they settled at the mouth of the Morthond. There was already a primitive harbour there of fisherfolk, but these in fear of the Eldar fled into the mountains.'[18]

In a note written in December 1972 or later, and among the last writings of my father's on the subject of Middle-earth, there is a discussion of the Elvish strain in Men, as to its being observable in the beardlessness of those who were so descended (it was a characteristic of all Elves to be beardless); and it is here noted in connection with the princely house of

Dol Amroth that 'this line had a special Elvish strain, according to its own legends' (with a reference to the speeches between Legolas and Imrahil in *The Return of the King* V 9, cited above).

As Legolas' mention of Nimrodel shows, there was an ancient Elvish port near Dol Amroth, and a small settlement of Silvan Elves there from Lórien. The legend of the prince's line was that one of their earliest fathers had wedded an Elf-maiden: in some versions it was indeed (evidently improbably) said to have been Nimrodel herself. In other tales, and more probably, it was one of Nimrodel's companions who was lost in the upper mountain glens.

This latter version of the legend appears in more detailed form in a note appended to an unpublished genealogy of the line of Dol Amroth from Angelimar, the twentieth prince, father of Adrahil, father of Imrahil, prince of Dol Amroth at the time of the War of the Ring:

> In the tradition of his house Angelimar was the twentieth in unbroken descent from Galador, first Lord of Dol Amroth (c. Third Age 2004–2129). According to the same traditions Galador was the son of Imrazôr the Númenórean, who dwelt in Belfalas, and the Elven-lady Mithrellas. She was one of the companions of Nimrodel, among many of the Elves that fled to the coast about the year 1980 of the Third Age, when evil arose in Moria; and Nimrodel and her maidens strayed in the wooded hills, and were lost. But in this tale it is said that Imrazôr harboured Mithrellas, and took her to wife. But when she had borne him a son, Galador, and a daughter, Gilmith, she slipped away by night and he saw her no more. But though Mithrellas was of the lesser Silvan race (and not of the High Elves or the Grey) it was ever held that the house and kin of the Lords of Dol Amroth was noble by blood as they were fair in face and mind.

The Elessar

In unpublished writing there is little else to be found concerning the history of Celeborn and Galadriel, save for a very rough manuscript of four pages titled 'The Elessar'. It is in the first stage of composition, but bears a few pencilled emendations; there are no other versions. It reads, with some very slight editorial emendation, as follows:

> There was in Gondolin a jewel-smith named Enerdhil, the greatest of that craft among the Noldor after the death of Fëanor.

Enerdhil loved all green things that grew, and his greatest joy was to see the sunlight through the leaves of trees. And it came into his heart to make a jewel within which the clear light of the sun should be imprisoned, but the jewel should be green as leaves. And he made this thing, and even the Noldor marvelled at it. For it is said that those who looked through this stone saw things that were withered or burned healed again or as they were in the grace of their youth, and that the hands of one who held it brought to all that they touched healing from hurt. This gem Enerdhil gave to Idril the King's daughter, and she wore it upon her breast; and so it was saved from the burning of Gondolin. And before Idril set sail she said to Eärendil her son: 'The Elessar I leave with thee, for there are grievous hurts to Middle-earth which thou maybe shalt heal. But to none other shalt thou deliver it.' And indeed at Sirion's Haven there were many hurts to heal both of Men and Elves, and of beasts that fled thither from the horror of the North; and while Eärendil dwelt there they were healed and prospered, and all things were for a while green and fair. But when Eärendil began his great voyages upon the Sea he wore the Elessar upon his breast, for amongst all his searchings the thought was always before him: that he might perhaps find Idril again; and his first memory of Middle-earth was the green stone above her breast, as she sang above his cradle while Gondolin was still in flower. So it was that the Elessar passed away, when Eärendil returned no more to Middle-earth.

In ages after there was again an Elessar, and of this two things are said, though which is true only those Wise could say who now are gone. For some say that the second was indeed only the first returned, by the grace of the Valar; and that Olórin (who was known in Middle-earth as Mithrandir) brought it with him out of the West. And on a time Olórin came to Galadriel, who dwelt now under the trees of Greenwood the Great; and they had long speech together. For the years of her exile began to lie heavy on the Lady of the Noldor, and she longed for news of her kin and for the blessed land of her birth, and yet was unwilling to forsake Middle-earth [this sentence was changed to read: but was not permitted yet to forsake Middle-earth]. And when Olórin had told her many tidings she sighed, and said: 'I grieve in Middle-earth, for leaves fall and flowers fade; and my heart yearns, remembering trees and grass that do not die. I would have these in my home.' Then Olórin said: 'Would you then have the Elessar?'

And Galadriel said: 'Where now is the Stone of Eärendil?

And Enerdhil is gone who made it.' 'Who knows?' said Olórin. 'Surely,' said Galadriel, 'they have passed over Sea, as almost all fair things beside. And must Middle-earth then fade and perish for ever?' 'That is its fate,' said Olórin. 'Yet for a little while that might be amended, if the Elessar should return. For a little, until the Days of Men are come.' 'If – and yet how could that be,' said Galadriel. 'For surely the Valar are now removed and Middle-earth is far from their thought, and all who cling to it are under a shadow.'

'It is not so,' said Olórin. 'Their eyes are not dimmed nor their hearts hardened. In token of which look upon this!' And he held before her the Elessar, and she looked on it and wondered. And Olórin said: 'This I bring to you from Yavanna. Use it as you may, and for a while you shall make the land of your dwelling the fairest place in Middle-earth. But it is not for you to possess. You shall hand it on when the time comes. For before you grow weary, and at last forsake Middle-earth one shall come who is to receive it, and his name shall be that of the stone: Elessar he shall be called.'[19]

The other tale runs so: that long ago, ere Sauron deluded the smiths of Eregion, Galadriel came there, and she said to Celebrimbor, the chief of the Elven-smiths: 'I am grieved in Middle-earth, for leaves fall and flowers fade that I have loved, so that the land of my dwelling is filled with regret that no Spring can redress.'

'How otherwise can it be for the Eldar, if they cling to Middle-earth?' said Celebrimbor. 'Will you then pass over Sea?'

'Nay,' she said. 'Angrod is gone, and Aegnor is gone, and Felagund is no more. Of Finarfin's children I am the last.[20] But my heart is still proud. What wrong did the golden house of Finarfin do that I should ask the pardon of the Valar, or be content with an isle in the sea whose native land was Aman the Blessed? Here I am mightier.'

'What would you then?' said Celebrimbor.

'I would have trees and grass about me that do not die – here in the land that is mine,' she answered. 'What has become of the skill of the Eldar?' And Celebrimbor said: 'Where now is the Stone of Eärendil? And Enerdhil who made it is gone.' 'They have passed over Sea,' said Galadriel, 'with almost all fair things else. But must then Middle-earth fade and perish for ever?'

'That is its fate, I deem,' said Celebrimbor. 'But you know that I love you (though you turned to Celeborn of the Trees), and for that love I will do what I can, if haply by my art your grief can be lessened.' But he did not say to Galadriel that he himself was of Gondolin long ago, and a friend of Enerdhil, though his friend in most things outrivalled him. Yet if Enerdhil had not been then Celebrimbor would have been more renowned. Therefore he took thought, and began a long and delicate labour, and so for Galadriel he made the greatest of his works (save the Three Rings only). And it is said that more subtle and clear was the green gem that he made than that of Enerdhil, but yet its light had less power. For whereas that of Enerdhil was lit by the Sun in its youth, already many years had passed ere Celebrimbor began his work, and nowhere in Middle-earth was the light as clear as it had been, for though Morgoth had been thrust out into the Void and could not enter again, his far shadow lay upon it. Radiant nonetheless was the Elessar of Celebrimbor; and he set it within a great brooch of silver in the likeness of an eagle rising upon outspread wings.[21] Wielding the Elessar all things grew fair about Galadriel, until the coming of the Shadow to the Forest. But afterwards when Nenya, chief of the Three,[22] was sent to her by Celebrimbor, she needed it (as she thought) no more, and she gave it to Celebrían her daughter, and so it came to Arwen and to Aragorn who was called Elessar.

At the end is written:

The Elessar was made in Gondolin by Celebrimbor, and so came to Idril and so to Eärendil. But that passed away. But the second Elessar was made also by Celebrimbor in Eregion at the request of the Lady Galadriel (whom he loved), and it was not under the One, being made before Sauron rose again.

This narrative goes with 'Concerning Galadriel and Celeborn' in certain features, and was probably written at about the same time, or a little earlier. Celebrimbor is here again a jewel-smith of Gondolin, rather than one of the Fëanorians (cf. p. 235); and Galadriel is spoken of as being *unwilling* to forsake Middle-earth (cf. p. 234) – though the text was later emended and the conception of the ban introduced, and at a later point in the narrative she speaks of the pardon of the Valar.

Enerdhil appears in no other writing; and the concluding words of the text show that Celebrimbor was to displace him as the maker of the Elessar in Gondolin. Of Celebrimbor's love for Galadriel there is no trace elsewhere. In 'Concerning Galadriel and Celeborn' the suggestion is that he came to Eregion with them (p. 235); but in that text, as in *The Silmarillion*, Galadriel met Celeborn in Doriath, and it is difficult to understand

Celebrimbor's words 'though you turned to Celeborn of the Trees'. Obscure also is the reference to Galadriel's dwelling 'under the trees of Greenwood the Great'. This might be taken as a loose use (nowhere else evidenced) of the expression to include the woods of Lórien, on the other side of Anduin; but 'the coming of the Shadow to the Forest' undoubtedly refers to the arising of Sauron in Dol Guldur, which in Appendix A (III) to *The Lord of the Rings* is called 'the Shadow in the Forest'. This may imply that Galadriel's power at one time extended into the southern parts of Greenwood the Great; and support for this may be found in 'Concerning Galadriel and Celeborn', p. 236, where the realm of Lórinand (Lórien) is said to have 'extended into the forests on both sides of the Great River, including the region where afterwards was Dol Guldur'. It is possible, also, that the same conception underlay the statement in Appendix B to *The Lord of the Rings*, in the headnote to the Tale of Years of the Second Age, as it appeared in the first edition: 'many of the Sindar passed eastward and established realms in the forests far away. The chief of these were Thranduil in the north of Greenwood the Great, and Celeborn in the south of the forest.' In the revised edition this remark about Celeborn was omitted, and instead there appears a reference to his dwelling in Lindon (cited above, p. 228).

Lastly, it may be remarked that the healing power here ascribed to the Elessar at the Havens of Sirion is in *The Silmarillion* (p. 247) attributed to the Silmaril.

NOTES

1   See Appendix E, p. 266.

2   In a note in unpublished material the Elves of Harlindon, or Lindon south of the Lune, are said to have been largely of Sindarin origin, and the region to have been a fief under the rule of Celeborn. It is natural to associate this with the statement in Appendix B; but the reference may possibly be to a later period, for the movements and dwelling-places of Celeborn and Galadriel after the fall of Eregion in 1697 are extremely obscure.

3   Cf. *The Fellowship of the Ring* I 2: 'The ancient East–West Road ran through the Shire to its end at the Grey Havens, and dwarves had always used it on their way to their mines in the Blue Mountains.'

4   It is said in Appendix A (III) to *The Lord of the Rings* that the ancient cities of Nogrod and Belegost were ruined in the breaking of Thangorodrim; but in the Tale of Years in Appendix B: 'c. 40 Many Dwarves leaving their old cities in Ered Luin go to Moria and swell its numbers.'

5   In a note to the text it is explained that *Lórinand* was the Nandorin name of this region (afterwards called *Lórien* and *Lothlórien*), and

contained the Elvish word meaning 'golden light': 'valley of gold'. The Quenya form would be *Laurenandë*, the Sindarin *Glornan* or *Nan Laur*. Both here and elsewhere the meaning of the name is explained by reference to the golden mallorn-trees of Lothlórien; but they were brought there by Galadriel (for the story of their origin see pp. 167–8), and in another, later, discussion the name *Lórinand* is said to have been itself a transformation, after the introduction of the mallorns, of a yet older name *Lindórinand*, 'Vale of the Land of the Singers'. Since the Elves of this land were in origin Teleri, there is here no doubt present the name by which the Teleri called themselves, *Lindar*, 'the Singers'. From many other discussions of the names of Lothlórien, to some extent at variance among themselves, it emerges that all the later names were probably due to Galadriel herself, combining different elements: *laurë* 'gold', *nan(d)* 'valley', *ndor* 'land', *lin-* 'sing'; and in *Laurelindórinan* 'Valley of Singing Gold' (which Treebeard told the Hobbits was the earlier name) deliberately echoing the name of the Golden Tree that grew in Valinor, 'for which, as is plain, Galadriel's longing increased year by year to, at last, an overwhelming regret'.

Lórien itself was originally the Quenya name of a region in Valinor, often used as the name of the Vala (Irmo) to whom it belonged: 'a place of rest and shadowy trees and fountains, a retreat from cares and griefs'. The further change from *Lórinand* 'Valley of Gold' to *Lórien* 'may well be due to Galadriel herself', for 'the resemblance cannot be accidental. She had endeavoured to make Lórien a refuge and an island of peace and beauty, a memorial of ancient days, but was now filled with regret and misgiving, knowing that the golden dream was hastening to a grey awakening. It may be noted that Treebeard interpreted *Lothlórien* as "Dreamflower".'

In 'Concerning Galadriel and Celeborn' I have retained the name *Lórinand* throughout, although when it was written Lórinand was intended as the original and ancient Nandorin name of the region, and the story of the introduction of the mallorns by Galadriel had not yet been devised.

6   This is a later emendation; the text as originally written stated that Lórinand was ruled by native princes.

7   In an isolated and undateable note it is said that although the name *Sauron* is used earlier than this in the Tale of Years, his name, implying identity with the great lieutenant of Morgoth in *The Silmarillion*, was not actually known until about the year 1600 of the Second Age, the time of the forging of the One Ring. The mysterious power of hostility, to Elves and Edain, was perceived soon after the year 500, and among the Númenóreans first by Aldarion towards the end of the eighth century (about the time when he established the haven of Vinyalondë, p. 176). But it had no known centre. Sauron

endeavoured to keep distinct his two sides: *enemy* and *tempter*. When he came among the Noldor he adopted a specious fair form (a kind of simulated anticipation of the later Istari), and a fair name: *Artano* 'high-smith', or *Aulendil*, meaning one who is devoted to the service of the Vala Aulë. (In *Of the Rings of Power*, p. 287, the name that Sauron gave to himself at this time was *Annatar*, the Lord of Gifts; but that name is not mentioned here.) The note goes on to say that Galadriel was not deceived, saying that this *Aulendil* was not in the train of Aulë in Valinor; 'but this is not decisive, since Aulë existed before the "Building of Arda", and the probability is that Sauron was in fact one of the Aulëan Maiar, corrupted "before Arda began" by Melkor'. With this compare the opening sentences in *Of the Rings of Power*: 'Of old there was Sauron the Maia. . . . In the beginning of Arda Melkor seduced him to his allegiance.'

8 In a letter written in September 1954 my father said: 'At the beginning of the Second Age he [Sauron] was still beautiful to look at, or could still assume a beautiful visible shape – and was not indeed wholly evil, not unless all "reformers" who want to hurry up with "reconstruction" and "reorganization" are wholly evil, even before pride and the lust to exert their will eat them up. The particular branch of the High Elves concerned, the Noldor or Loremasters, were always vulnerable on the side of "science and technology", as we should call it: they wanted to have the knowledge that Sauron genuinely had, and those of Eregion refused the warnings of Gil-galad and Elrond. The particular "desire" of the Eregion Elves – an "allegory" if you like of a love of machinery, and technical devices – is also symbolized by their special friendship with the Dwarves of Moria.'

9 Galadriel cannot have made use of the powers of Nenya until a much later time, after the loss of the Ruling Ring; but it must be admitted that the text does not at all suggest this (although she is said just above to have advised Celebrimbor that the Elven Rings should never be used).

10 The text was emended to read 'the first White Council'. In the Tale of Years the formation of the White Council is given under the year 2463 of the Third Age; but it may be that the name of the Council of the Third Age deliberately echoed that of this Council held long before, the more especially as several of the chief members of the one had been members of the other.

11 Earlier in this narrative (p. 237) it is said that Gil-galad gave Narya, the Red Ring, to Círdan as soon as he himself received it from Celebrimbor, and this agrees with the statements in Appendix B to *The Lord of the Rings* and in *Of the Rings of Power*, that Círdan held it from the beginning. The statement here, at variance with the others, was added in the margin of the text.

12 On the Silvan Elves and their speech see Appendix A, p. 256.

13 See Appendix C, p. 260, on the boundaries of Lórien.

14 The origin of the name *Dor-en-Ernil* is nowhere given; its only other occurrence is on the large map of Rohan, Gondor, and Mordor in *The Lord of the Rings*. On that map it is placed on the other side of the mountains from Dol Amroth, but its occurrence in the present context suggests that *Ernil* was the Prince of Dol Amroth (which might be supposed in any case).

15 See Appendix B, p. 257, on the Sindarin princes of the Silvan Elves.

16 The explanation supposes that the first element in the name *Amroth* is the same Elvish word as Quenya *amba* 'up', found also in Sindarin *amon*, a hill or mountain with steep sides; while the second element is a derivative from a stem *rath-* meaning 'climb' (whence also the noun *rath*, which in the Númenórean Sindarin used in Gondor in the naming of places and persons was applied to all the longer roadways and street of Minas Tirith, nearly all of which were on an incline: so *Rath Dínen*, the Silent Street, leading down from the Citadel to the Tombs of the Kings).

17 In the 'Brief Recounting' of the legend of Amroth and Nimrodel it is said that Amroth dwelt in the trees of Cerin Amroth 'because of his love for Nimrodel' (p. 240).

18 The place of the Elvish haven in Belfalas is marked with the name *Edhellond* ('Elf-haven', see the Appendix to *The Silmarillion* under *edhel* and *lond*) on the decorated map of Middle-earth by Pauline Baynes; but I have found no other occurrence of this name. See Appendix D, p. 261. Cf. *The Adventures of Tom Bombadil* (1962), p. 8: 'In the Langstrand and Dol Amroth there were many traditions of the ancient Elvish dwellings, and of the haven at the mouth of the Morthond from which "westward ships" had sailed as far back as the fall of Eregion in the Second Age.'

19 This chimes with the passage in *The Fellowship of the Ring* II 8, where Galadriel, giving the green stone to Aragorn, said: 'In this hour take the name that was foretold for you, Elessar, the Elfstone of the house of Elendil!'

20 The text here and again immediately below has *Finrod*, which I have changed to *Finarfin* to avoid confusion. Before the revised edition of *The Lord of the Rings* was published in 1966 my father changed Finrod to Finarfin, while his son Felagund, previously called Inglor Felagund, became Finrod Felagund. Two passages in the Appendices B and F were accordingly emended for the revised edition. – It is noteworthy that Orodreth, King of Nargothrond after Finrod Felagund, is not here named by Galadriel among her brothers. For a reason unknown to me, my father displaced the second King of Nargothrond and made him a member of the same family in the next generation; but this and associated genealogical changes were never incorporated in the narratives of *The Silmarillion*.

21 Compare the description of the Elfstone in *The Fellowship of the Ring* II 8: 'Then [Galadriel] lifted from her lap a great stone of a clear green, set in a silver brooch that was wrought in the likeness of an eagle with outspread wings; and as she held it up the gem flashed like the sun through the leaves of spring.'

22 But in *The Return of the King* VI 9, where the Blue Ring is seen on Elrond's finger, it is called 'Vilya, the mightiest of the Three'.

APPENDICES

APPENDIX A

THE SILVAN ELVES AND THEIR SPEECH

According to *The Silmarillion* (p. 94) some of the Nandor, the Telerin Elves who abandoned the march of the Eldar on the eastern side of the Misty Mountains, 'dwelt age-long in the woods of the Vale of the Great River' (while others, it is said, went down Anduin to its mouths, and yet others entered Eriador: from these last came the Green-elves of Ossiriand).

In a late etymological discussion of the names Galadriel, Celeborn, and Lórien the Silvan Elves of Mirkwood and Lórien are specifically declared to be descended from the Telerin Elves who remained in the Vale of Anduin:

> The Silvan Elves (*Tawarwaith*) were in origin Teleri, and so remoter kin of the Sindar, though even longer separated from them than the Teleri of Valinor. They were descended from those of the Teleri who, on the Great Journey, were daunted by the Misty Mountains and lingered in the Vale of Anduin, and so never reached Beleriand or the Sea. They were thus closer akin to the Nandor (otherwise called the Green-elves) of Ossiriand, who eventually crossed the mountains and came at last into Beleriand.

The Silvan Elves hid themselves in woodland fastnesses beyond the Misty Mountains, and became small and scattered peoples, hardly to be distinguished from Avari;

> but they still remembered that they were in origin Eldar, members of the Third Clan, and they welcomed those of the Noldor and especially the Sindar who did not pass over the Sea but migrated eastward [i.e. at the beginning of the Second Age]. Under the leadership of these they became again ordered folk and increased in wisdom. Thranduil father of Legolas of the Nine Walkers was Sindarin, and that tongue was used in his house, though not by all his folk.

In Lórien, where many of the people were Sindar in origin, or Noldor, survivors from Eregion [see p. 243], Sindarin had become the language of all the people. In what way their Sindarin differed from the forms of Beleriand – see *The Fellowship of the Ring* II 6, where Frodo reports that the speech of the Silvan folk that they used among themselves was unlike that of the West – is not of course now known. It probably differed in little more than what would now be popularly called 'accent': mainly differences of vowel-sounds and intonation sufficient to mislead one who, as Frodo, was not well acquainted with purer Sindarin. There may of course also have been some local words and other features ultimately due to the influence of the former Silvan tongue. Lórien had long been much isolated from the outside world. Certainly some names preserved from its past, such as *Amroth* and *Nimrodel*, cannot be fully explained from Sindarin, though fitting it in form. *Caras* seems to be an old word for a moated fortress, not found in Sindarin. *Lórien* is probably an alteration of an older name now lost [though earlier the original Silvan or Nandorin name was stated to be *Lórinand*; see p. 252, note 5].

With these remarks on Silvan names compare Appendix F (I) to *The Lord of the Rings*, section 'Of the Elves', footnote (appearing only in the revised edition).

Another general statement concerning Silvan Elvish is found in a linguistic-historical discussion dating from the same late period as that just cited:

Although the dialects of the Silvan Elves, when they again met their long separated kindred, had so far diverged from Sindarin as to be hardly intelligible, little study was needed to reveal their kinship as Eldarin tongues. Though the comparison of the Silvan dialects with their own speech greatly interested the loremasters, especially those of Noldorin origin, little is now known of the Silvan Elvish. The Silvan Elves had invented no forms of writing, and those who learned this art from the Sindar wrote in Sindarin as well as they could. By the end of the Third Age the Silvan tongues had probably ceased to be spoken in the two regions that had importance at the time of the War of the Ring: Lórien and the realm of Thranduil in northern Mirkwood. All that survived of them in the records was a few words and several names of persons and places.

APPENDIX B

THE SINDARIN PRINCES OF THE SILVAN ELVES

In Appendix B to *The Lord of the Rings*, in the headnote to the Tale of Years of the Second Age, it is said that 'before the building of the Barad-dûr many of the Sindar passed eastward, and some established realms in the forests far away, where their people were mostly Silvan Elves. Thranduil, king in the north of Greenwood the Great, was one of these.' Something more of the history of these Sindarin princes of the Silvan Elves is found in my father's late philological writings. Thus in one essay Thranduil's realm is said to have

extended into the woods surrounding the Lonely Mountain and growing along the west shores of the Long Lake, before the coming of the Dwarves exiled from Moria and the invasion of the Dragon. The Elvish folk of this realm had migrated from the south, being the kin and neighbours of the Elves of Lórien; but they had dwelt in Greenwood the Great east of Anduin. In the Second Age their king, Oropher [the father of Thranduil, father of Legolas], had withdrawn northward beyond the Gladden Fields. This he did to be free from the power and encroachments of the Dwarves of Moria, which had grown to be the greatest of the mansions of the Dwarves recorded in history; and also he resented the intrusions of Celeborn and Galadriel into Lórien. But as yet there was little to fear between the Greenwood and the Mountains and there was constant intercourse between his people and their kin across the River, until the War of the Last Alliance.

Despite the desire of the Silvan Elves to meddle as little as might be in the affairs of the Noldor and Sindar, or of any other peoples, Dwarves, Men, or Orcs, Oropher had the wisdom to foresee that peace would not return unless Sauron was overcome. He therefore assembled a great army of his now numerous people, and joining with the lesser army of Malgalad of Lórien he led the host of the Silvan Elves to battle. The Silvan Elves were hardy and valiant, but ill-equipped with armour or weapons in comparison with the Eldar of the West; also they were independent, and not disposed to place themselves under the supreme command of Gil-galad. Their losses were thus more grievous than they need have been, even in that terrible war. Malgalad and more than half his following perished in the great battle of the Dagorlad, being cut off from the main host and driven into the Dead Marshes. Oropher was slain in the first assault upon Mordor, rushing forward at the head of his most doughty warriors before Gil-galad had given the signal for the advance. Thranduil his son survived, but when the war ended and Sauron was slain (as it seemed) he led back home barely a third of the army that had marched to war.

Malgalad of Lórien occurs nowhere else, and is not said here to be the father of Amroth. On the other hand, Amdír father of Amroth is twice (pp. 240 and 243 above) said to have been slain in the Battle of Dagorlad, and it seems therefore that Malgalad can be simply equated with Amdír. But which name replaced the other I cannot say. This essay continues:

A long peace followed in which the numbers of the Silvan Elves grew

again; but they were unquiet and anxious, feeling the change of the
world that the Third Age would bring. Men also were increasing in
numbers and in power. The dominion of the Númenórean kings of
Gondor was reaching out northwards towards the borders of Lórien
and the Greenwood. The Free Men of the North (so called by the Elves
because they were not under the rule of the Dúnedain, and had not for
the most part been subjected by Sauron or his servants) were spreading
southwards: mostly east of the Greenwood, though some were estab-
lishing themselves in the eaves of the forest and the grasslands of the
Vales of Anduin. More ominous were rumours from the further East:
the Wild Men were restless. Former servants and worshippers of
Sauron, they were released now from his tyranny, but not from the
evil and darkness that he had set in their hearts. Cruel wars raged
among them, from which some were withdrawing westward, with
minds filled with hatred, regarding all that dwelt in the West as enemies
to be slain and plundered. But there was in Thranduil's heart a still
deeper shadow. He had seen the horror of Mordor and could not forget
it. If ever he looked south its memory dimmed the light of the Sun,
and though he knew that it was now broken and deserted and under
the vigilance of the Kings of Men, fear spoke in his heart that it was
not conquered for ever: it would arise again.

In another passage written at the same time as the foregoing it is said
that when a thousand years of the Third Age had passed and the Shadow
fell upon Greenwood the Great, the Silvan Elves ruled by Thranduil

> retreated before it as it spread ever northward, until at last Thranduil
> established his realm in the north-east of the forest and delved there
> a fortress and great halls underground. Oropher was of Sindarin origin,
> and no doubt Thranduil his son was following the example of King
> Thingol long before, in Doriath; though his halls were not to be
> compared with Menegroth. He had not the arts nor the wealth nor the
> aid of the Dwarves; and compared with the Elves of Doriath his Silvan
> folk were rude and rustic. Oropher had come among them with only a
> handful of Sindar, and they were soon merged with the Silvan Elves,
> adopting their language and taking names of Silvan form and style.
> This they did deliberately; for they (and other similar adventurers
> forgotten in the legends or only briefly named) came from Doriath
> after its ruin, and had no desire to leave Middle-earth, nor to be
> merged with the other Sindar of Beleriand, dominated by the Noldorin
> Exiles for whom the folk of Doriath had no great love. They wished
> indeed to become Silvan folk and to return, as they said, to the simple
> life natural to the Elves before the invitation of the Valar had disturbed
> it.

Nowhere (I believe) is it made clear how the adoption of the Silvan speech by the Sindarin rulers of the Silvan Elves of Mirkwood, as described here, is to be related to the statement cited on p. 257 that by the end of the Third Age Silvan Elvish had ceased to be spoken in Thranduil's realm. See further note 14 to 'The Disaster of the Gladden Fields', p. 280.

APPENDIX C

THE BOUNDARIES OF LÓRIEN

In Appendix A (I, iv) to *The Lord of the Rings* the kingdom of Gondor at the summit of its power in the days of King Hyarmendacil I (Third Age 1015-1149) is said to have extended northwards 'to Celebrant and the southern eaves of Mirkwood'. This my father stated several times to be in error: the correct reading should be 'to the Field of Celebrant'. According to his late writing on the interrelations of the languages of Middle-earth,

The river Celebrant (Silverlode) was within the borders of the realm of Lórien, and the effective bounds of the kingdom of Gondor in the north (west of Anduin) was the river Limlight. The whole of the grasslands between Silverlode and Limlight, into which the woods of Lórien formerly extended further south, were known in Lórien as Parth Celebrant (i.e. the field, or enclosed grassland, of Silverlode) and regarded as part of its realm, though not inhabited by its Elvish folk beyond the eaves of the woods. In later days Gondor built a bridge over the upper Limlight, and often occupied the narrow land between the lower Limlight and Anduin as part of its eastern defences, since the great loops of the Anduin (where it came down swiftly past Lórien and entered low flat lands before its descent again into the chasm of the Emyn Muil) had many shallows and wide shoals over which a determined and well-equipped enemy could force a crossing by rafts or pontoons, especially in the two westward bends, known as the North and South Undeeps. It was to this land that the name Parth Celebrant was applied in Gondor; hence its use in defining the ancient northern boundary. In the time of the War of the Ring, when all the land north of the White Mountains (save Anórien) as far as the Limlight had become part of the Kingdom of Rohan, the name Parth (Field of) Celebrant was only used of the great battle in which Eorl the Young destroyed the invaders of Gondor [see p. 299].

In another essay my father noted that whereas east and west the land of Lórien was bounded by Anduin and by the mountains (and he says nothing about any extension of the realm of Lórien across the Anduin, see p. 252), it had no clearly defined borders northward and southward.

Of old the Galadhrim had claimed to govern the woods as far as the falls in the Silverlode where Frodo was bathed; southward it had extended far beyond the Silverlode into more open woodland of smaller trees that merged into Fangorn Forest, though the heart of the realm had always been in the angle between Silverlode and Anduin where Caras Galadhon stood. There were no visible borders between Lórien and Fangorn, but neither the Ents nor the Galadhrim ever passed them. For legend reported that Fangorn himself had met the King of the Galadhrim in ancient days, and Fangorn had said: 'I know mine, and you know yours; let neither side molest what is the other's. But if an Elf should wish to walk in my land for his pleasure he will be welcome; and if an Ent should be seen in your land fear no evil.' Long years had passed, however, since Ent or Elf had set foot in the other land.

APPENDIX D

THE PORT OF LOND DAER

It was told in 'Concerning Galadriel and Celeborn' that in the war against Sauron in Eriador at the end of the seventeenth century of the Second Age the Númenórean admiral Ciryatur put a strong force ashore at the mouth of the Gwathló (Greyflood), where there was 'a small Númenórean harbour' (p. 239). This seems to be the first reference to that port, of which a good deal is told in later writings.

The fullest account is in the philological essay concerning the names of rivers which has already been cited in connection with the legend of Amroth and Nimrodel (pp. 242 ff.). In this essay the name Gwathló is discussed as follows:

The river Gwathló is translated 'Greyflood'. But *gwath* is a Sindarin word for 'shadow', in the sense of dim light, owing to cloud or mist, or in deep valleys. This does not seem to fit the geography. The wide lands divided by the Gwathló into the regions called by the Númenóreans Minhiriath ('Between the Rivers', Baranduin and Gwathló) and Enedwaith ('Middle-folk') were mainly plains, open and mountainless. At the point of the confluence of Glanduin and Mitheithel [Hoarwell] the land was almost flat, and the waters became sluggish and tended to spread into fenland.* But some hundred miles below Tharbad the slope

* The Glanduin ('border-river') flowed down from the Misty Mountains south of Moria to join the Mitheithel above Tharbad. On the original map to *The Lord of the Rings* the name was not marked (it only occurs once in the book, in Appendix A (I, iii)). It seems that in 1969 my father communicated to Miss Pauline Baynes certain additional names for inclusion in her decorated map of Middle-earth: 'Edhellond' (referred to above, p. 255, note 18), 'Andrast', 'Drúwaith Iaur (Old Púkel-land)', 'Lond Daer (ruins)',

increased. The Gwathló, however, never became swift, and ships of smaller draught could without difficulty sail or be rowed as far as Tharbad. The origin of the name Gwathló must be sought in history. In the time of the War of the Ring the lands were still in places well-wooded, especially in Minhiriath and in the south-east of Enedwaith; but most of the plains were grasslands. Since the Great Plague of the year 1636 of the Third Age Minhiriath had been almost entirely deserted, though a few secretive hunter-folk lived in the woods. In Enedwaith the remnants of the Dunlendings lived in the east, in the foothills of the Misty Mountains; and a fairly numerous but barbarous fisher-folk dwelt between the mouths of the Gwathló and the Angren (Isen).

But in the earlier days, at the time of the first explorations of the Númenóreans, the situation was quite different. Minhiriath and Enedwaith were occupied by vast and almost continuous forests, except in the central region of the Great Fens. The changes that followed were largely due to the operations of Tar-Aldarion, the Mariner-king, who formed a friendship and alliance with Gil-galad. Aldarion had a great hunger for timber, desiring to make Númenor into a great naval power; his felling of trees in Númenor had caused great dissensions. In voyages down the coasts he saw with wonder the great forests, and he chose the estuary of the Gwathló for the site of a new haven entirely under Númenórean control (Gondor of course did not yet exist). There he began great works, that continued to be extended after his days. This entry into Eriador later proved of great importance in the war against Sauron (Second Age 1693–1701); but it was in origin a timber-port and ship-building harbour. The native people were fairly numerous and warlike, but they were forest-dwellers, scattered communities without central leadership. They were in awe of the Númenóreans, but they did not become hostile until the tree-felling became devastating. Then they attacked and ambushed the Númenóreans when they could, and the Númenóreans treated them as enemies, and became ruthless in their fellings, giving no thought to husbandry or replanting. The fellings had at first been along both banks of the Gwathló, and timber had been floated down to the haven (Lond Daer); but now the Númenóreans drove great tracks and roads into the forests northwards and southwards from the Gwathló, and the native folk that survived fled from Minhiriath into the dark woods of the great Cape of Eryn Vorn, south of the mouth of the Baranduin, which they dared not

_____

'Eryn Vorn', 'R.Adorn', 'Swanfleet', and 'R.Glanduin'. The last three of these names were then written into the original map that accompanies the book, but why this was done I have been unable to discover; and while 'R.Adorn' is correctly placed, 'Swanfleet' and 'River Glandin' [*sic*] are blunderingly placed against the upper course of the Isen. For the correct interpretation of the relation between the names *Glanduin* and *Swanfleet* see pp. 264-5.

cross, even if they could, for fear of the Elvenfolk. From Enedwaith they took refuge in the eastern mountains where afterwards was Dunland; they did not cross the Isen nor take refuge in the great promontory between Isen and Lefnui that formed the north arm of the Bay of Belfalas [Ras Morthil or Andrast: see p. 214, note 6], because of the 'Púkel-men'. . . . [For the continuation of this passage see p. 383.] The devastation wrought by the Númenóreans was incalculable. For long years these lands were their chief source of timber, not only for their ship-yards at Lond Daer and elsewhere, but also for Númenor itself. Shiploads innumerable passed west over the sea. The denuding of the lands was increased during the war in Eriador; for the exiled natives welcomed Sauron and hoped for his victory over the Men of the Sea. Sauron knew of the importance to his enemies of the Great Haven and its ship-yards, and he used these haters of Númenor as spies and guides for his raiders. He had not enough force to spare for any assault upon the forts at the Haven or along the banks of the Gwathló, but his raiders made much havoc on the fringe of the forests, setting fire in the woods and burning many of the great wood-stores of the Númenóreans.

When Sauron was at last defeated and driven east out of Eriador most of the old forests had been destroyed. The Gwathló flowed through a land that was far and wide on either bank a desert, treeless but un-tilled. That was not so when it first received its name from the hardy explorers of Tar-Aldarion's ship who ventured to pass up the river in small boats. As soon as the seaward region of salt airs and great winds was passed the forest drew down to the river-banks, and wide though the waters were the huge trees cast great shadows on the river, under which the boats of the adventurers crept silently up into the unknown land. So the first name they gave to it was 'River of Shadow', *Gwath-hîr*, *Gwathir*. But later they penetrated northward as far as the beginning of the great fenlands; though it was still long before they had the need or sufficient men to undertake the great works of drainage and dyke-building that made a great port on the site where Tharbad stood in the days of the Two Kingdoms. The Sindarin word that they used for the fenland was *lô*, earlier *loga* [from a stem *log-* meaning 'wet, soaked, swampy']; and they thought at first that it was the source of the forest-river, not yet knowing the Mitheithel that came down out of the mountains in the north, and gathering the waters of the Bruinen [Loudwater] and Glanduin poured flood-waters into the plain. The name *Gwathir* was thus changed to *Gwathló*, the shadowy river from the fens.

The Gwathló was one of the few geographical names that became generally known to others than mariners in Númenor, and received an Adûnaic translation. This was *Agathurush*.

The history of Lond Daer and Tharbad is also mentioned in this same essay in a discussion of the name *Glanduin*:

Glanduin means 'border-river'. It was the name first given (in the Second Age), since the river was the southern boundary of Eregion, beyond which pre-Númenórean and generally unfriendly peoples lived, such as the ancestors of the Dunlendings. Later it, with the Gwathló formed by its confluence with the Mitheithel, formed the southern boundary of the North Kingdom. The land beyond, between the Gwathló and the Isen (Sîr Angren) was called Enedwaith ('Middle-folk'); it belonged to neither kingdom and received no permanent settlements of men of Númenórean origin. But the great North–South Road, which was the chief route of communication between the Two Kingdoms except by sea, ran through it from Tharbad to the Fords of Isen (Ethraid Engrin). Before the decay of the North Kingdom and the disasters that befell Gondor, indeed until the coming of the Great Plague in Third Age 1636, both kingdoms shared an interest in this region, and together built and maintained the Bridge of Tharbad and the long causeways that carried the road to it on either side of the Gwathló and Mitheithel across the fens in the plains of Minhiriath and Enedwaith.* A considerable garrison of soldiers, mariners and engineers had been kept there until the seventeenth century of the Third Age. But from then onwards the region fell quickly into decay; and long before the time of *The Lord of the Rings* had gone back into wild fen-lands. When Boromir made his great journey from Gondor to Rivendell – the courage and hardihood required is not fully recognized in the narrative – the North–South Road no longer existed except for the crumbling remains of the causeways, by which a hazardous approach to Tharbad might be achieved, only to find ruins on dwindling mounds, and a dangerous ford formed by the ruins of the bridge, impassable if the river had not been there slow and shallow – but wide.

If the name Glanduin was remembered at all it would only be in Rivendell; and it would apply only to the upper course of the river where it still ran swiftly, soon to be lost in the plains and disappear in the fens: a network of swamps, pools, and eyots, where the only in-habitants were hosts of swans, and many other water-birds. If the river had any name it was in the language of the Dunlendings. In

---

* In the early days of the kingdoms the most expeditious route from one to the other (except for great armaments) was found to be by sea to the ancient port at the head of the estuary of the Gwathló and so to the river-port of Tharbad, and thence by the Road. The ancient sea-port and its great quays were ruinous, but with long labour a port capable of receiving seagoing vessels had been made at Tharbad, and a fort raised there on great earthworks on both sides of the river, to guard the once famed Bridge of Tharbad. The ancient port was one of the earliest ports of the Númenóreans, begun by the renowned mariner-king Tar-Aldarion, and later enlarged and fortified. It was called Lond Daer Enedh, the Great Middle Haven (as being between Lindon in the North and Pelargir on the Anduin). [Author's note.]

The Return of the King VI 6 it is called the Swanfleet river (not River), simply as being the river that went down into Nîn-in-Eilph, 'the Waterlands of the Swans'.*

It was my father's intention to enter, in a revised map of *The Lord of the Rings*, *Glanduin* as the name of the upper course of the river, and to mark the fens as such, with the name *Nîn-in-Eilph* (or *Swanfleet*). In the event his intention came to be misunderstood, for on Pauline Baynes' map the lower course is marked as 'R.Swanfleet', while on the map in the book, as noted above (p. 262), the names are placed against the wrong river.

It may be noted that Tharbad is referred to as 'a ruined town' in *The Fellowship of the Ring* II 3, and that Boromir in Lothlórien told that he lost his horse at Tharbad, at the fording of the Greyflood (*ibid.* II 8). In the Tale of Years the ruining and desertion of Tharbad is dated to the year 2912 of the Third Age, when great floods devastated Enedwaith and Minhiriath.

From these discussions it can be seen that the conception of the Númenórean harbour at the mouth of the Gwathló had been expanded since the time when 'Concerning Galadriel and Celeborn' was written, from 'a small Númenórean harbour' to Lond Daer, the Great Haven. It is of course the Vinyalondë or New Haven of 'Aldarion and Erendis' (p. 176), though that name does not appear in the discussions just cited. It is said in 'Aldarion and Erendis' (p. 206) that the works that Aldarion began again at Vinyalondë after he became King 'were never completed'. This probably means no more than that they were never completed by him; for the later history of Lond Daer presupposes that the haven was at length restored, and made secure from the assaults of the sea, and indeed the same passage in 'Aldarion and Erendis' goes on to say that Aldarion 'laid the foundation for the achievement of Tar-Minastir long years after, in the first war with Sauron, and but for his works the fleets of Númenor could not have brought their power in time to the right place – as he foresaw'.

The statement in the discussion of *Glanduin* above that the port was called Lond Daer Enedh 'the Great Middle Haven', as being between the havens of Lindon in the North and Pelargir on the Anduin, must refer to a time long after the Númenórean intervention in the war against Sauron in Eriador; for according to the Tale of Years Pelargir was not built until the year 2350 of the Second Age, and became the chief haven of the Faithful Númenóreans.

---

* Sindarin *alph*, a swan, plural *eilph*; Quenya *alqua*, as in *Alqualondë*. The Telerin branch of Eldarin shifted original *kw* to *p* (but original *p* remained unshifted). The much-changed Sindarin of Middle-earth turned the stops to spirants after *l* and *r*. Thus original *alkwa* became *alpa* in Telerin, and *alf* (transcribed *alph*) in Sindarin.

APPENDIX E

THE NAMES OF CELEBORN AND GALADRIEL

It is said in an essay concerning the customs of name-giving among the Eldar in Valinor that they had two 'given names' (*essi*), of which the first was given at birth by the father; and this one usually recalled the father's own name, resembling it in sense or form, or might even be actually the same as the father's, to which some distinguishing prefix might be added later, when the child was full-grown. The second name was given later, sometimes much later but sometimes soon after the birth, by the mother; and these mother-names had great significance, for the mothers of the Eldar had insight into the characters and abilities of their children, and many also had the gift of prophetic foresight. In addition, any of the Eldar might acquire an *epessë* ('after-name'), not necessarily given by their own kin, a nickname – mostly given as a title of admiration or honour; and an *epessë* might become the name generally used and recognised in later song and history (as was the case, for instance, with Ereinion, always known by his *epessë* Gil-galad).

Thus the name *Alatáriel*, which, according to the late version of the story of their relationship (p. 231), was given to Galadriel by Celeborn in Aman, was an *epessë* (for its etymology see the Appendix to *The Silmarillion*, entry *kal-*), which she chose to use in Middle-earth, rendered into Sindarin as *Galadriel*, rather than her 'father-name' *Artanis*, or her 'mother-name' *Nerwen*.

It is only of course in the late version that Celeborn appears with a High-elven, rather than Sindarin, name: *Teleporno*. This is stated to be actually Telerin in form; the ancient stem of the Elvish word for 'silver' was *kyelep-*, becoming *celeb* in Sindarin, *telep-*, *telpe* in Telerin, and *tyelep-*, *tyelpe* in Quenya. But in Quenya the form *telpe* became usual, through the influence of Telerin; for the Teleri prized silver above gold, and their skill as silversmiths was esteemed even by the Noldor. Thus *Telperion* was more commonly used than *Tyelperion* as the name of the White Tree of Valinor. (*Alatáriel* was also Telerin; its Quenya form was *Altáriel*.)

The name Celeborn when first devised was intended to mean 'Silver Tree'; it was also the name of the Tree of Tol Eressëa (*The Silmarillion* p. 59). Celeborn's close kin had 'tree-names' (p. 233): Galadhon his father, Galathil his brother, and Nimloth his niece, who bore the same name as the White Tree of Númenor. In my father's latest philological writings, however, the meaning 'Silver Tree' was abandoned: the second element of *Celeborn* (as the name of a person) was derived from the ancient adjectival form *ornā* 'uprising, tall', rather than from the related noun *ornë* 'tree'. (*Ornë* was originally applied to straighter and more slender trees such as birches, whereas stouter, more spreading trees such as oaks and beeches were called in the ancient language *galadā* 'great growth';

but this distinction was not always observed in Quenya and disappeared in Sindarin, where all trees came to be called *galadh*, and *orn* fell out of common use, surviving only in verse and songs and in many names both of persons and of trees.) That Celeborn was tall is mentioned in a note to the discussion of Númenórean Linear Measures, p. 286.

On occasional confusion of Galadriel's name with the word *galadh* my father wrote:

When Celeborn and Galadriel became the rulers of the Elves of Lórien (who were mainly in origin Silvan Elves and called themselves the Galadhrim) the name of Galadriel became associated with trees, an association that was aided by the name of her husband, which also appeared to contain a tree-word; so that outside Lórien among those whose memories of the ancient days and Galadriel's history had grown dim her name was often altered to Galadhriel. Not in Lórien itself.

It may be mentioned here that *Galadhrim* is the correct spelling of the name of the Elves of Lórien, and similarly *Caras Galadhon*. My father originally altered the voiced form of *th* (as in Modern English *then*) in Elvish names to *d*, since (as he wrote) *dh* is not used in English and looks uncouth. Afterwards he changed his mind on the point, but *Galadrim* and *Caras Galadon* remained uncorrected until after the appearance of the revised edition of *The Lord of the Rings* (in recent reprints the change has been made). These names are wrongly spelt in the entry *alda* in the Appendix to *The Silmarillion*.

PART THREE

THE THIRD AGE

I

THE DISASTER OF
THE GLADDEN FIELDS

After the fall of Sauron, Isildur, the son and heir of Elendil, returned to Gondor. There he assumed the Elendilmir[1] as King of Arnor, and proclaimed his sovereign lordship over all the Dúnedain in the North and in the South; for he was a man of great pride and vigour. He remained for a year in Gondor, restoring its order and defining its bounds;[2] but the greater part of the army of Arnor returned to Eriador by the Númenórean road from the Fords of Isen to Fornost.

When he at last felt free to return to his own realm he was in haste, and he wished to go first to Imladris; for he had left his wife and youngest son there,[3] and he had moreover an urgent need for the counsel of Elrond. He therefore determined to make his way north from Osgiliath up the Vales of Anduin to Cirith Forn en Andrath, the high-climbing pass of the North, that led down to Imladris.[4] He knew the land well, for he had journeyed there often before the War of the Alliance, and had marched that way to the war with men of eastern Arnor in the company of Elrond.[5]

It was a long journey, but the only other way, west and then north to the road-meeting in Arnor, and then east to Imladris, was far longer.[6] As swift, maybe, for mounted men, but he had no horses fit for riding;[7] safer, maybe, in former days, but Sauron was vanquished, and the people of the Vales had been his allies in victory. He had no fear, save for weather and weariness, but these men must endure whom need sends far abroad in Middle-earth.[8]

So it was, as is told in the legends of later days, that the second year of the Third Age was waning when Isildur set forth from Osgiliath early in Ivanneth,[9] expecting to reach Imladris in forty days, by mid-Narbeleth, ere winter drew nigh in the North. At the Eastgate of the Bridge on a bright morning Meneldil[10] bade him farewell. 'Go now with good speed, and may the Sun of your setting out not cease to shine on your road!'

With Isildur went his three sons, Elendur, Aratan, and Ciryon,[11] and his Guard of two hundred knights and soldiers, stern men of Arnor and war-hardened. Of their journey nothing is told until they had passed over the Dagorlad, and on northward into the wide and empty lands south of Greenwood the Great. On the twentieth day, as they came within far sight of the forest crowning the highlands before them with a distant gleam of the red and gold of Ivanneth, the sky became overcast and a dark wind came up from the Sea of Rhûn laden with rain. The rain lasted for four days; so when they came to the entrance to the Vales, between Lórien and Amon Lanc,[12] Isildur turned away from the Anduin, swollen with swift water, and went up the steep slopes on its eastern side to gain the ancient paths of the Silvan Elves that ran near the eaves of the Forest.

So it came to pass that late in the afternoon of the thirtieth day of their journey they were passing the north borders of the Gladden Fields,[13] marching along a path that led to Thranduil's realm,[14] as it then was. The fair day was waning; above the distant mountains clouds were gathering, reddened by the misty sun as it drew down towards them; the deeps of the valley were already in grey shadow. The Dúnedain were singing, for their day's march was near its end, and three parts of the long road to Imladris were behind them. To their right the Forest loomed above them at the top of steep slopes running down to their path, below which the descent into the valley-bottom was gentler.

Suddenly as the sun plunged into cloud they heard the hideous cries of Orcs, and saw them issuing from the Forest and moving down the slopes, yelling their war-cries.[15] In the dimmed light their number could only be guessed, but the Dúnedain were plainly many times, even to ten times, outnumbered. Isildur commanded a *thangail*[16] to be drawn up, a shield-wall of two serried ranks that could be bent back at either end if outflanked, until at need it became a closed ring. If the land had been flat or the slope in his favour he would have formed his company into a *dirnaith*[16] and charged the Orcs, hoping by the great strength of the Dúnedain and their weapons to cleave a way through them and scatter them in dismay; but that could not now be done. A shadow of foreboding fell upon his heart.

'The vengeance of Sauron lives on, though he may be dead,' he said to Elendur, who stood beside him. 'There is cunning and design here! We have no hope of help: Moria and Lórien are now far behind, and Thranduil four days' march ahead.' 'And we bear burdens of worth beyond all reckoning,' said Elendur; for he was in his father's confidence.

The Orcs were now drawing near. Isildur turned to his esquire: 'Ohtar,'[17] he said, 'I give this now into your keeping'; and he delivered to him the great sheath and the shards of Narsil, Elendil's sword. 'Save it from capture by all means that you can find, and at all costs; even at the cost of being held a coward who deserted me. Take your companion with you and flee! Go! I command you!' Then Ohtar knelt and kissed his hand, and the two young men fled down into the dark valley.[18]

If the keen-eyed Orcs marked their flight they took no heed. They halted briefly, preparing their assault. First they let fly a hail of arrows, and then suddenly with a great shout they did as Isildur would have done, and hurled a great mass of their chief warriors down the last slope against the Dúnedain, expecting to break up their shield-wall. But it stood firm. The arrows had been unavailing against the Númenórean armour. The great Men towered above the tallest Orcs, and their swords and spears far outreached the weapons of their enemies. The onslaught faltered, broke, and retreated, leaving the defenders little harmed, unshaken, behind piles of fallen Orcs.

It seemed to Isildur that the enemy was withdrawing towards the Forest. He looked back. The red rim of the sun gleamed out from the clouds as it went down behind the mountains; night would soon be falling. He gave orders to resume the march at once, but to bend their course down towards the lower and flatter ground where the Orcs would have less advantage.[19] Maybe he believed that after their costly repulse they would give way, though their scouts might follow him during the night and watch his camp. That was the manner of Orcs, who were most often dismayed when their prey could turn and bite.

But he was mistaken. There was not only cunning in the attack, but fierce and relentless hatred. The Orcs of the Mountains were stiffened and commanded by grim servants of Barad-dûr, sent out long before to watch the passes,[20] and though it was unknown to them the Ring, cut from his black hand two years before, was still laden with Sauron's evil will and called to all his servants for their aid. The Dúnedain had gone scarcely a mile when the Orcs moved again. This time they did not charge, but used all their forces. They came down on a wide front, which bent into a crescent and soon closed into an unbroken ring about the Dúnedain. They were silent now, and kept at a distance out of the range of the dreaded steel-bows of Númenor,[21] though the light was fast failing, and Isildur had all too few archers for his need.[22] He halted.

There was a pause, though the most keen-eyed among the Dúnedain said that the Orcs were moving inwards, stealthily, step by step. Elendur went to his father, who was standing dark and alone, as if lost in thought. '*Atarinya*,' he said, 'what of the power that would cow these foul creatures and command them to obey you? Is it then of no avail?'

'Alas, it is not, *senya*. I cannot use it. I dread the pain of touching it.[23] And I have not yet found the strength to bend it to my will. It needs one greater than I now know myself to be. My pride has fallen. It should go to the Keepers of the Three.'

At that moment there came a sudden blast of horns, and the Orcs closed in on all sides, flinging themselves against the Dúnedain with reckless ferocity. Night had come, and hope faded. Men were falling; for some of the greater Orcs leaped up, two at a time, and dead or alive with their weight bore down a Dúnedan, so that other strong claws could drag him out and slay him. The Orcs might pay five to one in this exchange, but it was too cheap. Ciryon was slain in this way and Aratan mortally wounded in an attempt to rescue him.

Elendur, not yet harmed, sought Isildur. He was rallying the men on the east side where the assault was heaviest, for the Orcs still feared the Elendilmir that he bore on his brow and avoided him. Elendur touched him on the shoulder and he turned fiercely, thinking an Orc had crept behind.

'My King,' said Elendur, 'Ciryon is dead and Aratan is dying. Your last counsellor must advise, nay command you, as you commanded Ohtar. Go! Take your burden, and at all costs bring it to the Keepers: even at the cost of abandoning your men and me!'

'King's son,' said Isildur, 'I knew that I must do so; but I feared the pain. Nor could I go without your leave. Forgive me, and my pride that has brought you to this doom.'[24] Elendur kissed him. 'Go! Go now!' he said.

Isildur turned west, and drawing up the Ring that hung in a wallet from a fine chain about his neck, he set it upon his finger with a cry of pain, and was never seen again by any eye upon Middle-earth. But the Elendilmir of the West could not be quenched, and suddenly it blazed forth red and wrathful as a burning star. Men and Orcs gave way in fear; and Isildur, drawing a hood over his head, vanished into the night.[25]

Of what befell the Dúnedain only this was later known: ere long they all lay dead, save one, a young esquire stunned and buried under fallen men. So perished Elendur, who should afterwards have been King, and as all foretold who knew him, in his strength and wisdom, and his majesty without pride, one of the greatest, the fairest of the seed of Elendil, most like to his grandsire.[26]

Now of Isildur it is told that he was in great pain and anguish of heart, but at first he ran like a stag from the hounds, until he came to the bottom of the valley. There he halted, to make sure that he was not pursued; for Orcs could track a fugitive in the dark by scent, and needed no eyes. Then he went on more warily, for wide flats stretched on into the gloom before him, rough and pathless, with many traps for wandering feet.

So it was that he came at last to the banks of Anduin at the dead of night, and he was weary; for he had made a journey that the Dúnedain on such ground could have made no quicker, marching without halt and by day.[27] The river was swirling dark and swift before him. He stood for a while, alone and in despair. Then in haste he cast off all his armour and weapons, save a short sword at his belt,[28] and plunged into the water. He was a man of strength and endurance that few even of the Dúnedain of that age could equal, but he had little hope to gain the other shore. Before he had gone far he was forced to turn almost north against the current; and strive as he might he was ever swept down towards the tangles of the Gladden Fields. They were nearer than he had thought,[29] and even as he felt the stream slacken and had almost won across he found himself struggling among great rushes and clinging weeds. There suddenly he knew that the Ring had gone. By chance, or chance well used, it had left his hand and gone where he could never hope to find it again. At first so overwhelming was his sense of loss that he struggled no more, and would have sunk and drowned. But swift as it had come the mood passed. The pain had left him. A great burden had been taken away. His feet found the river bed, and heaving himself up out of the mud he floundered through the reeds to a marshy islet close to the western shore. There he rose up out of the water: only a mortal man, a small creature lost and abandoned in the wilds of Middle-earth. But to the night-eyed Orcs that lurked there on the watch he loomed up, a monstrous shadow of fear, with a piercing eye like a star. They loosed their poisoned arrows at it, and fled. Needlessly, for Isildur unarmed was pierced through heart and throat, and without a cry he fell back into the water. No trace of his body was ever found by Elves or Men. So passed the first victim of the malice of the masterless Ring: Isildur, second King of all the Dúnedain, lord of Arnor and Gondor, and in that age of the World the last.

The sources of the legend of Isildur's death

There were eye-witnesses of the event. Ohtar and his companion escaped, bearing with them the shards of Narsil. The tale mentions a young man who survived the slaughter: he was Elendur's esquire, named Estelmo, and was one of the last to fall, but was stunned by a club, and not slain, and was found alive under Elendur's body. He heard the words of Isildur and Elendur at their parting. There were rescuers who came on the scene too late, but in time to disturb the Orcs and prevent their mutilation of the bodies: for there were certain Woodmen who got news to Thranduil by runners, and also themselves gathered a force to ambush the Orcs – of which they got wind, and scattered, for though victorious their losses had been great, and almost all of the great Orcs had fallen: they attempted no such attack again for long years after.

The story of the last hours of Isildur and his death was due to surmise: but well-founded. The legend in its full form was not composed until the reign of Elessar in the Fourth Age, when other evidence was discovered. Up to then it had been known, firstly, that Isildur had the Ring, and had fled towards the River; secondly, that his mail, helm, shield and great sword (but nothing else) had been found on the bank not far above the Gladden Fields; thirdly, that the Orcs had left watchers on the west bank armed with bows to intercept any who might escape the battle and flee to the River (for traces of their camps were found, one close to the borders of the Gladden Fields); and fourthly, that Isildur and the Ring, separately or together, must have been lost in the River, for if Isildur had reached the west shore wearing the Ring he should have eluded the watch, and so hardy a man of great endurance could not have failed to come then to Lórien or Moria before he foundered. Though it was a long journey, each of the Dúnedain carried in a sealed wallet on his belt a small phial of cordial and wafers of a waybread that would sustain life in him for many days – not indeed the *miruvor*[30] or the *lembas* of the Eldar, but like them, for the medicine and other arts of Númenor were potent and not yet forgotten. No belt or wallet was among the gear discarded by Isildur.

Long afterwards, as the Third Age of the Elvish World waned and the War of the Ring approached, it was revealed to the Council of Elrond that the Ring had been found, sunk near the edge of the Gladden Fields and close to the western bank; though no trace of Isildur's body was ever discovered. They were also then aware that Saruman had been secretly searching in the same region; but though he had not found the Ring (which had long before been carried off), they did not yet know what else he might have discovered.

But King Elessar, when he was crowned in Gondor, began the re-ordering of his realm, and one of his first tasks was the restoration of Orthanc, where he proposed to set up again the *palantir* recovered from Saruman. Then all the secrets of the tower were searched. Many things of worth were found, jewels and heirlooms of Eorl, filched from Edoras by the agency of Wormtongue during King Théoden's decline, and other such things, more ancient and beautiful, from mounds and tombs far and wide. Saruman in his degradation had become not a dragon but a jackdaw. At last behind a hidden door that they could not have found or opened had not Elessar had the aid of Gimli the Dwarf a steel closet was revealed. Maybe it had been intended to receive the Ring; but it was almost bare. In a casket on a high shelf two things were laid. One was a small case of gold, attached to a fine chain; it was empty, and bore no letter or token, but beyond all doubt it had once borne the Ring about Isildur's neck. Next to it lay a treasure without price, long mourned as lost for ever: the Elendilmir itself, the white star of Elvish crystal upon a fillet of *mithril*[31] that had descended from Silmarien to Elendil, and had been taken by him as the token of royalty in the North Kingdom.[32] Every king and the chieftains that followed them in Arnor had borne the Elendilmir down even to Elessar himself; but though it was a jewel of great beauty, made by Elven-smiths in Imladris for Valandil Isildur's son, it had not the anciency nor potency of the one that had been lost when Isildur fled into the dark and came back no more.

Elessar took it up with reverence, and when he returned to the North and took up again the full kingship of Arnor Arwen bound it upon his brow, and men were silent in amaze to see its splendour. But Elessar did not again imperil it, and wore it only on high days in the North Kingdom. Otherwise, when in kingly raiment he bore the Elendilmir which had descended to him. 'And this also is a thing of reverence,' he said, 'and above my worth; forty heads have worn it before.'[33]

When men considered this secret hoard more closely, they were dismayed. For it seemed to them that these things, and certainly the Elendilmir, could not have been found, unless they had been upon Isildur's body when he sank; but if that had been in deep water of strong flow they would in time have been swept far away. Therefore Isildur must have fallen not into the deep stream but into shallow water, no more than shoulder-high. Why then, though an Age had passed, were there no traces of his bones? Had Saruman found them, and scorned them – burned them with dishonour in one of his furnaces? If that were so, it was a shameful deed; but not his worst.

NOTES

1   The Elendilmir is named in a footnote to Appendix A (I, iii) to *The Lord of the Rings*: the Kings of Arnor wore no crown, 'but bore a single white gem, the Elendilmir, Star of Elendil, bound on their brows with a silver fillet'. This note gives references to other mentions of the Star of Elendil in the course of the narrative. There were in fact not one but two gems of this name; see p. 277.

2   As is related in the Tale of Cirion and Eorl, drawing on older histories, now mostly lost, for its account of the events that led to the Oath of Eorl and the alliance of Gondor with the Rohirrim. [Author's note.] – See p. 308.

3   Isildur's youngest son was Valandil, third King of Arnor: see *Of the Rings of Power* in *The Silmarillion*, pp. 295–6. In Appendix A (I, ii) to *The Lord of the Rings* it is stated that he was born in Imladris.

4   This pass is named only here by an Elvish name. At Rivendell long after Gimli the Dwarf referred to it as the High Pass: 'If it were not for the Beornings, the passage from Dale to Rivendell would long ago have become impossible. They are valiant men and keep open the High Pass and the Ford of Carrock.' (*The Fellowship of the Ring* II 1.) It was in this pass that Thorin Oakenshield and his company were captured by Orcs (*The Hobbit* Chapter 4). *Andrath* no doubt means 'long climb': see p. 255, note 16.

5   Cf. *Of the Rings of Power* in *The Silmarillion*, p. 295: '[Isildur] marched north from Gondor by the way that Elendil had come.'

6   Three hundred leagues and more [i.e., by the route which Isildur intended to take], and for the most part without made roads; in those days the only Númenórean roads were the great road linking Gondor and Arnor, through Calenardhon, then north over the Gwathló at Tharbad, and so at last to Fornost; and the East–West Road from the Grey Havens to Imladris. These roads crossed at a point [Bree] west of Amon Sûl (Weathertop), by Númenórean road-measurements three hundred and ninety-two leagues from Osgiliath, and then east to Imladris one hundred and sixteen: five hundred and eight leagues in all. [Author's note.] – See the Appendix on Númenórean Linear Measures, p. 285.

7   The Númenóreans in their own land possessed horses, which they esteemed [see the 'Description of Númenor', p. 169]. But they did not use them in war; for all their wars were overseas. Also they were of great stature and strength, and their fully-equipped soldiers were accustomed to bear heavy armour and weapons. In their settlements on the shores of Middle-earth they acquired and bred horses, but used them little for riding, except in sport and pleasure. In war they were used only by couriers, and by bodies of light-armed archers (often not of Númenórean race). In the War of the Alliance such

horses as they used had suffered great losses, and few were available in Osgiliath. [Author's note.]

8 They needed some baggage and provisions in houseless country; for they did not expect to find any dwellings of Elves or Men, until they reached Thranduil's realm, almost at their journey's end. On the march each man carried with him two days' provisions (other than the 'need-wallet' mentioned in the text [p. 276]); the rest, and other baggage, was carried by small sturdy horses, of a kind, it was said, that had first been found, wild and free, in the wide plains south and east of the Greenwood. They had been tamed; but though they would carry heavy burdens (at walking pace), they would not allow any man to ride them. Of these they had only ten. [Author's note.]

9 *Yavannië* 5, according to the Númenórean 'King's Reckoning', still kept with little change in the Shire Calendar. *Yavannië* (*Ivanneth*) thus corresponded to *Halimath*, our September; and *Narbeleth* to our October. Forty days (till *Narbeleth* 15) was sufficient, if all went well. The journey was probably at least three hundred and eight leagues as marched; but the soldiers of the Dúnedain, tall men of great strength and endurance, were accustomed to move fully-armed at eight leagues a day 'with ease': when they went in eight spells of a league, with short breaks at the end of each league (*lár*, Sindarin *daur*, originally meaning a stop or pause), and one hour near midday. This made a 'march' of about ten and a half hours, in which they were walking eight hours. This pace they could maintain for long periods with adequate provision. In haste they could move much faster, at twelve leagues a day (or in great need more), but for shorter periods. At the date of the disaster, in the latitude of Imladris (which they were approaching), there were at least eleven hours of daylight in open country; but at midwinter less than eight. Long journeys were not, however, undertaken in the North between the beginning of *Hithui* (*Hísimë*, November) and the end of *Nínui* (*Nénimë*, February) in time of peace. [Author's note.] – A detailed account of the Calendars in use in Middle-earth is given in Appendix D to *The Lord of the Rings*.

10 Meneldil was the nephew of Isildur, son of Isildur's younger brother Anárion, slain in the siege of Barad-dûr. Isildur had established Meneldil as King of Gondor. He was a man of courtesy, but far-seeing, and he did not reveal his thoughts. He was in fact well-pleased by the departure of Isildur and his sons, and hoped that affairs in the North would keep them long occupied. [Author's note.] – It is stated in unpublished annals concerning the Heirs of Elendil that Meneldil was the fourth child of Anárion, that he was born in the year 3318 of the Second Age, and that he was the last man to be born in Númenor. The note just cited is the only reference to his character.

11 All three had fought in the War of the Alliance, but Aratan and

Ciryon had not been in the invasion of Mordor and the siege of Barad-dûr, for Isildur had sent them to man his fortress of Minas Ithil, lest Sauron should escape Gil-galad and Elendil and seek to force a way through Cirith Dúath (later called Cirith Ungol) and take vengeance on the Dúnedain before he was overcome. Elendur, Isildur's heir and dear to him, had accompanied his father throughout the war (save the last challenge upon Orodruin) and he was in Isildur's full confidence. [Author's note.] – It is stated in the annals mentioned in the last note that Isildur's eldest son was born in Númenor in the year 3299 of the Second Age (Isildur himself was born in 3209).

12 *Amon Lanc*, 'Naked Hill,' was the highest point in the highland at the south-west corner of the Greenwood, and was so called because no trees grew on its summit. In later days it was Dol Guldur, the first stronghold of Sauron after his awakening. [Author's note.]

13 The Gladden Fields (*Loeg Ningloron*). In the Elder Days, when the Silvan Elves first settled there, they were a lake formed in a deep depression into which the Anduin poured from the North down the swiftest part of its course, a long descent of some seventy miles, and there mingled with the torrent of the Gladden River (*Sîr Ninglor*) hastening from the Mountains. The lake had been wider west of Anduin, for the eastern side of the valley was steeper; but on the east it probably reached as far as the feet of the long slopes down from the Forest (then still wooded), its reedy borders being marked by the gentler slope, just below the path that Isildur was following. The lake had become a great marsh, through which the river wandered in a wilderness of islets, and wide beds of reed and rush, and armies of yellow iris that grew taller than a man and gave their name to all the region and to the river from the Mountains about whose lower course they grew most thickly. But the marsh had receded to the east, and from the foot of the lower slopes there were now wide flats, grown with grass and small rushes, on which men could walk. [Author's note.]

14 Long before the War of the Alliance, Oropher, King of the Silvan Elves east of Anduin, being disturbed by rumours of the rising power of Sauron, had left their ancient dwellings about Amon Lanc, across the river from their kin in Lórien. Three times he had moved northwards, and at the end of the Second Age he dwelt in the western glens of the Emyn Duir, and his numerous people lived and roamed in the woods and vales westward as far as Anduin, north of the ancient Dwarf-Road (*Men-i-Naugrim*). He had joined the Alliance, but was slain in the assault upon the Gates of Mordor. Thranduil his son had returned with the remnant of the army of the Silvan Elves in the year before Isildur's march.

The Emyn Duir (Dark Mountains) were a group of high hills in the north-east of the Forest, so called because dense fir-woods grew upon their slopes; but they were not yet of evil name. In later days when the shadow of Sauron spread through Greenwood the Great, and changed its name from Eryn Galen to Taur-nu-Fuin (translated Mirkwood), the Emyn Duir became a haunt of many of his most evil creatures, and were called Emyn-nu-Fuin, the Mountains of Mirkwood. [Author's note.] – On Oropher see Appendix B to 'The History of Galadriel and Celeborn'; in one of the passages there cited Oropher's retreat northwards within the Greenwood is ascribed to his desire to move out of range of the Dwarves of Khazad-dûm and of Celeborn and Galadriel in Lórien.

The Elvish names of the Mountains of Mirkwood are not found elsewhere. In Appendix F (II) to *The Lord of the Rings* the Elvish name of Mirkwood is Taur-e-Ndaedelos 'forest of the great fear'; the name given here, Taur-nu-Fuin 'forest under night', was the later name of Dorthonion, the forested highland on the northern borders of Beleriand in the Elder Days. The application of the same name, Taur-nu-Fuin, to both Mirkwood and Dorthonion is notable, in the light of the close relation of my father's pictures of them: see *Pictures by J. R. R. Tolkien*, 1979, note to no. 37. – After the end of the War of the Ring Thranduil and Celeborn renamed Mirkwood once more, calling it Eryn Lasgalen, the Wood of Greenleaves (Appendix B to *The Lord of the Rings*).

Men-i-Naugrim, the Dwarf Road, is the Old Forest Road described in *The Hobbit*, Chapter 7. In the earlier draft of this section of the present narrative there is a note referring to 'the ancient Forest Road that led down from the Pass of Imladris and crossed Anduin by a bridge (that had been enlarged and strengthened for the passage of the armies of the Alliance), and so over the eastern valley into the Greenwood. The Anduin could not be bridged at any lower point; for a few miles below the Forest Road the land fell steeply and the river became very swift, until it reached the great basin of the Gladden Fields. Beyond the Fields it quickened again, and was then a great flood fed by many streams, of which the names are forgotten save those of the larger: the Gladden (Sîr Ninglor), Silverlode (Celebrant), and Limlight (Limlaith).' In *The Hobbit* the Forest Road traversed the great river by the Old Ford, and there is no mention of there having once been a bridge at the crossing.

15 A different tradition of the event is represented in the brief account given in *Of the Rings of Power* (*The Silmarillion* p. 295): 'Isildur was overwhelmed by a host of Orcs that lay in wait in the Misty Mountains; and they descended upon him at unawares in his camp between the Greenwood and the Great River, nigh to Loeg Ningloron, the Gladden Fields, for he was heedless and set no guard, deeming that all his foes were overthrown.'

16 *Thangail* 'shield-fence' was the name of this formation in Sindarin,

the normal spoken language of Elendil's people; its 'official' name
in Quenya was *sandastan* 'shield-barrier', derived from primitive
thandā 'shield' and *stama-* 'bar, exclude'. The Sindarin word used
a different second element: *cail*, a fence or palisade of spikes and
sharp stakes. This, in primitive form *keglē*, was derived from a
stem *keg-* 'snag, barb', seen also in the primitive word *kegyā* 'hedge',
whence Sindarin *cai* (cf. the *Morgai* in Mordor).

The *dírnaith*, Quenya *nernehta* 'man-spearhead', was a wedge-
formation, launched over a short distance against an enemy massing
but not yet arrayed, or against a defensive formation on open ground.
Quenya *nehte*, Sindarin *naith* was applied to any formation or pro-
jection tapering to a point: a spearhead, gore, wedge, narrow promontory (root *nek* 'narrow'); cf. the Naith of Lórien, the land at the
angle of the Celebrant and Anduin, which at the actual junction of
the rivers was narrower and more pointed than can be shown on a
small-scale map. [Author's note.]

17 *Ohtar* is the only name used in the legends; but it is probably only
the title of address that Isildur used at this tragic moment, hiding
his feelings under formality. *Ohtar* 'warrior, soldier' was the title
of all who, though fully trained and experienced, had not yet been
admitted to the rank of *roquen*, 'knight'. But Ohtar was dear to Isildur
and of his own kin. [Author's note.]

18 In the earlier draft Isildur directed Ohtar to take two companions
with him. In *Of the Rings of Power* (*The Silmarillion* p. 295) and in
The Fellowship of the Ring II 2 it is told that 'three men only came
ever back over the mountains'. In the text given here the implication
is that the third was Estelmo, Elendur's esquire, who survived the
battle (see pp. 275–6).

19 They had passed the deep depression of the Gladden Fields, beyond
which the ground on the east side of Anduin (which flowed in a deep
channel) was firmer and drier, for the lie of the land changed. It
began to climb northwards until as it neared the Forest Road and
Thranduil's country it was almost level with the eaves of the Greenwood. This Isildur knew well. [Author's note.]

20 There can be no doubt that Sauron, well-informed of the Alliance,
had sent out such Orc-troops of the Red Eye as he could spare, to
do what they could to harry any forces that attempted to shorten
their road by crossing the Mountains. In the event the main might
of Gil-galad, together with Isildur and part of the Men of Arnor,
had come over the Passes of Imladris and Caradhras, and the Orcs
were dismayed and hid themselves. But they remained alert and
watchful, determined to attack any companies of Elves or Men that
they outnumbered. Thranduil they had let pass, for even his diminished
army was far too strong for them; but they bided their time, for the
most part hidden in the Forest, while others lurked along the river-

banks. It is unlikely that any news of Sauron's fall had reached them, for he had been straitly besieged in Mordor and all his forces had been destroyed. If any few had escaped, they had fled far to the East with the Ringwraiths. This small detachment in the North, of no account, was forgotten. Probably they thought that Sauron had been victorious, and the war-scarred army of Thranduil was retreating to hide in fastnesses of the Forest. Thus they would be emboldened and eager to win their master's praise, though they had not been in the main battles. But it was not his praise they would have won, if any had lived long enough to see his revival. No tortures would have satisfied his anger with the bungling fools who had let slip the greatest prize in Middle-earth; even though they could know nothing of the One Ring, which save to Sauron himself was known only to the Nine Ringwraiths, its slaves. Yet many have thought that the ferocity and determination of their assault on Isildur was in part due to the Ring. It was little more than two years since it had left his hand, and though it was swiftly cooling it was still heavy with his evil will, and seeking all means to return to its lord (as it did again when he recovered and was re-housed). So, it is thought, although they did not understand it the Orc-chiefs were filled with a fierce desire to destroy the Dúnedain and capture their leader. Nonetheless it proved in the event that the War of the Ring was lost at the Disaster of the Gladden Fields. [Author's note.]

21 On the bows of the Númenóreans see the 'Description of Númenor', p. 170.

22 No more than twenty, it is said; for no such need had been expected. [Author's note.]

23 Compare the words of the scroll which Isildur wrote concerning the Ring before he departed from Gondor on his last journey, and which Gandalf reported to the Council of Elrond in Rivendell: 'It was hot when I first took it, hot as a glede, and my hand was scorched, so that I doubt if ever again I shall be free of the pain of it. Yet even as I write it is cooled and seemeth to shrink . . .' (The Fellowship of the Ring II 2).

24 The pride that led him to keep the Ring against the counsel of Elrond and Círdan that it should be destroyed in the fires of Orodruin (The Fellowship of the Ring II 2, and Of the Rings of Power, in The Silmarillion, p. 295).

25 The meaning, sufficiently remarkable, of this passage appears to be that the light of the Elendilmir was proof against the invisibility conferred by the One Ring when worn, if its light would be visible were the Ring not worn; but when Isildur covered his head with a hood its light was extinguished.

26 It is said that in later days those (such as Elrond) whose memories recalled him were struck by the great likeness to him, in body and

mind, of King Elessar, the victor in the War of the Ring, in which both the Ring and Sauron were ended for ever. Elessar was according to the records of the Dúnedain the descendant in the thirty-eighth degree of Elendur's brother Valandil. So long was it before he was avenged. [Author's note.]

27 Seven leagues or more from the place of battle. Night had fallen when he fled; he reached Anduin at midnight or near it. [Author's note.]

28 This was of a kind called *eket*: a short stabbing sword with a broad blade, pointed and two-edged, from a foot to one and a half feet long. [Author's note.]

29 The place of the last stand had been a mile or more beyond their northern border, but maybe in the dark the fall of the land had bent his course somewhat to the south. [Author's note.]

30 A flask of *miruvor*, 'the cordial of Imladris', was given to Gandalf by Elrond when the company set out from Rivendell (*The Fellowship of the Ring* II 3); see also *The Road Goes Ever On*, p. 61.

31 For that metal was found in Númenor. [Author's note.] – In 'The Line of Elros' (p. 221) Tar-Telemmaitë, the fifteenth Ruler of Númenor, is said to have been called so (i.e. 'silver-handed') because of his love of silver, 'and he bade his servants to seek ever for *mithril*'. But Gandalf said that *mithril* was found in Moria 'alone in the world' (*The Fellowship of the Ring* II 4).

32 It is told in 'Aldarion and Erendis' (p. 184) that Erendis caused the diamond which Aldarion brought to her from Middle-earth 'to be set as a star in a silver fillet; and at her asking he bound it on her forehead'. For this reason she was known as Tar-Elestirnë, the Lady of the Star-brow; 'and thus came, it is said, the manner of the Kings and Queens afterward to wear as a star a white jewel upon the brow, and they had no crown' (p. 215, note 18). This tradition cannot be unconnected with that of the Elendilmir, a star-like gem borne on the brow as a token of royalty in Arnor; but the original Elendilmir itself, since it belonged to Silmarien, was in existence in Númenor (whatever its origin may have been) before Aldarion brought Erendis' jewel from Middle-earth, and they cannot be the same.

33 The actual number was thirty-eight, since the second Elendilmir was made for Valandil (cf. note 26 above). – In the Tale of Years in Appendix B to *The Lord of the Rings* the entry for the year 16 of the Fourth Age (given under Shire Reckoning 1436) states that when King Elessar came to the Brandywine Bridge to greet his friends he gave the Star of the Dúnedain to Master Samwise, while his daughter Elanor was made a maid of honour to Queen Arwen. On the basis of this record Mr Robert Foster says in *The Complete Guide to Middle-earth* that 'the Star [of Elendil] was worn on the brow of the Kings of the North-kingdom until Elessar gave it to Sam Gamgee in

Fourth Age 16'. The clear implication of the present passage is that King Elessar retained indefinitely the Elendilmir that was made for Valandil; and it seems to me in any case out of the question that he would have made a gift of it to the Mayor of the Shire, however greatly he esteemed him. The Elendilmir is called by several names: the Star of Elendil, the Star of the North, the Star of the North-kingdom; and the Star of the Dúnedain (occurring only in this entry in the Tale of Years) is assumed to be yet another both in Robert Foster's *Guide* and in J. E. A. Tyler's *Tolkien Companion*. I have found no other reference to it; but it seems to me to be almost certain that it was not, and that Master Samwise received some different (and more suitable) distinction.

APPENDIX

NÚMENÓREAN LINEAR MEASURES

A note associated with the passage in 'The Disaster of the Gladden Fields' concerning the different routes from Osgiliath to Imladris (pp. 271 and 278, note 6) runs as follows:

Measures of distance are converted as nearly as possible into modern terms. 'League' is used because it was the longest measurement of distance: in Númenórean reckoning (which was decimal) five thousand *rangar* (full paces) made a *lár*, which was very nearly three of our miles. *Lár* meant 'pause', because except in forced marches a brief halt was usually made after this distance had been covered [see note 9 above]. The Númenórean *ranga* was slightly longer than our yard, approximately thirty-eight inches, owing to their greater stature. Therefore five thousand *rangar* would be almost exactly the equivalent of 5280 yards, our 'league': 5277 yards, two feet and four inches, supposing the equivalence to be exact. This cannot be determined, being based on the lengths given in histories of various things and distances that can be compared with those of our time. Account has to be taken both of the great stature of the Númenóreans (since hands, feet, fingers and paces are likely to be the origin of names of units of length), and also of the variations from these averages or norms in the process of fixing and organising a measurement system both for daily use and for exact calculations. Thus two *rangar* was often called 'man-high', which at thirty-eight inches gives an average height of six feet four inches; but this was at a later date, when the stature of the Dúnedain appears to have decreased, and also was not intended to be an accurate statement of the observed average of male stature among them, but was an approximate length expressed in the well-known unit *ranga*. (The *ranga* is often said to have been the length of the stride, from rear heel to front toe, of a full-grown man marching swiftly but at ease; a full stride 'might be well nigh a *ranga* and a half'.) It is however said of the great people of the past that they were more than man-high. Elendil was said to be 'more than man-high by nearly half a *ranga*'; but he was accounted the tallest of all the Númenóreans who escaped the Downfall [and was indeed generally known as Elendil the Tall]. The Eldar of the Elder Days were also very tall. Galadriel, 'the tallest of all the women of the Eldar of whom tales tell', was said to be man-high, but it is noted 'according to the measure of the Dúnedain and the men of old', indicating a height of about six feet four inches.

The Rohirrim were generally shorter, for in their far-off ancestry they had been mingled with men of broader and heavier build. Éomer was said to have been tall, of like height with Aragorn; but he with other descendants of King Thengel were taller than the norm of Rohan, deriving this characteristic (together in some cases with darker hair) from Morwen, Thengel's wife, a lady of Gondor of high Númenórean descent.

A note to the foregoing text adds some information concerning Morwen to what is given in *The Lord of the Rings* (Appendix A (II), 'The Kings of the Mark'):

She was known as Morwen of Lossarnach, for she dwelt there; but she did not belong to the people of that land. Her father had removed thither, for love of its flowering vales, from Belfalas; he was a descendant of a former Prince of that fief, and thus a kinsman of Prince Imrahil. His kinship with Éomer of Rohan, though distant, was recognised by Imrahil, and great friendship grew between them. Éomer wedded Imrahil's daughter [Lothíriel], and their son, Elfwine the Fair, had a striking likeness to his mother's father.

Another note remarks of Celeborn that he was 'a Linda of Valinor' (that is, one of the Teleri, whose own name for themselves was Lindar, the Singers), and that

he was held by them to be tall, as his name indicated ('silver-tall'); but the Teleri were in general somewhat less in build and stature than the Noldor.

This is the late version of the story of Celeborn's origin, and of the meaning of his name; see pp. 233, 266.

In another place my father wrote of Hobbit stature in relation to that of the Númenóreans, and of the origin of the name Halflings:

The remarks [on the stature of Hobbits] in the Prologue to *The Lord of the Rings* are unnecessarily vague and complicated, owing to the inclusion of references to survivals of the race in later times; but as far as *The Lord of the Rings* is concerned they boil down to this: the Hobbits of the Shire were in height between three and four feet, never less and seldom more. They did not of course call themselves Halflings; this was the Númenórean name for them. It evidently referred to their height in comparison with Númenórean men, and was approximately accurate when given. It was applied first to the Harfoots, who became known to the rulers of Arnor in the eleventh century [cf. the entry for 1050 in the Tale of Years], and then later also to Fallohides and Stoors. The Kingdoms of the North and the South remained in close communication at that time, and indeed until much later, and each was well informed of all events in the other region, especially of the migration of peoples of all kinds. Thus though no 'halfling', so far as is known, had ever actually appeared in Gondor before Peregrin Took, the existence of this people within the kingdom of Arthedain was known in Gondor, and they were given the name Halfling, or in Sindarin *perian*. As soon as Frodo was brought to Boromir's notice [at the Council of Elrond] he recognised him as a member of this race. He had probably until then regarded them as creatures of what we should call fairy-tales or folklore. It seems plain from Pippin's reception in Gondor that in fact 'halflings' were remembered there.

In another version of this note more is said of the diminishing stature of both Halflings and Númenóreans:

> The dwindling of the Dúnedain was not a normal tendency, shared by peoples whose proper home was Middle-earth; but due to the loss of their ancient land far in the West, nearest of all mortal lands to the Undying Realm. The much later dwindling of hobbits must be due to a change in their state and way of life; they became a fugitive and secret people, driven (as Men, the Big Folk, became more and more numerous, usurping the more fertile and habitable lands) to refuge in forest or wilderness: a wandering and poor folk, forgetful of their arts, living a precarious life absorbed in the search for food, and fearful of being seen.

II

CIRION AND EORL
AND THE FRIENDSHIP OF
GONDOR AND ROHAN

(i)

The Northmen and the Wainriders

The Chronicle of Cirion and Eorl[1] begins only with the first meeting of Cirion, Steward of Gondor, and Eorl, Lord of the Éothéod, after the Battle of the Field of Celebrant was over and the invaders of Gondor destroyed. But there were lays and legends of the great ride of the Rohirrim from the North both in Rohan and in Gondor, from which accounts that appear in later Chronicles,[2] together with much other matter concerning the Éothéod, were taken. These are here drawn together briefly in chronicle form.

The Éothéod were first known by that name in the days of King Calimehtar of Gondor (who died in the year 1936 of the Third Age), at which time they were a small people living in the Vales of Anduin between the Carrock and the Gladden Fields, for the most part on the west side of the river. They were a remnant of the Northmen, who had formerly been a numerous and powerful confederation of peoples living in the wide plains between Mirkwood and the River Running, great breeders of horses and riders renowned for their skill and endurance, though their settled homes were in the eaves of the Forest, and especially in the East Bight, which had largely been made by their felling of trees.[3]

These Northmen were descendants of the same race of Men as those who in the First Age passed into the West of Middle-earth and became the allies of the Eldar in their wars with Morgoth.[4] They were therefore from afar off kinsmen of the Dúnedain or Númenóreans, and there was great friendship between them and the people of Gondor. They were in fact a bulwark of Gondor, keeping its northern and eastern frontiers from invasion; though that was not fully realised by the Kings until the bulwark was weakened and at last destroyed. The waning of the Northmen of Rhovanion began with the Great Plague, which appeared there in the winter of the year 1635 and soon spread to Gondor. In Gondor the mortality was great, especially among those who dwelt in cities. It was greater in Rhovanion, for though its people lived mostly in the open and had no great cities, the Plague came with a cold winter when horses and men were driven into shelter and their low wooden houses and stables were thronged; moreover they were little skilled in the arts of healing and medicine, of which much was still known in Gondor, preserved from the wisdom of Númenor. When the Plague passed it is said that more than half of the folk of Rhovanion had perished, and of their horses also.

They were slow to recover; but their weakness was not tested for a long time. No doubt the peoples further east had been equally afflicted, so that the enemies of Gondor came chiefly from the south or over sea. But when the invasions of the Wainriders began and involved Gondor in wars that lasted for almost a hundred years, the Northmen bore the brunt of the first assaults. King Narmacil II took a great army north into the plains south of Mirkwood, and gathered all that he could of the scattered remnants of the Northmen; but he was defeated, and himself fell in battle. The remnant of his army retreated over the Dagorlad into Ithilien, and Gondor abandoned all lands east of the Anduin save Ithilien.[5]

As for the Northmen, a few, it is said, fled over the Celduin (River Running) and were merged with the folk of Dale under Erebor (with whom they were akin), some took refuge in Gondor, and others were gathered by Marhwini son of Marhari (who fell in the rearguard action after the Battle of the Plains).[6] Passing north between Mirkwood and Anduin they settled in the Vales of Anduin, where they were joined by many fugitives who came through the Forest. This was the beginning of the Éothéod,[7] though nothing was known of it in Gondor for many years. Most of the Northmen were reduced to servitude, and all their former lands were occupied by the Wainriders.[8]

But at length King Calimehtar, son of Narmacil II, being free from other dangers,[9] determined to avenge the defeat of the Battle of the Plains. Messengers came to him from Marhwini warning him that the Wainriders were plotting to raid Calenardhon over the Undeeps;[10] but they said also that a revolt of the Northmen who had been enslaved was being prepared and would burst into flame if the Wainriders became involved in war. Calimehtar therefore, as soon as he could, led an army out of Ithilien, taking care that its approach should be well known to the enemy. The Wainriders came down with all the strength that they could spare, and Calimehtar gave way before them, drawing them away from their homes. At length battle was joined upon the Dagorlad, and the result was long in doubt. But at its height horsemen that Calimehtar had sent over the Undeeps (left unguarded by the enemy) joined with a great *éored*[11] led by Marhwini assailed the Wainriders in flank and rear. The victory of Gondor was overwhelming – though not in the event decisive. When the enemy broke and were soon in disordered flight north towards their homes Calimehtar, wisely for his part, did not pursue them. They had left well nigh a third of their host dead to rot upon the Dagorlad among the bones of other and nobler battles of the past. But the horsemen of Marhwini harried the fugitives and inflicted great loss upon them in their long rout over the plains, until they were within far sight of Mirkwood. There they left them, taunting them: 'Fly east not north, folk of Sauron! See, the homes you stole are in flames!' For there was a great smoke going up.

The revolt planned and assisted by Marhwini had indeed broken out; desperate outlaws coming out of the Forest had roused the slaves, and together had succeeded in burning many of the dwellings of the Wainriders, and their storehouses, and their fortified camps of wagons. But most of them had perished in the attempt; for they were ill-armed, and the enemy had not left their homes undefended: their youths and old men were aided by the younger women, who in that people were also trained in arms and fought fiercely in defence of their homes and their children. Thus in the end Marhwini was obliged to retire again to his land beside the Anduin, and the Northmen of his race never again returned to their former homes. Calimehtar withdrew to Gondor, which enjoyed for a time (from 1899 to 1944) a respite from war before the great assault in which the line of its kings came near to its end.

Nonetheless the alliance of Calimehtar and Marhwini had not been in vain. If the strength of the Wainriders of Rhovanion had not been broken, that assault would have come sooner and in greater force, and the realm of Gondor might have been destroyed. But the greatest effect of the alliance lay far in the future which none could then foresee: the two great rides of the Rohirrim to the salvation of Gondor, the coming of Eorl to the Field of Celebrant, and the horns of King Théoden upon the Pelennor but for which the return of the King would have been in vain.[12]

In the meanwhile the Wainriders licked their wounds, and plotted their revenge. Beyond the reach of the arms of Gondor, in lands east of the Sea of Rhûn from which no tidings came to its Kings, their kinsfolk spread and multiplied, and they were eager for conquests and booty and filled with hatred of Gondor which stood in their way. It was long, however, before they moved. On the one hand they feared the might of Gondor, and knowing nothing of what passed west of Anduin they believed that its realm was larger and more populous than it was in truth at that time. On the other hand the eastern Wainriders had been spreading southward, beyond Mordor, and were in conflict with the peoples of Khand and their neighbours further south. Eventually a peace and alliance was agreed between these enemies of Gondor, and an attack was prepared that should be made at the same time from north and south.

Little or nothing, of course, was known of these designs and movements in Gondor. What is here said was deduced from the events long afterwards by historians, to whom it was also clear that the hatred of Gondor, and the alliance of its enemies in concerted action (for which they themselves had neither the will nor the wisdom) was due to the machinations of Sauron. Forthwini, son of Marhwini, indeed warned King Ondoher (who succeeded his father Calimehtar in the year 1936) that the Wainriders of Rhovanion were recovering from their weakness and fear, and that he suspected that they were receiving new strength from the East, for he was much troubled by raids into the south of his land that came both up the river and through the Narrows of the Forest.[13] But Gondor could do no more at that time than gather and train as great an army as it could find or afford. Thus when the assault came at last it did not find Gondor unprepared, though its strength was less than it needed.

Ondoher was aware that his southern enemies were preparing for war, and he had the wisdom to divide his forces into a northern army and a southern. The latter was the smaller, for the danger from that quarter was held to be less.[14] It was under the command of Eärnil, a member of the Royal House, being a descendant of King Telumehtar, father of Narmacil II. His base was at Pelargir. The northern army was commanded by King Ondoher himself. This had always been the custom of Gondor, that the King, if he willed, should command his army in a major battle, provided that an heir with undisputed claim to the throne was left behind. Ondoher came of a warlike line, and was loved and esteemed by his army, and he had two sons, both of age to bear arms: Artamir the elder, and Faramir some three years younger.

News of the oncoming of the enemy reached Pelargir on the ninth day of Cermië in the year 1944. Eärnil had already made his dispositions: he had crossed the Anduin with half his force, and leaving by design the Fords of the Poros undefended had encamped some forty miles north in South Ithilien. King Ondoher had purposed to lead his host north through Ithilien and deploy it on the Dagorlad, a field of ill omen for the enemies of Gondor. (At that time the forts upon the line of the Anduin north of Sarn Gebir that had been built by Narmacil I were still in repair and manned by sufficient soldiers from Calenardhon to prevent any attempt of an enemy to cross the river at the Undeeps.) But the news of the northern assault did not reach Ondoher until the morning of the twelfth day of Cermië, by which time the enemy was already drawing near, whereas the army of Gondor had been moving more slowly than it would if Ondoher had received earlier warning, and its vanguard had not yet reached the Gates of Mordor. The main force was leading with the King and his Guards, followed by the soldiers of the Right Wing and the Left Wing which would take up their places when they passed out of Ithilien and approached the Dagorlad. There they expected the assault to come from the North or North-east, as it had before in the Battle of the Plains and in the victory of Calimehtar on the Dagorlad.

But it was not so. The Wainriders had mustered a great host by the southern shores of the inland Sea of Rhûn, strengthened by men of their kinsfolk in Rhovanion and from their new allies in Khand. When all was ready they set out for Gondor from the East, moving with all the speed they could along the line of the Ered Lithui, where their approach was not observed until too late. So it came to pass that the head of the army of Gondor had only drawn level with the Gates of Mordor (the Morannon) when a great dust borne on a wind from the East announced the oncoming of the enemy vanguard.[15] This was composed not only of the war-chariots of the Wainriders but also of a force of cavalry far greater than any that had been expected. Ondoher had only time to turn and face the assault with his right flank close to the Morannon, and to send word to Minohtar, Captain of the Right Wing behind, to cover his left flank as swiftly as he could, when the chariots and horsemen crashed into his disordered line. Of the confusion of the disaster that followed few clear reports were ever brought to Gondor.

Ondoher was utterly unprepared to meet a charge of horsemen and chariots in great weight. With his Guard and his banner he had hastily taken up a position on a low knoll, but this was of no avail.[16] The main charge was hurled against his banner, and it was captured, his Guard was almost annihilated, and he himself was slain and his son Artamir at his side. Their bodies were never recovered. The assault of the enemy passed over them and about both sides of the knoll, driving deep into the disordered ranks of Gondor, hurling them back in confusion upon those behind, and scattering and pursuing many others westward into the Dead Marshes.

Minohtar took command. He was a man both valiant and war-wise. The first fury of the onslaught was spent, with far less loss and greater success than the enemy had looked for. The cavalry and chariots now withdrew, for the main host of the Wainriders was approaching. In such time as he had Minohtar, raising his own banner, rallied the remaining men of the Centre and those of his own command that were at hand. He at once sent messengers to Adrahil of Dol Amroth,[17] the Captain of the Left Wing, commanding him to withdraw with all the speed he could both his own command and those at the rear of the Right Wing who had not yet been engaged. With these forces he was to take up a defensive position between Cair Andros (which was manned) and the mountains of Ephel Dúath, where owing to the great eastward loop of the Anduin the land was at its narrowest, to cover as long as he could the approaches to Minas Tirith. Minohtar himself, to allow time for this retreat, would form a rearguard and attempt to stem the advance of the main host of the Wainriders. Adrahil should at once send messengers to find Eärnil, if they could, and inform him of the disaster of the Morannon and of the position of the retreating northern army.

When the main host of the Wainriders advanced to the attack it was then two hours after noon, and Minohtar had withdrawn his line to the head of the great North Road of Ithilien, half a mile beyond the point where it turned east to the Watch-towers of the Morannon. The first triumph of the Wainriders was now the beginning of their undoing. Ignorant of the numbers and ordering of the defending army they had launched their first onslaught too soon, before the greater part of that army had come out of the narrow land of Ithilien, and the charge of their chariots and cavalry had met with a success far swifter and more overwhelming than they had expected. Their main onslaught was then too long delayed, and they could no longer use their greater numbers with full effect according to the tactics they had intended, being accustomed to warfare in open lands. It may well be supposed that elated by the fall of the King and the rout of a large part of the opposing Centre, they believed that they had already overthrown the defending army, and that their own main army had little more to do than advance to the invasion and occupation of Gondor. If that were so, they were deceived.

The Wainriders came on in little order, still exultant and singing songs of victory, seeing as yet no signs of any defenders to oppose them, until they found that the road into Gondor turned south into a narrow land of trees under the shadow of the dark Ephel Dúath, where an army could march, or ride, in good order only down a great highway. Before them it ran on through a deep cutting . . .

Here the text abruptly breaks off, and the notes and jottings for its continuation are for the most part illegible. It is possible to make out, however, that men of the Éothéod fought with Ondoher; and also that Ondoher's second son Faramir was ordered to remain in Minas Tirith as regent, for it was not permitted by the law that both his sons should go into battle at the same time (a similar observation is made earlier in the narrative, p. 291). But Faramir did not do so; he went to the war in disguise, and was slain. The writing is here almost impossible to decipher, but it seems that Faramir joined the Éothéod and was caught with a party of them as they retreated towards the Dead Marshes. The leader of the Éothéod (whose name is indecipherable after the first element Marh-) came to their rescue, but Faramir died in his arms, and it was only when he searched his body that he found tokens that showed that he was the Prince. The leader of the Éothéod then went to join Minohtar at the head of the North Road in Ithilien, who at that very moment was giving an order for a message to be taken to the Prince in Minas Tirith, who was now the King. It was then that the leader of the Éothéod gave him the news that the Prince had gone disguised to the battle, and had been slain.

The presence of the Éothéod and the part played by their leader may explain the inclusion in this narrative, ostensibly to be an account of the beginnings of the friendship of Gondor and the Rohirrim, of this elaborate story of the battle between the army of Gondor and the Wainriders.

The concluding passage of the fully-written text gives the impression that the host of the Wainriders were about to receive a check to their exaltation and elation as they came down the highway into the deep cutting; but the notes at the end show that they were not long held up by the rearguard defence of Minohtar. 'The Wainriders poured relentlessly into Ithilien', and 'late on the thirteenth day of Cermië they overwhelmed Minohtar', who was slain by an arrow. He is here said to have been King Ondoher's sister-son. 'His men carried him out of the fray, and all that remained of the rearguard fled southwards to find Adrahil.' The chief commander of the Wainriders then called a halt to the advance, and held a feast. Nothing more can be made out; but the brief account in Appendix A to *The Lord of the Rings* tells how Eärnil came up from the south and routed them:

In 1944 King Ondoher and both his sons, Artamir and Faramir, fell in battle north of the Morannon, and the enemy poured into Ithilien.

But Eärnil, Captain of the Southern Army, won a great victory in South Ithilien and destroyed the army of Harad that had crossed the River Poros. Hastening north, he gathered to him all that he could of the retreating Northern Army and came up against the main camp of the Wainriders, while they were feasting and revelling, believing that Gondor was overthrown and that nothing remained but to take the spoil. Eärnil stormed the camp and set fire to the wains, and drove the enemy in a great rout out of Ithilien. A great part of those who fled before him perished in the Dead Marshes.

In the Tale of Years the victory of Eärnil is called the Battle of the Camp. After the deaths of Ondoher and both his sons at the Morannon Arvedui, last king of the northern realm, laid claim to the crown of Gondor; but his claim was rejected, and in the year following the Battle of the Camp Eärnil became King. His son was Eärnur, who died in Minas Morgul after accepting the challenge of the Lord of the Nazgûl, and was the last of the Kings of the southern realm.

(ii)

The Ride of Eorl

While the Éothéod still dwelt in their former home[18] they were well-known to Gondor as a people of good trust, from whom they received news of all that passed in that region. They were a remnant of the Northmen, who were held to be akin in ages past to the Dúnedain, and in the days of the great Kings had been their allies and contributed much of their blood to the people of Gondor. It was thus of great concern to Gondor when the Éothéod removed into the far North, in the days of Eärnil II, last but one of the Kings of the southern realm.[19]

The new land of the Éothéod lay north of Mirkwood, between the Misty Mountains westward and the Forest River eastward. Southward it extended to the confluence of the two short rivers that they named Greylin and Langwell. Greylin flowed down from Ered Mithrin, the Grey Mountains, but Langwell came from the Misty Mountains, and this name it bore because it was the source of Anduin, which from its junction with Greylin they called Langflood.[20]

Messengers still passed between Gondor and the Éothéod after their departure; but it was some four hundred and fifty of our miles between the confluence of Greylin and Langwell (where was their only fortified *burg*) and the inflow of Limlight into Anduin, in a direct line as a bird might fly, and much more for those who journeyed on earth; and in like manner some eight hundred miles to Minas Tirith.

The Chronicle of Cirion and Eorl reports no events before the Battle of the Field of Celebrant; but from other sources they may be made out to have been of this sort.

The wide lands south of Mirkwood, from the Brown Lands to the Sea of Rhûn, which offered no obstacle to invaders from the East until they came to Anduin, were a chief source of concern and unease to the rulers of Gondor. But during the Watchful Peace[21] the forts along the Anduin, especially on the west shore of the Undeeps, had been unmanned and neglected.[22] After that time Gondor was assailed both by Orcs out of Mordor (which had long been unguarded) and by the Corsairs of Umbar, and had neither men nor opportunity for manning the line of Anduin north of the Emyn Muil.

Cirion became Steward of Gondor in the year 2489. The menace from the North was ever in his mind, and he gave much thought to ways that might be devised against the threat of invasion from that quarter, as the strength of Gondor diminished. He put a few men into the old forts to keep watch on the Undeeps, and sent scouts and spies into the lands between Mirkwood and Dagorlad. He was thus soon aware that new and dangerous enemies coming out of the East were steadily drifting in from beyond the Sea of Rhûn. They were slaying or driving north up the River Running and into the Forest the remnant of the Northmen, friends of Gondor that still dwelt east of Mirkwood.[23] But he could do nothing to aid them, and it became more and more dangerous to gather news; too many of his scouts never returned.

It was thus not until the winter of the year 2509 was past that Cirion became aware that a great movement against Gondor was being prepared: hosts of men were mustering all along the southern eaves of Mirkwood. They were only rudely armed, and had no great number of horses for riding, using horses mainly for draught, since they had many large wains, as had the Wainriders (to whom they were no doubt akin) that assailed Gondor in the last days of the Kings. But what they lacked in gear of war they made up in numbers, so far as could be guessed.

In this peril Cirion's thought turned at last in desperation to the Éothéod, and he determined to send messengers to them. But they would have to go through Calenardhon and over the Undeeps, and then through lands already watched and patrolled by the Balchoth[24] before they could reach the Vales of Anduin. This would mean a ride of some four hundred and fifty miles to the Undeeps, and more than five hundred thence to the Éothéod, and from the Undeeps they would be forced to go warily and mostly by night until they had passed the shadow of Dol Guldur. Cirion had little hope that any of them would get through. He called for volunteers, and choosing six riders of great courage and endurance he sent them out in pairs with a day's interval between them. Each bore a message learned by heart, and also a small stone incised with the seal of the Stewards,[25] that he should deliver to the Lord of the Éothéod in person, if he succeeded in reaching that land. The message was addressed to Eorl son of Léod, for Cirion knew that he had succeeded his father some years before, when he was but a youth of sixteen, and though now no more than five and twenty was praised in all such tidings as reached Gondor as a man of great courage and wise beyond his years. Yet Cirion had but faint hope that even if the message were received it would be answered. He had no claim on the Éothéod beyond their ancient friendship with Gondor to bring them from so far away with any strength that would avail. The tidings that the Balchoth were destroying the last of their kin in the South, if they did not know it already, might give weight to his appeal, if the Éothéod themselves were not threatened by any attack. Cirion said no more,[26] and ordered what strength he had to meet the storm. He gathered as great a force as he could, and taking command of it himself made ready as swiftly as might be to lead it north to Calenardhon. Hallas his son he left in command at Minas Tirith.

The first pair of messengers left on the tenth day of Súlimë; and in the event it was one of these, alone of all the six, who got through to the Éothéod. He was Borondir, a great rider of a family that claimed descent from a captain of the Northmen in the service of the Kings of old.[27] Of the others no tidings were ever heard, save of Borondir's companion. He was slain by arrows in ambush as they passed near Dol Guldur, from which Borondir escaped by fortune and the speed of his horse. He was pursued as far north as the Gladden Fields, and often waylaid by men that came out of the Forest and forced him to ride far out of the direct way. He came at last to the Éothéod after fifteen days, for the last two without food; and he was so spent that he could scarce speak his message to Eorl.

It was then the twenty-fifth day of Súlimë. Eorl took counsel with himself in silence; but not for long. Soon he rose, and he said: 'I will come. If the Mundburg falls, whither shall we flee from the Darkness?' Then he took Borondir's hand in token of his promise.

Eorl at once summoned his council of Elders, and began to prepare for the great riding. But this took many days, for the host had to be gathered and mustered, and thought taken for the ordering of the people and the defence of the land. At that time the Éothéod were at peace and had no fear of war: though it might prove otherwise when it became known that their lord had ridden away to battle far off in the South. Nonetheless Eorl saw well that nothing less than his full strength would serve, and he must risk all or draw back and break his promise.

At last the whole host was assembled; and only a few hundreds were left behind to support the men unfitted for such a desperate venture by youth or age. It was then the sixth day of the month of Víressë. On that day in silence the great *éohere* set out, leaving fear behind, and taking with them small hope; for they knew not what lay before them, either on the road or at its end. It is said that Eorl led forth some seven thousand fully-armed riders and some hundreds of horsed archers. At his right hand rode Borondir, to serve as guide so far as he might, since he had lately passed through the lands. But this great host was not threatened or assailed during its long journey down the Vales of Anduin. Such folk of good or evil kind as saw it approach fled out of its path for fear of its might and splendour. As it drew southward and passed by southern Mirkwood (below the great East Bight), which was now infested by the Balchoth, still there was no sign of men, in force or in scouting parties, to bar their road or to spy upon their coming. In part this was due to events unknown to them, which had come to pass since Borondir set out; but other powers also were at work. For when at last the host drew near to Dol Guldur, Eorl turned away westward for fear of the dark shadow and cloud that flowed out from it, and then he rode on within sight of Anduin. Many of the riders turned their eyes thither, half in fear and half in hope to glimpse from afar the shimmer of the Dwimordene, the perilous land that in legends of their people was said to shine like gold in the springtime. But now it seemed shrouded in a gleaming mist; and to their dismay the mist passed over the river and flowed over the land before them.

Eorl did not halt. 'Ride on!' he commanded. 'There is no other way to take. After so long a road shall we be held back from battle by a river-mist?'

As they drew nearer they saw that the white mist was driving back the glooms of Dol Guldur, and soon they passed into it, riding slowly at first and warily; but under its canopy all things were lit with a clear and shadowless light, while to left and right they were guarded as it were by white walls of secrecy.

'The Lady of the Golden Wood is on our side, it seems,' said Borondir.

'Maybe,' said Eorl. 'But at least I will trust the wisdom of Felaróf.[28] He scents no evil. His heart is high, and his weariness is healed: he strains to be given his head. So be it! For never have I had more need of secrecy and speed.'

Then Felaróf sprang forward, and all the host behind followed like a great wind, but in a strange silence, as if their hooves did not beat upon the ground. So they rode on, as fresh and eager as on the morning of their setting-out, during that day and the next; but at dawn of the third day they rose from their rest, and suddenly the mist was gone, and they saw that they were far out in the open lands. On their right the Anduin lay near, but they had almost passed its great eastward loop,[29] and the Undeeps were in sight. It was the morning of the fifteenth day of Víressë, and they had come there at a speed beyond hope.[30]

Here the text ends, with a note that a description of the Battle of the Field of Celebrant was to follow. In Appendix A (II) to *The Lord of the Rings* there is a summary account of the war:

A great host of wild men from the North-east swept over Rhovanion and coming down out of the Brown-lands crossed the Anduin on rafts. At the same time by chance or design the Orcs (who at that time before their war with the Dwarves were in great strength) made a descent from the Mountains. The invaders overran Calenardhon, and Cirion, Steward of Gondor, sent north for help . . .

When Eorl and his Riders came to the Field of Celebrant

the northern army of Gondor was in peril. Defeated in the Wold and cut off from the south, it had been driven across the Limlight, and was then suddenly assailed by the Orc-host that pressed it towards the Anduin. All hope was lost when, unlooked for, the Riders came out of the North and broke upon the rear of the enemy. Then the fortunes of battle were reversed, and the enemy was driven with slaughter over Limlight. Eorl led his men in pursuit, and so great was the fear that went before the horsemen of the North that the invaders of the Wold were also thrown into panic, and the Riders hunted them over the plains of Calenardhon.

A similar, briefer, account is given elsewhere in Appendix A (I, iv). From neither is the course of the battle perhaps perfectly clear, but it seems certain that the Riders, having passed over the Undeeps, then crossed the Limlight (see note 27, p. 313) and fell upon the rear of the enemy at the Field of Celebrant; and that 'the enemy was driven with slaughter over Limlight' means that the Balchoth were driven back southwards into the Wold.

(iii)

Cirion and Eorl

The story is preceded by a note on the Halifirien, westernmost of the beacons of Gondor along the line of Ered Nimrais.

The Halifirien[31] was the highest of the beacons, and like Eilenach, the next in height, appeared to stand up alone out of a great wood; for behind it there was a deep cleft, the dark Firien-dale, in the long northward spur of Ered Nimrais, of which it was the highest point. Out of the cleft it rose like a sheer wall, but its outer slopes, especially northwards, were long and nowhere steep, and trees grew upon them almost to its summit. As they descended the trees became ever more dense, especially along the Mering Stream (which rose in the cleft) and northwards out into the plain through which the Stream flowed into the Entwash. The great West Road passed through a long cutting in the wood, to avoid the wet land beyond its northern eaves; but this road had been made in ancient days,[32] and after the departure of Isildur no tree was ever felled in the Firien Wood, except only by the Beacon-wardens whose task it was to keep open the great road and the path towards the summit of the hill. This path turned from the Road near to its entrance into the Wood, and wound its way up to the end of the trees, beyond which there was an ancient stairway of stone leading to the beacon-site, a wide circle levelled by those who had made the stair. The Beacon-wardens were the only inhabitants of the Wood, save wild beasts; they housed in lodges in the trees near the summit, but they did not stay long, unless held there by foul weather, and they came and went in turns of duty. For the most part they were glad to return home. Not because of the peril of the wild beasts, nor did any evil shadow out of dark days lie upon the Wood; but beneath the sounds of the winds, the cries of birds and beasts, or at times the noise of horsemen riding in haste upon the Road, there lay a silence, and a man would find himself speaking to his comrades in a whisper, as if he expected to hear the echo of a great voice that called from far away and long ago.

The name Halifirien meant in the language of the Rohirrim 'holy mountain'.[33] Before their coming it was known in Sindarin as Amon Anwar, 'Hill of Awe'; for what reason was not known in Gondor, except only (as later appeared) to the ruling King or Steward. For the few men who ever ventured to leave the Road and wander under the trees the Wood itself seemed reason enough: in the Common Speech it was called 'the Whispering Wood'. In the great days of Gondor no beacon was built on the Hill while the *palantíri* still maintained communication between Osgiliath and the three towers of the realm[34] without need of messages or signals. In later days little aid could be expected from the North as the people of Calenardhon declined, nor was armed force sent thither as Minas Tirith became more and more hard put to it to hold the line of the Anduin and guard its southern coast. In Anórien many people still dwelt and had the task of guarding the northern approaches, either out of Calenardhon or across the Anduin at Cair Andros. For communication with them the three oldest beacons (Amon Dîn, Eilenach, and Min-Rimmon) were built and maintained,[35] but though the line of the Mering Stream was fortified (between the impassable marshes of its confluence with the Entwash and the bridge where the Road passed westward out of the Firien Wood) it was not permitted that any fort or beacon should be set upon Amon Anwar.

In the days of Cirion the Steward there came a great assault by the Balchoth, who allied with Orcs crossed the Anduin into the Wold and began the conquest of Calenardhon. From this deadly peril, which would have brought ruin upon Gondor, the coming of Eorl the Young and the Rohirrim rescued the realm.

When the war was over men wondered in what way the Steward would honour Eorl and reward him, and expected that a great feast would be held in Minas Tirith at which this would be revealed. But Cirion was a man who kept his own counsel. As the diminished army of Gondor made its way south he was accompanied by Eorl and an *éored*[36] of the Riders of the North. When they came to the Mering Stream Cirion turned to Eorl and said, to men's wonder:

'Farewell now, Eorl, son of Léod. I will return to my home, where much needs to be set in order. Calenardhon I commit to your care for this time, if you are not in haste to return to your own realm. In three months' time I will meet you here again, and then we will take counsel together.'

'I will come,' Eorl answered; and so they parted.

As soon as Cirion came to Minas Tirith he summoned some of his
most trusted servants. 'Go now to the Whispering Wood,' he said.
'There you must re-open the ancient path to Amon Anwar. It is
long overgrown; but the entrance is still marked by a standing stone
beside the Road, at that point where the northern region of the Wood
closes in upon it. The path turns this way and that, but at each turn
there is a standing stone. Following these you will come at length
to the end of the trees and find a stone stair that leads on upwards.
I charge you to go no further. Do this work as swiftly as you may and
then return to me. Fell no trees; only clear a way by which a few
men on foot can easily pass upwards. Leave the entrance by the Road
still shrouded, so that none that use the Road may be tempted to
use the path before I come there myself. Tell no one whither you go
or what you have done. If any ask, say only that the Lord Steward
wishes for a place to be made ready for his meeting with the Lord
of the Riders.'

In due time Cirion set out with Hallas his son and the Lord of
Dol Amroth, and two others of his Council; and he met Eorl at the
crossing of the Mering Stream. With Eorl were three of his chief
captains. 'Let us go now to the place that I have prepared,' said
Cirion. Then they left a guard of Riders at the bridge and turned
back into the tree-shadowed Road, and came to the standing stone.
There they left their horses and another strong guard of soldiers of
Gondor; and Cirion standing by the stone turned to his companions
and said: 'I go now to the Hill of Awe. Follow me, if you will. With
me shall come an esquire, and another with Eorl, to bear our arms;
all others shall go unarmed as witnesses of our words and deeds in
the high place. The path has been made ready, though none have
used it since I came here with my father.'

Then Cirion led Eorl into the trees and the others followed in
order; and after they had passed the first of the inner stones their
voices were stilled and they walked warily as if unwilling to make
any sound. So they came at last to the upper slopes of the Hill and
passed through a belt of white birches and saw the stone stair going
up to the summit. After the shadow of the Wood the sun seemed
hot and bright, for it was the month of Úrimë; yet the crown of the
Hill was green, as if the year were still in Lótessë.

At the foot of the stair there was a small shelf or cove made in the
hillside with low turf-banks. There the company sat for a while, until
Cirion rose and from his esquire took the white wand of office and the
white mantle of the Stewards of Gondor. Then standing on the first
step of the stair he broke the silence, saying in a low but clear voice:

'I will now declare what I have resolved, with the authority of the Stewards of the Kings, to offer to Eorl son of Léod, Lord of the Éothéod, in recognition of the valour of his people and of the help beyond hope that he brought to Gondor in time of dire need. To Eorl I will give in free gift all the great land of Calenardhon from Anduin to Isen. There, if he will, he shall be king, and his heirs after him, and his people shall dwell in freedom while the authority of the Stewards endures, until the Great King returns.[37] No bond shall be laid upon them other than their own laws and will, save in this only: they shall live in perpetual friendship with Gondor and its enemies shall be their enemies while both realms endure. But the same bond shall be laid also on the people of Gondor.'

Then Eorl stood up, but remained for some time silent. For he was amazed by the great generosity of the gift and the noble terms in which it had been offered; and he saw the wisdom of Cirion both on his own behalf as ruler of Gondor, seeking to protect what remained of his realm, and as a friend of the Éothéod of whose needs he was aware. For they were now grown to a people too numerous for their land in the North and longed to return south to their former home, but they were restrained by the fear of Dol Guldur. But in Calenardhon they would have room beyond hope, and yet be far from the shadows of Mirkwood.

Yet beyond wisdom and policy both Cirion and Eorl were moved at that time by the great friendship that bound their peoples together, and by the love that was between them as true men. On the part of Cirion the love was that of a wise father, old in the cares of the world, for a son in the strength and hope of his youth; while in Cirion Eorl saw the highest and noblest man of the world that he knew, and the wisest, on whom sat the majesty of the Kings of Men of long ago.

At last, when Eorl had swiftly passed all these things through his thought, he spoke, saying: 'Lord Steward of the Great King, the gift that you offer I accept for myself and for my people. It far exceeds any reward that our deeds could have earned, if they had not themselves been a free gift of friendship. But now I will seal that friendship with an oath that shall not be forgotten.'

'Then let us go now to the high place,' said Cirion, 'and before these witnesses take such oaths as seem fitting.'

Then Cirion went up the stair with Eorl and the others followed; and when they came to the summit they saw there a wide oval place of level turf, unfenced, but at its eastern end there stood a low mound on which grew the white flowers of *alfirin*,[38] and the westering sun touched them with gold. Then the Lord of Dol Amroth, chief of those in the company of Cirion, went towards the mound and saw, lying on the grass before it and yet unmarred by weed or weather, a black stone; and on the stone three letters were engraved. Then he said to Cirion:

'Is this then a tomb? But what great man of old lies here?'

'Have you not read the letters?' said Cirion.

'I have,' said the Prince,[39] 'and therefore I wonder; for the letters are *lambe, ando, lambe,* but there is no tomb for Elendil, nor has any man since his day dared to use that name.'[40]

'Nonetheless this is his tomb,' said Cirion; 'and from it comes the awe that dwells on this hill and in the woods below. From Isildur who raised it to Meneldil who succeeded him, and so down all the line of the Kings, and down the line of the Stewards even to myself, this tomb has been kept a secret by Isildur's command. For he said: "Here is the mid-point of the Kingdom of the South,[41] and here shall the memorial of Elendil the Faithful abide in the keeping of the Valar, while the Kingdom endures. This hill shall be a hallow, and let no man disturb its peace and silence, unless he be an heir of Elendil." I have brought you here, so that the oaths here taken may seem of deepest solemnity to ourselves and to our heirs upon either side.'

Then all those present stood a while in silence with bowed heads, until Cirion said to Eorl: 'If you are ready, take now your oath in such manner as seems to you fitting according to the customs of your people.'

Eorl then stood forth, and taking his spear from his esquire he set it upright in the ground. Then he drew his sword and cast it up shining in the sun, and catching it again he stepped forward and laid the blade upon the mound, but with his hand still about the hilts. He spoke then in a great voice the Oath of Eorl. This he said in the tongue of the Éothéod, which in the Common Speech is interpreted:[42]

Hear now all peoples who bow not to the Shadow in the East, by the gift of the Lord of the Mundburg we will come to dwell in the land that he names Calenardhon, and therefore I vow in my own name and on behalf of the Éothéod of the North that between us and the Great People of the West there shall be friendship for ever: their enemies shall be our enemies, their need shall be our need, and whatsoever evil, or threat, or assault may come upon them we will aid them to the utmost end of our strength. This vow shall descend to my heirs, all such as may come after me in our new land, and let them keep it in faith unbroken, lest the Shadow fall upon them and they become accursed.

Then Eorl sheathed his sword and bowed and went back to his captains.

Cirion then made answer. Standing to his full height he laid his hand upon the tomb and in his right hand held up the white wand of the Stewards, and spoke words that filled those who heard them with awe. For as he stood up the sun went down in flame in the West and his white robe seemed to be on fire; and after he had vowed that Gondor should be bound by a like bond of friendship and aid in all need, he lifted up his voice and said in Quenya:

> *Vanda sina termaruva Elenna·nóreo alcar enyalien ar Elendil Vorondo voronwë. Nai tiruvantes i hárar mahalmassen mi Númen ar i Eru i or ilyë mahalmar eä tennoio.*[43]

And again he said the Common Speech:

This oath shall stand in memory of the glory of the Land of the Star, and of the faith of Elendil the Faithful, in the keeping of those who sit upon the thrones of the West and of the One who is above all thrones for ever.

Such an oath had not been heard in Middle-earth since Elendil himself had sworn alliance with Gil-galad King of the Eldar.[44]

When all was done and the shadows of evening were falling Cirion and Eorl with their company went down again in silence through the darkling Wood, and came back to the camp by the Mering Stream where tents had been prepared for them. After they had eaten Cirion and Eorl, with the Prince of Dol Amroth and Éomund the chief captain of the host of the Éothéod, sat together and defined the boundaries of the authority of the King of the Éothéod and the Steward of Gondor.

The bounds of the realm of Eorl were to be: in the West the river Angren from its junction with the Adorn and thence northwards to the outer fences of Agrenost, and thence westwards and northwards along the eaves of Fangorn Forest to the river Limlight; and that river was its northern boundary, for the land beyond had never been claimed by Gondor.[45] In the east its bounds were the Anduin and the west-cliff of the Emyn Muil down to the marshes of the Mouths of Onodló, and beyond that river the stream of the Glanhír that flowed through the Wood of Anwar to join the Onodló; and in the south its bounds were the Ered Nimrais as far as the end of their northward arm, but all those vales and inlets that opened northwards were to belong to the Éothéod, as well as the land south of the Hithaeglir that lay between the rivers Angren and Adorn.[46]

In all these regions Gondor still retained under its own command only the fortress of Angrenost, within which was the third Tower of Gondor, the impregnable Orthanc where was held the fourth of the *palantíri* of the southern realm. In the days of Cirion Angrenost was still manned by a guard of Gondorians, but these had become a small settled people, ruled by an hereditary Captain, and the keys of Orthanc were in the keeping of the Steward of Gondor. The 'outer fences' named in the description of the bounds of the realm of Eorl were a wall and dyke running some two miles south of the gates of Angrenost, between the hills in which the Misty Mountains ended; beyond them were the tilled lands of the people of the fortress.

It was agreed also that the Great Road which had formerly run through Anórien and Calenardhon to Athrad Angren (the Fords of Isen),[47] and thence northwards on its way to Arnor, should be open to all travellers of either people without hindrance in time of peace, and its maintenance should from the Mering Stream to the Fords of Isen be in the care of the Éothéod.

By this pact only a small part of the Wood of Anwar, west of the Mering Stream, was included in the realm of Eorl; but Cirion declared that the Hill of Anwar was now a hallowed place of both peoples, and the Eorlings and the Stewards should henceforward share its guard and maintenance. In later days, however, as the Rohirrim grew in power and numbers, while Gondor declined and was ever threatened from the East and by sea, the wardens of Anwar were provided entirely by the people of Eastfold, and the Wood became by custom part of the royal domain of the Kings of the Mark. The Hill they named the Halifirien, and the Wood the Firienholt.[48]

In later times the day of the Oath-taking was reckoned as the first day of the new kingdom, when Eorl took the title of King of the Mark of the Riders. But in the event it was some while before the Rohirrim took possession of the land, and during his life Eorl was known as Lord of the Éothéod and King of Calenardhon. The term Mark signified a borderland, especially one serving as a defence of the inner lands of a realm. The Sindarin names Rohan for the Mark and Rohirrim for the people were devised first by Hallas, son and successor of Cirion, but were often used not only in Gondor but by the Éothéod themselves.[49]

The day after the Oath-taking Cirion and Eorl embraced and took their leave unwillingly. For Eorl said: 'Lord Steward, I have much to do in haste. This land is now rid of enemies; but they are not destroyed at the root, and beyond Anduin and under the eaves of Mirkwood we know not yet what peril lurks. I sent yestereve three messengers north, riders brave and skilled, in the hope that one at least will reach my home before me. For I must now return myself, and with some strength; my land was left with few men, those too young and those too old; and if they are to make so great a journey our women and children, with such goods as we cannot spare, must be guarded, and only the Lord of the Éothéod himself will they follow. I will leave behind me all the strength that I can spare, well nigh half of the host that is now in Calenardhon. Some companies of horsed archers there shall be, to go where need calls, if any bands of the enemy still lurk in the land; but the main force shall remain in the North-east to guard above all the place where the Balchoth made a crossing of the Anduin out of the Brown Lands; for there is still the greatest danger, and there also is my chief hope, if I return, of leading my people into their new land with as little grief and loss as may be. If I return, I say: but be assured that I shall return, for the keeping of my oath, unless disaster befall us and I perish with my people on the long road. For that must be on the east side of Anduin ever under the threat of Mirkwood, and at last must pass through the vale that is haunted by the shadow of the hill that you name Dol Guldur. On the west side there is no road for horsemen, nor for a great host of people and wains, even were not the Mountains infested by Orcs; and none can pass, few or many, through the Dwimordene where dwells the White Lady and weaves nets that no mortal can pass.[50] By the east road will I come, as I came to Celebrant; and may those whom we called in witness of our oaths have us in their keeping. Let us part now in hope! Have I your leave?'

'Indeed you have my leave,' said Cirion, 'since I see now that it cannot be otherwise. I perceive that in our peril I have given too little thought to the dangers that you have faced and the wonder of your coming beyond hope over the long leagues from the North. The reward that I offered in joy and fullness of heart at our deliverance now seems little. But I believe that the words of my oath, which I had not forethought ere I spoke them, were not put into my mouth in vain. We will part then in hope.'

After the manner of the Chronicles no doubt much of what is here put into the mouths of Eorl and Cirion at their parting was said and considered in the debate of the night before; but it is certain that Cirion said at parting his words concerning the inspiration of his oath, for he was a man of little pride and of great courage and generosity of heart, the noblest of the Stewards of Gondor.

(iv)

The Tradition of Isildur

It is said that when Isildur returned from the War of the Last Alliance he remained for a time in Gondor, ordering the realm and instructing Meneldil his nephew, before he himself departed to take up the kingship of Arnor. With Meneldil and a company of trusted friends he made a journey about the borders of all the lands to which Gondor laid claim; and as they were returning from the northern bound to Anórien they came to the high hill that was then called Eilenaer but was afterwards called Amon Anwar, 'Hill of Awe'.[51] That was near to the centre of the lands of Gondor. They made a path through the dense woods of its northward slopes, and so came to its summit, which was green and treeless. There they made a level space, and at its eastward end they raised a mound; within the mound Isildur laid a casket that he bore with him. Then he said: 'This is a tomb and memorial of Elendil the Faithful. Here it shall stand at the mid-point of the Kingdom of the South in the keeping of the Valar, while the Kingdom endures; and this place shall be a hallow that none shall profane. Let no man disturb its silence and peace, unless he be an heir of Elendil.'

They made a stone stair from the fringe of the woods up to the crown of the hill; and Isildur said: 'Up this stair let no man climb, save the King, and those that he brings with him, if he bids them follow him.' Then all those present were sworn to secrecy; but Isildur gave this counsel to Meneldil, that the King should visit the hallow from time to time, and especially when he felt the need of wisdom in days of danger or distress; and thither also he should bring his heir, when he was full-grown to manhood, and tell him of the making of the hallow, and reveal to him the secrets of the realm and other matters that he should know.

Meneldil followed Isildur's counsel, and all the Kings that came after him, until Rómendacil I (the fifth after Meneldil). In his time Gondor was first assailed by Easterlings;[52] and lest the tradition should be broken because of war or sudden death or other misfortune, he caused the 'Tradition of Isildur' to be set down in a sealed scroll, together with other things that a new King should know; and this scroll was delivered by the Steward to the King before his crowning.[53] This delivery was from then onwards always performed, though the custom of visiting the hallow of Amon Anwar with his heir was maintained by nearly all the Kings of Gondor.

When the days of the Kings came to an end and Gondor was ruled by the Stewards descended from Húrin, the steward of King Minardil, it was held that all the rights and duties of the Kings were theirs 'until the Great King returns'. But in the matter of the 'Tradition of Isildur' they alone were the judges, since it was known only to them. They judged that by the words 'an heir of Elendil' Isildur had meant one of the royal line descended from Elendil who had inherited the throne: but that he did not foresee the rule of the Stewards. If then Mardil had exercised the authority of the King in his absence,[54] the heirs of Mardil who had inherited the Stewardship had the same right and duty until a King returned; each Steward therefore had the right to visit the hallow when he would and to admit to it those who came with him, as he thought fit. As for the words 'while the Kingdom endures', they said that Gondor remained a 'kingdom', ruled by a vice-regent, and that the words must therefore be held to mean 'as long as the state of Gondor endures'.

Nonetheless, the Stewards, partly from awe, and partly from the cares of the kingdom, went very seldom to the hallow on the Hill of Anwar, except when they took their heir to the hill-top, according to the custom of the Kings. Sometimes it remained for several years unvisited, and as Isildur had prayed it was in the keeping of the Valar; for though the woods might grow tangled and be avoided by men because of the silence, so that the upward path was lost, still when the way was re-opened the hallow was found unweathered and unprofaned, ever-green and at peace under the sky, until the Kingdom of Gondor was changed.

For it came to pass that Cirion, the twelfth of the Ruling Stewards, was faced by a new and great danger: invaders threatened the conquest of all the lands of Gondor north of the White Mountains, and if that were to happen the downfall and destruction of the whole kingdom must soon follow. As is known in the histories, this peril was averted only by the aid of the Rohirrim; and to them Cirion with great wisdom granted all the northern lands, save Anórien, to be under their own rule and king, though in perpetual alliance with Gondor. There were no longer sufficient men in the realm to people the northward region, nor even to maintain in force the line of forts along the Anduin that had guarded its eastward boundary. Cirion gave long thought to this matter before he granted Calenardhon to the Horsemen of the North; and he judged that its cession must change wholly the 'Tradition of Isildur' with regard to the hallow of Amon Anwar. To that place he brought the Lord of the Rohirrim, and there by the mound of Elendil he with the greatest solemnity took the Oath of Eorl, and was answered by the Oath of Cirion, confirming for ever the alliance of the Kingdoms of the Rohirrim and of Gondor. But when this was done, and Eorl had returned to the North to bring back all his people to their new dwelling, Cirion removed the tomb of Elendil. For he judged that the 'Tradition of Isildur' was now made void. The hallow was no longer 'at the mid-point of the Kingdom of the South', but on the borders of another realm; and moreover the words 'while the Kingdom endures' referred to the Kingdom as it was when Isildur spoke, after surveying its bounds and defining them. It was true that other parts of the Kingdom had been lost since that day: Minas Ithil was in the hands of the Nazgûl, and Ithilien was desolate; but Gondor had not relinquished its claim to them. Calenardhon it had resigned for ever under oath. The casket therefore that Isildur had set within the mound Cirion removed to the Hallows of Minas Tirith; but the green mound remained as the memorial of a memorial. Nonetheless, even when it had become the site of a great beacon, the Hill of Anwar was still a place of reverence to Gondor and to the Rohirrim, who named it in their own tongue Halifirien, the Holy Mount.

NOTES

1 No writing is extant with this title, but no doubt the narrative given in the third section ('Cirion and Eorl', p. 300) represents a part of it.

2 Such as the Book of the Kings. [Author's note.] – This work was referred to in the opening passage of Appendix A to *The Lord of the Rings*, as being (with *The Book of the Stewards* and the *Akallabêth*) among the records of Gondor that were opened to Frodo and Peregrin by King Elessar; but in the revised edition the reference was removed.

3 The East Bight, not named elsewhere, was the great indentation in the eastern border of Mirkwood seen in the map to *The Lord of the Rings*.

4 The Northmen appear to have been most nearly akin to the third and greatest of the peoples of the Elf-friends, ruled by the House of Hador. [Author's note.]

5 The escape of the army of Gondor from total destruction was in part due to the courage and loyalty of the horsemen of the Northmen under Marhari (a descendant of Vidugavia 'King of Rhovanion') who acted as rearguard. But the forces of Gondor had inflicted such losses on the Wainriders that they had not strength enough to press their invasion, until reinforced from the East, and were content for the time to complete their conquest of Rhovanion. [Author's note.] – It is told in Appendix A (I, iv) to *The Lord of the Rings* that Vidugavia, who called himself King of Rhovanion, was the most powerful of the princes of the Northmen; he was shown favour by Rómendacil II King of Gondor (died 1366), whom he had aided in war against the Easterlings, and the marriage of Rómendacil's son Valacar to Vidugavia's daughter Vidumavi led to the destructive Kin-strife in Gondor in the fifteenth century.

6 It is an interesting fact, not referred to I believe in any of my father's writings, that the names of the early kings and princes of the Northmen and the Éothéod are Gothic in form, not Old English (Anglo-Saxon) as in the case of Léod, Eorl, and the later Rohirrim. *Vidugavia* is Latinized in spelling, representing Gothic *Widugauja* ('wood-dweller'), a recorded Gothic name, and similarly *Vidumavi* Gothic *Widumawi* ('wood-maiden'). *Marhwini* and *Marhari* contain the Gothic word *marh* 'horse', corresponding to Old English *mearh*, plural *mearas*, the word used in *The Lord of the Rings* for the horses of Rohan; *wini* 'friend' corresponds to Old English *winë*, seen in the names of several of the Kings of the Mark. Since, as is explained in Appendix F (II), the language of Rohan was 'made to resemble ancient English', the names of the ancestors of the Rohirrim are cast into the forms of the earliest recorded Germanic language.

7 As was the form of the name in later days. [Author's note.] – This is Old English, 'horse-people'; see note 36.

8 The foregoing narrative does not contradict the accounts in Appendix A (I, iv and II) to *The Lord of the Rings*, though it is much briefer. Nothing is said here of the war fought against the Easterlings in the thirteenth century by Minalcar (who took the name of Rómendacil II), the absorption of many Northmen into the armies of Gondor by that king, or of the marriage of his son Valacar to a princess of the Northmen and the Kin-strife of Gondor that resulted from it; but it adds certain features which are not mentioned in *The Lord of the Rings*: that the waning of the Northmen of Rhovanion was due to the Great Plague; that the battle in which King Narmacil II was slain in the year 1856, said in Appendix A to have been 'beyond Anduin', was in the wide lands south of Mirkwood, and was known as the Battle of the Plains; and that his great army was saved from annihilation by the Wainriders through the rearguard defence of Marhari, descendant of Vidugavia. It is also made clearer here that it was after the

Battle of the Plains that the Éothéod, a remnant of the Northmen,
became a distinct people, dwelling in the Vales of Anduin between
the Carrock and the Gladden Fields.

9 His grandfather Telumehtar had captured Umbar and broken the
power of the Corsairs, and the peoples of Harad were at this period
engaged in wars and feuds of their own. [Author's note.] – The taking
of Umbar by Telumehtar Umbardacil was in the year 1810.

10 The great westward bends of the Anduin east of Fangorn Forest; see
the first citation given in Appendix C to 'The History of Galadriel
and Celeborn', p. 260.

11 On the word *éored* see note 36.

12 This story is very much fuller than the summary account in Appendix
A (I, iv) to *The Lord of the Rings*: 'Calimehtar, son of Narmacil II,
helped by a revolt in Rhovanion, avenged his father with a great
victory over the Easterlings upon Dagorlad in 1899, and for a while
the peril was averted.'

13 The Narrows of the Forest must refer to the narrow 'waist' of
Mirkwood in the south, caused by the indentation of the East Bight
(see note 3).

14 Justly. For an attack proceeding from Near Harad – unless it had
assistance from Umbar, which was not at that time available – could
more easily be resisted and contained. It could not cross the Anduin,
and as it went north passed into a narrowing land between the river
and the mountains. [Author's note.]

15 An isolated note associated with the text remarks that at this period
the Morannon was still in the control of Gondor, and the two Watch-
towers east and west of it (the Towers of the Teeth) were still manned.
The road through Ithilien was still in full repair as far as the Morannon;
and there it met a road going north towards the Dagorlad, and another
going east along the line of Ered Lithui. [Neither of these roads is
marked on the maps to *The Lord of the Rings*.] The eastward road
extended to a point north of the site of Barad-dûr; it had never been
completed further, and what had been made was now long neglected.
Nonetheless its first fifty miles, which had once been fully constructed,
greatly speeded the Wainriders' approach.

16 Historians surmised that it was the same hill as that upon which
King Elessar made his stand in the last battle against Sauron with
which the Third Age ended. But if so it was still only a natural
upswelling that offered little obstacle to horsemen and had not yet
been piled up by the labour of Orcs. [Author's note.] – The passages
in *The Return of the King* (V 10) here referred to tell that 'Aragorn
now set the host in such array as could best be contrived, and they
were drawn up on two great hills of blasted stone and earth that orcs
had piled in years of labour,' and that Aragorn with Gandalf stood

on the one while the banners of Rohan and Dol Amroth were raised on the other.

17 On the presence of Adrahil of Dol Amroth see note 39.

18 Their former home: in the Vales of Anduin between the Carrock and the Gladden Fields, see p. 289.

19 The cause of the northward migration of the Éothéod is given in Appendix A (II) to *The Lord of the Rings*: '[The forefathers of Eorl] loved best the plains, and delighted in horses and all feats of horsemanship, but there were many men in the middle vales of Anduin in those days, and moreover the shadow of Dol Guldur was lengthening; when therefore they heard of the overthrow of the Witch-king [in the year 1975], they sought more room in the North, and drove away the remnants of the people of Angmar on the east side of the Mountains. But in the days of Léod, father of Eorl, they had grown to be a numerous people and were again somewhat straitened in the land of their home.' The leader of the migration of the Éothéod was named Frumgar; and in the Tale of Years its date is given as 1977.

20 These rivers, unnamed, are marked on the map to *The Lord of the Rings*. The Greylin is there shown as having two tributary branches.

21 The Watchful Peace lasted from the years 2063 to 2460, when Sauron was absent from Dol Guldur.

22 For the forts along the Anduin see p. 292, and for the Undeeps p. 260.

23 From an earlier passage in this text (p. 290) one gains the impression that there were no Northmen left in the lands east of Mirkwood after the victory of Calimehtar over the Wainriders on the Dagorlad in the year 1899.

24 So these people were then called in Gondor: a mixed word of popular speech, from Westron *balc* 'horrible' and Sindarin *hoth* 'horde', applied to such peoples as the Orcs. [Author's note.] – See the entry *hoth* in the Appendix to *The Silmarillion*.

25 The letters R · ND · R surmounted by three stars, signifying *arandur* (king's servant), steward. [Author's note.]

26 He did not speak of the thought that he had also in mind: that the Éothéod were, as he had learned, restless, finding their northern lands too narrow and infertile to support their numbers, which had much increased. [Author's note.]

27 His name was long remembered in the song of *Rochon Methestel* (Rider of the Last Hope) as Borondir Udalraph (Borondir the Stirrupless), for he rode back with the *éoherë* at the right hand of Eorl, and was the first to cross the Limlight and cleave a path to the aid of Cirion. He fell at last on the Field of Celebrant defending his lord, to the great grief of Gondor and the Éothéod, and was afterwards laid in tomb in the Hallows of Minas Tirith. [Author's note.]

28 Eorl's horse. In Appendix A (II) to *The Lord of the Rings* it is told that Eorl's father Léod, who was a tamer of wild horses, was thrown by Felaróf when he dared to mount him, and so he met his death. Afterwards Eorl demanded of the horse that he surrender his freedom till his life's end in wergild for his father; and Felaróf submitted, though he would allow no man but Eorl to mount him. He understood all that men said, and was as long-lived as they, as were his descendants, the *mearas*, 'who would bear no one but the King of the Mark or his sons, until the time of Shadowfax'. *Felaróf* is a word of the Anglo-Saxon poetic vocabulary, though not in fact recorded in the extant poetry: 'very valiant, very strong'.

29 Between the inflow of the Limlight and the Undeeps. [Author's note.] – This seems certainly in contradiction to the first citation given in Appendix C to 'The History of Galadriel and Celeborn', p. 260, where 'the North and South Undeeps' are 'the two westward bends' of the Anduin, into the northmost of which the Limlight flowed in.

30 In nine days they had covered more than five hundred miles in a direct line, probably more than six hundred as they rode. Though there were no great natural obstacles on the east side of Anduin, much of the land was now desolate, and roads or horse-paths running southward were lost or little used; only for short periods were they able to ride at speed, and they needed also to husband their own strength and their horses', since they expected battle as soon as they reached the Undeeps. [Author's note.]

31 The Halifirien is twice mentioned in *The Lord of the Rings*. In *The Return of the King* I 1, when Pippin, riding with Gandalf on Shadowfax to Minas Tirith, cried out that he saw fires, Gandalf replied: 'The beacons of Gondor are alight, calling for aid. War is kindled. See, there is fire on Amon Dîn, and flame on Eilenach; and there they go speeding west: Nardol, Erelas, Min-Rimmon, Calenhad, and the Halifirien on the borders of Rohan.' In I 3 the Riders of Rohan on their way to Minas Tirith passed through the Fenmarch 'where to their right great oakwoods climbed on the skirts of the hills under the shades of dark Halifirien by the borders of Gondor'. See the large-scale map of Gondor and Rohan in *The Lord of the Rings*.

32 It was the great Númenórean road linking the Two Kingdoms, crossing the Isen at the Fords of Isen and the Greyflood at Tharbad and then on northwards to Fornost; elsewhere called the North–South Road. See p. 264.

33 This is a modernized spelling for Anglo-Saxon *hálig-firgen*; similarly Firien-dale for *firgen-dæl*, Firien Wood for *firgen-wudu*. [Author's note.] – The *g* in the Anglo-Saxon word *firgen* 'mountain' came to be pronounced as a modern *y*.

34 Minas Ithil, Minas Anor, and Orthanc.

35 It is said elsewhere, in a note on the names of the beacons, that 'the full beacon system, that was still operating in the War of the Ring, can have been no older than the settlement of the Rohirrim in Calenardhon some five hundred years before; for its principal function was to warn the Rohirrim that Gondor was in danger, or (more rarely) the reverse'.

36 According to a note on the ordering of the Rohirrim, the *éored* 'had no precisely fixed number, but in Rohan it was only applied to Riders, fully trained for war: men serving for a term, or in some cases permanently, in the King's Host. Any considerable body of such men, riding as a unit in exercise or on service, was called an *éored*. But after the recovery of the Rohirrim and the reorganization of their forces in the days of King Folcwine, a hundred years before the War of the Ring, a "full *éored*" in battle order was reckoned to contain not less than 120 men (including the Captain), and to be one hundredth part of the Full Muster of the Riders of the Mark, not including those of the King's Household. [The *éored* with which Éomer pursued the Orcs, *The Two Towers* III 2, had 120 Riders: Legolas counted 105 when they were far away, and Éomer said that fifteen men had been lost in battle with the Orcs.] No such host, of course, had ever ridden all together to war beyond the Mark; but Théoden's claim that he might, in this great peril, have led out an expedition of ten thousand Riders (*The Return of the King* V 3) was no doubt justified. The Rohirrim had increased since the days of Folcwine, and before the attacks of Saruman a Full Muster would probably have produced many more than twelve thousand Riders, so that Rohan would not have been denuded entirely of trained defenders. In the event, owing to losses in the western war, the hastiness of the Muster, and the threat from North and East, Théoden only led out a host of some six thousand spears, though this was still the greatest riding of the Rohirrim that was recorded since the coming of Eorl.'

The full muster of the cavalry was called *éoherë* (see note 49). These words, and also *Éothéod*, are of course Anglo-Saxon in form, since the true language of Rohan is everywhere thus translated (see note 6 above): they contain as their first element *eoh* 'horse'. *Éored*, *éorod* is a recorded Anglo-Saxon word, its second element derived from *rád* 'riding'; in *éoherë* the second element is *herë* 'host, army'. *Éothéod* has *théod* 'people' or 'land', and is used both of the Riders themselves and of their country. (Anglo-Saxon *eorl* in the name Eorl the Young is a wholly unrelated word.)

37 This was always said in the days of the Stewards, in any solemn pronouncement, though by the time of Cirion (the twelfth Ruling Steward) it had become a formula that few believed would ever come to pass. [Author's note.]

38 *alfirin*: the *simbelmynë* of the Kings' mounds below Edoras, and the
    uilos that Tuor saw in the great ravine of Gondolin in the Elder Days;
    see p. 55, note 27. *Alfirin* is named, but apparently of a different
    flower, in a verse that Legolas sang in Minas Tirith (*The Return of
    the King* V 9): 'The golden bells are shaken of mallos and alfirin /
    In the green fields of Lebennin.'

39 The Lord of Dol Amroth had this title. It was given to his ancestors
    by Elendil, with whom they had kinship. They were a family of the
    Faithful who had sailed from Númenor before the Downfall and had
    settled in the land of Belfalas, between the mouths of Ringló and
    Gilrain, with a stronghold upon the high promontory of Dol Amroth
    (named after the last King of Lórien). [Author's note.] – Elsewhere it is
    said (p. 248) that according to the tradition of their house the first Lord
    of Dol Amroth was Galador (c. Third Age 2004–2129), the son of
    Imrazôr the Númenórean, who dwelt in Belfalas, and the Elven-lady
    Mithrellas, one of the companions of Nimrodel. The note just cited
    seems to suggest that this family of the Faithful settled in Belfalas
    with a stronghold on Dol Amroth before the Downfall of Númenor;
    and if that is so, the two statements can only be reconciled on the
    supposition that the line of the Princes, and indeed the place of their
    dwelling, went back more than two thousand years before Galador's
    day, and that Galador was called the first Lord of Dol Amroth
    because it was not until his time (after the drowning of Amroth in the
    year 1981) that Dol Amroth was so named. A further difficulty is the
    presence of an Adrahil of Dol Amroth (clearly an ancestor of Adrahil
    the father of Imrahil, Lord of Dol Amroth at the time of the War
    of the Ring) as a commander of the forces of Gondor in the battle
    against the Wainriders in the year 1944 (pp. 293–4); but it may be
    supposed that this earlier Adrahil was not called 'of Dol Amroth' at
    that time.
        While not impossible, these explanations to save consistency seem
    to me to be less likely that than of two distinct and independent
    'traditions' of the origins of the Lords of Dol Amroth.

40 The letters were ᴛᴘᴛ (L · ND · L): Elendil's name without
    vowel-marks, which he used as a badge, and a device upon his
    seals. [Author's note.]

41 Amon Anwar was in fact the high place nearest to the centre of a
    line from the inflow of the Limlight down to the southern cape of
    Tol Falas; and the distance from it to the Fords of Isen was equal
    to its distance from Minas Tirith. [Author's note.]

42 Though imperfectly; for it was in ancient terms and made in the
    forms of verse and high speech that were used by the Rohirrim, in
    which Eorl had great skill. [Author's note.] – There seems not to be
    any other version of the Oath of Eorl extant apart from that in the
    Common Speech given in the text.

43 *Vanda*: an oath, pledge, solemn promise. *ter-maruva*: *ter* 'through', *mar-* 'abide, be settled or fixed'; future tense. *Elenna·nóreo*: genitive case, dependent on *alcar*, of *Elenna·nórë* 'the land named Starwards'. *alcar*: 'glory'. *enyalien*: *en-* 'again', *yal-* 'summon', in infinitive (or gerundial) form *en-yalië*, here in dative 'for the re-calling', but governing a direct object, *alcar*: thus 'to recall or "commemorate" the glory'. *Vorondo*: genitive of *voronda* 'steadfast in allegiance, in keeping oath or promise, faithful'; adjectives used as a 'title' or frequently used attribute of a name are placed after the name, and as is usual in Quenya in the case of two declinable names in apposition only the last is declined. [Another reading gives the adjective as *vórimo* genitive of *vórima*, with the same meaning as *voronda*.] *voronwë*: 'steadfastness, loyalty, faithfulness', the object of *enyalien*.

    Nai: 'be it that, may it be that'; *Nai tiruvantes*: 'be it that they will guard it', i.e. 'may they guard it' (*-nte*, inflexion of 3 plural where no subject is previously mentioned). *i hárar*: 'they who are sitting upon'. *mahalmassen*: locative plural of *mahalma* 'throne'. *mi*: 'in the'. *Númen*: 'West'. *i Eru i*: 'the One who'. *eä*: 'is'. *tennoio*: *tenna* 'up to, as far as', *oio* 'an endless period'; *tennoio* 'for ever'. [Author's notes.]

44 And was not used again until King Elessar returned and renewed the bond in that same place with the King of the Rohirrim, Éomer the eighteenth descended from Eorl. It had been held lawful only for the King of Númenor to call Eru to witness, and then only on the most grave and solemn occasions. The line of the Kings had come to an end in Ar-Pharazôn who perished in the Downfall; but Elendil Voronda was descended from Tar-Elendil the fourth King, and was held to be the rightful lord of the Faithful, who had taken no part in the rebellion of the Kings and had been preserved from destruction. Cirion was the Steward of the Kings descended from Elendil, and so far as Gondor was concerned had as regent all their powers – until the King should come again. Nonetheless his oath astounded those who heard it, and filled them with awe, and was alone (over and above the venerable tomb) sufficient to hallow the place where it was spoken. [Author's note.] – Elendil's name Voronda, 'the Faithful', which appears also in Cirion's Oath, was in this note first written Voronwë, which in the Oath is a noun, meaning 'faithfulness, steadfastness'. But in Appendix A (I, ii) to *The Lord of the Rings* Mardil, the first Ruling Steward of Gondor, is called 'Mardil Voronwë "the Steadfast" '; and in the First Age the Elf of Gondolin who guided Tuor from Vinyamar was named Voronwë, which in the Index to *The Silmarillion* I likewise translated 'the Steadfast'.

45 See the first citation in Appendix C to 'The History of Galadriel and Celeborn', p. 260.

46 These names are given in Sindarin according to the usage of Gondor;

but many of them were named anew by the Éothéod, being alterations
of the older names to fit their own tongue, or translations of them,
or names of their own making. In the narrative of *The Lord of the
Rings* the names in the language of the Rohirrim are mostly used.
Thus Angren=Isen; Angrenost=Isengard; Fangorn (which is also
used)=Entwood; Onodló=Entwash; Glanhír=Mering Stream (both
mean 'boundary stream'). [Author's note.] – The name of the river
Limlight is perplexed. There are two versions of the text and note
at this point, from one of which it seems that the Sindarin name was
Limlich, adapted in the language of Rohan as *Limliht* ('modernized'
as *Limlight*). In the other (later) version, *Limlich* is emended, puzzlingly,
to *Limliht* in the text, so that this becomes the Sindarin form. Elsewhere (p. 281) the Sindarin name of this river is given as *Limlaith*.
In view of this uncertainty I have given *Limlight* in the text. Whatever
the original Sindarin name may have been, it is at least clear that the
Rohan form was an alteration of it and not a translation, and that
its meaning was not known (although in a note written much earlier
than any of the foregoing the name *Limlight* is said to be a partial
translation of Elvish *Limlint* 'swift-light'). The Sindarin names of
the Entwash and the Mering Stream are only found here; with
Onodló compare *Onodrim, Eynd*, the Ents (*The Lord of the Rings*,
Appendix F, 'Of Other Races').

47   *Athrad Angren*: see p. 264, where the Sindarin name for the Fords
of Isen is given as Ethraid Engrin. It seems then that both singular
and plural forms of the name of the Ford(s) existed.

48   Elsewhere the wood is always called the Firien Wood (a shortening
from Halifirien Wood). Firienholt – a word recorded in Anglo-Saxon
poetry (*firgenholt*) – means the same: 'mountain wood'. See note 33.

49   Their proper form was *Rochand* and *Rochir-rim*, and they were spelt
as *Rochand*, or *Rochan*, and *Rochirrim* in the records of Gondor. They
contain Sindarin *roch* 'horse', translating the *éo-* in *Éothéod* and in
many personal names of the Rohirrim [see note 36]. In *Rochand* the
Sindarin ending *-nd* (*-and, -end, -ond*) was added; it was commonly
used in the names of regions or countries, but the *-d* was usually
dropped in speech, especially in long names, such as *Calenardhon,
Ithilien, Lamedon*, etc. *Rochirrim* was modelled on *éo-herë*, the term
used by the Éothéod for the full muster of their cavalry in time of
war; it was made from *roch*+Sindarin *hîr* 'lord, master' (entirely
unconnected with [the Anglo-Saxon word] *herë*). In the names of
peoples Sindarin *rim* 'great number, host' (Quenya *rimbë*) was
commonly used to form collective plurals, as in *Eledhrim* (*Edhelrim*)
'all Elves', *Onodrim* 'the Ent-folk', *Nogothrim* 'all Dwarves, the
Dwarf-people'. The language of the Rohirrim contained the sound
here represented by *ch* (a back spirant as *ch* in Welsh), and, though
it was infrequent in the middle of words between vowels, it presented

them with no difficulty. But the Common Speech did not possess it, and in pronouncing Sindarin (in which it was very frequent) the people of Gondor, unless learned, represented it by *h* in the middle of words and by *k* at the end of them (where it was most forcibly pronounced in correct Sindarin). Thus arose the names *Rohan* and *Rohirrim* as used in *The Lord of the Rings*. [Author's note.]

50 Eorl appears to have been unconvinced by the token of the White Lady's goodwill; see p. 299.

51 *Eilenaer* was a name of pre-Númenórean origin, evidently related to *Eilenach*. [Author's note.] – According to a note on the beacons, Eilenach was 'probably an alien name: not Sindarin, Númenórean, or Common Speech. . . . Both Eilenach and Eilenaer were notable features. Eilenach was the highest point of the Drúadan Forest. It could be seen far to the West, and its function in the days of the beacons was to transmit the warning of Amon Dîn; but it was not suitable for a large beacon-fire, there being little space on its sharp summit. Hence the name Nardol "Fire-hilltop" of the next beacon westward; it was on the end of a high ridge, originally part of the Drúadan Forest, but long deprived of trees by masons and quarriers who came up the Stonewain Valley. Nardol was manned by a guard, who also protected the quarries; it was well-stored with fuel and at need a great blaze could be lit, visible on a clear night even as far as the last beacon (Halifirien) some hundred and twenty miles to the westward.'

In the same note it is stated that 'Amon Dîn "the silent hill" was perhaps the oldest, with the original function of a fortified outpost of Minas Tirith, from which its beacon could be seen, to keep watch over the passage into North Ithilien from Dagorlad and any attempt by enemies to cross the Anduin at or near Cair Andros. Why it was given this name is not recorded. Probably because it was distinctive, a rocky and barren hill standing out and isolated from the heavily wooded hills of the Drúadan Forest (Tawar-in-Drúedain), little visited by men, beasts or birds.'

52 According to Appendix A (I, iv) to *The Lord of the Rings* it was in the days of Ostoher, the fourth king after Meneldil, that Gondor was first attacked by wild men out of the East; 'but Tarostar, his son, defeated them and drove them out, and took the name Rómendacil "East-victor" '.

53 It was also Rómendacil I who established the office of Steward (*Arandur* 'king's servant'), but he was chosen by the King as a man of high trust and wisdom, usually advanced in years since he was not permitted to go to war or to leave the realm. He was never a member of the Royal House. [Author's note.]

54 Mardil was the first of the Ruling Stewards of Gondor. He was the Steward to Eärnur the last King, who disappeared in Minas Morgul

in the year 2050. 'It was believed in Gondor that the faithless enemy had trapped the King, and that he had died in torment in Minas Morgul; but since there were no witnesses of his death, Mardil the Good Steward ruled Gondor in his name for many years' (*The Lord of the Rings*, Appendix A (I, iv)).

III

THE QUEST OF EREBOR

This story depends for its full understanding on the narrative given in Appendix A (III, *Durin's Folk*) to *The Lord of the Rings*, of which this is an outline:

The Dwarves Thrór and his son Thráin (together with Thráin's son Thorin, afterwards called Oakenshield) escaped from the Lonely Mountain (Erebor) by a secret door when the dragon Smaug descended upon it. Thrór returned to Moria, after giving to Thráin the last of the Seven Rings of the Dwarves, and was killed there by the Orc Azog, who branded his name on Thrór's brow. It was this that led to the War of the Dwarves and the Orcs, which ended in the great Battle of Azanulbizar (Nanduhirion) before the East-gate of Moria in the year 2799. Afterwards Thráin and Thorin Oakenshield dwelt in the Ered Luin, but in the year 2841 Thráin set out from there to return to the Lonely Mountain. While wandering in the lands east of Anduin he was captured and imprisoned in Dol Guldur, where the ring was taken from him. In 2850 Gandalf entered Dol Guldur and discovered that its master was indeed Sauron; and there he came upon Thráin before he died.

There is more than one version of 'The Quest of Erebor', as is explained in an Appendix following the text, where also substantial extracts from an earlier version are given.

I have not found any writing preceding the opening words of the present text ('He would say no more that day'). The 'He' of the opening sentence is Gandalf, 'we' are Frodo, Peregrin, Meriadoc, and Gimli, and 'I' is Frodo, the recorder of the conversation; the scene is a house in Minas Tirith, after the coronation of King Elessar (see p. 329).

He would say no more that day. But later we brought the matter up again, and he told us the whole strange story; how he came to arrange the journey to Erebor, why he thought of Bilbo, and how he persuaded the proud Thorin Oakenshield to take him into his company. I cannot remember all the tale now, but we gathered that to begin with Gandalf was thinking only of the defence of the West against the Shadow.

'I was very troubled at that time,' he said, 'for Saruman was hindering all my plans. I knew that Sauron had arisen again and would soon declare himself, and I knew that he was preparing for a great war. How would he begin? Would he try first to re-occupy Mordor, or would he first attack the chief strongholds of his enemies? I thought then, and I am sure now, that to attack Lórien and Rivendell, as soon as he was strong enough, was his original plan. It would have been a much better plan for him, and much worse for us.

'You may think that Rivendell was out of his reach, but I did not think so. The state of things in the North was very bad. The Kingdom under the Mountain and the strong Men of Dale were no more. To resist any force that Sauron might send to regain the northern passes in the mountains and the old lands of Angmar there were only the Dwarves of the Iron Hills, and behind them lay a desolation and a Dragon. The Dragon Sauron might use with terrible effect. Often I said to myself: "I must find some means of dealing with Smaug. But a direct stroke against Dol Guldur is needed still more. We must disturb Sauron's plans. I must make the Council see that."

'Those were my dark thoughts as I jogged along the road. I was tired, and I was going to the Shire for a short rest, after being away from it for more than twenty years. I thought that if I put them out of my mind for a while I might perhaps find some way of dealing with these troubles. And so I did indeed, though I was not allowed to put them out of my mind.

'For just as I was nearing Bree I was overtaken by Thorin Oakenshield,[1] who lived then in exile beyond the north-western borders of the Shire. To my surprise he spoke to me; and it was at that moment that the tide began to turn.

'He was troubled too, so troubled that he actually asked for my advice. So I went with him to his halls in the Blue Mountains, and I listened to his long tale. I soon understood that his heart was hot with brooding on his wrongs, and the loss of the treasure of his forefathers, and burdened too with the duty of revenge upon Smaug that he had inherited. Dwarves take such duties very seriously.

'I promised to help him if I could. I was as eager as he was to see the end of Smaug, but Thorin was all for plans of battle and war, as if he were really King Thorin the Second, and I could see no hope in that. So I left him and went off to the Shire, and picked up the threads of news. It was a strange business. I did no more than follow the lead of "chance", and made many mistakes on the way.

'Somehow I had been attracted by Bilbo long before, as a child, and a young hobbit: he had not quite come of age when I had last seen him. He had stayed in my mind ever since, with his eagerness and his bright eyes, and his love of tales, and his questions about the wide world outside the Shire. As soon as I entered the Shire I heard news of him. He was getting talked about, it seemed. Both his parents had died early for Shire-folk, at about eighty; and he had never married. He was already growing a bit queer, they said, and went off for days by himself. He could be seen talking to strangers, even Dwarves.

'"Even Dwarves!" Suddenly in my mind these three things came together: the great Dragon with his lust, and his keen hearing and scent; the sturdy heavy-booted Dwarves with their old burning grudge; and the quick, soft-footed Hobbit, sick at heart (I guessed) for a sight of the wide world. I laughed at myself; but I went off at once to have a look at Bilbo, to see what twenty years had done to him, and whether he was as promising as gossip seemed to make out. But he was not at home. They shook their heads in Hobbiton when I asked after him. "Off again," said one hobbit. It was Holman, the gardener, I believe.[2] "Off again. He'll go right off one of these days, if he isn't careful. Why, I asked him where he was going, and when he would be back, and *I don't know* he says; and then he looks at me queerly. *It depends if I meet any, Holman*, he says. *It's the Elves' New Year tomorrow!*[3] A pity, and him so kind a body. You wouldn't find a better from the Downs to the River."

'"Better and better!" I thought. "I think I shall risk it." Time was getting short. I had to be with the White Council in August at the latest, or Saruman would have his way and nothing would be done. And quite apart from greater matters, that might prove fatal to the quest: the power in Dol Guldur would not leave any attempt on Erebor unhindered, unless he had something else to deal with.

'So I rode off back to Thorin in haste, to tackle the difficult task of persuading him to put aside his lofty designs and go secretly – and take Bilbo with him. Without seeing Bilbo first. It was a mistake, and nearly proved disastrous. For Bilbo had changed, of course. At least, he was getting rather greedy and fat, and his old desires had dwindled down to a sort of private dream. Nothing could have been more dismaying than to find it actually in danger of coming true! He was altogether bewildered, and made a complete fool of himself. Thorin would have left in a rage, but for another strange chance, which I will mention in a moment.

'But you know how things went, at any rate as Bilbo saw them. The story would sound rather different, if I had written it. For one thing he did not realize at all how fatuous the Dwarves thought him, nor how angry they were with me. Thorin was much more indignant and contemptuous than he perceived. He was indeed contemptuous from the beginning, and thought then that I had planned the whole affair simply so as to make a mock of him. It was only the map and the key that saved the situation.

'But I had not thought of them for years. It was not until I got to the Shire and had time to reflect on Thorin's tale that I suddenly remembered the strange chance that had put them in my hands; and it began now to look less like chance. I remembered a dangerous journey of mine, ninety-one years before, when I had entered Dol Guldur in disguise, and had found there an unhappy Dwarf dying in the pits. I had no idea who he was. He had a map that had belonged to Durin's folk in Moria, and a key that seemed to go with it, though he was too far gone to explain it. And he said that he had possessed a great Ring.

'Nearly all his ravings were of that. *The last of the Seven* he said over and over again. But all these things he might have come by in many ways. He might have been a messenger caught as he fled, or even a thief trapped by a greater thief. But he gave the map and the key to me. "For my son," he said; and then he died, and soon after I escaped myself. I stowed the things away, and by some warning of my heart I kept them always with me, safe, but soon almost forgotten. I had other business in Dol Guldur more important and perilous than all the treasure of Erebor.

'Now I remembered it all again, and it seemed clear that I had heard the last words of Thráin the Second,[4] though he did not name himself or his son; and Thorin, of course, did not know what had become of his father, nor did he ever mention "the last of the Seven Rings". I had the plan and the key of the secret entrance to Erebor, by which Thrór and Thráin had escaped, according to Thorin's tale. And I had kept them, though without any design of my own, until the moment when they would prove most useful.

'Fortunately, I did not make any mistake in my use of them. I kept them up my sleeve, as you say in the Shire, until things looked quite hopeless. As soon as Thorin saw them he really made up his mind to follow my plan, as far as a secret expedition went at any rate. Whatever he thought of Bilbo he would have set out himself. The existence of a secret door, only discoverable by Dwarves, made it seem at least possible to find out something of the Dragon's doings, perhaps even to recover some gold, or some heirloom to ease his heart's longings.

'But that was not enough for me. I knew in my heart that Bilbo must go with him, or the whole quest would be a failure – or, as I should say now, the far more important events by the way would not come to pass. So I had still to persuade Thorin to take him. There were many difficulties on the road afterwards, but for me this was the most difficult part of the whole affair. Though I argued with him far into the night after Bilbo had retired, it was not finally settled until early the next morning.

'Thorin was contemptuous and suspicious. "He is soft," he snorted. "Soft as the mud of his Shire, and silly. His mother died too soon. You are playing some crooked game of your own, Master Gandalf. I am sure that you have other purposes than helping me."

' "You are quite right," I said. "If I had no other purposes, I should not be helping you at all. Great as your affairs may seem to you, they are only a small strand in the great web. I am concerned with many strands. But that should make my advice more weighty, not less." I spoke at last with great heat. "Listen to me, Thorin Oakenshield!" I said. "If this hobbit goes with you, you will succeed. If not, you will fail. A foresight is on me, and I am warning you."

' "I know your fame," Thorin answered. "I hope it is merited. But this foolish business of your hobbit makes me wonder whether it is foresight that is on you, and you are not crazed rather than foreseeing. So many cares may have disordered your wits."

' "They have certainly been enough to do so," I said. "And among them I find most exasperating a proud Dwarf who seeks advice from me (without claim on me that I know of), and then rewards me with insolence. Go your own ways, Thorin Oakenshield, if you will. But if you flout my advice, you will walk to disaster. And you will get neither counsel nor aid from me again until the Shadow falls on you. And curb your pride and your greed, or you will fall at the end of whatever path you take, though your hands be full of gold."

'He blenched a little at that; but his eyes smouldered. "Do not threaten me!" he said. "I will use my own judgement in this matter, as in all that concerns me."

' "Do so then!" I said. "I can say no more – unless it is this: I do not give my love or trust lightly, Thorin; but I am fond of this hobbit, and wish him well. Treat him well, and you shall have my friendship to the end of your days."

'I said that without hope of persuading him; but I could have said nothing better. Dwarves understand devotion to friends and gratitude to those who help them. "Very well," Thorin said at last after a silence. "He shall set out with my company, if he dares (which I doubt). But if you insist on burdening me with him, you must come too and look after your darling."

' "Good!" I answered. "I will come, and stay with you as long as I can: at least until you have discovered his worth." It proved well in the end, but at the time I was troubled, for I had the urgent matter of the White Council on my hands.

'So it was that the Quest of Erebor set out. I do not suppose that when it started Thorin had any real hope of destroying Smaug. There was no hope. Yet it happened. But alas! Thorin did not live to enjoy his triumph or his treasure. Pride and greed overcame him in spite of my warning." '

'But surely,' I said, 'he might have fallen in battle anyway? There would have been an attack of Orcs, however generous Thorin had been with his treasure.'

'That is true,' said Gandalf. 'Poor Thorin! He was a great Dwarf of a great House, whatever his faults; and though he fell at the end of the journey, it was largely due to him that the Kingdom under the Mountain was restored, as I desired. But Dáin Ironfoot was a worthy successor. And now we hear that he fell fighting before Erebor again, even while we fought here. I should call it a heavy loss, if it was not a wonder rather that in his great age[5] he could still wield his axe as mightily as they say he did, standing over the body of King Brand before the Gate of Erebor until the darkness fell.

'It might all have gone very differently indeed. The main attack was diverted southwards, it is true; and yet even so with his far-stretched right hand Sauron could have done terrible harm in the North, while we defended Gondor, if King Brand and King Dáin had not stood in his path. When you think of the great Battle of Pelennor, do not forget the Battle of Dale. Think of what might have been. Dragon-fire and savage swords in Eriador! There might be no Queen in Gondor. We might now only hope to return from the victory here to ruin and ash. But that has been averted – because I met Thorin Oakenshield one evening on the edge of spring not far from Bree. A chance-meeting, as we say in Middle-earth.'

NOTES

1 The meeting of Gandalf with Thorin is related also in Appendix A (III) to *The Lord of the Rings*, and there the date is given: 15 March, 2941. There is the slight difference between the two accounts that in Appendix A the meeting took place in the inn at Bree and not on

the road. Gandalf had last visited the Shire twenty years before, thus in 2921, when Bilbo was thirty-one: Gandalf says later that he had not quite come of age [at thirty-three] when he last saw him.

2 Holman the gardener: Holman Greenhand, to whom Hamfast Gamgee (Sam's father, the Gaffer) was apprenticed: *The Fellowship of the Ring* I 1, and Appendix C.

3 The Elvish solar year (*loa*) began with the day called *yestarë*, which was the day before the first day of *tuilë* (Spring); and in the Calendar of Imladris *yestarë* 'corresponded more or less with Shire April 6'. (*The Lord of the Rings*, Appendix D.)

4 Thráin the Second: Thráin the First, Thorin's distant ancestor, escaped from Moria in the year 1981 and became the first King under the Mountain. (*The Lord of the Rings*, Appendix A (III).)

5 Dáin II Ironfoot was born in the year 2767; at the Battle of Azanulbizar (Nanduhirion) in 2799 he slew before the East-gate of Moria the great Orc Azog, and so avenged Thrór, Thorin's grandfather. He died in the Battle of Dale in 3019. (*The Lord of the Rings*, Appendices A (III) and B.) Frodo learnt from Glóin at Rivendell that 'Dáin was still King under the Mountain, and was now old (having passed his two hundred and fiftieth year), venerable, and fabulously rich'. (*The Fellowship of the Ring* II 1.)

APPENDIX

Note on the texts of 'The Quest of Erebor'

The textual situation in this piece is complex and hard to unravel. The earliest version is a complete but rough and much-emended manuscript, which I will here call A; it bears the title 'The History of Gandalf's Dealings with Thráin and Thorin Oakenshield'. From this a typescript, B, was made, with a great deal of further alteration, though mostly of a very minor kind. This is entitled 'The Quest of Erebor', and also 'Gandalf's Account of how he came to arrange the Expedition to Erebor and send Bilbo with the Dwarves'. Some extensive extracts from the typescript text are given below.

In addition to A and B ('the earlier version'), there is another manuscript, C, untitled, which tells the story in a more economical and tightly-constructed form, omitting a good deal from the first version and introducing some new elements, but also (particularly in the latter part) largely retaining the original writing. It seems to me to be quite certain that C is later than B, and C is the version that has been given above, although some writing has apparently been lost from the beginning, setting the scene in Minas Tirith for Gandalf's recollections.

The opening paragraphs of B (given below) are almost identical with a passage in Appendix A (III, *Durin's Folk*) to *The Lord of the Rings*, and obviously depend on the narrative concerning Thrór and Thráin that precedes them in Appendix A; while the ending of 'The Quest of Erebor' is also found in almost exactly the same words in Appendix A (III), here again in the mouth of Gandalf, speaking to Frodo and Gimli in Minas Tirith. In view of the letter cited in the Introduction (p. 11) it is clear that my father wrote 'The Quest of Erebor' to stand as part of the narrative of *Durin's Folk* in Appendix A.

Extracts from the earlier version

The typescript B of the earlier version begins thus:

So Thorin Oakenshield became the Heir of Durin, but an heir without hope. At the sack of Erebor he had been too young to bear arms, but at Azanulbizar he had fought in the van of the assault; and when Thráin was lost he was ninety-five, a great Dwarf of proud bearing. He had no Ring, and (for that reason maybe) he seemed content to remain in Eriador. There he laboured long, and gained such wealth as he could; and his people were increased by many of the wandering Folk of Durin that heard of his dwelling and came to him. Now they had fair halls in the mountains, and store of goods, and their days did not seem so hard, though in their songs they spoke ever of the Lonely Mountain far away, and the treasure and the bliss of the Great Hall in the light of the Arkenstone.

The years lengthened. The embers in the heart of Thorin grew hot again, as he brooded on the wrongs of his House and of the vengeance upon the Dragon that was bequeathed to him. He thought of weapons and armies and alliances, as his great hammer rang in the forge; but the armies were dispersed and the alliances broken and the axes of his people were few; and a great anger without hope burned him, as he smote the red iron on the anvil.

Gandalf had not yet played any part in the fortunes of Durin's House. He had not had many dealings with the Dwarves; though he was a friend to those of good will, and liked well the exiles of Durin's Folk who lived in the West. But on a time it chanced that he was passing through Eriador (going to the Shire, which he had not seen for some years) when he fell in with Thorin Oakenshield, and they talked together on the road, and rested for the night at Bree.

In the morning Thorin said to Gandalf: 'I have much on my mind, and they say you are wise and know more than most of what goes on in the world. Will you come home with me and hear me, and give me your counsel?'

To this Gandalf agreed, and when they came to Thorin's hall he sat long with him and heard all the tale of his wrongs.

From this meeting there followed many deeds and events of great moment: indeed the finding of the One Ring, and its coming to the Shire, and the choosing of the Ringbearer. Many therefore have supposed that Gandalf foresaw all these things, and chose his time for the meeting with Thorin. Yet we believe that it was not so. For in his tale of the War of the Ring Frodo the Ringbearer left a record of Gandalf's words on this very point. This is what he wrote:

In place of the words 'This is what he wrote' A, the earliest manuscript, has: 'That passage was omitted from the tale, since it seemed long; but most of it we now set out here.'

After the crowning we stayed in a fair house in Minas Tirith with Gandalf, and he was very merry, and though we asked him questions about all that came into our minds his patience seemed as endless as his knowledge. I cannot now recall most of the things that he told us; often we did not understand them. But I remember this conversation very clearly. Gimli was there with us, and he said to Peregrin:

'There is a thing I must do one of these days: I must visit that Shire of yours.* Not to see more Hobbits! I doubt if I could learn anything about them that I do not know already. But no Dwarf of the House of Durin could fail to look with wonder on that land. Did not the recovery of the Kingship under the Mountain, and the fall of Smaug, begin there? Not to mention the end of Barad-dûr, though both were strangely woven together. Strangely, very strangely,' he said, and paused.

Then looking hard at Gandalf he went on: 'But who wove the web? I do not think I have ever considered that before. Did you plan all this then, Gandalf? If not, why did you lead Thorin Oakenshield to such an unlikely door? To find the Ring and bring it far away into the West for hiding, and then to choose the Ringbearer – and to restore the Mountain Kingdom as a mere deed by the way: was not that your design?'

Gandalf did not answer at once. He stood up, and looked out of the window, west, seawards; and the sun was then setting, and a glow was in his face. He stood so a long while silent. But at last he turned to Gimli and said: 'I do not know the answer. For I have changed since those days, and I am no longer trammelled by the burden of Middle-earth as I was then. In those days I should have answered you with words like those I used to Frodo, only last year in the spring. Only last year! But such measures are meaningless. In that far distant time I said to a small and frightened hobbit: Bilbo was *meant* to find the

---

* Gimli must at least have passed through the Shire on journeys from his original home in the Blue Mountains (see p. 336).

Ring, and *not* by its maker, and you therefore were *meant* to bear it. And I might have added: and I was *meant* to guide you both to those points.

'To do that I used in my waking mind only such means as were allowed to me, doing what lay to my hand according to such reasons as I had. But what I knew in my heart, or knew before I stepped on these grey shores: that is another matter. Olórin I was in the West that is forgotten, and only to those who are there shall I speak more openly.'

A has here: 'and only to those who are there (or who may, perhaps, return thither with me) shall I speak more openly.'

Then I said: 'I understand you a little better now, Gandalf, than I did before. Though I suppose that, whether *meant* or not, Bilbo might have refused to leave home, and so might I. You could not compel us. You were not even allowed to try. But I am still curious to know why you did what you did, as you were then, an old grey man as you seemed.'

Gandalf then explained to them his doubts at that time concerning Sauron's first move, and his fears for Lórien and Rivendell (cf. p. 322). In this version, after saying that a direct stroke against Sauron was even more urgent than the question of Smaug, he went on:

'That is why, to jump forward, I went off as soon as the expedition against Smaug was well started, and persuaded the Council to attack Dol Guldur first, before he attacked Lórien. We did, and Sauron fled. But he was always ahead of us in his plans. I must confess that I thought he really had retreated again, and that we might have another spell of watchful peace. But it did not last long. Sauron decided to take the next step. He returned at once to Mordor, and in ten years he declared himself.

'Then everything grew dark. And yet that was not his original plan; and it was in the end a mistake. Resistance still had somewhere where it could take counsel free from the Shadow. How could the Ringbearer have escaped, if there had been no Lórien or Rivendell? And those places might have fallen, I think, if Sauron had thrown all his power against them first, and not spent more than half of it in the assault on Gondor.

'Well, there you have it. That was my chief reason. But it is one thing to see what needs doing, and quite another to find the means. I was beginning to be seriously troubled about the situation in the North when I met Thorin Oakenshield one day: in the middle of March 2941, I think. I heard all his tale, and I thought: "Well, here is an enemy of Smaug at any rate! And one worthy of help. I must do what I can. I should have thought of Dwarves before."'

'And then there was the Shire-folk. I began to have a warm place in my heart for them in the Long Winter, which none of you can remember.* They were very hard put to it then: one of the worst pinches they have been in, dying of cold, and starving in the dreadful dearth that followed. But that was the time to see their courage, and their pity one for another. It was by their pity as much as by their tough uncomplaining courage that they survived. I wanted them still to survive. But I saw that the Westlands were in for another very bad time again, sooner or later, though of quite a different sort: pitiless war. To come through that I thought they would need something more than they now had. It is not easy to say what. Well, they would want to know a bit more, understand a bit clearer what it was all about, and where they stood.

'They had begun to forget: forget their own beginnings and legends, forget what little they had known about the greatness of the world. It was not yet gone, but it was getting buried: the memory of the high and the perilous. But you cannot teach that sort of thing to a whole people quickly. There was not time. And anyway you must begin at some point, with some one person. I dare say he was "chosen" and I was only chosen to choose him; but I picked out Bilbo.'

'Now that is just what I want to know,' said Peregrin. 'Why did you do that?'

'How would you select any one Hobbit for such a purpose?' said Gandalf. 'I had not time to sort them all out; but I knew the Shire very well by that time, although when I met Thorin I had been away for more than twenty years on less pleasant business. So naturally thinking over the Hobbits that I knew, I said to myself: "I want a dash of the Took" (but not too much, Master Peregrin) "and I want a good foundation of the stolider sort, a Baggins perhaps." That pointed at once to Bilbo. And I had known him once very well, almost up to his coming of age, better than he knew me. I liked him then. And now I found that he was "unattached" – to jump on again, for of course I did not know all this until I went back to the Shire. I learned that he had never married. I thought that odd, though I guessed why it was; and the reason that I guessed was *not* the one that most of the Hobbits gave me: that he had early been left very well off and his own master. No, I guessed that he wanted to remain "unattached" for some reason deep down which he did not understand himself – or would not acknowledge, for it alarmed him. He wanted, all the same, to be free to go when the chance came, or he had made up his courage. I remembered how he used to pester me with questions when he was a youngster about the Hobbits that had occasionally "gone off", as they said in the Shire. There were at least two of his uncles on the Took side that had done so.'

* There is an account of the Long Winter of 2758-9 as it affected Rohan in Appendix A (II) to *The Lord of the Rings*; and the entry in the Tale of Years mentions that 'Gandalf came to the aid of the Shirefolk'.

These uncles were Hildifons Took, who 'went off on a journey and never returned', and Isengar Took (the youngest of the Old Took's twelve children), who was 'said to have "gone to sea" in his youth' (*The Lord of the Rings* Appendix C, Family Tree of Took of Great Smials).

When Gandalf accepted Thorin's invitation to go with him to his home in the Blue Mountains

'we actually passed through the Shire, though Thorin would not stop long enough for that to be useful. Indeed I think it was annoyance with his haughty disregard of the Hobbits that first put into my head the idea of entangling him with them. As far as he was concerned they were just food-growers who happened to work the fields on either side of the Dwarves' ancestral road to the Mountains.'

In this earlier version Gandalf gave a long account of how, after his visit to the Shire, he returned to Thorin and persuaded him 'to put aside his lofty designs and go secretly – and take Bilbo with him' – which sentence is all that is said of it in the later version (p. 323).

'At last I made up my mind, and I went back to Thorin. I found him in conclave with some of his kinsfolk. Balin and Glóin were there, and several others.

' "Well, what have you got to say?" Thorin asked me as soon as I came in.

' "This first," I answered. "Your own ideas are those of a king, Thorin Oakenshield; but your kingdom is gone. If it is to be restored, which I doubt, it must be from small beginnings. Far away here, I wonder if you fully realize the strength of a great Dragon. But that is not all: there is a Shadow growing fast in the world far more terrible. They will help one another." And they certainly would have done so, if I had not attacked Dol Guldur at the same time. "Open war would be quite useless; and anyway it is impossible for you to arrange it. You will have to try something simpler and yet bolder, indeed something desperate."

' "You are both vague and disquieting," said Thorin. "Speak more plainly!"

' "Well, for one thing," I said, "you will have to go on this quest yourself, and you will have to go *secretly*. No messengers, heralds, or challenges for you, Thorin Oakenshield. At most you can take with you a few kinsmen or faithful followers. But you will need something more, something unexpected."

' "Name it!" said Thorin.

' "One moment!" I said. "You hope to deal with a Dragon; and he is not only very great, but he is now also old and very cunning. From the beginning of your adventure you must allow for this: his memory, and his sense of smell."

' "Naturally," said Thorin. "Dwarves have had more dealings with

Dragons than most, and you are not instructing the ignorant."

' "Very good," I answered; "but your own plans did not seem to me to consider this point. My plan is one of stealth. *Stealth.* * Smaug does not lie on his costly bed without dreams, Thorin Oakenshield. He dreams of Dwarves! You may be sure that he explores his hall day by day, night by night, until he is sure that no faintest air of a Dwarf is near, before he goes to his sleep: his half-sleep, prick-eared for the sound of – Dwarf-feet."

' "You make your *stealth* sound as difficult and hopeless as any open attack," said Balin. "Impossibly difficult!"

' "Yes, it is difficult," I answered. "But not *impossibly* difficult, or I would not waste my time here. I would say *absurdly* difficult. So I am going to suggest an absurd solution to the problem. Take a Hobbit with you! Smaug has probably never heard of Hobbits, and he has certainly never smelt them."

' "What!" cried Glóin. "One of those simpletons down in the Shire? What use on earth, or under it, could he possibly be? Let him smell as he may, he would never dare to come within smelling distance of the nakedest dragonet new from the shell!"

' "Now, now!" I said, "that is quite unfair. You do not know much about the Shire-folk, Glóin. I suppose you think them simple, because they are generous and do not haggle; and think them timid because you never sell them any weapons. You are mistaken. Anyway, there is one that I have my eye on as a companion for you, Thorin. He is neat-handed and clever, though shrewd, and far from rash. And I think he has courage. Great courage, I guess, according to the way of his people. They are, you might say, 'brave at a pinch'. You have to put these Hobbits in a tight place before you find out what is in them."

' "The test cannot be made," Thorin answered. "As far as I have observed, they do all that they can to avoid tight places."

' "Quite true," I said. "They are a very sensible people. But this Hobbit is rather unusual. I think he could be persuaded to go into a tight place. I believe that in his heart he really desires to – to have, as he would put it, an adventure."

' "Not at my expense!" said Thorin, rising and striding about angrily. "This is not advice, it is foolery! I fail to see what any Hobbit, good or bad, could do that would repay me for a day's keep, even if he could be persuaded to start."

' "Fail to see! You would fail to hear it, more likely," I answered. "Hobbits move without effort more quietly than any Dwarf in the world could manage, though his life depended on it. They are, I suppose, the

---

* At this point a sentence in the manuscript, A, was perhaps unintentionally omitted in the typescript, in view of Gandalf's subsequent remark about Smaug's never having smelt a Hobbit: 'Also a scent that cannot be placed, at least not by Smaug, the enemy of Dwarves.'

most soft-footed of all mortal kinds. You do not seem to have observed that, at any rate, Thorin Oakenshield, as you tramped through the Shire, making a noise (I may say) that the inhabitants could hear a mile away. When I said that you would need stealth, I meant it: professional stealth."

' "Professional stealth?" cried Balin, taking up my words rather differently than I had meant them. "Do you mean a trained treasure-seeker? Can they still be found?"

'I hesitated. This was a new turn, and I was not sure how to take it. "I think so," I said at last. "For a reward they will go in where you dare not, or at any rate cannot, and get what you desire."

'Thorin's eyes glistened as the memories of lost treasures moved in his mind; but "A paid thief, you mean," he said scornfully. "That might be considered, if the reward was not too high. But what has all this to do with one of those villagers? They drink out of clay, and they cannot tell a gem from a bead of glass."

' "I wish you would not always speak so confidently without knowledge," I said sharply. "These villagers have lived in the Shire some fourteen hundred years, and they have learned many things in the time. They had dealings with the Elves, and with the Dwarves, a thousand years before Smaug came to Erebor. None of them are wealthy as your forefathers reckoned it, but you will find some of their dwellings have fairer things in them than you can boast here, Thorin. The Hobbit that I have in mind has ornaments of gold, and eats with silver tools, and drinks wine out of shapely crystal."

' "Ah! I see your drift at last," said Balin. "He is a thief, then? That is why you recommend him?"

'At that I fear I lost my temper and my caution. This Dwarvish conceit that no one can have or make anything "of value" save themselves, and that all fine things in other hands must have been got, if not stolen, from the Dwarves at some time, was more than I could stand at that moment. "A thief?" I said, laughing. "Why yes, a professional thief, of course! How else would a Hobbit come by a silver spoon? I will put the thief's mark on his door, and then you will find it." Then being angry I got up, and I said with a warmth that surprised myself: "You must look for that door, Thorin Oakenshield! I am *serious*." And suddenly I felt that I was indeed in hot earnest. This queer notion of mine was not a joke, it was *right*. It was desperately important that it should be carried out. The Dwarves must bend their stiff necks.

' "Listen to me, Durin's Folk!" I cried. "If you persuade this Hobbit to join you, you will succeed. If you do not, you will fail. If you refuse even to try, then I have finished with you. You will get no more advice or help from me until the Shadow falls on you!"

'Thorin turned and looked at me in astonishment, as well he might. "Strong words!" he said. "Very well, I will come. Some foresight is on you, if you are not merely crazed."

' "Good!" I said. "But you must come with good will, not merely in the hope of proving me a fool. You must be patient and not easily put off, if neither the courage nor the desire for adventure that I speak of are plain to see at first sight. He will deny them. He will try to back out; but *you must not* let him."

' "Haggling will not help him, if that is what you mean," said Thorin. "I will offer him a fair reward for anything that he recovers, and no more."

'It was not what I meant, but it seemed useless to say so. "There is one other thing," I went on; "you must make all your plans and preparations beforehand. Get everything ready! Once persuaded he must have no time for second thoughts. You must go straight from the Shire, east on your quest."

' "He sounds a very strange creature, this thief of yours," said a young Dwarf called Fili (Thorin's nephew, as I afterwards learned). "What is his name, or the one that he uses?"

' "Hobbits use their real names," I said. "The only one that he has is Bilbo Baggins."

' "What a name!" said Fili, and laughed.

' "He thinks it very respectable," I said. "And it fits well enough; for he is a middle-aged bachelor, and getting a bit flabby and fat. Food is perhaps at present his main interest. He keeps a very good larder, I am told, and maybe more than one. At least you will be well entertained."

' "That is enough," said Thorin. "If I had not given my word, I would not come now. I am in no mood to be made a fool of. For I am serious also. Deadly serious, and my heart is hot within me."

'I took no notice of this. "Look now, Thorin," I said, "April is passing and Spring is here. Make everything ready as soon as you can. I have some business to do, but I shall be back in a week. When I return, if all is in order, I will ride on ahead to prepare the ground. Then we will all visit him together on the following day."

'And with that I took my leave, not wishing to give Thorin more chance of second thoughts than Bilbo was to have. The rest of the story is well known to you – from Bilbo's point of view. If I had written the account, it would have sounded rather different. He did not know all that went on: the care, for instance, that I took so that the coming of a large party of Dwarves to Bywater, off the main road and their usual beat, should not come to his ears too soon.

'It was on the morning of Tuesday, April the 25th, 2941, that I called to see Bilbo; and though I knew more or less what to expect, I must say that my confidence was shaken. I saw that things would be far more difficult than I had thought. But I persevered. Next day, Wednesday, April the 26th, I brought Thorin and his companions to Bag End; with great difficulty so far as Thorin was concerned – he hung back at the last. And of course Bilbo was completely bewildered and behaved ridiculously. Everything in fact went extremely badly for me from the beginning; and that unfortunate business about the "professional thief", which the Dwarves had got firmly into their heads, only made matters worse. I was thankful that I had told Thorin we should all stay the night at Bag End, since we should need time to discuss ways and means. It gave me a last chance. If Thorin had left Bag End before I could see him alone, my plan would have been ruined.'

It will be seen that some elements of this conversation were in the later version taken up into the argument between Gandalf and Thorin at Bag End.

From this point the narrative in the later version follows the earlier very closely, which is not therefore further cited here, except for a passage at the end. In the earlier, when Gandalf ceased speaking, Frodo records that Gimli laughed.

'It still sounds absurd,' he said, 'even now that all has turned out more than well. I knew Thorin, of course; and I wish I had been there, but I was away at the time of your first visit to us. And I was not allowed to go on the quest: too young, they said, though at sixty-two I thought myself fit for anything. Well, I am glad to have heard the full tale. If it is full. I do not really suppose that even now you are telling us all you know.'

'Of course not,' said Gandalf.

And after this Meriadoc questioned Gandalf further about Thráin's map and key; and in the course of his reply (most of which is retained in the later version, at a different point in the narrative) Gandalf said:

'It was nine years after Thráin had left his people that I found him, and he had then been in the pits of Dol Guldur for five years at least. I do not know how he endured so long, nor how he had kept these things hidden through all his torments. I think that the Dark Power had desired nothing from him except the Ring only, and when he had taken that he troubled no further, but just flung the broken prisoner into the pits to rave until he died. A small oversight; but it proved fatal. Small oversights often do.'

IV

THE HUNT FOR THE RING

(i)

Of the Journey of the Black Riders
according to the account that Gandalf
gave to Frodo

Gollum was captured in Mordor in the year 3017 and taken to
Barad-dûr, and there questioned and tormented. When he had
learned what he could from him, Sauron released him and sent him
forth again. He did not trust Gollum, for he divined something
indomitable in him, which could not be overcome, even by the
Shadow of Fear, except by destroying him. But Sauron perceived
the depth of Gollum's malice towards those that had 'robbed' him,
and guessing that he would go in search of them to avenge himself,
Sauron hoped that his spies would thus be led to the Ring.

Gollum, however, was before long captured by Aragorn, and taken
to Northern Mirkwood; and though he was followed, he could not
be rescued before he was in safe keeping. Now Sauron had never
paid heed to the 'halflings', even if he had heard of them, and he did
not yet know where their land lay. From Gollum, even under pain,
he could not get any clear account, both because Gollum indeed had
no certain knowledge himself, and because what he knew he falsified.
Ultimately indomitable he was, except by death, as Sauron guessed,
both from his halfling nature, and from a cause which Sauron did
not fully comprehend, being himself consumed by lust for the Ring.
Then he became filled with a hatred of Sauron even greater than his
terror, seeing in him truly his greatest enemy and rival. Thus it was
that he dared to pretend that he believed that the land of the Halflings
was near to the places where he had once dwelt beside the banks of
the Gladden.

Now Sauron learning of the capture of Gollum by the chiefs of
his enemies was in great haste and fear. Yet all his ordinary spies and
emissaries could bring him no tidings. And this was due largely both
to the vigilance of the Dúnedain and to the treachery of Saruman,
whose own servants either waylaid or misled the servants of Sauron.

Of this Sauron became aware, but his arm was not yet long enough to reach Saruman in Isengard. Therefore he hid his knowledge of Saruman's double-dealing and concealed his wrath, biding his time, and preparing for the great war in which he planned to sweep all his enemies into the western sea. At length he resolved that no others would serve him in this case but his mightiest servants, the Ringwraiths, who had no will but his own, being each utterly subservient to the ring that had enslaved him, which Sauron held.

Now few could withstand even one of these fell creatures, and (as Sauron deemed) none could withstand them when gathered together under their terrible captain, the Lord of Morgul. Yet this weakness they had for Sauron's present purpose: so great was the terror that went with them (even invisible and unclad) that their coming forth might soon be perceived and their mission be guessed by the Wise.

So it was that Sauron prepared two strokes – in which many after saw the beginnings of the War of the Ring. They were made together. The Orcs assailed the realm of Thranduil, with orders to recapture Gollum; and the Lord of Morgul was sent forth openly to battle against Gondor. These things were done towards the end of June 3018. Thus Sauron tested the strength and preparedness of Denethor, and found them more than he had hoped. But that troubled him little, since he had used little force in the assault, and his chief purpose was that the coming forth of the Nazgûl should appear only as part of his policy of war against Gondor.

Therefore when Osgiliath was taken and the bridge broken Sauron stayed the assault, and the Nazgûl were ordered to begin the search for the Ring. But Sauron did not underesteem the powers and vigilance of the Wise, and the Nazgûl were commanded to act as secretly as they could. Now at that time the Chieftain of the Ringwraiths dwelt in Minas Morgul with six companions, while the second to the Chief, Khamûl the Shadow of the East, abode in Dol Guldur as Sauron's lieutenant, with one other as his messenger.[1]

The Lord of Morgul therefore led his companions over Anduin, unclad and unmounted, and invisible to eyes, and yet a terror to all living things that they passed near. It was, maybe, on the first day of July that they went forth. They passed slowly and in stealth, through Anórien, and over the Entwade, and so into the Wold, and rumour of darkness and a dread of men knew not what went before them. They reached the west-shores of Anduin a little north of Sarn Gebir, as they had trysted; and there received horses and raiment that were secretly ferried over the River. This was (it is thought) about the seventeenth of July. Then they passed northward seeking for the Shire, the land of the Halflings.

About the twenty-second of July they met their companions, the Nazgûl of Dol Guldur, in the Field of Celebrant. There they learned that Gollum had eluded both the Orcs that recaptured him, and the Elves that pursued them, and had vanished.[2] They were told also by Khamûl that no dwelling of Halflings could be discovered in the Vales of Anduin, and that the villages of the Stoors by the Gladden had long been deserted. But the Lord of Morgul, seeing no better counsel, determined still to seek northward, hoping maybe to come upon Gollum as well as to discover the Shire. That this would prove to be not far from the hated land of Lórien seemed to him not unlikely, if it was not indeed within the fences of Galadriel. But the power of the White Ring he would not defy, nor enter yet into Lórien. Passing therefore between Lórien and the Mountains the Nine rode ever on into the North; and terror went before them and lingered behind them; but they did not find what they sought nor learn any news that availed them.

At length they returned; but the summer was now far waned, and the wrath and fear of Sauron was mounting. When they came back to the Wold September had come; and there they met messengers from Barad-dûr conveying threats from their Master that filled even the Morgul-lord with dismay. For Sauron had now learned of the words of prophecy heard in Gondor, and the going forth of Boromir, of Saruman's deeds, and the capture of Gandalf. From these things he concluded indeed that neither Saruman nor any other of the Wise had possession yet of the Ring, but that Saruman at least knew where it might be hidden. Speed alone would now serve, and secrecy must be abandoned.

The Ringwraiths therefore were ordered to go straight to Isengard. They rode then through Rohan in haste, and the terror of their passing was so great that many folk fled from the land, and went wildly away north and west, believing that war out of the East was coming on the heels of the black horses.

Two days after Gandalf had departed from Orthanc, the Lord of Morgul halted before the Gate of Isengard. Then Saruman, already filled with wrath and fear by the escape of Gandalf, perceived the peril of standing between enemies, a known traitor to both. His dread was great, for his hope of deceiving Sauron, or at the least of receiving his favour in victory, was utterly lost. Now either he himself must gain the Ring or come to ruin and torment. But he was wary and cunning still, and he had ordered Isengard against just such an evil chance. The Circle of Isengard was too strong for even the Lord of Morgul and his company to assail without great force of war. Therefore to his challenge and demands he received only the answer of the voice of Saruman, that spoke by some art as though it came from the Gate itself.

'It is not a land that you look for,' it said. 'I know what you seek, though you do not name it. I have it not, as surely its servants perceive without telling; for if I had it, then you would bow before me and call me Lord. And if I knew where this thing was hid, I should not be here, but long gone before you to take it. There is one only whom I guess to have this knowledge: Mithrandir, enemy of Sauron. And since it is but two days since he departed from Isengard, seek him nearby.'

Such was still the power of the voice of Saruman that even the Lord of the Nazgûl did not question what it said, whether it was false or short of the full truth; but straightway he rode from the Gate and began to hunt for Gandalf in Rohan. Thus it was that on the evening of the next day the Black Riders came upon Gríma Wormtongue as he hastened to bring word to Saruman that Gandalf was come to Edoras, and had warned King Théoden of the treacherous designs of Isengard. In that hour the Wormtongue came near to death by terror; but being inured to treachery he would have told all that he knew under less threat.

'Yea, yea, verily I can tell you, Lord,' he said. 'I have overheard their speech together in Isengard. The land of the Halflings: it was thence that Gandalf came, and desires to return. He seeks now only a horse.

'Spare me! I speak as swiftly as I may. West through the Gap of Rohan yonder, and then north and a little west, until the next great river bars the way; the Greyflood it is called. Thence from the crossing at Tharbad the old road will lead you to the borders. "The Shire", they call it.

'Yea, verily, Saruman knows of it. Goods came to him from that land down the road. Spare me, Lord! Indeed I will say naught of our meeting to any that live.'

The Lord of the Nazgûl spared the life of the Wormtongue, not out of pity, but because he deemed that so great a terror was upon him that he would never dare to speak of their encounter (as proved true), and he saw that the creature was evil and was likely to do great harm yet to Saruman, if he lived. So he left him lying on the ground, and rode away, and did not trouble to go back to Isengard. Sauron's vengeance could wait.

Now he divided his company into four pairs, and they rode separately, but he himself went ahead with the swiftest pair. Thus they passed west out of Rohan, and explored the desolation of Enedwaith, and came at last to Tharbad. Thence they rode through Minhiriath, and even though they were not yet assembled a rumour of dread spread about them, and the creatures of the wild hid themselves, and lonely men fled away. But some fugitives on the road they captured; and to the delight of the Captain two proved to be spies and servants of Saruman. One of them had been used much in the traffic between Isengard and the Shire, and though he had not himself been beyond the Southfarthing he had charts prepared by Saruman which clearly depicted and described the Shire. These the Nazgûl took, and then sent him on to Bree to continue spying; but warned him that he was now in the service of Mordor, and that if ever he tried to return to Isengard they would slay him with torture.

Night was waning on the twenty-second day of September when drawing together again they came to Sarn Ford and the southernmost borders of the Shire. They found them guarded, for the Rangers barred their way. But this was a task beyond the power of the Dúnedain; and maybe it would still have proved so even if their captain, Aragorn, had been with them. But he was away to the north, upon the East Road near Bree; and the hearts even of the Dúnedain misgave them. Some fled northward, hoping to bear news to Aragorn, but they were pursued and slain or driven away into the wild. Some still dared to bar the ford, and held it while day lasted, but at night the Lord of Morgul swept them away, and the Black Riders passed into the Shire; and ere the cocks crowed in the small hours of the twenty-third day of September some were riding north through the land, even as Gandalf upon Shadowfax was riding over Rohan far behind.

(ii)

Other Versions of the Story

I have chosen to give the version printed above as being the most finished as a narrative; but there is much other writing that bears on these events, adding to or modifying the story in important particulars. These manuscripts are confusing and their relations obscure, though they all doubtless derive from the same period, and it is sufficient to note the existence of two other primary accounts beside the one printed (here called for convenience 'A'). A second version ('B') agrees very largely with A in its narrative structure, but a third ('C'), in the form of a plot-outline beginning at a later point in the story, introduces some substantial differences, and this I am inclined to think is the latest in order of composition. In addition there is some material ('D') more particularly concerned with Gollum's part in the events, and various other notes bearing on this part of the history.

In D it is said that what Gollum revealed to Sauron of the Ring and the place of its finding was sufficient to warn Sauron that this was indeed the One, but that of its present whereabouts he could only discover that it was stolen by a creature named *Baggins* in the Misty Mountains, and that *Baggins* came from a land called *Shire*. Sauron's fears were much allayed when he perceived from Gollum's account that *Baggins* must have been a creature of the same sort.

Gollum would not know the term 'Hobbit', which was local and not a universal Westron word. He would probably not use 'Halfling' since he was one himself, and Hobbits disliked the name. That is why the Black Riders seem to have had two main pieces of information only to go on: *Shire* and *Baggins*.

From all the accounts it is clear that Gollum did at least know in which direction the Shire lay; but though no doubt more could have been wrung from him by torture, Sauron plainly had no inkling that *Baggins* came from a region far removed from the Misty Mountains or that Gollum knew where it was, and assumed that he would be found in the Vales of Anduin, in the same region as Gollum himself had once lived.

This was a very small and natural error – but possibly the most important mistake that Sauron made in the whole affair. But for it, the Black Riders would have reached the Shire weeks sooner.

In the text B more is told of the journey of Aragorn with the captive Gollum northwards to the realm of Thranduil, and more consideration is given to Sauron's doubts about the use of the Ringwraiths in the search for the Ring.

[After his release from Mordor] Gollum soon disappeared into the Dead Marshes, where Sauron's emissaries could not or would not follow him. No other spies of Sauron could bring him any news. (Sauron probably had very little power yet in Eriador, and few agents there; and such as he sent were often hindered or misled by the servants of Saruman). At length therefore he resolved to use the Ringwraiths. He had been reluctant to do so, until he knew precisely where the Ring was, for several reasons. They were by far the most powerful of his servants, and the most suitable for such a mission, since they were entirely enslaved to their Nine Rings, which he now himself held; they were quite incapable of acting against his will, and if one of them, even the Witch-king their captain, had seized the One Ring, he would have brought it back to his Master. But they had disadvantages, until open war began (for which Sauron was not yet ready). All except the Witch-king were apt to stray when alone by daylight; and all, again save the Witch-king, feared water, and were unwilling, except in dire need, to enter it or to cross streams unless dryshod by a bridge.[3] Moreover, their chief weapon was terror. This was actually greater when they were unclad and invisible; and it was greater also when they were gathered together. So any mission on which they were sent could hardly be conducted with secrecy; while the passage of Anduin and other rivers presented an obstacle. For such reasons Sauron long hesitated, since he did not desire that his chief enemies should become aware of his servants' errand. It must be supposed that Sauron did not know at first that anyone save Gollum and 'the thief Baggins' had any knowledge of the Ring. Until Gandalf came and questioned him[4] Gollum did not know that Gandalf had any connexion with Bilbo, he had not even known of Gandalf's existence.

But when Sauron learned of Gollum's capture by his enemies the situation was drastically changed. When and how this happened cannot of course be known for certain. Probably long after the event. According to Aragorn Gollum was taken at nightfall on February 1st. Hoping to escape detection by any of Sauron's spies he drove Gollum through the north end of the Emyn Muil, and crossed Anduin just above Sarn Gebir. Driftwood was often cast up there on the shoals by the east shore, and binding Gollum to a log he swam across with him, and continued his journey north by tracks as westerly as he could find, through the skirts of Fangorn, and so over Limlight, then over Nimrodel and Silverlode through the eaves of Lórien,[5] and then on, avoiding Moria and Dimrill Dale, over Gladden until he came near the Carrock. There he crossed Anduin again, with the help of the Beornings, and passed into the Forest. The whole journey, on foot, was not much short of nine hundred miles, and this Aragorn accomplished with weariness in fifty days, reaching Thranduil on the twenty-first of March.[6]

It is thus most likely that the first news of Gollum would be learned by the servants of Dol Guldur after Aragorn entered the Forest; for though the power of Dol Guldur was supposed to come to an end at the Old Forest Road, its spies were many in the wood. The news evidently did not reach the Nazgûl commander of Dol Guldur for some time, and he probably did not inform Barad-dûr until he had tried to learn more of Gollum's whereabouts. It would then no doubt be late in April before Sauron heard that Gollum had been seen again, apparently captive in the hands of a Man. This might mean little. Neither Sauron nor any of his servants yet knew of Aragorn or who he was. But evidently later (since the lands of Thranduil would now be closely watched), possibly a month later, Sauron heard the disquieting news that the Wise were aware of Gollum, and that Gandalf had passed into Thranduil's realm.

Sauron must then have been filled with anger and alarm. He resolved to use the Ringwraiths as soon as he could, for speed rather than secrecy was now important. Hoping to alarm his enemies and disturb their counsels with the fear of war (which he did not intend to make for some time), he attacked Thranduil and Gondor at about the same time.[7] He had these two additional objects: to capture or kill Gollum, or at least to deprive his enemies of him; and to force the passage of the bridge of Osgiliath, so that the Nazgûl could cross, while testing the strength of Gondor.

In the event Gollum escaped. But the passage of the bridge was effected. The forces there used were probably much less than men in Gondor thought. In the panic of the first assault, when the Witch-king was allowed to reveal himself briefly in his full terror,[8] the Nazgûl crossed the bridge at night and dispersed northwards. Without belittling the valour of Gondor, which indeed Sauron found greater far than he had hoped, it is clear that Boromir and Faramir were able to drive back the enemy and destroy the bridge, only because the attack had now served its main purpose.

My father nowhere explained the Ringwraiths' fear of water. In the account just cited it is made a chief motive in Sauron's assault on Osgiliath, and it reappears in detailed notes on the movements of the Black Riders in the Shire: thus of the Rider (who was in fact Khamûl of Dol Guldur, see note 1) seen on the far side of Bucklebury Ferry just after the Hobbits had crossed (*The Fellowship of the Ring* I 5) it is said that 'he was well aware that the Ring had crossed the river; but the river was a barrier to his sense of its movement', and that the Nazgûl would not touch the 'Elvish' waters of Baranduin. But it is not made clear how they crossed other rivers that lay in their path, such as the Greyflood, where there was only 'a dangerous ford formed by the ruins of the bridge' (p. 264). My father did indeed note that the idea was difficult to sustain.

The account of the vain journey of the Nazgûl up the Vales of Anduin is much the same in version B as in that printed in full above (A), but with the difference that in B the Stoor settlements were not entirely deserted at that time; and such of the Stoors as dwelt there were slain or driven away by the Nazgûl.[9] In all the texts the precise dates are slightly at variance both with each other and with those given in the Tale of Years; these differences are here neglected.

In D is found an account of how Gollum fared after his escape from the Orcs of Dol Guldur and before the Fellowship entered the West-gate of Moria. This is in a rough state and has required some slight editorial revision.

It seems clear that pursued both by Elves and Orcs Gollum crossed the Anduin, probably by swimming, and so eluded the hunt of Sauron; but being still hunted by Elves, and not yet daring to pass near Lórien (only the lure of the Ring itself made him dare to do this afterwards), he hid himself in Moria.[10] That was probably in the autumn of the year; after which all trace of him was lost.

What then happened to Gollum cannot of course be known for certain. He was peculiarly fitted to survive in such straits, though at cost of great misery; but he was in great peril of discovery by the servants of Sauron that lurked in Moria,[11] especially since such bare necessity of food as he must have he could only get by thieving dangerously. No doubt he had intended to use Moria simply as a secret passage westward, his purpose being to find 'Shire' himself as quickly as he could; but he became lost, and it was a very long time before he found his way about. It thus seems probable that he had not long made his way towards the West-gate when the Nine Walkers arrived. He knew nothing, of course, about the action of the doors. To him they would seem huge and immovable; and though they had no lock or bar and opened outwards to a thrust, he did not discover that. In any case he was now far away from any source of food, for the Orcs were mostly in the East-end of Moria, and was become weak and desperate, so that even if he had known all about the doors he still could not have thrust them open.[12] It was thus a piece of singular good fortune for Gollum that the Nine Walkers arrived when they did.

The story of the coming of the Black Riders to Isengard in September 3018, and their subsequent capture of Gríma Wormtongue, as told in A and B, is much altered in version C, which takes up the narrative only at their return southward over the Limlight. In A and B it was two days after Gandalf's escape from Orthanc that the Nazgûl came to Isengard; Saruman told them that Gandalf was gone, and denied all knowledge of the Shire,[13] but was betrayed by Gríma whom they captured on the following day as he hastened to Isengard with news of Gandalf's coming to Edoras. In C, on the other hand, the Black Riders arrived at the Gate of Isengard while Gandalf was still a prisoner in the tower. In this account, Saruman, in fear and despair, and perceiving the full horror of service to Mordor, resolved suddenly to yield to Gandalf, and to beg for his pardon and help. Temporizing at the Gate, he admitted that he had Gandalf within, and said that he would go and try to discover what he knew; if that were unavailing, he would deliver Gandalf up to them. Then Saruman hastened to the summit of Orthanc – and found Gandalf gone. Away south against the setting moon he saw a great Eagle flying towards Edoras.

Now Saruman's case was worse. If Gandalf had escaped there was still a real chance that Sauron would not get the Ring, and would be defeated. In his heart Saruman recognized the great power and the strange 'good fortune' that went with Gandalf. But now he was left alone to deal with the Nine. His mood changed, and his pride reasserted itself in anger at Gandalf's escape from impenetrable Isengard, and in a fury of jealousy. He went back to the Gate, and he lied, saying that he had made Gandalf confess. He did not admit that this was his own knowledge, not being aware of how much Sauron knew of his mind and heart.[14] 'I will report this myself to the Lord of Barad-dûr,' he said loftily, 'to whom I speak from afar on great matters that concern us. But all that you need to know on the mission that he has given you is where "the Shire" lies. That, says Mithrandir, is northwest from here some six hundred miles, on the borders of the seaward Elvish country.' To his pleasure Saruman saw that even the Witch-king did not relish that. You must cross Isen by the Fords, and then rounding the Mountains' end make for Tharbad upon Greyflood. Go with speed, and I will report to your Master that you have done so.'

This skilful speech convinced even the Witch-king for the moment that Saruman was a faithful ally, high in Sauron's confidence. At once the Riders left the Gate and rode in haste to the Fords of Isen. Behind them Saruman sent out wolves and Orcs in vain pursuit of Gandalf; but in this he had other purposes also, to impress his power upon the Nazgûl, perhaps also to prevent them from lingering near, and in his anger he wished to do some injury to Rohan, and to increase the fear of him which his agent Wormtongue was building up in Théoden's heart. Wormtongue had been in Isengard not long since, and was then on his way back to Edoras; among the pursuers were some bearing messages to him.

When he was rid of the Riders Saruman retired to Orthanc, and sat in earnest and dreadful thought. It seems that he resolved still to temporize, and still to hope to get the Ring for himself. He thought that the direction of the Riders to the Shire might hinder them rather than help them, for he knew of the guard of the Rangers, and he believed also (knowing of the oracular dream-words and of Boromir's mission) that the Ring had gone and was already on the way to Rivendell. At once he marshalled and sent out into Eriador all the spies, spy-birds, and agents that he could muster.

In this version the element of Gríma's capture by the Ringwraiths and his betrayal of Saruman is thus absent; for of course there is insufficient time by this account for Gandalf to reach Edoras and attempt to warn King Théoden, and for Gríma in his turn to set out for Isengard to warn Saruman, before the Black Riders were already gone from Rohan.[15] The revelation of Saruman's lying to them here comes about through the man whom they captured and found to be bearing maps of the Shire (p. 341); and more is told of this man and of Saruman's dealings with the Shire.

When the Black Riders were far across Enedwaith and drawing near at last to Tharbad, they had what was for them a great stroke of good fortune, but disastrous for Saruman,[16] and deadly perilous for Frodo.

Saruman had long taken an interest in the Shire – because Gandalf did, and he was suspicious of him; and because (again in secret imitation of Gandalf) he had taken to the 'Halflings' leaf', and needed supplies, but in pride (having once scoffed at Gandalf's use of the weed) kept this as secret as he could. Latterly other motives were added. He liked to extend his power, especially into Gandalf's province, and he found that the money he could provide for the purchase of 'leaf' was giving him power, and was corrupting some of the Hobbits, especially the Bracegirdles, who owned many plantations, and so also the Sackville-Bagginses.[17] But also he had begun to feel certain that in some way the Shire was connected with the Ring in Gandalf's mind. Why this strong guard upon it? He therefore began to collect detailed information about the Shire, its chief persons and families, its roads, and other matters. For this he used Hobbits within the Shire, in the pay of the Bracegirdles and the Sackville-Bagginses, but his agents were Men, of Dunlendish origin. When Gandalf had refused to treat with him Saruman had redoubled his efforts. The Rangers were suspicious, but did not actually refuse entry to the servants of Saruman – for Gandalf was not at liberty to warn them, and when he had gone off to Isengard Saruman was still recognised as an ally.

Some while ago one of Saruman's most trusted servants (yet a ruffianly fellow, an outlaw driven from Dunland, where many said that he had Orc-blood) had returned from the borders of the Shire, where he had been negotiating for the purchase of 'leaf' and other supplies. Saruman was beginning to store Isengard against war. This man was now on his way back to continue the business, and to arrange for the transport of many goods before autumn failed.[18] He had orders also to get into the Shire if possible and learn if there had been any departures of persons well-known recently. He was well supplied with maps, lists of names, and notes concerning the Shire.

This Dunlending was overtaken by several of the Black Riders as they approached the Tharbad crossing. In an extremity of terror he was haled to the Witch-king and questioned. He saved his life by betraying Saruman. The Witch-king thus learned that Saruman knew well all along where the Shire was, and knew much about it, which he could and should have told to Sauron's servants if he had been a true ally. The Witch-king also obtained much information, including some about the only name that interested him: *Baggins*. It was for this reason that Hobbiton was singled out as one of the points for immediate visit and enquiry.

The Witch-king had now a clearer understanding of the matter. He had known something of the country long ago, in his wars with the Dúnedain, and especially of the Tyrn Gorthad of Cardolan, now the Barrow-downs, whose evil wights had been sent there by himself.[19] Seeing that his Master suspected some move between the Shire and Rivendell, he saw also that Bree (the position of which he knew) would be an important point, at least for information.[20] He put therefore the Shadow of Fear on the Dunlending, and sent him on to Bree as an agent. He was the squint-eyed southerner at the Inn.[21]

In version B it is noted that the Black Captain did not know whether the Ring was still in the Shire; that he had to find out. The Shire was too large for a violent onslaught such as he had made on the Stoors; he must use as much stealth and as little terror as he could, and yet also guard the eastern borders. Therefore he sent some of the Riders into the Shire, with orders to disperse while traversing it; and of these Khamûl was to find Hobbiton (see note 1), where 'Baggins' lived, according to Saruman's papers. But the Black Captain established a camp at Andrath, where the Greenway passed in a defile between the Barrow-downs and the South Downs;[22] and from there some others were sent to watch and patrol the eastern borders, while he himself visited the Barrow-downs. In notes on the movements of the Black Riders at that time it is said that the Black Captain stayed there for some days, and the Barrow-wights were roused, and all things of evil spirit, hostile to Elves and Men, were on the watch with malice in the Old Forest and on the Barrow-downs.

(iii)

Concerning Gandalf, Saruman and the Shire

Another set of papers from the same period consists of a large number of unfinished accounts of Saruman's earlier dealings with the Shire, especially as they concerned the 'Halflings' leaf', a matter that is

touched on in connection with the 'squint-eyed southerner' (see pp.
347–8). The following text is one version among many, but though
briefer than some is the most finished.

Saruman soon became jealous of Gandalf, and this rivalry turned at
last to a hatred, the deeper for being concealed, and the more bitter
in that Saruman knew in his heart that the Grey Wanderer had the
greater strength, and the greater influence upon the dwellers in
Middle-earth, even though he hid his power and desired neither
fear nor reverence. Saruman did not revere him, but he grew to fear
him, being ever uncertain how much Gandalf perceived of his inner
mind, troubled more by his silences than by his words. So it was
that openly he treated Gandalf with less respect than did others of
the Wise, and was ever ready to gainsay him or to make little of his
counsels; while secretly he noted and pondered all that he said,
setting a watch, so far as he was able, upon all his movements.

It was in this way that Saruman came to give thought to the
Halflings and the Shire, which otherwise he would have deemed
beneath his notice. He had at first no thought that the interest of
his rival in this people had any connexion with the great concerns
of the Council, least of all with the Rings of Power. For indeed in
the beginning it had no such connexion, and was due only to Gandalf's
love for the Little People, unless his heart had some deep premonition
beyond his waking thought. For many years he visited the Shire
openly, and would speak of its people to any who would listen; and
Saruman would smile, as at the idle tales of an old land-rover, but
he took heed nonetheless.

Seeing then that Gandalf thought the Shire worth visiting,
Saruman himself visited it, but disguised and in the utmost secrecy,
until he had explored and noted all its ways and lands, and thought
then he had learned all that there was to know of it. And even when
it seemed to him no longer wise nor profitable to go thither, he still
had spies and servants that went in or kept an eye upon its borders.
For he was still suspicious. He was himself so far fallen that he
believed all others of the Council had each their deep and far-
reaching policies for their own enhancement, to which all that they
did must in some way refer. So when long after he learned something
of the finding of Gollum's Ring by the Halfling, he could believe
only that Gandalf had known of this all the time; and this was his
greatest grievance, since all that concerned the Rings he deemed his
especial province. That Gandalf's mistrust of him was merited and
just in no way lessened his anger.

Yet in truth Saruman's spying and great secrecy had not in the beginning any evil purpose, but was no more than a folly born of pride. Small matters, unworthy it would seem to be reported, may yet prove of great moment ere the end. Now truth to tell, observing Gandalf's love of the herb that he called 'pipe-weed' (for which, he said, if for nothing else, the Little People should be honoured), Saruman had affected to scoff at it, but in private he made trial of it, and soon began to use it; and for this reason the Shire remained important to him. Yet he dreaded lest this should be discovered, and his own mockery turned against him, so that he would be laughed at for imitating Gandalf, and scorned for doing so by stealth. This then was the reason for his great secrecy in all his dealings with the Shire, even from the first before any shadow of doubt had fallen upon it, and it was little guarded, free for those who wished to enter. For this reason also Saruman ceased to go thither in person; for it came to his knowledge that he had not been all unobserved by the keen-eyed Halflings, and some, seeing the figure as it were of an old man clad in grey or russet stealing through the woods or passing through the dusk, had mistaken him for Gandalf.

After that Saruman went no more to the Shire, fearing that such tales might spread and come maybe to the ears of Gandalf. But Gandalf knew of these vists, and guessed their object, and he laughed, thinking this the most harmless of Saruman's secrets; but he said nothing to others, for it was never his wish that any one should be put to shame. Nonetheless he was not ill-pleased when the visits of Saruman ceased, doubting him already, though he could not himself yet foresee that a time would come when Saruman's knowledge of the Shire would prove perilous and of the greatest service to the Enemy, bringing victory to within a nail's breadth of his grasp.

In another version there is a description of the occasion when Saruman openly scoffed at Gandalf's use of the 'pipe-weed':

Now because of his dislike and fear, in the later days Saruman avoided Gandalf, and they seldom met, except at the assemblies of the White Council. It was at the great Council held in 2851 that the 'Halflings' leaf' was first spoken of, and the matter was noted with amusement at the time, though it was afterwards remembered in a different light. The Council met in Rivendell, and Gandalf sat apart, silent, but smoking prodigiously (a thing he had never done before on such an occasion), while Saruman spoke against him, and urged that contrary to Gandalf's advice Dol Guldur should not yet be molested. Both the silence and the smoke seemed greatly to annoy Saruman, and before the Council dispersed he said to Gandalf: 'When weighty matters are in debate, Mithrandir, I wonder a little that you should play with your toys of fire and smoke, while others are in earnest speech.'

But Gandalf laughed, and replied: 'You would not wonder, if you used this herb yourself. You might find that smoke blown out cleared your mind of shadows within. Anyway, it gives patience, to listen to error without anger. But it is not one of my toys. It is an art of the Little People away in the West: merry and worthy folk, though not of much account, perhaps, in your high policies.'

Saruman was little appeased by this answer (for he hated mockery, however gentle), and he said then coldly: 'You jest, Lord Mithrandir, as is your way. I know well enough that you have become a curious explorer of the small: weeds, wild things, and childish folk. Your time is your own to spend, if you have nothing worthier to do; and your friends you may make as you please. But to me the days are too dark for wanderers' tales, and I have no time for the simples of peasants.'

Gandalf did not laugh again; and he did not answer, but looking keenly at Saruman he drew on his pipe and sent out a great ring of smoke with many smaller rings that followed it. Then he put up his hand, as if to grasp them, and they vanished. With that he got up and left Saruman without another word; but Saruman stood for some time silent, and his face was dark with doubt and displeasure.

This story appears in half a dozen different manuscripts, and in one of them it is said that Saruman was suspicious,

doubting whether he read rightly the purport of Gandalf's gesture with the rings of smoke (above all whether it showed any connexion between the Halflings and the great matter of the Rings of Power, unlikely though that might seem); and doubting that one so great could concern himself with such a people as the Halflngs for their own sake merely.

In another (struck through) Gandalf's purpose is made explicit:

It was a strange chance, that being angered by his insolence Gandalf chose this way of showing to Saruman his suspicion that desire to possess them had begun to enter into his policies and his study of the lore of the Rings; and of warning him that they would elude him.

For it cannot be doubted that Gandalf had as yet no thought that the Halflings (and still less their smoking) had any connection with the Rings.[23] If he had had any such thought, then certainly he would not have done then what he did. Yet later when the Halflings did indeed become involved in this greatest matter, Saruman could believe only that Gandalf had known or foreknown this, and had concealed the knowledge from him and from the Council – for just such a purpose as Saruman would conceive: to gain possession and to forestall him.

In the Tale of Years the entry for 2851 refers to the meeting of the White Council in that year, when Gandalf urged an attack on Dol Guldur but was overruled by Saruman; and a footnote to the entry reads: 'It afterwards became clear that Saruman had then begun to desire to possess the One Ring himself, and hoped that it might reveal itself, seeking its master, if Sauron were let be for a time.' The foregoing story shows that Gandalf himself suspected Saruman of this at the time of the Council of 2851; though my father afterwards commented that it appears from Gandalf's story to the Council of Elrond of his meeting with Radagast that he did not seriously suspect Saruman of treachery (or of desiring the Ring for himself) until he was imprisoned in Orthanc.

NOTES

1 According to the entry in the Tale of Years for 2951 Sauron sent three, not two, of the Nazgûl to reoccupy Dol Guldur. The two statements can be reconciled on the assumption that one of the Ringwraiths of Dol Guldur returned afterwards to Minas Morgul, but I think it more likely that the formulation of the present text was superseded when the Tale of Years was compiled; and it may be noted that in a rejected version of the present passage there was only one Nazgûl in Dol Guldur (not named as Khamûl, but referred to as 'the Second Chief (the Black Easterling)'), while one remained with Sauron as his chief messenger. – From notes recounting in detail the movements of the Black Riders in the Shire it emerges that it was Khamûl who came to Hobbiton and spoke to Gaffer Gamgee, who followed the Hobbits along the road to Stock, and who narrowly missed them at the Bucklebury Ferry (see p. 344). The Rider who accompanied him, whom he summoned by cries on the ridge above Woodhall, and with whom he visited Farmer Maggot, was 'his companion from Dol Guldur'. Of Khamûl it is said here that he was the most ready of all the Nazgûl, after the Black Captain himself,

to perceive the presence of the Ring, but also the one whose power was most confused and diminished by daylight.

2   He had indeed in his terror of the Nazgûl dared to hide in Moria. [Author's note.]

3   At the Ford of Bruinen only the Witch-king and two others, with the lure of the Ring straight before them, had dared to enter the river; the others were driven into it by Glorfindel and Aragorn. [Author's note.]

4   Gandalf, as he recounted to the Council of Elrond, questioned Gollum while he was imprisoned by the Elves of Thranduil.

5   Gandalf told the Council of Elrond that after he left Minas Tirith 'messages came to me out of Lórien that Aragorn had passed that way, and that he had found the creature called Gollum'.

6   Gandalf arrived two days later, and left on the 29th of March early in the morning. After the Carrock he had a horse, but he had the High Pass over the Mountains to cross. He got a fresh horse at Rivendell, and making the greatest speed he could he reached Hobbiton late on the 12th of April, after a journey of nearly eight hundred miles. [Author's note.]

7   Both here and in the Tale of Years the assault on Osgiliath is dated the 20th of June.

8   This statement no doubt relates to Boromir's account of the battle at Osgiliath which he gave to the Council of Elrond: 'A power was there that we have not felt before. Some said that it could be seen, like a great black horseman, a dark shadow under the moon.'

9   In a letter written in 1959 my father said: 'Between 2463 [when Déagol the Stoor found the One Ring, according to the Tale of Years] and the beginning of Gandalf's special enquiries concerning the Ring (nearly 500 years later) they [the Stoors] appear indeed to have died out altogether (except of course for Sméagol); or to have fled from the shadow of Dol Guldur.'

10 According to the author's note given in Note 2 above, Gollum fled into Moria from terror of the Nazgûl; cf. also the suggestion on p. 339 that one of the purposes of the Lord of Morgul in riding on northward beyond the Gladden was the hope of finding Gollum.

11 These were in fact not very numerous, it would seem; but sufficient to keep any intruders out, if no better armed or prepared than Balin's company, and not in great numbers. [Author's note.]

12 According to the Dwarves this needed usually the thrust of two; only a very strong Dwarf could open them single-handed. Before the desertion of Moria doorwards were kept inside the West-gate, and one at least was always there. In this way a single person (and so any intruder or person trying to escape) could not get out without permission. [Author's note.]

13   In A Saruman denied knowledge of where the Ring was hid; in B he 'denied all knowledge of the land that they sought'. But this is probably no more than a difference of wording.

14   Earlier in this version it is said that Sauron had at this time, by means of the *palantíri*, at last begun to daunt Saruman, and could in any case often read his thought even when he withheld information. Thus Sauron was aware that Saruman had some guess at the place where the Ring was; and Saruman actually revealed that he had got as his prisoner Gandalf, who knew the most.

15   The entry for the 18th of September 3018 in the Tale of Years reads: 'Gandalf escapes from Orthanc in the early hours. The Black Riders cross the Fords of Isen.' Laconic as this entry is, giving no hint that the Riders visited Isengard, it seems to be based on the story told in version C.

16   No indication is given in any of these texts of what passed between Sauron and Saruman as a result of the latter's unmasking.

17   Lobelia Bracegirdle married Otho Sackville-Baggins; their son was Lotho, who seized control of the Shire at the time of the War of the Ring, and was then known as 'the Chief'. Farmer Cotton referred in conversation with Frodo to Lotho's property in leaf-plantations in the Southfarthing (*The Return of the King* VI 8).

18   The usual way was by the crossing of Tharbad to Dunland (rather than direct to Isengard), whence goods were sent more secretly on to Saruman. [Author's note.]

19   Cf. *The Lord of the Rings*, Appendix A (I, iii, *The North-kingdom and the Dúnedain*): 'It was at this time [during the Great Plague that reached Gondor in 1636] that an end came of the Dúnedain of Cardolan, and evil spirits out of Angmar and Rhudaur entered into the deserted mounds and dwelt there.'

20   Since the Black Captain knew so much, it is perhaps strange that he had had so little idea of where the Shire, the land of the Halflings, lay; according to the Tale of Years there were already Hobbits settled in Bree at the beginning of the fourteenth century of the Third Age, when the Witch-king came north to Angmar.

21   See *The Fellowship of the Ring* I, 9. When Strider and the Hobbits left Bree (*ibid.* I, 11) Frodo caught a glimpse of the Dunlending ('a sallow face with sly, slanting eyes') in Bill Ferny's house on the outskirts of Bree, and thought: 'He looks more than half like a goblin.'

22   Cf. Gandalf's words at the Council of Elrond: 'Their Captain remained in secret away south of Bree.'

23   As the concluding sentence of this quotation shows, the meaning is: 'Gandalf had as yet no thought that the Halflings would have in the future any connexion with the Rings.' The meeting of the White Council in 2851 took place ninety years before Bilbo found the Ring.

V

THE BATTLES OF
THE FORDS OF ISEN

The chief obstacles to an easy conquest of Rohan by Saruman were
Théodred and Éomer: they were vigorous men, devoted to the King,
and high in his affections, as his only son and his sister-son; and
they did all that they could to thwart the influence over him that
Gríma gained when the King's health began to fail. This occurred
early in the year 3014, when Théoden was sixty-six; his malady may
thus have been due to natural causes, though the Rohirrim commonly
lived till near or beyond their eightieth year. But it may well have
been induced or increased by subtle poisons, administered by Gríma.
In any case Théoden's sense of weakness and dependence on Gríma
was largely due to the cunning and skill of this evil counsellor's
suggestions. It was his policy to bring his chief opponents into dis-
credit with Théoden, and if possible to get rid of them. It proved
impossible to set them at odds with one another: Théoden before
his 'sickness' had been much loved by all his kin and people, and the
loyalty of Théodred and Éomer remained steadfast, even in his
apparent dotage. Éomer also was not an ambitious man, and his love
and respect for Théodred (thirteen years older than he) was only
second to his love of his foster-father.[1] Gríma therefore tried to play
them one against the other in the mind of Théoden, representing
Éomer as ever eager to increase his own authority and to act without
consulting the King or his Heir. In this he had some success, which
bore fruit when Saruman at last succeeded in achieving the death of
Théodred.

It was clearly seen in Rohan, when the true accounts of the battles
at the Fords were known, that Saruman had given special orders that
Théodred should at all costs be slain. At the first battle all his
fiercest warriors were engaged in reckless assaults upon Théodred
and his guard, disregarding other events of the battle, which might
otherwise have resulted in a much more damaging defeat for the
Rohirrim. When Théodred was at last slain Saruman's commander
(no doubt under orders) seemed satisfied for the time being, and
Saruman made the mistake, fatal as it proved, of not immediately

throwing in more forces and proceeding at once to a massive invasion of Westfold;[2] though the valour of Grimbold and Elfhelm contributed to his delay. If the invasion of Westfold had begun five days earlier, there can be little doubt that the reinforcements from Edoras would never have come near Helm's Deep, but would have been surrounded and overwhelmed in the open plain; if indeed Edoras had not itself been attacked and captured before the arrival of Gandalf.[3]

It has been said that the valour of Grimbold and Elfhelm contributed to Saruman's delay, which proved disastrous for him. The above account perhaps underestimates its importance.

The Isen came down swiftly from its sources above Isengard, but in the flat land of the Gap it became slow until it turned west; then it flowed on through country falling by long slopes down into the low-lying coast-lands of furthest Gondor and the Enedwaith, and it became deep and rapid. Just above this westward bend were the Fords of Isen. There the river was broad and shallow, passing in two arms about a large eyot, over a stony shelf covered with stones and pebbles brought down from the north. Only here, south of Isengard, was it possible for large forces, especially those heavily armed or mounted, to cross the river. Saruman thus had this advantage: he could send his troops down either side of the Isen and attack the Fords, if they were held against him, from both sides. Any force of his west of Isen could if necessary retreat upon Isengard. On the other hand, Théodred might send men across the Fords, either in sufficient strength to engage Saruman's troops or to defend the western bridgehead; but if they were worsted, they would have no retreat except back over the Fords with the enemy at their heels, and possibly also awaiting them on the eastern bank. South and west along the Isen they had no way home,[4] unless they were provisioned for a long journey into Western Gondor.

Saruman's attack was not unforeseen, but it came sooner than was expected. Théodred's scouts had warned him of a mustering of troops before the Gates of Isengard, mainly (as it seemed) on the west side of Isen. He therefore manned the approaches, east and west, to the Fords with sturdy men on foot from the levies of Westfold. Leaving three companies of Riders, together with horse-herds and spare mounts, on the east bank, he himself passed over with the main strength of his cavalry: eight companies and a company of archers, intending to overthrow Saruman's army before it was fully prepared.

But Saruman had not revealed his intentions nor the full strength of his forces. They were already on the march when Théodred set out. Some twenty miles north of the Fords he encountered their vanguard and scattered it with loss. But when he rode on to attack the main host the resistance stiffened. The enemy was in fact in positions prepared for the event, behind trenches manned by pike-men, and Théodred in the leading *éored* was brought to a stand and almost surrounded, for new forces hastening from Isengard were now outflanking him upon the west.

He was extricated by the onset of the companies coming up behind him; but as he looked eastward he was dismayed. It had been a dim and misty morning, but the mists were now rolling back through the Gap on a breeze from the west, and away east of the river he descried other forces now hasting towards the Fords, though their strength could not be guessed. He at once ordered a retreat. This the Riders, well trained in the manoeuvre, managed in good order and with little further loss; but the enemy was not shaken off or long outdistanced, for the retreat was often delayed, when the rearguard under Grimbold was obliged to turn at bay and drive back the most eager of their pursuers.

When Théodred gained the Fords the day was waning. He set Grimbold in command of the garrison of the west bank, stiffened with fifty dismounted Riders. The rest of his Riders and all the horses he at once sent across the river, save his own company: with these on foot he manned the eyot, to cover the retreat of Grimbold if he was driven back. This was barely done when disaster came. Saruman's eastern force came down with unexpected speed; it was much smaller than the western force, but more dangerous. In its van were some Dunlending horsemen and a great pack of the dreadful Orcish wolfriders, feared by horses.[5] Behind them came two battalions of the fierce Uruks, heavily armed but trained to move at great speed for many miles. The horsemen and wolfriders fell on the horse-herds and picketed horses and slew or dispersed them. The garrison of the east bank, surprised by the sudden assault of the massed Uruks, was swept away, and the Riders that had just crossed from the west were caught still in disarray, and though they fought desperately they were driven from the Fords along the line of the Isen with the Uruks in pursuit.

As soon as the enemy had gained possession of the eastern end of the Fords there appeared a company of men or orc-men (evidently dispatched for the purpose), ferocious, mail-clad, and armed with axes. They hastened to the eyot and assailed it from both sides. At the same time Grimbold on the west bank was attacked by Saruman's forces on that side of the Isen. As he looked eastward, dismayed by the sounds of battle and the hideous orc-cries of victory, he saw the

axe-men driving Théodred's men from the shores of the eyot towards
the low knoll in its centre, and he heard Théodred's great voice
crying *To me, Eorlingas!* At once Grimbold, taking a few men that
stood near him, ran back to the eyot. So fierce was his onset from
the rear of the attackers that Grimbold, a man of great strength and
stature, clove his way through, till with two others he reached
Théodred standing at bay on the knoll. Too late. As he came to his
side Théodred fell, hewn down by a great orc-man. Grimbold slew
him and stood over the body of Théodred, thinking him dead; and
there he would himself soon have died, but for the coming of Elfhelm.

Elfhelm had been riding in haste along the horse-road from Edoras,
leading four companies in answer to Théodred's summons; he was
expecting battle, but not yet for some days. But near the junction of
the horse-road with the road down from the Deeping[6] his outriders
on the right flank reported that two wolfriders had been seen abroad
on the fields. Sensing that things were amiss, he did not turn aside
to Helm's Deep for the night as he had intended but rode with all
speed towards the Fords. The horse-road turned north-west after
its meeting with the Deeping-road, but again bent sharply west when
level with the Fords, which it approached by a straight path of some
two miles long. Elfhelm thus heard and saw nothing of the fighting
between the retreating garrison and the Uruks south of the Fords.
The sun had sunk and light was failing when he drew near the last
bend in the road, and there encountered some horses running wild
and a few fugitives who told him of the disaster. Though his men
and horses were now weary he rode as fast as he could along the
straight, and as he came in sight of the east bank he ordered his
companies to charge.

It was the turn of the Isengarders to be surprised. They heard the
thunder of hooves, and saw coming like black shadows against the
darkening East a great host (as it seemed) with Elfhelm at its head,
and beside him a white standard borne as a guide to those that
followed. Few stood their ground. Most fled northwards, pursued
by two of Elfhelm's companies. The others he dismounted to guard
the east bank, but at once with the men of his own company rushed
to the eyot. The axemen were now caught between the surviving
defenders and the onslaught of Elfhelm, with both banks still held
by the Rohirrim. They fought on, but before the end were slain to
a man. Elfhelm himself, however, sprang up towards the knoll;
and there he found Grimbold fighting two great axemen for possession
of Théodred's body. One Elfhelm at once slew, and the other fell
before Grimbold.

They stooped then to lift the body, and found that Théodred still breathed; but he lived only long enough to speak his last words: *Let me lie here – to keep the Fords till Éomer comes!* Night fell. A harsh horn sounded, and then all was silent. The attack on the west bank ceased, and the enemy there faded away into the dark. The Rohirrim held the Fords of Isen; but their losses were heavy, not least in horses; the King's son was dead, and they were leaderless, and did not know what might yet befall.

When after a cold and sleepless night the grey light returned there was no sign of the Isengarders, save those many that they left dead upon the field. Wolves were howling far off, waiting for the living men to depart. Many men scattered by the sudden assault of the Isengarders began to return, some still mounted, some leading horses recaptured. Later in the morning most of Théodred's Riders that had been driven south down the river by a battalion of black Uruks came back battle-worn but in good order. They had a like tale to tell. They came to a stand on a low hill and prepared to defend it. Though they had drawn off part of the attacking force of Isengard, retreat south unprovisioned was in the end hopeless. The Uruks had resisted any attempt to burst eastwards, and were driving them towards the now hostile country of the Dunlendish 'west-march'. But as the Riders prepared to resist their assault, though it was now full night, a horn was sounded; and soon they discovered that the enemy had gone. They had too few horses to attempt any pursuit, or even to act as scouts, so far as that would have availed by night. After some time they began cautiously to advance north again, but met no opposition. They thought that the Uruks had gone back to reinforce their hold on the Fords, and expected there to meet in battle again, and they wondered much to find the Rohirrim in command. It was not till later that they discovered whither the Uruks had gone.

So ended the First Battle of the Fords of Isen. Of the Second Battle no such clear accounts were ever made, owing to the much greater events that immediately followed. Erkenbrand of Westfold assumed command of the West-mark when news of the fall of Théodred reached him in the Hornburg on the next day. He sent errand-riders to Edoras to announce this and to bear to Théoden his son's last words, adding his own prayer that Éomer should be sent at once with all help that could be spared.[7] 'Let the defence of Edoras be made here in the West,' he said, 'and not wait till it is itself besieged.' But Gríma used the curtness of this advice to further his policy of delay. It was not until his defeat by Gandalf that any action was taken. The reinforcements with Éomer and the King himself set out in the afternoon of March the 2nd, but that night the Second Battle of the Fords was fought and lost, and the invasion of Rohan began.

Erkenbrand did not at once himself proceed to the battle-field. All was in confusion. He did not know what forces he could muster in haste; nor could he yet estimate the losses that Théodred's troops had actually suffered. He judged rightly that invasion was imminent, but that Saruman would not dare to pass on eastward to attack Edoras while the fortress of the Hornburg was unreduced, if it was manned and well stored. With this business and the gathering of such men of Westfold as he could, he was occupied for three days. The command in the field he gave to Grimbold, until he could come himself; but he assumed no command over Elfhelm and his Riders, who belonged to the Muster of Edoras. The two commanders were, however, friends and both loyal and wise men, and there was no dissension between them; the ordering of their forces was a compromise between their differing opinions. Elfhelm held that the Fords were no longer important, but rather a snare to entrap men better placed elsewhere, since Saruman could clearly send forces down either side of the Isen as suited his purpose; and his immediate purpose would undoubtedly be to overrun Westfold and invest the Hornburg, before any effective help could come from Edoras. His army, or most of it, would therefore come down the east side of the Isen; for though by that way, over rougher ground without roads, their approach would be slower, they would not have to force the passage of the Fords. Elfhelm therefore advised that the Fords should be abandoned; all the available men on foot should be assembled on the east side, and placed in a position to hold up the advance of the enemy: a long line of rising ground running from west to east some few miles north of the Fords; but the cavalry should be withdrawn eastward to a point from which, when the advancing enemy was engaged with the defence, a charge with the greatest impact could be delivered on their flank and drive them into the river. 'Let Isen be their snare and not ours!'

Grimbold on the other hand was not willing to abandon the Fords. This was in part due to the tradition of Westfold in which he and Erkenbrand had been bred; but was not without some reason. 'We do not know,' he said, 'what force Saruman has still at his command. But if it is indeed his purpose to ravage Westfold and drive its defenders into Helm's Deep and there contain them, then it must be very great. He is unlikely to display it all at once. As soon as he guesses or discovers how we have disposed our defence, he will certainly send great strength at all speed down the road from Isengard, and crossing the undefended Fords come in our rear, if we are all gathered northwards.'

In the end Grimbold manned the western end of the Fords with the greater part of his foot-soldiers; there they were in a strong position in the earth-forts that guarded the approaches. He remained with the rest of his men, including what remained to him of Théodred's cavalry, on the east bank. The eyot he left bare.[8] Elfhelm however withdrew his Riders and took up his position on the line where he had wished the main defence to stand; his purpose was to descry as soon as could be any attack coming down on the east of the river and to disperse it before it could reach the Fords.

All went ill, as most likely it would have done in any case: Saruman's strength was too great. He began his attack by day, and before noon of March the 2nd a strong force of his best fighters, coming down by the Road from Isengard, attacked the forts on the west of the Fords. This force was in fact only a small part of those that he had in hand, no more than he deemed sufficient to dispose of the weakened defence. But the garrison of the Fords, though greatly outnumbered, resisted stubbornly. At length, however, when both the forts were heavily engaged, a troop of Uruks forced the passage between them and began to cross the Fords. Grimbold, trusting in Elfhelm to hold off attack on the east side, came across with all the men he had left and flung them back – for a while. But the enemy commander then threw in a battalion that had not been committed, and broke the defences. Grimbold was obliged to withdraw across the Isen. It was then near sunset. He had suffered much loss, but had inflicted far heavier losses on the enemy (mostly Orcs), and he still held the east bank strongly. The enemy did not attempt to cross the Fords and fight their way up the steep slopes to dislodge him; not yet.

Elfhelm had been unable to take part in this action. In the dusk he withdrew his companies and retired towards Grimbold's camp, setting his men in groups at some distance from it to act as a screen against attack from north and east. From southwards they expected no evil, and hoped for succour. After the retreat across the Fords errand-riders had been dispatched at once to Erkenbrand and to Edoras telling of their plight. Fearing, indeed knowing, that greater evil would befall them ere long, unless help beyond hope reached them swiftly, the defenders prepared to do what they could to hold up Saruman's advance before they were overwhelmed.[9] The greater part stood to arms, only a few at a time attempting to snatch such brief rest and sleep as they could. Grimbold and Elfhelm were sleepless, awaiting the dawn and dreading what it might bring.

They did not have to wait so long. It was not yet midnight when points of red light were seen coming from the north and already drawing near on the west of the river. It was the vanguard of the whole remaining forces of Saruman that he was now committing to battle for the conquest of Westfold.[10] They came on at great speed, and suddenly all the host burst into flame, as it seemed. Hundreds of torches were kindled from those borne by the leaders of troops, and gathering into their stream the forces already manning the west bank they swept over the Fords like a river of fire with a great clamour of hate. A great company of bowmen might have made them rue the light of their torches, but Grimbold had only a handful of archers. He could not hold the east bank, and withdrew from it, forming a great shieldwall about his camp. Soon it was surrounded, and the attackers cast torches among them, and some they sent high over the heads of the shieldwall, hoping to kindle fires among the stores and terrify such horses as Grimbold still had. But the shieldwall held. Then, since the Orcs were of less avail in such fighting because of their stature, fierce companies of the Dunlendish hillmen were thrown against it. But for all their hatred the Dunlendings were still afraid of the Rohirrim if they met face to face, and they were also less skilled in warfare and less well armed.[11] The shieldwall still held.

In vain Grimbold looked for help to come from Elfhelm. None came. At last then he determined to carry out if he could the plan that he had already made, if he should find himself in just such a desperate position. He had at length recognised the wisdom of Elfhelm, and understood that though his men might fight on till all were slain, and would if he ordered it, such valour would not help Erkenbrand: any man that could break out and escape southwards would be more useful, though he might seem inglorious.

The night had been overcast and dark, but now the waxing moon began to glimmer through drifting cloud. A wind was moving from the East: the forerunner of the great storm that when day came would pass over Rohan and burst over Helm's Deep the next night. Grimbold was aware suddenly that most of the torches had been extinguished and the fury of the assault had abated.[12] He therefore at once mounted those riders for whom horses were available, not many more than half an *éored*, and placed them under the command of Dúnhere.[13] The shieldwall was opened on the east side and the Riders passed through, driving back their assailants on that side;

then dividing and wheeling round they charged the enemy to the north and south of the camp. The sudden manoeuvre was for a space successful. The enemy was confused and dismayed; many thought at first that a large force of Riders had come from the east. Grimbold himself remained on foot with a rearguard of picked men, already chosen, and covered for the moment by these and the Riders under Dúnhere the remainder retreated with what speed they could. But Saruman's commander soon perceived that the shieldwall was broken and the defenders in flight. Fortunately the moon was overtaken by cloud and all was dark again, and he was in haste. He did not allow his troops to press the pursuit of the fugitives far into the darkness, now that the Fords were captured. He gathered his force as best he could and made for the road southward. So it was that the greater part of Grimbold's men survived. They were scattered in the night, but, as he had ordered, they made their ways away from the Road, east of the great turn where it bent west towards the Isen. They were relieved but amazed to encounter no enemies, not knowing that a large army had already some hours before passed southward and that Isengard was now guarded by little but its own strength of wall and gate.[14]

It was for this reason that no help had come from Elfhelm. More than half of Saruman's force had actually been sent down east of Isen. They came on more slowly than the western division, for the land was rougher and without roads; and they bore no lights. But before them, swift and silent, went several troops of the dreaded wolfriders. Before Elfhelm had any warning of the approach of enemies on his side of the river the wolfriders were between him and Grimbold's camp; and they were also attempting to surround each of his small groups of Riders. It was dark and all his force was in disarray. He gathered all that he could into a close body of horsemen, but he was obliged to retreat eastward. He could not reach Grimbold, though he knew that he was in straits and had been about to come to his aid when attacked by the wolfriders. But he also guessed rightly that the wolfriders were only the forerunners of a force far too great for him to oppose that would make for the southward road. The night was wearing away; he could only await the dawn.

What followed is less clear, since only Gandalf had full knowledge of it. He received news of the disaster only in the late afternoon of March the 3rd.[15] The King was then at a point not far east of the junction of the Road with the branch going to the Hornburg. From there it was about ninety miles in a direct line to Isengard; and

Gandalf must have ridden there with the greatest speed that Shadow-fax could command. He reached Isengard in the early darkness,[16] and left again in no more than twenty minutes. Both on the outward journey, when his direct route would take him close to the Fords, and on his return south to find Erkenbrand, he must have met Grimbold and Elfhelm. They were convinced that he was acting for the King, not only by his appearance on Shadowfax, but also by his knowledge of the name of the errand-rider, Ceorl, and the message that he brought; and they took as orders the advice that he gave.[17] Grimbold's men he sent southward to join Erkenbrand . . .

NOTES

1 Éomer was the son of Théoden's sister Théodwyn, and of Éomund of Eastfold, chief Marshal of the Mark. Éomund was slain by Orcs in 3002, and Théodwyn died soon after; their children Éomer and Éowyn were then taken to live in King Théoden's house, together with Théodred, the King's only child. (*The Lord of the Rings*, Appendix A (II).)

2 The Ents are here left out of account, as they were by all save Gandalf. But unless Gandalf could have brought about the rising of the Ents several days earlier (as from the narrative was plainly not possible), it would not have saved Rohan. The Ents might have destroyed Isengard, and even captured Saruman (if after victory he had not himself followed his army). The Ents and Huorns, with the aid of such Riders of the East-mark as had not yet been engaged, might have destroyed the forces of Saruman in Rohan, but the Mark would have been in ruins, and leaderless. Even if the Red Arrow had found any one with authority to receive it, the call from Gondor would not have been heeded – or at most a few companies of weary men would have reached Minas Tirith, too late except to perish with it. [Author's note.] – For the Red Arrow see *The Return of the King* I 3, where it was brought to Théoden by an errand-rider from Gondor as a token of the need of Minas Tirith.

3 The first battle of the Fords of Isen, in which Théodred was slain, was fought on the 25th of February; Gandalf reached Edoras seven days later, on the 2nd of March. (*The Lord of the Rings*, Appendix B, year 3019.) See note 7.

4 Beyond the Gap the land between Isen and Adorn was nominally part of the realm of Rohan; but though Folcwine had reclaimed it, driving out the Dunlendings that had occupied it, the people that remained were largely of mixed blood, and their loyalty to Edoras was weak: the slaying of their lord, Freca, by King Helm was still

remembered. Indeed at this time they were more disposed to side with Saruman, and many of their warriors had joined Saruman's forces. In any case there was no way into their land from the west except for bold swimmers. [Author's note.] – The region between Isen and Adorn was declared to be a part of the realm of Eorl at the time of the Oath of Cirion and Eorl: see p. 305.

In the year 2754 Helm Hammerhand, King of the Mark, slew with his fist his arrogant vassal Freca, lord of lands on either side of the Adorn; see *The Lord of the Rings*, Appendix A (II).

5 They were very swift and skilled in avoiding ordered men in close array, being used mostly to destroy isolated groups or to hunt down fugitives; but at need they would pass with reckless ferocity through any gaps in companies of horsemen, slashing at the bellies of the horses. [Author's note.]

6 The Deeping: this is so written and is clearly correct, since it occurs again later. My father noted elsewhere that the Deeping-coomb (and Deeping-stream) should be so spelt, rather than Deeping Coomb, 'since *Deeping* is not a verbal ending but one indicating relationship: the coomb or deep valley belonging to the *Deep* (*Helm's Deep*) to which it led up'. (Notes on Nomenclature to assist translators, published in *A Tolkien Compass*, edited by Jared Lobdell, 1975, page 181.)

7 The messages did not reach Edoras until about noon on February the 27th. Gandalf came there early in the morning of March the 2nd (February had thirty days!): it was thus, as Gríma said, not then fully five days since news of Théodred's death had reached the King. [Author's note.] – The reference is to *The Two Towers*, III 6.

8 It is told that he set up on stakes all about the eyot the heads of the axemen that had been slain there, but above the hasty mound of Théodred in the middle was set his banner. 'That will be defence enough,' he said. [Author's note.]

9 This, it is said, was Grimbold's resolve. Elfhelm would not desert him, but had he himself been in command, he would have abandoned the Fords under cover of night and withdrawn southwards to meet Erkenbrand and swell the forces still available for the defence of the Deeping-coomb and the Hornburg. [Author's note.]

10 This was the great host that Meriadoc saw leaving Isengard, as he related afterwards to Aragorn, Legolas and Gimli (*The Two Towers* III 9): 'I saw the enemy go: endless lines of marching Orcs; and troops of them mounted on great wolves. And there were battalions of Men, too. Many of them carried torches, and in the flare I could see their faces. . . . They took an hour to pass out of the gates. Some went off down the highway to the Fords, and some turned away and went eastward. A bridge has been built down there, about a mile away, where the river runs in a very deep channel.'

11   They were without body-armour, having only among them a few
     hauberks gained by theft or in loot. The Rohirrim had the advantage
     in being supplied by the metal-workers of Gondor. In Isengard as
     yet only the heavy and clumsy mail of the Orcs was made, by them
     for their own uses. [Author's note.]

12   It seems that Grimbold's valiant defence had not been altogether
     unavailing. It had been unexpected, and Saruman's commander was
     late: he had been delayed for some hours, whereas it was intended
     that he should sweep over the Fords, scatter the weak defences, and
     without waiting to pursue them hasten to the road and proceed then
     south to join in the assault on the Deeping. He was now in doubt.
     He awaited, maybe, some signal from the other army that had been
     sent down the east side of the Isen. [Author's note.]

13   A valiant captain, nephew of Erkenbrand. By courage and skill in
     arms he survived the disaster of the Fords, but fell in the Battle of
     the Pelennor, to the great grief of Westfold. [Author's note.] –
     Dúnhere was Lord of Harrowdale (*The Return of the King* V 3).

14   This sentence is not very clear, but in view of what follows it seems
     to refer to that part of the great army out of Isengard that came down
     the east side of the Isen.

15   The news was brought by the Rider named Ceorl, who returning
     from the Fords fell in with Gandalf, Théoden and Éomer as they
     rode west with reinforcements from Edoras: *The Two Towers* III 7.

16   As the narrative suggests, Gandalf must already have made contact
     with Treebeard, and knew that the patience of the Ents was at an
     end; and he had also read the meaning of Legolas' words (*The Two
     Towers* III 7, at the beginning of the chapter): Isengard was veiled
     in an impenetrable shadow, the Ents had already surrounded it.
     [Author's note.]

17   When Gandalf came with Théoden and Éomer to the Fords of Isen
     after the Battle of the Hornburg he explained to them: 'Some men
     I sent with Grimbold of Westfold to join Erkenbrand. Some I set
     to make this burial. They have now followed your marshal, Elfhelm.
     I sent him with many Riders to Edoras.' (*The Two Towers* III 8.)
     The present text ends in the middle of the next sentence.

APPENDIX

(i)

In writing associated with the present text some further particulars are
given concerning the Marshals of the Mark in the year 3019 and after
the end of the War of the Ring:

Marshal of the Mark (or Riddermark) was the highest military rank and the title of the King's lieutenants (originally three), commanders of the royal forces of fully equipped and trained Riders. The First Marshal's ward was the capital, Edoras, and the adjacent King's Lands (including Harrowdale). He commanded the Riders of the Muster of Edoras, drawn from this ward, and from some parts of the West-mark and East-mark* for which Edoras was the most convenient place of assembly. The Second and Third Marshals were assigned commands according to the needs of the time. In the beginning of the year 3019 the threat from Saruman was the most urgent, and the Second Marshal, the King's son Théodred, had command over the West-mark with his base at Helm's Deep; the Third Marshal, the King's nephew Éomer, had as his ward the East-mark with his base at his home, Aldburg in the Folde.†

In the days of Théoden there was no man appointed to the office of First Marshal. He came to the throne as a young man (at the age of thirty-two), vigorous and of martial spirit, and a great horseman. If war came, he would himself command the Muster of Edoras; but his kingdom was at peace for many years, and he rode with his knights and his Muster only on exercises and in displays; though the shadow of Mordor reawakened grew ever greater from his childhood to his old age. In this peace the Riders and other armed men of the garrison of Edoras were governed by an officer of the rank of marshal (in the years 3012–19 this was Elfhelm). When Théoden became, as it seemed, prematurely old, this situation continued, and there was no effective central command: a state of affairs encouraged by his counsellor Gríma. The King, becoming decrepit and seldom leaving his house, fell into the habit of issuing orders to Háma, Captain of his Household, to Elfhelm, and even to the Marshals of the Mark, by the mouth of Gríma Wormtongue. This was resented, but the orders were obeyed, within Edoras. As far as fighting was concerned, when the war with Saruman began Théodred without orders assumed general command. He summoned a muster of Edoras, and drew away a large part of its Riders, under Elfhelm, to strengthen the Muster of Westfold and help it to resist the invasion.

In times of war or unquiet each Marshal of the Mark had under his immediate orders, as part of his 'household' (that is, quartered under arms at his residence) an *éored* ready for battle which he could use in

* These were terms only used with reference to military organisation. Their boundary was the Snowbourn River to its junction with the Entwash, and thence north along the Entwash. [Author's note.]

† Here Eorl had his house; it passed after Brego son of Eorl removed to Edoras into the hands of Eofor, third son of Brego, from whom Éomund, father of Éomer, claimed descent. The Folde was part of the King's Lands, but Aldburg remained the most convenient base for the Muster of the East-mark. [Author's note.]

an emergency at his own discretion. This was what Éomer had in fact done;* but the charge against him, urged by Gríma, was that the King had in this case forbidden him to take any of the still uncommitted forces of the East-mark from Edoras, which was insufficiently defended; that he knew of the disaster at the Fords of Isen and the death of Théodred before he pursued the Orcs into the remote Wold; and that he had also against general orders allowed strangers to go free, and had even lent them horses.

After the fall of Théodred command in the West-mark (again without orders from Edoras) was assumed by Erkenbrand, Lord of Deeping-coomb and of much other land in Westfold. He had in youth been, as most lords, an officer in the King's Riders, but he was so no longer. He was, however, the chief lord in the West-mark, and since its people were in peril it was his right and duty to gather all those among them able to bear arms to resist invasion. He thus took command also of the Riders of the Western Muster; but Elfhelm remained in independent command of the Riders of the Muster of Edoras that Théodred had summoned to his assistance.

After the healing of Théoden by Gandalf, the situation changed. The King again took command in person. Éomer was reinstated, and became virtually First Marshal, ready to take command if the King fell or his strength failed; but the title was not used, and in the presence of the King in arms he could only advise and not issue orders. The part he actually played was thus much the same as that of Aragorn: a redoubtable champion among the companions of the King.†

When the Full Muster was made in Harrowdale, and the 'line of journey' and order of battle considered and as far as possible determined,‡ Éomer remained in this position, riding with the King (as commander of the leading *éored*, the King's Company) and acting as his chief counsellor. Elfhelm became a Marshal of the Mark, leading the first *éored* of the Muster of the East-mark. Grimbold (not previously mentioned in the narrative) had the function, but not the title, of the

---

* I.e., when Éomer pursued the Orcs, captors of Meriadoc and Peregrin, who had come down into Rohan from the Emyn Muil. The words that Éomer used to Aragorn were: 'I led forth my *éored*, men of my own household' (*The Two Towers* III 2).

† Those who did not know of the events at court naturally assumed that the reinforcements sent west were under Éomer's command as the only remaining Marshal of the Mark. [Author's note.] – The reference here is to the words of Ceorl, the Rider who met the reinforcements coming from Edoras and told them what had happened in the Second Battle of the Fords of Isen (*The Two Towers* III 7).

‡ Théoden called a council of 'the marshals and captains' at once, and before he took a meal; but it is not described, since Meriadoc was not present ('I wonder what they are all talking about.'). [Author's note.] – The reference is to *The Return of the King* V 3.

Third Marshal, and commanded the Muster of the Westmark.* Grimbold fell in the Battle of the Pelennor Fields, and Elfhelm became the lieutenant of Éomer as King; he was left in command of all the Rohirrim in Gondor when Éomer went to the Black Gate, and he routed the hostile army that had invaded Anórien (*The Return of the King* V, end of chapter 9 and beginning of 10). He is named as one of the chief witnesses of Aragorn's coronation (*ibid.* VI 5).

It is recorded that after Théoden's funeral, when Éomer reordered his realm, Erkenbrand was made Marshal of the West-mark, and Elfhelm Marshal of the East-mark, and these titles were maintained, instead of Second and Third Marshal, neither having precedence over the other. In time of war a special appointment was made to the office of Underking: its holder either ruled the realm in the King's absence with the army, or took command in the field if for any reason the King remained at home. In peace the office was only filled when the King because of sickness or old age deputed his authority; the holder was then naturally the Heir to the throne, if he was a man of sufficient age. But in war the Council was unwilling that an old King should send his Heir to battle beyond the realm, unless he had at least one other son.

(ii)

A long note to the text (at the place where the differing views of the commanders on the importance of the Fords of Isen is discussed, pages 360-1) is given here. The first part of it largely repeats history that is given elsewhere in this book, but I have thought it best to give it in full.

In ancient days the southern and eastern bounds of the North Kingdom had been the Greyflood; the western bounds of the South Kingdom was the Isen. To the land between (the Enedwaith or 'middle region') few Númenóreans had ever come, and none had settled there. In the days of the Kings it was part of the realm of Gondor,† but it was of little concern to them, except for the patrolling and upkeep of the great Royal Road. This went all the way from Osgiliath and Minas Tirith to Fornost in the far North, crossed the Fords of Isen and

* Grimbold was a lesser marshal of the Riders of West-mark in Théodred's command, and was given this position, as a man of valour in both the battles at the Fords, because Erkenbrand was an older man, and the King felt the need of one of dignity and authority to leave behind in command of such forces as could be spared for the defence of Rohan. [Author's note.] – Grimbold is not mentioned in the narrative of *The Lord of the Rings* until the final ordering of the Rohirrim before Minas Tirith (*The Return of the King*, V 5).

† The statement that Enedwaith was in the days of the Kings part of the realm of Gondor seems to conflict with that immediately preceding, that 'the western bounds of the South Kingdom was the Isen'. Elsewhere (see p. 264) it is said that Enedwaith 'belonged to neither kingdom'.

passed through Enedwaith, keeping to the higher land in the centre and north-east until it had to descend to the west lands about the lower Greyflood, which it crossed on a raised causeway leading to a great bridge at Tharbad. In those days the region was little peopled. In the marshlands of the mouths of Greyflood and Isen lived a few tribes of 'Wild Men', fishers and fowlers, but akin in race and speech to the Drúedain of the woods of Anórien.* In the foothills of the western side of the Misty Mountains lived the remnants of the people that the Rohirrim later called the Dunlendings: a sullen folk, akin to the ancient inhabitants of the White Mountain valleys whom Isildur cursed.† They had little love of Gondor, but though hardy and bold enough were too few and too much in awe of the might of the Kings to trouble them, or to turn their eyes away from the East, whence all their chief perils came. The Dunlendings suffered, like all the peoples of Arnor and Gondor, in the Great Plague of the years 1636–7 of the Third Age, but less than most, since they dwelt apart and had few dealings with other men. When the days of the Kings ended (1975–2050) and the waning of Gondor began, they ceased in fact to be subjects of Gondor; the Royal Road was unkept in Enedwaith, and the Bridge of Tharbad becoming ruinous was replaced only by a dangerous ford. The bounds of Gondor were the Isen, and the Gap of Calenardhon (as it was then called). The Gap was watched by the fortresses of Aglarond (the Hornburg) and Angrenost (Isengard), and the Fords of Isen, the only easy entrance to Gondor, were ever guarded against any incursion from the 'Wild Lands'.

But during the Watchful Peace (from 2063 to 2460) the people of Calenardhon dwindled: the more vigorous, year by year, went eastward to hold the line of the Anduin; those that remained became rustic and far removed from the concerns of Minas Tirith. The garrisons of the forts were not renewed, and were left to the care of local hereditary

---

* Cf. p. 262, where it is said that 'a fairly numerous but barbarous fisher-folk dwelt between the mouths of the Gwathló and the Angren (Isen)'. No mention is made there of any connection between these people and the Drúedain, though the latter are said to have dwelt (and to have survived there into the Third Age) in the promontory of Andrast, south of the mouths of Isen (p. 384 and note 13).

† Cf. *The Lord of the Rings* Appendix F (Of Men): 'The Dunlendings were a remnant of the peoples that had dwelt in the vales of the White Mountains in ages past. The Dead Men of Dunharrow were of their kin. But in the Dark Years others had removed to the southern dales of the Misty Mountains, and thence some had passed into the empty lands as far north as the Barrow-downs. From them came the Men of Bree; but long before these had become subjects of the North Kingdom of Arnor and had taken. up the Westron tongue. Only in Dunland did Men of this race hold to their old speech and manners: a secret folk, unfriendly to the Dúnedain, hating the Rohirrim.'

chieftains whose subjects were of more and more mixed blood. For the Dunlendings drifted steadily and unchecked over the Isen. Thus it was, when the attacks on Gondor from the East were renewed, and Orcs and Easterlings overran Calenardhon and besieged the forts, which would not have long held out. Then the Rohirrim came, and after the victory of Eorl on the Field of Celebrant in the year 2510 his numerous and warlike people with great wealth of horses swept into Calenardhon, driving out or destroying the eastern invaders. Cirion the Steward gave them possession of Calenardhon, which was thenceforth called the Riddermark, or in Gondor Rochand (later Rohan). The Rohirrim at once began the settlement of this region, though during the reign of Eorl their eastern bounds along the Emyn Muil and Anduin were still under attack. But under Brego and Aldor the Dunlendings were rooted out again and driven away beyond the Isen, and the Fords of Isen were guarded. Thus the Rohirrim earned the hatred of the Dunlendings, which was not appeased until the return of the King, then far off in the future. Whenever the Rohirrim were weak or in trouble the Dunlendings renewed their attacks.

No alliance of peoples was ever more faithfully kept on both sides than the alliance of Gondor and Rohan under the Oath of Cirion and Eorl; nor were any guardians of the wide grassy plains of Rohan more suited to their land than the Riders of the Mark. Nonetheless there was a grave weakness in their situation, as was most clearly shown in the days of the War of the Ring when it came near to causing the ruin of Rohan and of Gondor. This was due to many things. Above all, the eyes of Gondor had ever been eastward, whence all their perils came; the enmity of the 'wild' Dunlendings seemed of small account to the Stewards. Another point was that the Stewards retained under their own rule the Tower of Orthanc and the Ring of Isengard (Angrenost); the keys of Orthanc were taken to Minas Tirith, the Tower was shut, and the Ring of Isengard remained manned only by an hereditary Gondorian chieftain and his small people, to whom were joined the old hereditary guards of Aglarond. The fortress there was repaired with the aid of masons of Gondor and then committed to the Rohirrim.* From it the guards of the Fords were supplied. For the most part their settled dwellings were about the feet of the White Mountains and in the glens and valleys of the south. To the northern bounds of the Westfold they went seldom and only at need, regarding the eaves of Fangorn (the Entwood) and the frowning walls of Isengard with dread. They meddled little with the 'Lord of Isengard' and his secret folk, whom they believed to be dealers in dark magic. And to

---

* By whom it was called *Glǽmscrafu*, but the fortress Súthburg, and after King Helm's day the Hornburg. [Author's note.] – *Glǽmscrafu* (in which the *sc* is pronounced as *sh*) is Anglo-Saxon, 'caves of radiance', with the same meaning as *Aglarond*.

Isengard the emissaries from Minas Tirith came ever more seldom, until they ceased; it seemed that amidst their cares the Stewards had forgotten the Tower, though they held the keys.

Yet the western frontier and the line of the Isen was naturally commanded by Isengard, and this had evidently been well understood by the Kings of Gondor. The Isen flowed down from its sources along the eastern wall of the Ring, and as it went on southwards it was still a young river that offered no great obstacle to invaders, though its waters were still very swift and strangely cold. But the Great Gate of Angrenost opened west of Isen, and if the fortress were well manned enemies from the westlands must be in great strength if they thought to pass on into Westfold. Moreover Angrenost was less than half the distance of Aglarond from the Fords, to which a wide horseroad ran from the Gates, for most of the way over level ground. The dread that haunted the great Tower, and fear of the glooms of Fangorn that lay behind, might protect it for a while, but if it were unmanned and neglected, as it was in the latter days of the Stewards, that protection would not long avail.

So it proved. In the reign of King Déor (2699 to 2718) the Rohirrim found that to keep a watch on the Fords was not enough. Since neither Rohan nor Gondor gave heed to this far corner of the realm, it was not known until later what had happened there. The line of the Gondorian chieftains of Angrenost had failed, and the command of the fortress passed into the hands of a family of the people. These, as has been said, were already long before of mixed blood, and they were now more friendly disposed to the Dunlendings than to the 'wild Northmen' who had usurped the land; with Minas Tirith far away they no longer had any concern. After the death of King Aldor, who had driven out the last of the Dunlendings and even raided their lands in Enedwaith by way of reprisal, the Dunlendings unmarked by Rohan but with the connivance of Isengard began to filter into northern Westfold again, making settlements in the mountain glens west and east of Isengard and even in the southern eaves of Fangorn. In the reign of Déor they became openly hostile, raiding the herds and studs of the Rohirrim in Westfold. It was soon clear to the Rohirrim that these raiders had not crossed the Isen either by the Fords or at any point far south of Isengard, for the Fords were guarded.* Déor therefore led an expedition northwards, and was met by a host of Dunlendings. These he overcame; but he was dismayed to find that Isengard was also hostile. Thinking that he had relieved Isengard of a Dunlendish siege, he sent messengers to its Gates with words of good will, but the Gates were shut upon them and the only answer they got was by bowshot. As was later known,

---

* Attacks were often made on the garrison of the west bank, but these were not pressed: they were in fact only made to distract the attention of the Rohirrim from the north. [Author's note.]

the Dunlendings, having been admitted as friends, had seized the Ring of Isengard, slaying the few survivors of its ancient guards who were not (as were most) willing to merge with the Dunlendish folk. Déor sent word at once to the Steward in Minas Tirith (at that time, in the year 2710, Egalmoth), but he was unable to send help, and the Dunlendings remained in occupation of Isengard until, reduced by the great famine after the Long Winter (2758–9) they were starved out and capitulated to Fréaláf (afterwards first King of the Second Line). But Déor had no power to storm or besiege Isengard, and for many years the Rohirrim had to keep a strong force of Riders in the north of Westfold; this was maintained until the great invasions of 2758.*

It can thus be readily understood that when Saruman offered to take command of Isengard and repair it and reorder it as part of the defences of the West he was welcomed both by King Fréaláf and by Beren the Steward. So when Saruman took up his abode in Isengard, and Beren gave to him the keys of Orthanc, the Rohirrim returned to their policy of guarding the Fords of Isen, as the most vulnerable point in their western frontier.

There can be little doubt that Saruman made his offer in good faith, or at least with good will towards the defence of the West, so long as he himself remained the chief person in that defence, and the head of its council. He was wise, and perceived clearly that Isengard with its position and its great strength, natural and by craft, was of utmost importance. The line of the Isen, between the pincers of Isengard and the Hornburg, was a bulwark against invasion from the East (whether incited and guided by Sauron, or otherwise), either aiming at encircling Gondor or at invading Eriador. But in the end he turned to evil and became an enemy; and yet the Rohirrim, though they had warnings of his growing malice towards them, continued to put their main strength in the west at the Fords, until Saruman in open war showed them that the Fords were small protection without Isengard and still less against it.

* An account of these invasions of Gondor and Rohan is given in *The Lord of the Rings* Appendix A (I, iv and II).

PART FOUR

I

THE DRÚEDAIN

The Folk of Haleth were strangers to the other Atani, speaking an alien language; and though united with them in alliance with the Eldar, they remained a people apart. Among themselves they adhered to their own language, and though of necessity they learned Sindarin for communication with the Eldar and the other Atani, many spoke it haltingly, and some of those who seldom went beyond the borders of their own woods did not use it at all. They did not willingly adopt new things or customs, and retained many practices that seemed strange to the Eldar and the other Atani, with whom they had few dealings except in war. Nonetheless they were esteemed as loyal allies and redoubtable warriors, though the companies that they sent to battle beyond their borders were small. For they were and remained to their end a small people, chiefly concerned to protect their own woodlands, and they excelled in forest warfare. Indeed for long even those Orcs specially trained for this dared not set foot near their borders. One of the strange practices spoken of was that many of their warriors were women, though few of these went abroad to fight in the great battles. This custom was evidently ancient;[1] for their chieftainess Haleth was a renowned Amazon with a picked bodyguard of women.[2]

The strangest of all the customs of the Folk of Haleth was the presence among them of people of a wholly different kind,[3] the like of which neither the Eldar in Beleriand nor the other Atani had ever seen before. They were not many, a few hundreds maybe, living apart in families or small tribes, but in friendship, as members of the same community.[4] The Folk of Haleth called them by the name *drûg*, that being a word of their own language. To the eyes of Elves and other Men they were unlovely in looks: they were stumpy (some four foot high) but very broad, with heavy buttocks and short thick legs; their wide faces had deep-set eyes with heavy brows, and flat noses, and grew no hair below their eyebrows, except in a few men (who were proud of the distinction) a small tail of black hair in the midst of the chin. Their features were usually impassive, the most mobile being their wide mouths; and the movement of their wary eyes could not be observed save from close at hand, for they were so black that the pupils could not be distinguished, but in anger they glowed red. Their voices were deep and guttural, but their laughter was a surprise: it was rich and rolling, and set all who heard it, Elves or Men, laughing too for its pure merriment untainted by scorn or malice.[5] In peace they often laughed at work or play when other Men might sing. But they could be relentless enemies, and when once aroused their red wrath was slow to cool, though it showed no sign save the light in their eyes; for they fought in silence and did not exult in victory, not even over Orcs, the only creatures for whom their hatred was implacable.

The Eldar called them Drúedain, admitting them to the rank of Atani,[6] for they were much loved while they lasted. Alas! they were not long-lived, and were ever few in number, and their losses were heavy in their feud with the Orcs, who returned their hatred and delighted to capture them and torture them. When the victories of Morgoth destroyed all the realms and strongholds of Elves and Men in Beleriand, it is said that they had dwindled to a few families, mostly of women and children, some of whom came to the last refuges at the Mouths of Sirion.[7]

In their earlier days they had been of great service to those among whom they dwelt, and they were much sought after; though few would ever leave the land of the Folk of Haleth.[8] They had a marvellous skill as trackers of all living creatures, and they taught to their friends what they could of their craft; but their pupils did not equal them, for the Drúedain used their scent, like hounds save that they were also keen-eyed. They boasted that they could smell an Orc to windward further away than other Men could see them, and could follow its scent for weeks except through running water. Their knowledge of all growing things was almost equal to that of the Elves (though untaught by them); and it is said that if they removed to a new country they knew within a short time all things that grew there, great or minute, and gave names to those that were new to them, discerning those that were poisonous, or useful as food.[9]

The Drúedain, as also the other Atani, had no form of writing until they met the Eldar; but the runes and scripts of the Eldar were never learned by them. They came no nearer to writing by their own invention than the use of a number of signs, for the most part simple, for the marking of trails or the giving of information and warning. In the far distant past they appear already to have had small tools of flint for scraping and cutting, and these they still used, although the Atani had a knowledge of metals and some smith-craft before they came to Beleriand,[10] for metals were hard to come by and forged weapons and tools very costly. But when in Beleriand by association with the Eldar and in traffic with the Dwarves of Ered Lindon these things became more common, the Drúedain showed great talent for carving in wood or stone. They already had a know-ledge of pigments, derived chiefly from plants, and they drew pictures and patterns on wood or flat surfaces of stone; and sometimes they would scrape knobs of wood into faces that could be painted. But with sharper and stronger tools they delighted in carving figures of men and beasts, whether toys and ornaments or large images, to which the most skilled among them could give vivid semblance of life. Sometimes these images were strange and fantastic, or even fearful: among the grim jests to which they put their skill was the making of Orc-figures which they set at the borders of the land, shaped as if fleeing from it, shrieking in terror. They made also images of themselves and placed them at the entrances to tracks or at turnings of woodland paths. These they called 'watch-stones'; of which the most notable were set near the Crossings of Teiglin, each representing a Drúadan, larger than the life, squatting heavily upon a dead Orc. These figures served not merely as insults to their enemies; for the Orcs feared them and believed them to be filled with the malice of the *Oghor-hai* (for so they named the Drúedain), and able to hold communication with them. Therefore they seldom dared to touch them, or to try to destroy them, and unless in great numbers would turn back at a 'watch-stone' and go no further.

But among the powers of this strange people perhaps most to be remarked was their capacity of utter silence and stillness, which they could at times endure for many days on end, sitting with their legs crossed, their hands upon their knees or in their laps, and their eyes closed or looking at the ground. Concerning this a tale was related among the Folk of Haleth:

On a time, one of the most skilled in stone-carving among the Drûgs made an image of his father, who had died; and he set it up by a pathway near to their dwelling. Then he sat down beside it and passed into a deep silence of recollection. It chanced that not long after a forester came by on a journey to a distant village, and seeing two Drûgs he bowed and wished them good day. But he received no answer, and he stood for some time in surprise, looking closely at them. Then he went on his way, saying to himself: 'Great skill have they in stone-work, but I have never seen any more lifelike.' Three days later he returned, and being very weary he sat down and propped his back against one of the figures. His cloak he cast about its shoulders to dry, for it had been raining, but the sun was now shining hot. There he fell asleep; but after a while he was wakened by a voice from the figure behind him. 'I hope you are rested,' it said, 'but if you wish for more sleep, I beg you to move to the other one. He will never need to stretch his legs again; and I find your cloak too hot in the sun.'

It is said that the Drúedain would often sit thus in times of grief or loss, but sometimes for pleasure in thought, or in the making of plans. But they could also use this stillness when on guard; and then they would sit or stand, hidden in shadow, and though their eyes might seem closed or staring with a blank gaze nothing passed or came near that was not marked and remembered. So intense was their unseen vigilance that it could be felt as a hostile menace by intruders, who retreated in fear before any warning was given; but if any evil thing passed on, then they would utter as a signal a shrill whistle, painful to endure close at hand and heard far off. The service of the Drúedain as guards was much esteemed by the Folk of Haleth in times of peril; and if such guards were not to be had they would have figures carved in their likeness to set near their houses, believing that (being made by the Drúedain themselves for the purpose) they would hold some of the menace of the living men.

Indeed, though they held the Drúedain in love and trust, many of the Folk of Haleth believed that they possessed uncanny and magical powers; and among their tales of marvels there were several that told of such things. One of these is recorded here.

The Faithful Stone

On a time there was a Drûg named Aghan, well-known as a leech. He had a great friendship with Barach, a forester of the Folk, who lived in a house in the woods two miles or more from the nearest village. The dwellings of Aghan's family were nearer, and he spent most of his time with Barach and his wife, and was much loved by their children. There came a time of trouble, for a number of daring Orcs had secretly entered the woods nearby, and were scattered in twos and threes, waylaying any that went abroad alone, and at night attacking houses far from neighbours. The household of Barach were not much afraid, for Aghan stayed with them at night and kept watch outside. But one morning he came to Barach

and said: 'Friend, I have ill news from my kin, and I fear I must
leave you a while. My brother has been wounded, and he lies now
in pain and calls for me, since I have skill in treating Orc-wounds.
I will return as soon as I may.' Barach was greatly troubled, and
his wife and children wept, but Aghan said: 'I will do what I can.
I have had a watch-stone brought here and set near your house.'
Barach went out with Aghan and looked at the watch-stone. It was
large and heavy and sat under some bushes not far from his doors.
Aghan laid his hand upon it, and after a silence said: 'See, I have
left with it some of my powers. May it keep you from harm!'

Nothing untoward happened for two nights, but on the third
night Barach heard the shrill warning call of the Drûgs – or
dreamed that he heard it, for it roused no one else. Leaving his
bed he took his bow from the wall and went to a narrow window;
and he saw two Orcs setting fuel against his house and preparing
to kindle it. Then Barach was shaken with fear, for marauding
Orcs carried with them brimstone or some other devilish stuff that
was quickly inflamed and not quenched with water. Recovering
himself he bent his bow, but at that moment, just as the flames
leapt up, he saw a Drûg come running up behind the Orcs. One
he felled with a blow of his fist, and the other fled; then he plunged
barefoot into the fire, scattering the burning fuel and stamping on
the Orc-flames that ran along the ground. Barach made for the
doors, but when he had unbarred them and sprang out the Drûg
had disappeared. There was no sign of the smitten Orc. The fire
was dead, and there remained only a smoke and a stench.

Barach went back indoors to comfort his family, who had been
roused by the noises and the burning reek; but when it was daylight he went out again and looked about. He found that the watch-
stone had gone, but he kept that to himself. 'Tonight I must be
the watchman,' he thought; but later in the day Aghan came back,
and was welcomed with joy. He was wearing high buskins such
as the Drûgs sometimes wore in hard country, among thorns or
rocks, and he was weary. But he was smiling, and seemed pleased;
and he said: 'I bring good news. My brother is no longer in pain
and will not die, for I came in time to withstand the venom. And
now I learn that the marauders have been slain, or else fled. How
have you fared?'

'We are still alive,' said Barach. 'But come with me, and I will
show you and tell you more.' Then he led Aghan to the place of
the fire and told him of the attack in the night. 'The watch-stone
has gone – Orc-work, I guess. What have you to say to that?'

'I will speak, when I have looked and thought longer,' said Aghan; and then he went hither and thither scanning the ground, and Barach followed him. At length Aghan led him to a thicket at the edge of the clearing in which the house stood. There the watch-stone was, sitting on a dead Orc; but its legs were all blackened and cracked, and one of its feet had split off and lay loose at its side. Aghan looked grieved; but he said: 'Ah well! He did what he could. And better that his legs should trample Orc-fire than mine.'

Then he sat down and unlaced his buskins, and Barach saw that under them there were bandages on his legs. Aghan undid them. 'They are healing already,' he said. 'I had kept vigil by my brother for two nights, and last night I slept. I woke before morning came, and I was in pain, and found my legs blistered. Then I guessed what had happened. Alas! If some power passes from you to a thing that you have made, then you must take a share in its hurts.'[11]

Further notes on the Drúedain

My father was at pains to emphasize the radical difference between the Drúedain and the Hobbits. They were of quite different physical shape and appearance. The Drúedain were taller, and of heavier and stronger build. Their facial features were unlovely (judged by general human standards); and while the head-hair of the Hobbits was abundant (but close and curly) the Drúedain had only sparse and lank hair on their heads and none at all on their legs and feet. They were at times merry and gay, like Hobbits, but they had a grimmer side to their nature and could be sardonic and ruthless; and they had, or were credited with, strange or magical powers. They were moreover a frugal people, eating sparingly even in times of plenty and drinking nothing but water. In some ways they resembled rather the Dwarves: in build and stature and endurance; in their skill in carving stone; in the grim side of their character; and in their strange powers. But the 'magic' skills with which the Dwarves were credited were quite different; and the Dwarves were far grimmer, and also long-lived, whereas the Drúedain were short-lived compared with other kinds of Men.

Only once, in an isolated note, is anything said explicitly concerning the relationship between the Drúedain of Beleriand in the First Age, who guarded the houses of the Folk of Haleth in the Forest of Brethil, and the remote ancestors of Ghân-buri-Ghân, who guided the Rohirrim down the Stonewain Valley on their way to Minas Tirith (*The Return of the King* V 5), or the makers of the images on the road to Dunharrow (*ibid.* V 3).[12] This note states:

An emigrant branch of the Drúedain accompanied the Folk of Haleth at the end of the First Age, and dwelt in the Forest [of Brethil] with them. But most of them had remained in the White Mountains, in spite of their persecution by later-arrived Men, who had relapsed into the service of the Dark.

It is also said here that the identity of the statues of Dunharrow with the remnants of the Drúath (perceived by Meriadoc Brandybuck when he first set eyes on Ghân-buri-Ghân) was originally recognized in Gondor, though at the time of the establishment of the Númenórean kingdom by Isildur they survived only in the Drúadan Forest and in the Drúwaith Iaur (see below).

We can thus if we wish elaborate the ancient legend of the coming of the Edain in *The Silmarillion* (pp. 140–3) by the addition of the Drúedain, descending out of Ered Lindon into Ossiriand with the Haladin (the Folk of Haleth). Another note says that historians in Gondor believed that the first Men to cross the Anduin were indeed the Drúedain. They came (it was believed) from lands south of Mordor, but before they reached the coasts of Haradwaith they turned north into Ithilien, and eventually finding a way across the Anduin (probably near Cair Andros) settled in the values of the White Mountains and the wooded lands at their northern feet. 'They were a secretive people, suspicious of other kinds of Men by whom they had been harried and persecuted as long as they could remember, and they had wandered west seeking a land where they could be hidden and have peace.' But nothing more is said, here or elsewhere, concerning the history of their association with the Folk of Haleth.

In an essay, cited previously, on the names of rivers in Middle-earth there is a glimpse of the Drúedain in the Second Age. It is said here (see p. 263) that the native people of Enedwaith, fleeing from the devastations of the Númenóreans along the course of the Gwathló,

did not cross the Isen nor take refuge in the great promontory between Isen and Lefnui that formed the north arm of the Bay of Belfalas, because of the 'Púkel-men', who were a secret and fell people, tireless and silent hunters, using poisoned darts. They said that they had always been there, and had formerly lived also in the White Mountains. In ages past they had paid no heed to the Great Dark One (Morgoth), nor did they later ally themselves with Sauron; for they hated all invaders from the East. From the East, they said, had come the tall Men who drove them from the White Mountains, and they were wicked at heart. Maybe even in the days of the War of the Ring some of the Drû-folk lingered in the mountains of Andrast, the western outlier of the White Mountains, but only the remnant in the woods of Anórien were known to the people of Gondor.

This region between Isen and Lefnui was the Drúwaith Iaur, and in yet another scrap of writing on this subject it is stated that the word *Iaur* 'old' in this name does not mean 'original' but 'former':

The 'Púkel-men' occupied the White Mountains (on both sides) in the First Age. When the occupation of the coastlands by the Númenóreans began in the Second Age they survived in the mountains of the promontory [of Andrast], which was never occupied by the Númenóreans. Another remnant survived at the eastern end of the range [in Anórien]. At the end of the Third Age the latter, much reduced in numbers, were believed to be the only survivors; hence the other region was called 'the Old Púkel-wilderness' (Drúwaith Iaur). It remained a 'wilderness' and was not inhabited by Men of Gondor or of Rohan, and was seldom entered by any of them; but Men of the Anfalas believed that some of the old 'Wild Men' still lived there secretly.[13]

But in Rohan the identity of the statues of Dunharrow called 'Púkel-men' with the 'Wild Men' of the Drúadan Forest was not recognized, neither was their 'humanity': hence the reference by Ghân-buri-Ghân to persecution of the 'Wild Men' by the Rohirrim in the past ['leave Wild Men alone in the woods and do not hunt them like beasts any more']. Since Ghân-buri-Ghân was attempting to use the Common Speech he called his people 'Wild Men' (not without irony); but this was not of course their own name for themselves.[14]

NOTES

1 Not due to their special situation in Beleriand, and maybe rather a cause of their small numbers than its result. They increased in numbers far more slowly than the other Atani, hardly more than was sufficient to replace the wastage of war; yet many of their women (who were fewer than the men) remained unwed. [Author's note.]

2 In *The Silmarillion* Bëor described the Haladin (afterwards called the People or Folk of Haleth) to Felagund as 'a people from whom we are sundered in speech' (p. 142). It is said also that 'they remained a people apart' (p. 146), and that they were of smaller stature than the men of the House of Bëor; 'they used few words, and did not love great concourse of men; and many among them delighted in solitude,

wandering free in the greenwoods while the wonder of the lands of the Eldar was new upon them' (p. 148). Nothing is said in *The Silmarillion* about the Amazonian element in their society, other than that the Lady Haleth was a warrior and the leader of the people, nor of their adherence to their own language in Beleriand.

3 Though they spoke the same language (after their fashion). They retained however a number of words of their own. [Author's note.]

4 After the fashion in which in the Third Age the Men and Hobbits of Bree lived together; though there was no kinship between the Drûg-folk and the Hobbits. [Author's note.]

5 To the unfriendly who, not knowing them well, declared that Morgoth must have bred the Orcs from such a stock the Eldar answered: 'Doubtless Morgoth, since he can make no living thing, bred Orcs from various kinds of Men, but the Drúedain must have escaped his Shadow; for their laughter and the laughter of Orcs are as different as is the light of Aman from the darkness of Angband.' But some thought, nonetheless, that there had been a remote kinship, which accounted for their special enmity. Orcs and Drûgs each regarded the other as renegades. [Author's note.] – In *The Silmarillion* the Orcs are said to have been bred by Melkor from captured Elves in the beginning of their days (p. 50; cf. pp. 93–4); but this was only one of several diverse speculations on the origin of the Orcs. It may be noted that in *The Return of the King* V 5 the laughter of Ghân-buri-Ghân is described: 'At that old Ghân made a curious gurgling noise, and it seemed that he was laughing.' He is described as having a scanty beard that 'straggled on his lumpy chin like dry moss', and dark eyes that showed nothing.

6 It is stated in isolated notes that their own name for themselves was *Drughu* (in which the *gh* represents a spirantal sound). This name adopted into Sindarin in Beleriand became *Drû* (plurals *Drúin* and *Drúath*); but when the Eldar discovered that the Drû-folk were steadfast enemies of Morgoth, and especially of the Orcs, the 'title' *adan* was added, and they were called *Drúedain* (singular *Drúadan*), to mark both their humanity and friendship with the Eldar, and their racial difference from the people of the Three Houses of the Edain. *Drû* was then only used in compounds such as *Drúnos* 'a family of the Drû-folk', *Drúwaith* 'the wilderness of the Drû-folk'. In Quenya *Drughu* became *Rú*, and *Rúatan*, plural *Rúatani*. For their other names in later times (Wild Men, Woses, Púkel-men) see p. 384 and note 14.

7 In the annals of Númenor it is said that this remnant was permitted to sail over sea with the Atani, and in the peace of the new land throve and increased again, but took no more part in war, for they dreaded the sea. What happened to them later is only recorded in one of the few legends that survived the Downfall, the story of the

first sailings of the Númenóreans back to Middle-earth, known as *The Mariner's Wife*. In a copy of this written and preserved in Gondor there is a note by the scribe on a passage in which the Drúedain in the household of King Aldarion the Mariner are mentioned: it relates that the Drúedain, who were ever noted for their strange foresight, were disturbed to hear of his voyages, foreboding that evil would come of them, and begged him to go no more. But they did not succeed, since neither his father nor his wife could prevail on him to change his courses, and the Drúedain departed in distress. From that time onward the Drúedain of Númenor became restless, and despite their fear of the sea one by one, or in twos and threes, they would beg for passages in the great ships that sailed to the North-western shores of Middle-earth. If any asked 'Why would you go, and whither?' they answered: 'The Great Isle no longer feels sure under our feet, and we wish to return to the lands whence we came.' Thus their numbers dwindled again slowly through the long years, and none were left when Elendil escaped from the Downfall: the last had fled the land when Sauron was brought to it. [Author's note.] – There is no trace, either in the materials relating to the story of Aldarion and Erendis or elsewhere, of the presence of Drúedain in Númenor apart from the foregoing, save for a detached note which says that 'the Edain who at the end of the War of the Jewels sailed over sea to Númenor contained few remnants of the Folk of Haleth, and the very few Drúedain that accompanied them died out long before the Downfall'.

8   A few lived in the household of Húrin of the House of Hador, for he had dwelt among the Folk of Haleth in his youth and had kinship with their lord. [Author's note.] – On the relationship of Húrin to the Folk of Haleth see *The Silmarillion* p. 158. – It was my father's intention ultimately to transform Sador, the old serving-man in Húrin's house in Dor-lómin, into a Drûg.

9   They had a law against the use of all poisons for the hurt of any living creatures, even those who had done them injury – save only Orcs, whose poisoned darts they countered with others more deadly. [Author's note.] – Elfhelm told Meriadoc Brandybuck that the Wild Men used poisoned arrows (*The Return of the King* V 5), and the same was believed of them by the inhabitants of Enedwaith in the Second Age (p. 383). At a later point in this essay something is told of the dwellings of the Drúedain, which it is convenient to cite here. Living among the Folk of Haleth, who were a woodland people, 'they were content to live in tents or shelters, lightly built round the trunks of large trees, for they were a hardy race. In their former homes, according to their own tales, they had used caves in the mountains, but mainly as store-houses, only occupied as dwellings and sleeping-places in severe weather. They had similar refuges in

Beleriand to which all but the most hardy retreated in times of storm or bitter winter; but these places were guarded and not even their closest friends among the Folk of Haleth were welcomed there.'

10 Acquired according to their legends from the Dwarves. [Author's note.]

11 Of this story my father remarked: 'The tales, such as *The Faithful Stone*, that speak of their transferring part of their "powers" to their artefacts, remind one in miniature of Sauron's transference of power to the foundations of the Barad-dûr and to the Ruling Ring.'

12 'At each turn of the road there were great standing stones that had been carved in the likeness of men, huge and clumsy-limbed, squatting cross-legged with their stumpy arms folded on fat bellies. Some in the wearing of the years had lost all features save the dark holes of their eyes that still stared sadly at the passers-by.'

13 The name *Drúwaith Iaur* (*Old Púkel-land*) appears on Miss Pauline Baynes' decorated map of Middle-earth (see p. 261), placed well to the north of the mountains of the promontory of Andrast. My father stated however that the name was inserted by him and was correctly placed. – A marginal jotting states that after the Battles of the Fords of Isen it was found that many Drúedain did indeed survive in the Drúwaith Iaur, for they came forth from the caves where they dwelt to attack remnants of Saruman's forces that had been driven away southwards. – In a passage cited on p. 370 there is a reference to tribes of 'Wild Men', fishers and fowlers, on the coasts of Enedwaith, who were akin in race and speech to the Drúedain of Anórien.

14 Once in *The Lord of the Rings* the term 'Woses' is used, when Elfhelm said to Meriadoc Brandybuck: 'You hear the Woses, the Wild Men of the Woods.' *Wose* is a modernization (in this case, the form that the word would have had now if it still existed in the language) of an Anglo-Saxon word *wása*, which is actually found only in the compound *wudu-wása* 'wild man of the woods'. (Saeros the Elf of Doriath called Túrin a 'woodwose', pp. 80–1 above. The word survived long in English and was eventually corrupted into 'woodhouse'.) The actual word employed by the Rohirrim (of which 'wose' is a translation, according to the method employed throughout) is once mentioned: *róg*, plural *rógin*.

It seems that the term 'Púkel-men' (again a translation: it represents Anglo-Saxon *púcel* 'goblin, demon', a relative of the word *púca* from which *Puck* is derived) was only used in Rohan of the images of Dunharrow.

II

THE ISTARI

The fullest account of the Istari was written, as it appears, in 1954 (see the Introduction, p. 12, for an account of its origin). I give it here in full, and will refer to it subsequently as 'the essay on the Istari'.

Wizard is a translation of Quenya istar (Sindarin *ithron*): one of the members of an 'order' (as they called it), claiming to possess, and exhibiting, eminent knowledge of the history and nature of the World. The translation (though suitable in its relation to 'wise' and other ancient words of knowing, similar to that of *istar* in Quenya) is not perhaps happy, since the *Heren Istarion* or 'Order of Wizards' was quite distinct from the 'wizards' and 'magicians' of later legend; they belonged solely to the Third Age and then departed, and none save maybe Elrond, Círdan, and Galadriel discovered of what kind they were or whence they came.

Among Men they were supposed (at first) by those that had dealings with them to be Men who had acquired lore and arts by long and secret study. They first appeared in Middle-earth about the year 1000 of the Third Age, but for long they went about in simple guise, as it were of Men already old in years but hale in body, travellers and wanderers, gaining knowledge of Middle-earth and all that dwelt therein, but revealing to none their powers and purposes. In that time Men saw them seldom and heeded them little. But as the shadow of Sauron began to grow and take shape again, they became more active, and sought ever to contest the growth of the Shadow, and to move Elves and Men to beware of their peril. Then far and wide rumour of their comings and goings, and their meddling in many matters, was noised among Men; and Men perceived that they did not die, but remained the same (unless it were that they aged somewhat in looks), while the fathers and sons of Men passed away. Men, therefore, grew to fear them, even when they loved them, and they were held to be of the Elven-race (with whom, indeed, they often consorted).

Yet they were not so. For they came from over the Sea out of the Uttermost West; though this was for long known only to Círdan,

Guardian of the Third Ring, master of the Grey Havens, who saw their landings upon the western shores. Emissaries they were from the Lords of the West, the Valar, who still took counsel for the governance of Middle-earth, and when the shadow of Sauron began first to stir again took this means of resisting him. For with the consent of Eru they sent members of their own high order, but clad in bodies as of Men, real and not feigned, but subject to the fears and pains and weariness of earth, able to hunger and thirst and be slain; though because of their noble spirits they did not die, and aged only by the cares and labours of many long years. And this the Valar did, desiring to amend the errors of old, especially that they had attempted to guard and seclude the Eldar by their own might and glory fully revealed; whereas now their emissaries were forbidden to reveal themselves in forms of majesty, or to seek to rule the wills of Men or Elves by open display of power, but coming in shapes weak and humble were bidden to advise and persuade Men and Elves to good, and to seek to unite in love and understanding all those whom Sauron, should he come again, would endeavour to dominate and corrupt.

Of this Order the number is unknown; but of those that came to the North of Middle-earth, where there was most hope (because of the remnant of the Dúnedain and of the Eldar that abode there), the chiefs were five. The first to come was one of noble mien and bearing, with raven hair, and a fair voice, and he was clad in white; great skill he had in works of hand, and he was regarded by well-nigh all, even by the Eldar, as the head of the Order.[1] Others there were also: two clad in sea-blue, and one in earthen brown; and last came one who seemed the least, less tall than the others, and in looks more aged, grey-haired and grey-clad, and leaning on a staff. But Círdan from their first meeting at the Grey Havens divined in him the greatest spirit and the wisest; and he welcomed him with reverence, and he gave to his keeping the Third Ring, Narya the Red.

'For,' said he, 'great labours and perils lie before you, and lest your task prove too great and wearisome, take this Ring for your aid and comfort. It was entrusted to me only to keep secret, and here upon the West-shores it is idle; but I deem that in days ere long to come it should be in nobler hands than mine, that may wield it for the kindling of all hearts to courage.'[2] And the Grey Messenger took the Ring, and kept it ever secret; yet the White Messenger (who was skilled to uncover all secrets) after a time became aware of this gift, and begrudged it, and it was the beginning of the hidden ill-will that he bore to the Grey, which afterwards became manifest.

Now the White Messenger in later days became known among Elves as Curunír, the Man of Craft, in the tongues of Northern Men Saruman; but that was after he returned from his many journeys and came into the realm of Gondor and there abode. Of the Blue little was known in the West, and they had no names save *Ithryn Luin* 'the Blue Wizards'; for they passed into the East with Curunír, but they never returned, and whether they remained in the East, pursuing there the purposes for which they were sent; or perished; or as some hold were ensnared by Sauron and became his servants, is not now known.[3] But none of these chances were impossible to be; for, strange indeed though this may seem, the Istari, being clad in bodies of Middle-earth, might even as Men and Elves fall away from their purposes, and do evil, forgetting the good in the search for power to effect it.

A separate passage written in the margin no doubt belongs here:

For it is said indeed that being embodied the Istari had need to learn much anew by slow experience, and though they knew whence they came the memory of the Blessed Realm was to them a vision from afar off, for which (so long as they remained true to their mission) they yearned exceedingly. Thus by enduring of free will the pangs of exile and the deceits of Sauron they might redress the evils of that time.

Indeed, of all the Istari, one only remained faithful, and he was the last-comer. For Radagast, the fourth, became enamoured of the many beasts and birds that dwelt in Middle-earth, and forsook Elves and Men, and spent his days among the wild creatures. Thus he got his name (which is in the tongue of Númenor of old, and signifies, it is said, 'tender of beasts').[4] And Curunír 'Lân, Saruman the White, fell from his high errand, and becoming proud and impatient and enamoured of power sought to have his own will by force, and to oust Sauron; but he was ensnared by that dark spirit, mightier than he.

But the last-comer was named among the Elves Mithrandir, the Grey Pilgrim, for he dwelt in no place, and gathered to himself neither wealth nor followers, but ever went to and fro in the Westlands from Gondor to Angmar, and from Lindon to Lórien, befriending all folk in times of need. Warm and eager was his spirit (and it was enhanced by the ring Narya), for he was the Enemy of Sauron, opposing the fire that devours and wastes with the fire that kindles, and succours in wanhope and distress; but his joy, and his swift wrath, were veiled in garments grey as ash, so that only those that knew him well glimpsed the flame that was within. Merry he could be, and kindly to the young and simple, and yet quick at times to sharp speech and the rebuking of folly; but he was not proud, and sought neither power nor praise, and thus far and wide he was beloved among all those that were not themselves proud. Mostly he journeyed unwearingly on foot, leaning on a staff; and so he was called among Men of the North Gandalf, 'the Elf of the Wand'. For they deemed him (though in error, as has been said) to be of Elven-kind, since he would at times work wonders among them, loving especially the beauty of fire; and yet such marvels he wrought mostly for mirth and delight, and desired not that any should hold him in awe or take his counsels out of fear.

Elsewhere it is told how it was that when Sauron rose again, he also arose and partly revealed his power, and becoming the chief mover of the resistance to Sauron was at last victorious, and brought all by vigilance and labour to that end which the Valar under the One that is above them had designed. Yet it is said that in the ending of the task for which he came he suffered greatly, and was slain, and being sent back from death for a brief while was clothed then in white, and became a radiant flame (yet veiled still save in great need). And when all was over and the Shadow of Sauron was removed, he departed for ever over the Sea. Whereas Curunír was cast down, and utterly humbled, and perished at last by the hand of an oppressed slave; and his spirit went whithersoever it was doomed to go, and to Middle-earth, whether naked or embodied, came never back.

In *The Lord of the Rings* the only general statement about the Istari is found in the headnote to the Tale of Years of the Third Age in Appendix B:

When maybe a thousand years had passed, and the first shadow had fallen on Greenwood the Great, the *Istari* or Wizards appeared in Middle-earth. It was afterwards said that they came out of the Far West and were messengers sent to contest the power of Sauron, and to unite all those who had the will to resist him; but they were forbidden to match his power with power, or to seek to dominate Elves or Men by force or fear.

They came therefore in the shape of Men, though they were

never young and aged only slowly, and they had many powers of mind and hand. They revealed their true names to few, but used such names as were given to them. The two highest of this order (of whom it is said there were five) were called by the Eldar Curunír, 'the Man of Skill', and Mithrandir, 'the Grey Pilgrim', but by Men in the North Saruman and Gandalf. Curunír journeyed often into the East, but dwelt at last in Isengard. Mithrandir was closest in friendship with the Eldar, and wandered mostly in the West, and never made for himself any lasting abode.

There follows an account of the guardianship of the Three Rings of the Elves, in which it is said that Círdan gave the Red Ring to Gandalf when he first came to the Grey Havens from over the Sea ('for Círdan saw further and deeper than any other in Middle-earth').

The essay on the Istari just cited thus tells much about them and their origin that does not appear in *The Lord of the Rings* (and also contains some incidental remarks of great interest about the Valar, their continuing concern for Middle-earth, and their recognition of ancient error, which cannot be discussed here). Most notable are the description of the Istari as 'members of their own high order' (the order of the Valar), and the statements about their physical embodiment.[5] But also to be remarked are the coming of the Istari to Middle-earth at different times; Círdan's perception that Gandalf was the greatest of them; Saruman's knowledge that Gandalf possessed the Red Ring, and his jealousy; the view taken of Radagast, that he did not remain faithful to his mission; the two other 'Blue Wizards', unnamed, who passed with Saruman into the East, but unlike him never returned into the Westlands; the number of the order of the Istari (said here to be unknown, though 'the chiefs' of those that came to the North of Middle-earth were five); the explanation of the names Gandalf and Radagast; and the Sindarin word *ithron*, plural *ithryn*.

The passage concerning the Istari in *Of the Rings of Power* (in *The Silmarillion*, p. 300) is very close indeed to the statement in Appendix B to *The Lord of the Rings* cited above, even in wording; but it does include this sentence, agreeing with the essay on the Istari:

Curunír was the eldest and came first, and after him came Mithrandir and Radagast, and others of the Istari who went into the East of Middle-earth, and do not come into these tales.

Most of the remaining writings about the Istari (as a group) are unhappily no more than very rapid jottings, often illegible. Of major interest, however, is a brief and very hasty sketch of a narrative, telling of a council of the Valar, summoned it seems by Manwë ('and maybe he called upon Eru for counsel?'), at which it was resolved to send out three emissaries to Middle-earth. 'Who would go? For they must be mighty, peers of Sauron, but must forgo might, and clothe themselves in flesh so as to treat on equality and win the trust of Elves and Men. But this would imperil them, dimming their wisdom and knowledge, and confusing them with fears, cares, and wearinesses coming from the flesh.' But two only came forward: Curumo, who was chosen by Aulë, and Alatar, who was sent by Oromë. Then Manwë asked, where was Olórin? And Olórin, who was clad in grey, and having just entered from a journey had seated himself at the edge of the council, asked what Manwë would have of him. Manwë replied that he wished Olórin to go as the third messenger to Middle-earth (and it is remarked in parentheses that 'Olórin was a lover of the Eldar that remained', apparently to explain Manwë's choice). But Olórin declared that he was too weak for such a task, and that he feared Sauron. Then Manwë said that that was all the more reason why he should go, and that he commanded Olórin (illegible words follow that seem to contain the word 'third'). But at that Varda looked up and said: 'Not as the third'; and Curumo remembered it.

The note ends with the statement that Curumo [Saruman] took Aiwendil [Radagast] because Yavanna begged him, and that Alatar took Pallando as a friend.[6]

On another page of jottings clearly belonging to the same period it is said that 'Curumo was obliged to take Aiwendil to please Yavanna wife of Aulë'. There are here also some rough tables relating the names of the Istari to the names of the Valar: Olórin to Manwë and Varda, Curumo to Aulë, Aiwendil to Yavanna, Alatar to Oromë, and Pallando also to Oromë (but this replaces Pallando to Mandos and Nienna).

The meaning of these relations between Istari and Valar is clearly, in the light of the brief narrative just cited, that each Istar was chosen by each Vala for his innate characteristics – perhaps even that they were members of the 'people' of that Vala, in the same sense as is said of Sauron in the *Valaquenta* (*The Silmarillion* p. 32) that 'in his beginning he was of the Maiar of Aulë, and he remained mighty in the lore of that people'. It is thus very notable that Curumo (Saruman) was chosen by Aulë. There is no hint of an explanation of why Yavanna's evident desire that the Istari should include in their number one with a particular love of the things of her making could only be achieved by imposing Radagast's company on Saruman; while the suggestion in the essay on the Istari (p. 390) that in becoming enamoured of the wild creatures of Middle-earth Radagast neglected the purpose for which he was sent is perhaps not perfectly in accord with the idea of his being specially chosen by Yavanna. Moreover both in the essay on the Istari and in *Of the Rings of Power* Saruman came first and he came alone. On the other hand it is possible to see a hint of the story of Radagast's unwelcome company in Saruman's extreme scorn for him, as related by Gandalf to the Council of Elrond:

' "Radagast the Brown!" laughed Saruman, and he no longer concealed his scorn. "Radagast the Bird-tamer! Radagast the Simple! Radagast the Fool! Yet he had just the wit to play the part that I set him." '

Whereas in the essay on the Istari it is said that the two who passed into the East had no names save *Ithryn Luin* 'the Blue Wizards' (meaning of course that they had no names in the West of Middle-earth), here they are named, as Alatar and Pallando, and are associated with Oromë, though no hint is given of the reason for this relationship. It might be (though this is the merest guess) that Oromë of all the Valar had the greatest knowledge of the further parts of Middle-earth, and that the Blue Wizards were destined to journey in those regions and to remain there.

Beyond the fact that these notes on the choosing of the Istari certainly date from after the completion of *The Lord of the Rings* I can find no evidence of their relation, in time of composition, to the essay on the Istari.[7]

I know of no other writings about the Istari save some very rough and in part uninterpretable notes that are certainly much later than any of the foregoing, and probably date from 1972:

We must assume that they [the Istari] were all Maiar, that is persons of the 'angelic' order, though not necessarily of the same rank. The Maiar were 'spirits', but capable of self-incarnation, and could take 'humane' (especially Elvish) forms. Saruman is said (e.g. by Gandalf himself) to have been the chief of the Istari – that is, higher in Valinórean stature than the others. Gandalf was evidently the next in order. Radagast is presented as a person of much less power and wisdom. Of the other two nothing is said in published work save the reference to the Five Wizards in the altercation between Gandalf and Saruman [*The Two Towers* III 10]. Now these Maiar were sent by the Valar at a crucial moment in the history of Middle-earth to enhance the resistance of the Elves of the West, waning in power, and of the uncorrupted Men of the West, greatly outnumbered by those of the East and South. It may be seen that they were free each to do what they could in this mission; that they were not commanded or supposed to act *together* as a small central body of power and wisdom; and that each had different powers and inclinations and were chosen by the Valar with this in mind.

Other writings are concerned exclusively with Gandalf (Olórin, Mithrandir). On the reverse of the isolated page containing the narrative of the choice of the Istari by the Valar appears the following very remarkable note:

Elendil and Gil-galad were partners; but this was 'the Last Alliance' of Elves and Men. In Sauron's final overthrow, Elves were not effectively concerned at the point of action. Legolas probably achieved least of the Nine Walkers. Galadriel, the greatest of the Eldar surviving in Middle-earth, was potent mainly in wisdom and goodness, as a director or counsellor in the struggle, unconquerable in *resistance* (especially in mind and spirit) but incapable of punitive *action*. In her scale she had become like Manwë with regard to the greater total action. Manwë, however, even after the Downfall of Númenor and the breaking of the old world, even in the Third Age when the Blessed Realm had been removed from the 'Circles of the World', was still not a mere observer. It is clearly from Valinor that the emissaries came who were called the Istari (or Wizards), and among them Gandalf, who proved to be the director and coordinator both of attack and defence.

Who was 'Gandalf'? It is said that in later days (when again a shadow of evil arose in the Kingdom) it was believed by many of the 'Faithful' of that time that 'Gandalf' was the last appearance of Manwë himself, before his final withdrawal to the watchtower of Taniquetil. (That Gandalf said that his name 'in the West' had been Olórin was, according to this belief, the adoption of an incognito, a mere by-name.) I do not (of course) know the truth of the matter, and if I did it would be a mistake to be more explicit than Gandalf was. But I think it was not so. Manwë will not descend from the Mountain until the Dagor Dagorath, and the coming of the End, when Melkor returns.[8] To the overthrow of Morgoth he sent his herald Eönwë. To the defeat of Sauron would he not then send some lesser (but mighty) spirit of the angelic people, one coëval and equal, doubtless, with Sauron in their beginnings, but not more? Olórin was his name. But of Olórin we shall never know more than he revealed in Gandalf.

This is followed by sixteen lines of a poem in alliterative verse:

Wilt thou learn the lore.   that was long secret
of the Five that came   from a far country?
One only returned.   Others never again

under Men's dominion   Middle-earth shall seek
until Dagor Dagorath   and the Doom cometh.
How hast thou heard it: the hidden counsel
of the Lords of the West   in the land of Aman?
The long roads are lost   that led thither,
and to mortal Men   Manwë speaks not.
From the West-that-was   a wind bore it
to the sleeper's ear,   in the silences
under night-shadow,   when news is brought
from lands forgotten   and lost ages
over seas of years   to the searching thought.
Not all are forgotten   by the Elder King.
Sauron he saw   as a slow menace. . . .

There is much here that bears on the larger question of the concern of Manwë and the Valar with the fate of Middle-earth after the Downfall of Númenor, which must fall quite outside the scope of this book.

After the words 'But of Olórin we shall never know more than he revealed in Gandalf' my father added later:

save that Olórin is a High-elven name, and must therefore have been given to him in Valinor by the Eldar, or be a 'translation' meant to be significant to them. In either case, what was the significance of the name, given or assumed? *Olor* is a word often translated 'dream', but that does not refer to (most) human 'dreams', certainly not the dreams of sleep. To the Eldar it included the vivid contents of their *memory*, as of their *imagination*: it referred in fact to *clear vision*, in the mind, of things not physically present at the body's situation. But not only to an idea, but to a full clothing of this in particular form and detail.

An isolated etymological note explains the meaning similarly:

olo-s: vision, 'phantasy': Common Elvish name for 'construction of the mind' not actually (pre)existing in Eä apart from the construction, but by the Eldar capable of being by Art (*Karmë*) made visible and sensible. *Olos* is usually applied to *fair* constructions having solely an artistic object (i.e. not having the object of deception, or of acquiring power).

Words deriving from this root are cited: Quenya *olos* 'dream, vision', plural *olozi/olori*; *ōla-* (impersonal) 'to dream'; *olosta* 'dreamy'. A reference is then made to *Olofantur*, which was the earlier 'true' name of Lórien, the Vala who was 'master of visions and dreams', before it was changed to *Irmo* in *The Silmarillion* (as *Nurufantur* was changed to *Námo* (Mandos): though the plural *Fëanturi* for these two 'brethren' survived in the *Valaquenta*).

These discussions of *olos, olor* are clearly to be connected with the passage in the *Valaquenta* (*The Silmarillion* pp. 30–1) where it is said that Olórin dwelt in Lórien in Valinor, and that

> though he loved the Elves, he walked among them unseen, or in form as one of them, and they did not know whence came the fair visions or the promptings of wisdom that he put into their hearts.

In an earlier version of this passage it is said that Olórin was 'counsellor of Irmo', and that in the hearts of those who hearkened to him awoke thoughts 'of fair things that had not yet been but might yet be made for the enrichment of Arda'.

There is a long note to elucidate the passage in *The Two Towers* IV 5 where Faramir at Henneth Annûn told that Gandalf had said:

> Many are my names in many countries. Mithrandir among the Elves, Tharkûn to the Dwarves; Olórin I was in my youth in the West that is forgotten,[9] in the South Incánus, in the North Gandalf; to the East I go not.

This note dates from before the publication of the second edition of *The Lord of the Rings* in 1966, and reads as follows:

> The date of Gandalf's arrival is uncertain. He came from beyond the Sea, apparently at about the same time as the first signs were noted of the re-arising of 'the Shadow': the reappearance and spread of evil things. But he is seldom mentioned in any annals or records during the second millennium of the Third Age. Probably he wandered long (in various guises), engaged not in deeds and events but in exploring the hearts of Elves and Men who had been and might still be expected to be opposed to Sauron. His own statement (or a version of it, and in any case not fully understood) is preserved that his name in youth was Olórin in the West, but he was called Mithrandir by the Elves (Grey Wanderer), Tharkûn by the Dwarves (said to mean 'Staff-man'), Incánus in the South, and Gandalf in the North, but 'to the East I go not'.
>
> 'The West' here plainly means the Far West beyond the Sea, not part of Middle-earth; the name Olórin is of High-Elven form. 'The

North' must refer to the North-western regions of Middle-earth, in which most of the inhabitants or speaking-peoples were and remained uncorrupted by Morgoth or Sauron. In those regions resistance would be strongest to the evils left behind by the Enemy, or to Sauron his servant, if he should reappear. The bounds of this region were naturally vague; its eastern frontier was roughly the River Carnen to its junction with Celduin (the River Running), and so to Núrnen, and thence south to the ancient confines of South Gondor. (It did not originally exclude Mordor, which was occupied by Sauron, although outside his original realms 'in the East', as a deliberate threat to the West and the Númenóreans.) 'The North' thus includes all this great area: roughly West to East from the Gulf of Lune to Núrnen, and North and South from Carn Dûm to the southern bounds of ancient Gondor between it and Near Harad. Beyond Núrnen Gandalf had never gone.

This passage is the only evidence that survives for his having extended his travels further South. Aragorn claims to have penetrated 'the far countries of Rhûn and Harad where the stars are strange' (*The Fellowship of the Ring* II 2).[10] It need not be supposed that Gandalf did so. These legends are North-centred – because it is represented as an historical fact that the struggle against Morgoth and his servants occurred mainly in the North, and especially the North-west, of Middle-earth, and that was so because the movement of Elves, and of Men afterwards escaping from Morgoth, had been inevitably *westward*, towards the Blessed Realm, and *north-westward* because at that point the shores of Middle-earth were nearest to Aman. *Harad* 'South' is thus a vague term, and although before its downfall Men of Númenor had explored the coasts of Middle-earth far southward, their settlements beyond Umbar had been absorbed, or being made by men already in Númenor corrupted by Sauron had become hostile and parts of Sauron's dominions. But the southern regions in touch with Gondor (and called by men of Gondor simply Harad 'South', Near or Far) were probably both more convertible to the 'Resistance', and also places where Sauron was most busy in the Third Age, since it was a source to him of man-power most readily used against Gondor. Into these regions Gandalf may well have journeyed in the earlier days of his labours.

But his main province was 'the North', and within it above all the North-west, Lindon, Eriador, and the Vales of Anduin. His alliance was primarily with Elrond and the northern Dúnedain (Rangers). Peculiar to him was his love and knowledge of the 'Halflings', because his wisdom had presage of their ultimate importance, and at the same time he perceived their inherent worth. Gondor attracted his attention less, for the same reason that made it more interesting to Saruman: it was a centre of knowledge and power. Its rulers by ancestry and all their traditions were irrevocably opposed to Sauron, certainly politically: their realm arose as a threat to him, and continued to exist only in so far and so long as his threat to them could be resisted by armed force. Gandalf could do little to guide their proud rulers or to instruct them, and it was only in the decay of their power, when they were ennobled by courage and steadfastness in what seemed a losing cause, that he began to be deeply concerned with them.

The name *Incánus* is apparently 'alien', that is neither Westron, nor Elvish (Sindarin or Quenya), nor explicable by the surviving tongues of Northern Men. A note in the Thain's Book says that it is a form adapted to Quenya of a word in the tongue of the Haradrim meaning simply 'North-spy' (*Inkā + nūs*).[11]

Gandalf is a substitution in the English narrative on the same lines as the treatment of Hobbit and Dwarf names. It is an actual Norse name (found applied to a Dwarf in *Völuspá*)[12] used by me since it appears to contain *gandr*, a staff, especially one used in 'magic', and might be supposed to mean 'Elvish wight with a (magic) staff'. Gandalf was not an Elf, but would be by Men associated with them, since his alliance and friendship with Elves was well-known. Since the name is attributed to 'the North' in general, *Gandalf* must be supposed to represent a Westron name, but one made up of elements not derived from Elvish tongues.

A wholly different view of the meaning of Gandalf's words 'in the South Incánus', and of the etymology of the name, is taken in a note written in 1967:

It is very unclear what was meant by 'in the South'. Gandalf disclaimed ever visiting 'the East', but actually he appears to have confined his journeys and guardianship to the western lands, inhabited by Elves and peoples in general hostile to Sauron. At any rate it seems unlikely that he ever journeyed or stayed long enough in the Harad (or Far Harad!) to have there acquired a special name in any of the alien languages of those little known regions. The South should thus mean Gondor (at its widest those lands under the suzerainty of Gondor at the height of its power). At the time of this Tale, however, we find Gandalf always called Mithrandir in Gondor (by men of rank or Númenórean origin, as Denethor, Faramir, etc.).

This is Sindarin, and given as the name used by the Elves; but men of rank in Gondor knew and used this language. The 'popular' name in the Westron or Common Speech was evidently one meaning 'Greymantle', but having been devised long before was now in an archaic form. This is maybe represented by the *Greyhame* used by Éomer in Rohan.

My father concluded here that 'in the South' did refer to Gondor, and that Incánus was (like Olórin) a Quenya name, but one devised in Gondor in earlier times while Quenya was still much used by the learned, and was the language of many historical records, as it had been in Númenor.

Gandalf, it is said in the Tale of Years, appeared in the West early in the eleventh century of the Third Age. If we assume that he first visited Gondor, sufficiently often and for long enough to acquire a name or names there – say in the reign of Atanatar Alcarin, about 1800 years before the War of the Ring – it would be possible to take Incánus as a Quenya name devised for him which later became obsolete, and was remembered only by the learned.

On this assumption an etymology is proposed from the Quenya elements *in(id)*- 'mind' and *kan*- 'ruler', especially in *cáno*, *cánu* 'ruler, governor, chieftain' (which latter constitutes the second element in the names *Turgon* and *Fingon*). In this note my father referred to the Latin word *incánus* 'grey-haired' in such a way as to suggest that this was the actual origin of this name of Gandalf's when *The Lord of the Rings* was written, which if true would be very surprising; and at the end of the discussion he remarked that the coincidence in form of the Quenya name and the Latin word must be regarded as an 'accident', in the same way that Sindarin *Orthanc* 'forked height' happens to coincide with the Anglo-Saxon word *orþanc* 'cunning device', which is the translation of the actual name in the language of the Rohirrim.

NOTES

1 In *The Two Towers* III 8 it is said that Saruman was 'accounted by many the chief of Wizards', and at the Council of Elrond (*The Fellowship of the Ring* II 2) Gandalf explicitly stated this: 'Saruman the White is the greatest of my order.'

2 Another version of Círdan's words to Gandalf on giving him the Ring of Fire at the Grey Havens is found in *Of the Rings of Power* (*The Silmarillion* p. 304), and in closely similar words in Appendix B

to *The Lord of the Rings* (headnote to the Tale of Years of the Third Age).

3   In a letter written in 1958 my father said that he knew nothing clearly about 'the other two', since they were not concerned in the history of the North-west of Middle-earth. 'I think,' he wrote, 'they went as emissaries to distant regions, East and South, far out of Númenórean range: missionaries to enemy-occupied lands, as it were. What success they had I do not know; but I fear that they failed, as Saruman did, though doubtless in different ways; and I suspect they were founders or beginners of secret cults and "magic" traditions that outlasted the fall of Sauron.'

4   In a very late note on the names of the Istari Radagast is said to be a name deriving from the Men of the Vales of Anduin, 'not now clearly interpretable'. Rhosgobel, called 'the old home of Radagast' in *The Fellowship of the Ring* II 3, is said to have been 'in the forest borders between the Carrock and the Old Forest Road'.

5   It appears indeed from the mention of Olórin in the *Valaquenta* (*The Silmarillion* pp 30–1) that the Istari were Maiar; for Olórin was Gandalf.

6   *Curumo* would seem to be Saruman's name in Quenya, recorded nowhere else; *Curunír* was the Sindarin form. *Saruman*, his name among Northern men, contains the Anglo-Saxon word *searu, saru* 'skill, cunning, cunning device'. *Aiwendil* must mean 'lover of birds'; cf. *Linaewen* 'lake of birds' in Nevrast (see the Appendix to *The Silmarillion*, entry *lin* (*I*).) For the meaning of *Radagast* see p. 390 and note 4. *Pallando*, despite the spelling, perhaps contains *palan* 'afar', as in *palantír* and in *Palarran* 'Far Wanderer', the name of Aldarion's ship.

7   In a letter written in 1956 my father said that 'There is hardly any reference in *The Lord of the Rings* to things that do not actually *exist*, on its own plane (of secondary or sub-creational reality)', and added in a footnote to this: 'The cats of Queen Berúthiel and the names of the other two wizards (five minus Saruman, Gandalf, Radagast) are all that I recollect.' (In Moria Aragorn said of Gandalf that 'He is surer of finding the way home in a blind night than the cats of Queen Berúthiel' (*The Fellowship of the Ring* II 4).)

Even the story of Queen Berúthiel does exist, however, if only in a very 'primitive' outline, in one part illegible. She was the nefarious, solitary, and loveless wife of Tarannon, twelfth King of Gondor (Third Age 830–913) and first of the 'Ship-kings', who took the crown in the name of Falastur 'Lord of the Coasts', and was the first childless king (*The Lord of the Rings*, Appendix A, I, ii and iv). Berúthiel lived in the King's House in Osgiliath, hating the sounds and smells of the sea and the house that Tarannon built below

Pelargir 'upon arches whose feet stood deep in the wide waters of Ethir Anduin'; she hated all making, all colours and elaborate adornment, wearing only black and silver and living in bare chambers, and the gardens of the house in Osgiliath were filled with tormented sculptures beneath cypresses and yews. She had nine black cats and one white, her slaves, with whom she conversed, or read their memories, setting them to discover all the dark secrets of Gondor, so that she knew those things 'that men wish most to keep hidden', setting the white cat to spy upon the black, and tormenting them. No man in Gondor dared touch them; all were afraid of them, and cursed when they saw them pass. What follows is almost wholly illegible in the unique manuscript, except for the ending, which states that her name was erased from the Book of the Kings ('but the memory of men is not wholly shut in books, and the cats of Queen Berúthiel never passed wholly out of men's speech'), and that King Tarannon had her set on a ship alone with her cats and set adrift on the sea before a north wind. The ship was last seen flying past Umbar under a sickle moon, with a cat at the masthead and another as a figure-head on the prow.

8 This is a reference to 'the Second Prophecy of Mandos', which does not appear in *The Silmarillion*; its elucidation cannot be attempted here, since it would require some account of the history of the mythology in relation to the published version.

9 Gandalf said again 'Olórin I was in the West that is forgotten' when he spoke to the Hobbits and Gimli in Minas Tirith after the coronation of King Elessar: see 'The Quest of Erebor', p. 330.

10 The 'strange stars' apply strictly only to the Harad, and must mean that Aragorn travelled or voyaged some distance into the southern hemisphere. [Author's note.]

11 A mark over the last letter of *Inkā-nūs* suggests that the final consonant was *sh*.

12 One of the poems of the collection of very ancient Norse poetry known as the 'Poetic Edda' or the 'Elder Edda'.

III

THE PALANTÍRI

The *palantíri* were no doubt never matters of common use or common knowledge, even in Númenor. In Middle-earth they were kept in guarded rooms, high in strong towers, only kings and rulers, and their appointed wardens, had access to them, and they were never consulted, nor exhibited, publicly. But until the passing of the Kings they were not sinister secrets. Their use involved no peril, and no king or other person authorized to survey them would have hesitated to reveal the source of his knowledge of the deeds or opinions of distant rulers, if obtained through the Stones.[1]

After the days of the Kings, and the loss of Minas Ithil, there is no further mention of their open and official use. There was no answering Stone left in the North after the shipwreck of Arvedui Last-king in the year 1975.[2] In 2002 the Ithil-stone was lost. There then remained only the Anor-stone in Minas Tirith and the Orthanc-stone.[3]

Two things contributed then to the neglect of the Stones, and their passing out of the general memory of the people. The first was ignorance of what had happened to the Ithil-stone: it was reasonably assumed that it was destroyed by the defenders before Minas Ithil was captured and sacked;[4] but it was clearly possible that it had been seized and had come into the possession of Sauron, and some of the wiser and more farseeing may have considered this. It would appear that they did so, and realized that the Stone would be of little use to him for the damage of Gondor, unless it made contact with another Stone that was in accord with it.[5] It was for this reason, it may be supposed, that the Anor-stone, about which all the records of the Stewards are silent until the War of the Ring, was kept as a closely-guarded secret, accessible only to the Ruling Stewards and never by them used (it seems) until Denethor II.

The second reason was the decay of Gondor, and the waning of interest in or knowledge of ancient history among all but a few even of the high men of the realm, except in so far as it concerned their genealogies: their descent and kinship. Gondor after the Kings declined into a 'Middle Age' of fading knowledge, and simpler skills.

Communications depended on messengers and errand-riders, or in times of urgency upon beacons, and if the Stones of Anor and Orthanc were still guarded as treasures out of the past, known to exist only by a few, the Seven Stones of old were by the people generally forgotten, and the rhymes of lore that spoke of them were if remembered no longer understood; their operations were transformed in legend into the Elvish powers of the ancient kings with their piercing eyes, and the swift birdlike spirits that attended on them, bringing them news or bearing their messages.

The Orthanc-stone appears to have been at this time long disregarded by the Stewards: it was no longer of any use to them, and was secure in its impregnable tower. Even if it too had not been overshadowed by the doubt concerning the Ithil-stone, it stood in a region with which Gondor became less and less directly concerned. Calenardhon, never densely populated, had been devastated by the Dark Plague of 1636, and thereafter steadily denuded of inhabitants of Númenórean descent by migration to Ithilien and lands nearer Anduin. Isengard remained a personal possession of the Stewards, but Orthanc itself became deserted, and eventually it was closed and its keys removed to Minas Tirith. If Beren the Steward considered the Stone at all when he gave these to Saruman, he probably thought that it could be in no safer hands than those of the head of the Council opposed to Sauron.

Saruman had no doubt from his investigations[6] gained a special knowledge of the Stones, things that would attract his attention, and had become convinced that the Orthanc-stone was still intact in its tower. He acquired the keys of Orthanc in 2759, nominally as warden of the tower and lieutenant of the Steward of Gondor. At that time the matter of the Orthanc-stone would hardly concern the White Council. Only Saruman, having gained the favour of the Stewards, had yet made sufficient study of the records of Gondor to perceive the interest of the *palantíri* and the possible uses of those that survived; but of this he said nothing to his colleagues. Owing to Saruman's jealousy and hatred of Gandalf he ceased to cooperate with the Council, which last met in 2953. Without any formal declaration Saruman then seized Isengard as his own domain and paid no further attention to Gondor. The Council no doubt disapproved of this; but Saruman was a free agent, and had the right, if he wished, to act independently according to his own policy in the resistance to Sauron.[7]

The Council in general must independently have known of the

Stones and their ancient dispositions, but they did not regard them as of much present importance: they were things that belonged to the history of the Kingdoms of the Dúnedain, marvellous and admirable, but mostly now lost or rendered of little use. It must be remembered that the Stones were originally 'innocent', serving no evil purpose. It was Sauron who made them sinister, and instruments of domination and deceit.

Though (warned by Gandalf) the Council may have begun to doubt Saruman's designs as regarded the Rings, not even Gandalf knew that he had become an ally, or servant, of Sauron. This Gandalf only discovered in July 3018. But, although Gandalf had in latter years enlarged his own and the Council's knowledge of Gondor's history by study of its documents, his and their chief concern was still with the Ring: the possibilities latent in the Stones were not realized. It is evident that at the time of the War of the Ring the Council had not long become aware of the doubt concerning the fate of the Ithil-stone, and failed (understandably even in such persons as Elrond, Galadriel, and Gandalf, under the weight of their cares) to appreciate its significance, to consider what might be the result if Sauron became possessed of one of the Stones, and anyone else should then make use of another. It needed the demonstration on Dol Baran of the effects of the Orthanc-stone on Peregrin to reveal suddenly that the 'link' between Isengard and Barad-dûr (seen to exist after it was discovered that forces of Isengard had been joined with others directed by Sauron in the attack on the Fellowship at Parth Galen) was in fact the Orthanc-stone – and one other *palantír*.

In his talk to Peregrin as they rode on Shadowfax from Dol Baran (*The Two Towers* III 11) Gandalf's immediate object was to give the Hobbit some idea of the history of the *palantíri*, so that he might begin to realize the ancientry, dignity, and power of things that he had presumed to meddle with. He was not concerned to exhibit his own processes of discovery and deduction, except in its last point: to explain how Sauron came to have control of them, so that they were perilous for *anyone*, however exalted, to use. But Gandalf's mind was at the same time earnestly busy with the Stones, considering the bearings of the revelation at Dol Baran upon many things that he had observed and pondered: such as the wide knowledge of events far away possessed by Denethor, and his appearance of premature old age, first observable when he was not much above sixty years old, although he belonged to a race and family that still normally had longer lives than other men. Undoubtedly Gandalf's haste to reach

Minas Tirith, in addition to the urgency of the time and the imminence of war, was quickened by his sudden fear that Denethor also had made use of a *palantír*, the Anor-stone, and his desire to judge what effect this had had on him: whether in the crucial test of desperate war it would not prove that he (like Saruman) was no longer to be trusted and might surrender to Mordor. Gandalf's dealings with Denethor on arrival in Minas Tirith, and in the following days, and all things that they are reported to have said to one another, must be viewed in the light of this doubt in Gandalf's mind.[8]

The importance of the *palantír* of Minas Tirith in his thoughts thus dated only from Peregrin's experience on Dol Baran. But his knowledge or guesses concerning its existence were, of course, much earlier. Little is known of Gandalf's history until the end of the Watchful Peace (2460) and the formation of the White Council (2463), and his special interest in Gondor seems only to have been shown after Bilbo's finding of the Ring (2941) and Sauron's open return to Mordor (2951).[9] His attention was then (as was Saruman's) concentrated on the Ring of Isildur; but in his reading in the archives of Minas Tirith he may be assumed to have learned much about the *palantíri* of Gondor, though with less immediate appreciation of their possible significance than that shown by Saruman, whose mind was in contrast to Gandalf's always more attracted by artefacts and instruments of power than by persons. Gandalf all the same probably at that time already knew more than did Saruman about the nature and ultimate origin of the *palantíri*, since all that concerned the ancient realm of Arnor and the later history of those regions was his special province, and he was in close alliance with Elrond.

But the Anor-stone had become a secret: no mention of its fate after the fall of Minas Ithil appeared in any of the annals or records of the Stewards. History would indeed make it clear that neither Orthanc nor the White Tower in Minas Tirith had ever been captured or sacked by enemies, and it might therefore be supposed that the Stones were most probably intact and remained in their ancient sites; but it could not be certain that they had not been removed by the Stewards, and perhaps 'buried deep'[10] in some secret treasure-chamber, even one in some last hidden refuge in the mountains, comparable to Dunharrow.

Gandalf should have been reported as saying that he did not *think* that Denethor had presumed to use it, until his wisdom failed.[11] He could not state it as a known fact, for when and why Denethor had dared to use the Stone was and remains a matter of conjecture.

Gandalf might well think as he did on the matter, but it is probable, considering Denethor and what is said about him, that he began to use the Anor-stone many years before 3019, and earlier than Saruman ventured or thought it useful to use the Stone of Orthanc. Denethor succeeded to the Stewardship in 2984, being then fifty-four years old: a masterful man, both wise and learned beyond the measure of those days, and strong-willed, confident in his own powers, and dauntless. His 'grimness' was first observable to others after his wife Finduilas died in 2988, but it seems fairly plain that he had *at once* turned to the Stone as soon as he came to power, having long studied the matter of the *palantíri* and the traditions regarding them and their use preserved in the special archives of the Stewards, available beside the Ruling Steward only to his heir. During the end of the rule of his father, Ecthelion II, he must have greatly desired to consult the Stone, as anxiety in Gondor increased, while his own position was weakened by the fame of 'Thorongil'[12] and the favour shown to him by his father. At least one of his motives must have been jealousy of Thorongil, and hostility to Gandalf, to whom, during the ascendancy of Thorongil, his father paid much attention; Denethor desired to surpass these 'usurpers' in knowledge and information, and also if possible to keep an eye on them when they were elsewhere.

The breaking strain of Denethor's confrontation of Sauron must be distinguished from the general strain of using the Stone.[13] The latter Denethor thought that he could endure (and not without reason); confrontation with Sauron almost certainly did not occur for many years, and was probably never originally contemplated by Denethor. For the uses of the *palantíri*, and the distinction between their solitary use for 'seeing' and their use for communication with another respondent Stone and its 'surveyor', see pp. 410–11. Denethor could, after he had acquired the skill, learn much of distant events by the use of the Anor-stone alone, and even after Sauron became aware of his operations he could still do so, as long as he retained the strength to control his Stone to his own purposes, in spite of Sauron's attempt to 'wrench' the Anor-stone always towards himself. It must also be considered that the Stones were only a small item in Sauron's vast designs and operations: a means of dominating and deluding two of his opponents, but he would not (and could not) have the Ithil-stone under perpetual observation. It was not his way to commit such instruments to the use of subordinates; nor had he any servant whose mental powers were superior to Saruman's or even Denethor's.

In the case of Denethor, the Steward was strengthened, even against Sauron himself, by the fact that the Stones were far more amenable to legitimate users: most of all to true 'Heirs of Elendil' (as Aragorn), but also to one with inherited authority (as Denethor), as compared to Saruman, or Sauron. It may be noted that the effects were different. Saruman fell under the domination of Sauron and desired his victory, or no longer opposed it. Denethor remained steadfast in his rejection of Sauron, but was made to believe that his victory was inevitable, and so fell into despair. The reasons for this difference were no doubt that in the first place Denethor was a man of great strength of will, and maintained the integrity of his personality until the final blow of the (apparently) mortal wound of his only surviving son. He was proud, but this was by no means merely personal: he loved Gondor and its people, and deemed himself appointed by destiny to lead them in this desperate time. And in the second place the Anor-stone was his *by right*, and nothing but expediency was against his use of it in his grave anxieties. He must have guessed that the Ithil-stone was in evil hands, and risked contact with it, trusting his strength. His trust was not entirely unjustified. Sauron failed to dominate him and could only influence him by deceits. Probably he did not at first look towards Mordor, but was content with such 'far views' as the Stone would afford; hence his surprising knowledge of events far off. Whether he ever thus made contact with the Orthanc-stone and Saruman is not told; probably he did, and did so with profit to himself. Sauron could not break in on these conferences: only the surveyor using the Master Stone of Osgiliath could 'eavesdrop'. While two of the other Stones were in response, the third would find them both blank.[14]

There must have been a considerable lore concerning the *palantíri* preserved in Gondor by the Kings and Stewards, and handed down even after use was no longer made of them. These Stones were an inalienable gift to Elendil and his heirs, to whom alone they belonged by right; but this does not mean that they could only be used rightfully by one of these 'heirs'. They could be used lawfully by anyone authorized by either the 'heir of Anárion' or the 'heir of Isildur', that is, a lawful King of Gondor or Arnor. Actually they must normally have been used by such deputies. Each Stone had its own warden, one of whose duties was to 'survey the Stone' at regular intervals, or when commanded, or in times of need. Other persons also were appointed to visit the Stones, and ministers of the Crown concerned with 'intelligence' made regular and special inspections of them, reporting the information so gained to the King and Council, or to the King privately, as the matter demanded. In Gondor latterly, as the office of Steward rose in importance and became hereditary, providing as it were a permanent 'understudy' to the King, and an immediate viceroy at need, the command and use of the Stones seems mainly to have been in the hands of the Stewards, and the traditions concerning their nature and use to have been guarded and transmitted in their House. Since the Stewardship had become hereditary from 1998 onwards,[15] so the authority to use, or again to depute the use, of the Stones, was lawfully transmitted in their line, and belonged therefore fully to Denethor.[16]

It must however be noted with regard to the narrative of *The Lord of the Rings* that over and above such deputed authority, even hereditary, any 'heir of Elendil' (that is, a recognized descendant occupying a throne or lordship in the Númenórean realms by virtue of this descent) had the *right* to use any of the *palantíri*. Aragorn thus claimed the right to take the Orthanc-stone into his possession, since it was now, for the time being, without owner or warden; and also because he was *de jure* the rightful King of both Gondor and Arnor, and could, if he willed, for just cause withdraw all previous grants to himself.

The 'lore of the Stones' is now forgotten, and can only be partly recovered by conjecture and from things recorded about them. They were perfect spheres, appearing when at rest to be made of solid glass or crystal deep black in hue. At smallest they were about a foot in diameter, but some, certainly the Stones of Osgiliath and Amon Sûl, were much larger and could not be lifted by one man. Originally they were placed in sites suitable to their sizes and intended uses, standing on low round tables of black marble in a central cup or depression, in which they could at need be revolved by hand. They were very heavy but perfectly smooth, and would suffer no damage if by accident or malice they were unseated and rolled off their tables. They were indeed unbreakable by any violence then controlled by men, though some believed that great heat, such as that of Orodruin, might shatter them, and surmised that this had been the fate of the Ithil-stone in the fall of Barad-dûr.

Though without any external markings of any kind they had permanent *poles*, and were originally so placed in their sites that they stood 'upright': their diameters from pole to pole pointed to the earth's centre, but the permanent nether pole must then be at the bottom. The faces along the circumference in this position were the viewing faces, receiving the visions from the outside, but transmitting them to the eye of a 'surveyor' upon the far side. A surveyor, therefore, who wished to look west would place himself on the east side of the Stone, and if he wished to shift his vision northward must move to his left, southward. But the minor Stones, those of Orthanc, Ithil, and Anor, and probably Annúminas, had also fixed orientation in their original situation, so that (for example) their west face would only look west and turned in other directions was blank. If a Stone became unseated or disturbed it could be re-set by observation, and it was then useful to revolve it. But when removed and cast down, as was the Orthanc-stone, it was not so easy to set right. So it was 'by chance' as Men call it (as Gandalf would have said) that Peregrin, fumbling with the Stone, must have set it on the ground more or less 'upright', and sitting westward of it have had the fixed east-looking face in the proper position. The major Stones were not so fixed: their circumference could be revolved and they could still 'see' in any direction.[17]

Alone the *palantíri* could only 'see': they did not transmit sound. Ungoverned by a directing mind they were wayward, and their 'visions' were (apparently at least) haphazard. From a high place their westward face, for instance, would look to vast distance, its vision blurred and distorted to either side and above and below, and its foreground obscured by things behind receding in ever-diminishing clarity. Also, what they 'saw' was directed or hindered by chance, by darkness, or by 'shrouding' (see below). The vision of the *palantíri* was not 'blinded' or 'occluded' by physical obstacles, but only by darkness; so they could look *through* a mountain as they could look *through* a patch of dark or shadow, but see nothing within that did not receive some light. They could see through walls but see nothing within rooms, caves, or vaults unless some light fell on it; and they could not themselves provide or project light. It was possible to guard against their sight by the process called 'shrouding', by which certain things or areas would be seen in a Stone only as a shadow or a deep mist. How this was done (by those aware of the Stones and the possibility of being watched by them) is one of the lost mysteries of the *palantíri*.[18]

A viewer could by his will cause the vision of the Stone to *concentrate* on some point, on or near its direct line.[19] The uncontrolled 'visions' were small, especially in the minor Stones, though they were much larger to the eye of a beholder who placed himself at some distance from the surface of the *palantír* (about three feet at best). But controlled by the will of a skilled and strong surveyor, remoter things could be enlarged, brought as it were nearer and clearer, while their background was almost suppressed. Thus a man at a considerable distance might be seen as a tiny figure, half an inch high, difficult to pick out against a landscape or a concourse of other men; but concentration could enlarge and clarify the vision till he was seen in clear if reduced detail like a picture apparently a foot or more in height, and recognized if he was known to the surveyor. Great concentration might even enlarge some detail that interested the surveyor, so that it could be seen (for instance) if he had a ring on his hand.

But this 'concentration' was very tiring and might become exhausting. Consequently it was only undertaken when information was urgently desired, and chance (aided by other information maybe) enabled the surveyor to pick out items (significant for him and his immediate concern) from the welter of the Stone's visions. For example, Denethor sitting before the Anor-stone anxious about Rohan, and deciding whether or not at once to order the kindling of the beacons and the sending out of the 'arrow', might place himself in a direct line looking north-west by west through Rohan, passing close to Edoras and on towards the Fords of Isen. At that time there might be visible movements of men in that line. If so, he could concentrate on (say) a group, see them as Riders, and finally discover some figure known to him: Gandalf, for instance, riding with the reinforcements to Helm's Deep, and suddenly breaking away and racing northwards.[20]

The *palantíri* could not themselves survey men's minds, at unawares or unwilling; for the transference of thought depended on the *wills* of the user on either side, and thought (received as speech)[21] was only transmittable by one Stone to another in accord.

NOTES

1   Doubtless they were used in the consultations between Arnor and Gondor in the year 1944 concerning the succession to the Crown. The 'messages' received in Gondor in 1973, telling of the dire straits of the Northern Kingdom, was possibly their last use until the approach of the War of the Ring. [Author's note.]

2   With Arvedui were lost the Stones of Annúminas and Amon Sûl (Weathertop). The third *palantír* of the North was that in the tower Elostirion on Emyn Beraid, which had special properties (see note 16).

3   The Stone of Osgiliath had been lost in the waters of Anduin in 1437, during the civil war of the Kin-strife.

4   On the destructibility of the *palantíri* see p. 409. In the entry in the Tale of Years for 2002, and also in Appendix A (I, iv), it is stated as

a fact that the *palantír* was captured in the fall of Minas Ithil; but my father noted that these annals were made after the War of the Ring, and that the statement, however certain, was a deduction. The Ithil-stone was never found again, and probably perished in the ruin of Barad-dûr; see p. 409.

5   By themselves the Stones could only *see*: scenes or figures in distant places, or in the past. These were without explanation; and at any rate for men of later days it was difficult to direct what visions should be revealed by the will or desire of a surveyor. But when another mind occupied a Stone in accord, thought could be 'transferred' (received as 'speech'), and visions of the things in the mind of the surveyor of one Stone could be seen by the other surveyor. [See further pp. 410–11 and note 21.] These powers were originally used mainly in consultation, for the purpose of exchanging news necessary to government, or advice and opinions; less often in simple friendship and pleasure or in greetings and condolence. It was only Sauron who used a Stone for the transference of his superior will, dominating the weaker surveyor and forcing him to reveal hidden thought and to submit to commands. [Author's note.]

6   Cf. Gandalf's remarks to the Council of Elrond concerning Saruman's long study of the scrolls and books of Minas Tirith.

7   For any more 'worldly' policy of power and warlike strength Isengard was well placed, being the key to the Gap of Rohan. This was a weak point in the defences of the West, especially since the decay of Gondor. Through it hostile spies and emissaries could pass in secret, or eventually, as in the former Age, forces of war. The Council seems to have been unaware, since for many years Isengard had been closely guarded, of what went on within its Ring. The use, and possibly special breeding, of Orcs was kept secret, and cannot have begun much before 2990 at earliest. The orc-troops seem never to have been used beyond the territory of Isengard before the attack on Rohan. Had the Council known of this they would, of course, at once have realized that Saruman had become evil. [Author's note.]

8   Denethor was evidently aware of Gandalf's guesses and suspicions, and at once both angered and sardonically amused by them. Note his words to Gandalf at their meeting in Minas Tirith (*The Return of the King* V 1): 'I know already sufficient of these deeds for my own counsel against the menace of the East', and especially his mocking words that followed: 'Yea; for though the Stones be lost, they say, still the lords of Gondor have keener sight than lesser men, and many messages come to them.' Quite apart from the *palantíri*, Denethor was a man of great mental powers, and a quick reader of thoughts behind faces and words, but he may well also have actually seen in the Anor-stone visions of events in Rohan and Isengard. [Author's note.] – See further p. 411.

9   Note the passage in *The Two Towers* IV 5 where Faramir (who was
    born in 2983) recollected seeing Gandalf in Minas Tirith when he
    was a child, and again two or three times later; and said that it was
    interest in records that brought him. The last time would have been
    in 3017, when Gandalf found the scroll of Isildur. [Author's note.]

10 This is a reference to Gandalf's words to Peregrin (*The Two Towers*
    III 11): 'Who knows where the lost Stones of Arnor and Gondor now
    lie, buried, or drowned deep?'

11 This is a reference to Gandalf's words after the death of Denethor
    in *The Return of the King* V 7, at the end of the chapter. My father's
    emendation (arising from the present discussion) of 'Denethor did
    not presume to use it' to 'Denethor would not presume to use it'
    was (apparently by mere oversight) not incorporated in the revised
    edition. See the Introduction, p. 13.

12 Thorongil ('Eagle of the Star') was the name given to Aragorn when
    he served in disguise Ecthelion II of Gondor; see *The Lord of the
    Rings*, Appendix A (I, iv, *The Stewards*).

13 The use of the *palantíri* was a mental strain, especially on men of
    later days not trained to the task, and no doubt in addition to his
    anxieties this strain contributed to Denethor's 'grimness'. It was
    probably felt earlier by his wife than by others and increased her
    unhappiness, to the hastening of her death. [Author's note.]

14 An unplaced marginal note observes that Saruman's integrity 'had
    been undermined by purely personal pride and lust for the domination
    of his own will. His study of the Rings had caused this, for his pride
    believed that he could use them, or It, in defiance of any other will.
    He, having lost any devotion to other persons or causes, was open to
    the domination of a superior will, to its threats, and to its display of
    power.' And moreover he had himself no *right* to the Orthanc-stone.

15 1998 was the year of the death of Pelendur, Steward of Gondor. 'After
    the days of Pelendur the Stewardship became hereditary as a kingship,
    from father to son or nearest kin,' *The Lord of the Rings*, Appendix
    A, I, iv, *The Stewards*.

16 The case was different in Arnor. Lawful possession of the Stones
    belonged to the King (who normally used the Stone of Annúminas);
    but the Kingdom became divided and the high-kingship was in
    dispute. The Kings of Arthedain, who were plainly those with the
    just claim, maintained a special warden at Amon Sûl, whose Stone
    was held to be the chief of the Northern *palantíri*, being the largest
    and most powerful and the one through which communication with
    Gondor was mainly conducted. After the destruction of Amon Sûl
    by Angmar in 1409 both Stones were placed at Fornost, where the
    King of Arthedain dwelt. These were lost in the shipwreck of
    Arvedui, and no deputy was left with any authority direct or inherited

to use the Stones. One only remained in the North, the Elendil Stone on Emyn Beraid, but this was one of special properties, and not employable in communications. Hereditary right to use it would no doubt still reside in the 'heir of Isildur', the recognized chieftain of the Dúnedain, and descendant of Arvedui. But it is not known whether any of them, including Aragorn, ever looked into it, desiring to gaze into the lost West. This Stone and its tower were maintained and guarded by Círdan and the Elves of Lindon. [Author's note.] – It is told in Appendix A (I, iii) to *The Lord of the Rings* that the *palantír* of Emyn Beraid 'was unlike the others and not in accord with them; it looked only to the Sea. Elendil set it there so that he could look back with "straight sight" and see Eressëa in the vanished West; but the bent seas below covered Númenor for ever.' Elendil's vision of Eressëa in the *palantír* of Emyn Beraid is told of also in *Of the Rings of Power* (*The Silmarillion* p. 292); 'it is believed that thus he would at whiles see far away even the Tower of Avallónë upon Eressëa, where the Master-stone abode, and yet abides'. It is notable that in the present account there is no reference to this Master-stone.

17 A later, detached note denies that the *palantíri* were polarized or oriented, but gives no further detail.

18 The later note referred to in note 17 treats some of these aspects of the *palantíri* slightly differently; in particular the concept of 'shrouding' seems differently employed. This note, very hasty and somewhat obscure, reads in part: 'They retained the images received, so that each contained within itself a multiplicity of images and scenes, some from a remote past. They could not "see" in the dark; that is, things that were in the dark were not recorded by them. They themselves could be and usually were kept in the dark, because it was much easier then to see the scenes that they presented, and as the centuries passed to limit their "overcrowding". How they were thus "shrouded" was kept secret and so is now unknown. They were not "blinded" by physical obstacles, as a wall, a hill, or a wood, so long as the distant objects were themselves in light. It was said, or guessed, by later commentators that the Stones were placed in their original sites in spherical cases that were locked to prevent their misuse by the unauthorized; but that this casing also performed the office of shrouding them and making them quiescent. The cases must therefore have been made of some metal or other substance not now known.' Marginal jottings associated with this note are partly illegible, but so much can be made out, that the remoter the past the clearer the view, while for distant viewing there was a 'proper distance', varying with the Stones, at which distant objects were clearer. The greater *palantíri* could look much further than the lesser; for the lesser the 'proper distance' was of the order of five hundred miles, as between the Orthanc-stone and that of Anor. 'Ithil was too near, but was

largely used for [illegible words], not for personal contacts with Minas Anor.'

19 The orientation was not, of course, divided into separate 'quarters' but continuous; so that its *direct* line of vision to a surveyor sitting south-east would be to the north-west, and so on. [Author's note.]

20 See *The Two Towers* III 7.

21 In a detached note this aspect is more explicitly described: 'Two persons, each using a Stone "in accord" with the other, could converse, but not by sound, which the Stones did not transmit. Looking one at the other they would exchange "thought" – not their full or true thought, or their intentions, but "silent speech", the thoughts they wished to transmit (already formalized in linguistic form in their minds or actually spoken aloud), which would be received by their respondents and of course immediately transformed into "speech", and only reportable as such.'

INDEX

This Index, as noted in the Introduction, covers not only the main texts but also the Notes and Appendices, since much original material appears in these latter. As a result a good many references are trivial, but I have thought it more useful, as it is certainly easier, to aim at completeness. The only intentional exceptions are a very few cases (as *Morgoth, Númenor*) where I have used the word *passim* to cover certain sections of the book, and the absence of references for *Elves, Men, Orcs,* and *Middle-earth.* In many cases the references include pages where a person or place is mentioned but not by name (thus the mention on p. 232 of 'the haven where Círdan was lord' is given under *Mithlond*). Asterisks are used to indicate names, nearly a quarter of the total, that have not been published in my father's works (they are thus also set against the names, listed in the footnote on pp. 261–2, that appeared on Miss Pauline Baynes' map of Middle-earth). The brief defining statements are not restricted to matters actually mentioned in the book; and occasionally I have added notes on the meaning of hitherto untranslated names.

This Index is not a model of consistency in presentation, but its deficiency in this respect may be partly excused in view of the interlacing ramification of names (including variant translations, partial translations, names that are equivalent in reference but not in meaning), which makes such consistency extremely difficult or impossible to achieve: as may be seen from such a series as *Eilenaer, Halifirien, Amon Anwar, Anwar, Hill of Anwar, Hill of Awe, Wood of Anwar, Firienholt, Firien Wood, Whispering Wood.* As a general rule I have included references for translations of Elvish names under the Elvish entry (as *Langstrand* under *Anfalas*), with a cross-reference, but I have departed from this in particular cases, where the 'translated' names (as *Mirkwood, Isengard*) are generally used and familiar.

Amdír King of Lórien, slain in the Battle of Dagorlad; father of Amroth. 240, 243–4, 258. See *Malgalad*.

Amon Anwar Sindarin name of Halifirien, seventh of the beacons of Gondor in Ered Nimrais. 301–2, 308–10, 316. Translated *Hill of Awe* 301–2, 308, and partially as *Hill of Anwar* 306, 309–10; also simply *Anwar* 306. See *Eilenaer, Halifirien, Wood of Anwar*.

Amon Darthir A peak in the range of Ered Wethrin south of Dor-lómin. 68, 148.

Amon Dîn 'The Silent Hill', first of the beacons of Gondor in Ered Nimrais. 301, 314, 319

Amon Ereb 'The Lonely Hill' in East Beleriand. 77

Amon Ethir The great earthwork raised by Finrod Felagund to the east of the Doors of Nargothrond. 116–19. Translated *the Spyhill* 116–17.

Amon Lanc 'The Naked Hill' in the south of Greenwood the Great, afterwards called *Dol Guldur*, q.v. 272, 280

Amon Obel A hill in the Forest of Brethil, on which was built Ephel Brandir. 104, 110, 123, 125, 136

Amon Rûdh 'The Bald Hill', a lonely height in the lands south of Brethil; abode of Mîm, and lair of Túrin's outlaw band. 98–100, 148, 150–4. See *Sharbhund*.

Amon Sûl 'Hill of the Wind', a round bare hill at the southern end of the Weather Hills in Eriador. 278, 409, 411, 413. Called in Bree *Weathertop* 278, 411

Amon Uilos Sindarin name of *Oiolossë*, q.v. 55

Amroth Sindarin Elf, King of Lórien, lover of Nimrodel; drowned in the Bay of Belfalas. 234, 237–8, 240–6, 255, 257–8, 261, 316. *The country of Amroth* (coast of Belfalas near Dol Amroth) 175, 214. *Amroth's Haven*, see *Edhellond*.

Anach Pass leading down from Taur-nu-Fuin (Dorthonion) at the western end of Ered Gorgoroth. 54, 95

Anar Quenya name of the Sun. 22, 29–30

Anárion (1) See *Tar-Anárion*.

Anárion (2) Younger son of Elendil, who with his father and his brother Isildur escaped from the Drowning of Númenor and founded in Middle-earth the Númenórean realms in exile; lord of Minas Anor; slain in the siege of Barad-dûr. 215, 279. *Heir of Anárion* 408

Anardil The given name of Tar-Aldarion. 173, 199, 212, 219; with suffix of endearment, *Anardilya* 174. [The sixth King of Gondor was also named *Anardil*.]

Ancalimë See *Tar-Ancalimë*. The name was also given by Aldarion to the tree from Eressëa that he planted in Armenelos 202

Andrast 'Long Cape', the mountainous promontory between the rivers Isen and Lefnui. 214, 261, 263, 370, 383–4, 387. See *Ras Morthil, Drúwaith Iaur*.

Andrath 'Long Climb', defile between the Barrow-downs and the South Downs through which the North–South Road (Greenway) passed. 348

Andróg Man of Dor-lómin, a leader of the outlaw-band (*Gaurwaith*) that Túrin joined. 85–90, 92–102, 148, 151–2, 154

Androth Caves in the hills of Mithrim where Tuor dwelt with the Grey-elves and afterwards as a solitary outlaw. 18–19

Anduin 'The Long River' east of the Misty Mountains; also *the River*, *the Great River*. Frequently in *the Vale(s) of Anduin*. 168, 236, 243, 245–7, 252, 256, 258–61, 264–5, Part 3 §§ I and II *passim*, 321, 338–9, 342–3, 345–6, 370–1, 383, 398, 401, 404, 411. See *Ethir Anduin*, *Langflood*.

Andúnië 'Sunset', city and haven on the west coast of Númenor. 167, 169, 173, 182, 185, 189, 193, 214–15, 217, 220, 223. *Bay of Andúnië* 167. *Lord(s) of Andúnië* 171, 173, 182, 215, 217, 219, 223

Andustar The western promontory of Númenor. 165, 167, 217. Translated *the Westlands* 165, 169, 181, 185, 189, 194, 196, 215. *Lady of the Westlands*, Erendis, 180

Anfalas Fief of Gondor; coastal region between the mouths of the rivers Lefnui and Morthond. 384. In Westron translated *Langstrand* 255

Anfauglith Name of the plain of Ard-galen after its desolation by Morgoth in the Dagor Bragollach. 17, 58

Angband The great fortress of Morgoth in the North-west of Middle-earth. 18, 37, 51, 55, 58, 66–7, 75, 78–9, 81, 89–90, 94, 128, 149, 153–9, 161, 195, 232, 385. *The Siege of Angband* 34, 53, 155

Angelimar Twentieth Prince of Dol Amroth, grandfather of Imrahil. 248

Anglachel Beleg's sword. 148. See *Gurthang*.

Angmar The Witch-realm ruled by the Lord of the Nazgûl at the northern end of the Misty Mountains. 313, 322, 354, 390, 413

Angren Sindarin name of the Isen, q.v. (also *Sîr Angren*, River Isen). 175, 214, 262, 264, 305–6, 318, 370. See *Athrad Angren*.

Angrenost Sindarin name of Isengard, q.v. 305–6, 318, 370–2

Angrod Noldorin prince, the third son of Finarfin; slain in the Dagor Bragollach. 52, 159, 231, 250

Annael Grey-elf of Mithrim, fosterfather of Tuor. 17–21, 25, 56

Annatar 'Lord of Gifts', name given to himself by Sauron in the Second Age. 236, 254. See *Artano*, *Aulendil*.

Annon-in-Gelydh Entrance to a subterranean watercourse in the western hills of Dor-lómin, leading to Cirith Ninniach. 18. Translated *Gate of the Noldor* 18–21, 51, 162

Annúminas 'Tower of the West', ancient seat of the Kings of Arnor beside Lake Nenuial; afterwards restored by King Elessar. 410–11, 413

Anórien Region of Gondor north of Ered Nimrais. 260, 301, 306, 308–9, 338, 369–70, 384, 387

Anor-stone, *Stone of Anor* The *palantír* of Minas Anor. 403–4, 406–8, 410–12, 414

Anwar See *Amon Anwar*.

Ar-Abattârik Adûnaic name of Tar-Ardamin. 222

Ar-Adûnakhôr   Twentieth Ruler of Númenor; named in Quenya *Tar-Herunúmen*. 218, 222, 226–7

Aragorn   Thirty-ninth Heir of Isildur in the direct line; King of the reunited realms of Arnor and Gondor after the War of the Ring; wedded Arwen, daughter of Elrond. 251, 255, 286, 312, 337, 341–4, 353, 365, 368–9, 398, 401–2, 408–9, 413–14. See *Elessar, Elfstone, Strider, Thorongil*.

*Arandor   The 'Kingsland' of Númenor. 165, 169

*Arandur   'King's servant, minister', Quenya term for the Stewards of Gondor. 313, 319

Aranrúth   'King's Ire', Thingol's sword. 171

Aranwë   Elf of Gondolin, father of Voronwë. 32, 45. *Aranwion*, son of Aranwë. 50

Aratan   Second son of Isildur, slain at the Gladden Fields. 271, 274, 279

*Ar-Belzagar   Adûnaic name of Tar-Calmacil. 222

Arda   'The Realm', name of the Earth as the Kingdom of Manwë. 67–8, 156, 173, 201, 254, 397

Aredhel   Sister of Turgon and mother of Maeglin. 54

Ar-Gimilzôr   Twenty-third Ruler of Númenor; named in Quenya *Tar-Telemnar*. 223, 227

Ar-Inziladûn   Adûnaic name of Tar-Palantir. 223, 227

Arkenstone   The great jewel of the Lonely Mountain. 328

Armenelos   City of the Kings in Númenor. 165, 169, 173, 175–7, 181, 183–6, 189–90, 192–3, 195–9, 201, 203–5, 208, 218

Arminas   Noldorin Elf, who with Gelmir came upon Tuor at Annon-in-Gelydh, and afterwards went to Nargothrond to warn Orodreth of its peril. 21–2, 51–2, 159–62

Arnor   The northern realm of the Númenóreans in Middle-earth. 173, 271, 275, 277–8, 282, 284, 287, 306, 308, 370, 406, 408–9, 411, 413. *The North(ern) Kingdom, Northern Realm* 264, 277, 284–5, 287, 295, 369–70, 411

Aros   The southern river of Doriath. 77

Ar-Pharazôn   Twenty-fifth and last Ruler of Númenor, who perished in the Downfall; named in Quenya *Tar-Calion*. 165, 215, 224, 317

*Arroch   The horse of Húrin of Dor-lómin. 70

Ar-Sakalthôr   Twenty-second Ruler of Númenor; named in Quenya *Tar-Falassion*. 223

Artamir   Elder son of Ondoher King of Gondor; slain in battle with the Wainriders. 291–2, 294–5

*Artanis   Name given to Galadriel by her father. 231, 266

*Artano   'High-smith', name given to himself by Sauron in the Second Age. 254. See *Annatar, Aulendil*.

Arthedain   One of the three kingdoms into which Arnor was divided in the ninth century of the Third Age; bounded by the rivers Baranduin and Lhûn, extending eastwards to the Weather Hills, and with its chief place at Fornost. 287, 413

Balrogs See *Gothmog*.

**Barach* A forester of the People of Haleth in the story of 'The Faithful Stone'. 380–2

Barad-dûr 'The Dark Tower' of Sauron in Mordor. 257–8, 272, 279–80, 312, 329, 337, 339, 344, 387, 405, 409, 412. *Lord of Barad-dûr*, Sauron, 346

Barad Eithel 'Tower of the Well', the fortress of the Noldor at Eithel Sirion. 65

Baragund Father of Morwen the wife of Húrin; nephew of Barahir and one of his twelve companions on Dorthonion. 57, 63, 215–16

Barahir Father of Beren; rescued Finrod Felagund in the Dagor Bragollach, and received from him his ring; slain on Dorthonion. 63. *The Ring of Barahir* 171–2

Baranduin 'The long gold-brown river' in Eriador, in the Shire called the Brandywine. 175, 239, 261–2, 344. *Brandywine* 214, *Brandywine Bridge* 284; *the River* 323

Bar-en-Danwedh 'House of Ransom', the name that Mîm gave to his dwelling on Amon Rûdh when he yielded it to Túrin. 100–1, 104, 148, 150–2. See *Echad i Sedryn*.

**Bar-en-Nibin-noeg* 'House of the Petty-dwarves', Mîm's dwelling on Amon Rûdh. 100

**Bar Erib* A stronghold in Dor-Cúarthol, not far south of Amon Rûdh. 153

Barrow-downs Downs east of the Old Forest, on which were great burial-mounds said to have been built in the First Age by the forefathers of the Edain before they entered Beleriand. 348, 370. See *Tyrn Gorthad*.

Barrow-wights Evil spirits dwelling in the burial-mounds on the Barrow-downs. 348, 354

Battle of Azanulbizar See *Azanulbizar*.

Battle of Dagorlad See *Dagorlad*.

Battle of Dale Battle of the War of the Ring in which Sauron's northern army defeated the Men of Dale and the Dwarves of Erebor. 326–7

Battle of the Camp The victory of Eärnil II of Gondor over the Wainriders in Ithilien in Third Age 1944. 295

Battle of the Field of Celebrant. See *Field of Celebrant*.

**Battle of the Gwathló* The rout of Sauron by the Númenóreans in Second Age 1700. 239

Battle of the Hornburg Assault on the Hornburg by the army of Saruman in the War of the Ring. 366

Battle of the Pelennor (*Fields*) See *Pelennor*.

**Battle of the Plains* The defeat of Narmacil II of Gondor by the Wainriders in the lands south of Mirkwood in Third Age 1856. 289, 292, 311–12

Battle of Tumhalad See *Tumhalad*.

Battle Plain See *Dagorlad*.

Battles of the Fords of Isen Two battles fought during the War of the

Ring between Riders of Rohan and Saruman's forces out of Isengard. *The First Battle* described 355–9, referred to 364; *the Second Battle* described 359–63, referred to 368; other references 355, 366, 368–9, 387

Bauglir 'The Constrainer', a name of Morgoth. 66

Bay of Balar See *Balar.*

Bay of Belfalas See *Belfalas.*

Beacons of Gondor 300–1, 314–15, 319

Beleg Elf of Doriath; a great archer, and chief of Thingol's marchwardens; friend and companion of Túrin, by whom he was slain. 37, 51, 54, 73–4, 77, 79–80, 82–5, 90–6, 134, 145, 147–8, 151–4. Called *Cúthalion* 79, 94, translated *(the) Strongbow* 73, 77, 82, 90, 95

Belegaer 'The Great Sea' of the West, between Middle-earth and Aman. 24, 34. *The Great Sea* 20, 24–5, 30, 35, 171, 174–5, 179, 181, 184, 200, 241, 247; in many other passages called simply *the Sea.*

Belegost One of the two cities of the Dwarves in the Blue Mountains. 55, 75, 128, 146, 235, 252

Belegund Father of Rían wife of Huor; nephew of Barahir and one of his twelve companions on Dorthonion. 58, 215

Beleriand Lands west of the Blue Mountains in the Elder Days. 17, 20, 22, 25–6, 33, 44, 58, 63, 67–8, 73, 85, 125, 146, 156, 171, 214–15, 228–9, 231–3, 247, 256–7, 259, 281, 377–9, 382, 384–5, 387. *East Beleriand* (divided from West Beleriand by the river Sirion) 75, 147. *Tongue of Beleriand*, see *Sindarin. First Battle of Beleriand* 77. Adjective *Beleriandic* 236, 244

Belfalas Fief of Gondor; coastal region looking on to the great bay of the same name. 240, 243, 247–8, 255, 286, 316. *Bay of Belfalas* 175, 214, 242, 245–7, 263, 383

Bëor Leader of the first Men to enter Beleriand, progenitor of the First House of the Edain. 384. *House of, People of, Bëor* 57, 63–4, 147, 161, 171, 177, 214–15, 384; *Bëorian(s)* 215, 225

Beornings Men of the upper Vales of Anduin. 278, 343

*Beregar Man from the Westlands of Númenor, descended from the House of Bëor; father of Erendis. 177, 181, 183, 185, 190, 193–4

Beren (1) Man of the House of Bëor, who cut the Silmaril from Morgoth's crown, and alone of mortal Men returned from the dead. 57–8, 63, 74, 77, 79, 84, 116, 157, 161, 171. Called after his return from Angband *Erchamion* 77, translated *One-hand* 57, 171; and *Camlost* 'Empty-handed' 161

Beren (2) Nineteenth Ruling Steward of Gondor, who gave the keys of Orthanc to Saruman. 373, 404

*Bereth Sister of Baragund and Belegund and ancestress of Erendis. 215–16

Berúthiel Queen of Tarannon Falastur, twelfth King of Gondor. 401–2

Bilbo Baggins Hobbit of the Shire, finder of the One Ring. 321–7, 329–35, 343, 354, 406. See *Baggins.*

Celebrant   River rising in Mirrormere and flowing through Lothlórien to join Anduin. 260, 281–2. Translated *Silverlode* 245, 260–1, 281, 343. See *Field of Celebrant*.

Celebrían   Daughter of Celeborn and Galadriel, wedded to Elrond. 234, 237, 240, 244, 251

Celebrimbor   'Hand of Silver', greatest of the smiths of Eregion, maker of the Three Rings of the Elves; slain by Sauron. 235–8, 244, 250–2, 254

Celebros   'Silver Foam' or 'Silver Rain', a stream in Brethil falling down to Teiglin near the Crossings. 123, 127, 130, 136

Celegorm   The third son of Fëanor. 54, 235

Celon   River in East Beleriand, rising in the Hill of Himring. 77

Celos   One of the rivers of Lebennin in Gondor; tributary of the Sirith. ('The name must be derived from the root *kelu-* "flow out swiftly", formed with an ending *-sse*, *-ssa*, seen in Quenya *kelussë* "freshet, water falling out swiftly from a rocky spring".') 243

Ceorl   Rider of Rohan who brought news of the Second Battle of the Fords of Isen. 364, 366, 368

Cerin Amroth   'Amroth's Mound' in Lórien. 216, 240, 246, 255

Cermië   Quenya name of the seventh month according to the Númenórean calendar, corresponding to July. 291–2, 294

Children of Aulë   The Dwarves. 235

Children of Earth   Elves and Men. 29

Children of Ilúvatar   Elves and Men. 156. *The Elder Children*, Elves, 62

Children of the World   Elves and Men. 56

Circles of the World   67, 242, 395

Círdan   Called 'the Shipwright'; Telerin Elf, 'Lord of the Havens' of the Falas; at their destruction after the Nirnaeth Arnoediad escaped with Gil-galad to the Isle of Balar; during the Second and Third Ages keeper of the Grey Havens in the Gulf of Lhûn; at the coming of Mithrandir entrusted to him Narya, the Ring of Fire. 20, 32, 34–5, 51–2, 53, 55, 156, 159–60, 162, 171, 174–6, 200, 205, 232, 237, 239, 247, 254, 283, 388–9, 392, 400, 414

Cirion   Twelfth Ruling Steward of Gondor, who granted Calenardhon to the Rohirrim after the Battle of the Field of Celebrant in Third Age 2510. 278, 288, 296–7, 299, 301–10, 313, 315, 317, 371. *Chronicle of, Tale of, Cirion and Eorl* 278, 288, 296, 310. *Oath of Cirion* 310, 317, 365, 371; words of the oath 305, 317

Cirith Dúath   'Shadow Cleft', former name of Cirith Ungol, q.v. 280

Cirith Forn en Andrath   'The High-climbing Pass of the North' over the Misty Mountains east of Rivendell. 271, 278. Called *the High Pass* 278, 353, and *the Pass of Imladris* 281–2.

Cirith Ninniach   'Rainbow Cleft', name given by Tuor to the ravine leading from the western hills of Dor-lómin to the Firth of Drengist. 23, 46

Cirith Ungol   'Spider's Cleft', pass over the Ephel Dúath above Minas Morghul. 280. See *Cirith Dúath*.

Dungortheb For *Nan Dungortheb*, 'Valley of Dreadful Death', between the precipices of Ered Gorgoroth and the Girdle of Melian. 41

Dunharrow Fortified refuge in Ered Nimrais above Harrowdale, approached by a climbing road at each turn of which were set the statues called Púkel-men. 382–4, 387, 406. *Dead Men of Dunharrow*, Men of Ered Nimrais who were cursed by Isildur for breaking their oath of allegiance to him. 370

Dúnhere Rider of Rohan, Lord of Harrowdale; fought at the Fords of Isen and at the Pelennor Fields, where he was slain. 362–3, 366

Dunland A country about the west-skirts of the Misty Mountains at their far southern end, inhabited by the Dunlendings. 263, 347, 354, 370

Dunlendings Inhabitants of Dunland, remnants of an old race of Men that once lived in the valleys of Ered Nimrais; akin to the Dead Men of Dunharrow and to the Breelanders. 262, 264, 362, 364, 366, 370–3. *The Dunlending*, Saruman's agent, the 'squint-eyed southerner' in the inn at Bree, 348–9, 354. Adjectives *Dunlending*, 357, and *Dunlendish*, 347, 359, 362, 372–3

Durin I Eldest of the the Seven Fathers of the Dwarves. *Heir of Durin*, Thorin Oakenshield, 328. *Durin's Folk* 238, 324, 328, 334; *Durin's House, House of Durin* 328–9

Durin III King of Durin's Folk in Khazad-dûm at the time of Sauron's assault on Eregion. 238

Dwarf-road (i) The road leading down into Beleriand from Nogrod and Belegost and crossing Gelion at Sarn Athrad. 75 (ii) Translating *Men-i-Naugrim*, a name of the Old Forest Road (see *Roads*). 280

Dwarves 55, 75, 97–9, 102–3, 128, 146, 235–8, 241, 252, 254, 258–9, 281, 299, 318, 321–4, 326–8, 330, 332–6, 353, 379, 382, 387, 397, 399. See *Petty-dwarves*.

*Dweller in the Deep, of the Deep See *Ulmo*.

Dwimordene 'Phantom-vale', name of Lórien among the Rohirrim. 298, 307

Eä The World, the material Universe; *Eä*, meaning in Elvish 'It is' or 'Let it be', was the word of Ilúvatar when the World began its existence. 173, 396

Eagles Of the Crissaegrim, 42–3, 55. Of Númenor, 166, 169 (see *Witnesses of Manwë*). With reference to Gwaihir, who rescued Gandalf from Orthanc, 346

*Eambar Ship built by Tar-Aldarion for his dwelling-place, on which was the Guildhouse of the Venturers. (The name doubtless means 'Sea-dwelling'.) 176, 178, 180, 182, 190, 201, 214

Eärendil Son of Tuor and Idril Turgon's daughter, born in Gondolin; wedded Elwing daughter of Dior Thingol's Heir; father of Elrond and Elros; sailed with Elwing to Aman and pleaded for help against Morgoth (see 156); set to sail the skies in his ship Vingilot bearing

Esgalduin The river of Doriath, dividing the forests of Neldoreth and Region and flowing into Sirion. 74, 82, 120

Estelmo Elendur's esquire, who survived the disaster of the Gladden Fields. 276, 282

Estolad The land south of Nan Elmoth in East Beleriand where the Men of the followings of Bëor and Marach dwelt after they had crossed the Blue Mountains. 77

Ethir Anduin 'Outflow of Anduin', the delta of the Great River in the Bay of Belfalas. 240, 242, 402

Ethraid Engrin Sindarin name (also in singular form *Athrad Angren*) of the Fords of Isen, q.v. 264, 318

Evendim See *Nenuial.*

Evermind See *simbelmynë.*

Evil Breath A wind out of Angband that brought sickness to Dor-lómin, from which Túrin's sister Urwen (Lalaith) died. 58–9, 61

Exiles, The The rebellious Noldor who returned to Middle-earth from Aman. 20, 55, 229, 259

Faelivrin Name given to Finduilas by Gwindor. 37, 54

Fair Folk The Eldar. 72

Faithful, The (i) Those Númenóreans who were not estranged from the Eldar and continued to reverence the Valar in the days of Tar-Ancalimon and later kings. 222–3, 265, 316–17. (ii) 'The Faithful' of the Fourth Age. 395

Falas The western coasts of Beleriand, south of Nevrast. 33–4, 51. *Havens of the Falas* 247

Falastur 'Lord of the Coasts', name of Tarannon, twelfth King of Gondor. 401

Falathrim Telerin Elves of the Falas, whose lord was Círdan. 33

Fallohides One of the three peoples into which the Hobbits were divided, described in the Prologue (1) to *The Lord of the Rings*. 287

Fangorn (i) The oldest of the Ents and the guardian of Fangorn Forest. 261. Translated *Treebeard* 253, 366. (ii) The Forest of Fangorn, at the south-eastern end of the Misty Mountains, about the upper waters of the rivers Entwash and Limlight. 241, 261, 305, 312, 318, 343, 371–2. See *Entwood.*

Faramir (1) Younger son of Ondoher King of Gondor; slain in battle with the Wainriders. 291, 294–5

Faramir (2) Younger son of Denethor II, Steward of Gondor; Captain of the Rangers of Ithilien; after the War of the Ring Prince of Ithilien and Steward of Gondor. 344, 397, 399, 408, 413

Far Harad See *Harad.*

Faroth See *Taur-en-Faroth.*

Fëanor Eldest son of Finwë, half-brother of Fingolfin and Finarfin; leader of the Noldor in their rebellion against the Valar; maker of the

Silmarils and of the *palantíri*. 23, 76, 229–33, 235–6, 248. *Sons of Fëanor* 146; *Fëanorians* 251. *Fëanorian lamps* 22, 51, 154

Fëanturi 'Masters of Spirits', the Valar Námo (Mandos) and Irmo (Lórien). 397. See *Nurufantur, Olofantur.*

Felagund The name by which Finrod was known after the establishment of Nargothrond; for references see *Finrod*. *Doors of Felagund* 116–17, 119

Felaróf The horse of Eorl the Young. 299, 314

Fell Winter The winter of the year 495 from the rising of the Moon, after the fall of Nargothrond. 25, 28, 36, 38, 42, 52, 112

Fenmarch Region of Rohan west of the Mering Stream. 314

Ferny A family of Men in Bree. *Bill Ferny* 354

Field of Celebrant Partial translation of *Parth Celebrant*, q.v. The grasslands between the rivers Silverlode (Celebrant) and Limlight; in restricted sense of Gondor, the land between the lower Limlight and Anduin. *Field of Celebrant* is often used of the *Battle of the Field of Celebrant*, the victory of Cirion and Eorl over the Balchoth in Third Age 2510, references to which are included here. 260, 288, 290, 296, 299–300, 307 (*Celebrant*), 313, 339, 371

Fíli Dwarf of the House of Durin; nephew and companion of Thorin Oakenshield; slain in the Battle of Five Armies. 335

Finarfin Third son of Finwë, the younger of Fëanor's half-brothers; remained in Aman after the Flight of the Noldor and ruled the remnant of his people in Tirion; father of Finrod, Orodreth, Angrod, Aegnor, and Galadriel. 229–30; other references are to Finarfin's house, kin, people, or children: 21, 52, 157, 159, 229, 231, 234, 250, 255

Finduilas (*1*) Daughter of Orodreth, loved by Gwindor; captured in the sack of Nargothrond, killed by Orcs at the Crossings of Teiglin and buried in the Haudh-en-Elleth. 37, 54, 108–9, 111–12, 122, 130, 143, 150, 157–9

Finduilas (*2*) Daughter of Adrahil, Prince of Dol Amroth; wife of Denethor II, Steward of Gondor, mother of Boromir and Faramir. 407, 413

Fingolfin Second son of Finwë, the elder of Fëanor's half-brothers; High King of the Noldor in Beleriand, dwelling in Hithlum; slain by Morgoth in single combat; father of Fingon, Turgon, and Aredhel. 43, 55–60, 215. *House of, people of, Fingolfin* 45, 68, 157; *son of Fingolfin*, Turgon, 18, 45

Fingon Eldest son of Fingolfin; High King of the Noldor in Beleriand after his father; slain by Gothmog in the Nirnaeth Arnoediad; father of Gil-galad. 18, 59–60, 63, 65–6, 75, 146, 400. *Son of Fingon*, Gil-galad, 199

Finrod Eldest son of Finarfin; founder and King of Nargothrond, whence his name *Felagund* 'cave-hewer'; died in defence of Beren in the dungeons of Tol-in-Gaurhoth. 38, 54, 229–30. *Finrod Felagund* 234,

255; *Felagund* 87, 112, 116–17, 250, 384. [Rejected name of *Finarfin* 255]

Finwë King of the Noldor in Aman; father of Fëanor, Fingolfin, and Finarfin; slain by Morgoth at Formenos. 230

*Firien-dale Cleft in which the Mering Stream rose. 300, 314

*Firienholt Another name for the Firien Wood, of the same meaning. 306, 318

Firien Wood In full *Halifirien Wood*; in Ered Nimrais about the Mering Stream and on the slopes of the Halifirien. 300–1, 314, 318. Also called *Firienholt*, q.v.; *the Whispering Wood* 301–2; and *the Wood of Anwar* 306

Firth of Drengist See *Drengist.*

flet Old English word meaning 'floor'; a *talan*, q.v. 245–6

Folcwine Fourteenth King of Rohan, great-grandfather of Théoden; reconquered the west-march of Rohan between Adorn and Isen. 315, 364

Folde A region of Rohan about Edoras, part of the King's Lands. 367

Ford of Carrock Ford over Anduin between the Carrock and the east bank of the river; but probably here referring to the Old Ford, where the Old Forest Road crossed Anduin, south of the Ford of Carrock. 278

Fords of Isen Crossing of the Isen by the great Númenórean road linking Gondor and Arnor; called in Sindarin *Athrad Angren* and *Ethraid Engrin*, q.v. 264, 271, 306, 314, 316, 318, 346, 354, 356–66, 368–73, 411; see also *Battles of the Fords of Isen.*

Fords of the Poros Crossing of the river Poros on the Harad Road. 291

Forest River River flowing from Ered Mithrin through northern Mirkwood and into the Long Lake. 295

Forest Road See *Roads.*

Fornost 'Northern Fortress', in full *Fornost Erain* 'Norbury of the Kings', later seat of the Kings of Arnor on the North Downs, after the abandonment of Annúminas. 271, 278, 314, 369, 413

*Forostar The northern promontory of Númenor. 165, 167, 169, 173. Translated *the Northlands* 165, 169, *the north country* 174

*Forthwini Son of Marhwini; leader of the Éothéod in the time of King Ondoher of Gondor. 291

*Forweg Man of Dor-lómin, captain of the outlaw-band (*Gaurwaith*) that Túrin joined; slain by Túrin. 85–9, 147–8

Fréalaf Tenth King of Rohan, nephew of King Helm Hammerhand. 373

Freca A vassal of King Helm Hammerhand, slain by him. 364–5

*Free Men of the North See *Northmen.*

Frodo Frodo Baggins, Hobbit of the Shire; the Ringbearer in the War of the Ring. 148, 216, 228–9, 231, 246, 257, 261, 287, 310, 321, 326–30, 336, 347, 354

Frumgar Leader of the northward migration of the Éothéod out of the Vales of Anduin. 313

Galadhon Father of Celeborn. 233, 266

Galadhrim The Elves of Lórien. 245–6, 260–1, 267

Galador First Lord of Dol Amroth, son of Imrazôr the Númenórean and the Elf Mithrellas. 248, 316

Galadriel Daughter of Finarfin; one of the leaders of the Noldorin rebellion against the Valar (see 232); wife of Celeborn, with whom she remained in Middle-earth after the end of the First Age; Lady of Lothlórien. 168, 206, 228–38, 240, 243–5, 249–56, 258, 266–7, 281, 286, 339, 388, 395, 405. Called *Lady of the Noldor* 249, *Lady of the Golden Wood* 299, *the White Lady* 307, 319; see also *Al(a)táriel*, *Artanis*, *Nerwen*.

Galathil Brother of Celeborn and father of Nimloth the mother of Elwing. 233, 266

Galdor Called *the Tall*; son of Hador Goldenhead and Lord of Dor-lómin after him; father of Húrin and Huor; slain at Eithel Sirion. 21, 57, 60, 66, 75, 79, 105

Gamgee A family of Hobbits of the Shire. See *Elanor, Hamfast, Samwise*.

Gamil Zirak Called *the Old*; Dwarf smith, master of Telchar of Nogrod. 76

Gandalf One of the Istari (Wizards), member of the Fellowship of the Ring. *Gandalf* ('Elf of the Wand') was his name among Northern Men; see 391, 399. 54–5, 235, 283–4, 312, 314, Part 3 §§ III and IV *passim*, 356, 360, 363–6, 368, Part 4 §§ II and III *passim*. See *Olórin, Mithrandir, Incánus, Tharkûn, Greyhame*.

Gap of Rohan, the Gap The opening, some 20 miles wide, between the last end of the Misty Mountains and the north-thrust spur of the White Mountains, through which flowed the river Isen. 340, 356–7, 364, 370, 412; *Gap of Calenardhon* 370

Gate of the Noldor See *Annon-in-Gelydh*.

Gates of Mordor See *Morannon*.

Gaurwaith The outlaw-band on the western borders of Doriath that Túrin joined, and of which he became the captain. 85, 87, 90. Translated *Wolf-men* 85, 90

Gelmir Noldorin Elf, who with Arminas came upon Tuor at Annon-in-Gelydh and afterwards went to Nargothrond to warn Orodreth of its peril. 21–2, 51–2, 159–62

Gethron Man of Húrin's household who with Grithnir accompanied Túrin to Doriath and afterwards returned to Dor-lómin. 71, 73–4

Ghân-buri-Ghân Chieftain of the Drúedain or 'Wild Men' of Drúadan Forest. 382–5; *Ghân* 385

Gil-galad 'Star of Radiance', the name by which Ereinion son of Fingon was known. After the death of Turgon he became the last High King of the Noldor in Middle-earth, and remained in Lindon after the end of the First Age; leader with Elendil of the Last Alliance of Elves and Men and slain with him in combat with Sauron. 148, 168, 174–5, 185, 199, 203, 206, 212–13, 217, 219–20, 236–9, 243–4, 247, 254, 258, 262,

to the lands west of Sirion. 130, 377, 385. *House of, People of, Folk of, Men of, Haleth* 63, 85, 87, 110–11, 129, 134, 377–80, 382–4, 386–7. See *Brethil, Halethrim.*

*Halethrim The People of Haleth. 140

Halflings Hobbits; translation of Sindarin *periannath.* 286–7, 337, 339, 342, 349–52, 354, 398. *Land of the Halflings* 339–40, 354; *Halflings' Leaf* 347–8, 350. See *Perian.*

Halifirien 'Holy Mount', name in Rohan of *Amon Anwar,* q.v. 300–1, 306, 310, 314, 319. *Halifirien Wood* 318. See *Eilenaer.*

Halimath The ninth month in the Shire Calendar. 279. See *Yavannië, Ivanneth.*

*Hallacar Son of Hallatan of Hyarastorni; wedded Tar-Ancalimë, first Ruling Queen of Númenor, with whom he was at strife. 211–12, 220. See *Mámandil.*

Hallas Son of Cirion; thirteenth Ruling Steward of Gondor; deviser of the names *Rohan* and *Rohirrim.* 297, 302, 307

*Hallatan Lord of Hyarastorni in the Mittalmar (Inlands) of Númenor; cousin of Tar-Aldarion. 197–9, 204, 206, 209, 211, 217, 220. Called *the Sheep-lord* 195

Halmir Lord of the Haladin, father of Haldir. 57

Háma Captain of the household of King Théoden. 367

Hamfast Gamgee Sam Gamgee's father. (The name *Hamfast* is Anglo-Saxon *hām-fæst,* literally 'home-fixed', 'home-firm'.) 327. Called *Gaffer Gamgee* and *the Gaffer,* 327, 352

Handir Lord of the Haladin, son of Haldir and Glóredhel. 91. *Son of Handir,* Brandir the Lame, 110, 129, 138, 141

Harad 'The South', used vaguely of countries far south of Gondor and Mordor. 181, 236, 295, 312, 398–9, 402. *Near Harad* 312, 398; *Far Harad* 398–9

Haradrim Men of the Harad. 399

Haradwaith 'South-folk', the Harad. 383

Hareth Daughter of Halmir of Brethil, wedded Galdor of Dor-lómin; mother of Húrin and Huor. 57, 63

Harfoots One of the three peoples into which the Hobbits were divided (see *Fallohides*). 287

Harlindon Lindon south of the Gulf of Lhûn. 252

Harrowdale Valley at the head of the Snowbourn, under the walls of Dunharrow. 366–8

*Hatholdir Man of Númenor, friend of Tar-Meneldur; father of Orchaldor. 173

Haudh-en-Elleth The mound in which Finduilas of Nargothrond was buried near the Crossings of Teiglin. (It is not clear what relation *Elleth,* rendered 'Elf-maid' and always so spelt, bears to *Eledh* 'Elda' seen in Morwen's name *Eledhwen.*) 112, 122, 124, 130, 137–8, 143. Translated *Mound of the Elf-maid* 112

Haudh-en-Ndengin 'Mound of the Slain' in the desert of Anfauglith,

*lairelossë 'Summer-snow-white', fragrant evergreen tree brought to Númenor by the Eldar of Eressëa. 167

Lalaith 'Laughter', name by which Urwen Húrin's daughter was called, from the stream that flowed past Húrin's house. 57–61, 147, 157. See Nen Lalaith.

Lamedon Region about the upper waters of the rivers Ciril and Ringló under the southern slopes of Ered Nimrais. 318

Lammoth Region north of the Firth of Drengist, between Ered Lómin and the Sea. 23, 52

*Land of Gift See Númenor, Yôzâyan.

Land of the Star Númenor; translation of Quenya Elenna·nórë in the Oath of Cirion. 305

Land of Willows See Nan-tathren.

*Langflood Name of Anduin among the Éothéod. 295

Langstrand See Anfalas.

*Langwell 'Source of the Langflood', name given by the Éothéod to the river from the northern Misty Mountains which after its junction with Greylin they called Langflood (Anduin). 295

*lár A league (very nearly three miles). 279, 285

*Larnach One of the Woodmen in the lands south of Teiglin. 88, 90. Daughter of Larnach 88–90

Last Alliance The league made at the end of the Second Age between Elendil and Gil-galad to defeat Sauron; also the Alliance, the War of the (Last) Alliance. 237, 239, 243, 245, 258, 271, 278–82, 308, 395

Laurelin 'Song of Gold', the younger of the Two Trees of Valinor. 49, 168, 230. Called the Tree of the Sun 49, the Golden Tree of Valinor 168, 253

Laurelindorinan 'Valley of Singing Gold', see Lórien (2).

Laurenandë See Lórien (2).

*laurinquë Yellow-flowered tree of the Hyarrostar in Númenor. 168

Lebennin 'Five Rivers' (those being Erui, Sirith, Celos, Serni, and Gilrain), land between Ered Nimrais and Ethir Anduin; one of the 'faithful fiefs' of Gondor. 242, 316

Lefnui River flowing to the sea from the western end of Ered Nimrais. (The name means 'fifth', i.e. after Erui, Sirith, Serni, and Morthond, the rivers of Gondor that flowed into Anduin or the Bay of Belfalas.) 263, 383–4

Legolas Sindarin Elf of Northern Mirkwood, son of Thranduil; one of the Fellowship of the Ring. 171, 246, 248, 256, 258, 315–16, 365–6, 395

lembas Sindarin name of the waybread of the Eldar. 148, 152, 276. Waybread (of the Elves) 33, 38, 152

Léod Lord of the Éothéod, father of Eorl the Young. 297, 301, 303, 311, 313–14

Lhûn River in the west of Eriador issuing in the Gulf of Lhûn. 239. Gulf of Lhûn 213. Frequently in an adapted spelling Lune, q.v.

Northern Waste Region of cold in the far North of Middle-earth (also called *Forodwaith*, see Introduction p. 14). 242

*Northlands (of Númenor) See *Forostar*.

Northmen The horsemen of Rhovanion, allies of Gondor, ancestrally related to the Edain; from them derived the *Éothéod*, q.v. 288–90, 295–7, 310–13; with reference to the Rohirrim 372. *Free Men of the North* 258

North–South Road See *Roads*.

*Núath, Woods of Woods extending westward from the upper waters of the river Narog. 36, 53

*Númellótë 'Flower of the West' = *Inziladûn*. 227

*Númendil Seventeenth Lord of Andúnië. 223

Númenor (In full Quenya form *Númenórë*, 199.) 'Westernesse', 'Westland', the great island prepared by the Valar as a dwelling-place for the Edain after the ending of the First Age. 52, 56, Part 2 §§ I-III *passim*, 236, 239, 247, 262–3, 265, 272, 276, 279–80, 284, 287–8, 316–17, 385–6, 398, 400, 403, 414. Called *the Great Isle* 386, *Isle of Kings* 199, *Isle of Westernesse* 183, *Land of Gift* 165, 167, 201, *Land of the Star* 305; and see *Akallabêth*, *Elenna·nórë*, *Yôzâyan*. References to the *Downfall of Númenor* are given in a separate entry.

Númenóreans The Men of Númenor. (The following references include *Númenórean* used as an adjective.) Part 2 §§ I-III *passim* (see especially 206–7, 224–5), 236, 239, 247–8, 253, 255, 258, 261–5, 273, 278–9, 283, 285–8, 314, 369, 383–4, 386, 398–9, 401, 404, 409. *Kings of Men* 27, 200, 259, 303; *Men of the Sea* 170, 263; and see *Dúnedain*. *Númenórean tongue, speech*, see *Adûnaic*.

*Númerrámar 'West-wings', the ship of Vëantur in which Aldarion made his first voyage to Middle-earth. 175

*Nunduinë River in the west of Númenor, flowing into the sea at Eldalondë. 168

*Núneth Mother of Erendis. 183, 186, 190–1, 193, 198

Núrnen 'Sad Water', inland sea in the south of Mordor. 398

*Nurufantur One of the *Fëanturi*, q.v.; the earlier 'true' name of Mandos, before it was replaced by Námo. 397. See *Olofantur*.

Ohtar Esquire of Isildur, who brought the shards of Narsil to Imladris. (On the name *Ohtar* 'warrior' see 282). 272–5, 282

*Oghor-hai Name given to the Drúedain by Orcs. 379

*oiolairë 'Ever-summer', an evergreen tree brought to Númenor by the Eldar of Eressëa, from which was cut the Bough of Return set upon the Númenórean ships. (*Corollairë*, the Green Mound of the Trees in Valinor, was also called *Coron Oiolairë*: Appendix to *The Silmarillion*, entry *coron*). 167, 179, 187–8, 192, 205, 215. *Bough of Return* 179–80, 192

Oiolossë 'Ever-snow-white', the Mountain of Manwë in Aman. 55. See *Amon Uilos*, *Taniquetil*.

*Old Company Name given to the original members of Túrin's band in Dor-Cúarthol. 153

Ossë Maia of the Sea, vassal of Ulmo. 30, 32, 53, 156, 178–9, 181, 214

Ossiriand 'Land of Seven Rivers' between the river Gelion and the Blue Mountains in the Eldar Days. 77, 234, 256, 383. See *Lindon.*

Ost-in-Edhil The city of the Elves in Eregion. 236

Ostoher Seventh King of Gondor. 319

palantíri (Singular *palantír*). The seven Seeing Stones brought by Elendil and his sons from Númenor; made by Fëanor in Aman. 276, 301, 306, 354, 401, 403–15 (in Part 4 § III frequently referred to as the *Stone(s)*).

*Palarran 'Far-Wanderer', a great ship built by Tar-Aldarion. 178–9, 187–8, 212, 401

*Pallando One of the Blue Wizards (*Ithryn Luin*). 393–4, 401

*Parmaitë Name given to Tar-Elendil. (Quenya *parma* 'book'; the second element is no doubt *-maitë* '-handed', cf. *Tar-Telemmaitë*). 219

Parth Celebrant 'Field (grassland) of Silverlode'; Sindarin name usually translated *Field of Celebrant*, q.v. 260

Parth Galen 'Green Sward', a grassy place on the northern slopes of Amon Hen by the shore of Nen Hithoel. 405

Pass of Caradhras See *Caradhras.*

Pass of Imladris See *Cirith Forn en Andrath.*

Pelargir City and haven on the delta of Anduin. 264–5, 291, 402

Pelendur Steward of Gondor. 413

Pelennor (*Fields*) 'Fenced Land', the 'townlands' of Minas Tirith, guarded by the wall of Rammas Echor, on which was fought the greatest battle of the War of the Ring. 290, 326, 366, 369

Pelóri The mountains on the coast of Aman. 36

Peregrin Took Hobbit of the Shire, one of the Fellowship of the Ring. 287, 310, 321, 329, 331, 368, 405–6, 410, 413. Called *Pippin* 287, 314

Perian Sindarin word translated *Halfling*, q.v.; plural *periannath*. 287

Petty-dwarves A race of Dwarves in Beleriand described in *The Silmarillion* p. 204. 100, 148, 150. See *Nibin-noeg, Noegyth Nibin.*

Pillar, The See *Meneltarma.*

Pippin See *Peregrin Took.*

Poros River flowing down from the Ephel Dúath to join Anduin above its delta. 295. See *Fords of the Poros.*

Púkel-men Name in Rohan for the images on the road to Dunharrow, but also used as a general equivalent to *Drúedain*, q.v. 263, 383–5, 387. See *Old Púkel-land.*

Quendi Original Elvish name for all Elves. 225

Quenya The ancient tongue, common to all Elves, in the form that it took in Valinor; brought to Middle-earth by the Noldorin exiles, but abandoned by them as a daily speech, save in Gondolin (see 55); for its use in Númenor see 216. 55, 216, 218, 221–2, 253, 255, 265–7, 282, 305, 317–18, 385, 388, 396, 399–401. *High Speech of the Noldor* 44, *of the West* 55; *High-elven* 112, 216, 218, 266, 396–7

Rivendell   Translation of Sindarin *Imladris*, q.v.; Elrond's dwelling in a deep valley of the Misty Mountains. 238, 264, 278, 283–4, 322, 327, 330, 347–8, 350, 353

Rivil   Stream falling northwards from Dorthonion and flowing into Sirion at the Fen of Serech. 66

Roads   (1) In Beleriand in the Elder Days: (i) The highway from Tol Sirion to Nargothrond by the Crossings of Teiglin. 38–9, 54, 91–2, 130, 149; called *the old South Road* 96. (ii) *The East Road*, from Mount Taras in the West, crossing Sirion at the Brithiach and Aros at the Arossiach, perhaps leading to Himring. 41, 54. (iii) See *Dwarf-road (i)*.

(2) East of the Blue Mountains: (i) The great Númenórean road linking the Two Kingdoms, by Tharbad and the Fords of Isen; called *the North–South Road* 264, 314, and (east of the Fords of Isen) *the West Road* 300; also *the Great Road* 306, *the Royal Road* 369–70, *the horseroad* 358, *the Greenway* (q.v.) 348; other references 271, 278, 300, 302, 314, 340, 363, 366. (ii) The branch road from (i) going to the Hornburg 358, 363 (see *Deeping-road*). (iii) The road from Isengard to the Fords of Isen 361, 365, 372. (iv) The Númenórean road from the Grey Havens of Rivendell, traversing the Shire; called *the East–West Road* 252, 278, *the East Road* 341; other references 271, 332, 335. (v) The road descending from the Pass of Imladris, crossing Anduin at the Old Ford, and traversing Mirkwood; called *the Old Forest Road* 281, 344, 401, *the Forest Road* 281–2, and *Men-i-Naugrim, the Dwarf-road*, q.v. (vi) Númenórean roads east of Anduin: the road through Ithilien 294, 312, called *the North Road* 293–4; roads east and north from the Morannon 312

Rochan(d)   See *Rohan*.

Rochon Methestel   'Rider of the Last Hope', the name of a song made concerning Borondir Udalraph, q.v. 313

Róg   The actual name (plural *Rógin*) of the Drúedain in the language of the Rohirrim, represented by the translation *Woses*. 387

Rohan   Form in Gondor of the Sindarin name *Rochan(d)* (318, 371), 'the Horse-country', the great grassy plain originally the northern part of Gondor, and then called *Calenardhon*, q.v. (For the name see 318.) 55, 237, 255, 260, 286, 288, 306, 311, 313–15, 318–19, 331, 339–41, 346–7, 355, 360, 362, 364, 368–9, 371–3, 384, 387, 400, 411–12. See *Mark, The*; *Gap of Rohan*; *Rohirrim*.

Rohirrim   'The Horse-lords' of Rohan. 55, 278, 286, 288, 290, 294, 301, 306–7, 309–11, 315–19, 355, 358–9, 362, 366, 369–73, 382, 384, 387, 400. *Riders of Rohan* 314–15, 356–7, 359–64, 366–9, 371, 373, 411. See *Eorlings*, *Éothéod*.

Rómendacil I   Tarostar, eighth King of Gondor, who took the title of *Rómendacil* 'East-victor' after his repulse of the first attacks on Gondor by Easterlings. 308, 319

Rómendacil II   Minalcar, for many years Regent and afterwards nine-

was continued to the sea after its confluence with Gilrain. Its mouth was blocked with shingles, and at any rate in later times ships approaching Anduin and making for Pelargir went by the eastern side of Tol Falas and took the sea-way passage made by the Númenóreans in the midst of the Delta of Anduin.') 243

Shadowfax The great horse of Rohan ridden by Gandalf in the War of the Ring. 314, 341, 364, 405

*Shadowy Isles Probably a name for the *Enchanted Isles*, q.v. 30, 52

Shadowy Mountains See *Ered Wethrin*.

*Sharbhund Name among the Petty-dwarves for *Amon Rûdh*, q.v. 98

Shire, The The chief dwelling-place of Hobbits in the west of Eriador. 234, 252, 287, 322–5, 327–9, 331–5, 339–42, 344–50, 352, 354. *Shire Calendar, Reckoning*, 279, 284. *Shire-folk* 323, 331, 333

Silmarien Daughter of Tar-Elendil; mother of Valandil first Lord of Andúnië and ancestress of Elendil the Tall. 171, 173, 208, 215, 219, 225, 277, 284

Silmarils The three jewels made by Fëanor before the destruction of the Two Trees of Valinor, and filled with their light. 52, 230, 233, 252. See *War of the Jewels*.

Silvan Elves Nandorin Elves who never passed west of the Misty Mountains but remained in the Vale of Anduin and in Greenwood the Great. 214, 240–1, 243, 245, 247–8, 256–60, 267, 272, 280. *Silvan Elvish, Silvan tongue* 241, 257, 259–60. See *Tawarwaith*.

Silverlode See *Celebrant*.

simbelmynë A small white flower, also called *alfirin* and *uilos*, q.v. 55, 316. Translated *Evermind* 48, 55

Sindar The Grey-elves; name applied to all the Elves of Telerin origin whom the returning Noldor found in Beleriand, save for the Green-elves of Ossiriand. 48, 228, 236, 247, 252, 256–9. *Grey-elves* 17–19, 21, 34, 68, 93, 100, 103, 234, 248

Sindarin Of the Sindar: 233, 240, 243–4, 252, 256, 258–60. Of the tongue of the Sindar: 54–5, 76, 148, 215–16, 231, 243, 247, 253, 255, 257, 261, 263, 265–7, 279, 281–2, 287, 301, 306, 313, 317–19, 377, 385, 388, 392, 399–400. *Tongue of Beleriand* 44, 215, *Grey-elven tongue* 146

*Sîr Angren See *Angren*.

*Siril The chief river of Númenor, flowing southwards from the Meneltarma. 168

Sirion The great river of Beleriand. 34–5, 38, 40–2, 54, 56, 78, 109, 114, 116, 120, 147. *Fens of Sirion* 147; *Havens of Sirion, Sirion's Haven*, see *Havens*; *Mouths of Sirion* 20, 34, 51, 53, 121, 159–60, 378; *Pass(es) of Sirion* 18, 110, 160; *Springs of Sirion* 160; *Vale (Valley) of Sirion* 28, 39, 43, 73, 96, 99, 109, 147–8

*Sîr Ninglor Sindarin name of the *Gladden River*, q.v. 280–1

Smaug The great Dragon of Erebor. In many references called *the Dragon*. 258, 321–4, 326, 328–30, 332–4

Sméagol Gollum. 353

Snowbourn River rising under the Starkhorn and flowing out down Harrowdale and past Edoras. 367

Sorontil 'Eagle-horn', a great height on the coast of the northern promontory of Númenor. 167

Soronto Númenórean, son of Tar-Aldarion's sister Ailinel and cousin of Tar-Ancalimë. 173, 208–9, 211, 213, 220, 225–6

South Downs Hills in Eriador south of Bree. 348

Southern Realm See *Gondor*.

Southfarthing One of the divisions of the Shire. 341, 354

South Kingdom See *Gondor*.

Spyhill See *Amon Ethir*.

Star (of Eärendil) See *Earendil*; *Land of the Star*, see *Númenor*.

Star of Elendil, *Star of the North (Kingdom)* See *Elendilmir*.

Stewards of Gondor 297, 302–6, 308–9, 315, 317, 319, 371–2, 403–4, 406–9, 413. *Book of the Stewards* 310. See *Arandur*.

Stock A village in the Shire, at the north end of the Marish. 352

Stone of Eärendil See *Elessar (1)*.

Stones, The See *palantíri*.

Stonewain Valley Valley in the Drúadan Forest at the eastern end of Ered Nimrais. (The name is a translation of *Imrath Gondraich*; *imrath* means 'a long narrow valley with a road or watercourse running through it lengthwise'.) 319, 382

Stoors One of the three peoples into which the Hobbits were divided; see *Fallohides*. 287, 339, 345, 348, 353

Strawheads Contemptuous name among the Easterlings in Hithlum for the People of Hador. 69

Strider The name of Aragorn in Bree. 354

Strongbow See *Beleg*.

Súlimë Quenya name of the third month according to the Númenórean calendar, corresponding to March. 21, 297. See *Gwaeron*.

Súrion See *Tar-Súrion*.

Súthburg Former name of the Hornburg. 371

Swanfleet See *Nîn-in-Eilph*.

talan (Plural *telain*). The wooden platforms in the trees of Lothlórien on which the Galadhrim dwelt. 245–6. See *flet*.

Talath Dirnen The plain north of Nargothrond, called *the Guarded Plain*. 92

taniquelassë Fragrant evergreen tree brought to Númenor by the Eldar of Eressëa. 167

Taniquetil The Mountain of Manwë in Aman. 30, 395. See *Amon Uilos*, *Oiolossë*.

Tar-Alcarin Seventeenth Ruler of Númenor. 222

Tar-Aldarion Sixth Ruler of Númenor, the Mariner King; by the Guild of Venturers called *the (Great) Captain*. 168, 171, 173–206, 208–9, 212–17, 219–20, 224–5, 227, 236, 239, 253, 262–5, 284, 386, 401. See *Anardil*.

Tar-Amandil Third Ruler of Númenor, grandson of Elros Tar-Minyatur.
217, 219, 225

Tar-Anárion Eighth Ruler of Númenor, son of Tar-Ancalimë and
Hallacar of Hyarastorni. 211–12, 217, 220. *Daughters of Tar-Anárion*
212, 220

Tar-Ancalimë Seventh Ruler of Númenor and the first Ruling Queen,
daughter of Tar-Aldarion and Erendis. 190–5, 197–8, 202–4, 206–9,
211–12, 217, 219–20, 225. See *Emerwen.*

Tar-Ancalimon Fourteenth Ruler of Númenor. 169, 221, 224, 226

*Tar-Anducal Name taken as Ruler of Númenor by Herucalmo, who
usurped the throne on the death of Tar-Vanimeldë his wife. 222

Tarannon Twelfth King of Gondor. 401–2. See *Falastur.*

*Tar-Ardamin Nineteenth Ruler of Númenor, called in Adûnaic Ar-
Abattârik. 222, 227

Taras Mountain on a promontory of Nevrast, beneath which was
Vinyamar, the ancient dwelling of Turgon. 26–7, 33, 36, 41, 54

*Taras-ness The headland from which Mount Taras rose. 28

Tar-Atanamir Thirteenth Ruler of Númenor, called *the Great* and *the
Unwilling.* 169, 216, 218, 221, 226–7

Tar-Calion Quenya name of Ar-Pharazôn. 224

Tar-Calmacil Eighteenth Ruler of Númenor, called in Adûnaic *Ar-
Belzagar.* 222–3, 226–7

Tar-Ciryatan Twelfth Ruler of Númenor. 221

Tar-Elendil Fourth Ruler of Númenor, father of Silmarien and Meneldur.
171–3, 175, 208, 214–15, 219, 225, 317. See *Parmaitë.*

*Tar-Elestirnë 'Lady of the Star-brow', name given to Erendis. 184, 205, 284

*Tar-Falassion Quenya name of Ar-Sakalthôr. 223

Tar-Herunúmen Quenya name of Ar-Adûnakhôr. 216, 218, 222

*Tar-Hostamir Quenya name of Ar-Zimrathon. 222

*Tarmasundar 'Roots of the Pillar', the five ridges extending from the
base of the Meneltarma. 166

Tar-Meneldur Fifth Ruler of Númenor, astronomer, father of Tar-
Aldarion. 167, 171, 173–81, 183–4, 186–8, 192–3, 195–206, 208, 212,
214–15, 219, 225, 236, 386. See *Elentirmo, Írimon.*

Tar-Minastir Eleventh Ruler of Númenor, who sent the fleet against
Sauron. 206, 220, 223, 226, 239, 265

Tar-Minyatur Name of Elros as first Ruler of Númenor. 52, 169, 177,
208, 211, 218

Tar-Míriel Daughter of Tar-Palantir; forced into marriage by Ar-
Pharazôn, and as his queen named in Adûnaic *Ar-Zimraphel.* 224, 227

Tarostar Given name of Rómendacil I, q.v. 319

Tar-Palantir Twenty-fourth Ruler of Númenor, who repented of the
ways of the Kings and took his name in Quenya: 'He who looks afar';
named in Adûnaic (*Ar-*) *Inziladûn.* 223–4, 227

Tar-Súrion Ninth Ruler of Númenor. 212, 220, 226

Tar-Telemmaitë Fifteenth Ruler of Númenor, so named ('Silver-handed')
for his love of silver. 221, 284

Théodred Son of Théoden King of Rohan; slain in the First Battle of the Fords of Isen. 355–61, 364–5, 367–9

Théodwyn Daughter of Thengel King of Rohan, mother of Éomer and Éowyn. 364

Thingol 'Grey-cloak' (Quenya *Singollo*), the name by which Elwë (Sindarin Elu), leader with his brother Olwë of the host of the Teleri from Cuiviénen and afterwards King of Doriath, was known in Beleriand. 55–7, 63, 70–2, 74–85, 90, 93–5, 112–14, 119–21, 143, 147–9, 153, 171, 228–9, 231–4, 259. See *Elu, Elwë*.

Thorin Oakenshield Dwarf of the House of Durin, King in exile, leader of the expedition to Erebor; slain in the Battle of Five Armies. 278, 321–36

Thorondor Lord of the Eagles of the Crissaegrim. 43, 48, 55

Thorongil 'Eagle of the Star', name of Aragorn in Gondor when he served Ecthelion II. 407, 413

Thrain I Dwarf of the House of Durin, first King under the Mountain. 327

Thrain II Dwarf of the House of Durin, King in exile, father of Thorin Oakenshield; died in the dungeons of Dol Guldur. 321, 324, 327–8, 336

Thranduil Sindarin Elf, King of the Silvan Elves in northern Mirkwood; father of Legolas. 243–4, 252, 256–60, 272, 276, 279–83, 338, 342–4, 353

Thrór Dwarf of the House of Durin, King under the Mountain at the coming of Smaug, father of Thrain II; killed in Moria by the Orc Azog. 321, 324, 327–8

*Thurin Name given to Túrin in Nargothrond by Finduilas; translated *the Secret*. 157, 159

Tinúviel See *Lúthien*.

Tol Eressëa See *Eressëa*.

Tol Falas Island in the Bay of Belfalas close to Ethir Anduin. 316

Tol-in-Gaurhoth 'Isle of Werewolves', later name of Tol Sirion, the island in the river in the Pass of Sirion on which Finrod built the tower of Minas Tirith. 54. *Sauron's Isle* 160

Tol Uinen Island in the Bay of Rómenna on the east coast of Númenor. 176, 182

Took Name of a family of Hobbits in the Westfarthing of the Shire. 331. See *Peregrin, Hildifons, Isengar, Old Took*.

Tower Hills See *Emyn Beraid*.

Towers of the Teeth The watchtowers east and west of the Morannon, q.v. 312

Treebeard See *Fangorn*.

Tree of Tol Eressëa See *Celeborn (1)*.

tuilë The first season ('spring') in the *loa*, q.v. 327

Tumhalad Valley in West Beleriand between the rivers Ginglith and Narog where the host of Nargothrond was defeated. 155, 159

Tuor Son of Huor and Rían; with Voronwë came to Gondolin bearing